Tapestry

Tapestry

Christopher Largent

© Copyright Christopher Largent 2015
All rights reserved.

ISBN: 1514860821
ISBN 13: 9781514860823
Library of Congress Control Number: 2015910956
CreateSpace Independent Publishing Platform
North Charleston, South Carolina

Dedicated to my brothers.

TABLE OF CONTENTS

1 Assassins · 1
2 A Hermit for Healing · 29
3 Archery and Poison · 67
4 The Ends of Princes · 82
5 The Warrior of the Bear · 111
6 The Duke and His Emissary · 125
7 A Journey to an Assassin · 141
8 The Monk, the Courtier, and the Lady · · · · · · · · · · · · · 164
9 A Winter's God · 189
10 Northern Peril · 198
11 A Question of Killing · 228
12 Kings and Diplomats · 245
13 Poison and a Bear · 278
14 A Chase Around the World · 290
15 Hervor · 315
16 The End of the World · 348
17 Red Angels · 369
18 Visions · 389
19 The Death of a King · 436
20 Rapid Returns · 459
21 The Duke, the King, and the Killer · · · · · · · · · · · · · · 472
22 The Secret · 500
23 Engagements · 517
24 Death of a Lady · 525

25	The Last Assassin	531
26	Gideon's Army	548
27	A Marriage	562
28	Statecraft	575
29	Strategies	622
30	Hiatus	653
31	The Battle	668
32	The Tapestry	764
	Acknowledgements	777
	Glossary of Characters	779
	About the Author	791

CHAPTER 1

ASSASSINS

A.D. 1035

What surprised me was William's face as he gazed through the tower window at the men sent to kill him — no fear, only curiosity about the assassins shouting and the horses stamping outside the castle gate.

As his mother reached the window behind him, her face too was calm.

Edward's was not, nor was mine. As the gate lowered — by treasonous prearrangement — I could see my fear reflected in Edward's glance. The informant had told the truth.

With the Duke and his knights away in Rouen, Edward was our only protector. His longsword hung from a belt slung over his shoulder, but he was no match for six mounted men.

He jerked Arlette and William back into the room. "Come away — quickly!"

The castle gate continued to creak open.

William set his jaw, making his seven-year-old face as stern as he could. He thrust his hand to his waist. "I have my knife."

Edward ignored him. "Arlette," he whispered to William's mother, "into the hiding chamber. God will conceal us!"

She had already lit a candle from the fireplace, and her arm encircled her son. "Come, William." She turned to me. "Lod, you must go."

Edward leaned to put his hands on my shoulders. "Yes, Lod, flee. If you're found with us, you'll be killed. Go! No one will harm a lame boy, and the Lord will protect you."

The three of them slipped through the secret door near the fireplace.

I sprang for the chamber door and stumbled. Silently cursing myself for leaving my crutch in the castle yard, I hopped toward the stairs and leaped downward. Their twisting dizzied me, causing me to trip over my bad foot. I caught myself on the hand rope. Using it as a crutch, I skipped down the steps two at a time, but each hop was agony. My shoes, their leather worn, offered little protection even for my good foot.

At last wood gave way to earth. Panting, I searched the castle yard.

The courtiers' children had vanished, herded to safety. Tucked under the upper walk, the storehouses became wooden faces with their eyes and mouths clamped shut. No wagons or carts remained. Even the castle guards had disappeared.

Across the yard my crutch leaned against a bolted doorway.

At the yard's far end, the gate opened.

I heard a voice behind me: "The wine barrels. Look right." When I glanced around, no one was nearby. To my right, though, were indeed leaking wine barrels, and I hurled myself behind them. The wine-keeper had piled straw around them to cover the seeping wine. I dug under the straw, clawing at the ground.

As I tried to quiet my breathing, hoofs struck the center of the yard. Feet thumped onto earth. Metal weapons cracked through wood.

"Kill the lame boy, too! Neither must escape!"

The barrel in front of me exploded. I half-stifled a cry. A spear thrust through the splintered wood. The straw reddened with wine.

A second spear struck the earth in front of me. I cried out and scrambled away.

"Over here!" A call sounded from the other side of the yard.

The spear vanished, and I heard running footfalls. Away from me.

A moment later, a scream came from the far courtyard, followed by another. Children's screams — and the shrieks of women.

Then grunts, a muffled command, fading hoof beats, and silence.

I lay still on the ground for a long time. When I heard no sound close to me, I crawled from the straw.

My eyes followed the smashed boxes and barrels, shattered doors and windows to the doorway opposite me. Courtiers moaned and swayed around two still bodies. My crutch sprawled nearby.

Trembling, I wiped wine from my eyes and looked upward. Edward and Arlette peered from the tower window. Edward's head twisted toward the dust-filled castle entrance, while Arlette gazed at the dead children below. William stood between them, frowning.

Within three days, the bells of Falaise announced the arrival of Duke Robert.

"He must have ceased preparations for the pilgrimage," Arlette said as she stepped away from the fireplace to join William.

Below, the village dogs barked, and I hobbled to the window, nudging William to let me have a better view. He stepped aside and pointed.

Just inside the gate, the dogs yapped at the heels of seven knights. Ahead of them the Duke pulled his horse to a stop.

A few moments later Duke Robert appeared in the doorway, breathing heavily. Caked mud flecked his riding cloak, and the leather of his shoes was stained. He seized Arlette and William in his arms.

Eventually, he released them and put a huge hand on my shoulder. "Were you harmed, Lod?"

"No, my lord," I said. I wanted to tell him about the assassin's command to kill a lame boy, but the words would not come.

At the Duke's urging, Arlette and William described the attack, the disappearance of the castle guards, and the deaths of two boys, one of whom had been mistaken for William.

"Did you recognize anything?" Duke Robert asked. "The assassins' shields or armor?"

"We saw them only from a distance," Arlette said, her arm still resting on his. "The men weren't outlaws."

"Hirelings of nobles," the Duke said, "again ... or ..."

I blurted out, "My lord, I heard the voice of one of the assassins. He wasn't a Norman."

He looked down at me. "How do you know?"

"He shouted ... something ... and his voice sounded strange."

The Duke knelt to face me. "Was his accent Saxon, like Prince Edward's? Could the man have come from England?"

I shook my head.

"Like the Franks of Paris? Or the Lombard priests?"

I had heard the speech of the Franks when they visited Duke Robert. The priests who taught me Latin were Lombards from the Italian cities south of the Alps. The killer's voice resembled none of these.

Duke Robert frowned. He rose, speaking to himself, "A Northerner then. Denmark or Norway. God help us." He turned to William and Arlette. "Come. You too, Lod. We hold court in the castle yard."

The court produced little more knowledge than we had given the Duke.

The workers in the courtyard had fled when a terrified messenger dashed into the tower to warn Arlette, William, and Prince Edward.

Every castle official had been traveling at the time of the attack. The assigned guards had fallen asleep outside the walls.

Under a new beard grown for pilgrimage, Duke Robert's face reddened with anger.

It softened, though, as Prince Edward strode toward the ducal chair.

Edward's white skin seemed even paler against his black cloak. Some priests called him "albus," in Latin, an albino, though his hair was no lighter than any other Saxon's, the Duke had told me.

The Duke nodded toward him. "I'm in your debt again, cousin. You guarded my son and his mother as I would have myself."

"A service I was pleased to perform." Edward bent his long neck as if praying. "It was unheroic, however. I regret the loss of two innocent lives."

Duke Robert shook his head. "The loss was out of your hands."

"In God's hands," Edward said, "and the children rest with the Virgin Mother. Their sacrifice and that of their parents will be praised by men and angels. They have given the highest measure for their future Duke. The saints and the Savior will reward them. In heaven, they will be..."

I glanced at Duke Robert as Edward continued. The Duke listened patiently. Knowing that Edward's holy speeches could stretch into hours, I shuffled restlessly.

The Duke caught my movement out of the corner of his eye. He shifted in his chair.

"Cousin," he said when Edward paused, "we still need to discover who is behind these attacks. Did you recognize any markings?"

"No, I regret to say, but only barons can afford to hire these ruffians. We know of their jealousy and their connection with Canute's northern empire. Young William — "

Duke Robert interrupted him again. "Unhappily, the nobles will soon realize what their hirelings have not accomplished. Will you wait on me in the great hall at the noon bell?"

Edward bowed and was gone.

From the far end of the courtyard strode a tall man in a black robe, its hood raised, hiding his face, except for a white beard. He approached the Duke without any of the usual courtesies.

The Duke waved him forward as he waved us away. He also lowered his voice, so that I could barely make out what the two men were saying.

The Duke's voice was the louder of the two. "Northern nobles trying to kill my son again? Or something else? The Empire?"

From under the hood: "It could be either … worshippers of Thor are half of your problem … Empire … the other half."

The Duke leaned further forward. "What have your spies told you?"

"This Pope imitates old Roman rulers … violent … wants an empire …. He tolerates no obstacles … realms where the local ruler allows the local churches to be independent … Normandy is an example he does not wish spread abroad. So far, he can't penetrate …"

Duke Robert paused. "Because Thor worship is practiced here?"

A pause and a louder reply, "Because he does not control you."

Duke Robert sighed. "I'm going on a pilgrimage. I'm giving my lands to …" He sighed again.

I almost thought I heard a laugh from under the hood and then, plainly: "Reverence for your religion is not capitulation to Pope Benedict, Robert. He wants to control the world, as do the forces allied with him and the Holy Roman Empire."

"For this he would murder my heir?"

A quieter reply again: "Never openly … forces behind the papal throne … and this Pope is violent, cruel … For the Empire, who is Pope matters little, but this Pope suits the powers…"

"Would the Pope ally himself with Thor-worshippers to bring Normandy into the Empire?"

"I'm not sure … whether I think the Empire would deal with Thor-worshippers … but this Pope and this Empire are more dangerous than you imagine."

The Duke sighed deeply. "Then the danger might be greater … William, even Lod's life is threatened."

I felt myself shudder.

The hooded man sounded surprised. "Lod?"

"The assassins came for both boys."

There was silence for a moment. Then the man spoke again. "Unless you can convince … intend to move Normandy into the Holy Roman Empire … great danger for all Normans." Then, distinctly: "The Pope and the Holy Roman Empire are snarling beasts at your back … Canute's Danish Empire to your north, even though Canute himself has just died."

Duke Robert whispered something that I did not hear.

The hooded man nodded, turned, and strode slowly across the courtyard toward the castle gate.

The Duke looked startled as he noticed us, as if he had been unaware that we remained nearby. He leaned toward Arlette, putting his hand on hers. "My lady, would you please escort William and Lod upstairs?"

Arlette rose and took each of us by the hand. She led us back up to William's chamber.

As we mounted the stairs, I glanced over my shoulder to see the Duke lean across the arm of his chair. I heard him summon the guards who had abandoned their posts.

Back in William's room, I asked his mother, "Who is that man in the black cloak? Is he a priest?"

Arlette looked at me for a moment and then said, "He's a friend."

William stepped between us and faced his mother. "What will my father do to the guards? Punish them?" He frowned. "They should be punished."

Arlette drew the hood of her blue cloak over her head. "That's not something for you to know or see. Don't think about it. And don't ask Robert — either of you."

As usual, she failed to be stern. Nonetheless, she stooped to put her arms around us.

William put one of his hands on her face. "Are the two dead boys in heaven? Lod says God has taken them."

"That's what the priests told me," I said.

Arlette took William's hand. "The priests are right. The boys are in heaven. Now I must return to the yard."

She slipped from the room. William stood gazing after her for a moment.

I nudged him. "Will you ask Duke Robert why those men wanted to kill me?"

"Why don't you ask him? You're older. And you always ask questions."

"This is different. Besides, he's your father."

William returned to thinking.

"They wanted to kill me," I said.

"Me, too."

"I'm a commoner, William."

He shrugged. "Maybe not you then. Three other cripples live in the village."

"I'm the only one who's here every day. And …"

"Yes?"

"I heard a voice telling me to hide behind the wine barrels, but no one was there."

He stared at me for a long time. "Was it God?"

"Why would God talk to me? Or even care about a lame villager? Can you ask your father about it?"

He kept staring. Eventually he said, "All right."

A guard escorted him back to the yard, while I fidgeted in his room. I shuffled to the window to gaze out at the fields and woods surrounding Falaise village.

Placing my crutch on the window ledge, I traced Falaise stream as it meandered through the village. I searched the road where we had first spotted the armed riders. Then I leaned forward, almost too far.

In the distance, I could see a figure in black turn off the road and slip into the woods.

Behind me, the door swung open — hard. William ran across the room and snatched up his green cloak, the one that his father had given him on his seventh birthday. We called it "the Duke cloak."

"Did you tell him?" I asked.

He threw the cloak over his shoulders and stared at me for a time. "The villagers say it was a miracle."

"What?"

"The wine from the barrels. They say it was blood."

"It was burgundy. What about the voice?"

"My father says the Eucharist wine is burgundy. Burgundy is the blood of the Savior. He didn't say anything about the voice."

"What did he say about the men looking for a lame boy?"

"I should give you a new name."

"What? What does that have to do with —?"

"Do you know what 'Lod' means? 'Bastard' the villagers say."

I didn't know what a bastard was. "What about the man who wants to kill me?"

"The name isn't safe. And the men attacked on Friday. Fridays are unlucky."

"Why would anyone want to kill me? Did the Duke say anything about that?"

William tilted his head and gave me his earnest look. "My father says we must hide in the village on Fridays. And I must give you a new name."

"Why does Duke Robert care about my name?"

"With a new name, assassins won't know you. That's clear."

It wasn't clear to me. "I don't want a new name."

William drew the Duke cloak around his neck. "You need one. My father says so. A new name will protect you."

I sighed. I'd get nothing from him until he executed the ducal command.

"Someday, when I'm Duke of Normandy," he said, "I'll be a great ruler. Like Charlemagne. I'll need wise men. Like Charlemagne's." He studied me for a moment. "You'll be my wise man at court. Like Alcuin of York. He was Charlemagne's wise man."

A Falaise commoner could not be a wise man at court, I told him.

He ignored me. "Alcuin," he said to himself. "Alcuin doesn't sound Norman. But it's a good name." He hesitated. "Maybe it shouldn't be so long. I don't think my father would approve. A courtier's name longer than a duke's? No."

"I'm not a courtier."

He paid no attention. "We'll shorten it." He pondered the possibilities. "Al. Al." He wrinkled his nose. "It sounds like a peasant."

"I am a peasant."

"Cuin." He said. "Cuin. I like that. Cuin. I declare that from this day, you are to be named Cuin."

"I'll be anyone you wish. What about the killers?"

"My father says the name will take care of that. The rest, he says, is a secret."

When Edward paid his evening visit to William's chamber, he too brushed aside my questions about the assassins. He seemed interested only in William's name for me.

He stroked the beard he was nursing and nodded approval. "It's only right that you receive a new name, freeing you from the stain of your … unfortunate birth."

I didn't know what "unfortunate birth" meant. I knew that Prince Edward worried more than Normans about how people were born. He often fretted that Duke Robert had never wed Lady Arlette. That made William's birth "unfortunate" too.

"God blessed you by his miracle," he said. "Your new name reflects that. The Danes, though, will stop at nothing —"

He stopped himself, put his hand on my shoulder, and smiled down at me. Then he marched to the church to pray, which he did at that hour every evening, even without miracles.

That night, I dreamed of a dark figure looming over me, brandishing a knife. As I stared at the knife and its curved blade with blood running down it, I thought I saw the head of a huge dragon swinging around toward me. Then both were gone.

Remaining in Falaise to protect us, Duke Robert renewed preparations for his pilgrimage to Jerusalem. He and his companions would wear the roughly woven robes customary for pilgrims, so his knights were being measured by Falaise's tailor. They shifted impatiently, until the Duke himself appeared and began jesting with them.

I perched on a nearby bench. The priests, busy with plans for the new court church, had postponed my lessons. So I had the afternoon to watch the tailor wrestle with his pins and to laugh at the Duke's jests.

Not far away, servants packed skins of wine and jars of dried food for the journey. Next to these they stacked boxes of gold, pearls, and gemstones. I gaped at them.

Striding over to me, Duke Robert poked my ribs. "Would you like to have some of those?"

I didn't know what to say.

The Duke looked me up and down for a moment. "How old are you now, Cuin?"

I paused, not yet accustomed to my new name. "This is my ninth year, my lord."

"Well, you're probably too young to know what to do with jewels and gold. Except to buy more apples."

I glanced up hopefully. "And oranges."

He smiled.

I looked over at the servants again. "Why are you going to the Holy Land, sire?"

He tilted his head. "I'm on a quest."

"What kind of quest, if you don't mind my asking?"

"I never mind your questions. The quest, well, I don't know all of it myself, but I need to discover something about myself. And the world. There are secrets out there, and I'd like to know more about them. My brother knew some of the secrets and died as a consequence. That alone would be enough to drive me."

"I'm sorry he died."

He put his hand on my shoulder. "I'm sorry, too. I'm also sorry I can't give these jewels to you or any other Norman. The priests have dedicated them to God, and I shall need every piece of them to pursue my quest in the Holy Land." He paused. "I do know where there are more apples and the best oranges in Normandy — in Rouen. Shall I take you there?"

"Rouen? Would you, my lord?"

"Tomorrow, if you wish."

"Thank you!"

"It's settled then." He patted my shoulder and turned back toward his men.

As he marched away, William appeared beside me and whispered, "Do you know why he's taking us to Rouen?"

"It has apples and oranges and the Duke's largest house."

"Besides that."

"There's a festival there?"

William shook his head. "We're not safe here. The assassins will find out."

"I thought my name would protect me."

"It will protect you better in Rouen."

"Is it safe in Rouen?"

He patted his belt. "If not, I have my knife."

Rouen, as I had guessed, was having a festival. It had been a safe guess. Few days passed in Normandy without some sort of festival. The day we arrived, though, as Duke Robert informed us over the din, a market day and a holiday coincided.

The city was full of people. Artisans in orange tunics and yellow hose haggled with buyers, mostly women in blue or gray gowns with green mantles, their hair covered by white wimples.

Merchants in fur-trimmed cloaks boasted of their goods to passersby, even to the occasional black-frocked priests.

Moneychangers called to customers over their copper scales, while nobles in jeweled and feathered robes looked down their noses at everyone.

At the same time, a holiday procession jostled through the markets. As it passed, townspeople joined the singing and dancing. Even the stone and wood shopfronts — their horizontal shutters open to display wares — seemed to wave the banners that hung beside their signboards.

In the commotion, people paid scant attention to us, except for having to yield to the wagon and bow to the Duke. In his turn, Duke Robert greeted priests, nuns, fair-goers, and shop owners.

One tiny knot of nobles, wearing long cloaks over oddly patterned tunics, stared at William. Duke Robert gazed back. They bowed briefly to him and then turned away. As they turned, I noticed upside down crosses sewn into several of their tunics.

"Some of the barons of Western Normandy," Arlette said to William. "They fear that your father will name you …"

She dropped her voice, so that I heard no more.

But I was puzzled. Normans in the West, the priests had told me, were unconverted. They worshipped Thor and Odin, not Christ. Why then would they have crosses on their clothes? Why were the crosses upside down?

I stared at them as they disappeared behind us.

Soon after, we rolled through the town gate, and knights and nobles scurried to greet Duke Robert. They soon surrounded him, and he was swept away from us.

I leaped from the wagon to escape the wooden torture-seat. It had beaten at my posterior parts all the way from Falaise. As I hit the earth, I scarcely noticed the pain in my bad foot. Too much hurt elsewhere.

William handed my crutch to me and jumped to the ground.

"Do you have any pennies?" I asked him. "I'm hungry."

"The kitchen cooks will feed us. We shouldn't wander away."

"I'm starving. And no one will bother me." I waved toward the crowds. "Or notice me."

William frowned.

"Just a few pennies," I said. "I'd love to buy some sweets. I'll bring you some."

He grinned. "Sweets. All right. My father gave me these. You may have them."

He pulled some silver pennies from the leather pouch at his belt and dropped them into my hand. I thanked him and hobbled through the residence entrance before any zealous guard decided to close it.

I skipped past the pillory outside the wall. It had been emptied of criminals, and I recalled Duke Robert saying that he wished to show visiting merchants how safe the city was and how leniently he handled dishonest traders.

As I entered the town, the noisy buyers created a wall with no openings for a young boy. But first one person then another glanced at my crutch, stepped aside, and pulled others from my path. As a result, I progressed quickly.

And quick progress was necessary. I noticed a tall man moving behind me wherever I went. Someone was following me.

I turned a quick corner to avoid him. Why was he following me? Or was I imagining that he was?

My thoughts were interrupted by odors of fish and brackish water. This street led to the Seine, which would be crowded with merchants unloading ships. There would be no bakers there.

It would also be a dead end, with my follower behind me, cutting off any other turns.

I hurried onto the next side street and quickly pulled in my breath — butchers. The stench revealed that even on festival days, they threw animals' blood and offal into their street-drains.

The third street had the pungency that came from linen making. No self-respecting pastry-maker would place his shop here.

I spotted the tall man behind me again.

I was being followed.

As I hobbled forward, I noticed a beggar perched on a wooden-wheeled trolley. I paused to give him a penny. His eyes widened as he saw the silver, and he blessed me.

Around us floated the smell of burning charcoal, identifying the blacksmith's home, so the armorers, helmet-makers, and swordsmiths would be housed down this street.

The beggar must once have been a warrior. He may have lost his legs in battle and now hoped that those purchasing weapons would reward him for his past valor.

The beggar grinned at me. "What are you searching for, my young friend?"

"A baker, sir. I'm on an errand for the Duke's residence."

"The ducal residence? Well, then you'd better head for the best merchants." Pointing eastward, he said, "The best shops are there, and they'll trade well for silver."

As I adjusted my crutch to leave, he caught my sleeve. "Don't mention ducal chores to the Western merchants, though. They don't favor Duke Robert, and the price will go hard for you." He glanced in the direction behind me. "There's a man watching you, son. Is he one of the Duke's?"

"I don't know. I don't think so. He's just following me, and it makes me afraid."

"Move on then. I'll direct him away from you."

I hurried to the eastern end of the main street, where the beggar had directed me. It did boast the best shops, as he had said. Surely no assassin would dare harm me here.

I gaped at the bright colors and fine carvings decorating the tailor's store, a silversmith's home, and the wool-dealer's shop, all more grand than anything in Falaise.

In front of the wine store, a gold-clad wine crier with a fancy hat shouted prices and offered samples. He had cornered one of the oddly dressed nobles whom Arlette had identified as Western.

Again I noticed an upside down cross on the Western noble's tunic and wondered at it. The noble turned and stared at me menacingly. I averted my face and skipped away as quickly as I could.

The people issuing from the next side street had their cloaks pulled over their noses. I smiled. The foul odor belonged to the tanners' district.

I did not mind the smell of tanning, because Arlette's father — William's grandfather — was a tanner in Falaise. He was a nice man, and William and I visited him often. A Falaise courtier's son once taunted William about his "commoner mother and smelly, tanner grandfather." William had thrashed him.

At last, I located a baker and pastry-maker. I traded some pennies for an armload of bread and pastries and began to munch on the pastry closest to my mouth.

Before I had swallowed once, a hand seized my shoulder.

"Here, now!" a gruff voice said. "No running away!"

I glanced up to see the tall man who had been following me, but the hand and voice belonged to one of Duke Robert's knights.

"You've given me a chase," he growled. "Come along. You shouldn't have left the Duke's lodging, and we're going back."

I offered him a pastry, and his temper sweetened.

That same evening, the town bell summoned the barons, knights, and prelates to the great hall. Some momentous event was about to unfold.

Not wanting to sit on any surface — my posterior still sore from the wagon ride — I stood along the walls with the ladies and villagers and tried not to trip any with my crutch.

Since I had already felled one otherwise dignified woman, I pressed my back against a wall hanging and tried to look helpless.

When Duke Robert's entrance was announced, I inched along the wall toward William. He stood, clad in his new blue tunic and black leggings, beside his father's carved stone chair. His knife was at his waist as usual, but now it rested in a jeweled sheath. The "Duke cloak" hung from his shoulders, fastened by a jeweled pin.

Duke Robert strode into the hall, dressed in scarlet with a gold cloak trimmed in fox fur. Spotting me, he frowned and waved me away.

Perhaps I had been too close to the ducal throne. Perhaps he had seen my crutch trip the noblewoman. I squeezed my way to the back of the room. Soon I could not see William or Duke Robert at all.

Blocking my view were barons and bishops, their jeweled sword sheaths and fur-trimmed cloaks draped over massive shoulders. Their newly shaved faces had huge noses and eyes, while their hair fell in great swaths across enormous heads. Except for the monks' tonsures, the backs of their heads were shaved in the Norman fashion, making their ears seem monstrously long.

The farthest nobles from the Duke were the Western barons. Again dressed in their oddly patterned cloaks and tunics, including the mysterious upside down crosses, they spoke among themselves in low tones.

A shout from the front of the hall silenced everyone. With much clanking and groaning, the nobles knelt onto the earthen floor, which had been covered with new rushes for the ceremony.

I could now see Duke Robert, standing with his hand up. He lowered himself onto the ducal chair, silently studying the bowed heads of the nobles. Behind his chair stood a richly dressed priest, the powerful Archbishop of Rouen, I guessed.

The Duke set William between his knees and began to speak in the loud voice that I had heard him use during ceremonies. "I have no intention of leaving you without a Duke, should I fail to return from Jerusalem. I expect no danger, but mine might be a mission less safe than that of other pilgrims. So, I request that you elect my son overlord in my place."

He paused. The Western barons with the upside down crosses exchanged frowns.

"He's young," the Duke said, "but he will grow. His courage has already been tested." He stared hard at the nobles. "More than once. And by more enemies than you."

The nobles seemed to become the statues they resembled.

Duke Robert continued, "If God pleases, he shall become a gallant and good ruler. He is of your blood, of your upbringing. I thus declare him my heir and bequeath him the whole of Normandy."

The barons murmured among themselves. Then, slowly, one at a time, they drew themselves up and stepped forward. Each one knelt before William and thrust his clasped hands out. With his father guiding him, William placed one hand over, the other under each baron's extended hands.

Then the noble swore a loyalty oath on a jeweled relic box held by the bishop.

The Western barons, their jaws set, approached the front of the hall. Whatever threats they had in their minds, I thought, some Eastern barons had worse. Among the local nobles, after all, was the man who had hired the assassins, either for himself or for the Pope and the Holy Roman Empire.

My mind began to work, and my fear mounted. I held my breath. I imagined a jealous noble pulling his knife and eliminating Duke Robert's only heir.

None did, though. Before evening's last bell, the Duke-to-be had received the fealty of all the lords, Eastern and Western.

"Do you know why my father waved you away?" William asked me, as we lay on our beds in a guarded section of the ducal residence's upper level.

I looked away. "No."

"He doesn't want us to be seen together. Especially when other people are around. He told me we shouldn't have ridden openly through the streets today."

I rolled over and faced him. "Why?"

"Because the killers may see us together. Your crutch was behind us in the cart."

"Where was I supposed to put it?"

"We should have hidden it. We should have disguised you. As a girl." William chuckled. "A girl."

"You won't disguise me as a girl. If he wants someone to be a girl, you be it. You're younger."

"I'm to be the Duke, so you have to be the girl." He chuckled again.

I leaped onto his bed, tickling him. He shrieked with laughter, and the guards dashed around the separating partition, swords drawn.

Arlette appeared soon after. We were ordered back to bed and to sleep.

For the next few weeks the Duke commanded us to remain in the residence while he finished his pilgrimage preparations. What the preparations were I could not tell, but they involved meeting with many nobles, bishops, and Rouen's archbishop, who was also the Duke's uncle.

The nobles and archbishop were disturbed about the pilgrimage for some reason.

William and I roamed the residence grounds, which at first seemed a large space to fill small days. No guards accompanied us, although one of the dogs often trotted alongside.

"My father wants to replace all the wood with stone," William told me as we watched the masons and carpenters work on that first day of our wanderings.

I sneezed as stone dust reached my nostrils. "Why?"

"Wood burns. It isn't as strong as stone. And" — he thrust his broad face toward me, gripping his knife — "there are always rebellions."

I nodded to show that I appreciated the problem, though I really did not. "William, do you know what your father is talking about? With these nobles? They look worried."

William shook his head. "The Danes. The Norwegians. Vikings. They're coming." He stared at me earnestly. "That's why they want us dead. So they can take us over and slaughter us. The same as years ago. That includes you and me."

"Why me?"

He shook his head to disapprove of the question. "It's a secret."

I spent my first few days in the residence library. Because William could neither read nor write and did not want to learn, he soon disappeared. I always found him later at the courtyard drills conducted by the weapons-masters.

The shadow of assassins seemed to hang over us, and William drilled with weapons more and more earnestly.

As spring warmed — and spring had been unusually warm — the meals, the high point of our days, moved into the open air, where we listened to stories told by visiting nobles, priests, or pilgrims.

The pilgrim's tales were the most interesting, so I was glad that Duke Robert extended them with his questions.

The pilgrims described wearying treks on horseback, sometimes with long detours to avoid warring nobles. They spoke of struggling over the Alps, sitting for weeks on wooden trailers pulled by oxen over neglected Roman roads, long since robbed of their paving.

I recalled my wagon trip and ached in sympathy.

Pressing from hamlet to hamlet, the travelers wrestled with the local dialects to order beef, eggs, and cheese at the inns. All the while, they feared avalanches, common even in summer, as well as the ever-present outlaws.

"Spirits and monsters also inhabit the Alps," one aging pilgrim said. "I've seen one, high in the mountains. It was over two feet long with a red, hairy head, almost like a cat's — glowing eyes, a snake's tongue, scaly legs, and a long, hairy tail."

My mouth fell open, but the Duke leaned toward Arlette and whispered, "Why does he think that appearance odd? Many Western nobles fit that description."

Once I asked a pilgrim whether he had gone all the way to the Holy Land.

"Oh, yes, my boy," he replied, pointing to one of the badges on his cloak. "I survived a sea voyage from Venice to Jaffa, terrible and dangerous, with monsters all around. And the storms! The storms made me wish I had been eaten by the monsters."

I widened my eyes. "Did you see monsters?"

"Many, my boy, many — with scales and teeth and huge tails." He turned to shake his head at the Duke. "The greatest monster, though, was the ship's captain. He insisted on sailing farther into the ocean than was necessary, never putting into harbors for fresh bread, water, or meat. He then made us pay an outrageous fare — 80 ducats for a trip that should have cost 30 — and only because he insisted on sailing along the edge of the world to frighten us. We could see it in the distance."

"Did he get you to Jaffa?" Duke Robert asked.

The old pilgrim huffed. "Eventually, but the innkeepers there and in all the southern lands — unlike those in the Alps, our Savior bless them — put too much water in the wine and made us pay for broken, stinking, flea-ridden beds. I can tell you that I delivered many of my kin from Hellfire with what I endured on that trip. 'Through my suffering, they are healed.'"

Other pilgrims described the shrines they had visited all over the world: those of the Black Virgins in Chartres, St. James in Compostela, and Saints Peter and Paul in Rome.

Many spoke of the miracles that occurred at the shrines: healings of the blind and lame (they glanced at me), of madness and leprosy, of fevers and toothaches.

They recounted stories of the Blessed Virgin. One woman pilgrim told of a Flemish monk who, painting a picture of Heaven and Hell in his abbey, refused to paint the devil as a handsome man after Satan himself appeared and demanded that he do so. Furious, Satan pulled away his scaffold. As the monk fell, a statue of the Virgin reached out and held him until help arrived.

Duke Robert glanced at me and said, "I hear that your crutch pulls away the scaffolding from the carpenters on the residence walls." He pointed at it. "Could the devil be in there?"

William chuckled. "The devil in the crutch."

I gave both of them a sour look.

What seemed most moving to the pilgrims were the sacred relics. With awe they spoke of having kissed or touched an article of clothing, a bit of hair, a tooth, a foot, a finger bone, or even the entire arm of a saint.

They proudly displayed the badges they had bought on each pilgrimage: shells from Compostela, a tin head of John the Baptist from Amiens, a holy napkin from Rome, a leaden image of the Black Madonna from Rocamadour.

It was when they described the Holy Land itself that we — and Duke Robert — listened most intently.

"The Holy Land," a noble-turned-monk said, "... barren now, just rocks. Once it had trees and great cities, but the ancient demons destroyed those. Now there are only scrub bushes, squat trees, and decaying walls. Along the roads, we saw many ruined villages. We visited some ... to offer goods in exchange for some old, old things."

He pulled stone pieces from his cloak. "See here? Bits of plates. This is an ancient knife. And this comb that may have belonged to the original Christians, perhaps to an apostle. Or even to our Savior Himself."

While I wondered whether the Savior ever combed his hair, the monk's companion, a former knight, added, with a glance at the Duke, "Be warned, though. It is dangerous country. A man can die of thirst easily. Water is scarce, and the wells that we found were few. There are worse terrors, too. In the mountains near Bethlehem, brigands rob and kill pilgrims who are not escorted by Saracen chiefs. Robbers also stalk the road from Jerusalem to Galilee."

Duke Robert shook his head and whistled through his teeth. He did that whenever something amazed him, and he did it often while listening to pilgrims.

Then he asked, "What of Jerusalem itself?"

The monk's smile returned. "Ah, Jerusalem." He gazed over everyone's heads at nothing. "The sight of Jerusalem is burned into my memory. It stands on a low hill. As I approached it from the mountains, I saw what all travelers first see: the leaden roof of the Temple of Solomon — or what's left of the Temple. The city itself has stone walls and houses, narrow passageways. People drape cloth from poles above the streets for shade. And everyone wears robes and headdresses to protect themselves from the sun. The sun burns and burns."

He fell silent for a moment. "Of course, what's most marvelous about Jerusalem is its holiness, its relics. It holds the arm of St. George, the burned, powdered flesh of St. Lawrence, and the staff of St. Nicholas." He paused. "And we saw the ear of St. Paul."

While we gaped in amazement, he continued, "That's not all. We saw one of the jars in which Our Lord had turned water to wine. And one of Goliath's teeth. The tooth weighs twelve pounds, we were told."

I saw William make a slow biting motion.

"Did you have trouble getting into the city?" Duke Robert asked. "Will the followers of Muhammad let visitors see the sacred sites?"

"That's to their credit," the monk said. "Though the Saracens control the city, they administer it fairly. At least, they're fair with Christian pilgrims. We were allowed to see the Pillar of Pilate in the Praetorium. And to place our hands in the hole where the cross was set in Golgotha, the Hill of the Skull."

"Also," his companion added, coming back to life, "we kissed the floor of the tomb where the body of the Healer had been placed. We also kissed the rock from which He ascended into Heaven. Along with other pilgrims, we crawled on our knees along the road to Calvary. Crawled the whole way. And put most of our silver in the box nearby — our last penance in the Holy Land."

Crawling along a stony road on knees struck me as penance enough for any sin. What crime these men might have committed to have to add silver was beyond my imagining. As the Falaise priests said, though, there are many great sinners in the world.

Rouen delighted us for the first week and held our interest for the second. By the third week, though, the daily routine seemed monotonous, and even the Duke's jokes could not enliven it.

I had read all the books that I could understand. The cathedral priests had stopped teaching to oversee the building of a new chapel. Fewer pilgrims arrived with tales to recount.

The Duke was having sharper arguments with the bishops and his uncle, the archbishop, so he was less available.

William seemed to miss only hunting, but he found a substitute in weapons training. Soon he was training the entire day.

I had nothing to fill the days, and I realized that we would never leave the residence. William and I would grow old without seeing the outside world again. I would perish, and my headstone would read: he died in Rouen, never having explored the world.

It was the morning of St. Augustine's Day — not the African Augustine but the one that Pope Gregory sent north to England.

I was kicking my way down the winding steps that led to the residence yard, using my crutch to send stones cascading before me. As I did, I sang a village song that I had heard at the Duke's dinners.

"I hope you don't plan to be a singer," a thin voice interrupted me.

I looked up and gasped. For a moment the dark shape from my dreams loomed before me. I blinked, and the shape vanished.

Standing at the foot of the steps was Guy, William's cousin, and behind him a guard.

Guy tilted his head up at me. Wrapped in a gold-trimmed red cloak, he was doing something crooked with his mouth that he probably thought was smiling.

"Oh, hello," I said, finishing my descent. "No, I only sing when no one is around."

"Well, I was around, and it was an ordeal."

I could never decide whether Guy, who was exactly my age, intended to ridicule me or fling harmless barbs. Since he was William's favorite friend, I remained determinedly nice to him.

"Are you looking for William?" I asked. To his nod, I replied, "He's training in the outer yard with the sword-master."

I could not understand why Guy would want to join William. Guy seemed frail, and I thought that swordsmanship would be his last interest.

Guy nodded his thanks. "It was nice seeing you again, briefly. I'll be going, so you can sing. When I'm far enough away, of course."

Guy may have intended to insult me, but he had also done me an unintended favor. The guard accompanying him had temporarily left a side door unguarded.

I glanced around to see if anyone noticed. I was alone. I hurried through the door.

I was free.

No festival filled the city this day. The pillory in front of the residence was doing normal duty. It held a baker with a loaf of bread strung around his neck.

I felt sorry for him, but the priests said the law about uniform bread sizes protected everyone. Nonetheless, I stared at his blank face for a long time. Perhaps I could free him. Perhaps he would reward me with —

A sound off to my right interrupted my thoughts. A tall, black-bearded man, hooded and robed in dark gray, had dropped something that clattered against the stones serving as a drain for the residence's wine merchant.

The man knelt to retrieve the object, muttering to himself in a language I did not recognize.

The object was a curved-bladed knife with a red line running down the blade.

Just then I thought I heard a hissing voice next to me say, "Hide!" though no one was near me.

The weapon and the voice unnerved me, so I slipped down a side street and took the next several turns I found. Though there was no festival, enough townspeople stood in the streets to hide my retreat.

At the next turn, though, I spotted the hooded man again. I hobbled quickly into another street and rounded another corner.

The row of shops before me faced the Seine as it flowed to the south. I didn't recognize this part of the city, but I recognized its smell: tanning. For a moment, I felt safe. I relaxed my gait and adjusted the crutch under my arm.

As I glanced behind me, the hooded man was there, striding towards me.

I ducked behind a pile of treated skins from which I could risk a longer look down the street.

At the far end, the hooded man leaned forward to talk to a merchant. The merchant, hands on hips, pointed down the street in my direction.

"Hello," a voice above me said.

Startled, I looked up to see a smiling face over a brown and orange tunic. Arms ran from the tunic, at the end of which were a tanner's knife and a skin, its hair partly scraped away.

"Are you playing hide-and-seek?"

"That man in the hood is following me. I don't know who he is."

The tanner's smile turned wry. "You haven't stolen something from him, have you?"

"No! I've just come from the Duke's residence, and — "

"Are you with the Duke and his son?"

"Here from Falaise. Yes, sir."

"And with the Duke's lady, the tanner's daughter?"

I nodded, glancing back at the hooded man.

He now strode down the street, staring through the opened shutters of the shops and stealing in and out of the doors.

I gazed up at the tanner. "Can you help me?"

"Of course. Come with me."

He took me inside his shop, where he spoke to his apprentice, a boy not much older than I. "Hide this young gentleman's crutch."

As I protested that I was not a gentleman, he lifted me over stacks of skins and placed me between two of them. He put a tanned skin over my head.

"I hope you don't mind the smell. This one's already been rubbed with dung. No one will look under it, though, that's for certain!"

Before I had time to answer, I heard the apprentice cough loudly and the tanner's voice say, "Good morning. Would you like to buy a hide?"

"I search for boy. Have you seen?"

Neither the voice nor the speech pattern was Norman. It seemed familiar, though. And menacing.

"The only boy here is my apprentice, whom you see."

A pause. "He comes from Duke's home. Crippled boy with crutch. Came this way."

"We didn't see any boy."

"I saw him here."

The tanner's voice turned hostile. "You're a Northerner, aren't you?"

"Norwegian."

"Well, Norwegian, come with me." A pause. Then the tanner's voice, farther away: "Do you see that blockade built part-way into the river? Do you know why that blockade is there?"

A grunted "No."

"It was built years ago to keep Northerners such as you from sailing farther south after they sacked Rouen. It was never finished. So the Vikings killed up and down the Seine. They murdered old men, women, and children. Duke Robert had the blockade partly rebuilt to remind everyone what happened. Though we were once Northerners, too, the blockade reminds us how differently we now conduct our lives."

Another pause. The tanner's voice again: "Let me say it to you this way. The other tanners and I look at the blockade every day as we work. Every day. And we think of your Northern axes stained with the blood of Norman men, women, and children. Shall I call the others and tell them I found a Norwegian warrior, searching for a Norman child?"

I waited, holding my breath.

The skin over my head raised, and the tanner grinned at me as I rose. "He's gone."

"I'm very grateful."

The tanner grinned. "I was happy to help you, young sir."

He lifted me out, and the apprentice handed me my crutch.

I thanked them again and added, "I'm not a sir of any type. I happen to know Duke Robert only because of Lady Arlette. She lets me come to the castle to play with William. I'm a commoner from Falaise."

"Nevertheless, it was my pleasure to help a friend of the present and future Duke." The tanner gave me a short bow.

Recalling my manners, I said, "I'm in your debt."

The tanner leaned toward me. "I'd be careful of that Northerner, though. He's a fighter. With a scar on his face to prove it. And I saw a long knife under his robe. I'll take you back to the residence."

"You don't need to — " I began, but he would hear no refusals.

Despite my fears about the Duke's reaction, though, I was happy to have the escort.

As Duke Robert listened to the tanner's story, he eyed me. I shifted on my crutch, feeling anxious.

After the tanner left — generously rewarded — I was sure the Duke would punish me. He motioned me toward his chair.

I must have looked frightened, because he said, "Don't be afraid. It's all right. It's over now."

I managed to say, "I just wanted to see the town."

"It's all right," he repeated. "When I asked you to stay in the residence, I — "

At that moment, William raced into the hall, a short sword in his hand. "You were attacked?"

My voice felt unsteady, but I said, "No, followed."

William lowered his sword. "Are you all right?"

I nodded.

He sniffed at me. "Have you been tanning?"

"A tanner rescued him," the Duke said.

William straightened. "From what?"

"A Northern warrior followed me."

Duke Robert drew William toward him with one arm, me with the other.

"Listen, both of you. You aren't safe here, except inside the residence." He looked at me, but I looked at the floor. "I know you won't understand this, because Normandy hasn't been invaded for years, but it's not safe here. There are Northern kings who want this land and will kill to get it — kill me, kill both of you, kill any Norman who stands in their way. That's why it worries me that the man looking for you, Cuin, is a Northerner."

Imitating his father, William whistled through his teeth. He looked at me. "How did you get out?"

"Guy left a door open."

The Duke pondered a moment and then said to me, "Though God has protected you from the warrior, Cuin — and we know you are especially protected by God — we cannot take risks. We will no longer remain here. We leave tomorrow morning. Until then, remain near one of my knights."

He pushed us gently away. "Now, William, see that Cuin gets a bath."

The next morning we headed south. I borrowed a cushion from the Duke's residence. Since God was occupied in protecting me from the Norwegian warrior, I decided to protect myself from wagon-seats.

As we traveled, Duke Robert drew his horse beside William and spoke to him. After a few minutes, he lifted his voice to tell me that his men had been unable to locate the Norwegian warrior before we left, but that they would keep searching Rouen.

"Perhaps he was just a traveler, my lord, and wanted to talk to me about something."

"Perhaps." He rode silently for a moment. Then he said, "Cuin, there's something particular I want you to remember when I'm gone. I have a friend, a hermit, who can help you. He can teach you. Can you remember that? In the event that I don't return?"

"Yes, my lord. But you'll be coming back soon, won't you?"

"I hope so." He watched my face for a moment and then shared a jest. I had heard it already, but I laughed anyway.

The next day, we reached Falaise.

Soon after, he was gone.

CHAPTER 2

A HERMIT FOR HEALING

A.D. 1035

Summer had arrived in Falaise village, sunny and apparently safe. The barons' oaths had bound them to William, and none dared violate them — at least, as Prince Edward said, until they could find a legal way of getting around them.

Just before he left, the Duke had exchanged words with Edward about assassins serving the Holy Roman Empire and the Pope, but none had appeared.

Within a few weeks, a messenger informed us that Duke Robert's pilgrimage had already taken him over the Alps, headed south.

In late spring — what the priests called St. Erasmus of Formia's Day — Arlette and Edward decided to revisit Rouen. They took William with them, depriving me of my opponent for horseshoes and bowling.

In Falaise as in Rouen, the priests busied themselves with the new church, so I was excused from Latin studies.

I returned to one of my village families. In gratitude for their taking me in, I gathered twigs, dung, and moss for winter fires, my usual offerings.

They in turn rewarded me not only with hearty meals and new straw for my bed but also with gossip I had missed.

The "miracle of the wine barrels" remained the major event. I was treated with unusual reverence, though everyone assumed the killers had sought only William. The two boys who died "had sacrificed their lives for their Duke and been taken up by the Blessed Virgin."

The only other news came from the priests' clerk as he paced through the village on Sunday, dipping his sprinkler in the holy water stoup and shaking it at us.

"A stranger?" he replied to my question. "Yes, I've seen one recently. He wasn't a Norman, though. He had a Northern accent. He was tall, had long black hair and a black beard, a scar, and wore a gray-colored cloak with … well, there might have been blue in it, too. Strange garment. It almost wasn't there, if you know what I mean."

I didn't know.

The clerk's voice dropped. "That blue-gray cloak seemed not of this world. There was something sinister about it. And about him. When I tried to sprinkle him with holy water, he ran. You would have thought that I was throwing poison. The priests said he belonged to the old religion. I think he was" — his voice fell to a whisper — "a demon."

For a few days I stayed close to the village. Then on St. Barnabas's Day, I resumed my gathering, filling a sack draped from my crutch. The summer had turned hot, so the midday bell found me stretched out on a familiar, maple-shaded rock, from which I could stare at the sky.

"Don't get up." The voice from behind startled me. I sat up and spun around to see a white-haired, white-bearded face wrinkled in a smile.

"You're the lame boy who's been taken in at the castle, aren't you?"

I breathed a sigh of relief. This was no assassin. I recognized the black-robed man I had seen talking to the Duke after the assassins' attack.

Nonetheless the smile and cheerful tone annoyed me. Being lame deserved more sympathy. It was trouble enough.

The robe he wore I took to be Benedictine, so I replied with respect, "Yes, sir. I visit the castle sometimes."

"Gathering, lad?"

"Tinder for the winter fires, sir — for the villagers."

"A clever system you've got there. Perhaps you'll gather for me."

Custom decreed that I do as he ask, which annoyed me more. Indicating my burdened sack, I said, "I have a full sack here and — "

"Later then. I'm in no hurry." He pointed with his left hand. "My hut's over that hill. I'll expect you this afternoon. I'll offer you something in return, too."

I should have consented silently. Instead I blurted out, "Can't you do your own gathering?" My village upbringing struggled against my castle training. "I'm sorry, sir. I meant to say, how do you usually get kindling?"

He nodded, his smile intact. "Oh, I find some sympathetic villager or traveler. I don't have the time, and it's a nuisance to do myself."

Using his left hand, he pulled his right arm from the pouch of his robe. The arm dropped lifelessly. He lifted his right sleeve to expose a scar twisting from the elbow to the shoulder. He returned the arm to its pouch, nodded a farewell, and left.

I dragged my bulging sack to one of my adopted mothers and asked about the stranger.

She paused from her gardening to thrust out her lower lip. "That's Garrad the hermit. Friend of the Duke. Related to the family in some way or another. Trained as a warrior when he was young. Studied in monasteries in the North. Don't know whether he's really a monk, though. Studied in the South, too, with some famous teacher."

"How did his arm get — ?" "He's a healer. Can't fix his own arm, though. Well, that's to be expected. It's useless, you know."

"I saw it."

"Vikings, they say. When he was in England. I've heard it was a Berserker."

"Berserker?"

"From the North. Vicious fighters. Like animals they fight. Until they kill or get killed." Her wrinkles deepened into a frown, and she shuddered. She let down the skirts of her robe, which she had hiked up to garden. "They let him keep the arm, though. I've heard they chop them off most times." She wiped her hands on the skirt. "If Garrad favors you, listen to him. He knows more about everything than anyone I know."

My curiosity overcame my annoyance — and I recalled the Duke's insistence that his friend, a hermit, could help me.

By dusk I had refilled the sack and presented it at the entrance to what appeared to be a massive rock.

The hermit flung open the door. "Cuin returned. With a full sack. You have my gratitude." Using his good left arm, he lifted the bag and placed it just inside the door. "My name, by the way, is Garrad."

He extended his left hand. I thought it strange for a grown man to offer a handshake to a boy, but I took it nonetheless. He smiled and drew me inside the dwelling.

The hut — for it was a hut built into the side of the hill — smelled of smoke and spices. It was as large as some houses in the village, more spacious than it appeared from the outside. Herbs hung in bunches from the ceiling. Jars, bowls, and pouches lined the shelves along one wall.

On a nearby table, I noticed books, pieces of parchment, and leather with Latin markings on them. I opened one of the books, but the hermit closed it. "Only with clean hands."

I nodded. Nearby, a sand-filled hourglass had almost run out. When I reached to turn it over, he said, "Leave it as it is, please."

"I'm sorry," I mumbled.

He smiled and patted my back. "Don't be concerned. It's the way with all new things. You'll get accustomed to this place in time. Then it will seem ordinary."

I stared up at him. This hermit was a nice man.

"Here," he said, patting a table-sized stone jutting from the middle of the room, "what do you think of this?"

I stared at it a moment. "Is it a table? It seems so high."

"It was here when I built the hut. It's been a companion ever since."

A stone as a companion seemed strange, but I said nothing. My attention was drawn to a robin limping around the northeast corner of the hut with one of its wings bound.

"Boneset," the hermit said. "I'm treating her with boneset. Diluted, of course." He watched me a moment. "Are you hungry?"

"Yes, sir."

"Garrad," he corrected me. "I'm not a knight or a noble. Please call me Garrad."

"Yes, sir — Garrad."

On a small wooden table near the fireplace, he laid out cups of an herbal brew I didn't recognize and a meal of greens.

As I ate, he talked about them. "You like these, good. They're more than nourishing. This fennel can stop cramps, if you know how to apply it. This parsley strengthens weak stomachs and stops coughs. The mint aids digestion and heals dog bites."

He paused and gazed at the fireplace for a moment. "You've heard about the heat?"

I had indeed heard the villagers' complain about the heat. Even travelers carried tales about it. "The stifling air," they said, "is causing sickness all over Normandy."

He squinted at me. "I visit the towns and abbeys when they need additional healers. With the heat, I should go this summer. If I had your help, I could leave earlier."

I stopped eating to stare at him. I knew nothing about healing, and I certainly did not look studious, as the priests often commented.

"I don't know how I can help, sir."

"Garrad," he corrected me again. "I'll train you." He pursed his lips. "And we'll visit villages and abbeys all over Normandy."

I pondered a moment. It was true that, with William, Arlette, and Edward gone, I had little to do. Certainly traveling and learning about healing appealed to me more than gathering dung. Besides, this man prepared good food.

The following morning, I arrived at the hut and listened for sounds inside. I heard nothing, so I squatted on a rock to wait.

As I studied the hut, I was surprised that I had not noticed it before. It was not far from the village.

On the other hand, it seemed to grow from the rocky hill behind it, which it resembled. A person could walk by and not spot it. From all sides but the front, it appeared to be one of many boulders among the trees. Even its windows, covered with oiled parchment, were hidden by twisting vines.

A low whistle interrupted my thoughts. It was followed by a call, almost lost in the morning breeze: "Cuin, over here."

I turned to see the hermit bent over a sandy patch of earth, his left hand caressing some pale green leaves and straw-colored flowers. "Come, we have a great deal to do."

I grabbed my crutch and hurried over to him. Dropping onto my knees, I reached for some heart-shaped leaves.

"Not those. They're wood sorrel, stickwort. It's the wrong phase of the moon to pick stickwort. Over here. I have already spoken to the spirits of these Carolina plants, which I have been cultivating for some time. They're thistles, named after Charlemagne, who received them from an angel to cure a plague. Come."

We collected herbs all morning. By the time the noon bell rang from the distant castle church, we had gathered over thirty different kinds, or so the hermit assured me. Returning to the hut, he hung some to dry and soaked others in brandy. Still others he began to blend with beeswax.

"With these we make salves. Put this one on the rock for me, please."

He showed me how to prepare powders, using the herbs that had already dried in the hut, while those that had been soaking in brandy and wine we would make into tinctures.

"We save the wine we pour off and blend it with brandy. A few sips of this will keep us healthy through the winter. And warm."

With every plant we prepared, he told me to repeat its name and mentioned many others: blessed thistle, yarrow also called soldier's wound wort, wormwood, rest harrow, bishop's wort, shepherd's purse, and St. John's wort.

Some were familiar, because the castle cooks and my village mothers used them. Many were foreign to me, though, and soon their names, the times to gather them, the ways they combined, and the ailments they healed began to swim in my head.

"Let's have something to eat," he said, and I smiled gratefully.

As we strode back into the forest to collect more herbs later, I squinted up at Garrad. "I never knew that healing was so complicated."

He patted my shoulder with his good hand. "Don't be concerned. As you use herbs over the years, they'll become easier to remember. I'll teach you an astrological system to organize all you need to know. Soon you'll even understand poisons."

I paused to shift my crutch. "Poisons?"

"Yes, some parts of plants can kill. I use hellebore roots to kill troublesome rats around the village, though not all rats are troublesome. And this mushroom" — he leaned over to pluck a yellowish plant from the base of a nearby elm — "is fatal for humans. If I ate this now, I'd be dead in a day. But remember the healer's rule, 'Beside the poison grows the antidote'."

"What's the antidote for that?" I pointed to the mushroom, afraid to touch it.

He shrugged. "This one's a mystery to everybody, as far as I know. There are poisons, as the saying goes, for which the only antidote is prayer."

We prepared remedies for several weeks, and Garrad showed me how to talk to each herb, asking its permission for use in healing. At first, I thought he was jesting or using a device to help me learn herbs, but he seemed serious and insisted that I "commune silently with the plant."

Then, if I had a scratch or bruise, he made one of the herbs I had communed with into a salve and applied it. If it was effective, he would say that now we knew for certain that this herb wanted to work with me.

He used the same procedure in preparing tinctures for many ailments, including indigestion — a foul-tasting mixture of mint, dandelion, and bitterwort. I seldom had trouble digesting anything, but I obliged him, so that the three would become my helpers.

He showed me how to apply remedies to animals, beginning with the broken-winged robin. We worked on her for several weeks — he insisted it was female, though I did not know how he knew — until she could fly again.

I also found a cat who had been scratched in a midnight fracas and a dog whose eyes had become red and runny. After I asked permission from the plants, we treated them with vervain poultices and fennel. Within a week, both had recovered, and I had two more herbal helpers.

"Now," Garrad said, "you need human patients, and Falaise is full of them."

Armed with sacks of salves, tinctures, and decoctions, we ventured into the village.

No one seemed surprised to see Garrad or to see me helping him. Everyone seemed to know him.

Marie, a young village widow who often took me in, assisted us as if she had been working with him for years.

I shrugged off my ignorance, assuming I had been in the castle whenever Garrad visited the village and so coincidentally had never met him. He was a hermit, after all.

We were soon busy with villagers' complaints, including those of their dogs, goats, and pigs. With both the human and nonhuman patients, I recalled more and more of what I learned, as Garrad had predicted.

The villagers in turn expressed their gratitude. We received, in addition to thanks, bread, wine, pastries, cloth for tunics, and, from William's grandfather, tanned leather for shoes. One of my adopted mothers gave us wheat cakes with honey.

At the last home we visited, though, I encountered my first deep gash. One of my village playmates had fallen against a stone, and his thigh had torn open.

I felt as if I would retch. Garrad assumed that a friend's pain bothered me, so he promptly administered a brandy-based mixture of crushed poppy seeds and mandrake, which induced sleep.

My face must have continued to reflect my distress.

Garrad glanced at me as he treated the wound. "Whatever illness you confront, just do what needs to be done. Focus on that. Concentrate. Make treating the injury like a prayer. Contact the herb and keep your whole mind on what it can do." He finished binding the wound. "In time, you'll find that you can even cut and lance, as the barber-surgeons do."

I shuddered and shook my head. I would rather try every poultice and tincture in the world than take a knife to flesh. I could not even tolerate the castle cooks slaughtering animals outside the kitchen.

Marie watched my face and then touched Garrad's good arm. "Cutting isn't likely to be one of Cuin's talents."

He rose and smiled at her and then me. "Perhaps not."

Back at the hut, Garrad instructed me to study the healing books he had, particularly those from the medical school at Salernum, south of the Alps. He had copied them while studying at a monastery there.

The books covered details of disease, health, diet, and body care. They also outlined surgical methods. Their teachings impressed me but did not persuade me that I could do surgery.

Midsummer gave way to August, and our time to leave approached. I had been so engrossed in healing that the terrors dominating my life a few months earlier seemed distant and dreamlike.

On the eve of St. Lawrence's Day, though, as I emerged later than usual from the forest onto the village road, I felt uneasy.

The sky darkened around me. Only a strip of sunset remained.

If I had counted the days in the week correctly, it was Friday. Unlucky Friday.

The road was empty, so I pressed home, my foot rested from the day's labors. The road dust and occasional grass clumps made the walk easy. The sky shifted from red to purple, fading toward black.

I was not far from the village when I heard footsteps. I glanced around, hoping to see a familiar villager.

Instead, a gray-robed figure strode behind me, its hooded head barely visible against the darkening sky. It was taller than any villager I knew.

A chill crept along my back. I thought I heard a voice. I disregarded custom and ignored it. Gripping my crutch tightly, I swung my legs more quickly toward the village.

The figure called out, clearly now, "Here, boy! Stop!"

The accent was not Norman. I pretended not to hear and quickened my pace even more.

Again, the figure cried, "You, boy! I want speech with you!"

The voice was now unmistakable. It belonged to the hooded Norwegian warrior in Rouen.

I limped faster. He might not be an assassin, but I had no desire to find out what he wanted.

The figure shouted more loudly, "Stop, you lame boy! Stop!"

With a shock, I heard the voice that had rung in my nightmares since the attack on William: the assassin calling for my death.

The killer and the Norwegian warrior in Rouen were the same man.

I heard rapid footfalls behind me. I threw aside my crutch and ran. My leg throbbed as it pounded against the road. My head and breath beat together. My chest heaved. Pain stabbed my foot.

The last curve to the village broke. Houses stood within a few yards. But a makeshift market, abandoned for supper, blocked the way.

A voice seemed to come from it, whispering, almost hissing: "Bakehouse woodbox."

I ducked under a cart and hurled myself around the first house. I skirted the backs of homes toward the bakehouse.

Leaping behind the bakehouse, I tore open the lid of its woodbox and hurled myself in.

I wriggled under the kindling, much of which I had collected myself. Holding my breath, I tensed every muscle into motionlessness.

Nothing. Then a voice. A second voice. Louder and louder.

The word "lame" rose again and again. The voices died down.

I remained unmoving. Long minutes passed as I heard only my own breathing.

The lid of the woodbox flew open. I gasped.

"You can come out now. He's gone." The grinning, red face of Walter, one of my adopted fathers, peered down at me. "You're lucky that I was the only person who saw you jump in here. What did you do to that stranger, Cuin? Rob him?"

He lifted me out. I shook so badly and my foot hurt so much that he picked me up to carry me.

He frowned as I told him that the attacker was a Northern warrior who had followed me from Rouen.

He put me down. "I thought you were staying with the widow Marie this week. What were you doing in the forest so late?"

I swallowed against a parched throat. "Working with the hermit."

"Then we're going back to his hut. It's the best place for you to hide. I'll tell Marie. Get on my back. We'll find your crutch as we go."

When we reached the hut, I discovered that Walter, too — though he had not been someone we had healed during our village visits — knew Garrad well. He told me to repeat my story.

As I did, Garrad frowned. When I finished, he touched my shoulder. "Are you all right?"

"I'm frightened, and my foot hurts."

He laid a straw bed in a corner. "Lie down here."

Then he and Walter stepped outside the door. I heard their voices humming but could not make out what they were saying.

The only word I recognized was "Magnus." I didn't know anyone named Magnus.

Garrad slipped back inside the door and dropped the wooden bar into its holders.

"This may not be necessary," he said. I felt safer, though. "Now let's tend to you."

He rubbed arnica salve on my foot and fed me a tea of all-heal.

I dropped my head onto the straw-filled mat and fell asleep immediately.

My dreams, though, were invaded by the assassin's voice and menacing shape. Several times I awoke, sweating and crying.

Each time Garrad was leaning over me, his good hand on my head. "It's all right. Go back to sleep."

When the morning breeze slipped through the window near me, carrying with it the first bell from the castle church, I felt relieved.

Over breakfast, I asked Garrad, "Why does that warrior want to kill me? All the way from Norway. The priests say it's very far. I don't know anyone far away. Duke Robert says Northerners want to kill all of us. Why?"

"What Robert means is that Northern warriors may raid here again as they did in the last century. That's how Normans came to be here. Do you know the history?"

The priests had told me, but such stories didn't always stay with me.

He continued, "Norwegian and Danish warriors — the villagers call them Vikings — attacked this region about a hundred years ago. They were so vicious that the King in Paris feared they would kill everyone in his realm. To prevent that, the King made a pact with one of the Viking leaders, a man named Rollo."

"Is that a Northern name?"

"No, it's what the French King called him. Rolf was his Northern name. In return for land, Rollo, or Rolf, and his men agreed to protect the rest of France from other Northern raiders. That's how Rollo became the first Duke of the land we now live in — the land of the Northmen, Normandy."

"Do you mean that William's father is a Norwegian or a Dane?"

"Yes. All of us are, at least partly. You are. I am."

"Do you mean I'm the same as the warrior who wants to kill me?"

"Not exactly. Some of us have different parents." He hesitated a long time. "Many other people have come to live in Normandy: English Saxons, Lombards from the South, and Franks from the East as well as Norwegians and Danes. But yes, you're a Northerner, too."

"Then why do they want to kill us?"

"It's not that they want to kill us. It's that the Northern kings have become strong enough to attack Normandy again. They already rule most of England, which is why Prince Edward is here."

"Why?"

"You don't know that story, either?"

"I think that Edward told me, but …"

He nodded. "I understand. Edward talks a great deal, and it's hard to recall everything he says. Well, Edward's father was once the Saxon king of England. The Danes overthrew his father and forced Edward and his brother to flee. Their mother was Norman, you see, the sister of William's grandfather. So Edward and his brother were welcome here."

"Where's Edward's mother? Was she killed?"

"No, she stayed in England."

"In England? With the Danes? Why?"

"It's too long a story for now. All you need to know is that the Danes control England, and they wish to control Normandy. The Norwegian king, Magnus, may wish to help them."

"Magnus? I heard that name last night when you and Walter …"

"Yes, we considered the possibility that the man after you is an assassin sent by King Magnus of Norway."

"Why? Why would this King want to kill me? I don't know him. I'm not a noble."

He dropped his head and said slowly, "I don't know."

I felt more afraid.

Then I remembered the voice, telling me to go to the bakehouse, the same voice that had advised me every time the assassin appeared.

"Garrad, do you ever hear voices talking to you when no one is around?"

"I do not, although I have heard of those who do. The ancient Greek philosopher Socrates did."

"Did his voice try to help him?"

"No, it simply warned him when he was about to do something dangerous. Why? Have you heard voices?"

"I'm not sure. I don't know whether I talk to myself … but some voice seems to offer help when I'm in trouble."

"That's good."

"Yes, it seems to be. I don't know what the voice is or where it comes from, though … or whether I will need it again."

He paused for a long time, staring at me, and then put his left hand on my arm. "Don't be concerned. Whoever this warrior is, whatever he wants, he will not find you. We'll pack today, leave tomorrow, and stay away until autumn. That will put him off your track. By the time the leaves fall, he'll be back in Norway fishing."

"I hope so."

By noon the next day, we had strapped our packs to a small donkey Garrad had borrowed from the castle stables. We had also covered the outside of the hut with branches and moss.

Slipping through the forest, we wound our way around Falaise, hidden from the village and castle and headed west.

For over a week, we traveled from one village to the next. Garrad walked tirelessly, but I often perched on the donkey to rest. With this method — and extra padding on my crutch — I gradually became accustomed to walking longer distances. An arnica wrap, which I used daily now, also strengthened my foot.

We healed wherever we were needed, which was almost everywhere. The summer's heat had created illness in Western Normandy, as it had done in Falaise.

Almost everyone knew Garrad. He introduced me to more monks, merchants, farmers, and knights than I could ever remember.

To my surprise, even abbots and barons — lords of great abbeys and manors — treated us as friends. Sickness, Garrad said, blurred distinctions of rank.

Sometimes I caught some of them, especially the monks, staring at me.

"They're all nice," I said as we pulled the donkey out of Domfront one morning. "Even to me."

Garrad laughed, though I didn't know why. "Yes," he eventually said, "even to you."

I noticed the upside-down crosses embroidered on the tunics of Western nobles. They reminded me of similar crosses I had seen on Western tunics in Rouen, which had puzzled me. I asked Garrad about them.

"What appears to be an upside-down cross is Thor's hammer," he replied.

"I thought the Western nobles wanted to kill William. They seem too polite to kill anyone."

"Yes, don't they? Well, the politeness comes from the cathedral schools, which have made inroads here despite the old religion. The schools have been growing since William's grandfather founded them, and the teachers — mostly Lombards from the South — have tried to inspire the nobles to stop squabbling. As you say, the teaching shows in the barons' manners. Nonetheless, they would rather rule their territories alone than answer to anyone, including William if he becomes Duke."

"According to the priests, the Western barons must answer to King Henry in Paris, though. If William were killed, wouldn't the King name someone else Duke? William might be a better Duke than anyone the King chooses. Why don't the nobles think of that? It might be better for them to leave William alone."

Garrad smiled broadly. "You reason like a diplomat. The priests would approve. The Western nobles still cling to the old religion, and they believe more in war than in diplomacy."

"The old religion tells them to make war?"

"It admires warriors."

"So do the priests."

He laughed. "That's true. I'll just say that the Northern religions admire warriors more. Besides, I suspect that there's more to this than just the Northern religions. There are also the Northern kings."

"What do they have to do with Norman barons?"

"More than it may appear. I believe that if the King of either Denmark or Norway gets a foothold in Normandy, he will conquer it and then move on Paris. From Rouen and Paris, he would strike west into the Empire and even south over the Alps."

I looked at him blankly.

"That would mean," he said, "that the Northerners would rule our world."

I thought of the Norwegian warrior chasing me. "That would be bad."

"Northerners are like Normans — some are good, some are not. However, I would not want the Northern religion's love of war to replace the teachings of the Healer. Right now, many Northerners are Christians. Religious Christians, I mean. That doesn't stop war, but it does curtail it."

"Are there other kinds of Christians who are not religious?"

"I think that's a long conversation. Let's just say that the Northern Kings are a threat. They're likely to be a threat for years. At the same time, the Holy Roman Empire, which is barely Christian, threatens us immediately."

"Will it be a threat for years, too?"

He smiled at me. "That's a good question for one so young. Yes, for many years."

To my relief, we saw no sign of the assassin. Garrad's assurances that even a Northern warrior could not find us seemed to be true.

Using extra caution, though, we traveled off the road, making our way through woodlands.

Garrad joked about finding our own fords across streams and rivers. "We'll pay fewer tolls, since the trees don't mind if we walk through them. That's the advantage of traveling with a donkey. A cart or wagon would tie us to the roads."

Traveling in the forest, though, made me anxious. We had slept mostly in villages or monasteries, so the first night we slept deep in the woods, I felt afraid.

"The priests say the forest is the home of the devil."

"The forest protects us," Garrad replied. "Forest sounds tell us whether we're being followed or not. They're our watchmen."

I peered anxiously at the massive, darkened trunks and branches all around us, their leaves blocking the stars.

He saw my look. "All right. I'll tell you which birds and insects to listen for. Are you paying attention?"

I nodded but continued to glance from side to side. Garrad began teaching me, but I heard little of what he said. In the days that followed, he had to repeat the lessons many times.

One evening, he asked me to sit with my back against a tree. "Recall how you contact plants. Do the same with this tree. Let yourself go into it. Feel its bark as if it is your skin and its sap as if it is your blood. Feel the wind move in the branches as if it is moving in your hair. Feel the leaves at the end of your fingertips."

Imagining myself as a tree was fun, so I had little trouble imagining that I was becoming the tree.

"Now," Garrad said, "whenever you're in a forest, remember what it's like to be a tree. Speak with the trees you meet. Ask permission to walk through their forests. Find out what they are feeling. You'll feel safer."

He was right.

By the time I was beginning to feel at ease in the forest, we had reached the ocean. Before us was the monastery on Mont St. Michel, surrounded by the sea.

My mouth fell open. I had seen the ocean only from a distance when we were in Avranches. Avranches, though, sat on an inlet on Normandy's western coast. As a result, the ocean was, as the monk who accompanied me noted, "well behaved." From Avranches, the calm of sky and sea was interrupted only by the island mountain, Mont St. Michel, and its islet, Tombelaine, far in the distance.

Here, however, far south of Avranches, Mont St. Michel loomed before us, and the ocean was not calm. The sea leaped in front of me like the master of the world. Whipped by storm winds, waves crashed against the mountain and its monastery.

The storm also attacked Tombelaine. As the waves hit the islet, arcs of water hurled themselves into the sky, which shrieked as if the water were wounding it.

Huddled in a shelter built for pilgrims en route to the abbey, I slid closer to Garrad.

Garrad raised his voice above the storm. "Don't be concerned. We'll sit the storm out here today. As for the monastery, it is safe. Mont St. Michel possesses a force from another world. No sea storm can conquer it. It has been invaded only once — by a fallen angel."

Against the black clouds, the mountain jutted upward. The abbey's stone walls thrust above the mount, unmoved by the storm. Gradually, as we watched, the sea abandoned its assault.

"We'll arrive on an auspicious day, as I hoped," Garrad said, as we sat near the fire that evening.

We stared from the shelter at the now silent bay, which drowned our passage to Mont St. Michel until the tide changed the next morning.

I pulled my blanket over my head. "Why is tomorrow auspicious?"

"It's St. Aubert's Day."

"Is there a story behind St. Aubert's Day?" I asked, hopefully.

"Yes."

"Good." I leaned back against the donkey, who huffed at me and then fell back to sleep.

"In ancient times," Garrad began, "the forest of Scissy covered this entire bay." He stretched his good arm out. "There wasn't any water here at all. Then, three hundred years ago, the archangel Michael appeared three times to St. Aubert, Bishop of Avranches. Each time, the archangel commanded the Bishop to build a sanctuary on the mountain, which in those days was called Mont Tombe."

"That's why the little island is called Tombelaine?"

"Yes, very good. In those days, because there was no water yet, Tombelaine was a small mountain sitting in the forest. So St. Aubert decided he would build a sanctuary. Of course, he needed holy relics to be housed there. So he sent emissaries south over the Alps to buy some. By the time the emissaries returned, the forest had vanished. Only Mont Tombe and Tombelaine remained, but now both stood in the middle of a bay."

"Where did the forest go?"

"Nowhere. It was still there. Instead of waiting for the men to clear the forest, though, the archangel had moved the sea."

I gazed at the mountain, silhouetted against a sky turning an ever deeper blue. The lights of the abbey shone from the mountain and reflected in the water.

"How can an archangel move a sea?"

Garrad laughed and continued, "About seventy years ago, William's grandfather established a Benedictine monastery on the mountain. He brought monks here from St. Wandrille and Monte Cassino. The older buildings here were repaired, and new ones added, but it was Duke Robert's brother, Richard, who initiated the building going on now. We'll see building tomorrow, even on St. Aubert's day, and since we'll have much to see, we should sleep now."

That night, I dreamed about William and his father, Duke Robert. They stood next to each other and glanced over their shoulders at a shadowy figure behind them. I could not see who it was.

Suddenly, a dragon head appeared, its voice hissing softly, almost gently, whispering "Michael." I was startled and almost afraid. Then I recognized the voice. It was the one that had warned me to hide under the wine barrels and in the bakehouse woodbox.

I awoke briefly and decided that I would tell no one that I thought a dragon was talking to me in both my dreams and my everyday life. Even to me, that sounded odd.

The next morning, we crossed the sandbar at low tide and climbed the mount's tree-lined slopes. Garrad pulled the donkey up the steep incline, while I picked my way with my crutch.

Even as I concentrated on the stones in the road, though, I could hear shouting, hammering, and sawing. The familiar smells of stone dust and hewn wood drifted toward us. The festivities of St. Aubert's Day had not slowed the early-morning work.

We passed through the monastery gate to see monks and builders — their black robes and brown tunics pulled through their belts — bent over wood, stone, and tile.

I saw common laborers, too, their plain tunics hanging over dusty leggings and shoes. They carried lead gutters and roof pieces up wooden scaffolding, which encased much of the abbey.

Dominating the work scene near the building was a giant crane, mounted on a wooden platform. Its arm reached along one wall and dangled a rope to the ground. As I stared at it, two men lashed a stack of roof stones to it. They shouted to the crane operator outside the wall.

Garrad, abandoning the donkey, hurried me up the steps to look over the wall. We arrived just in time to see the crane operator crack his whip over two oxen. The oxen heaved forward, and the windlass, around which the crane line was wrapped, creaked and began to turn. The crane line tightened, and the roof stones rose.

A tall man in a black cowled robe strode toward us. I took half a step behind Garrad.

"It's the Abbot," Garrad said.

The Abbot greeted Garrad warmly. "I'm delighted to see you again, my son. It's been too long since your last visit, and we can use your help." He leaned around Garrad. "Who's this?"

"A fellow Falaise villager and helper of mine. His name is Cuin."

"Greetings, young helper." The Abbot smiled at me and turned back to Garrad. "I must tell you that I've received a letter from our friend, Lanfranc. He is well, but Pavia is not. Another rebellion. I have written to tell him he should come north. He would be a splendid teacher here."

"Lanfranc is a teacher I studied with in the South," Garrad said to me. "The most famous teacher in all Lombardy. He lives in a Southern town called Pavia."

To the Abbot he said, "I hope he does come north. I invited him to do so myself some years ago, because I agree that his teaching would be well received here."

Garrad leaned forward to whisper something to the Abbot, who turned to me, his eyebrows raised.

"Well, then, you two will dine with us this afternoon and sit in the place of honor next to me. We're having a special meal, since it's St. Aubert's Day."

Whether Garrad had described our hunger or my appetite, I did not know, but I was grateful.

The afternoon meal was indeed special, full of meat and soups, vegetables and breads. Having sat through a special noon High Mass, running longer than the usual two hours to commemorate works of St. Aubert, the monks had eagerly taken their places at the dining hall's long table.

With the elaborate meal laid out before them, they smiled at their plates. I knew monks did not smile at their plates usually, both because they were not supposed to and because they had little reason to.

Yet even the Abbot glancing from between the two candles that marked his place at the head of the table, beamed at his charges and his food.

Of course, he and the brothers obeyed the Benedictine rule of silence throughout the meal, with one monk reading from the Psalter and reciting the life of St. Aubert. My Latin was good enough for me to hear him confirm what Garrad had told me about the saint.

When the meal ended, the Abbot leaned toward me. "Have you eaten enough, my son?"

I politely replied yes.

"There is more to come, though," he said. "It is St. Aubert's Day."

The serving monk put in front of each of us a small loaf of bread, laced with cinnamon and raisins. As I knew only too well from the meals at Rouen, cinnamon was costly and usually reserved for nobles. Like the brothers, I too now smiled at my plate.

The Abbot offered a prayer to St. Aubert, while the smell of cinnamon filled my nostrils. When he finished, the brothers intoned an "amen," and I blurted out, "The Lord bless St. Aubert."

The Abbot peered at me and smiled. "You may eat."

As I ate, slowly and happily, the Abbot glanced at me often.

When I had finished eating, he asked, "Do you know how the abbey and the mountain got their name?"

Finishing a last swallow, I replied, "Garrad has told me some of their history, Father."

"Do you know that it was here that the archangel Michael — St. Michael, we call him — fought Lucifer?"

"Is that why he wanted a sanctuary built here?"

The Abbot nodded. "You see, in the beginning, Lucifer was the governor of the heavens, seated right next to God, as you are to me now."

I widened my eyes. "Was he?"

"Yes, and the Lord commanded that no member of the heavenly court sit on the divine throne, even Lucifer the governor. One day when the Lord was absent, Lucifer, swollen with pride, sat down on the throne. St. Michael, angered at this audacity, commanded Lucifer to remove himself. Lucifer refused. So the archangel gathered his forces and drove Lucifer and his cohorts into the darkness, where the once-governor of the heavens became the ruler of Hell, Satan as he is called now."

The Abbot made the sign of the cross, as did all the monks. I made the sign too.

The Abbot continued, "There was an ancient castle on this mountain, long before an abbey ever stood here. In his battle, St. Michael lured Lucifer into it. Lucifer had lost his wings in the fighting, and he thought the castle would provide a refuge. St. Michael, though, boarded all the doors and windows. Realizing that he was trapped, Lucifer fled to the top of the castle and leaped off it, breaking his leg. That is why, to this day, the devil limps."

The news dismayed me. "He limps?"

The Abbot exchanged looks with Garrad. "Oh, but Satan's limp differs entirely from yours. Do you know how boys like you come to limp?"

I shook my head.

The Abbot took my chin, lifted my head, and pointed upward. "In Heaven, all who now limp were the trusted and beloved servants of God. When you left to be born, the Lord did not wish to part with you, so He grabbed you by the foot to hold you back. In the end, He reluctantly let you go to do your earthly service, but His mark remains. Every time you limp, you show how valued you were in the service of God."

I looked at Garrad, who nodded solemnly. I smiled at the Abbot.

"Now, my young friend," he said, "would you enjoy a tour of the abbey?"

"Oh, yes, Father. Thank you." I glanced at Garrad. "I usually help with the healing, though."

Garrad waved me on. "You should see the abbey. Take your healing sack with you in the event that you're needed, but enjoy the abbey."

The Abbot led me first through the church and its side chapels, which formed the bases for the church's transepts.

Carpenters were finishing the timber roofs spanning the stone walls. In the nave, stone was being cut, and the hammers rang against wedges. The noise hurt my ears, while the dust caught in my mouth and nose.

The Abbot seemed not to notice. "Those two short aisles," he shouted, pointing toward the western side of the nave, "are over a hundred years old. We've shored up the roof timbers, but the pillars remain untouched."

I tried to imagine how old the massive stone pillars must be, but I could not think back a hundred years.

"Now we shall see something even older."

He escorted me away from the noise, for which I was grateful. We descended a flight of stone steps into a rectangular, beamed building, which served both as the monks' exercise gallery and cloister. It smelled of fennel and mint, the leaves of which had been sprinkled on the floor to sweeten the air.

The Abbot greeted several monks and introduced me. Then he guided me through a door at the far end of the room.

"This leads down to the kitchens," he said, pointing at a stairway in front on us, and indeed, I could smell garlic and onion drifting up the steps.

To my regret, we took a different stairway to our left, dropping down slowly to an arched stone doorway.

The Abbot swung open a heavy wooden door, its crosspieces chinked and weathered. Behind the door was a crypt. My eyes gradually adjusted to its darkness, sliced at intervals by the light streaming in the narrow windows. Through them, I could glimpse the sea and sky.

In front of me, round pillars supported ribbed stone arches that crisscrossed the entire ceiling. Straw beds had been placed around the pillars and along the walls. The room was scented with rosemary.

"This crypt serves as our almshouse. It's also a hundred years old and more, though some of its stones — those in the outer wall, we believe — come from the chapels built here under the protection of St. Stephen. Over five hundred years ago."

I gaped at the unimaginably old rock.

"These stones," he said, pointing, "came from the old castle, the castle in which the archangel fought the devil thousands of years ago."

Staring at the stones, I hobbled over to them. I stretched out my hand to touch them.

"One of those may have been trodden on by St. Michael himself. Or Lucifer."

I drew my hand back. The Abbot smiled and led me to the chapels on the other side of the church.

During the entire afternoon, the only healing I did was pouring some pennywort juice in the ear of a monk with an earache and helping the abbey's infirmarian, who joined us in our walk, apply sassafras oil to the heads of several brothers with lice.

In one case — "particularly resistant," the infirmarian said — I applied an ointment Garrad and I had made from stavesacre seeds.

The Abbot added a sprinkling of holy water from a vial in his robe pocket and forgave the brothers "whatever sins had led to these judgments from God."

Garrad was nowhere to be seen.

The Abbot then excused himself, and I remained, talking with the infirmarian, an aged, pleasant-faced man with long, gnarled hands. We walked back up to the stone terrace.

I stared out across the sea. "It's safe here, isn't it?"

The infirmarian ran a hand over his tonsure. "Yes, it is. It always has been. Even during the Northern raids, no Viking warriors could get inside. If the raids begin again, this will be the safest place in Normandy."

"How did you get to be a monk here?"

"I was trained from childhood. I studied here after my parents were killed in a Northern raid."

"My parents are dead, too."

"I'm sorry." He put a long hand on my shoulder. "You have a fine friend in Garrad, though. There are few like him in the land."

"He's a nice man."

We fell silent, and then I asked, "Do you think the Northern raids will start again?"

He breathed in deeply. "From what the Abbot says, if either Normandy or England has weak leaders, the Kings of the North will attack. Of course, there is always a lingering fear of Hardraada's return to Norway. That would be terrible for us all, so I pray that he will remain in the South, in Byzantium."

"Who is Hardraada?"

"Hardraada is the name given to a Northern warrior who fights now for the Eastern Empire in Byzantium, where he has built a reputation for cleverness and ferocity. Even pilgrims from the East carry tales of him. He's in the line of the Kings of Norway, and if he ever returns, the North will again be dangerous to us in the South."

By suppertime, Garrad appeared but did not say what he had been doing. The Abbot thanked him for his help.

"You have aided us often," the Abbot said, "and we have offered you little."

"Fine meals and good company are more than ample thanks."

"God sees your work," the Abbot said. "Nonetheless, you shall have more tangible thanks, especially since it is St. Aubert's Day." He handed Garrad a small book. "I copied it myself several years ago."

From the way Garrad thanked him, it seemed that the book was more valuable than bread with cinnamon and raisins.

"All books are valuable," Garrad said, as we settled into our straw beds in the guesthouse that night. "This must have taken the Abbot months to copy."

"What is it?"

"A fine philosophical work by Boethius, the ancient philosopher. It's what he wrote during the time he spent in prison for crimes he did not commit. It's the last book he ever wrote."

"Why?"

"Like too many brave thinkers, he was tortured and executed. This book served as his last friend. He called it 'The Consolation of Philosophy.'"

We left the security of Mont St. Michel the next morning at low tide. I was genuinely sorry when the mountain disappeared beneath the trees that closed behind us.

As we traveled north along the western coast of Normandy and then struck eastward, I realized that many new farms had been cleared. Some villages were so new that Garrad was unknown, which made me anxious.

Worse, in the villages that clung to the Northern religion, I noticed shrines to Thor and Odin situated in oak groves. I imagined evil spirits lurking there, waiting to devour small, limping Christians.

Apparently fearless, Garrad introduced himself to everyone. I met settlers who had come from Brittany, Maine, France, Anjou, and Lombardy, south of the Alps, all drawn by the reputations of the Norman dukes as fair rulers.

One recent settler, having been a pilgrim for years, raised bushy eyebrows when he heard that Garrad and I were from Falaise. "Do you know Duke Robert?"

When Garrad said we did, the man became animated. "I saw him in the Holy Land. What a man! I liked him very much. He and his men were offering gifts everywhere."

I glanced up at Garrad

He seemed unmoved by the news. He only said to the former pilgrim, "Could you tell how he was faring?"

"He and his men seemed healthy, though no doubt dirtier than when you last saw them." The man smiled.

"Did you discover where he was going?"

"He had been to Jerusalem and was traveling north again, headed for Toulouse, he said. That destination confused me, I must confess. Toulouse is on the pilgrim route to St. James in Compostela, but Duke Robert said he had no interest in St. James. Why would he want to go to Toulouse and not go on to Compostela?"

Garrad turned to go. "I don't know. Thank you for your information, and we wish you good farming here."

When the man was out of earshot, I asked Garrad about Duke Robert going to the south of France.

"Yes, this is a conversation we would have sooner or later. Now is a good time."

I sat down, expecting another good story, even though Garrad looked more serious than he did when preparing to tell stories.

"You already know that Normandy faces a threat from the Northern kings. You also know that in some way, you are involved in that threat. How, we do not know, but someone wants you dead, and that someone seems to be from the North."

I was startled to hear him put this so bluntly.

"There is an even greater threat from the South — from the Church. To be specific, from the Pope."

"The Holy Father?"

"There is little fatherly about most Popes and even less holy. I say the Pope, because a dangerous force, a small group of individuals, controls the papacy for their own ends. End, I should say. That end is a Holy Roman Empire that is a return of the old, aggressive Roman Empire."

"These men behind the Pope want the Church to become an empire, like Rome? But — it's a church."

"The Christian Church as a religion is a church, yes. We see this religious church doing good work: stopping animal and human sacrifice, limiting war, reducing crime, spreading cathedral schools. However, the papacy as a political tool and the Holy Roman Empire as an empire are not religious in this sense."

"The Pope is not religious?"

Garrad smiled. "All right, let me rephrase that: whatever the character of the sitting Pope, the power behind the papacy is bent on empire. On amassing power. That power began to grow with Charlemagne converting by force, by the sword, where necessary, and by deceit where force failed. When the Millennium came — just over three decades ago — and the Savior did not return, the Church powers assumed that their empire would be the Second Coming, that the Church would take over the world within the next thousand years."

I could scarcely understand what I was hearing. "The spread of Christianity is not because of ..."

"Its message of hope and salvation? Is that what the priests teach you?"

"Yes. It isn't true?"

"It is, and it isn't. A reforming religion can spread naturally, growing because people see its potential and its saving force. An empire can hide behind that religion just by taking its name and then spread its power by force."

"So, that is what the powers behind the Holy Roman Empire ... and Pope Benedict ... are doing now?"

"For some time, we have suspected that the old powers — old families who trace themselves back to the Roman Empire — hide behind the religion and push themselves forward. Since the Millennium, they have become more open. They install whatever Pope they want, move one out, move another one in, hoping for the Pope who will take their orders or share their goals of empire. The sitting Pope now is particularly violent and venal — and dangerous."

"The Savior ...?"

"They have reinterpreted the return of the Savior as their own growing power, the power of an empire. A power that will rule the earth in a thousand years. Rule it absolutely and completely."

"These men want to take over the whole world? Using a religion?"

"It would be more accurate to say 'hiding behind a religion.' These old powers intend to take over the whole earth, using a Roman-style empire run by absolute tyrants. Even now, there are towns and cities where bishops and archbishops rule as absolute monarchs."

"How do we fit into this? The Normans?"

"The old Roman Empire includes what we call the land of the Normans. There are Normans, as you know, in southern Italy as well as here. So Normans attract the attention of the Holy Roman Empire and the Pope. The powers behind these two want an empire that spreads from Italy through Normandy. As a result, all rulers in these realms, rulers such as Duke Robert, must be controlled or eliminated."

"Killed?"

"Killing is not a problem for an empire. Destruction is an empire's definition of power."

"So Duke Robert …?"

"Robert will not capitulate to the Pope or the Holy Roman Empire — as many in the North will not — but when the attacks on William began, he announced to the world that he would give up his position and go on a pilgrimage."

"Hoping that would end the attacks on William?"

"Hoping that the threat from the South would stop long enough for us to deal with the threat from the North."

I shook my head. "I had no idea that Normandy was …"

"In such danger? We stand between two threats. If Normandy is to survive, we need to find ways to deal with both … and keep William and you alive."

That night I dreamed that Duke Robert stood next to a small woman I did not recognize. She was crying and pointing to a child behind her who seemed bent over. Above the child was the dragon's head. It stared at me for a long time and whispered something I could not hear.

As we continued our healing work, most Western Normans greeted us with blessings of Odin. They even offered, as payments for healing, amulets of Thor's hammer, which hung around their necks.

I recoiled from these at first, but Garrad accepted them.

If any villager noticed my reaction, Garrad said, "Please excuse my apprentice. He's shy." To me he said, "Don't be concerned. Remember, these are merely upside-down crosses. To these people, they have great significance, deep meaning."

I pondered what he had said. I also realized for the first time that Garrad referred to me as his apprentice. I had not thought of myself as an apprentice, since I had made no formal declaration nor signed any contract. I was his apprentice, though, in spite of that, and I liked it. A healer's apprentice.

Especially while the problems we encountered were limited to scratches, burns, stomach trouble, and sleeplessness.

At the next monastery we visited, however — one of the newer, smaller ones — several monks were being bled. Garrad had to lead me outside the infirmary.

I leaned against a tree.

"Breathe deeply," he said.

I swallowed hard. "What are they doing?"

"It's what I was doing at Mont St. Michel. The monks submit to bleeding twice a year, sometimes more. It cleanses them of wastes."

I grimaced.

"It's not as bad as you think. They must tolerate the ordeal, it's true. Many monks, though — former knights or mercenaries — have suffered worse. Besides, they rest a week in the infirmary. They can converse with the friends who recuperate with them."

That seemed small compensation to me.

"Remember, the daily schedule here is demanding. A church floor can be cold when you kneel on it in the middle of the night. The work — tending the fields, bringing in wood, carrying water, putting up all the new buildings we've seen — is hard. A little rest, for whatever reason, is welcome." He shook his head. "Besides, most of these monks are not good builders."

This was particularly true at Bec. Bec Abbey, not far from Brionne, was new and "particularly squalid," in Garrad's words.

"It holds ragged but pious monks whom St. Benedict himself would have admired. Here you will find real religious Christians, not empire builders. In fact, these men can't build much of anything."

When we arrived, the sad-faced Abbot asked us to bleed his monks. "I don't have an infirmary yet," he said, "nor an infirmarian. If the brothers become ill, I simply let them rest in their huts until God forgives their transgressions."

My eyes followed the wave of his hand toward the cluster of hovels. Garrad was certainly right about the poor building skills. Even I could see that the way the wood overlapped, from the bottom up rather than the top down, encouraged rain to leak in rather than run off.

Worse, the walls had barely any sod piled against them to keep out cold or heat. The few huts that had been sodden were falling apart. The straight wooden walls made the sod topple away from the buildings in bad weather.

Garrad agreed to do the bleeding. As usual, I asked whether I could be taken to the other sick monks.

"Despite his youth, Cuin is a good healer," Garrad said.

"I don't doubt it. Wouldn't our Lord have been a healer as a child?"

The Abbot — his name was Herluin — showed me the modest community. One hut served as a rough church, another a dining hall. A bakehouse site was being cleared.

He apologized for the shabbiness of the buildings. "My brothers and I were knights, not builders, but the Lord has provided for us."

I tried to be polite. "The huts seem fine ... for now."

The Abbot smiled at me and led me into one. Inside lay a monk who complained of fever and dizziness.

Abbot Herluin said to him, "God has sent a child angel to heal you."

I thought my character had been exaggerated, but I reached inside my leather sack, determined to prove my abilities.

The hut was unlit and dank. I spread mint leaves around and opened the door for light and air. A sweet-smelling forest breeze drifted in as I applied eucalyptus salve to the monk's chest and fed him a decoction of feverfew, boneset, and yarrow.

"It's pleasant here," I said.

"Ah, yes, the forest and the stream are charming," the Abbot replied. "Count Gilbert was kind to give us such lovely land."

Unusually kind, I thought. Except for Mont St. Michel, Brionne Forest was the most beautiful abbey setting I had seen. Garrad and I had hiked along the stream called Bec, from which the monastery took its name, on our way to the abbey. It was almost magically beautiful.

Situating huts in Bec's valley, though, guaranteed dampness, Garrad had remarked as we approached the monastery. The dampness contributed to the sicknesses the knight-monks suffered.

Garrad still had not finished his chore, so I asked, "Are there any other ailing monks, even with minor complaints?"

Abbot Herluin hesitated. "There is one."

We made our way through the trees to a lone hut where a tall man sprawled across his cot. On his upper back were long, once-bleeding welts. I winced at them.

They didn't seem minor, and I felt my stomach become queasy. I recalled Garrad's instructions to focus on my task, so I focused.

"What sun sign were you born under, brother?" I asked him.

"The sign of the Lion," he said.

I nodded. "Good. For you and these wounds, I will use rue and chamomile, which are ruled by the Sun and Leo."

I bathed the wounds with rue and scattered what was left of it — since it was particularly strong smelling — around the hut. Then I spread a comfrey and chamomile salve on the welts.

"How did he get these?" I whispered.

"Self-flagellation," Abbot Herluin replied.

I did not understand.

"To atone for his sins, he beat himself."

Frowning, I rose and spoke to the monk in my most adult voice. "You must not do that again."

As we climbed out of Bec's valley, Garrad told me that Count Gilbert, the lord of Brionne Castle, had indeed chartered the lands to the abbey.

Not as easily as the Abbot implied, though.

A formidable knight before he was an Abbot, Herluin had been sworn to Count Gilbert. After he received a vision from God, though, he had asked to be released from his vow.

Initially, Gilbert simply refused to lose his best fighter. Herluin responded by appearing at court in a villager's tunic astride a donkey. His fellow knights ridiculed him.

The count was humiliated and then infuriated. He joined in insulting Herluin, hoping the knight would abandon his peasant antics.

Herluin bore every gibe in silence.

Gilbert released him from service.

Herluin then set out to become a monk at one of the many local monasteries. To his amazement, abbey after abbey disregarded the Rule of St. Benedict. The monks behaved as ordinary villagers might, or worse, as courtiers did. Twice Herluin was beaten, driven away by the very brothers he wished to join.

"One night, he was about to give up becoming a monk. He would be a hermit. A fine choice, of course." Garrad grinned. "He stopped in an abbey church to pray. One of the brothers knelt there, praying and weeping. Herluin bowed down behind him and began praying himself. The two of them, Herluin's monks tell me, prayed on their knees in that little church all night. When Herluin left the next morning, the monk was still there. So Herluin decided that there were men who needed a place to retreat for prayer, a refuge from the world when it became hard. When Count Gilbert heard the story, he consented to give Herluin land for his abbey."

During the remaining days and nights on the road, Garrad decided — abruptly, I thought — to teach me the Northern tongues of Denmark and Norway as well as the four Saxon dialects of England.

"It's not as difficult an exercise as it may sound. Danish is the basic Northern language. Though the Norwegian and Icelandic versions are somewhat different, the Danes have ruled the North for such a long time that their language is universal there." Patting the donkey, he said, "We have talked about the Northern Empire that may spread even into Normandy. That empire is ruled by the Danes."

"Why should I learn these languages?"

"They're not difficult. In practice, since even the English tongues resemble the Danish, you're really learning only one language with variations."

"I don't mind learning a language, easy or not. I like learning languages. But why do I need to learn this one at all?"

"Well, you may travel beyond Normandy. The priests have taught you Latin, so you won't have trouble if you head south. You'll need more than Latin, though, if you travel north."

"Do you think that with my crutch I'll become a great traveler?"

He laughed and began teaching me.

That night I dreamed again of the dark figure with curved-bladed bloody knife. This time the figure seemed far away and less frightening. In front of him was a cross, which also appeared to be bleeding, while behind him glowed a huge upside-down cross, the hammer of Thor.

Then the dragon face appeared as it had in the earlier dreams, hissing softly. "I am not like their dragons. Not a lizard dragon of the North. I am a serpent dragon, and we never destroy …" Then his words faded in my sleep.

The next day, while I was concentrating on Danish, I stumbled over a rotten log. I had mistaken it for a newly fallen trunk and braced my crutch on it. When the log's crust collapsed, so did I.

Garrad picked me up. "You can avoid such tumbles, you know."

I grumbled that it was Friday, so luck was against me. "Besides, the forest isn't always friendly. Especially to a boy with a crutch."

"No, the forest is a friend."

I stared at the ground.

He patted my back. "This was only a case of inadequate training. Don't trust a log, rock, any handhold, or foothold until it's proven itself. If you haven't tested it, don't rely on it. That's true for people as well."

"How can I know what to trust before I walk on it? If I do walk on it, I'll fall in."

"You can learn how not to fall in. Walk more lightly. Bend your knees. Lift your feet."

"With a crutch — ?"

"Even with a crutch. Try."

I retrieved my crutch and for the next few miles practiced lifting my feet and treading lightly on the earth. Though I hurt my bad foot occasionally, the new method helped my walking, especially over the many bogs and marshes dotting Eastern Normandy's fields and forests.

Even around Falaise, when I played with friends, my crutch would sometimes slip into a quagmire. A companion would have to pull me out before I sank to my death.

Now, though, I skipped over miry ground. As soon as I felt its trembling beneath my feet, I lifted my crutch and skipped ahead until the earth felt firm again.

One day, though, my crutch slipped into a bog, and I stumbled. The mud dragged me down, seizing my legs almost up to my knees. I cried for help.

Garrad paused with the donkey and looked back at me. "Fall forward," he called out.

"Can't you grab me?"

"The donkey may wander away. Besides, you'll enjoy learning this. Fall forward."

I remained uncertain about the enjoyment, but I obeyed immediately. My body dropped into the bog. The reeking muck clutched at my clothes, but my feet began to rise.

"Keep your arms splayed out and crawl forward slowly."

I tried to crawl.

"Don't push your elbows and knees in. Pretend you're a snake. Slither."

I slithered. Before long my body lay on firm ground.

As I drew myself into a kneeling position, Garrad said, "Stay on your knees to get your crutch. That way you won't sink if you hit the bog again."

I stared at him. "Won't you get it for me?"

He shook his head. "Not with my arm. Besides, these are skills that could save your life someday. You need to master them. You'll be fine. Have no fear." After I retrieved the crutch, he said, "Well done. I'm impressed with your abilities."

I rose and hobbled over to him.

He drew away. "We'll wash you in the first stream we find. If you sink again, though, choose a place with less rot."

Between lessons in Danish, Garrad made more suggestions about walking so that I could avoid bogs. "Watch carefully where you walk and try to see as far as you can."

"I have my eyes open."

"I don't mean that. Study what's around you. Even at great distances. For example, do you see the crow on that young beech?" He pointed with his good hand.

I could barely see the beech.

"Focus on it. Don't strain. Allow your eyes to bring the picture to you in all its details. Gently."

I did as he instructed, and in fact a crow did perch on a branch of the beech.

"You can see more than you may think. It's simply a matter of practice."

"I'm not sure I want to practice anything more."

"All right, then, let's have a little contest. If you spot any animal before I do between here and Falaise, I'll make you new shoes when we reach home."

"From dyed leather?"

"Whatever color you want."

My eyesight improved quickly.

The concentration and extra work demanded by the new skills, though, made me weary by day's end. We slept under the trees next to a smoldering fire, and I scarcely had enough strength to eat. Nonetheless, I persevered.

Realizing that I was tired, Garrad told me more stories. Some I had not heard, many I had, but I enjoyed his recounting them.

He began with tales of Atlantis and the Seven Sages of the ancient Greek world. Then he told of St. Lawrence, who, while being grilled alive, joked with his torturers: "You can turn me over now. I'm done on that side."

He also mentioned teachers of the past, a great Sage of the Far East named Chrishna, whose teachings were brought west by Pythagoras. And the Enlightened One of India, the Buddha, whose ideas spread through the teachings of Apollonius of Tyana and Apollonius' long-time student, Damis.

I asked that he recite warrior's tales, especially about the Twelve Noble Peers in the court of Charlemagne, including Roland, Oliver, Ogier the Dane, and Archbishop Turpin, after which came stories of Alexander the Great, Julius Caesar, Alfred the Great, King Canute — the Dane who had conquered England — and of course Normandy's Duke Rolf, called Rollo by the French.

He told most of his warrior stories about Harald Hardraada, the Norwegian warrior who now fought in Byzantium. I recalled that Duke Robert had mentioned this man, as had the infirmarian at Mont St. Michel. Garrad seemed equally impressed.

Nearly seven feet tall, Hardraada was not only a powerful fighter but also clever and ruthless. Once, Garrad said, Hardraada broke a siege by tying burning cloths to birds, who then flew to their nests inside the city and set it ablaze. Another time, Hardraada staged his own death, lying in a closed coffin as he was carried into an enemy camp. He and his pallbearers slaughtered everyone, priests included. I shuddered.

"When this man returns to the North," Garrad said, "Normandy needs either his friendship — though it will be a miracle if we get it — or the protection of God."

Feeling frightened by Hardraada, I asked Garrad to abandon warrior tales. So he switched to the Man in the Moon, who had gathered sticks on the Sabbath and so was condemned to his lunar prison.

He told me about the elephant that Caliph Haroud al-Raschid had given to Charlemagne. About Charlemagne and flying chariots. About gray and green elves. About the Tall People who used to rule the world. Until I drifted off to sleep.

As we journeyed deeper into Eastern Normandy, we encountered the fever, especially in the larger towns. Garrad did not say what caused it, only that when the heat came to crowded areas, so did the fever.

Many villagers told us that evil spirits brought it, agents of Satan, dressed in black robes with long black swords or riding black horses. Others said that small gray demons with large black eyes and long fingers brought it, because they were seen at night invading the townspeople's homes.

The victims I saw in the disease's early stages complained of chills and aching. They suffered headaches, and pink rashes appeared on their bodies. After the rashes turned to brown spots, the fever dominated their entire bodies.

Spreading rue to cleanse the air, Garrad and I treated each symptom as it arose. We fed the victims teas and tinctures of golden seal, chamomile, bitterroot, myrrh, and, of course, angelica.

I remembered angelica, because Garrad had told me a long story about it, as he had many herbs. An angel had given angelica to a monk in a dream and told him to use it for any fever that spreads.

Because Garrad knew astrology, he could predict the time each stage of fever would last, the proper treatment for each person, and the success each one would have in recovering.

Some who had survived the fever in previous years had not recovered completely. They had relapses or worse, became mad. Crouching at the edge of towns in ragged tunics, they had the sign of a cross shaved into their hair, as did all madmen.

Garrad always stopped to rub nettle and eucalyptus oil onto their chests and temples. The oil would help madmen recover their sanity, Garrad said, provided God wanted them to return to society.

If any began to rave while he was applying the oil, Garrad asked me to hold their hands, rub the wrists gently, and speak quietly to them. At first, this frightened me, but it never failed to calm the person.

When I asked Garrad why it worked, he said, "You were born under the sign of the Water Bearer, Aquarius. A pure water-bearer can calm madmen by speaking to them or touching them. Usually."

"How do you know which day I was born? Even I don't know that."

He hesitated briefly. "I can tell from your personality."

In Exmes, the last town we visited, I saw my first leper. Though we had passed many leper colonies at a safe distance, this was the first leper I had seen so close — a man. He was dressed in a plain robe, and his face was completely covered with a draped cloth.

Sitting on a litter, he was being carried along a narrow street by four priests, considered immune by God's grace, who sang a Latin psalm as they bore their burden.

For a moment, the wind rose and lifted the shroud, exposing a huge, yellowish face with sunken eyes. I shrank behind Garrad.

The priests, looking alarmed, covered the man again. Then they carried him into a church.

"What's happening in there?"

"The priests are reading the service of the dead. At the end of the service they'll give the man his pair of claquers. Do you recall the noises we heard whenever we got near a leper colony? Claquers. Lepers must sound them when strangers are near."

"How will the man get out of town?"

"They'll carry him to the local colony, along with the others who are now among the dead."

"He's not dead."

"To the community he is. During the service, the priest forbids him to return to the town, enter a church, monastery, or market, to bathe himself, to have physical contact with any woman, or to even speak to someone unless he is downwind of the person."

"Is there anything we can do?"

"Not at this late stage. The Madonna lily's leaves and roots will cure some people, but when it gets this far, the priests say it's a curse sent by God for a terrible sin."

"Is that true?"

He looked down at me. "I don't know. I'm not God."

Two days later, St. Jude's Day, we crossed the Ante, the stream that led into Falaise. The healing journey around Normandy had ended.

I now had to discover whether Falaise was safe for me or not.

CHAPTER 3

ARCHERY AND POISON

A.D. 1035

Autumn arrived in the village before we did, and fallen leaves camouflaged Garrad's hut. The village roofs were similarly decorated, I noticed, as the villagers asked me about my trip and reported the summer gossip.

The most important news came from Walter. I found him repairing a hole in his roof thatch made by an over-eager squirrel.

He climbed down to greet me. "That Northern fellow who attacked you passed through again, a few weeks after you left. But with a blue cloak this time, trying to make us believe he wasn't the same man. No one else recognized him, but I did. I was clever, though, and didn't let him know that I saw through his disguise."

"Did he ask for me? Did he know my name?"

"No, he asked whether the village had any crippled boys. I told him that Falaise has several cripples, and this summer we sent them off to monasteries and cathedral schools to study, since they'd be no use in farming." Walter chuckled. "I said we sent them as far west as Avranches and as far east as Fecamp. If he's looking for you, that'll put him off the track for a long time."

I breathed deeply and thanked him.

"Do you know yet why he wishes you harm?"

"No, I wish I did." I paused. "Do you?"

"I? How would I know?" He glanced at his thatch. "Oh, there's another matter. Lady Arlette's here to visit her father, and I told her about your troubles. She wants to see you."

While Garrad remained in the village to visit the widow Marie, I hobbled toward the stone walls of Falaise castle — more stone than when I had left, I thought.

I found William and Arlette, huddled in conversation behind an enclosure in a corner of the great hall. They glanced up from their carved chairs. Arlette smiled and waved me toward them.

Grinning, William ran over to me. "How was your trip? I'm happy you're back safe. Do you like my new purple cloak? Did you see the stone walls? They're covering the wooden ones. How far did you go? Did you see the ocean?"

Arlette rose to hug me. "How was your journey, Cuin? Tell us about it."

As I described my travels and adventures, William whistled through his teeth, imitating Duke Robert. He seemed especially excited about the storm assaulting Mont St. Michel.

Arlette seemed distracted as I talked. Before long she interrupted me. "Did you encounter the Northern warrior again?"

"No."

She gave a short nod. "We've been discussing you, Cuin. When I was in the village recently, Walter told me about your being chased."

William frowned at me. "I heard about it, too."

Arlette continued, "We cannot allow killers to hunt you down."

"No," William said, putting his hand on the ever-present knife.

"I think he may be far away," I said, "from what Walter told me."

"He may come back," she replied. "Besides, William tells me that when the boys come here from Rouen, they bully you. That's not right."

The sons of Duke Robert's barons enjoyed pushing me into wet straw, mocking "the wine-barrels miracle." I didn't like it, but there was nothing I could do. I tried to shrug it off.

That did not satisfy Arlette. "Your life is in danger. Starting tomorrow, you begin training with William's weapons teachers."

I was less than enthusiastic. The instructors were less than that. A nine-year-old warrior would be a challenge under any conditions, and common law decreed that villagers not be trained in weaponry. Arlette had ordered them to teach me, though, so they reluctantly obeyed.

They discovered that their reluctance was unnecessary. I was harmless with a sword in my hand. Or a battle-axe. Or a spear. Whatever weapon I tried to wield, my bad foot failed to support it in fighting stances. Arlette frowned as I tumbled to the earth again and again.

The last heavy weapon they asked me to try was a chained mace. I almost hit myself in the head with it, and the teachers had to scramble for safety as the studded iron ball, which I unleashed as I stumbled, assumed a life of its own.

William suggested a bow. The teachers shook their heads. A peasant with a bow meant poaching.

They liked me, they said, but the law was the law. They crossed their arms and stood unmoving.

I rose, brushed the dirt from my tunic, and reached for my crutch, relieved that my lessons, abruptly begun, were as abruptly ended.

William, however, did not budge. He glowered at the instructors. Until his father returned, he was the Duke. They must obey him or suffer the consequences.

They ignored him.

He thrust a knife into his belt and gripped his sword in one hand, his shield in the other. The seven-year-old Duke stood armed against three grown teachers of weaponry.

I turned to Arlette. She was studying William as if she had never seen him before.

Then she drew the teachers aside and whispered something. I saw their eyes grow wide, then smiles form. To my astonishment and dismay, my training with the bow began immediately.

The teachers were still not hopeful, though. At the outset, they wondered how I could manage the required steadiness for archery. I could not. Putting weight on my deformed left foot brought pain almost immediately. To stand and shoot arrow after arrow was impossible.

Once again, I thought that I would be released from my trials.

"Can't you stay off that foot?" William asked, pointing.

I glared at him, hoping he would go away. He remained, staring at my foot.

One of the teachers, following this idea, suggested I shoot with my weight back on my good foot. Mumbling to myself, I obeyed.

Unhappily, the method worked. I notched the arrow as I leaned forward on my bad left foot, rapidly shifting back onto my right to relieve the pain and release the arrow.

The second teacher looked surprised but patted my shoulder.

The third teacher shook his head. "How will he ever hit anything swaying back and forth?"

"There's little hope of this succeeding," the first teacher said to Arlette.

"He will be trained in a weapon, and this is the only one he can handle," she said. "You must teach him."

So, for several days, I shot arrows all over the practice field. Everywhere. I heard the teachers mutter that they might be creating the first inadvertent poacher in Norman history.

Garrad passed by every morning to encourage me, while Guy, ever obnoxious, stopped by each afternoon to make fun of my wildness. He tried to draw William away to play but with no success. William was as determined as I was humiliated. He dragged me back to the practice field after the training sessions each morning and afternoon. Hour after hour, he kept me shooting.

My hands became sore. My forearm grew raw. When I complained, he commanded me to continue. "I'm the Duke until my father returns. Shoot."

"An unkind ruler," I said, quoting the priests, "breeds unhappy subjects."

"Shoot," he said.

The practice began to yield results. After a few weeks, I could hit targets — randomly.

William pressed me. "You should hit it every time."

Whenever I missed, I said, "This won't help me with assassins or bullies, you know."

In fact, when William wasn't with me in the castle, I discouraged bullies by exaggerating my limp and looking pathetic. I didn't carry a bow with me.

Nor would driving an arrow through a courtier's son have endeared me to the barons. I already had one enemy too many.

William would not be put off. "You can't just limp around. That won't work. The killer knows you limp."

I frowned at him. It annoyed me that William's logic was good, since he didn't study logic with the priests. I returned to practicing.

I was, however, unwilling to give up my admittedly cowardly methods of coping with bullies for what seemed an uncertain alternative.

I complained to Garrad. He replied by teaching me about flight paths of arrows in different winds.

When I carried my plight to Arlette, she presented me to an archery master from Kiev, a big, bearded man with rough hands. He made me practice more often than William had.

Each day he dragged me from the castle before the first morning bell. My fingers froze as I drove arrows through the chilly air at stuffed targets that reminded me of the straw bed I had left.

He also began to teach me how to craft my own bows. Because I had been making my own crutches for years, this was easier than archery practice, but it was still hard work.

Even as I lamented to myself how unpitied I was, Garrad's explanations and the daily drills improved my shooting. I began to hit the target almost every time. Not the center, of course.

But the center was what the archery teacher wanted.

"Focus on target center," he said in rough Norman French. "Little spot. I make little spot for you. See arrow hit little spot before you shoot. Feel arrow flight."

I thought he was mad and wondered whether I should rub his wrists or put nettle and eucalyptus oil on his temples. Before the first snows, though, I began to understand not only his words but also what he meant. Sometimes I could actually feel where an arrow was going before I released it — in almost any kind of wind.

And the winds became stronger and stronger. Winter's first snowfall ended my practice days.

On St. Nicholas's Day, Lady Arlette journeyed to Rouen for news of Duke Robert. She also intended to visit friends and attend to what ducal matters Robert had urged on her.

The nobles did not like her administering the dukedom, she told us, "in any way, even the least detail. They think I'm meddling. Especially the Western barons." She was not put off, however, and said she would continue to do as Robert had requested.

Arlette remained uncertain about Rouen's security, so she asked William to remain in Falaise castle with the elder Osbern, steward of the ducal household. Osbern had been William's protector for months and had kept him safe. William and I liked him and played with his son.

She also reminded William to hear Mass every morning and bathe once a week. I knew he would obey both commands without question, and that I too would be cleaner than I wanted to be. Fortunately, as she was leaving, she asked me to return to the village and stay out of sight. I happily agreed.

William and I waved our farewells as her cart bounced through the castle gate.

I stayed with Marie in the village until the winter fever arrived. Its assault was a lingering effect of the summer fever Garrad and I had battled. He warned me it might come, so the day I heard of its outbreak, I took refuge with him.

Not unexpectedly, he marched me back to the village. "The best training you can get now is curing this fever," he said.

We worked for a week, both of us staying in Marie's hut to be closer to the sick. Following the summer's debilitating heat, the fever struck with unusual force. Even with Marie's assistance and my growing knowledge, we did not defeat it easily. Three of my childhood friends and one adopted parent succumbed.

From childhood, I had seen babies die. I had also seen a few corpses on our healing trip. These villagers, though, were people I had grown up with. I felt sad and found that when I summoned up images of playing with my now departed friends, I cried. Marie comforted me and sent me to the priests, who also consoled me, explaining about the afterlife.

When I returned to help Garrad, he put his good hand on my shoulder as he usually did. "How are you feeling?"

"Better, thank you."

"Still sad? It's understandable. Let yourself feel sad as long as you need to."

I stared at the bodies laid out to be buried, their heads pointed east in Christian fashion.

"Garrad, what happens after a person dies?"

His breath frosted as he spoke. "What did the priests tell you?"

"That the poor and sick go to Heaven, where God repays them for their suffering."

"Then they've gone to Heaven."

"That's not bad then."

"It's good, from what I've heard."

In the evenings I blessed the sick, including the dead bodies. Because of the "miracle of the wine barrels," the villagers and mourning parents believed that I bore some divine favor. I didn't know what good my prayers could do, but the priests told me that praying never hurt.

Because the ground had frozen, the four bodies could not be buried yet. So the priests sprinkled them with holy water, and Garrad and I covered them with a layer of rue, ashes, and what dirt we could scratch from the freezing earth.

When we finally returned to his hut, I felt exhausted. I dragged my bed to the fire side of the great stone to catch the reflected heat. Stretched out, I gazed at the fire and listened to the wind. A snowstorm mounted outside.

Garrad decided to forgo any language lessons, but he did want to talk about history. Normally, I would have complained, but Garrad said that history was a good antidote for sadness.

"The Romans were fine builders," he was saying, "better than anyone before or since. Their roads ran all over Normandy, Flanders, the North, too. Most of the roads we trod this summer are over a thousand years old."

"So, the Roman Empire wasn't all bad —"

The door's bursting open interrupted me. In the doorway huddled the son of the steward Osbern. Snow swirled in behind him.

"Here, boy!" Garrad leaped up from his stool near the fire. "Close that door! You'll — " He stopped himself. "What's wrong, lad?"

Normally cheerful, young Osbern was crying, his face white, resisting the reddening of the cold.

"My father," he sobbed, "He's sick. I — "

"The village fever?" Garrad was already reaching for his cloak and leather sack.

"He's got stomach pains, and he's dizzy and — "

"Oh, God." Garrad hesitated a moment and then was upon him, ready to go. "Is William with him?"

The boy nodded, gulping.

"Is William sick too?"

Young Osbern shook his head.

"Cuin, bring your extra crutch."

I wanted to ask why, but Garrad had already seized young Osbern's hand and plunged through the door.

I wrapped one of Garrad's blankets around me and scurried after them, hobbling on one crutch and carrying the other.

Slipping on the icy rocks, I soon fell behind. I stumbled on, but the frozen ground stung my foot, slowing me even more. Garrad and young Osbern disappeared among black trees.

I could see nothing but snow. It was not deep yet, but the wind drove it into my face. Then the snow curtain parted, and Garrad's figure loomed in front of me. Motioning me onto his back, he grasped the crutches with his left hand, so I could hang from his neck. Young Osbern clung to his lifeless right arm. We pressed on through the snow.

The guard admitted us through an already opened castle gate. "There was a scuffle outside young William's bedchamber. The steward drove some assassin away, I was told, but then the steward fell ill."

"Who found him?" Garrad asked.

"The boy there." The guard indicated young Osbern. "He came to tell me. Since everyone else is hiding from the fever and the snow and I can't leave my post, I sent him to you."

"Good. No one else knows?"

The guard shook his head.

Garrad lowered me, and the three of us hurried to William's bedchamber.

William stood near the fireplace, staring wide-eyed at the bed. He shuffled toward us, draping himself in Garrad's arm.

"You're all right then?" Garrad asked him.

William nodded.

On the bed lay the steward's still form, closed like a fist. Young Osbern began to cry again. Garrad passed William to me and knelt by the bed.

"What happened?" I asked William.

"He kept an assassin away. A man with a knife, they told me. But then, after dinner," he stammered, "he had pains. He couldn't stand up — "

Garrad glanced at William. "Did you eat with him?"

"No. I was hunting. With the archery masters. We ate in the forest. I know I wasn't supposed to be hunting …" He dropped his head. "The snow brought us back."

"Your love of hunting saved your life."

I moved closer to Garrad. "Fever?"

"Poison. Deadly nightshade, it appears."

"Who would do this?" I asked, trying to pull my eyes from the corpse.

"I don't know." He frowned and shook his head, muttering something to himself about "North or South." Aloud, he said, "We're dealing with a determined assassin. So we must make him think he's succeeded — if only for now. That will give us time to hide William and find a new guardian." He straightened. "Do you recall where we put the bodies of the boys who died from the fever?"

"In the shallow grave," I whispered. "Just outside the castle wall."

"That's right. One of them is close to William's age?"

I nodded. "Thomas."

"You have a blanket. Can you bring Thomas's body here?"

I did not move. Of course, I would not refuse, but I never wanted to do anything less than rob a grave outside the castle walls on a dark, snowy night.

"I'm not sure I feel very well," I said.

"You won't be disturbing their spirits. Both you and the priests blessed them." He pulled a coin from the pouch on his robe and pushed it into my hand. "Give this to the guard at the gate. He'll let you out and back in without question."

I still hesitated.

"Just wrap the body in the blanket, taking care not to touch the skin."

I continued to stare at him.

"I'm sorry I can send only young Osbern with you, but no one else must know, and William and I have work to do here."

I was not sorry to have even distraught company. I led Osbern down the stairs, across the courtyard, and past the guard. I didn't know whether to take the guard into our confidence, but I had no choice. As I explained what we had to do, he nodded, grim-faced. I pressed the coin into his hand.

He returned it and said, "Thank your master, but there's no need." He patted a still sobbing Osbern on the head. "I'm sorry, lad." To me he said, "I'd help if I could leave my post, but, truth be told, I'd rather be here. Yours is not a task I'd want to perform."

I nodded, giving him a miserable look. I didn't want to perform it, either.

Osbern and I pushed through the snow to the shallow grave. Realizing we had difficult work, he stopped crying. He helped me scrape at the snow-and-ash crust. The smell of rue drifted past our noses, even in the cold. Soon we had unearthed the corpse of eight-year-old Thomas.

As we gazed down on the body, Osbern began to sob again. I felt my own wave of sadness. Our friend Thomas was gone. The priests always said that friends were a treasure greater than gold. Now I had one less friend. I was poorer by their standards, and I felt poorer. My eyes watered and stung in the night cold.

I shivered. "We have to get him ... back."

Osbern kept crying.

"The priests say this is just the shell of our friend. Like your father, he's gone to Heaven."

Osbern wasn't consoled.

"Think of this. God has given Thomas a chance to do a last service for his Duke, as your father did."

Wiping snow from his face, he sniffed and nodded.

With great care, we wrapped the body in the blanket and heaved it onto our shoulders. I shifted it onto my right shoulder, so that I could use my crutch to support my left foot.

We stumbled back to the castle past the guard, who crossed himself and helped us carry the body across the courtyard and up the tower stairs. But it was with clear relief that he returned to his post.

When we arrived at the chamber, Garrad took the body and unwrapped it at the foot of the bed. He placed William's hunting cloak around Thomas and put a pair of William's shoes on the dead boy's feet.

As Osbern and I caught our breath, he explained in a low voice, "It must appear that William was poisoned as well. The assassin won't know the difference between death by nightshade poisoning and death from fever. At least, that is what I hope. I also hope that Thomas will be mistaken for William. So William must disappear."

To that end, Garrad had given William a thoroughly uncourtlike appearance. He was smeared with fire-soot from his face to his shoes. Osbern and I received the same treatment.

"Now," Garrad said, "we'll hide William and Osbern with Walter in the village, while you, Cuin, will stay with me."

He gave William my extra crutch, and all four of us crept from the castle. Outside the walls, we straightened and made our way down the road.

To any watching eyes, Garrad would appear to be a peasant father escorting his three sons — two of them crippled — toward Falaise village on a snowy night.

The following morning, Garrad left the hut to visit the castle. He was gone most of the morning but returned with news before the noon bell. As he brushed the snow from his shoes, he told me that a newly hired cellarer's assistant had fled when the poisoning was discovered.

"I told the cellarer to say nothing to anyone else, and I put both bodies in the shallow grave. That's all we can do for poor Osbern for now."

"Did we fool the poisoner?"

"We can't be certain, nor can we take a risk." He pulled his stool near the fire. "Until a new guardian comes forward, we'll keep William in the village. He'll be safe. Even if assassins knew he was there, the only way they could get him would be to kill every boy in the village."

I gasped. "They wouldn't do that. Would they?"

"No, the Western barons wouldn't, but Southern powers might."

He rose, lifted his healing sack from its peg, and began to fill it.

"Are we going somewhere?"

"To the village. We must tell William and Osbern to stay in disguise and out of sight. Get your crutch and a heavy cloak. We'll do some healing this morning."

We forced the drifts away from the doors and announced our presence. In each house, we tended the sick. Garrad sprinkled rue and mint around to cut the smell of disease. We also checked smoke-holes. Garrad had taught me that smoke can kill if it is not let out, especially when snow clogs the thatch.

Healing at many homes, we were able to check on William without attracting unusual attention. We confirmed that William and Osbern were still hidden and that Walter was as determined to keep them safe as we were.

Word of William's survival spread, and Arlette returned briefly to comfort him. She traveled in disguise, though, and returned quickly to Rouen.

Within a few days, though, we wondered whether William would survive. A traveler stumbled into Falaise with the news that Duke Robert had died the previous summer at Nicaea in Bythinia, a country far away in Asia Minor.

I thought of the Duke and his jests and cried. Garrad was uncharacteristically silent for days.

William was moved to a guardian closer to Rouen and Arlette.

Huddling around their fires, the villagers gossiped about the death of Duke Robert and the precarious life of his son. They claimed that Duke Robert's own kinsmen had poisoned the Duke so they could divide Normandy among themselves.

We began to hear of fighting in the west of Normandy, as the barons there tried to seize more and more territory. Even nobles loyal to William tried to expand their property.

More attempts to poison William were uncovered by loyal courtiers. Some assassins, believing him to still be in Falaise, made attempts at the castle. During a trip to the castle kitchen, I discovered monkshood slipped in among the horseradishes, which it resembled. I sliced it open to reveal its poisonous, yellow inside.

Since the kitchen staff might have eaten some of it, I gave them horehound and insisted that they keep taking it, especially if they had nausea. It was the only time in my life that the cooks praised my habit of nibbling among the dishes they prepared.

With the attempts on Williams's life, I thought it odd that within a few months of the Duke's death, the barons elected William Duke with only a few dissenting voices.

When I said so to Garrad, he was silent for a long time. He had been filling our new winter leggings with dried moss for warmth. He broke off from this and stared at the fire.

"It's not as odd as you may think. First, William has the backing of the Archbishop of Rouen, his grand uncle, the most powerful and influential man in Normandy. The nobles may think that the Church powers back William."

"They would not want to stand against the Church?"

"Not unless they have to."

"They don't have to be Christians, but they don't want the Church as an enemy, especially the Holy Roman Empire. Is that right?"

Garrad smiled. "Yes, that's right. You do think like a diplomat. Now, where was I?"

"First, William has the backing of the archbishop," I repeated.

"Ah, yes. Second, Count Baldwin of Flanders, one of the richest and most powerful lords in the Western world — who owes us a favor — may help to defend William. Third, you may be thinking about the nobles fighting among themselves. Keep in mind that most Eastern barons are not related to the ducal family. They have nothing to gain if William is killed. So they want to fight each other, but not the Duke."

"The nobles related to William would like to see him dead, though. That's what they say in the village."

He nodded. "It's true that William's relatives would rather have him dead, as would the Western barons. The rest of the Norman nobles, however, are pleased to have a young, weak Duke. It gives them freer rein to steal from each other." He returned to his work. "Will you hold the end of this?"

"Is there any word from Lady Arlette?"

"No. I doubt we'll hear from her for some time. She has her own grieving to do. And she'll have ducal business to attend to, meeting with the Duke's council and King Henry."

"The King in Paris? Why?"

"He's the Duke's overlord, so he's protecting Normandy from outside attack until William is old enough, and he will now take in William for protection and training."

"He hasn't stopped any of the assassins."

"No. He's going to try to evaluate William's character while William is at his court. And he's probably waiting."

"For what?"

"To see who's going to take over Normandy."

A few weeks before the Christmas season, the weather turned warm, and Arlette and William did return for a visit.

A few days later, William unexpectedly appeared at Garrad's hut, asking me to join him in archery practice.

I was reluctant. "Is this a sociable invitation or a command?"

He was too enthusiastic to be put off. "I have an idea. I want to try something. It's about your foot. Come on!"

I didn't want to dampen William's spirits, especially because he had been less cheerful since the death of his father — even after the return of Lady Arlette. So I agreed to join him. With Garrad as escort, we reached the field just after the noon bell, and the day felt almost warm.

The Kiev teacher had set up straw targets and seemed as eager as William. Only Guy, standing a safe distance away, shouted taunts about my abilities. I ignored him and turned to face the Kiev teacher.

"Speed," the teacher said. "Duke William has fine idea. About speed."

"You sway to shoot," William said. "Just keep swaying and shooting."

"What?" Then I realized what he meant. "Why?"

"For speed," repeated the Kiev teacher. "Speed."

"I think what they're suggesting," Garrad said, "is that if you keep a continuous swaying motion, you can shoot arrow after arrow — rapidly."

"Will that work?"

Garrad tilted his head, thinking a moment. "Why not? If you can develop a fluid motion and still shoot, it should work. Of course, you need to draw and fix your arrows quickly, but you're already good at that — trying to shoot as quickly as possible to end the practice session. If you develop this swaying skill as well, you will shoot more rapidly than any other archer in the world."

"Shooting that fast, how am I to hit anything?"

I realized too late that I should not have asked the question.

William and the archery master replied almost in unison, "Practice."

CHAPTER 4

THE ENDS OF PRINCES

A.D. 1036

"Prince Alfred, I think, is more holy than Prince Edward," Garrad said as we marched toward the castle to meet with the two brothers.

His breath misted as he spoke. It was St. Enda's Day, and March had chill left in it, so much chill that I had been relieved when Edward summoned me to fetch Garrad. He had liberated me from archery practice in the castle.

"Do you think so?" I asked.

To me, Alfred seemed as gentle as his brother but acted less holy than Edward. Alfred laughed easily and often. He celebrated the saints' feasts after the holy services, while Edward participated only in the Mass.

Alfred also brought his lute to the great hall and serenaded the court with Norman and Saxon ballads. He sang the village songs and danced the village dances — not holy conduct in Edward's eyes. Alfred could also outdrink any Norman, as the Duke's knights said. I wasn't sure what that meant, but they regarded it as a great accomplishment and a worldly one.

Alfred even joined in games that William and I played. William usually defeated me, so Alfred took my side. When William complained, Alfred leaped upon him, tickling him. While William rolled on the ground laughing and shrieking at me to aid him, I made a great show of scouting the horizon, assuring William that I would protect him from any attackers who dared show their faces. Alfred would then congratulate me for being so loyal to the young Duke.

Prince Alfred seemed too much fun to be holy. Not for Garrad, though. "There's more life in him," he said.

I agreed that he was alive.

Garrad abandoned his explanation. "Tell me what the princes want. Why is Edward interrupting my afternoon reading?"

"He told me to tell you that it's a difficult and delicate matter. Those were his exact words. He told me to remember them."

"To what matter does he refer?"

"Lady Emma invites the princes back to England to take the throne, now that her husband, King Canute, is dead."

He paused to stare at me. "Yes. Canute died not long after Robert. Hmm. This is a delicate matter. Did Edward offer any opinion?"

"He doesn't trust any of that Danish brood."

"Yes, he would say something like that."

"Oh, he said exactly that. He said he especially didn't trust Emma the harlot. He didn't tell me to say that. I overheard it."

He chuckled. "No, I'm sure he didn't want you to say that or even hear it."

"Garrad, what's a harlot?"

"A prostitute, like the ones we saw at fairs on our trip last summer. Perhaps you didn't notice them. They're popular at fairs."

"Are they a special craft?"

He hesitated. "Not special. During fairs, women from many crafts become prostitutes, if they need the money and like the work."

"Are they a craft, though?"

"That depends …" He raised his eyebrows and took a breath. "Did Edward tell you anything else?"

"Yes, he said that he couldn't understand why Emma would want her Saxon sons to take the throne when she prefers her Danish son."

"I agree with him."

Using my crutch, I vaulted over a puddle. "Does that make her a harlot?"

"No. Let's leave the subject of harlots for now, please. Edward is referring to Lady Emma's wedding the Danish king, Canute, after having been married to Edward's father, King Ethelred."

I could scarcely believe what I'd heard. "Edward's mother married the man who defeated her husband?"

"A long time ago. It seems odd, I know."

I couldn't grasp what he said. "Do you mean that Edward's mother, a Saxon — "

"She's a Norman."

"That's right. Norman. She was married to the Saxon King, Edward and Alfred's father, and then married King Canute? A Dane? The enemy of her own husband?"

He shrugged. "Apparently Emma fell in love with Canute. She even let it be known publicly that she never liked Ethelred — though she had eight sons by him, including Edward and Alfred. Keep in mind that Ethelred was as ruthless as Emma was ambitious. For instance, when he first came to power, Ethelred had many Danes in his kingdom brutally killed. Emma must have found him a hard man to live with."

"Emma and King Canute had children?"

"A son and a daughter, and that son, Hardecanute, is her favorite."

"She likes him better than Edward and Alfred?"

"That's what Edward says. Apparently Emma hasn't been shy about expressing her fondness for Hardecanute publicly, and travelers have brought word to Edward." He paused to glance at the clouds and pull his hood over his head. "Remember, though, that Emma wouldn't prefer Ethelred because he was a Saxon or dislike Canute because he was a Dane. She is a Norman, after all, William's great aunt."

"Why should Emma like Hardecanute better than Edward or Alfred? They're nice."

"It has puzzled me, though Ethelred's character must play some part in her preference for her children by Canute. I've also been told that Emma always wanted to be the mother of a great king. And Canute's son Hardecanute could become a powerful king. He's at war with Magnus of Norway now, from what traders and pilgrims tell me, and if he takes Norway, he'll become King of Norway, Denmark, and England. Consider that. Edward or Alfred would be King of England and nothing more."

I thought about how long the princes had been in Normandy. "Do you think the Lady Emma left the princes here … to get rid of them?"

"I don't know. Lady Emma told her sons that she had brought them here to protect them from the Danes when Canute invaded England. Edward thinks there's more to it than that, and he never fails to remind us of his suspicions."

When we arrived at the castle, a guard escorted us to one end of the great hall where Edward paced and Alfred leaned against a wooden support pillar. A fire glowed in the fireplace, and Garrad and I pulled benches in front of it. Garrad piled on more wood.

Alfred greeted us pleasantly, while Edward continued to pace, preoccupied.

Abruptly he stopped and looked up. "Thank you for coming, Garrad. Thank you for fetching him, Cuin."

Garrad nodded again and said, "It's my pleasure to see you again, Prince."

Alfred, watching Garrad stir the fire to a blaze, strode toward it and sat next to us, leaning back in a wooden chair. He thrust his hands into his wide-sleeved tunic and stretched his feet toward the fire. His shoes, though dyed a cheerful red to match his tunic, were stained and worn at the heels. I recalled Garrad's saying that while the brothers had great nobility, they had little wealth.

Alfred smiled as he spoke to Edward. "I'm sure that Garrad, for all his pleasure at being here, would rather be reading." He turned to Garrad. "What are you working on now?"

"I've been given a new copy of Boethius's 'The Consolation of Philosophy'."

"A marvelous work!" Alfred said with his usual enthusiasm. "My own namesake, King Alfred, translated it into the Saxon tongue over a hundred years ago, though I was taught — "

Edward cut him off. "Garrad, the Lady Emma's letter invites Alfred or me or both of us to England, with a safe landing guaranteed by Godwin, Earl of Wessex. What do you make of that?"

"Earl Godwin is a powerful man."

"The most powerful of the Saxon lords," Edward replied, "a position he earned by aiding the Danes."

"He is a confidant of your mother, is he not?"

"Godwin is friendly with Emma," Edward said. "He's no fool, though, nor is he power-mad, neither of which I can say about my mother."

"If Earl Godwin guarantees our passage, can we not trust him?" Alfred asked.

"When I said that Godwin was not power-mad," Edward said, "I did not mean that I trust him. As Garrad correctly pointed out, he is friendly with our mother."

"I have heard," Garrad said, "that Godwin's family has a mixed reputation, if I may put it that way."

Edward produced a sound that resembled a huff. "If what you mean is, could we ever trust that family, you have asked the crucial question. They have long dominated the other Saxon families, but only because the Danes insure their power." Edward shook his head. "Godwin even gave his sons Danish names. If he hadn't been born a commoner, he would probably want to rule England himself. Or stand behind the Danes as they rule it."

Alfred rubbed his feet together and moved them even closer to the fire. "No one knows whether Godwin is a commoner."

"As I understand it," Garrad said, "Earl Godwin takes pains that his ancestry remains secret. Whether or not he has descended from even minor nobility is unknown."

Edward pointed at Garrad as he spoke to Alfred. "That is just what I mean. Why does Godwin hide his birth? Why is it a mystery?"

Alfred shrugged and looked at the fire. "Modesty?"

Garrad smiled. "Even I know that Godwin's family has no modest members." He rose. "May I see the letter you received? I don't wish to be privy to its contents. I just want to see its external markings."

Edward handed it to him. "You are free to examine the contents."

"Thank you. There's no need." Garrad studied the outside of the letter. "It has no seal."

Alfred raised his eyebrows. "Hasn't it?"

"No," Edward said, not quietly, "and this letter, lacking a royal seal, could come from anyone, including a ruffian with ransom on his mind."

"Godwin's not a ruffian," Alfred said. "Nor can I imagine that our mother — "

"Yes, our mother! Suppose she has written this letter. Why should we trust her?"

Edward threw open the window shutters and wrapped his black cloak around his shoulders. Garrad, Alfred, and I exchanged glances and drew closer to the fire.

"Are you inclined to ignore the letter?" Garrad asked Edward.

"Most assuredly."

Garrad turned to Alfred. "And you, Prince?"

Alfred shook his head and spoke slowly. "You must appreciate that I never expected to be offered a throne. I thought Canute would live longer. In any event, the throne should be Edward's."

Edward relaxed his frown to nod in appreciation.

"So," continued Alfred, "if Edward doesn't go, I believe it becomes my duty to do so."

Edward threw his arms open. "That would be madness, Alfred. This is what I feared. She's luring you. Don't you see? Garrad, tell him. You've had dealings with the Danes."

Garrad sighed and turned to Alfred. "The possibilities for treachery are greater than those for good will, Prince. If Lady Emma has her heart set on Hardecanute becoming King of England, this is her opportunity to dispose of you. Godwin's power has depended not on the Saxons in England but as your brother reminds us, on the Danes. He would likely support any treachery of Lady Emma's."

Edward nodded once, firmly. "That's what I was saying just before you came."

"Of course," Garrad added, "we have no clear indication of treachery, though I find the lack of a seal disquieting."

Alfred sat, unspeaking. All of us stared at him a long time.

Edward eventually spoke, more calmly. "Alfred, are you determined to go?"

"I believe we have a duty," Alfred said. "One of us must see whether there is even a chance we can reclaim the throne for the Saxons. And the Christians."

I realized that this afterthought was to appeal to Edward's piety.

"After all," Alfred continued, "Hardecanute is still in Denmark. If he hasn't been invited to return, perhaps our mother wants England to return to the Saxon Christians."

"Is there anything I can do to change your mind?" Edward asked.

"I'm sorry, no."

Edward turned to Garrad.

Garrad said, "I advise against the trip, Prince. I would rather you send a messenger."

"If this is treachery," Alfred said, "a messenger could be bribed. You know that. We would learn nothing that way."

"Unless the messenger were killed," Garrad said.

"I don't believe anyone will be killed. I believe that our mother is trying to work out some arrangement, so that one of us can have the throne or at least share it with Hardecanute. If Edward will not go, I must."

"If you must go, Prince, I advise caution," Garrad said. "Keep spies with you, and travel in disguise."

"I appreciate your concern," Alfred said, "but such precautions are unnecessary. I trust Godwin, and I am a prince."

"Perhaps," said Garrad, "but your life may depend on your judgement, and you haven't seen Earl Godwin in twenty years."

"No, but I recall him vividly."

"Then all I can say is that I hope Providence goes with you."

"Thank you."

Edward sighed loudly and stared out the window. "If you're intent on going, I'll raise a small fleet before you leave and sail from Avranches. That will draw the main Danish fleet south and west toward me. If anyone is planning to harm you, at least they'll lack the support of the fleet."

Alfred thanked him. "That precaution I accept."

"May God go with you," Edward said.

"Will he be harmed, do you think?" I asked Garrad as we returned to the hut.

"Alfred? I don't know. From what I've heard of Lady Emma and Godwin of Wessex, there could be treachery."

There was treachery. A messenger arrived from England a month after Alfred's departure with the terrible story, and two pilgrims confirmed it later in the summer.

Edward's pretended attack did draw the Danish fleet to the west long enough for Alfred to land safely in Kent. Alfred was greeted by a smiling Earl Godwin, who escorted him to the Wessex manor at Guildford. The support of Godwin and his Wessex knights seemed to put the throne within Alfred's reach.

Guildford, however, turned into Alfred's prison. He was seized by Danish forces, put on trial for violating the peace of the country, and hastily convicted.

Edward never tired of recounting the grisly events that followed: Prince Alfred was stripped naked and paraded over the Saxon lands to show "the barrenness of Saxon claims," his companions were either murdered or mutilated, and Alfred himself was blinded so savagely — the court's sentence — that he died.

"This," Edward said, "is what Danish rule has meant in England. When we can't trust the word of a noble, everything must fall apart. Terrible violence, terrible destruction will result. It will come here, too, I warn you. The Danes want Normandy."

I always cried silently as I listened to Edward, while William frowned, clenched his teeth, and gripped the handle of his knife.

We later heard that the Lady Emma had fled to Denmark, taking refuge with Hardecanute. The Falaise courtiers' suspicions shifted from her to Earl Godwin.

Edward blamed them both.

A.D. 1040

"I cannot participate in a competition against the barons' sons," I told William. "If I lose, they'll mock me as a commoner. If I win, they'll beat me."

"They'll do neither." William waved me to one side of the great hall. He pulled on the green Duke cloak and settled into the ducal chair. "We'll talk about it."

Striding into the great hall at that moment were two barons, draped in gold-embroidered robes and colorful tunics and leggings. Both had greatswords slung over their shoulders.

"We won't talk about it," I said, grabbing my crutch to escape.

"Cuin! This won't take long. So don't leave. That's a command."

I grumbled to myself but stepped quickly to avoid the barons and dropped onto a side bench.

Removing their swords and laying them on the floor, the nobles bowed and straightened before William. Neither looked at him with respect, I thought.

William seemed not to notice. He told the barons to state their positions clearly, one at a time, and without rancor. His tone seemed harsh, and I noted nervously that there were only two guards in the room, both of whom looked smaller than the barons.

Though William was tall, muscular, and looked older than his twelve years, I wasn't sure that his strength would be enough to aid the guards. At that moment, I wished that he would speak more kindly to his nobles.

The barons did state their cases clearly, each declaring that though William was not yet of age, they wanted him to hear their case. They had failed to reach a decision between the two of them and wished him as arbiter.

Their difference seemed to be about who would be the ward of a young woman with the common name of Mary. I didn't pay attention to her district or family name. Each baron argued that he should be the ward, that he had the legal right, that her district was close to his, and so on, until I began staring out the half-shuttered window looking for something interesting.

William's voice brought my attention back: "Why do you desire to take on this responsibility, my lords?"

I glanced at their faces. Both assumed looks of sincerity, almost sanctity. Both spoke about their sadness over the deaths of the woman's parents, their closeness to the family, and their fatherly affection for young Mary.

William leaned forward, watching both of them closely. "Mary now owns land. Also gold and jewels. Her ward would have the use of these until Mary came of age. Five years, I believe."

The barons looked less saintly and surprised. They nodded.

William settled back in his chair. "I have no way to decide between you, my lords. I shall let Mary choose her own guardian. That is my decision."

The barons glanced at each other.

William continued, "One promise I have wrung from Mary. Whichever of you she does not choose will receive from her thirty gold pieces. I shall add the same sum from my own chest. I shall also excuse all payments to the duchy for the five-year period. This for your willingness to settle the matter without arms."

The barons seemed surprised again, thanked William for his judgment, praised his generosity, bowed, and strode from the hall.

"You handled that well," I said, adjusting the crutch under my arm to approach his chair. "You've made two friends."

"I saw my father do this many times. I think it's the decision he would have made. I'm happy to make friends. Besides, I need the barons to stop fighting."

"Well, you're going to get a fight, if you force me to enter the archery competition this spring."

He rose, swung the Duke cloak from his shoulders and folded it on the ducal chair. "Don't be foolish. You can't win, but you can't lose, either."

"I don't understand you. Perhaps you should put the cloak back on. You don't make sense without it."

He took my arm and led me from the hall. "I have a plan."

"I was afraid you might have."

At first, his plan seemed to be that I practice more to prepare for the competition. I was less than happy about this and said so. He replied that I should keep practicing but concentrate on the rapid release of arrows.

"I'm less accurate that way".

"It's no matter. You don't have the accuracy to compete with the barons' sons. Work on your speed."

When the day of the competition arrived, St. Germanus's Day, I was more nervous than I had ever been. I had made a new bow for the occasion — more to keep my nervousness in check than to have something to show off.

I put on new black leggings, but I wore an old brown tunic, sure that the barons' sons would have me in the dirt before the noon bell.

The May sun was warm but not hot, and a fair formed around the arms competition. Garrad bought me cider and encouraged me, but I became more anxious as I watched the boys' contests in swords, spears, and maces. My hand shook as I tried to eat a pastry — an ominous sign.

Eventually the archery competition was announced, and I moved toward the field where targets had been set up.

William jumped up from his chair to intercept me. He pulled me behind a tree. "How do you feel?"

"Scared."

"Don't fear," he said, glancing around. Then, to my astonishment, he kicked the shin of my bad foot and seized my crutch, catching me as I fell. I cried out, and he pulled me from behind the tree into the open.

"My friends," he shouted to the assembled barons' sons nearby. "Cuin has twisted his foot. Injured it, I'm sorry to say. I'm excusing him from the marksmanship competition. I hope he can recover for speed-shooting."

"Have you gone mad?" I muttered to him.

He grinned at the young archers, waving them on.

"No. I'm showing you why you didn't need to wear this old tunic." He crumpled me onto the ground. "Just sit here. Rise only when the speed contest begins."

I couldn't understand what he was doing, and my shin ached. I should have been angry, but I was relieved to be sitting and not competing. Perhaps William's plan was that I would be willing to enter the competitions but never compete. Yes, that must be it. I wouldn't have to draw an arrow. I relaxed and leaned back against the tree.

As it turned out — or William made it appear so — all of the barons' sons were so talented in archery that everyone got some prize, from gifts of clothing to silver pennies. Young Osbern, of course, won the top prize, but even Guy won a handful of silver coins, and he was no marksman.

William turned from his prize-giving to announce the speed competition.

"Before we begin, though, I have requested that Cuin give us an exhibition. He's mastered a technique I suggested to him, something that allows him to shoot with his bad foot. Since he's just injured that foot, though, competing would be unfair, and I'll even ask him to make his exhibition brief."

For a moment I sat stunned. Then I heard a voice whispering as if from the tree itself, "There's no need to fear. You won't be competing with any baron's son."

Yes, I thought, all I need to do is shoot a few arrows and then sit down.

My head pounding and my knees shaking, I pulled myself up, slung my bow over my shoulder, and strapped my arrow sheath to my waist. Using my crutch heavily, I limped toward the targets, my shin feeling sore where William had kicked me. For a moment, I wished he had broken my leg.

I stepped to the shooting area and stared at the target. It seemed farther away than I remembered. Had someone moved it?

Dropping my crutch, I took my bow in my left hand and with my right fanned three arrows in my sheath. I notched a fourth carefully in my bow. My hand shook so badly that I wondered whether I would be able to shoot at all. I heard Guy in the crowd, ridiculing me.

Then another voice just behind me spoke. It was the Kiev teacher: "Concentrate. Focus. Feel flight. Feel arrow. Be arrow. Be target."

His voice seemed to run through my body, stilling the shaking. I took a deep breath and focused. For a moment the crowd and noise faded, and all I could see was the target. In my mind, the bow, arrows, and target seemed to become a single device, each part working with the others.

I found my arm pulling the arrow back. At the same time I leaned forward. I swayed back and released the arrow. Providence alone guided it.

After that, everything happened so quickly that I seemed to be somewhere else, watching the events. Before the first arrow struck, my hand was reaching for the second. I swayed forward as the first arrow hit its target. I notched the second arrow and swayed back to release it. My hand reached for the third. I shot, and I had the fourth in the air as the third hit the target.

For a moment the world became silent, like a tapestry hanging in a church. Then I heard myself panting, more from nervousness than effort.

In the distance I could see the target. The three arrows had grouped themselves at a respectable but not too great distance from the first. They appeared to be three courtier arrows standing around a Duke arrow, which rested precisely in the target's center.

Behind me the Falaise villagers shouted and screamed and clapped.

I heard Osbern in the crowd of barons' sons, yelling, "Well done! Well done!"

I turned to see even the courtiers' sons clapping. Except for the grinning Osbern, they seemed astonished and shouted to each other about my having turned warrior. Guy's mouth was open, but he too applauded.

Coming to my senses, I bowed.

William stepped toward me. "Would anyone like to challenge that? Or shall we just carry on at a slower speed?"

The villagers laughed, and Osbern shouted, "I'm happy if Cuin's bad foot keeps him out of our competition."

William smiled at him. "Let's agree that Cuin will remain in his own class of speed-archers."

I bowed to him, trying to look solemn. The Kiev teacher sprang forward to give me a crushing hug, followed by Garrad's good arm around my shoulders.

William was right. That day I did not need my old tunic.

After the competition, I felt that I would be able to handle the Northern assassin himself. Fortunately, he had not been seen for years, though rumors of a Northern warrior wandered through Falaise almost every season.

William was not as fortunate. Though more barons rallied to him, especially as they came to respect his judgments, the Western nobles remained hostile. The attempts on his life continued — four unsuccessful tries in as many years, though none involved poison.

As a result, Arlette continued to move William from Rouen to Falaise Castle to the village. He also traveled to the castle of any noble willing to risk protecting him.

That summer, my fourteenth, the willing noble was Count Gilbert. So in June on St. Silverius's Day, William, young Osbern, and I made the two-day journey to Count Gilbert's castle on an island in the Risle River near Brionne, not far from the monastery at Bec that the Count had made possible.

Our guardian was Edward, because Garrad wanted to remain in Falaise to visit Marie. In addition, Edward wanted to see Count Gilbert again. Gilbert was William's cousin twice removed, and that made him cousin to Prince Edward as well, though how many times removed I could not work out.

Edward told me again and again how friendly Gilbert was. And how religious.

I was curious about the man who had provided the land for Herluin's abbey at Bec with its poor knight-monks who had no building skills. As Garrad had recounted on our first healing trip, Gilbert had been reluctant to release Herluin from his knightly vows to pursue a monk's life. Eventually he had relented and even donated the beautiful Bec Valley for Herluin's new abbey.

So, as we bumped over the bridge leading to Brionne Castle, I wondered whether this Count was truly religious or whether Herluin had just worn him down.

I watched the Risle River flow beneath us and around one of the few all-stone castles in Normandy. It was Brionne Castle's stones and position in the middle of the Risle River that made it ideal for William's protection.

It was a beautiful castle, too, with grander spires than I had seen even in Rouen. The river, separating the fortress from its neighboring forest, made Brionne Castle one of the loveliest and, I thought, safest places in the world.

I recalled the serious face of Abbot Herluin as I dropped from the cart and watched Count Gilbert approach us, round-faced and smiling. The Count was a short, stocky man, looking as solid as his castle. His strides were direct and purposeful. Even his dress — a plain brown tunic, red leggings, and brown shoes — seemed straightforward.

He was friendly, as Edward had said. After greeting the others, Count Gilbert turned to me, his recently shaved face looking like a large, cheerful squash. He treated me almost as if I were a baron's son, shaking my hand and inviting me to visit Brionne whenever I wished. I thanked him several times.

He did not seem particularly religious, though.

"What you must keep in mind," Edward told me, as we strolled the stony castle yard, "is that Norman nobles love religion, whether they appear religious or not. They're devoted to religion, certainly more than Saxon nobles in England." He spat at the ground. "Normans have seen what civilizing effects the Church has wherever it goes. That's why Duke Robert encouraged his barons to rebuild the older monasteries and to give land to new ones."

I recalled the monastery of Mont St. Michel. "Even in the West, in spite of the Thor-worshipping nobles there. Garrad and I met many on our healing trip."

"Yes. If William continues the policies of his father and converts the Western nobles, Normandy could be spared the misery of the past." He looked down at me, his long face serious, even for him. "The invasions from the North were, after all, God's punishment for the Westerners' sins."

What sins those were, he did not say.

Nor did I have time to inquire during our visit. I spent most of my time in archery practice. As it turned out, Count Gilbert's court had an excellent archery teacher. When I expressed my interest, spurred on by William, the Count asked the master archer to work with me daily.

The teacher was a tall, pleasant man from the southern province of Maine, so I understood his French easily.

I took a few practice shots, and he smiled at my rocking motion.

When I looked embarrassed, he said, "I'm sorry. Please don't feel embarrassed by the unconventionality of your method. If you combine this method with accuracy and strength, it may benefit you."

"It does allow me to shoot more quickly."

"Please show me."

I demonstrated the speed I had used at the competition, and he nodded approvingly.

"That's good," he said. "Now you need greater accuracy and penetration."

"Penetration?"

"How deeply you drive your arrows into the target." He put his hand on my shoulder and upper arm. "We can work on your strength here. Let's begin, though, with accuracy. Please shoot four arrows as you just did."

I quickly drew and released four arrows. They hit the target, but all missed the center.

"That's good," he said. "At that speed, it's remarkable. Where are you looking when you shoot?"

"At the target."

"Any particular place on the target?"

"I look at the center for the first one. That's what my teacher in Falaise taught me. I don't know about the others. I suppose I just look at the target in general." I grinned at him. "I'm happy to hit it in general."

He grinned in reply. "I appreciate that, and it is an accomplishment. Will you, though, try something for me? Before you shoot, will you concentrate on the center until you feel it pulling you toward it?"

"Will it do that?"

"Try."

I did. At first, staring just made my eyes water, until the target became a blur. Then I blinked and tried again.

The teacher encouraged me. "Take deep breaths. Relax your arms and shoulders. Let the bow and arrow just rest in your hands. Don't try to shoot. See the center of the target only. Let it tell you when to shoot."

I tried again and before long, I felt the center closing on me. Without thinking, I raised the bow and shot an arrow. It hit the center.

"It works!"

"Yes. Now, keep your eyes focused on the center for all four arrows. Don't look away, and don't see the whole target. See only the center."

I relaxed and focused again. When I felt the center pull me, I shot three arrows in rapid succession. All three hit the center. The fourth missed, but I realized that I had let my focus shift from the center to the target as a whole.

"Good. This will be your practice while you're here. Before you begin, though, one more suggestion."

I sighed, wondering how much more I could handle, but he didn't say anything. He just strode to the target and moved it farther away.

As he returned, he said, "When you can hit the target at that distance, your penetration will have improved."

"How can I? It's so far!"

"Use everything your Falaise teacher has taught you. Use what you've just learned. Your body will adjust. In the meantime, I'll show you exercises for building the strength in your shoulders and arms."

I wrinkled my face. "Does that mean more practice?"

The teacher put his hands on both my shoulders. "You have power here that you're not using. When you can combine it with your speed and accuracy, you'll be one of the most formidable archers in the world. That is the purpose of practice from now on."

I stared at the distant target, placed more arrows in my sheath, and began to shoot.

That evening, as Edward and I rested in the great hall, Count Gilbert and three of his men returned. I glanced at them from a chamber window. I was not surprised that William had remained in the forest with Osbern; William would hunt all day, if he could.

The Count and his knights tarried in the courtyard, their voices rising through the window. They seemed to be arguing. Trying to ignore what we assumed to be a private matter, Edward and I rose to find something to do.

Looking awkward, Edward asked, "Would you like to —?" But his words were cut off.

Below us, the voices abruptly ceased, replaced by a clashing of metal. Edward and I frowned at each other and made for the window. He reached it before I did, glanced down, and uttered a cry. By the time I reached it, he had grabbed his sword and was racing toward the courtyard.

Outside, Count Gilbert's sword crossed another, wielded by one of his own knights. Another knight crouched nearby, sword ready. The body of a third lay near the Count.

Gilbert lunged at the first knight, slashing with his knife and then driving his sword into the knight's stomach. As the wounded man fell back, the other knight rushed at Gilbert. The Count dropped to one knee, swinging at the attacker's legs.

The blow found its mark. At the same time, though, the knight ran his sword through Gilbert. The Count fell forward. The knight, his leg bleeding, stumbled to the ground.

At that moment, Edward reached the knight and in a single move, knocked aside the knight's sword, driving his own through the knight's midsection. Guards from the tower and the front gate raced into view, their spears brandished.

I groaned and leaned back, feeling sick.

A few moments later, Edward reappeared in the great hall, his sword sheathed. One of the guards followed him.

He panted. "Cuin, quickly. We must find William in the forest. He's in danger. The guard thinks he knows where the hunting party may be."

"What happened?" I asked.

"Count Gilbert is dead. I'll tell you the rest as we go."

To the guard he said, "Carry Cuin to the cart. You lead us."

As we bounced through the woods on roads bumpier than the road to Bec Abbey, Edward told me what he had learned.

Over the noise of the cart, he shouted, "The guards overheard some of the argument. The three knights" — he paused as we hit a hole and bounced into the air — "were bribed to kill William. They tried to persuade Gilbert to join them. He refused."

"Are other knights seeking William's life?" I shouted.

"The guards couldn't tell. Let's pray not."

We hit another bump, and I felt it must have bruised my backside. "What will we do if they are?"

He kept his eyes ahead, gripping the horse's reins tightly. "Like St. Michael, we'll fight the devil in whatever form we find him."

The guard turned on his horse to call to us, "I see a falcon, and I hear dogs."

At the next bend in the road, we too heard dogs barking and a reply to the guard's shouts. Edward urged the horse ahead, and we spotted forms in the distance. In a small clearing stood William, Osbern, and a hunting party of a dozen knights.

"At least these knights can be trusted," Edward said in my ear. "If they had wanted to kill William, they would have done so by now."

As we reached the party, he jerked the cart to a halt, and I gripped the seat, suffering my last blow. He leaped from the cart and ran to William, who blinked in surprise at him.

"Cousin," Edward said, "Count Gilbert has been murdered by three of his knights." He swung his eyes toward the other knights.

William's mouth fell open, and his hand went to his knife. "What? Why?"

"There was a plot to kill you, and Gilbert would not aid it. He killed two of the knights, and I killed the third. We cannot return to the castle, however, until we know who is behind this and whether any others are seeking your life."

William crossed himself, and the rest of the party did the same.

"What shall we do?" William asked.

Edward drew him away from the others, toward where I sat in the cart. "We'll be safe at Bec Abbey."

In the morning, Edward appeared at the abbey. He still wore his riding cloak, and I wondered whether he had slept at all. Under his white beard, his long face looked paler than usual.

"I've sent knights back to Brionne Castle to secure it," he said.

"Where's William?"

"Since it's sunny, he's getting ready to ride. We're returning to Falaise with three of Gilbert's knights. I think that's the safest place for us. William can hide in the village." He touched my shoulder. "Come. The others are waiting."

William and the knights were saddling horses not far from Herluin's rough quarters. The cart stood nearby, a horse already hitched to it.

William was thanking Abbot Herluin, and I heard the Abbot say, "It is we who are indebted to the Dukes of Normandy."

"Nonetheless," William replied, "I will not forget your kindness."

Herluin turned to me, almost smiling. "Ah, master Cuin, good morning." His face turned sad again. "May I have a private word with you?"

I nodded and stepped behind an oak with him.

"Though I have no wish to trouble you, I feel I must speak. On your last visit, Garrad confided to me that there have been threats on your life. With the death of Count Gilbert, I feel I must say something that I hesitated to tell you during your recent visit."

"Has it something to do with the Count?"

"Not directly. I realize now, though, that there are men determined to destroy the young Duke and anyone close to him."

"Do you mean me?"

"I'm afraid so. I think you should know that a Northern warrior passed through here a few weeks ago asking about a crippled boy from Falaise. He posed as a monk, but my brothers and I were not fooled." He smiled. "We may not know building, but we know warriors. This man was a warrior."

"What did you tell him?"

He looked pained for a moment. "I hated to lie, so I wrestled with what to say for a long time. In the end, though, I believe that God directed me to behave as the Wise Men did with Herod. I told him that we knew of no such boy, but that Falaise villagers often sent their crippled children to a monastery at Fecamp in the north of Normandy. I calculated that if you and Garrad had embarked on a healing trip, you would be going in the opposite direction."

"That's right. Did he believe you?"

"From his displeasure at having to travel so great a distance, I feel certain that he did. I'm sorry to have to frighten you, though."

I groped for words. "Thank you, Father. I appreciate knowing, and I'll tell Garrad. You have done me a great service."

The Abbot put his hand on my head and blessed me. He added, "St. Michael will go with you. I see him hovering over your head."

"Good," I said without thinking. Any angel hovering anywhere around me made me feel safer.

A.D. 1041

Edward was leaving. Garrad and I were summoned to Rouen for the farewell meeting.

"What's happened?" I asked Garrad as we hurriedly packed.

"According to the messenger, Lady Emma recently returned to England with her Danish son Hardecanute as her escort. And — this will not surprise you — the Witan, the electing Council, chose Hardecanute to be King, urged no doubt by Lady Emma and Hardecanute himself." He glanced at me. "You had better take the heavy leggings I made for you."

I bent over my bag, filling it with extra clothes against the winter chill and extra blankets for the seat on the donkey cart we were borrowing from Falaise Castle's stables. I added the leggings.

"Edward is really returning to England?"

"Lady Emma and Hardecanute need him to assure the Saxon nobles of their good will and to allay suspicions that they were involved in Alfred's death. So, Edward is making a public arrival in London in the presence of most of the Saxon nobles, those who can afford to attend, that is."

"Edward will have to be very careful. I still can't ..." My thoughts drifted to Alfred's horrible death.

Garrad nodded. "That's true. Edward has survived in a foreign land for most of his life, though, and he knows the ways of the North. That's why he's arriving openly in London. He has also taken the precaution of inviting all Church authorities in the North to be present at his coronation."

As we left Falaise behind, Garrad leaned toward me in the cart. "There are some surprises about all this that I didn't mention."

"Lady Emma wants to be declared queen again?"

He laughed as he adjusted the reins in his good hand. "The surprise would be if she didn't want to be queen. No, listen to this: Hardecanute ordered Earl Godwin of Wessex to stand trial for killing Prince Alfred."

I almost fell off the seat as I twisted to stare at him. "I assumed that Lady Emma and Earl Godwin were in league with Hardecanute."

"You're not alone. Hear the conclusion, though: Godwin swore his innocence, and many earls spoke for him. In Saxon law, that was sufficient to acquit him of guilt."

"Hardecanute believed that?"

"Perhaps his credulity was strengthened by the fact that Godwin presented him with a newly built dragon-ship embellished with gold and manned by eighty warriors."

I adjusted the blanket I was sitting on as we hit a rock. "Was that a bribe?"

Garrad smiled. "It was a gift to a new king. Of course, a somewhat lavish gift. The messenger told me that each of the eighty warriors had a golden helmet, a gilded axe, a gilded spear, and six-ounce gold bracelets on each arm."

I shook my head. "Is Hardecanute in league with Godwin after all?"

"Perhaps. He is Emma's son. Or perhaps he's simply a king who knows innocence when he sees it." He laughed at his own jest. "At least, he's a clever king. He apparently secured Emma's approval to invite Edward back to court to share the kingship."

"Edward will be King with Hardecanute? Can that be?"

"Yes, and if I were Hardecanute, I'd have made the same arrangement. Many of the older nobles don't like Hardecanute, while the Church authorities love Edward. Moreover, Hardecanute has taxed the nobles heavily, which they resent. Edward is just the man Hardecanute needs as co-ruler to keep the Pope and the Holy Roman Empire at bay and keep the nobles loyal to whoever is King of England."

That night, I dreamed of a large dragon-ship, and even in the dream I realized it was the ship Earl Godwin had given Hardecanute. Then the dragon's head appeared over the ship, saying, "This is not my kind. We are not lizard-dragons like this, butchering …" Then I fell back in to a deep sleep.

It was St. Romanus's Day when we reached Rouen, and I heard the bells calling people to late-afternoon Mass. Garrad and I found William and Edward in the castle's great hall, where we soon huddled next to a fire to ward off the late winter chill. William sat near me, while Edward did his usual pacing.

As I stretched my hands toward the warmth, Edward was saying, "I am the seventh of my father's sons, the last left alive. This is what was meant to be, divine Providence. It was foretold at my birth, and God has spoken to me in a dream." He paused to gaze out the window. His black, fur-lined robe apparently kept out the cold better than my wool cloak. "This is my opportunity to win the throne. This is the time. If I go to England now, I'll return the throne to Christian Saxons."

"Aren't the Danes in England also Christians?" I asked.

"Some are, some aren't," he replied. He turned to smile at me. "That's not my only reason for returning, though. I believe that Hardecanute and I can end the fighting among the earls." His face hardened. "Hardecanute has shown that he is not completely controlled by my mother. I doubt she wanted her friend Godwin put on trial."

Garrad turned from the fire. "The trial could have been a ruse, Prince. It did — in law if not in truth — prove Godwin's innocence. That could have been what Godwin and Emma wanted."

Edward gazed at him and sighed. "Yes, that's possible. I have tried to keep treachery from my considerations, though, since I must work with Hardecanute. I have also kept the Church authorities close and closely informed."

Garrad nodded. "It's how I would think myself, if I were convinced that Hardecanute would work with me."

Edward crossed to the fire and put his arm on Garrad's shoulder. "You're right, of course. A good advisor, as always. I have not forgotten my brother's death, though, and if I did not have other advisors who assure me that Hardecanute would work with me, I would not be going."

Garrad smiled. "Why, Prince, you don't employ spies, do you?"

William, staring at Edward, asked, "Do you have spies in England?"

"I will just say, cousin, that during my exile, I have traveled much, as you know. I have learned the ways of courts here, in Paris, in Flanders, even in Rome. I can easily grasp the workings of Hardecanute's court from a traveler's slightest comment."

"You are certain of Hardecanute's friendship then?" Garrad asked.

"I have learned that he is not friendly to Wessex. Of course, he must tolerate Godwin and his sons. He also needs the support of the other earls, especially Mercia and Northumbria, who favor me. Above all, I know that I must return the throne to the Saxons and undo whatever plots my mother hatches to keep England in Denmark's empire."

Garrad nodded. "Your mother often seems as formidable as the Danish Empire she plots for."

"She is, and if she succeeds, the Danes come here next."

"That is a concern of mine," Garrad said.

Edward's face softened suddenly, and he gazed at each of us in turn. "Do you know that I have known you, all of you, nearly all my life?" He sighed. "For over thirty years, I have known no other home. I shall miss Normandy. I shall miss all of you."

William rose and extended a hand. As William had grown into his teen years, he and Edward had become friends. They both loved hunting and often hunted together. William sometimes wore the same solemn look as Edward and imitated his piety. He was even dressed in black and scarlet for the farewell.

"We'll miss you, cousin," William said. "we'll miss your help and wisdom. I hope we'll still have that — even from a distance."

Edward smiled at him. "God willing, yes."

As we hurried to the stables to reclaim our donkey cart, I asked Garrad why he had not tried to prevent Edward's sailing to England. "Won't they do to him what they did to Alfred?"

Garrad threw back the hood of his brown cloak. "In the first place, we don't know who was responsible for Alfred's death."

"You said that Earl Godwin — "

"All I did was repeat stories about Godwin. I don't know him, and I can't be sure what happened. I know that since Canute first strengthened Wessex, Godwin has been at the center of power struggles. I don't know for certain, however, whether Godwin caused any treachery."

"Alfred was killed. Someone killed him."

He leaned toward me as we walked. "The messenger told Edward a few things that you and William didn't hear. I did hear them. Edward has reasons other than birth prophecies, his dream, and the Church's support to return to England, though these would have been sufficient for him."

"Other reasons than the ones he told us?"

Garrad lowered his voice as we walked, though few people were on the streets. "Those are his intentions. His reasons are different. You see, the messenger told us that the Christian Saxon lords will protect Edward. They now have an opportunity to regain control of their lands, to force the Danes out of England, so they want a Saxon king who has the support of the Church."

"By that, they mean the Holy Roman Empire, Pope Benedict, and the powers behind the Pope."

He smiled. "Yes, you've retained what I told you. Edward is perceived by the Pope as loyal, someone he can draw into the Empire as an ally."

"Hardecanute is also King, though."

"The Saxon lords have assured Edward that the new King won't remain long in England."

"Why not?"

"One possibility is that he may be drawn away to battles in the North. Hardecanute is King of both Denmark and England, though he has a regent holding the throne in Denmark just now. That regent is at war with King Magnus of Norway. Because the regent hasn't the men or ships to defeat Norway, he'll likely lose Denmark to Magnus. Hardecanute must then either leave England to regain Denmark or wait for Magnus to attack him in England."

"Would Magnus attack England?"

"You know what I've told you: both the Northern kings, Danish and Norwegian, want England. If King Magnus takes Denmark, he'll look to England."

"If Hardecanute returns to Denmark, does that leave England to Edward?"

"Yes, but if Hardecanute doesn't go, the Saxons will be desperate to get rid of him. He is too great a prize for Magnus to leave alone. Either way, they want him off the throne, and they are determined to assure his absence."

"How?"

He glanced at me but said nothing.

I stopped and gaped at him. "They wouldn't kill him, would they? A king?"

"Kings fall ill."

I stood where I was, trying to grasp what he was suggesting. "Would they" — I lowered my head and my voice — "Would they poison him?" I leaned on my crutch heavily. "I can scarcely believe that Christian nobles would poison their King."

Garrad glanced around and urged me to a walk again. "Cuin, poisoning kings isn't uncommon. Roman emperors and their heirs died of poison more often than they died of old age."

"Poisoning a king, though … "

I pondered this as we hitched the donkey to the cart and began bouncing through the streets of Rouen. We reached the gate and passed under it.

As we came out the other side, I saw movement out of the corner of my eye and turned to see a man running toward us. He seemed to have come from a makeshift hovel leaning against the outside of the city wall.

"Stop!" he shouted. "Stop! You're the one! You're the one who'll save us! Stop! You're the one!"

As Garrad pulled the donkey up, one of the castle guards sprang from inside the walls and seized the man. The man struggled briefly and then fell limp in the guard's grasp.

"He's mad," the guard explained to Garrad. "He hasn't harmed anyone, so we give him food and wood for his fire. I hope he hasn't frightened you."

The madman raised his head to gape at me, his mouth hanging open.

"No, he hasn't," Garrad said, getting down from the cart. "Thank you for your pains." He glanced from the man to me. To the guard he said, "Please release him. I may be able to help."

"Yes, sir," the guard replied, "I recognize you, master Garrad, and the lad here." He turned to the man. "Will you be quiet?"

The man said nothing, and the guard moved away from him, watching. "I think he'll give you no trouble now."

Garrad lifted his healing pouch from the cart and pulled out what I was sure would be nettle and eucalyptus salve. "Cuin, come here."

I eased myself down and took the man's hands, as I had done before with madmen. Abruptly the man began to cry out again and startled me.

"You're the one! Rouen is taken, and you're the one!"

"Look into his eyes, and rub his wrists," Garrad said.

I obeyed, and the man fell quiet again.

"I'm not as mad as you think," he said softly, which startled me almost as much as his crying out.

"I know," Garrad said. "You have visions?"

The man frowned. "Visions. Yes. Visions."

"What do you see now?" Garrad asked.

The man began crying out again, "Rouen is taken! Rouen is taken! There's no home for me! No one gives me wood for my fire!" He stared at me again. "He's the one! He's the one! He can save us."

"This boy?" Garrad asked. "How?"

The man panted. "He ... he's a priest, no, a monk, no, a priest, and he ... he has a ..." He began to cry. "He has a bear."

I kept rubbing his wrists. "What does he mean? Why is he crying?"

"He's crying because he can't make sense of his vision. It's probably why he was considered mad in the first place. He doesn't know how to interpret what he sees."

The man nodded through his crying.

"He sees, but he can't understand, so the vision brings him ... despair."

The man fell silent and stared at Garrad.

"Now," Garrad said, "look into his eyes again and try to see his vision."

"How can I do that?"

"Let your thoughts drift away until none are left. Then let his vision come into your mind."

I tried to follow his instructions, and even as I gazed at the man's wild face, I found my mind going blank.

"What do you see?"

"Nothing."

The man stopped crying and swallowed hard. He shifted to study me.

Garrad put his good hand on my back. "Now do you have any impressions? Feelings? Anything?"

I paused. "Yes. Something about walls. The walls of Rouen. They're very high, higher than they are now."

"Rouen is taken by some enemy, so the walls seem higher to him. What else?"

"The Bible and a name. Gideon. Gideon from the Old Testament."

"Yes, that's why he said you're a priest. You've been trained by the priests to read the Bible. Anything else about Gideon?"

"No."

"The bear?"

"There's a man. He's tall and bearded. I can't see his face clearly. He's been wounded somehow. Perhaps he has a scar. He's the bear."

"What do you mean?"

"I'm not sure. He keeps changing into a bear and back again." My mind went blank again, and I returned to normal, feeling the day's cold on my hands and face. "That's all I see."

Garrad shook his head. "A bear. A Berserker warrior perhaps? How would you be traveling with a Berserker warrior?" He rubbed more salve on the man's temples and helped him back to his hovel. As he did, I heard him say, "The boy will be back to help you and Rouen. Have no fear. The blessings of God be on you for your visions."

The night we reached Falaise, my sleep in Garrad's hut was invaded by nightmares. I awoke often, trying to shake them.

I saw what seemed to be Heaven and Hell. A bearded figure — was it God? — sat brooding on a throne surrounded by robed creatures — where they angels? Below him, a mustached, long-haired devil and his demons plotted mischief. The bearded figure turned into Edward, sitting on a wooden throne surrounded by courtiers, whispering. The devil dissolved into a blonde, mustached lord with his warriors, waving swords.

Then William appeared. He was surrounded by a sea of spears, which engulfed the long-haired lord and his knights. The wooden throne then rose above the sea of spears. It was now empty, and William sat down on it, his sword beside him. The dragon's voice ended the dream with, "He's a king now."

I awoke to find Garrad perched on my bed, staring at me. To my surprise, I was sitting up, my eyes open. "I was dreaming."

"I could tell. What did you see?"

"I saw Edward and William, both kings. William was sitting on Edward's throne."

"What did the lord look like?"

"I couldn't tell. He had light hair and a mustache."

"A Saxon."

I was confused. "What kind of dream was that? It seemed so real."

"A vision of the future. Like the madman's vision."

"Am I going mad?"

He rose, patting the great stone. "No. Visions happen here. That's why I built in this place. I had my first vision sitting against this rock. Unlike the madman, you can learn to interpret what you see."

"What does the vision mean?"

He did not reply for a time. Then he said, "I think we should visit Lanfranc. He's in Avranches."

CHAPTER 5

THE WARRIOR OF THE BEAR

A.D. 1041

Trying to throw off the winter afternoon's chill, we paced before the entrance to the schoolrooms of Avranches Cathedral. The school had been founded by Garrad's friend, the lawyer Lanfranc, who had traveled to Normandy from Pavia a few years earlier. He was the "famous teacher" I had heard about from the priests, the Abbot of Mont St. Michel, and my Falaise village families.

Adjoining the stone church, the schoolrooms included rows of small chambers off a wood-beamed main hall. On the hall's floor, the students sat, as I did in Falaise, for training in grammar, rhetoric, and logic. I could detect the scent of rosemary, which I too wore around my neck to improve my memory.

For the Christmas season, new rushes had been strewn on the floor. The walls had also been recently decorated. New garlands had been hung — vines twisted with pine branches to hold dried oranges, apples, and rose petals.

Between these decorations hung less festive grammar charts, but even these had been encircled with garlands of pine boughs.

In one corner of the hall stood a paradise tree — a fir covered in red apples, reminiscent of the apple eaten by Eve — evidence, Garrad said, that at least one of the teachers came from the German Saxon states.

A tall, hooded monk, whose face I could not see, nodded that he would find "the master" for us. He disappeared through a door.

"The master." The phrase made me wonder what the famous Lombard teacher would look like. Garrad had told me of their first meeting in Pavia. Even then, Lanfanc's fame as a lawyer and teacher attracted students. Garrad had often remarked that Lanfranc knew the law better than anyone in the world.

Born in Pavia, I thought to myself, so Lanfranc would be be short and balding, like the Roman priests who visited Rouen. Maybe tall, since he was wise. He would be either short or tall.

Balding, certainly. Older than Garrad, I guessed, to be so intelligent, and with an otherworldly air. The Roman clerics always had an otherworldly air, and Pavia was not that far from Rome. Both were south of the Alps, after all.

My musing was interrupted by the approach of two men. Both had the hoods of their brown woolen robes thrown back as they walked. They spoke in low tones, their breath misty. Both were tall.

The older one, who appeared older than Garrad, I took to be Lanfranc. He had white hair and a rough voice.

I only glanced at his companion — too young for a wise man, with curly brown hair, an animated face, and a voice to match. A gray cat trotted at his feet.

I scrutinized the older man. His skin was lighter than I thought Lanfranc's would be, and he was thin, hawk-nosed, and solemn. Here was the otherworldly effect. A scar ran across his balding forehead down to his left eye.

I thought it odd that a famous teacher should have what appeared to be a battle scar. Yet Garrad had lost the use of his arm in battle. Perhaps they had fought together. That would be a story.

Oddly, I found myself unable to take my eyes off him. He seemed familiar, though I could not recall where I might have met him. On a healing journey perhaps?

To my surprise, he returned my gaze with a glare, aimed first at my face and then at my crutch. I had pictured Lanfranc restrained but friendly, especially at Christmastime, but certainly sympathetic of a cripple. Hostility seemed out of place.

Abruptly, the older man spun and marched away, leaving the younger man to greet us.

"Garrad, it's been too long since our last meeting." The cheerful face beamed at Garrad then at me. "Cuin, I'm delighted to meet you at last." He stretched out his hand. "I hope you're staying for our celebration. You've come at a marvelous season. We have a wickedly good time before Christmas. Our Christmas play is elegant, and the feast after Christmas Mass will please any palate." He glanced down the passageway, then winked at us. "Now that Voldred is gone, we can have some wine. He's sincere enough but a bit sour. He's been here only a few months, so let's hope he hasn't turned the wine sour, too!" He laughed, slapping Garrad on the shoulder.

My mouth dropped open. This was Lanfranc. This was the "master", the "wise man." Younger than Garrad. And grinning and garrulous.

He took my arm and led us through the school's center hall. With the accent of Pavia coloring his French, he continued to talk in a stream of not-quite-funny comments and Latin puns, at which he laughed uproariously.

Perhaps the journey over the Alps had done it to him. He had left Pavia a wise man and arrived a fool.

After the evening meal, we rested on wooden chairs in front of an enormous fireplace. I pulled my chair as close as I could. Even with the fire, I felt chilled. The winds invaded the cathedral rooms, checked only by shutters and cotton wall-hangings.

I tugged on my cloak and tried to concentrate on Lanfranc, as he chatted and stroked the gray cat in his lap.

My attention, though, was drawn away by the iron spits, pots, and tiered grates in front of me. Just to the left of them was a baking oven. Lingering odors inspired visions of breads and pastries, which even now would be hidden somewhere for the Christmas feast. I wondered where.

What drew me most was the soup left over from dinner, still bubbling in a huge side pot, simmering for the following day's meals. Its aroma mingled with the smell of burning wood.

As I tried to identify the herbs in the soup, a movement caught the corner of my eye. A shadow stirred in the hall behind Lanfranc. When I turned my head toward it, the shadow fell still.

A few moments later, a tall figure strode past the door — the older, hostile monk, the one with the scar. Voldred, Lanfranc had called him. The name did not sound Norman.

Lanfranc's voice invaded my thoughts. "… Cuin's dream," he was saying as he turned to me.

I stared at him. "Um, what are you talking about, sir?"

"What we just mentioned while you were daydreaming about food," Garrad said. "Lanfranc's travels after he left Pavia may help us understand your vision."

"I'm sorry."

Lanfranc smiled. "There's no need to be. Our cook here rivals some of the best I recall from Pavia."

"If it's not an impolite question," I said, "why did you leave?"

He sighed, and his face became surprisingly serious. "Pavia, like too many states south of the Alps, is wracked by power struggles. The nobles and the Church both want to rule, though powers behind the Pope want an empire even more than the nobles." He glanced at Garrad, who nodded slightly. "My family was in the political arena, you see. Though I avoided politics — and my parents had died when I was young — my larger family's involvement tended to identify me with their faction."

"That was why," Garrad said to me, "many of us wrote asking him to come north."

Lanfranc smiled. "Yes, many of my friends feared for my safety. It would have gone ill for my students and family, however, if I'd simply fled. Factions in power would have assumed that I was disapproving of them. Or plotting something. Being a public figure in Pavia had its drawbacks."

"So your taking the occasional trip north was something of a ruse," Garrad said. "When you finally did flee Pavia, no one could tell whether you were on pilgrimage, visiting former students, or just traveling for recreation."

"That was my strategy, yes. Fortunately, I have students as far north as Denmark. After I crossed the Alps, I made my way to Rouen and from Rouen struck north to see former students in Flanders. I enjoyed my visits so much that I pushed on to Denmark. I took the Army Road over the Danework and arrived in a trading town called Hedeby. In one of the inns there, I happened to share a table with a goldsmith, who told me a fascinating story — a story which may be related to your dream, Cuin. As you probably know, at the turn of the millennium, the whole of Iceland adopted the Christian faith."

Garrad nodded at me. "To settle a quarrel."

"A quarrel?"

"I don't wish to interrupt Lanfranc's story —" Garrad began.

"Please do," Lanfranc said. "Cuin may someday need to know the history of the North."

"Thank you, Master Lanfranc." Garrad turned to me. "Previously Icelanders worshipped Thor, Frey and Freya, and Odin — the old gods, the warrior gods."

"The same ones Western Normans worship?"

"The same. The warrior gods, though, were not without opponents. Christian missionaries sent by Norway's King Olaf, Magnus's father, aggressively converted everyone they could. Soon Iceland had a vocal Christian minority, which continued aggressive conversions."

Lanfranc leaned toward me. "By 'aggressive,' he means that they destroyed the sanctuaries of the old gods, burned all writings they found, and killed the occasional poet who wrote verses against them."

"Yes, unhappily. The missionaries didn't enhance the Savior's reputation by their actions, but they did impress the warriors of the North. By the turn of the new millennium, the two religions were at such odds that it seemed they might have a war. To avoid bloodshed, they brought their dispute to a summer assembly, an Althing — where Iceland's laws are made and debated. It's customary to do this, and the two sides asked the Lawspeaker to mediate."

Lanfranc sat back. "Though Icelanders are fierce warriors, they have an impressive tradition for settling conflicts peacefully, one that other Christian countries should emulate."

Garrad nodded at him. "Both sides were passionate about their causes, but they agreed to abide by the Lawspeaker's decision."

"Whichever religion this Lawspeaker happened to like?" I said.

"Lawspeakers take their charges seriously, and this one took days of contemplation to decide."

"Besides," Lanfranc said, "Icelanders, like Normans, respect the power of law. According to the account I heard, the parties said that to divide the law would be to divide the peace, a sentiment which I as a lawyer appreciate."

"The result," Garrad said, "was that the old religion was set aside. The Lawspeaker decided that all Icelanders should become Christian, though practitioners of the old religion were tolerated, as long as they kept their practice private. That ended the quarrel as well as any violence it had caused to that point."

Lanfranc chuckled. "All who converted were to be baptized, while all unbaptized Christians should also undergo baptism — to bind all of them together in one religious body. The waters at the assembly were so cold, though, that many waited until they could find hot springs on the way home."

"Iceland is full of hot springs and bubbling pools," Garrad said. He turned to Lanfranc. "Of course, you've seen them, Master Lanfranc, and that brings us back to your story. You were telling us about your meeting with a goldsmith."

"Yes. While in Hedeby, the Danish trading town, I struck up a conversation with a young goldsmith. He had been born in Iceland. He told me that a famous Icelandic prophet converted at that historic assembly, the one Garrad just described. This prophet's conversion included a vision from God, a vision that showed the crowns of the North bowing to a crown in the South. But — and here is what surprised the goldsmith — not the Holy Roman Emperor's crown."

"The Danish crown?" Garrad asked. "Until his recent death, King Canute ruled the entire North."

"Not the Danish crown, either. A different crown." Lanfranc paused to pet the gray cat in his lap. "The Four Crowns prophecy, the prophet called it — and was so convinced of its significance that he passed it on to King Olaf, who recounted it to his son Magnus. According to what the goldsmith overheard, King Magnus treats the Four Crowns Prophecy with great seriousness, almost horror."

"Why?" I asked. "What does it mean?"

"No one is certain," Lanfranc said, "but for Magnus's dismay, it is enough that Northern crowns bow to a Southern crown. In the present age, of course, Northerners bow to no one. Most of the world north of the Alps —"

"Lands not claimed by the Holy Roman Empire, that is —" Garrad said.

Lanfranc nodded and continued, "Yes, most land not claimed by the Empire is under a Northern king. Until he died a few years ago, that King was Canute of Denmark, as Garrad said. So, you see, Cuin, if your vision suggests that William could play some role in England's future, his could be the Southern crown that defeats the Northern ones. I know that a duke doesn't wear a crown but this could be symbolic. I don't —"

A noise in the doorway cut him off. He glanced toward it, squinted, and rose. The gray cat jumped down from his lap.

Staring at the doorway and exchanging glances with Garrad, he eventually said, "Let's finish our discussion in my quarters."

Leaning against a snow squall, we crossed a narrow passage behind the schoolrooms and pushed through a rough wooden door.

Inside, Lanfranc lit two candles to reveal a small room with two chairs, a low table, and a bed. The walls, wooden and drafty, were decorated with winter garlands, which made the room smell of fir.

We shivered from the chill, so Lanfranc hastily prepared a fire.

While he worked, he said, "Some of the cathedral servants haven't been here long. Even Voldred, the monk you saw me with, has come recently, as I mentioned. I don't know which monks here I can trust."

"About what?" I asked, watching my breath turn into mist in the dark air.

"Here in Western Normandy," Lanfranc replied, "it's better to have no political position about the Northern lands. The Western nobles still feel a kinship with their Northern ancestors. I don't want to repeat my Pavia troubles."

"With many Western nobles still being Thor-worshippers," Garrad said to me, "political opinions of Christian teachers are a concern. The nobles want to know which Christians favor their Northern connections and which do not."

I looked at Lanfranc. "Do Western nobles spy on you, Master Lanfranc?"

"I suspect they do. So it's best we have our discussions here."

He finished the fire and invited Garrad to take the only other chair in the room. Like a good student, I sat on the dirt floor with a cotton mat under me, my crutch at my side.

Lanfranc rubbed his hands over the fire. "Now, where were we? Oh, yes, William and the crown of England. It seems that one interpretation of your dream is that William will either help Edward in England or even become a co-ruler in England."

"Excuse me," I said, "but William is just surviving assassins now. Even his control of Normandy is not assured. Why would he want to rule a foreign country?"

Lanfranc nodded. "It does seem unlikely."

Garrad leaned toward the fire, staring at it. "I agree that William would not want to rule a foreign country. Perhaps he may enter into an alliance with Edward or Edward's successor."

Lanfranc studied Garrad's face. "Some idea has got hold of you, I see."

Garrad smiled faintly. "Yes. Assuming that Edward becomes King, what would happen if William were to succeed him, perhaps with another ruler?"

"As co-ruler in England?"

"It has happened before in England's history."

Lanfranc nodded. "So it has. Well, let's consider the situation. If Edward becomes King, he has no need of a co-ruler, certainly not a Norman one."

"Agreed."

"So, you are speculating about what happens after Edward's death."

"Yes."

"Well, there would be many candidates for the succession in England. Why would the Saxon Witan want William, unless the other ruler were only partially acceptable?"

"The Witan?" I asked. "The word means ... 'wise'?"

"The Witan is the Council of Saxon nobles who choose the successor to the English throne." Lanfranc smiled. "I'm impressed with your knowledge of the Saxon dialect. The full name of the Council in Saxon would be 'Witangemot,' meaning 'a meeting of wise men.'"

"I appreciate that this Witan choice seems improbable," Garrad said. "However, what if William were in a position to join England to Normandy? That could free England of Northern rule. A co-ruler might look on William as a desirable partner."

Lanfranc smiled. "It is a pleasant prospect: William and his co-ruler in England as a wall against Northern invasions." He paused for a moment. "Surely only an extraordinary series of events could create such a situation. William could never invade England and be accepted as King."

"I agree. A partnership perhaps?"

Lanfranc fell silent for a moment. "As you say, it would not be the first time that there were two kings in England."

"This is part of the reason for our journey. I wanted to ask about William's legal position. What would be necessary for him as Duke of Normandy to have a legal claim to the throne of England, even as a co-ruler?"

"Do any family connections exist?"

"His blood connection is through Lady Emma, Edward's mother. She's a Norman, William's great aunt."

Lanfranc ran a hand over his stubbly beard. "You're assuming that Edward won't have any children."

"I have good reason to believe that he won't. It's not well known, but he's taken a vow of celibacy. Since he may soon be sole King in England and expected to marry, I'm sure he does not want the vow trumpeted about."

"In that case, Duke William would need two things to convince England's Council to elect him. First, he would need to be designated by Edward or at least favored by Edward as a co-ruler. Second, he would need either the backing of a powerful lord in England — because of the peculiarities of Saxon law — or a marriage to someone in the line of Saxon kings."

"A marriage." Garrad stared at the fire. "What about the fact that William is illegitimate?"

"It may be a factor, but Saxons, like Normans, don't care that much —" Lanfranc broke off, gaping at the shuttered window behind him.

Over the crackling of the fire and the rush of the wind sprang an unearthly howl. The shutter rattled under a blow.

Then dull thuds rained on the door. Another, louder blow fell on the shutter, and its wooden bar, bolting it from the inside, shook.

Lanfranc sprang to his feet and jerked his chair in front of the door. Garrad did the same and grabbed my crutch, brandishing it in his good hand. Lanfranc snatched a knife from under his straw mattress. I crawled closer to the fire, ready to seize a firebrand.

The blows fell faster, and the unearthly howling filled the air.

Abruptly the pounding and howling stopped. We heard cries, far away then coming closer, accompanied by footfalls.

Moments later, a voice rang through the door. "Master Lanfranc! It's the night guard! Are you there?"

Lanfranc moved the chairs and swung the door open to six men in hooded scarlet robes and black hats, brandishing spears and firebrands.

"We heard that accursed sound and came as fast as we could," one of them said. "Are you all right?"

"Yes, thank you. We're unharmed. You've done us a great service."

"It seems that we chased off a thief — or a demon. A tall one, but we didn't see his face. I've never heard such a howl, though."

"Nor have I," Lanfranc said.

"We'll keep our rounds close by tonight, and we'll be watching your house for a few nights."

Lanfranc thanked him again and closed the door. He turned to us. "I think we should sleep in the cathedral rooms tonight."

"So do I," Garrad said. "I've heard howling like that before."

"You have?" I glanced at him, wondering where he could have ever encountered such a demonic sound.

"It's a Berserker's howl."

We spent what was left of the night huddled near a small fireplace in a heavily-beamed, stone room high in the cathedral.

I was frightened and had trouble falling asleep. As I did, though, I realized that the day that was ending was Friday. Unlucky Friday.

The morning bell drove us from our now chilled sanctuary, and we took refuge in a stone chapel adjacent to the cathedral nave. Fortunately, a fire had been laid, and we lit it.

The snow, a lean one, had stopped at daybreak, so Lanfranc and Garrad decided that we should leave that morning.

"We can't be certain who the attacker was or what he wanted," Garrad said to me. "He may just have been a thief adopting a Berserker howl."

"What is a Berserker?"

"In the old war religion, a Berserker is a warrior who binds himself to the god Odin. He receives special training to become a fierce fighter. He believes that in battle he possesses the strength and spirit of an animal."

"What sort of animal?"

Lanfranc strode in at that moment, greeted us, and urged Garrad to finish his explanation.

"A wolf or a bear," Garrad said. "The name 'berserker,' as I understand it, means 'bear-skin.' Berserkers fight with only a bearskin or wolfskin on them, sometimes naked. In battle, they howl the way you heard last night, imitating a wild beast. When they work themselves up into the Berserker Rage, neither fire nor steel can harm them — or so it is said. Fortunately for us, the attacker last night didn't have time to get himself completely into the Rage. Or he wasn't a true Berserker."

I shuddered. "Have you ever seen a Berserker ... in the Rage?"

"Once."

"Were you afraid?"

"Not as afraid as I should have been." He nodded at his limp right arm.

Lanfranc shifted in his chair to face me. "Don't take Garrad's comment too lightly, Cuin. As far as I know, Garrad is the only warrior to have faced Berserkers alone and lived. Even in the South, Garrad's battle with the Berserkers is legendary. I heard that even with one arm, he was more formidable than most warriors with two. You can, therefore, imagine my surprise when he turned up as a student of law and philosophy."

Garrad changed the subject. "Do you have any idea why we were attacked last night?"

"No. The man may have wanted me. It was my house. Whether a Berserker seeks my life or either of yours, though, Avranches is not safe for any of us."

"Will you leave the school?" Garrad asked.

"It may be best. I'll either visit Falaise or send word about where I am."

To my delight, Garrad asked me to fetch the package while he continued his discussions with Lanfranc privately.

I slipped down the side corridor along the nave as quietly as I could, though my crutch occasionally clicked on the stone.

A few people knelt in the main part of the nave, saying Christmas prayers. Above their heads draped red, yellow, and green wall-hangings, telling stories of saints. Priests scurried along the opposite corridor, some heading for the chapels, others preparing for the Christmas ceremonies. Everything smelled of pine.

Missing a Christmas feast in a cathedral distressed me, but I was consoled when a smiling cook promised that the food package included sweets.

I noticed some small cakes on a table nearby, and when the cook turned away, I stuffed two of them into the pocket of my tunic. Surely missing the feast entitled me to a few extra pastries.

Garrad waited for me just outside the kitchen, where he was bidding Lanfranc farewell. Lanfranc was saying something about "the warrior Hardraada," but he broke off when I appeared.

Lanfranc gave me a grinning farewell, and in a few moments we were tramping east from Avranches.

The forest on either side of the road had filled with snow more than once in December. Nonetheless, two tracks in the road remained packed by carts' wheels and horses' hoofs, while the leathered feet of travelers tramped down the middle.

Several groups on their way to Avranches passed us, both mounted and on foot, gaily dressed and singing. The town would have a bustling as well as a holy Christmas.

When the travelers had finally disappeared, I asked Garrad, "Did Lanfranc say something about Hardraada? Does he know him?"

"No." Garrad seemed preoccupied and answered distractedly, "Lanfranc said only that Hardraada is still in Byzantium, but he may be coming north soon."

"Why — ?" I began, but he shook his head. He apparently did not want his thoughts disturbed.

At the next bend in the road, he stopped. He inspected the woods, stretching his head from side to side. With his walking-stick, he poked at the snow-crust along the road.

Then he pointed at a frozen stream, coming down the hill from a bank on our right. It wound down the hill and ran along the road.

Without saying anything, Garrad strode toward it and motioned me to follow.

I watched him labor up the hill, his legs straddling the stream so that his feet stayed on its solidly iced edges. I did the same, using my crutch as an anchor in the snow. Nonetheless, I stumbled and almost fell several times on the rough ice. I marveled at Garrad's agility.

When we reached the hill's crest, he glanced behind us and muttered something under his breath. Seizing a nearby fallen branch, he motioned for me to hide behind a boulder and then disappeared back over the hill.

I peeked after him as he slid down to the road. Then he remounted the hill, brushing away any footprints not masked by the icy stream. He regained the crest of the hill, threw the branch away, and knelt down beside me, his finger over his lips.

Before long, I heard a thudding sound, faint at first, then louder. It was a horse, just one, moving along the road. The hoofbeats approached and without pausing continued down the road, fading from our hearing.

Garrad peered over the hill, using his good hand to lift my head at the same time. We could just glimpse a tall, gray-cloaked man on a black horse disappearing around a bend in the road. At his side hung a huge sword.

"He's been following us since we left Avranches. He may be a traveler. Or a local baron's man. Whoever he is, we'll let him ride on a distance before we set out again."

"How did you hear him?"

He smiled. "You'd have heard him too if you hadn't filled your mind with Hardraada. And Christmas sweets. Never fear, though. We'll have plenty of those when we return to Falaise. Marie offered to feed us if we missed the feast in Avranches. She had some feelings about our journey. She's intuitive that way." He leaned back against the bank. "Speaking of that, where are the little cakes you stole from Lanfranc's kitchen? We can eat them while the horseman gets ahead of us."

I felt my face get hot. I assumed that no one had seen me take the pastries.

He smiled. "If you're going to be a thief, you're going to have to pay the price when you're caught. This time the price is sharing the loot with me."

As I reached into my tunic, he added, "Do extra penance when you get home. The Lord probably doesn't care about a few cakes. However, you don't want anything to come between you and Him on Judgement Day."

CHAPTER 6

THE DUKE AND HIS EMISSARY

A.D. 1042

In William's fourteenth year, he was knighted in Rouen. We celebrated with more Norman cider than my sixteen-year-old body was prepared for, and Garrad had to feed me a special herbal brew to resurrect me. Having experienced such misery once, I swore I never would again.

Nonetheless, I did have three important events to celebrate — and even the madman at the gate had become calm and quiet to join us.

First, William had survived to become the seventh Duke of Normandy. Assassination attempts by his own kinsmen and Western nobles had failed — for fourteen years — and Garrad felt they would now abate.

Second, Falaise, briefly claimed by a rebellious baron, had been recaptured. From Rouen, where Garrad and I had spent the "year of the rebellion," we learned that Falaise had been little affected, and that Marie, my families, and his hut were safe. At a special feast, we celebrated the good news and the fact that William was now officially Duke of all Normandy.

Third, Edward had been crowned King of England. Hardecanute, King of England and Denmark and Lady Emma's last Danish son, had died — a sudden illness, the messengers said — and the Saxon Witan had elected Edward King unanimously. Even Godwin had seemed to abandon his Danish leanings and welcome Edward.

Early in June on St. Ephraem's Day, William appeared unexpectedly at Garrad's hut. He was alone and dressed in a plain brown tunic and leggings, looking common — traveling incognito, I supposed.

He seldom visited now, so we prepared a small feast. Within a few hours, Garrad and I had laid out a meal of soup, fruit, nuts, and Garrad's special mead. William had put together some greens, but I had to help him season them. Mixing herbs was not a talent of his.

In spite of eating more than Garrad and I combined — William was now taller than either of us — he seemed pensive. Even as he thanked us for what we had prepared, he looked disturbed.

He stretched his long legs out, resting his back against the great stone, and we joined him. Garrad stared out the window. I stared at William.

"I need to talk to someone about the fighting," William said, "and I can trust few people in Rouen. Most courtiers are allied to one baron or another."

I replied, "I was promised a position as an advisor years ago, when I received my name. You may talk to me."

William smiled at me but with little mirth. "That's why I came. The problems with the barons have gotten worse. I'm not sure what to do."

"We had heard," Garrad said, "that they stopped paying their dues and were refusing to render you military service. Travelers have reported that they also encroach on ducal territory and steal each other's property."

William glanced at him, his eyes narrowing. "Do you have spies, Garrad?"

"I have informants, of course. I'm not sure I would call them spies."

"Would they bring me information, if you asked them?"

"Some would. Others don't trust anyone in power. I'm sure you could develop a network of your own informants, though. It's not difficult."

"I'd like to know what's happening in Normandy. I don't want to have to wait for pilgrims or travelers to arrive with bad news."

"Is the news very bad?" I asked.

William nodded. "The nobles ... they do, as Garrad says, hold back dues and service. That, however, is a minor problem. Their violence is the major one. They battle each other to expand their borders."

"They steal each other's land?"

William looked hard at me. "You must have heard about it on your travels. The barons even murder each other. They turn on their own families if they think land is involved. Last Sunday, one of them strangled his wife on the way home from church. In full view of everyone. He thought she was plotting with his son, conspiring against him. He didn't even offer penance for the bloodshed." He dropped his head onto his chest.

"They're still not fully human then?" Garrad tilted his head at William.

William stared back. "No."

"I'm not sure what you mean," I said.

Garrad began slowly, "The nobles are not, shall I say, complete human beings."

"Are they demons?"

"You could say that, yes. They are partly demons."

"Trying to be humans," William said.

I hesitated. "You're a noble."

"Only half-noble," Garrad said. "His mother was a commoner."

I still did not understand. "Are all nobles part demon?"

Garrad paused. "Not all."

William interrupted the exchange. "I don't know how to stop it. The violence."

Both of them fell silent for a moment.

"Have you thought about the Truce of God?" Garrad asked.

"Some bishops think we should put it into effect here. Aquitaine and Burgundy have. I heard that it has helped there."

"Do you have any reason to think it wouldn't help here?"

Before William could reply, I asked, "What is the Truce of God?"

"About fifteen years ago," Garrad replied, "the Pope called a synod of prelates and barons worried about violence on this side of the Alps. They decided a ban should be placed on fighting. So the Pope declared the Truce of God, which calls for the cessation of all violence between Vespers on Wednesday evening and Prime on Monday. It also prohibits fighting during Lent, Advent, Easter, and Christmas. The Pope excommunicates anyone who doesn't obey."

Excommunication — just thinking of it made me shudder. "Has he had to excommunicate anyone?"

"I hear that he has in Burgundy," Garrad said.

William shook his head slowly. "We gain from the Truce only if we can enforce it, and even Aquitaine and Burgundy have had troubles. Problems get worse when the Truce is not in force. The nobles even use legal pretexts to kill." He was silent for a time. "There was a mutilation this week, a punishment for a minor crime, worse than what happened to Prince Alfred. It's what drove me here."

Garrad watched William closely. "Let's think it through. What weapons do you have at your disposal?"

William shrugged. "A few alliances with Eastern barons. The support of King Henry in Paris."

"I'm not certain that you can depend on Henry."

"That's what my barons say. Henry will help us only when it serves his interests to do so."

"You may have other weapons," Garrad said.

I stared at Garrad. "What are they?"

"Let's consider the situation. The barons, the Christian ones, that is, love two things besides fighting — God and the law. Wherever nobles accept the Truce, they do so because it contains both. Of course, the Truce solves only half the problem, that is, for only half the week."

William nodded. "We can't just ban fighting. We need to stop it at its roots."

"I agree," Garrad said. "So, let's consider the situation closely. Why do nobles fight? I don't ask about their less than human character. I want to inquire into the reason they fight …"

"Land for their children?" I said.

William clenched his teeth. "Murdering for land is against the laws of God."

Garrad raised his eyebrows. "Hmm. Yes, you're right. That may just be the key to the matter." He leaned toward William. "The nobles fight over land in spite of the laws, though they love the law. So either they're ignorant of the law, or the law is not properly administered."

This sounded like an insult to William's governing, so I quickly added, "Maybe they have nothing else to do."

"The younger ones have little else to resort to," Garrad said. "Younger sons know they won't inherit much. So they use any excuse to steal land. However, they still need some excuse, even if it's ignorance of the law. As for the older nobles, either they don't know the law, or they don't respect its administration."

William listened, staring at Garrad intently, but said nothing.

Garrad leaned toward William and continued, "Consider: first, the nobles don't know the laws of God or the laws that should bind them to you. Second, the administration of the law is inadequate. Do you see a common thread in these circumstances?"

I did not, but William stirred. "Yes. Learning. My father talked to me about education often."

Garrad smiled. "Yes, education. About God and the law together."

"I don't see how that would help," I said.

Garrad leaned back to look at me. "If the sons of nobles go to cathedral schools, where they are trained not only in the seven liberal arts but also in law and theology, then they are no longer bored and useless. They have something to do, something useful: administer the law. Think of Lanfranc's students: they're trained to be clerks and scribes and lawyers and magistrates."

William sat up. "Yes, they would enforce the law everywhere else. It's a good idea. My father and grandfather supported the cathedrals and their schools."

"Yes, they did. Not just because they were Christians and surely not to support the Pope."

"Why would the nobles send their sons to cathedral schools?" I asked.

"Duke William will give them a reason," Garrad replied. "Our gracious Duke, with a reputation for magnificence that rivals his father's, will promise the younger sons positions at court on the condition that they are properly educated. There they will help Duke William enforce the law and keep the peace, especially in the new towns that are growing up all over Normandy. The older barons will be delighted to place their sons in important positions, and they won't have to steal land for them."

"Wouldn't the Pope approve, too?" I asked.

Garrad nodded at me. "You think like a diplomat."

William drew his knees up to his chest and stared out the window.

After a while, he said, "It could work."

At first, it did not work. William was back in Falaise within a few weeks to report that the greater nobles and the bishops they controlled had rejected the Truce of God. The fighting worsened.

William refused to give up, however. "I've begun giving gifts to cathedrals with schools. I've offered positions at court to any baron's son who attends them." He smiled. "The schools will be receiving new students as we speak. Now we must pray for rapid teaching."

Garrad and I were to do more than just pray, though. As we prepared to go on another summer healing tour, William instructed us to carry his message of education to every church and cathedral. We were also to urge noble families we healed to send their children to the new schools.

Garrad was at the castle conferring one last time with William, while I took out our summer traveling clothes and put our winter clothes away. I scattered dried rose petals on the winter clothes and packed them in our wooden chests at the back of the hut. Combining with the sweet woodruff I had strewn about, the aroma almost drew me outside to daydream under a tree.

Before I could abandon my chores, though, the door swung open, and Garrad appeared.

"I've received a letter from Lanfranc," he said, waving it in the air with his good hand. "He says the roof of the dormitory at Bec Abbey has blown off."

"Herluin's abbey?"

"Yes, and the walls of the cloister and its wooden pillars have fallen down." Garrad shook his head. "Those knights could never build anything properly."

"How does Lanfranc know?"

"He's now at Bec. He intends to go into seclusion there. He writes that he must learn how to pray."

I dropped the clothes I was folding. "Lanfranc is just the teacher William needs. What sense does it make for him to go into a disease-infested monastery to pray?"

"He says there have been changes in his life."

"My life has changed, too, but I can pray about it at night and have the rest of the day to work."

"He must do what he thinks is best. He must depend on God, as we must."

I sat down on my bed. I could not argue with that — though I wanted to.

"Can't we talk to Lanfranc? Persuade him to go into seclusion when he's older, perhaps ten or twenty years older?"

He joined me in packing the winter clothes. "We have enough to do here. We must postpone our trip. There's been another assassination attempt at the castle."

"Was anyone harmed?"

"No, but we must find a way to end these attacks on William."

"How?"

A.D. 1043

"It will have to be a single weapon … the castle soldiers, but not openly … no unnecessary killing … not a Friday."

I shook my head. Trying to eavesdrop on William and his mother as they planned some secret activity, I could catch only a few phrases here and there before they would shrink into some corner to whisper.

It annoyed me, because eavesdropping at the castle was usually easy.

A few years after Duke Robert's death, Lady Arlette had married the Count of Conteville. Sometimes, while her new husband hunted, she visited Falaise.

Recently, the visits had become more frequent. And more secret.

At first, I thought that she and William were planning a grand hunt. I had even made a new bow for the occasion, but the bow remained unused for days, though William insisted that I keep it with me at all times and practice constantly.

Then I noticed the oddness of the preparations. Hunts were court affairs, public, even celebrative. For this event, the courtiers and villagers had been ordered away. By the end of a week's preparation, the castle seemed nearly empty.

Nor did hunts require moving hay bales and wagons around the castle yard in strange formations. Or forging a huge sword, fit for an unusually tall, muscular young man.

Nor did hunts demand William's practicing a new fighting maneuver, one that not even I was permitted to witness.

Garrad would say nothing except that he would be staying with Marie and her family in the village for a few days and that I should remain in the castle. I knew, though that he had consulted with Lady Arlette and William before and during the preparations.

Before I could discover what they were planning, a Monday afternoon arrived, and I noticed it was Monday afternoon, because William commented — twice — that the Truce of God was not in effect on Monday afternoons. Even though the Truce had been rejected in council, William was determined to observe it.

He and I stood alone in the castle yard. I assumed from his dress that he planned a late-day practice session with the weapons-masters. He wore his chained mail shirt over a wide-sleeved, brown tunic, a conical helmet, and thick cotton leggings covered with leather.

My bow hung over my shoulder, my quiver of arrows at my waist. "Do you mean for me to join you at practice today? Do you have something new for me to try with my bow, shooting while standing on my head, perhaps?"

"I have something to tell you," he began. Then he held up his hand. "Horses. Do you hear?"

I opened my mouth to say yes, but he spun away from me, striding toward the far end of the castle yard.

At the same moment, blows rained on the castle gate.

Unsheathing the huge sword, William called back to me, "Assassins. Garrad's spies were right. Even to the day and hour."

Assassins. I froze.

"Take three arrows," he commanded as he walked. "Stand behind the wine barrels. Don't shoot unless I tell you to."

I stared at him. For a moment he looked like a giant, gripping his sword and spreading his feet in a fighting stance.

He glanced at me. "Go on, Cuin."

I strung my bow, snatched three arrows from the quiver, and limped behind the barrels.

William reached the far end of the yard and faced the gate. As I swung my eyes from him to the gate, I noticed Arlette, watching from the stone tower, as she had all those years ago when assassins had sought both my life and his.

I gripped my bow tightly and put an arrow to it.

With a crash, the gate fell open, as if its ropes had suddenly failed. I jumped, startled, and then watched in terror as five men galloped into the castle yard.

Five.

Surely Arlette, and Garrad had not counted on so many. In the past there had been two or three. But five. William's sword and my arrows could bring down only four. If they didn't kill us first.

As I watched the riders close on William, I realized that I had never shot a human being. My hands shook.

The narrowness of the gate made the riders enter it singly. The hay bales stacked along the entryway forced them into a line. As a result, they bore down on William one at a time.

I steadied my hands and raised my bow.

William lifted the sword in front of him.

When the first lance came within a few feet of him, William lunged suddenly to his right, forcing the attacker to swing the weapon over his mount's head. As the lance was re-aimed, William sprang forward at his full height. Leaping, he parried the lance in a circular motion, closing with a blow to the attacker's neck. The sword drove in deeply between the man's armor and helmet. He thudded to the earth.

I felt the thud in my stomach and feared I might be sick.

Without hesitating, William repeated the motion. He struck the second attacker with the flat of the sword, unseating him. The third fell the same way.

The two remaining attackers jerked their mounts to a halt.

William stood in front of them, dust rising around his legs, his sword raised and pointed at the assassins.

"If you leave my castle in peace," a youthful, deep voice said loudly, "there will be no more honor or life lost on this day."

The would-be assassins looked from their two stunned companions to the dead one, his bloody neck just visible beneath the swirling dust. They stared at William.

Then they jerked their reins and pulled their horses' heads about, casting nervous glances around them.

As they galloped from the castle yard, I saw their eyes fall on what had been hidden earlier. In positions on the wall crouched the castle guards, their bows notched with arrows.

The two unseated attackers stirred to find William standing over them, sword brandished.

"I have no quarrel with you," he said. "If you swear never to attack me, my family, or my friends again, you may go in peace. If not, I will kill you where you lie."

They swore.

"Take this back to those who hired you," William said. "There is no assassin who can kill me. I have divine protection from poisoners, and I have my sword for such as you. Report that, and tell your masters that if they are wise, they will join me rather than try to kill me. They have nothing to gain and everything to lose by opposing me."

In a few moments, these attackers too had ridden back through the gate.

I emerged from behind my barrels. William watched the two men flee. He breathed heavily and then shook his head.

Guards raced from behind the hay bales toward the dead man. I glanced at him and took a deep breath to make the sick feeling pass.

"Are you all right?" I asked William.

He nodded but kept his eyes on the guards and the fallen assassin. Eventually, he said, "I should go up."

I watched him ascend the tower stairs where Arlette leaned against the wall outside the hiding-tower.

I stared at the fallen assassin, now being lifted by the guards. He didn't appear to be very old. Perhaps twenty. Perhaps less. I studied his face as it rose above the guards' shoulders. It stared at nothing at all. It was no longer the face of a killer, though. It belonged to an ordinary man, his final task badly done.

A.D. 1044

"Who?" I asked, stirring the coals in the fireplace.

The previous summer's healing tour had gone so well — and William's education ideas so well received — that I thought Garrad would be looking forward to this summer. As winter ended, though, he had seemed unusually anxious. I had returned from an afternoon visit to the castle to find him almost irritable, a rare state for Garrad.

"Harald, son of Sigurd, called Hardraada," he replied as he scattered pennyroyal around my bed. I had imported fleas from the castle. "King Magnus's uncle. Don't you recall? Stay away from those castle dogs until they get rid of their fleas."

"Hardraada, yes, of course I remember. I don't play with the dogs. They play with me."

"Hardraada will leave Byzantium soon. I've heard stories from pilgrims all winter."

"Hardraada. Hardraada. That's not really a name, is it? I remember this. It's a title or ..." I now had an opportunity to impress Garrad with how I'd mastered the Northern languages. "It means ... um ..."

He rose, shifting his lifeless arm into the pouch of his robe. "Pay attention, Cuin. Hardraada has argued with the Byzantine Empress in the past, but this seems to be their farewell argument."

"Hardraada." I made out its Norwegian roots. "Hard counsel?"

"Or 'ruthless'— 'Hardraada' can mean either. You recall correctly. It's not a name. Nor does anyone call him that to his face. It's an epithet used by those who have fought with him and against him. Face to face, he's Prince Harald, Sigurd's son."

He unrolled a parchment map. "Look here."

I pulled myself up with my crutch and joined him at the table.

He traced a line with his good hand. "Hardraada will most likely return along this route. Through the land of the Rus. He will stop in Kiev to collect his booty."

"Booty? I don't understand. I thought Hardraada was a mercenary for the Empress."

"He is. Or was."

"The priests have told me that mercenaries owe all their booty to their lords."

"That's one of the things Hardraada and the Empress have quarreled about. While other mercenaries give their loot to her, Hardraada smuggles everything back to Yaroslav, Prince of Kiev. So when Hardraada returns, he returns as the richest man in the North. Think of it: a vicious fighter, a cunning strategist, a natural leader, and possessing more gold, silver, and jewels than any Northern ruler."

"Will the raids begin again? As in the time of the 'Great Army' of Vikings?"

Garrad straightened. "Unless we do something about them, yes."

"The tanner in Rouen who saved me from the assassin said that the mill wheels on the Seine couldn't turn for years, because they were jammed by corpses. He said the entire river was red around the city."

"He recalled the events accurately." He put his good hand on my shoulder, which meant that he was about to say something important. "Do you see what we face? That's why we need an alliance with Hardraada. Or a way to head him off before he reaches Norway and joins forces with anyone, especially King Magnus."

"Will Hardraada respect an alliance?"

"He takes an oath just as seriously as we do. Convincing him to take it — that will be difficult. As it now stands, he has no reason to want an alliance with us. Normandy must have something to offer him in terms of power, and we have little enough of that now." He rolled up the map.

"What about King Magnus?"

He dropped his head toward the rolled map and stared at it blankly. "I don't know about Magnus."

"Could we get an alliance with him?"

"Like Hardraada, he has no reason to want one with us. We have failed in the past. Unless —" He paused.

"Unless what?"

"Magnus is at war with Denmark just now. If the war is costly enough, he may need both wealth and allies."

"Hardraada's loot will give Magnus what he needs to carry on any war."

He turned to search my face. "Yes, as you say: Hardraada's loot would give him the wealth to carry on any war. Including one against Normandy." He paused. "How would you like a trip to Rouen?"

"Fine. What are we going for?"

"It's time to lay some plans with William."

As we traveled, we stopped at villages and monasteries to find respite from the early-spring chill and to cure illnesses. In the villages, I was amazed at how many new farms, houses, churches, and shops had sprung up where the year before had been only forests. At the churches and abbeys, I was impressed with the number of new students and the new buildings to house them.

Even at Bec, the monk-knights had improved their living quarters. Abbot Herluin was happy to see us, but Lanfranc remained in seclusion. He saw no one.

Outside Rouen, the always impressive Abbey of St. Ouen boasted new buildings and a higher outer wall. It also had more students and monks who needed bleeding, so Garrad was pressed into service.

As a consequence, I entered Rouen alone. Here, too, new houses were everywhere, and the castle continued to be reinforced. William had workmen putting stone on every wall and minarets on every tower.

William himself sat in the great hall on his ducal platform, instructing guards, reprimanding knights, and scheduling the services of nobles.

Along with his golden-threaded clothes, he wore the stern ducal expression I had seen since we were children. He would not relax it while a noble or knight stood in front of him. Indeed, his face softened only when merchants brought complaints about prices and standards or when villagers delivered wax, eggs, apples, flax, or cheese to pay their taxes.

I lowered myself onto a bench along the wall and studied the apples and cheese. As I longed for an apple, William judged cases brought by magistrates. He leaned first on one arm and then the other of his chair, keeping his frown in place.

Only once did it slip.

A noblewoman brought in a girl whom she had seized from a tenant. The girl's father had failed to deliver three sheep that he owed the noblewoman, so the noblewoman had taken the daughter as payment.

The father, a slanted-faced man who had not mended his tunic or bathed recently, demanded his daughter back.

The noblewoman insisted that the exchange was fair and that the girl would be brought up in a noble household and when the time arrived, married to a young knight.

When William asked the girl what she wanted, she murmured, "I'd love to marry a knight."

William smiled. Her father scowled at her, and she pulled away from him, clinging to the noblewoman's arm.

William allowed the girl to be taken into the noblewoman's household.

When the hall fell quiet — relatively, at least — I approached him. He broke into a full grin, greeted me cheerfully, and asked about our trip. As I spoke, he listened intently.

Knowing that he still struggled with warring nobles, I took the opportunity to praise his ducal administration. "The towns and monasteries between here and Falaise seem to be flourishing. There's new growth everywhere."

He nodded and asked, "How's your archery practice? How is your bow-making coming along?"

"My aim and strength continue to improve. My bows are beginning to impress even the Kiev teacher."

"Good. How is your foot?"

I hesitated, because William knew all about my foot. "It aches sometimes, as it always has."

"Yes." He studied me. "Will you accompany me to the stables when I finish here?"

At the stables, I discovered the motive behind his concern for my foot.

"You must learn to ride a horse," he said, as he dragged me toward a huge animal that he had just saddled and bridled.

I had avoided horses all my life, resisting both Garrad's and William's urgings to learn to ride. I had no intention of giving up that resistance now.

"Oh, no," I protested. "What about my foot? Besides, this animal is huge. Look at it! It could throw me, and I'd be killed, and all your training would be for nothing, and you'd have to find a new friend."

"Don't worry. You don't ride with your feet but with your legs. You'll get used to it as soon as you've tried it a few times."

"In the meantime, I may fall off and kill myself."

"Then you'll go to Heaven. You've said so yourself."

"Then I won't get my position as court advisor, and you promised that —"

"You're an advisor now, and this is a ducal command."

I knew I could not move William. So, resigned to a probable death, I let him lift me onto the enormous beast. He showed me how to flop over its back and swing my legs over, so that I could mount the creature on my own, despite my bad foot.

Earlier, I had wondered what made him saddle a horse himself rather than let a stableboy do it. Now I realized he wanted me to learn by watching him.

I silently reproached myself for not being alert to his intentions. It might have been the last mistake of my life.

William led the horse into a walk and then jogged with it into a trot. I was jostled all over the castle yard, flopping and flailing, to the amusement of the crowd that gathered in the courtyard. Did no one have work to do in this castle? And did no one have pity on cripples anymore?

When I grumbled to Garrad that evening, he rubbed my aching legs with St. Johns wort liniment and fed me a tea of cramp bark, prickly ash, and ginger.

"You should continue," he said.

"I don't see why."

"Duke William has better informants than I in the matter of Hardraada. Hardraada did estrange himself from the Byzantine Empress. He did travel north. He did stop in Kiev, where he promptly married the daughter of Prince Yaroslav. But—" he raised the forefinger of his good hand "— he has decided to remain in Kiev for at least a year. That gives us time."

"For what?"

"To train the emissary we're thinking of sending north to negotiate with Hardraada."

I shifted my legs and groaned at the pain. "Who's that?"

"We're thinking of sending you."

I thought he was joking. "A lame emissary — clever idea."

"Being lame, you'll be able to go anywhere, without arousing suspicion or fear. You'll move freely and easily."

"And slowly and clumsily."

"That's why you must learn to ride."

CHAPTER 7

A JOURNEY TO AN ASSASSIN

A.D. 1045

"My informants warned me that King Magnus's fleet left Norway twice to attack us," Garrad said. "Fortunately, battles with Denmark diverted him."

William frowned. "If Magnus' regent Sweyn hadn't usurped the Danish throne, Magnus's fleet would have been on our shores already. With our nobles fighting among themselves and refusing to render military service, a Norwegian army would have met no more resistance than a few local knights."

"The usurper Sweyn turns out to be Normandy's godsend," Garrad agreed. "Hardraada, however …"

"When Hardraada adds his huge wealth and experience to Magnus's ships and ambition," Osbern said, "we are doomed. What town in Normandy can stand against such a force?"

"Hardraada will not tarry in Kiev much longer," Garrad said. "He has already sent messages to Magnus and Sweyn."

They fell silent for a moment. The four of us sat in the private chamber off the great hall in Rouen Castle. It was late spring, St. Barnabas' Day.

A breeze pushed through the narrow window and reached the back of my neck. When I glanced up to see if anyone else had shivered, I realized that they were all staring at me.

"We need our emissary," Garrad said, "now."

"We've run out of training time," William said.

I stared back at them, tapping my fingers on my chair. "Are you planning something that involves me?"

William leaned forward, assuming his ducal air. "Normandy is in great danger."

"I'm more than willing to help," I said to him, "but I don't grasp what role you think I can play."

Garrad glanced at William. "He didn't hear us. He was probably daydreaming again." To me he said, "Cuin, to survive, Normandy needs your skills now. Threats to our safety that previously remained distant now press upon us."

I nodded. "I did hear that. I do understand that King Magnus may strike south. I do know that we are threatened by Norway."

"Denmark, too," Osbern added.

"I know about King Sweyn of Denmark," I reminded him. I looked at William. "I wasn't daydreaming. Well, yes I was, but I did hear you say that Sweyn's usurping the Danish throne is what keeps Magnus from attacking us. Magnus, who rules Norway and should rule Denmark, is busy fighting Sweyn, who stole Denmark from Magnus after Magnus appointed him regent there. I heard all of that, and I know all of that."

"Then you must see," William said, "that when Hardraada arrives in the North with his men and wealth and joins his cousin Magnus, the issue will be resolved. Magnus will defeat Sweyn, become sole king of Norway and Denmark, and attack us. With Hardraada's help."

"If you leave Rouen within the week," Osbern said, "you could be in Denmark by midsummer, Norway by autumn."

"At the latest," William said.

"It's nice of you to send me on a trip," I replied, "but I'm not sure what I'm supposed to do in the North. I appreciate that you want me as an emissary and that I have some training, but in the face of Hardraada's return, what good will I be?"

"Hardraada must not join Magnus," William said. "If he does, we at least need some promise from both of them not to attack Normandy."

"So, you are suggesting that I convince two seasoned warriors not to seize a prize that's waiting for them — a prize, I might add, that they might think naturally belongs to the North, since Normans were originally Danes and Norwegians."

"I suggest," Osbern said, "that you win Hardraada's favor."

William leaned toward me. "Or drive a wedge between Hardraada and Magnus."

"If you win Hardraada over," Osbern actually sounded hopeful, "we have nothing to fear."

"How?" I asked him. "Shall I save his life in battle, so that he's obligated both to me and Normandy?"

Osbern broke into a smile. "An excellent idea!"

"I was jesting." I paused to glance at each of them. "You don't really intend to send me north, do you?"

They stared at me.

"Has it occurred to you that I'm not a warrior? Will you send warriors with me?"

William shook his head. "That's too dangerous. We would have to send a large force with you — a small one would be of no use — and even if I could muster it, Hardraada, Magnus, or Sweyn would perceive it as an invasion. Even King Henry in Paris or Count Baldwin in Flanders might mistake it as a threat. No."

"Am I to go alone?"

"I have friends I intend to send with you," Garrad said.

"Do your friends have weapons?"

"They're wandering monks. Not quite monks. They're Goliards."

My mouth fell open. "The ones that sing outrageous songs? What will they threaten Hardraada with? Bad Latin?"

"They're more useful than you think," Garrad said. "Besides, we're not sending you to threaten Hardraada. You have skills beyond that. You know the Northern languages as well as Latin. You think quickly and speak cleverly. You reason like a diplomat. You're resourceful."

"You're also the best bowman in Normandy," Osbern said.

"And God protects you," William said.

I gaped at him. "You believe that?"

"I've seen too many circumstances in your life to doubt it."

I sighed. "Do you have any real, practical strategy for gaining Hardraada's favor?"

"You're a healer," Garrad said.

"What do you mean?"

"I think he means," William said, making his voice quiet, "that it would be possible for a healer of your talents to make Hardraada ill and then heal him."

I looked hard at William. "Do you really want me to try such a dangerous tactic?"

Garrad shrugged. "It may be all you can do."

I took a deep breath. "I'd rather save his life in battle."

Osbern nodded vigorously. "I still think that's the best idea."

I frowned at him.

"You must do something," William said. "While fighting among the nobles continues here, you remain our best hope. Winning Hardraada's favor or turning him against Magnus — however you manage it — appears to be our only way of saving Normandy. For now, we're not strong enough for any other strategy."

Osbern leaned toward me. "Saving Normandy is worth any risk you may have to take. After all, if you fail, you'll be killed along with the rest of us. By a Northern army back here in Normandy."

"Or by a rebel army," Garrad said. "That, too, is a real fear."

William glanced at him and clenched his jaw but nodded in agreement.

I leaned back in my chair. "I'll go, of course. What choice do I have? Particularly since the task of winning Hardraada's favor has been so clearly defined, and since I'll be so well protected by defrocked, singing monks."

As Garrad and I paced across the castle yard, he said, his voice low, "I didn't want to burden William further, but the fear of a rebellion is greater than he may realize. That's why I don't want to send Osbern or any of the knights with you. William needs all his supporters here. They don't have your talents, in any event."

"That does not encourage me." I looked at him. "What have you heard?"

"In northern and western Normandy, fighting among the barons has died down."

"That's good."

"For local villagers, yes. William is relieved, of course. The barons' partial truce, however, may become an alliance against William. If they find a legitimate contender to the ducal throne, they will attack him."

"Is there one?"

"His cousin."

"Guy? He's one of William's closest friends."

"He's also weak and ambitious, which is all the more reason I want you, as you pass through Flanders, to see Count Baldwin, if you can. Do you recall that William's father once aided him, and he owes us a favor?"

I nodded, "I also recall that he's one of the wealthiest, most powerful nobles in the Western world. Where may I find him? Flanders is large."

"He often holds court in fortified monasteries, and he's engaged in yet another battle with the Holy Roman Emperor."

"Do you really think that Count Baldwin will help William?"

"Yes, and we need his help," He put his good hand on my shoulder. "So, you see how vital your tasks are to our survival. Normandy's fate is truly in your hands."

"Are you certain that I —?"

"I also want you to get to know Baldwin's family, especially his daughter."

"Why?"

"Any contact that may end in marriage is useful."

I stopped, partially to rest my foot, which had begun to ache. "Is someone seeking a wife?"

"Wives can make good political alliances. Do you know, for instance, that Edward is marrying a Wessex woman?"

"Edward? Marrying one of Godwin's court ladies?"

"That's what I'm told. I suspected that Godwin would offer someone to Edward. As for Edward, it's a good tactic. He strengthens his hand with his principal enemy, Godwin. At the same time, he allies himself to the Saxons, particularly the Saxons who have the best relations with Danes in England."

"I'm having trouble imagining Edward married to anyone."

He smiled. "Yes, that does seem odd. I think he will keep his celibacy vow, though. I've heard that his wife has a similar vow. For similar reasons." What those reasons were he didn't say.

"Is Edward safe in England now?"

"Edward has courted the favor of the Pope, who is now engaged in a power struggle in Rome. So those factors are enough to keep Edward secure, at least as far as the Holy Roman Empire is concerned."

"Count Baldwin is not safe, though, as far as the Empire is concerned."

"He has enough wealth and power to stand his own ground."

"Where exactly in Flanders am I to find Count Baldwin? You mentioned fortified monasteries."

"As I calculate his movements, he'll be staying at the monastery of St. Vaast near Arras by the time you get there."

I was accustomed to Garrad's being informed of events elsewhere, but I never knew the sources of his information. "Well, if I can find the Count, I'll at least meet a friend before I have to confront Hardraada or Magnus."

Garrad stared hard at me for a moment. "Whether you realize it or not, this is what you have trained for all your life. You have traveled all over Normandy and met many people. You know healing and history and languages. You have a quick wit and are too intelligent to mistake foolhardiness for courage. You have the skills to be the best emissary in Normandy."

"Does that include my riding?"

"Except for that."

By week's end, I had finished my preparations, even down to the mugwort I carried in the pouch of my robe for good fortune on the roads.

Since I would be traveling with Goliards, I was disguised as a rumpled, outcast monk. I had to appear as disreputable as they had become — and as harmless. Even the tonsure that Garrad had shaved on my head was smaller than most and growing in by the time the Goliards arrived in Rouen.

"They're adequate bodyguards," Garrad said as he led me to the castle yard to meet them. "You need only traveling companions, though. The roads between Normandy and Denmark, carrying merchants to and from the trading cities and fairs, are safe during summer months. You won't need protection … until you meet Hardraada."

The Goliard leader Rolf knew Garrad well. As usual, they had already met in some unnamed place at some unrevealed time.

Standing in the courtyard of the castle, Rolf eyed me, smiling. He stepped toward me to finger the fraying cloth at my sleeves and study the stubble of my beard and tonsure. Both mirrored his appearance. He tilted his head sympathetically at my crutch.

Stepping back, he announced, "We'll take him!"

I glanced at Garrad and William. They smiled.

"I do agree that he looks like a monk," William said. "Perhaps you have finally found your calling, Cuin."

"Yes," Garrad said, "but what kind of monk would he make?"

"What kind, indeed?" Rolf said. "Do you know that we're the only monks in the world descended from the Philistine Goliath?"

Behind him, his dozen companions chuckled.

"That's what I've heard," I replied. "Does it mean that you'll turn into giants as we travel? That would be a useful trait."

He laughed. "A wit! Just what we need! No, lad. It means that we sing and drink and make love to any woman who will have us!"

I saw William gaze at the ground, and I did as well. Though most of my village friends had married long ago, my life — like William's — had been too focused on Normandy and avoiding assassins to allow for but a few affairs of the senses and none of the heart.

One of the Goliards struck a lute he carried, signaling the others to sing a Latin refrain, which they repeated in Norman French:

The farmer's daughter goes out at dawn with wool to spin and staff, and
in her flocks are colts and bulls and a heifer calf.
Hard she looks at the man of books alone in a grassy spot:
"What are you doing there, studious sir?
Come play with me — why not?"

The knights and guards in hearing distance shouted their approval. The chapel priests, standing just behind William, apparently thought of something to do elsewhere.

Rolf put his hands on his hips. "We're not merely frivolous, my friends! We're tellers of truth, and we call the bishops what they deserve to be called!"

Apparently, this was a cue for another lute chord and another song:

> *Bishops own God, lord and sire,*
> *Putting sacraments to hire.*
> *While secure in power they sit,*
> *Making mock at Holy Writ.*
> *Bad men they prefer to good,*
> *Loot is all their livelihood.*
> *Through the South their power extends,*
> *Every convent holds their friends!*

This was followed by general laughter, especially since the word for "friend" implied "lover."

Then one of the Goliards cried, "Nor do we overlook nobles!" and striding forward, sang by himself:

> *While rich men vaunt, the wise man grieves,*
> *For justice fallen among thieves:*
> *For courts that hear, to line the pockets,*
> *The lamest suits that shame their dockets.*
> *Wherever money's power is found,*
> *The poor man gets the run-around:*
> *Here's a case, let none deny it,*
> *Fixed before the court can try it.*
> *But when poor Codrus starts a suit,*
> *Case dismissed — he's destitute!*
> *The fingers of the great, it's funny,*
> *Are magnets for attracting money;*

> *Whenever profits are in view*
> *They put a price on all they do;*
> *And further, risking retribution,*
> *Assess a tax on absolution!*

The others clapped him on the back with cries of "Well sung!" and "Finely rendered!"

Some of the nobles behind William shifted and fingered their swords, but William laughed out loud, accompanied by Garrad.

Rolf scolded his companions that the season for gaiety should find them singing barbed songs. In response, they called down mock curses on themselves and broke into a song praising love.

The road to Denmark was going to be much longer than I had imagined.

The next morning, St. Silverius's Day, the Goliards and I stood at the entrance to the castle, mounted and ready to ride — those of us with mounts. Half of the Goliards walked, while the other half preferred donkeys.

I reluctantly perched myself on the pony Arlette had chosen for me. It was slow and small enough, she said, to make me feel secure. It was indeed slow and small, but I did not feel secure.

My too-large robe draped over me and the pony like a tent. Despite the heat, I wore cotton leggings covered with leather for protection from hours in the saddle and colder weather to come. As a result, my legs, protruding from the vast robe, appeared plump.

As he emerged from the great hall with Garrad and Arlette, William burst into laughter.

"I'm glad I don't strike terror into your heart, my lord," I said.

The effect was what I had hoped for. Secretly, though, I wanted to be a warrior setting off to battle. To that end, I had slung my bow and arrows over the horse's back, along with my crutch and healer's pouch.

William studied me. "Some monks are fighters, but don't you think a bow will make you more noticeable?"

"I will say that it's a gift for the lord of whatever region I'm passing through. This is the new one I've been working on. It looks like a gift."

He ran his hand over it. "It's beautiful. And long."

"I made it especially long. That will fortify my story. I look as if I'm too short to pull so long a bow."

"You look as if you're too short to get off your horse."

Arlette stepped forward to say good-bye. As always, her face changed little, but she made me lean forward to receive an embrace. I almost fell off the pony, which I took to be a bad sign.

William gave me a bag of silver pieces and grasped my hand. "Remember, whatever your outward appearance, you're the Duke's emissary on a critical mission. Farewell."

Garrad regretted that he could not accompany me. "I look forward to receiving word of you, though."

"I'll send messages back with any traveler I meet," I said. "I hope to deliver my own messages by winter."

Garrad shook my hand. "I hope so, too, but I'm sending you and the Goliards on a leisurely southern route to put any spy off your track. Once you're in the North — though I hope you work quickly — take whatever time you need to get the alliance with Hardraada. Or Magnus. Who knows? By then, I may join you. One thing more, Cuin: don't forget Count Baldwin. Duke William needs every friend you can win for him. Remember, Baldwin is fighting the Holy Roman Empire, so that puts him on our side, even though we have never openly defied the Pope or the Empire."

I nodded.

He paused and then said, "I don't wish to frighten you, but the assassin may still be —"

"I know. I've thought of that."

"Don't let anyone know your true identity unless you have to. We still don't know who sent the assassin or why."

"I'll be Brother Somebody wherever I am."

He smiled. "Good. God go with you, my friend."

The Goliards shouted that they must leave.

Garrad smiled at Rolf and said, "I'm sending Brother Augustine with you now."

Rolf looked at Garrad closely and nodded.

"Come then, Brother Augustine," he shouted.

The Goliards and I passed through the castle gate. I twisted to wave to William, Arlette, and Garrad. As we rode through the streets of Rouen, the Goliards began singing.

The first three days of traveling delighted me. Except for a passing shower, the days remained dry and warm and the evenings comfortable. The threat of an invading Northern army seemed remote, and the fears that lurked in the shadows of Rouen vanished in the sun.

I made a truce with the pony. "As long as you amble slowly," I said to him, "I'll stay up here."

Slow turned out to be his only speed. As he settled into calm plodding, I lost my fear of falling off him. I shifted my sitting position to avoid saddle-soreness, but each night I felt as if the saddle were still under me, and my legs ached.

Gradually, I grew relaxed enough to enjoy the ride. Though the sun burned the part of my head exposed by the tonsure, its light also slanted through the trees, creating restful shade and mottled patterns on the road, except where we found clearings.

Rolf commented that the untouched clearings might be the work of ancient Romans, the building stones stolen long ago, "or Viking outposts of the dark years here."

Where the clearings were farmed, we ate well. The Goliards' songs were popular, and every farmer seemed happy to part with bread, apples, or carrots as payment. Regardless of how late the hour was, though, we left the farmhouses to sleep in the forest, away from the road.

Though I doubted their abilities as bodyguards, the Goliards turned out to be pleasant companions, breaking into song less frequently than I had feared. They traveled in two groups, the mounted half riding behind me, the walkers in front.

Sometimes Rolf, astride his donkey, would trot forward to discuss our journey or spin tales about their founding bishop Golias, whom I knew to be a fiction.

As we passed the new farms and towns, I found many other people glad to talk with me. I exchanged gossip with farmers who cleared land or strode behind iron-wheeled plows, masons who hauled stones for churches, and carpenters who repaired causeways.

We often encountered merchants hurrying to trading towns or the summer fair at Troyes. They paused to grumble about tolls at bridges and river fords.

I talked most to the children playing in village streets, accompanied by dogs and cats. Their lack of fear reminded me that they had lived their few years free of the threat of Northern attack and assassins.

I wondered whether their later years would be free of this threat.

The Goliards chatted cheerfully during the day and sang loudly at night.

Until the end of the first week.

As we made camp in the forest that evening, they did not sing or speak, observing an almost frightening silence. If I opened my mouth, they shook their heads, waving me toward my makeshift bed, situated in the center of their own.

Only the next morning, after they had scouted the area and we were again on the road, did they again strum their lutes and sing to one another. Even then, they seemed to be listening for something. Soon they stopped all playing and singing.

I pulled my pony alongside Rolf's donkey. Like the others, he had been silent most of the morning.

"Why were you and the others so quiet last night?" I asked. "Today as well?"

He grinned. "Have you never heard of monks taking vows of silence?"

"You haven't seemed silent to me or monkish."

He poked at my robe. "When we're silent, we're listening. You may wish to, as well, because there's much to hear. Surely Garrad has taught you that."

He turned in his saddle. "For instance, can you hear that someone's behind us? We've been followed for the last two days. The birds and insects tell us that someone is trying to determine who we are without revealing himself."

I had noticed signs that other travelers were in the vicinity. "Another party on the road seems no reason for concern."

"Perhaps not. This traveler, though, has followed the same circular route that Garrad laid out for us. He also stops when we stop and avoids overtaking us."

"Perhaps he dislikes Goliards."

Rolf winked. "You mean he dislikes our singing. Perhaps it's time to find out." He called to his fellows, "Come, monks of Golias, let's announce ourselves. To our brothers everywhere, sing like Goliath!"

The others responded:

> *To our fellow Goliards, we call for cheerful meeting,*
> *The brotherhood of Golias, we send to you a greeting:*
> *Genuine Goliards are we, no other name will fit us,*
> *Fear you not to join our ranks, and to yours please admit us!*
> *At dinner hour we ask of you to share your ordinary,*
> *Ply us with the choicest wine — we pray you not be chary;*
> *If we exceed the measure of drink, prop us when we stagger,*
> *Whatever happens afterward, please tell no tongue-wagger!*

Rolf grinned. "Now let's see whether our traveler is a lover of wine and song."

For a moment, there was only silence. Then a howl pierced the air, rising slowly to a shriek.

The Goliards froze, staring at each other.

"What was that?" one asked.

Rolf and I replied together, "A Berserker howl."

Then he said to me, "You agree that a Berserker is not a normal traveler on the roads of Normandy."

I could feel my heart beginning to pound. "He may be seeking me."

The Goliards grouped around me.

"Why?" Rolf asked.

"Years ago, a Norwegian warrior, who may have been a Berserker, sought my life. I don't know why."

Following close on my words was the sound of galloping.

"If a Berserker does seek your life, we can't resist him," Rolf said quickly. "Those of us who are mounted will ride ahead, drawing him away. You flee with the others on foot. Lead the pony and erase his tracks as you go. Farewell, and God protect you!"

I jumped from the pony, grabbed my crutch, and scrambled after the Goliards into the forest. One of them led the pony, while another brushed away signs of our passage.

The galloping became louder.

We scrambled up a rise, over its top, and behind a boulder just as the galloping closed on where we had stood in the road.

It slowed and then halted.

We pressed ourselves against the boulder. I kept my eyes on the bow and arrows resting across the pony's back. I was ready to seize them if the Berserker came toward us.

We heard nothing for a long time. Then footsteps on the road. The rider was walking around.

My body began to shake.

The footsteps came into the forest and toward the rise.

I almost raised my hand toward the bow, but a voice seemed to whisper inside my head, "Don't move."

The footsteps stopped. There was silence for a long time. Then they moved away. We heard more footsteps, moving toward the opposite side of the road. Again silence for a long time.

Then footsteps again, a short grunting sound, and hoofbeats. The rider was following Rolf and the others.

I said in a voice just above a whisper, "I hope that the rider's stop gave Rolf and the others time to escape."

The Goliards nodded but still frowned.

One of them searched the forest and then cocked his head. "Listen. There is a river nearby. We can follow it to the next village and avoid the road." He turned to me and the others. "Let's pray that if this Berserker does catch our friends, he will not hurt them."

They stood silently for a moment, their heads drooped. Then they wound their way between oaks and elms, heading toward the sound of the river.

That night, as we camped by the water in a stand of willows, I lay awake, staring at the stars through the leaves. As I had done the entire day, I pondered the danger I had brought on my escort.

If the Berserker had in fact returned to kill me, then anything that happened to the Goliards would be on my soul.

If I voiced my concerns, though, the Goliards would cling to me. That would be the proper thing to do. In spite of their irreverent songs, the Goliards were proper in their duty.

So I decided that my duty was to slip away. The group on foot would then be safe from attack, while I sought the mounted band.

Silently, I raised myself from my blankets, rolled them into a bundle under one arm, and propped my crutch under the other. I stepped gingerly between the beds, limping toward the pony. All of Garrad's teaching about moving silently helped me not to arouse anyone.

The Goliard guarding the pony had himself fallen asleep. To my relief, the pony made only a slight huffing sound as I wrapped his reins around my crutch and pulled him through the forest.

As the Goliards had suggested, I followed the stream. In the distance I could see the village they mentioned. Day had just broken, and no traveler was in sight, so I remounted. As I rode, I prayed that Rolf and the other Goliards had eluded the Berserker warrior.

At this hour of the morning, the village was a sleepy one. Only a resident beggar in a dirty brown robe greeted me with an empty cup. I slid off the pony and gave him the last of the cider I carried in a clay jug. I gave him the jug too.

He sipped and grimaced at me, causing the hairs of his beard to shoot out from his face. "Excuse me, brother. What is this?"

"It's cider. It's all I have."

He eyed my crutch. "Ah, well. Thank you for the jug, anyway."

"Have you seen any riders here? A single horsemen or a group of Goliards?"

He nodded. "Last night a group of brothers passed through, but they weren't singing like Goliards. These were quiet as monks."

I thanked him and pressed on.

Soon I entered a wild countryside. No one else was on the road, and no new farms had been built along it. I silently thanked the ancient Romans and their road-making that I could pass through without having to clear away undergrowth, having to move only a few fallen branches.

I also thanked Garrad for teaching me foraging skills. I was able to eat well, finding nuts, berries, some edible leaves, and chewable bark each time I rested.

That night, I slept in the forest, far enough away from the pony that I would not be spotted if anyone found him. If he neighed at an intruder, however, the sound would alert me. I pressed the bow, arrows, and knife to my side.

My sleep, however, was fitful. Every owl or passing animal startled me. I sat up at any sound, my knife brandished. Then I sank down again, peering into the darkness until I dozed or some other noise alarmed me. I was grateful when the morning sun appeared through the trees.

By afternoon, though, I began to feel the effects of my lack of sleep. As I rode alone on a cleared road with the sun warming my back, I felt drowsy. My eyes drifted closed. I opened them, and they closed again. Perhaps, I thought, I don't need to open them …

A shower awakened me, the raindrops hitting my face as I leaned precariously to one side.

Something else had disturbed my sleep, too. I strained to listen.

The whispering voice was back: "Leave the road." It overlapped a drumming sound on the road behind me.

The Goliards were mounted, but they would be far ahead, and they rode six donkeys. This sound came from a single horse.

I pulled the pony off the road into a dense thicket and tied him behind a beech.

The hoofbeats behind me stopped.

I froze for a moment and then glanced around, taking in my surroundings. I had been riding in a valley cradled between steep banks. As I studied them, I could see that the banks, unlike the thicket, supported only sparse undergrowth around their trees.

I could climb a bank on foot and double-back on my trail. If the rider had sought shelter from the rain, he might rest where I could see him.

I slung the longbow and a quiver of arrows over my shoulder and grabbed my crutch. Seeing no one, I clambered up the slope to the northwest. I pulled myself along by grasping tree trunks.

Wherever I found smooth bark, though, its wetness slipped under my grasp. Even with my crutch, I struggled for footing among slick ferns. My hood, soaked, draped over my eyes. I had to throw it back, exposing my face to the rain.

Finally I reached the crest of the ridge and crept backward along it.

I wondered what I would do if the traveler turned out to be the Berserker. For all my secret desire to be a wandering warrior, I doubted that I could actually shoot anyone. Would my disguise save me?

The traveler, however, was not a warrior. He was a monk. At least, he wore a Benedictine's black robe. Having dismounted, he huddled against a spreading tree, the reins of his black horse wrapped around his wrist. Unfortunately, he had covered his head with his hood against the rain, so that I could not see his face.

Because I had met many monks on healing trips with Garrad, I wondered whether I knew this one. Perhaps he would be friendly. I did not want to risk another companion's life, but just now I would welcome a friend.

I leaned out from the elm that was hiding me. If only he would look up, I could see his face.

As if in answer to my wish, leaves rustled and a branch cracked behind me. Instinctively, I shrank behind the elm, while keeping the monk in view.

He leaped up, jerking a dagger from inside his robe. Double-edged, it curved three times before reaching its point. A crimson streak ran down it, as if it dripped blood.

Its bearer peered in my direction. He crossed the road toward where I trembled behind my elm. Had he seen me? I held my breath. The rain abruptly stopped. The woods fell silent. Except for the approaching footfalls.

I prayed many prayers, all adapted to keeping knife-bearers away from lame, stupid travelers with too much curiosity.

To my delight, my prayers were answered. An adventuresome buck — probably the source of the cracking branch — chose that moment to spring from the ridge behind me. It dashed down the slope, splaying its hoofs on the wet forest floor. It regained its balance and bolted across the road, thudding into the distance.

The knife-bearer grunted and strode away.

I sighed a heavenward thanks, waited a moment, and then, crouching and wrapping myself around the elm, risked another look.

The man had thrown back his hood. As he picked his way through the trees and muddy ferns, I could study his profile. It was long, angular ... and familiar.

The clouds drifted apart, and a single ray of sunlight fell on his forehead. A scar ridged across it down to the left eye. Though I had not seen the face in years, I recognized it. It belonged to the old monk from Lanfranc's school in Avranches.

I almost laughed with relief. This was one of Lanfranc's men.

I rose to identify myself, but some uneasiness prevented me. The old man — what had Lanfranc called him? — had been unfriendly during Garrad's and my stay in Avranches.

Now he turned up on the road to Flanders, and I did not know why. Had Garrad seen Lanfranc, and had Lanfranc arranged to have a protector follow me? Lanfranc, though, was at Bec, and Garrad had said nothing about visiting him.

Voldred — that was the name.

Why was he here, so far from Avranches? Was he at Bec with Lanfranc? If so, what was he doing in Flanders? And what was he doing with a knife that could almost have been the one from my childhood nightmares?

Too many questions remained unanswered for me to be uncautious. At the very least, journeying with a hostile companion held little appeal. And the image of the snakelike knife hung in my mind.

I decided to let him ride away.

That presented a problem, though. The rain had ended earlier than I expected — much earlier — and the buck's adventure had prevented my return to the pony. The monk Voldred mounted and urged his horse down the road. He would reach the pony before I did.

I silently cursed myself for not hiding it better. No wonder the Lord had to look after me. I behaved stupidly when left to myself.

I scrambled back through the forest, slipping like the buck sent in answer to my prayers.

By the time I reached the place where I had left the pony, Voldred had passed. The marks on the road revealed that he had urged his horse into a gallop.

The pony was gone.

At first, I thought Voldred must have taken it with him, but only one set of hoof prints wound down the road. My pony's hoofmarks led into the forest, accompanied by footprints.

Gripping my bow and knife, I followed them. Not far away, a path appeared. It curved around a low bluff, which blocked my view. From behind the bluff I heard a scuffling noise. I squeezed the knife handle. No one appeared. The noise stopped.

I lifted the knife and crept forward. Straining to see around the bluff, I discerned a form through the protruding roots and branches: the pony. He lifted his head, twitched his ears, and neighed at me.

"Quiet," I said.

Scouting the area, though, I found no one else who could hear him.

I wondered who had led the pony away from the road. The footprints of whoever had done so ran down the path in the opposite direction Voldred had ridden. I checked my provisions. Nothing had been stolen. I shook my head at the mystery.

If Garrad had calculated correctly, I was within a day's ride of Arras. At the monastery of St. Vaast, I would find refuge and possibly Count Baldwin, the friend of William's father. I mounted and rode on.

Unfortunately, I did not reach Arras that night. The Goliards and I must have ridden more leisurely than Garrad had estimated. Or perhaps I had struck too far south.

Watching the dusk turn gray and settle around the trees, I did not welcome another night in the forest. Besides, the pony would be tiring of foraged food and be hungry for oats. I was hungry for some different fare myself.

I turned onto an inland road until I found one of the sheep fields common to Flanders. A thatched farmhouse perched on its edge. Smoke sifted through the thatch. Outside the house, a young shepherd-farmer in a russet tunic relaxed on a wooden bench, enjoying the sunset.

As I neared, he rose.

I raised my hand in greeting, but he brandished a staff in return. I stopped, surprised. Villagers in the Lowlands revered monks, or so Garrad had told me. One on horseback with weapons may have seemed odd, but it did not warrant hostility.

I greeted the shepherd-farmer in the French dialect of this part of Flanders. I appended a Latin blessing.

The staff lowered, but the farmer challenged me, "Are you with the monk who rode through this morning?"

"I ride alone."

"Where are you from, and where are you bound?"

"I've come from the Abbey of St. Ouen near Rouen in Normandy, and I'm heading for St. Vaast in Arras. I'm a healer, and I have herbs to offer the infirmarian there." I held up my healer's pouch.

"Hmm. All right." He lowered his staff. "I'm sorry, brother. Forgive me, but you're not the first monk I've dealt with today, and the other was unfriendly."

He explained that an older, scarred Benedictine had ridden through earlier, demanding information about travelers. Though nearby Arras usually bustled with activity, no one had passed by, at least no one that the farmer had seen. This infuriated the monk, who then demanded livestock.

"I keep goats," the shepherd told me. "For the milk. This monk would have a goat or kill me. A horned goat. He even pulled a knife. A vicious-looking knife, too — as long as my arm."

"Was its blade curved, with a red marking?"

He nodded and thrust his head toward me. "Do monks carry knives like that?"

I shook my head. "No, but I've seen something similar, and it is terrifying."

"That's why I let him have the goat. I'll be at the monastery soon, you can be sure. They owe me."

"Is St. Vaast nearby?"

"Yes."

Over dinner, I asked for directions to the monastery.

As his family blinked and stared at me, the shepherd described the route. "It's easy to find. It's safe there, too. Of course, it wasn't always that way. My own grandfather saw the Vikings plunder it. They killed the monks first." He lifted an eyebrow at me. "We can praise the saints for the end of that time."

Early next morning — having given the shepherd a silver piece for his hospitality and the pony's oats — I thanked him, blessed his family, and rode toward St. Vaast.

I was uneasy, because the day was Friday, and I did not wish to have luck against me on this day.

I tried to think about the Abbey of St. Vaast. One decision I made was that if I found Brother Voldred there, I would confront him with his bad behavior. His rudeness reflected on all monks, even those of us disguised as monks.

The day being sunny and the road wide, I pressed on as quickly as the pony would go. I noticed storm clouds behind me and hoped to outdistance them.

As the sky grayed, the road narrowed into a forest path, wide enough for only one horse. Branches stretched across it, forming a green canopy. The effect was beautiful, but I ignored it, silently rehearsing the sermons I would give Voldred if I found him.

My silent preaching was interrupted by a pattern of sound-then-silence behind me. Once. Twice. Three times.

I was being followed.

Voldred? Had he doubled back overnight and found my trail?

I pulled the pony to a stop and peered down the road behind me.

Shortly a horse did appear, its rider obscured but for an outline behind overhanging branches. The horse, however, was not black but pale, almost white. The pursuer sat straighter in his saddle than Voldred, and he did not wear monk's robes. Along his legs — the only part of him I could see clearly — hung the scabbard of a huge sword.

I decided to make for Arras as quickly as I could. I urged the pony forward, quietly. The pony cared nothing for speed, though. We were condemned to trot through the forest, certainly not fast enough to outpace a horse.

I tugged the hood over my head. Branches clawed at it. The sky was swallowed by darkening clouds. Rain pelted on the leaves and my hood and robe. I drew my hands into my sleeves, trying to keep the reins dry. The drops fell larger and faster, until they pounded like a hundred galloping horses.

I glanced backward but could see only a sheet of rain.

I silently cursed the weather and the slow pony and then stole another backward glance. As I twisted to the front again, a soaked branch slapped my cheek. I cursed once more, this time out loud, and lashed at the offending leaves. They bounced away, brushing my shoulder as I rounded a bend in the path.

There, not far away, lay the town of Arras.

Now I did hear, even in the driving rain, galloping. I spun to see the pale horse hurtling at me, its rider, a blond-haired man, waving his sword and shouting.

I sprang from the pony, placing it between the assailant and me. I grabbed for my bow and arrows and jammed my crutch under my arm to brace myself.

Another horse thudded to a stop behind me. I turned. Voldred leaped from it.

"Thank God!" I exclaimed. "You're Brother Voldred, aren't you? I'm Cuin! I met you in —"

I was cut off as his face twisted, and he let out a shriek — the Berserker howl.

In an instant, I realized why, all those years ago in Avranches, his voice had seemed familiar. It belonged to the assassin.

The Norwegian warrior in Rouen and Falaise, the Berserker in Avranches, and the Berserker who had followed the Goliards: Voldred.

I lifted the bow to ward him off.

Snatching the curved knife from his robe, he slashed it down toward my chest. I swerved, using my bow to parry him, but the blow's force carried the blade into my forearm. Pain shot through it.

Wincing, I gripped the bow with both hands to meet the next attack.

He jerked the knife into the air again. At that moment the blond rider reached us. From his horse, he drove his sword down across Voldred's shoulder and back. Voldred whirled around, waving the snakelike knife.

The blond rider's momentum carried him beyond the knife blows. He reined his horse around to strike again.

Voldred slouched under the pain. He tried to lift the knife again, but only his hand moved.

Uttering a Northern curse, he stumbled toward his own mount.

Grimacing, he wrenched himself into his saddle and pulled another long knife from it. With effort, he hurled it at the blond rider.

The knife struck the rider in the chest, causing him to sway in his saddle. Nonetheless, he drove his horse toward Voldred and slashed again, this time cutting Voldred's other shoulder and arm.

Voldred slumped forward against his horse's neck, and the horse bolted, carrying him away from Arras.

Feeling dizzy, I sagged against the pony. The trees and houses began to spin, and I dropped to the ground.

As blackness descended, I saw the rider still in his saddle, a sword in his hand, the knife protruding from his chest.

CHAPTER 8

THE MONK, THE COURTIER, AND THE LADY

A.D. 1045

When I awoke, he was leaning over me. I stirred, but he pinned my arms.

From far away I heard a voice: "Lie still." It was a Saxon dialect.

I struggled to free myself.

"Lie still!" the voice, more muffled, commanded again.

I sank back into darkness.

My eyes opened. The blackness did not dissipate but gradually became gray. It was night.

Breathing was difficult. My body, aching, sank into the straw bed. Fresh straw, from the smell of it.

Too little straw, though. The last bed I had found so uncomfortable belonged to Bec Abbey, where Garrad and I had visited Abbot Herluin and Lanfranc. This had to be a monastery bed, one that would purge a monk's soul of a many sins for every night he slept on it.

Unexpectedly the image of an old woman wearing an odd cloak came into my mind. Then I recalled that I had been visited by vivid dreams about flying toward the stars and climbing huge trees to look at strangely shaped clouds. The old woman seemed to be in the background of all the dreams. I wondered momentarily whether my wound had disoriented my mind.

I twisted my head in the direction of a whispering sound — breathing. Peering into the darkness, I could discern a figure, slumped in a chair. It was the blond rider. He was sleeping.

With painful effort, I pushed myself into a sitting position. I tried to stand, but my legs failed to respond. I groped around the bottom of the bed to see whether my robe was there. The movement sent pain shooting through my left arm.

The blond man stirred, stared at me, and rose. He strode from the room and returned with a lighted candle.

"How do you feel?" he asked in the Saxon dialect I had heard earlier.

While I was deciding how to answer, he repeated the question in Norman French.

I was astonished. In the candlelight, his appearance was no different from a common mercenary, not unlike those hired to kill William. His tunic and shoes were undyed, and his leggings were brown. His blond hair had dried matted from the heavy rain, and his face was stubbly.

Saxons who spoke foreign languages were courtiers, Garrad had told me.

"Who are you?" I asked.

"A friend." He placed the candle in a wall-holder. "How do you feel?"

I remembered Voldred's other knife protruding from the blond man's chest. "You were struck with a knife."

"It lodged in my mail. I suffered only a bruise. How do you feel?"

He towered over me, seeming almost as tall as William but not much older. His voice was rough and bass.

I took a painful breath. "Not very well. Everything hurts, and I have trouble breathing."

"The monk tending you says the knife was poisoned."

I glanced at my bandaged left arm. "Where am I?"

"The infirmary at the monastery of St. Vaast."

I managed another breath. "And you are?"

"You may call me Tostig." The reply was proud enough to come from a courtier, though he did not insist on a title.

"What happened to the monk who attacked me?"

"I don't know. I didn't pursue him. I was more concerned about you."

I forced a deep breath, and my chest ached in response. "I'm in your debt —"

He interrupted me. "You are Cuin, aren't you?"

I was astonished again and must have looked it.

He explained, "Duke William told me about you."

"You know Duke William?"

"He sent me after you. I landed in Normandy on my way here. The Duke said he had recently dispatched an emissary, disguised as a monk, to Flanders. I promised I would look for you and offer my protection."

"You certainly did that, and I'm in your debt," I said. He nodded in response. "I must get word to the Duke, though, that my mission is delayed."

"I've already sent a messenger."

"I'm doubly indebted to you."

"Why did that monk want to kill you?"

"I don't think he's a monk, and I have no idea why he wants me dead."

He ran his hand over his stubbly beard and frowned. "Do you know him?"

"No. Do you?"

"I didn't speak with him. When I saw you were being followed, I watched from a distance, which was easy. That horse of yours doesn't move very fast."

I recalled the episode in the forest. "You moved my pony from the path."

"Yes." He shrugged. "You should have hidden it better. If the monk had seen it, what would you have done?"

"I thought of that too late."

"Too late indeed. I would have stayed to instruct you, but I had to reach my own horse, hidden farther down the path — well hidden. By the time I returned, you were gone. I followed, but you must have changed your route as you neared Arras, because I lost your trail. Only after spending the night here and then backtracking along the roads to Arras did I find you. Barely in time."

"I'm more in your debt than I—"

"You may repay me by taking more caution in the future. If you had been killed, my relation with Duke William would have suffered."

Mine too, I thought.

He continued, "I have a gift for the Duke's emissary — of gold." He pulled two arm-rings from a leather pouch at his belt. They shone brightly, even in the candlelight, and the work on them appeared to be intricate.

Most of my silver pieces were gone by now. "I'm sorry I have nothing to offer in return."

"It's unnecessary. Your Duke has been more than generous."

"Yes. William would be." I wanted to redeem myself somehow, so I showed him that I recognized his dialect. "You're Saxon."

He nodded and opened his mouth to identify the region.

"Mercia," I guessed.

He grimaced. "Wessex."

"Yes, of course. I'm a commoner myself, as William must have told you, though I'd prefer to maintain my disguise as a monk."

"I understand. You are traveling as —?"

"Brother Augustine of St. Ouen."

"Yes, now I recall that he mentioned your assumed name." He rose. "I will protect your secret with the brothers here ... Brother Augustine."

"Thank you, Tostig of Wessex," I said, trying to sound courtlike, "it's been my good fortune to meet you."

My breathing had become labored, though, so my voice sounded harsh. My eyelids began to droop.

He excused himself, and I fell asleep again.

I dreamed vivid dreams of Garrad and healing tours, William and archery practice, Osbern and poisonings, Count Gilbert's death, Edward and poor Alfred, Lanfranc and Herluin, assassins with curved, poisoned knives, and, I thought, a dragon.

I awoke to a monastery bell followed by a song outside my window. A single voice accompanied by a lute sang:

> *Down the broad, broad way I go,*
> *Young and unregretting.*
> *Wrap me in my vices up*
> *Virtue all forgetting.*
> *Greedier for all delights*
> *Than heaven to enter in.*
> *Since the soul in me is dead,*
> *Better save the skin!*

I twisted my head to see Rolf, the leader of the Goliards, stride through the door. I was so happy to see him that I tried to sit up, only to sink back onto the bed.

"You must rest and move slowly, my clever friend," he said as he perched on the chair next to the bed. "You have been poisoned, I hear."

The body pains returned, but I smiled as broadly as I could. "I'm delighted to see you alive, Rolf. How are the others? Were any harmed?"

"None. We're untouched. Everyone is safe. Look."

My eyes followed his gesture. Straining, I turned my head to see, peering in through my window, the grinning faces of the Goliard band. I lifted my right hand in greeting and received a chorus of cries and blessings in return.

I turned back to Rolf. "How did you escape the Berserker?"

He smiled. "We didn't. We confronted him."

"A Berserker?"

"Goliards are clever, too, you know. Our donkeys couldn't outpace a horse. So we prayed for time, which the warrior gave us, and a hawthorn tree, which the Lord gave us. Having found the hawthorn just off the road, we quickly hid the donkeys in the forest, rolled ourselves in dust, and climbed into the crotches of the tree, from which we loudly chanted prayers in our worst Latin."

I gaped at him.

"Berserkers, you know, are sworn to Odin in the old religion."

"I know. What's that got to do with hawthorn trees? Witches live in hawthorn trees —"

"That's it. We've heard stories, as you probably have, that the North is full of demons and witches. In the North, witches live in hawthorn trees. When the Berserker came upon us, he heard our chanting. With the bad Latin and the dust, I was sure he would take us for witches. I gazed at him — with otherworldly solemnity — and reached my hand toward him. Well" — he chuckled — "he spun the horse around and raced down the road with a speed that would startle the devil himself."

Though my chest resisted, I laughed. "So that's why he came back in my direction. You frightened him halfway back to Rouen."

"I'm sorry we sent him in your direction. I thought you were with the men who followed the stream. That's what we had planned."

"Planned?" I frowned at him. "You planned that? When? We didn't know that we'd be followed. Or was that when I wasn't listening?"

He leaned back in his chair. "We didn't plan it. Garrad did. He planned the entire route, including alternative ones if we had to leave the road."

"Yes, he would."

"He plans everything."

I studied the Goliard leader. "How long have you known Garrad? You're a Briton, aren't you? Where did you meet him?" I wondered if I was prying impolitely, so I added, "If you don't mind telling me."

"No, Goliards love to tell stories. As you guessed, I'm a Briton, but only by my father, whose family lived close to the border between Normandy and Brittany. My mother was a Norman, and she named me after Rolf, the first Duke of Normandy. When Garrad came north with the Norman force to help the English, I joined him. After his injury, he became a wanderer, until, as you know, he returned to Falaise to watch over the young son of the Duke."

"I didn't think Garrad watched William anymore than anyone else in Falaise. He advises William now, but —"

Rolf shifted in the chair and resumed his narrative. "I met him first in the south of England. Some of my friends and I were mercenaries. Looking for adventure, you know. Garrad was sixteen, I think, and we were a few years older. He could outfight any ten of us, so when he joined an expedition to fight Norwegians in the isles north of England, we followed him. That's where he lost the use of his arm."

I felt my body pains increasing and my eyes getting heavy, but my curiosity made me struggle to stay awake. "How did that happen? He's never told me, and I've only heard something about Berserkers."

"Berserkers, yes. That was a battle! The Norwegians had already won the day, but Garrad took on a band of Berserkers to guard our retreat. He was outnumbered three to one. By Berserkers! He kept the three at bay long enough for the rest of us to escape. Eventually, though, one of the Berserkers struck him in his sword-arm with an axe. They respected his skill so much, though, that they let him live and delivered him to a nearby abbey to be healed. The other mercenaries gave him up for dead, but I found him at the abbey and stayed with him while he recovered. That's when we decided to become pilgrims."

"Did you study in monasteries with him?"

"For a time. We tramped all the way from the north of England to the south. Then we traveled from Rouen to Pavia, where we met Lanfranc. Eventually, we went on to Rome. We even undertook a trek to Constantinople. What a place! The most beautiful walls, monuments, and cathedrals I've ever seen. But the smelliest city in Christendom! The whole place reeks of garlic and rotting fish. The locals, you know, put brown fish sauce over everything they eat." He wrinkled his nose.

"Garrad said he studied at Salernum too."

"Yes, we returned to Italy, and he went to Salernum, determined to study healing at the school there. He also returned to study with Lanfranc and to try to discover the origins of the Christian faith. I had lost my respect for the Church, though, having heard too many stories and studied too much history. I reminded Garrad that the Emperor Theodosius made it a crime punishable by death to even talk about other religions, and the Emperor Justinian did the same, and that those were the true origins of Christianity."

I nodded. Garrad had taught me the early history of the Roman state religion.

He continued, "By 500 in the Year of Our Lord, if a Roman or Byzantine citizen did not belong to the Roman Church or did not keep his mind exclusively on Church doctrines, especially if he decided to become a philosopher, he could be executed and usually was." He snorted. "Now, five hundred years later, the Church is little more than a military organization. Except for local priests, there's nothing religious about it that I can see."

I felt more tired, but I forced out, "Garrad once talked to me about the difference between religious Christianity and political empire-building in the name of Christianity."

"Yes, that's the problem now. The Empire and the papacy represent two powerful forces striving to dominate the world. To force the independent rulers to bow to them."

I felt more awake. "Like Duke Robert. Did the Church have Duke Robert killed?"

"I don't know, but I would not be shocked to discover that it did." He paused. "To resume my tale: when Garrad wanted to learn more about Church history, I moved on. Garrad and I never lost touch with each other, though. Indeed, when Garrad became involved in the ducal court, I served as …"

The tiredness returned. My eyelids drifted closed, and my head nodded forward.

Rolf rose. "I'll leave you now."

"Thank you … for everything."

When I awoke again, Tostig and a round-faced monk perched on my bed, staring. Tostig had washed and shaved and wore a green and yellow-striped tunic with yellow leggings. He looked more like a courtier. Indeed, his clothes and gold arm-rings made the monk's faded black robe and wooden cross appear all the more rough.

"Good morning," I said, though again my voice sounded forced and thus harsh.

"I'm glad you're conscious," Tostig said. "We've been waiting some time. This is Brother Berengar, the infirmarian here."

I sat up and nodded at the round-faced monk. "I am Augustine," I said and glanced at Tostig.

"You've had a struggle with death, I'm afraid, Brother Augustine," the infirmarian said.

My arm throbbed, my body ached, and breathing seemed difficult.

"I thank you for your efforts on my behalf, Brother Berengar."

"I wish I could have done more."

I put my hand to my chest. It felt clammy. I spotted a basin and towel on the table near the bed.

"Yes," Brother Berengar confirmed, "the infirmary novitiate has recently scrubbed your feet and upper body as part of the normal purification of the sick."

"Thank you, and please thank him for me."

Brother Berengar urged me to walk if I could. With Tostig supporting one arm and the infirmarian supporting the other, I was able to walk out of the room and down the hall.

Before long, we sat in the infirmary kitchen, where I downed as much beef and barley soup as the cook was willing to part with. In Normandy, meat was permitted in most infirmary kitchens, because infirmarians believed that it replenished the blood and warmed ailing bodies, though Garrad always disputed this belief, noting that reformed monasteries south of the Alps forbade meat. The infirmarians in Flanders apparently agreed with those in Normandy.

"Your Goliard friends," the cook said, "ate the same way you do. I'm happy not to have to feed them anymore."

I glanced up at him. "They're gone?"

He nodded.

Brother Berengar added, "When I told them that your recuperation may take the rest of the summer, they said they had to press on. They'll find you again, they promised."

"I hope my healing does not take that long. I have work to do in the North. But I'm sorry to lose my friends."

"I was sorry to send them on," Brother Berengar said, "but the poison will take time to leave you. Any substance potent enough to render you unconscious and affect your body for so long will not easily retreat."

"It must have been a combination of poisons," I said. "No single substance produces such pains. And the strange dreams I've been having. Henbane, thorn apple, and nightshade perhaps?"

Tostig looked at me sharply.

Brother Berengar cocked his head. "Do you know about poisons?"

I hesitated. "Well, some few … I have a friend who knows poisons, and he talks about them."

I silently reprimanded myself for showing off my knowledge. If Voldred survived his wounds — which I privately hoped he did not — he now knew me as Cuin of Falaise. I needed to re-establish my disguise as a simple monk.

While I was pondering, Brother Berengar sighed. "Well, the Count will be here from Lille within the week. His daughter and her attendant know a great deal about wounds and healing. They'll be more help to you than I. In the meantime, you should rest and eat." He watched me consume another bowl of soup. "Resting may be the greater challenge."

In fact, I slept long hours, deeply enough to hear none of the abbey bells. The dreams about the old woman continued, so I became accustomed to them. I even imagined that I got to know her and asked her questions.

Inwardly, I laughed at the idea of talking to someone in my dreams. Perhaps I was going a bit mad, like the poor man outside Rouen's gate. I did not mind the visions, though. Flying and visiting exotic worlds were pleasant activities.

While awake, I ate as often as I liked. Until someone arrived that knew more about wounds than I did, I certainly knew how to encourage poison to leave a body — with food.

I was also happy to wait for the Count and his daughter. They were just the people that Garrad wanted me to meet.

So I set myself a healing regimen of eating and sleeping, the latter of which always included more strange dreams.

The rest of the time, I wandered around the monastery. Probably because of Count Baldwin's disputes with the Holy Roman Empire, St. Vaast was enormous and fortified like a castle. Its stone-and-earth walls spread between niched guard-stations. Watchtowers rose at each corner, their window slits no wider than a spear head.

Even the inside walls were of heavy stone, the corridors lined with massive, rounded pillars. Huge wooden beams supported the roof.

Here, as the young shepherd-farmer had predicted, I felt safe.

Often, as I strolled through the arched passageways and around the grassy clearings leading to the center fountains, Tostig accompanied me, practicing his Flemish French and praising "the unmatched beauty of Wessex."

On one of these walks I asked him, "Why are you in Flanders … if the question isn't an intrusion? And how do you know Duke William?"

Except for Earl Godwin and his ambitious sons, I had never heard William mention any Wessex nobles, and he did not count Godwin's family as friends. Perhaps Tostig was the emissary of some lesser Wessex noble.

"I'm here to meet someone," he replied, "and I sought Duke William's advice on a diplomatic matter. King Edward suggested that I consult the Duke, privately and confidentially." He gave me a hard look. "My visit must remain confidential."

I was curious about his mission, but I replied, "You may be assured of my silence."

He nodded his appreciation.

"Then you know the King personally?" I asked.

"Of course. He just married … one of the Wessex ladies."

"He went through with the wedding then? I thought he might not, in the end."

He scrutinized me. "Did you know about the plans for the wedding?"

"Oh, yes," I tried to sound casual. "News about King Edward is always of interest in Normandy."

"The wedding negotiations were secret."

He stared at me, waiting for my reply. Again I had let my mouth run ahead of my caution. "Emissaries for Duke William sometimes know more than courtiers."

"Perhaps. I could see from the way Duke William spoke of you that you're more than an emissary. You also know more about dialects and poisons than a Norman courtier usually does. At least more than the Norman fools who accompanied King Edward to England. I will respect your privacy, though, as you respect mine."

I thanked him awkwardly and changed the subject. "You don't approve of the Normans in England?"

"They're not all bad, but I don't think they have adequate knowledge of our land." He paused. "King Edward's a good man, perhaps even chosen by God to be King, as some bishops claim. I admire him. I even like him. However, he's half-Norman and raised in Normandy. Like other Normans, I don't think he knows enough of English earldoms to be an adequate ruler."

He watched my reaction, so I tried to have none.

If he worried about offending me, though, his words did not indicate it. He continued, "He places Normans in positions they don't deserve. Then he takes Norman advice and ignores ours, but we tell him the truth, while Normans don't."

I decided to pursue a different line. "When you spoke with Duke William, did he mention the substance of my mission?"

"Not directly. It's plain that you're headed north for an alliance with a Northern king. With Hardraada now approaching the North, you'd be wise to develop a friendship with either King Sweyn of Denmark or King Magnus of Norway, though I'd choose Magnus if I were you. He's related to Hardraada, he's a brilliant fighter, and he's reputed to be a fine man. If you win his support, you may gain Hardraada's as well." He stared at one of the protecting walls. "If you fail, Normandy may fall to Hardraada."

That night I had not just a dream but a vision. I had never experienced a vision away from the rock in Garrad's hut.

I saw a King, a small man, standing beside a taller Duke Robert. At first, I was happy that the Duke was alive. Then I remembered that he wasn't and felt sad.

When I wondered who the short King was, I suddenly saw the dragon's face and heard it whisper, "Canute, once King of Denmark, Norway, and England."

King Canute seemed to offer a young woman to Duke Robert in marriage, but the young woman faded, and Arlette stood beside the Duke. Behind them, too far in the distance for me to recognize any features, stood two Norman boys. "Remember," the dragon hissed and was gone.

By the time Count Baldwin's party arrived, my aches were beginning to subside. Even so, they attacked me vigorously when I walked more than a few minutes. My breath came more easily, though I still panted after any movement.

Brother Berengar continued to fret that the wound was not closing as he thought it should. He muttered to himself as he walked from my room to consult Count Baldwin's court healer.

I lay my head back on the bed, trying not to think about the wound. Blood still made me queasy. Instead, I studied the wooden ceiling for the hundredth time, wondering how soon I would be able to ride again.

Not that I looked forward to returning to the pony's back, but I worried that Hardraada might join forces with Magnus before I found either of them.

Though my delay had made me anxious, no message had come from William or Garrad. Did they know something about Hardraada's movements that I did not? Was he perhaps not moving as quickly as they had thought?

Or did something occupy them in Normandy, something troublesome? This latter thought seemed sinister, and I frowned at it.

Brother Berengar interrupted my pondering. He pushed through my door, followed by two of the most beautiful women I had ever seen, both dressed in light blue surcoats over white tunics, their sleeves laced from the wrist to the elbow, visible through the wide sleeves of their surcoats.

One woman seemed about my height and age. She had blond hair, parted down the middle and hanging down her shoulders and back. She wore no necklaces or rings, and the belt over her surcoat was of white cotton.

The other woman, pink-cheeked with white blond hair, parted and braided, was younger and smaller. Trying not to stare, I marveled at how such tiny features could produce so graceful an effect. She wore two gold necklaces, a gold bracelet around each wrist, and a jeweled ring on each hand. Her belt was wool, sewn with silver thread and had a clasp set with garnets.

"This is the lady Matilda," the infirmarian said, gesturing toward the smaller woman, "the daughter of Count Baldwin." He indicated the taller woman. "This is Anette, her attendant. Anette's also the court healer, and she's Norman." He assumed, I supposed, that I had provincial attitudes and would be happy to meet a fellow Norman. In fact, I was.

While Lady Matilda drew the monk aside, Anette examined my arm. As her fingers pressed gently around the wound, I studied her. Her straight features and large eyes reminded me of most Norman women, but she was more beautiful than others I had met, even Arlette.

After studying the wound, she asked how I felt. Her Norman French lacked any Flemish accent, and I found her voice soothing. She inquired about every detail of my health, more than I would have disclosed to a stranger, especially a female one.

Her concern and objectivity reminded me of Garrad, and she asked the questions of an experienced healer. I felt that I could trust her.

Finally she rose to leave, speaking in low tones with Lady Matilda. She gave instructions to the infirmarian.

To me she said, "I shall have to soak this wound every day, several times a day, for several weeks. We will watch how it responds."

As eager as I was to continue my journey, this regimen seemed a pleasant prospect.

For the first few days that she worked on my arm, Anette was politely distant. We spoke about normal matters: the building of new churches, the condition of the town and its fields, the size of the year's crop, and the weather's long-term promise. She asked about Rouen and William, both of which I described at length, though she seemed reticent to discuss her own background.

When Lady Matilda visited, as she did daily, Anette rose and drew toward her, seeming relieved. She may have been happy to have propriety restored: a chaperone in the room.

For my part, I enjoyed her company and continued to be in awe of someone as skilled in healing as she was. I realized that she knew more than I did. Her training must have been longer than mine.

She tended my wound with poultices, using a few herbs unfamiliar to me. I asked her about them, and she explained where they grew, their uses, and how to harvest and prepare them. I was sure Garrad would have wanted me to absorb every word — indeed, to discuss familiar herbs with her and learn more about them.

I picked up a few insights, of course, but most of the time I found myself watching the light on her hair or the way she moved. I watched her eyes, which seemed sometimes gray, sometimes green. As she spoke, I watched her lips move and the expressions on her face, each of which seemed fascinating.

I was jerked back to the wound, though, every time she applied poultices. She made them hotter than any I had ever prepared. Though I was pleased to see her every day, I groaned inwardly every time she arrived from the infirmary kitchen with a cloth on a clay dish. Outwardly, I tried not to react, to assume the demeanor of a courageous knight wounded in battle, but whenever she scooped the scalding cloth onto my arm, my body jumped.

"I'm sorry," she said, "but I must make it hot."

"You've succeeded."

When she discovered that I had read books from the medical school at Salernum, she wanted to know all I could remember of them. I tried to sound knowledgeable, but I felt certain that my lesser knowledge must be obvious to her. Nonetheless, she appeared interested in whatever I said.

Since she knew more than I did, I decided that the best way to make a positive impression was humor. However, she only smiled politely at what I believed to be clever comments. She found the Goliard songs more amusing.

She finally laughed, though, when I quoted a couplet from the Salernum books about a patient's recuperating period:

> *Use three physicians still: first Doctor Quiet,*
> *Next Doctor Merryman, third Doctor Diet.*

Cast in the comical Latin verse typical of ancient southern thinkers, it represented precisely the regimen she had prescribed for me. After that, she appeared more at ease. Encouraged, I told her amusing stories about healing trips with Garrad.

When I mentioned my reaction to bleeding and surgery, she smiled, then agreed with a grimace. "I have never been fond of blood or bloody wounds, either. I know how to tend them, but I would rather deal with something else."

Nonetheless, when she spoke of "muscles", "nerves" and "organs", it was clear that here, too, she knew more than I. She hesitated to elaborate on this part of her training, though, so I returned to healing books and amusing stories.

On the afternoon of St. Thomas's Day, she surprised me by saying, "You are not a monk, are you?"

I should have lied to protect my disguise. Instead, I heard myself reply, "No, I'm not. How did you know?"

"Since childhood, I have had what you might call visions but of a particular kind. I see pictures of things as they really are. For instance, when I first looked at you, I saw an image of you in a light blue cloak, wearing the clothes of a villager. Why do you disguise yourself as a monk?"

"I use the robe to travel safely. I'm bound north. I don't know what my reception there may be."

"I would have thought your foot would be enough to protect you. Even Northmen are kind to the lame."

I felt my face get hot. Since we had not walked together, I had hoped that my deformity had gone undetected, something I had never hoped in my life.

She must have seen the misshapen foot when the novitiate was washing it. The monastic obsession with purifying everything seemed overdone to me. Now it was infuriating.

Worse, though, she compounded my embarrassment by examining my foot.

After pressing on it, she looked up at me. "It gives you pain to walk, doesn't it?"

I nodded.

"Perhaps it need not cause you pain. Lady Matilda and I have seen drawings of foot muscles. She has even seen the inside of a foot. Let me speak to her about it. If we can strengthen the muscles, they will bear your weight better. Perhaps less painfully."

My embarrassment was overcome by my surprise. Drawings of the insides of bodies were frowned on by the Church because of the methods required to get them. Bishops feared grave-robbing, and many priests denounced the "ghoulish practices" carried on for the medical schools.

Successes of physicians from the Salernum and Montpellier schools had softened some of the resistance, especially in the larger towns such as Rouen. The priests in Falaise, however, still preferred prayer to any human medicine, especially anatomy. As a result, even Garrad could not obtain drawings, though he wished that he could.

"Have you seen the inside of a foot?" I asked.

"No, I am not as brave as her ladyship."

I wondered how Lady Matilda, younger than both Anette and I, came to be so tough-minded and pondered it when she next visited me.

Maintaining her daily routine, she stopped in my room to inquire about my health. After consulting with Anette, she examined my foot. To my amazement, she even massaged it.

She pressed with more force than I would have expected in hands so delicate. At one point I started in pain.

"I'm sorry, my lady."

"It is to be expected." She turned to Anette. "Here is where the original damage is. Work along these muscles. Then correct his gait. You can see where he walks on the outside of his foot to compensate for the pain, but that only makes the foot worse." She looked back at me. "You will have to change your walk, Brother Augustine. You need to use your muscles in different ways, so your leg will ache initially. But over time, it will strengthen."

Lady Matilda was like no noblewoman I had ever met. She certainly did not seem like the daughter of a Count descended from both Charlemagne and the Saxon King Alfred the Great.

Not that she did not bear herself nobly and speak with confidence and refinement. She did. However, she spoke directly to everyone: monk, peasant, or courtier. Her concern for my health made me an equal while we discussed it.

I had experienced such equality with only one other noble — William.

The more I became acquainted with her, the more she reminded me of William. Their similarities had not struck me at first because of the physical differences. He stood taller than most men I knew, while she was smaller than any woman I knew.

Her character, though — her concentration, apparent fearlessness, and matter-of-fact concern — were similar to his.

I watched her closely as she probed my foot the following day. William and Matilda, I was thinking. I wonder whether they would —

She hit a sensitive spot. I yelped.

She stared at me, unblinking. "It does not hurt quite as much, though, does it?"

"Not quite."

"Good. Massage here, Anette. Hard. Apply hot poultices. Very hot."

Yes, she and William would be a perfect match.

During this time, Anette encouraged me, as Brother Berengar had, to roam the monastery grounds. She wanted me to test my endurance and to retrain my foot and leg muscles.

I was happy to comply, both because she sometimes joined me and because I wanted to feel healthy again.

Of course, I kept my head covered even in the heat. Infirmary patients were considered unclean and had to cover their heads when wandering the cloister. My crutch substituted for the cane that the sick used as a sign of their condition.

When Anette did not join me, I strolled alone — the brothers avoided the sick — or with Tostig. Since he left the monastery for days or weeks at a time, I often walked alone.

By early summer, I let the St. John's Eve festivities draw me high onto the monastery walls. By now I had been sufficiently purified that the brothers did not mind if I passed by them.

A few greeted me cheerfully as I labored upward. I gasped a greeting in return. The steps seemed never-ending, but they finally reached the walk near the top of the walls.

As I leaned over the wall, panting, I smelled the newly cut hay. No work would be done tonight, though. The gaily dressed Arras villagers danced and sang as they threw St. John's wort and other herbs — mugwort, vervain, figwort, fennel, chamomile, and milfoil — onto fires atop the hills.

The scent of hay was replaced by the herbal smoke that drifted over the countryside to protect the townspeople, their crops, and animals from ill fortune. From ancient times, Garrad had told me, the smoke of St. John's wort was so offensive to evil spirits that a single whiff would cause them to flee.

The smoke added a layer of color to the sunset, glowing over the treetops. I watched the celebration and the fading sun until the Prior's voice called me down.

"Come, Brother Augustine!" He waved his candle. "Dusk is the devil's time, and we must close ranks!"

Gradually my breathing, still labored, began to normalize. I ached less and had greater stamina for exercise. My foot bore more weight, and though my leg hurt more than usual, as Lady Matilda had predicted, it seemed stronger with every walk.

Then in mid-July, on St. Vulmar's Day, as I reached for my crutch, Anette appeared in the doorway and said, "Please leave it here."

I looked uncomprehending, so she added, "I will support you. Come, walk with me. I have another intuition."

I was so delighted to have her holding my arm that I did not even consider resisting. With her help I hobbled down the vaulted passageway outside my room and under the arbors in the center yard past the fountain. I scarcely noticed the pain in my foot. My entire concentration was on my arm where hers held it.

When we reached the orchard with its soft grass, she asked, "Can you walk along this row of trees without me?"

Except for childhood play and escaping from assassins, I had never tried to walk without my crutch. I felt odd without it. I would, however, do whatever she asked.

I hazarded one step. Then a second. Then another. Then a few more. My foot tolerated my weight.

"Does it hurt much?" she asked.

"No more than if I were using the crutch," I called back.

"Good. Do not turn your foot to the outside. Remember what Lady Matilda has taught you about walking."

"I'm trying to."

Staring down at my foot, I paced along the trees, rested for a moment on a turf bench and returned to her. Though my leg muscles trembled and ached, my foot hurt only slightly.

"I never believed I could do this."

"We'll keep working on it. You should massage it, too. Press hard wherever it hurts. For as long as you can endure the pain. Do the same all along your leg. We can also continue the hot poultices and these walks." She smiled. "I am pleased that you can give up your crutch. Before long, you will walk with almost no limp at all … so that next month you may escort me to the market in Arras."

Finally, on a sunny morning in August, St. Thaddeus's Day, I felt strong enough to journey to town and back without my crutch. I stuffed one of the gold arm-rings Tostig had given me into a pouch hanging from my belt. Limping only slightly, I marched from my room to find Anette.

It was market-day.

Looking elegant in a tan robe with wide, floral-trimmed sleeves, Anette took my arm, which had now become her habit, and held it until we neared the monastery gate. Then she dropped her hand, maintaining the pretense that she was a courtier being escorted to market by a protecting monk.

We nodded at several of the brothers and strode through the gate toward the town.

Established by the Abbot years earlier, the market of Arras supplied much of the monastery's wealth. Anette told me that tolls as well as trade filled the abbey treasury, making possible both the church's ornaments and the monks' aid to the poor.

As we walked, she pointed at farmers and merchants struggling under huge burdens, while their horses bore light loads. The abbey charged dues only on goods carried by animals.

Because the toll on an unshod horse was one denier — half the toll of a shod horse — most of the animals arrived in Arras without shoes.

I shook my head at the farmers, since I could not imagine carrying so much weight. My own body was all my foot could tolerate. Nonetheless, I walked with less pain than I ever had, though still with a limp.

No one in Arras, though, would see the limp. The dense crowds left no space to see anyone's feet. Even the beggars had been forced from the town gates to the outer edges of the makeshift stalls and platforms, where they banged on their cups and dishes, adding to the din.

The size of the market rivaled Rouen. In addition to the everyday storefronts, makeshift wooden stalls crowded the streets and outskirts of the town. The upper floors of the houses, which were built out over the streets, allowed only a little light into the street.

Under this roof, a mass of merchants, craftsmen, and buyers — Germans, Scots, Swedes, Icelanders, Portugese, Lombards, and, of course, the Syrian moneylenders who frequented every large fair — flowed sluggishly along the passageways, their patterned hats, headbands, and braids the only visible parts of them.

Anette and I pressed through the mass. She reattached herself to my arm as we passed shop after shop, staring at and smelling the wares.

In addition to daily goods, wine, salt, butter, and the famous blue Arras cloth and tapestries, dyed with the woad that grew all over Flanders, traders boasted merchandise that I had seen only on Rouen's busiest days: whale meat and reindeer horn from the Northern countries, gaming-pieces, silks, and brocades from Byzantium, glass beads and highly decorated pottery from the mountains of German Saxony.

I located a cloth merchant. With the gold arm-ring Tostig had given me, I bought blue Frisian cloth for Anette. I haggled poorly, but I did not need the skill. The merchant's eyes widened as I laid the arm-ring on his brass scales. He added an extra length of cloth to what I had purchased.

"It's mostly silver we see here," he said, eyeing my monk's robe. "Except for courtiers' goods." He clipped away the proper-weighted piece and returned the rest to me.

"The gold was a gift from a courtier," I told him. "I … um … helped him with his livestock."

His head bobbed, and he adopted a solemn look. "Curing livestock is a noble task."

I sniffed my way to a pastry shop, where Anette laughed at the quantity of sweets I bought.

Then we passed a wine-crier, and I requested the wine he was announcing. He looked surprised when I asked for Norman cider too, but he found a dusty flask of it.

We edged toward the far end of the town, elbowing our way out of the crowd. We settled onto a grassy hill to fill ourselves with pastries and drinks. Anette tasted the cider and smiled but turned down my offer of more.

I leaned backward onto my elbows, admiring the cloudless sky and nearby beeches reigning over fields of yellow and purple wildflowers. When I glanced at Anette, she too was gazing at the sky. I was about to say something when a sound drew my attention back toward the town — the shrill cry of a woman.

Not far from us a stall of jugglers and tumblers performed. The noise of their shouts and the crowd around them drowned out all sounds except for a pained, high-pitched cry.

The cry, however, did not issue from the performers. Or from the people pressed around them. I stood up.

Beyond the juggler's stall was a platform with men and women lined up on it. Much of their clothing was unfamiliar: brown woolen robes, white tunics with puffed sleeves, patterned dresses, and wide-brimmed hats. They were chained to each other at the neck.

Anette rose and stood beside me. "Slaves — Irish, Slavic, and some whose dress I do not recognize."

One of the women cried at us. I could not understand the words. I limped toward her. Anette retrieved the remaining pastries and wine and followed me.

As we neared the platform, I realized that the woman spoke a Saxon dialect. She wore a brown robe, similar to what I had seen in convents.

"Please," she called, "I am a nun. My sisters and I" — she indicated three women near her —"were captured by pagans in a raid. Please, Brother, help us."

I halted, unsure of what to do. The nun repeated her plea in Latin.

"From here," Anette said in my ear, "they go either north to Norwegian farms or south to rich Arabs. My intuition tells me south."

The woman continued, "Please, brother, please help us. I can prove who we are." She began singing psalms in Latin. The others joined her.

The slave-dealer, a bearded man with his arms folded over an ornate blue and yellow tunic, had been watching me.

I faced him. "May I buy the woman?"

He scanned my robe. "Are you as rich as you are frayed, Brother?" He spoke a rough Flemish French.

I laid what was left of the gold arm-ring on the table in front of him. He raised his eyebrows and stared at me for a moment. Removing his scales from their case, he put lead weights in one pan, the arm-ring in the other.

"Because it's gold, it's enough for her."

I felt my heart pound as I tried a deception. "And for her ailing companions?"

"Ailing?"

"I'm a healer, and I assure you that those three women will not only break out with fever within a week, but they will infect every other slave that you have."

He smiled. "Will they?"

I swallowed. "Yes."

He remained unmoved. I could think of nothing more to say.

Anette broke in. "From here, where will your trade take you?"

Still eyeing me, he answered, "South."

"To Cordova? Or Baghdad? The Church excommunicates traders who sell Christian slaves to the followers of Muhammad."

He glowered at her. "They're not Christians. They're heathen Slavs."

"The sick women are English Saxon nuns," I said. "From the east of England, probably Mercia."

He hesitated, biting his lower lip.

I pressed him. "They are Saxon Christians, and they are diseased. Look at them. They have dark circles under their eyes. They'll tell you they have trouble breathing. Their bodies have red rashes." I guessed that the heat would produce itching under the woolen robes. "I'm just trying to save your trade."

"I know what you're trying to do." He squinted at me and then the women. "For gold, you may have them anyway."

As the trader unlocked their neck chains, the four nuns wept and thanked us. I was eager to leave before the trader changed his mind, so I escorted them quickly from the platform and urged them toward St. Vaast.

Their health was in fact good, so the six of us trod briskly down the Arras road. If my foot ached, I did not notice it.

As we walked, Anette and I offered the pastries and wine to the nuns. They thanked us. Between bites, they told us that they had been taken from a monastery near Chester.

"In the earldom of Mercia," one named Edyth told us.

Anette smiled at me. I tried not to look proud for having guessed the correct region.

"We were seized by raiding Northmen and bargained away to this trader in Denmark. At the trading town of Hedeby. Though we pleaded with people at every market, the few who understood us lacked either the wealth or the will to free us. But we never abandoned hope. And God answered our prayers."

We reached St. Vaast and escorted the Chester nuns to the Abbot, who was entertaining Tostig.

When I told Tostig how I had spent his gift, he seemed annoyed. I pointed out that if he returned the nuns to England, they would pray for his soul as long as he lived and afterward. So would the entire monastery near Chester.

He nodded at this and asked the Abbot to lodge the nuns for him until his departure.

That night I had another vision. I was in an unfamiliar monastery, tending to a man with a head wound. He had blond hair and a mustache, and a crown had fallen from his head. The dragon's head appeared over both of us and whispered, "He dies only to be reborn, and you attend the rebirth."

CHAPTER 9

A WINTER'S GOD

A.D. 1045

In Rouen, I thought to myself as I lay on my hard monastery bed, the townspeople and monks would be celebrating St. Ouen's Day. Summer was slipping away, and I knew I should press north, but I postponed leaving.

The poison, I told myself, might cause a sudden weakness as I rode, but I didn't feel weak.

Of course, without Rolf and the Goliards, I lacked traveling companions. If Voldred had survived his wounds and was still seeking my life, though, I preferred traveling alone.

I worried about robbers. Yet I could easily reach the Army Road, which would be crowded with merchants and pilgrims headed north. What if things had changed in the North, though …?

I finally admitted to myself that I was torn between my duty and the companionship of Anette and the monks inside a walled monastery. I rolled over on my bed, determined to postpone my decision one more day.

A fever decided the issue. For two months it swept through the abbey. I helped to tend the sick, including Tostig. Weakened by constant travel, he fell ill quickly.

He struggled against the fever for two weeks, until a powder of imperial masterwort and some fennel tea that I administered cured him. He expressed his gratitude, but I told him that I owed him at least a little healing.

The Chester nuns, also weakened by their trials, were ill for several weeks, but Anette and I tended them successfully.

We even worked with Edyth and a younger nun named Agnes, teaching them what we knew of healing. While Edyth was interested and intelligent, Agnes was unusually talented at healing. Anette and I spent many days training her.

Count Baldwin, still battling the Holy Roman Emperor, had come and gone several times during the summer. Though I had spoken with him when he held court and once privately to win his good wishes for William, he had little time for diplomacy.

Now, to avoid the fever, he left St. Vaast, taking with him what remained of his court. Lady Matilda accompanied him.

Anette stayed behind to help the Chester nuns recover, and I stayed to help her and continue training the nuns Edyth and Agnes in healing.

The Count's sister, Lady Judith, also stayed, but since I had met her only once, I could not determine her reasons for remaining.

By the time we subdued the fever, autumn had arrived. Traveling north would mean risking death in a snowstorm.

Since no word had come from Normandy, I assumed that Hardraada had not yet reached the North. I requested permission to winter with the St. Vaast monks. The Abbot consented.

A few weeks later, when the Goliards returned to St. Vaast, as they had promised, I asked Rolf to carry a message to William and Garrad, to let them know that I would be traveling north the following spring.

"I have news of my own for them," Rolf said, "and I'll be happy to pass yours on. Perhaps my friends and I will return in time to escort you again."

I said I hoped so, but secretly I did not wish to endanger their lives a second time.

Anette and I resumed our strolls even through the early snowfalls, though they were shortened by the early darkness. As night intruded on afternoon, we often found ourselves being waved toward the visitors' dormitory by a torch-bearing monk. We heard again and again, "Darkness belongs to the devil. Go inside, please!" and had to hurry past the candles that would burn all night in the vaulted corridors.

We continued our discussions, too, which shifted from healing and local concerns to society's foibles. Because both of us were approaching our twentieth year, we felt qualified to analyze the behavior of abbots, mayors, bishops, and nobles. We exchanged opinions about how monasteries, parishes, and towns should be governed.

We also discussed the nature of God and good and evil and death and afterlife and Eastern religions and pagan philosophers. Anette probed issues so deeply, though, that her questions soon surpassed my understanding. My training with the Falaise priests lacked theological depth, I realized, and said so to her.

She replied that she, too, had more questions than answers. She suggested we get permission to use the winter to study in the abbey library, which contained works by St. Augustine, Boethius, Dionysius, and others, including Alcuin of York. The library, she told me, also housed an ancient Bible, perhaps only two or three copies removed from the original in St. Jerome's Latin.

We commenced our study but continued our walks while the weather permitted. Fortunately, the three Chester nuns, whom Tostig had not yet returned to England, joined us. Edyth, trained in theology, deepened our conversations.

The day we began to discuss the Last Judgment and God's mercy — St. Martin's Day — Edyth added more than theology. She related a remarkable tale.

"... told by a Norman priest visiting Chester," she glanced at me, "a Norman like our young Brother Augustine here, who will also visit us one day, so that we may repay him."

I smiled at her.

"The story is true. More than a vision or a dream, though it would inspire awe and reverence even as a vision or dream. It is one of the rare encounters of the living with the dead."

With a blazing fire keeping the early November cold from my back, I sat forward, resting my chin on my hands.

"The Norman priest — who told me the tale himself — was on his way home from visiting a sick man, a member of his parish. He hurried along the road, because the hour was late. On a night of the full moon. A priest knows that the devil's work can go on late on a night of the full moon."

All of us nodded and made the sign of the cross.

"Before he had traveled any great distance, the priest heard on the road behind him a noise like a great army. He turned to see what was overtaking him. Because of the moon's fullness, he could see the road clearly. Behind him a great crowd struggled along the road on foot, bearing on their necks and shoulders animals, clothes, furnishings, and household goods of all kinds — the sorts of things raiders take as plunder. All the travelers, though, wailed and lamented bitterly and urged those in front of them to quicken their pace.

"The priest recognized among the crowd many of his neighbors who had died. Surrounding them were local noblemen and noblewomen, also recently dead. One of the nobles was being goaded by a demon with red-hot spurs. A noblewoman rode a side-saddle studded with burning nails. To the priest's amazement, he even saw the Abbot of a nearby monastery in the group, being driven with the lash by two demons."

One of Edyth's sisters said, "The judgment of God is not the same as the judgment of men. God looks into the heart."

"What did the priest do?" The donkey-boy, the novitiate who supplied the wood, had paused to listen and blurted out the question, in spite of the silence imposed upon him by his daily discipline.

Edyth nodded at him. "You're right to inquire, young master. The priest, hoping to convince his living friends of the truth of what he had seen, tried to seize one of the horses that trotted by, one without a rider."

The donkey-boy gasped.

Edyth nodded again. "Yes, he himself was seized by one of the damned, a nobleman 'with a grip like fire,' the priest told me. By the grace of God, the nobleman did not carry him away. Rather, he wanted a favor from the priest. 'I'm being tormented,' the noble told him, 'because I lent money to a poor man, receiving his mill as a pledge, and when he was unable to pay, I seized the mill and passed it on to my heirs.' The noble opened his mouth wide, and it fell to his chest. 'Do you see?' he cried. 'In my mouth I carry a burning mill-shaft, heavier than the castle of Rouen. I beg you, please, tell my wife and son that they must return the mill to the poor man or his family.'"

Agnes the healer murmured in Latin, "May God have mercy on his soul."

Edyth continued, "The priest stood aghast at this, until a knight galloped up to him and waved a sword. The knight spoke to the priest sternly, 'You deserve to die and be swept along with us to share our punishment, because you tried to seize things that are ours. The Mass you sang today, however, has saved you. Otherwise, you would be riding my horse and bearing my arms.' The knight brandished his sword and spear, and the priest could see that they were red-hot. 'And the burning of my sword and spear against my flesh constantly offends my nostrils with an appalling stench,' the knight said. 'My only consolation is that because of a Mass my own priest said for me, I no longer carry my shield, which caused me unspeakable agonies. Go your way, and say Masses for all of us, so that we may be released from our burdens. For God is just, but He is also merciful.'"

The donkey-boy leaned against the stone, his mouth agape. Edyth sank back in her chair.

"Well, sisters and brothers, what do you say? Is the Lord's justice greater than His mercy, or is His mercy greater than his justice?"

By January, the Abbott and three brothers joined our talks, almost as if to compensate for the loss of Edyth, Agnes the healer, and the other Chester nuns. Tostig, now healthy and restless, announced his intention to return to England and take the nuns with him.

After he was cured, for which I had received another gold arm-ring, Tostig had spent most of his time with Lady Judith, the Count's half-sister. I often saw them strolling over the monastery grounds, coming to rest in the orchard.

Lady Judith was unmarried, and I suspected that Tostig's confidential mission might have something to do with a wedding.

Anette broached the subject with Lady Judith and confirmed my suspicions. There was to be a marriage between Wessex and Flanders, though that was all Lady Judith would say.

It was enough. Tostig, I surmised, had been chosen as his lord's emissary to begin negotiations with Count Baldwin. Of course, the negotiations would remain secret until Baldwin and Earl Godwin of Wessex publicly agreed to the match.

Apparently the early negotiations had been successful; Tostig was cheerful as he prepared to leave. He whistled and sang to himself as he packed his horse and shouted orders to the knights who would accompany him and the nuns to the coast.

His clothing had improved with every journey to England. Now he wore a fur cape, a blue tunic, yellow leggings, and fine, intricately stitched scarlet shoes. His sword sheath and saddle boasted more jewels than any knight had. His lord must be one of Wessex's wealthier nobles, I thought.

He seemed friendly as we parted. I helped him swing into his saddle and thanked him again for saving my life and for his gifts.

He glanced down at me. "I owe you thanks for healing me."

I risked a jest. "I'm a healer. I would have healed you if you had been a dog."

He laughed, and his breath turned to frost. "You sound like my brother. I'm almost tempted to journey north with you in the spring. Many years have passed since I saw my Danish cousins. I must return home, though." He bent to clasp my hand. "If your travels ever bring you to Wessex, you're welcome at court. I'll teach you to speak English more like a Saxon."

"I thought I spoke English exactly like a Saxon."

He laughed again, this time more loudly.

Edyth and Agnes also invited me to England. "You will love the country around Chester, and we will love to have you visit us."

I thanked them and said I hoped to be in England before many years passed. And I encouraged Agnes to keep up her healing studies.

Then the nuns, Tostig, and the knights rode through the abbey gate into the snow-covered landscape.

The Abbot, the monks, and Anette and I returned to our discussions.

As spring brightened, I offered to do compensatory work for the daily omission of Matins and Lauds — the Abbot had let me sleep in all winter — and to repay him for his kindness.

Because I was still very weak, I could only do work that allowed me to sit most of the time.

The Abbot looked up from his desk, his head haloed by the flowers blooming outside his window. "Can you read and write?"

"Yes, of course."

"Good. I can use an extra scribe for recording the villagers' tithes, though that's not a pressing need." He hesitated and then looked hopeful. "Can you copy?"

"Certainly," I lied. "I've done it often." How difficult could copying be?

Smiling, he rose and led me to the scriptorium. "I need every copyist I can find. I'm sorry I didn't know of your talents earlier. Not only do I wish to supply the abbey library with more works of theology, philosophy, and spiritual guidance, but I need books for gifts."

So, the next morning I lifted myself onto a high, narrow chair in the scriptorium next to a slitted window and bent over my writing board. As the Abbot ordered, I recited a silent prayer for accuracy.

Nodding to myself — I saw the other two copyists do this, and it looked wonderfully holy — I marked my lines with a ruler and awl and set to work with my quill.

After I smeared one uncleaned parchment with watery ink and broke a quill, the copyists hurried over to instruct me. They showed me how to scrape parchment clean, how to smooth it with pumice, how to mix my ink, and trim my quill.

Fortunately, my writing was acceptable, and I was slow enough to make few mistakes. Within a week, I had produced usable copies of ten anonymous sermons.

Pleased, the Abbot assigned me to Latin poetry, intended as a gift for a local noble. The poetry was from Horace and included three of his love poems. I had never read these, and several lines from "Kiss in Time" affected me deeply:

> *Now on the campus and the squares,*
> *When evening shades descend,*
> *Soft whisperings again are heard,*
> *And loving voices blend;*

> *And now the low delightful laugh*
> *Betrays the lurking maid,*
> *While from her slowly yielding arms*
> *The forfeiture is paid.*

The last stanza of "Love Unreasoning" also moved me:

> *Happy, happy, happy they*
> *Whose living love, untroubled by strife,*
> *Binds them till the last sad day,*
> *Nor parts them but with parting life.*

My gaze wandered out the window, until I caught the frown of one of the other copyists. I returned to work.

The next day, the Abbot appeared and placed another of Horace's poems, "The Golden Mean," on my writing board. He had scratched a mark beside three of the first four stanzas:

> *Live so that you never tempt the relentless sea,*
> *Nor press too close to the threatening shore;*
> *Beware extremes, and cling to the golden mean,*
> *that most priceless of treasures.*
> *Safely ensconced, you need not dread the house of poverty.*
> *Owning wisdom, you need not seek mansions that others envy.*
> *Secure in truth, protected by moderation,*
> *Fate cannot harm you. ...*
> *Let hope for a brighter tomorrow lighten any grief*
> *and knowledge of fortune's fickleness temper any joy.*
> *Bear the winters, knowing that, despite their fury,*
> *Jove will call them back.*

Under the poem was a book of the sermons of St. Augustine. It looked huge, and in fact I spent every morning of two months copying it.

Finally, my hands and back aching, I completed it. I leaned forward once more to write at the bottom of the last page the copyist's closing: "Explicit, Deo Gratias — Finished, thank God!"

CHAPTER 10

NORTHERN PERIL

A.D. 1046

When summer returned, so did my strength. So did Count Baldwin, Lady Judith, and the courtiers. The Count's visit was a brief one, though. He announced his intention to take the court south within the week. He wanted Anette to accompany them.

He also had a message for me.

"From Duke William," he said. "The messenger from your Duke, bearing fine gifts for my court, said to tell you that a giant strides toward you. I trust you understand."

"Yes, I do. Thank you." I recognized the reference to Hardraada, so I decided to leave for the North at the same time the count's party headed south.

The Count sighed. "You have the Pope and the Holy Roman Empire to your south and east, and the Danish empire to the north. Normandy seems vulnerable just now. I don't know how you will …" He broke off and looked at the flowers not far from the long bench on which we sat.

"I appreciate your concern, my lord." I didn't know how to reply to the Count's sympathetic concern. "At least, Edward is on the English throne now."

"Yes. He solved his Danish problem the same way I'm solving mine: by marrying into Earl Godwin's family." He looked down at his hands. "Godwin and his sons — the eyes and ears of the Danes in England. King Edward does not have allies in that family. They're closer to me, for instance, than to him. His marriage to Edith, Godwin's daughter, may gain some advantage for him."

"Excuse me, my lord, but did you say that King Edward has married Earl Godwin's daughter?"

"Yes. I suppose that, since you have been ill, you would not have heard of the wedding."

"Not of that particular wedding," I said, almost mumbling to myself.

"King Edward also courts the Pope, so the Holy Roman Empire is likely to leave him alone, though that puts us in opposing camps sometimes."

"Courts the Pope?"

"King Edward is the Pope's idea of a perfect king in a land full of heathen Danes and Saxons, which is the Pope's appraisal of England. King Edward is an ardent Christian. He's also respectful to the Pope in his exchanges with Rome."

"So the forces behind the Holy Roman Empire …"

"Which are such an annoyance to me …"

"… will leave Edward alone."

"Yes. He has a delicately balanced strategy in place, which might just keep his reign free of interference from the Church."

I nodded. "Now I understand why he was willing to return to England, join the Danish King, and marry a Saxon woman. He's solved for England all the problems we haven't yet solved for Normandy — how to keep the Danish and Holy Roman Empires at bay."

"Yes, though that solution may be temporary. When King Edward dies … I doubt even his heir, if he has one, could withstand Godwin's family. Godwin's son, Harold, is more ambitious than his father, and even the Danes in England admire him."

"Perhaps he could be separated from the Danes in some way."

"Drive a wedge. Yes, that would be good, if you could do it." The Count smiled. "It would serve my purposes, since Godwin's family and I are allied, and I have no wish to be part of the Danish Empire."

"I appreciate that sentiment."

He put his hand on my shoulder. "Your Duke has a fine emissary, but that emissary needs to watch the Pope, the Holy Roman Empire, King Magnus, the usurper Sweyn, and the family of Earl Godwin, especially Earl Harold, Godwin's son … closely."

"Yes, I will need many eyes."

He smiled again. "I do know that Harald Hardraada is a giant. There are many giants surrounding you and your Duke, my young friend."

When the day of parting came, I found Count Baldwin shouting orders to his men just inside the main gate. I bade him farewell.

Not far away Lady Matilda, dressed in scarlet and yellow, instructed the servants who packed her wagon. I took formal but pleasant leave of her.

"You've gained a servant for life, my lady," I said. "I don't know how else to thank you for ridding me of my crutch."

She replied as straightforwardly as William might. "You owe me no thanks. You and Anette did the difficult work. I merely offered my analysis."

I bowed to her. "I pray that Normandy may find a way to bless Flanders for your analysis."

Anette rested on a wooden bench nearby, watching us. She wore her blue surcoat and white cloak. I excused myself and strode over to her, trying to limp as little as possible.

"May I sit here?" I asked.

She gazed at me and said, "Yes, please do."

Everything I had planned to say left me. Eventually I shrugged and said, "I have no idea how to say good-bye. Or how to thank you for everything you've done for me."

"I am rewarded by your lack of a crutch and your friendship."

"I'll think of you whenever I heal anyone, whenever I walk anywhere, whenever I discuss politics or theology or government."

She touched my arm. "Cuin, promise me that you'll come to court — wherever we are — on your return."

I repeated the promise I had made in the winter. "Nothing would please me more than to see you in a few months or even weeks. Wherever the court is, I'll find it."

Her brow wrinkled in concern. "I do have a vision of your returning, but it isn't this autumn. Or the next."

This alarmed me, but I wanted to sound brave and sure. "Your vision has failed you this one time. I shall return soon."

"I hope so." She paused. "God be with you and bring you back."

I leaned back to reply but was struck dumb by the tears in her eyes.

At that moment, one of the Count's men appeared and offered her his arm. With a glance at me, she rose and allowed herself to be escorted to Lady Matilda's wagon. I followed.

A command rang out, and the party surged forward. As the wagon jostled through the gate, Anette turned to watch me. I raised my hand in farewell, and she did the same.

The wagon and the Count's men disappeared into the distance. I thought I could see Anette's face gazing back at me the whole time.

I turned for a final survey of the buildings, fountains, and arched passageways of the monastery. What had been a friendly refuge for a year seemed suddenly desolate.

I hurriedly thanked the Abbot and the Prior, Brother Berengar and the cooks. I shouted good-bye to the brothers as they worked in the garden. They glanced up from their planting to wave and call to me.

Then I mounted the pony and rode through the gate. St. Vaast's walls faded behind me.

I intended to ride directly to the Army Road. According to the Abbot, an old Roman path ran east from St. Vaast. If I stayed on it, I could reach the Army Road in a few days. I was looking forward to finding the much-traveled route with its pilgrims and merchants. The Abbot assured me that the Army Road would be crowded this time of year.

To throw off anyone who might be following me, though, I rode into the forest just north of the Roman path, hoping to keep it a few hundred feet to the south. This way, I would be safe until I reached friendly travelers.

Though my plan worked while I rode through Flanders, the countryside in Frisia refused to cooperate. The trees and undergrowth set themselves thickly against a straight path, and I encountered one bog after another. I had to dismount often to avoid a thicket or swamp.

There was an additional problem: glancing up at the sun by day and the stars by night, I discovered that the terrain was driving me north, away from the Roman path.

Of course, I benefited from the forest's food. The crusty bread, cheese, and dried fruit the St. Vaast cook had generously packed soon vanished. So I foraged for berries, groundnuts, roots and tubers, and seeds and accustomed the pony to similar fare.

With each foraging trip, though, my path shifted farther north.

One afternoon, when I mounted a hill and climbed a pine tree to locate the road or a village, nothing was in sight. I scoured the south and could see only treetops. The boggy forest had become a wilderness. I had lost the Roman path.

I cursed myself for wandering into the wilderness and almost began to understand why the St. Vaast monks called it "the devil's land."

I recalled my training with Garrad, though, and settled myself into the tree. I took a deep breath and tried to become the old pine. Did it have any messages for a hapless, dimwitted traveler?

In a few moments, I found my head twisting north, though I did not know why. My eyes opened wide. There, stretched before me, clouds piled above it, was the ocean. Though heading east every day to intersect the Army Road, I had drifted so far north that I had reached the Frisian coast.

As always, the ocean impressed me, even when it was relatively mild. I dismounted and after foraging for wood, constructed a lean-to and built a fire in front of it. As darkness fell, I watched the stars reflect in the ocean and then drifted off to sleep.

Awakening to a cloudless morning, I had an impulse to practice with the bow. Now that I was healthy and unencumbered by my disguise, I wanted to remind myself that I could handle such a long weapon.

It pulled differently from the shorter ones I had used, but it felt like an old friend within a few minutes. My arrows found any mark I chose, even at great distances. I felt more secure.

I mounted the pony and rode east along the coast.

Soon, however, I lost the ocean. First one marsh then another drove me inland. Reluctantly, I was journeying far south of any coastline. Even there, bogs and swamps slowed my progress.

Fortunately, Garrad had made me study his maps. Recalling them and watching the stars closely, I pressed north and soon came to what I was sure was the River Eider, whose northern branch, the Trene, would lead into Denmark — and one of its forks, the Rheide, would lead to the Danish trading town of Hedeby.

The pony and I picked our way through the trees and underbrush until we arrived at the Rheide. Near its eastern end, only about a day's ride away now, lay Hedeby. There Edyth and her sister nuns had been sold as slaves, there Lanfranc had heard Icelandic prophecies, and there I could get news.

I turned the horse's head east and silently practiced my Danish.

In a short time, I spotted a huge earthen wall in the distance, on the northern side of the Rheide: the Danework. It sprawled before me, marking the boundary between the southern, German end of the Holy Roman Empire and the Northern countries.

I had reached Denmark.

"Taller than a man but ten times that broad," Garrad had said, but the Danework looked even larger than that. It had been built two hundred years earlier by the Danish King Godfred to keep the German Saxons at bay. Danish kings had extended it over the years and built palisades and occasional guard-towers on top of it, with water-filled ditches along most of it.

I stared at the palisades rising in the distance like great wooden fences, the towers mounting them at intervals. This earth and wood defense stretched across Denmark's Jutland peninsula from sea to sea, broken only where rivers, such as the Trene and Rheide, offered natural defenses against invaders.

Now I had perilous work to do. Garrad had advised me to approach Hedeby from inside the Danework, from the north. The detour would take extra time, but it would hide the fact that I came from the south, adding deception to my disguise.

So my immediate task was to locate an opening not visible from a guarded tower. Fording the Rheide would be easy compared to crossing the Danework undetected.

I dismounted and climbed a nearby beech.

I spotted a gap in the palisade that had no watchtowers and no water-filled ditch. I could not understand why the Danes had left this area exposed to invasion, but I hoped it was an intentional oversight. I climbed down from the tree, remounted, and urged the pony toward the gap.

We left the forest's safety and entered a narrow, grassy meadow that stretched to the foot of the embankment.

Only a few feet into the meadow, though, the pony snorted and threw his head. I, too, smelled the offensive odor and tugged him to a halt. In front of us, swarms of flies hovered just above the ground. Off to the right and left were marsh marigolds, their shiny green leaves looking almost poisonous.

Retrieving my walking-staff, I slipped to the earth and began prodding the ground. Flies buzzed around my ankles and waist, and an acrid smell assaulted my nostrils.

Within a few feet, the staff sank half its length, and I had to struggle to free it. This was the reason the Danes needed no palisade at this point: a hidden bog provided the defense. From its stench, I realized that it had claimed animals and men in the performance of its duty.

Using the staff to poke the earth, I led the pony around the edge of the bog. I glanced upward. I had swung so far to the left that I was again below the wooden palisade. The gap I needed was now sharply to my right and almost straight up. From here, the pony and I would have to strike diagonally across the steep embankment to reach the gap.

It would be a hard climb, and we would be visible to guards for a longer time than I had hoped.

I had no choice, though. I took the pony's reins and began to lead him up the slope. We reached the edge of the palisade, skirted it, and stepped through the gap.

No guard was in sight. I searched the top of the Danework as it stretched both east and west. There were no guards anywhere.

I glanced down the embankment in front of me. Crossing my path below, a stony road traversed the length of the Danework. Stretching beyond the road was a meadow, its grasses swaying in the afternoon wind. Their straw color must have reminded the pony of hay, because he regained his energy, neighing and stamping.

"So you become a noble steed when the route is downhill," I said out loud — in Danish. "Well, this is the place to be fast as well as noble. We need to reach that forest before anyone sees us."

The pony's pace remained sluggish, though. It was late afternoon by the time we reached the safety of the trees. I breathed a sigh of relief. I caught myself thinking that it was unlucky Friday, but I had made it safely into the forest.

I pressed north until sundown. Then I turned eastward again, aiming at Hedeby. I used the mounds I had spotted as landmarks. Just after dusk, I glimpsed a wide, well-traveled route several hundred feet in front of me: the Army Road. I smiled at it and began to kick the pony forward.

At that moment, though, a black horse trotted into view from the south. Astride it was a black-robed figure.

"Many Benedictines probably pass through here," I said to the pony, "but there's one warrior-monk I don't want to meet. As a precaution, you and I will avoid any black robe we can."

As I spoke, the rider jerked his horse to a stop. His hood twisted in my direction, revealing only a void. The hood moved deliberately from side to side, as if searching the woods.

I wished I had hidden behind one of the rocks that dotted the forest. I remained motionless and silent, praying the pony would do the same.

The pony never moved. The monk rode on.

I breathed heavily in relief. "Well done! I'll never again call you fat and noisy."

As the pony paced forward, I spotted one of the bare mounds that I had encountered all afternoon. This one, though, stood atop a larger, tree-covered hill and dominated its neighbors.

Even in the fading light, I could discern lines etched on its bare surface, like farmers' drainage ditches, though neither as wide nor as deep. Some wood-and-stone structure mounted its summit.

What could its purpose be? I glanced at the Army Road in the distance. I could take some time to investigate the mound, which would allow the monk on the black horse to get even farther away from us.

I urged the pony up the oak-covered hill to the foot of the mound. Dismounting, I used my walking-staff to climb to its top.

As I ascended, I recognized scorch-marks on the ground. Someone had burned every plant to leave the mound bald except for the crisscross patterns. In the center of the patterns stood a table-sized stone slab, layered with wood covered by leather, probably to keep off dew and rain.

What was this place's purpose? I stood pondering and began to feel disconnected, as if I had somehow stepped outside of time.

Abruptly, I realized that I had lingered much longer than I intended. Darkness now deepened around me.

Before I could stir, though, a low chanting drifted up the hill. I smelled torches and spied light specks through the trees below.

Fortunately, the moon, still low in the sky, rested behind the light specks. I could see the silhouettes of a dozen forms with what appeared to be horns on their heads, winding up the hill. The faces, though, remained dark. Each figure carried a glowing torch.

The hissing voice, as if close to my ear, cried, "Hide!"

The guttural chanting grew louder. The tones violated the Church's harmonies, and their dissonances seemed to freeze my bones. For a brief time, I was afraid I could not move.

The voice now almost shrieked: "Hide!"

I grabbed the pony's reins, jerking him from the mound and down the opposite side of the tree-covered hill. To my relief, he did not snort or thud his hoofs on the earth. He picked his way as quickly as I did.

I paused to scan the mound. One torch burst over its black horizon. Then another. And another. The marchers had reached the top.

I pulled the pony behind three huddled oaks and tied him to one of them. Standing behind him, I stared back toward the mound.

Who were those people? Were they people at all? The priests in Falaise had often told me about demons that inhabited the wilderness, especially the Northern wilderness.

This, however, was not the wilderness. I was a few miles away from small villages and a large trading-town, Hedeby. More likely, this group belonged to one of the pagan communities that Garrad had told me about. Although Denmark had been Christian for a century, it tolerated the worship of Odin, Thor, and other gods.

What god did this group worship? What did the horns signify? What kind of ritual was occurring?

My curiosity overcame my fear. First crouching then crawling, I sneaked back up the hill. A boulder between two oaks provided a hiding-place. I bent behind it, peering into the darkness.

I counted thirteen shapes, apparently wearing horned masks. They wound themselves into a circle around the massive stone slab. For a long time, they swayed, mingled, and reassembled in the circle, accompanying their movements with throaty chants.

Their torches burned lower and offered only fading light. I rose and stretched forward on the rock for a better view.

The voices rose again, this time in Danish. I could only understand the names of old gods and a few phrases: "Thor's hammer, the thunder cross" and "Odin, the god who hung on the tree."

Whatever else these people intended to do with their rites, they at least worshipped the old Northern warrior gods.

Abruptly, the chanting hushed. The forms stiffened. One voice rang out.

This time I could not understand the words, nor could I identify the language. Other voices responded in what sounded like hoarse gibberish.

A group split away and vanished momentarily. They reappeared, holding some squirming form above their heads.

Suddenly, a blaze flashed from the altar.

I gasped involuntarily — out loud.

The firelight brightened the oaks near me. To any chanter who happened to look, I was plainly visible. I dropped below the rock.

But not before two horned figures spun and gestured toward me.

I glanced over the rock. All of the forms, now brightly illuminated, began to writhe. They howled and waved long knives in the air.

Abruptly, they jerked the knives down — in my direction.

At that moment, a hand clapped over my mouth, wrenching me backward. A voice hissed in my ear, "Don't make a sound. I'm going to release you, but don't speak."

The hand drew away. A face twisted around my shoulder, its left hand to its mouth to indicate silence. It was Garrad.

"Listen to me," he whispered. "We must leave. Quickly but quietly. Follow me."

The chanters fell silent. The only sound issuing from the hill was the fire's roar. Then a voice bawled something in a dialect I did not recognize. Others echoed it.

Garrad grabbed my robe at the shoulder. "I've moved your horse. He's safe. Come!"

Stooping low, I scrambled behind Garrad. He plunged through the forest, ducking from tree to tree and circling the hill as he descended.

He paused at intervals to pull away tree branches with his good hand. He peered into the darkness behind the branches, shook his head, and then resumed circling.

During one of his pauses, I glanced toward the mound. The chanters had fanned out. Three of them slunk down the hill toward us, their horned masks black before the firelight. They lifted their knives high.

Garrad seized my arm and dragged me after him. The three apparently had not seen us, but they soon closed on where we had stood.

We continued circling down the hill, though I did not know why. Since the chanters had fanned out, this maneuver could not save us.

I stumbled behind Garrad, panting. Sweat poured from my face and body, soaking my tunic.

Two chanters' shadows, cast by the firelight, inched toward our feet.

Garrad tugged at some tree branches in front of me. He grabbed me, pulled me into a shallow cave behind the branches, and crawled in after me.

Signaling me to be quiet, he rolled a nearby stone over the entrance, hiding all of it but a crack. Leaning against the rooted wall, he closed his eyes and seemed to fall asleep. I tried not to breathe or make a sound, but my lungs ached for air, and every part of my body trembled violently.

The chanters thrashed around outside the cave, shouting to each other. Their voices seemed near the cave entrance. Even nearer.

Then distant. Then close again. After what seemed hours, they drifted away.

Garrad opened his eyes. "To be safe, we'll stay here for the night. Go to sleep."

I had a hundred questions. I was too exhausted and frightened to utter a word, though. As my trembling subsided, I dozed off.

The next thing I felt was a hand shaking my shoulder.

Garrad leaned in the cave from the outside, his good hand reaching toward me. "Let's go. I've scouted outside. There's no sign of anyone."

I crawled from the cave, brushing past the oak and maple leaves that had concealed it. The stone covering its entrance was gone. It had been rolled to the back of the cave.

I stretched and stared at the forest, now hung in a mist, the tree trunks mere shadows around us.

Garrad set off at a jog down the hill. Feeling stiff in my joints, I stumbled after him. Soon we were trotting down the hill at an even pace. My foot and leg muscles had become so strong that even running — now or the night before — did not hurt them. Garrad seemed not to realize that I had no crutch.

Finally, we reached a clearing and halted. At its eastern edge yawned another, larger cave. Inside stood my pony. Next to him was a black horse.

Garrad drew close to me. "We're probably not in danger. We interrupted a local ritual last night, though, and we may be unwelcome. We can talk later."

We mounted and picked our way through the misty forest to the Army Road. We turned onto it where I had seen the rider the night before.

"It was you, then," I said, as the horses trotted along the damp road.

"Yes. I've been riding up and down this stretch for weeks, watching for you."

"How did you find me?"

"It wasn't easy. I almost missed you last night." With an amused look, he studied my now unkempt hair and beard. "Your disguise fooled me completely. If I hadn't heard a voice, I wouldn't have paused to look. Even then, I rode on until I heard the voice again and realized it was yours."

I thought I had been undetected the night before, as I had hidden and spoken to the pony. It never occurred to me that the rider might have the eyesight and hearing of Garrad.

"I tried to locate you before the ritual began. I found your pony and moved him. I knew that would prevent your riding away. I couldn't find you when I returned to the hill, though. I might have missed you altogether, except that when the chanters lit the fire, you nearly shouted."

I was chagrined that he had caught my one mistake, after all the care I had taken to be quiet on my journey. "It wasn't that loud."

"That's true, but they heard you."

"Who were they?"

"Danes, I suppose. Though not Christian ones."

"They sounded like worshippers of the warrior-gods. I heard something about Thor's thunder-cross and Odin's hanging on a tree. They also chanted sounds I didn't understand."

He nodded. "I heard the phrases, too. The other sounds probably had something to do with the moon-god. That would explain the mound in the middle of a forest."

"So it was some mixture of the warrior-religion and moon-worship?"

"Many local rituals are mixtures. Unlike Odin-worshippers, though, moon-worshippers keep their activities secret. That's why two men dressed as Benedictine monks would have been unwelcome."

"Were they sacrificing —?"

"A horned goat. That's the usual sacrifice for the moon-god. The goat's horns relate to the horns on their headdresses and the horns of the moon in its first quarter. Moon-worshippers feel that the early moon makes them fertile and powerful. They offer the goat's blood and horns to it." He smiled. "Your shout not only led me to you. It also saved the life of an unfortunate goat."

"The ritual was about the moon and fertility?"

"Many other things, too."

"What other things?"

He sighed. "I suppose you should know ... all right, some philosophy. What we refer to as our everyday life, is often limited, as you and I have often discussed. We experience only what is around us everyday, and that becomes our world. There are, however, many more worlds than our everyday one. In the ancient worlds, for instance, many different kinds of people existed:

some our size, of course, but also some very small and some very tall. Some appeared as we do, while some had ... unusual features."

"Are you saying that some of these tall or small people had horns?"

"Your thinking is as quick as ever. Yes, some had horns. Usually the Tall People would have these and sometimes were considered demons. Dangerous."

"Were they dangerous?"

"That's like asking me whether the people surrounding the Pope and the Holy Roman Emperor are dangerous. Some are, and some are not."

"These Tall People, did they rule the earth? You once told me stories about them."

"Yes, they were a power here. What's more, many Tall People still exist, though in our lands in these times, they hide themselves."

"Why?"

"Long ago, they first battled and then joined ... otherworldly demons who were bent on ruling the world."

"So, the Tall beings ... did bad things? Were a destructive force here?"

"Yes. Many, though, wished to repair what they had done. Many still try to help humanity."

"So, sacrificing a goat to the moon-god ..."

"May be an act of gratitude for and unity with the beneficent Tall People — as well as identifying with the natural, fluid processes we all live within, symbolized by the cyclical expanding and contracting of the moon, from a perfect sphere to a horned crescent."

Voldred's demanding that the Flemish farmer give him a horned goat passed through my mind. "Could the Berserker who tried to kill me involve himself in such a ritual? Even this particular ritual?"

"It's probable that he might participate in such rituals. It's possible that he might have been in this one, especially if he was following you. Was he?"

"I don't know. I didn't think so. I was wandering in the wilderness so long ..."

"Then he probably was not in last night's ritual."

"I hope not." I breathed heavily. "How did you know there would be a cave where we could hide?"

"I had been staying below in another, larger cave. Double caves were usual in the old religions — one lower down, one about halfway up the hill. Fortunately for us, the tradition was maintained here."

"Why didn't the worshippers find it then?"

"I hoped that they didn't know about it. The larger one showed no signs of use. No local people frequented it, nor were there signs of rituals. So I assumed the smaller cave had been neglected as well, probably hidden behind trees that had grown up over the years, concealing its entrance. In my travels, I've found many ancient sites overgrown and forgotten."

He glanced around. "We should slip off the road here. Traders will be coming along as we near Hedeby. I want to talk privately for a time."

We turned the horses' heads into the forest and rode until we found a large, flat stone on top of a bluff. To the south, the Danework was visible through the remnants of the morning fog. We dismounted and rested on the rock.

He inspected me. "Your crutch is gone. Lady Matilda and Anette must be better healers than I."

My mouth fell open. "How do you know about them?"

"Earl Tostig told me."

"*Earl* Tostig?"

"Yes, I spoke with him when he came to visit Duke William. It's hard to ignore a son of Godwin of Wessex."

"Son? Of Godwin? I thought he was a courtier." Garrad had once told me the Danish names of Earl Godwin's sons. I should have guessed Tostig's identity.

He put his good hand on my shoulder. "Didn't Tostig negotiate with Count Baldwin to marry the Count's half-sister?"

"Yes, but I thought he was acting for some Wessex lord."

"It's Tostig himself who wishes to marry Lady Judith. At some time in the future, at least. Tostig told Duke William that the wedding plans must be kept quiet for now, because they could upset the power balance in England. He also told us about your encounter with Voldred. I realized that Voldred must have been the Berserker who attacked Lanfranc's house in Avranches."

"Yes, and he was disguised as a monk when he stabbed me."

"How's your arm?"

"Except for aching in damp weather, it's fine."

"Good. Let's hope that Voldred leaves you alone now. If he was as badly wounded as Tostig described, he may be inspired to return home and stay there."

"Do you think that Tostig might have killed him?"

"It's possible, of course, but I'm afraid it's unlikely. Berserkers are hard to kill."

"I don't wish anyone to be killed. I would like to stop worrying about assassins, though, particularly this one."

Garrad stared at me a moment and then said, "After Duke William and I received your message, that you'd be leaving Arras this summer, I decided to come north to escort you and bring you news. Rolf and his Goliards accompanied me."

"Are they safe and well?"

"Yes. After they left you last summer, they scouted Norway for us. That's why we didn't urge you to press north. We learned from their scouting that there was nothing you could do, since neither Hardraada nor Magnus were anywhere I expected them to be."

"The Goliards act as spies for you?"

"They have for years, yes. They also mentioned Lady Matilda and Anette. It was Earl Tostig who told us that the ladies were healers. He also told us about your curing him of a fever and freeing the English nuns. I enjoyed that. In fact, it gave me an idea, and I asked Duke William for some gilded helmets to bring north."

I had already noted the bulging sack slung across his horse.

He continued. "I tried to catch you at Arras, but I was detained in the south of Flanders by the Count and his party."

"I didn't think you knew the Count."

"I didn't until then. The Goliards did, though. And I wanted to meet him. And his daughter."

"Lady Matilda, William's tiny counterpart in Flanders."

He smiled. "You discovered that, did you?"

"It would be difficult not to. Why? Does it make a difference?"

"We'll see. Anyway, it's what made me miss you. So the Goliards and I headed for the Army Road as quickly as we could. We couldn't find you there, and no one in Hedeby had seen you. Nonetheless, my inner senses told me you were near. So while the Goliards pressed on to Norway, I found a cave and waited and watched."

Without revealing that I had gotten lost, I detailed the route I had taken along the Frisian coast and how I had kept out of sight.

"A wise course," he said, "but I would have preferred you to have an escort."

"I didn't want to risk anyone else's life."

"I understand. I would have felt the same. Besides, your not being in Hedeby worked out well for me. I spoke to the local traders and learned many of the details about what the Goliards discovered when they left you last year: Prince Harald Hardraada, they said, returned to the North from Byzantium last winter."

I groaned. "I shouldn't have stayed so long in Flanders."

"Don't be concerned. Your being in the North would have served no purpose. You couldn't have known Hardraada's strategy. Even I didn't guess it."

I felt relieved. "What is his strategy?"

Garrad shielded his eyes with his good hand and gazed skyward. The morning haze had dissipated, revealing a sky so clear that it seemed to etch the pine and oak forest.

"Let's walk the horses back to the road. I'll tell you as we go. I would like to be in Hedeby soon for food."

I glanced at the sun directly overhead. "So would I."

As we guided the horses back through the trees, Garrad began speaking again. "Hardraada didn't return to his home country, Norway, as we thought he would. Instead, he went to Denmark and allied himself to Sweyn, the usurper."

"What? Sweyn? That doesn't make sense. Why would Hardraada, a Norwegian, join the Danish usurper? Why not join King Magnus, his own nephew, in Norway?"

Garrad smiled. "I sat in the cave asking myself that very question. If I have guessed correctly, I admire Hardraada's strategy. Consider this: Hardraada returned from Byzantium with more wealth than most kings but with few men and a small fleet. If he went to his nephew, King Magnus, he would be going as a supplicant."

"Because he has so few warriors and ships."

"And no land. Before he did anything else, he would have to buy ships and soldiers. That would mean losing his wealth without having gained any land."

"He would have to hope that Magnus offered him land."

"Yes. Exactly. Hardraada also knows that Magnus, loyal to his own Norwegian culture, wants to end the Danish domination of Norway. To do so, Magnus must have no rebellions at home. He must not be distracted from confronting Sweyn in Denmark."

"Would Magnus fear Hardraada as the potential leader of a rebellion?"

"Of course. So Magnus would be reluctant to give Hardraada any land."

"So Hardraada would have men and ships but no land, thus no hope of getting that land in Norway. By the time he had the land and sea forces he needed, he would have exhausted his wealth getting men and ships. I see."

"So, what does Hardraada do? He doesn't beg from his nephew Magnus. He doesn't use his own wealth to buy ships or soldiers."

"Instead, he joins Magnus's enemy, Sweyn."

"Yes. If Magnus doesn't wish to fight his own uncle and if he needs Hardraada's money — his wars against the Danes have been costly — he must negotiate to win his uncle away from Sweyn, the Danish King."

I shook my head. "That is clever. More clever than I could ever be. Allied to Magnus' enemy, Hardraada is in a position to ask for all the men, ships, and especially all the land he wants."

"Without having to drain his own wealth."

"Magnus would have to give Hardraada land to win him back from Sweyn. A clever plan."

"If it works." He gazed at me. "Hardraada might be more clever than you. He might not. You see, though, the adversary you're facing. Winning an agreement from him will not be easy."

"Yes, I know. We need the agreement with at least Hardraada to protect Normandy. Indeed, now I see that an agreement with Hardraada is more important than an agreement with both Magnus and Sweyn."

We reached the edge of the forest. Merchants and farmers — Danes, Norwegians, and Icelanders — crowded the Army Road, their wagons and horses laden with wares.

As we joined them, Garrad spoke casually to any in hearing distance, establishing our deception of having come from the North.

This gave me an opportunity to listen to the Northern tongues. I was pleased that I could understand everything that was said. As we approached the opening in the Danework, I decided to practice speaking the dialects out loud.

In Danish, I asked Garrad about Edward. "Tostig reported that Edward did marry. 'A Wessex lady', he said."

Garrad nodded. "Tostig's own sister."

"Edward married a daughter of Godwin? That's what Count Baldwin told me, but I could scarcely believe it."

"Yes," he said, smiling, "but like your spoken Danish, the marriage is far from perfect. At least, that's what we hear from the Normans who have returned from London and Winchester — and many have returned. Earl Godwin has pressured Edward to remove Normans from positions there."

Ignoring his jest, I persisted in Danish. "Why is Edward becoming friendly with Godwin? I thought he distrusted Godwin."

"He does, but he wants peace within the country. For that end, he needs all the help he can get, especially from a powerful earl such as Godwin. Keep in mind that Edward is worried about Magnus and Hardraada, just as we are. After you left Rouen, we heard that Edward stationed the royal fleet off Sandwich. There were rumors that Magnus might invade England."

"Did he?"

"The invasion never came. Edward retired the fleet to London for the winter, but he returned them to Sandwich before I set out."

"You left from Rouen then? How are things there?"

"Not well, but would prefer to discuss them privately. We're approaching the Danework, and we're about to become very public."

He was right. As we trotted through the opening in the Danework and turned east along its Connecting Rampart, merchants and farmers joined us from small side-roads on their way to Hedeby.

A v-shaped moat stretched along the southern side of the Connecting Rampart, and we rode beside it for much of the morning, never out of earshot of some Dane eager for news as well as for goods.

Garrad pointed. "There's Hedeby."

From where we sat on our horses, no town was visible — only an earth and wood embankment. Though I expected Hedeby to be enclosed in an embankment similar to the Danework, this circular rampart was massive. It loomed five times the height of a man. Huge wooden palisades reinforced both its top and bottom.

The tunnel-like opening in front of us was as tall as a church. Planked on its inner walls, the entrance stretched the full length of the horse-drawn wagon ahead of us.

The wagon clattered as it drew through the opening. The roadway had been paved with stones.

As we crossed the wooden bridge that led to the entrance, I peered down. A moat lay under us, surrounding the rampart. The blackness of the water proved that it was as deep as any in Normandy.

As we emerged on the village side of the entrance, I noticed soldiers off to my right. I understood their Danish well enough to hear that they were comparing weapons and battles. One brandished a sword, pointing to the copper and gold inlay on its double-edged blade. It was beautiful enough to be one of the famous Frankish swords, perhaps from Cologne itself.

Behind them was a cemetery, its stones and crosses interspersed with small mounds. Winding in from the left, a stream angled at the road and curved through the town, as if it had mistaken Hedeby for a meadow. A branch of it watered the cemetery, where birch trees shaded the gossiping soldiers.

At the village center, a second stone road, stretching north and south, crossed our path. Beyond it, the main road veered to the right, cutting down to the harbor.

Garrad leaned toward me. "Let's ride to the harbor so that you can see the entire town."

I nodded, and we urged our horses toward the water.

More sparse near the entrance, houses choked the harbor section. Some stood only as wide and tall as the small houses in Falaise. Many were larger.

Different building methods were jumbled together. Homes with vertical wall-planking stood next to ones with horizontal planking. Beside these stood houses built on wooden frames with panels of woven sticks and mud.

"They have been attacked often," Garrad replied to my questioning stare, "and houses in this damp weather last only about twenty years, even if they survive attacks. The inhabitants rebuild them with whatever happens to be the popular method."

As in Falaise, some houses had wooden roofs, but most were thatched with reeds. A few boasted stone roofs stretching down to the door tops.

To my surprise, the doors were very low. I imagined Northerners, like Voldred, to be huge, especially with Garrad's mention of Tall People in the North. Where I could see inside the houses — most villagers had flung their doors open to the air — I could see why the doors seemed low. The homes had sunken floors. Those whose floors were at street level showed a short board or stone threshold jutting upward.

When I asked Garrad about it, he said, "It's a cold trap. The raised threshold keeps cold air from flowing in from the street."

The houses were grouped inside fences, their outhouses huddled behind them and their gable ends facing the street. Planked walkways connected everything inside the fences. Some of the enclosures accommodated barns and stables. Some contained shops and storehouses. Most had wells.

As in Rouen or Arras, everyone here was too busy working or trading to notice us. We rode by men and women who carried bundles wrapped in colorful cloth or bent over crafts, singing to themselves. They repaired roofs, patched barns, groomed horses, pounded metal, shaped clay, and haggled over goods.

Inside the houses, the peasant women wove cloth and worked among the pots at the fireplace. They pushed scarves back from their heads to nod at us and wiped their hands on the apron they wore over the strapped woolen dresses that covered their chemises.

Many were preparing bread, and when I smelled the aromas from the baking ovens, I smiled.

Garrad noticed and said, "Does your nose detect anything different?"

I sniffed. "Yes. Something like … pine."

"Your sense of smell is as good as ever. At least for food. The commoners here use pine bark to fill out their grain. It's gritty and wears their teeth down, but it's tasty. Now you may appreciate how good you have it at Falaise and Rouen Castles."

I nodded, but I was curious to taste the coarser bread. Or any bread.

Shouting drew my attention to the right. A group of children played with dogs in the street. Near them sat older men and women, dressed in plain cloaks, watching. Chaperones perhaps. Or grandparents.

One child seized the ears of an old man seated before him and said something close to the man's face. The man burst into laughter. Not far away, a potter's apprentice watched the play longingly.

The only eyes on us were those of the town cats, who paused in their treks along the tops of fences to stare at us. They yawned and returned to their journeys. In the feline world, two Benedictines could not have been very interesting.

Through the cooking odors, I smelled mostly fish. At the harbor where the rampart opened to the sea, I sniffed the air and recalled Mont St. Michel and the Frisian coast.

In this protected harbor, though, bogs such as I had seen in Frisia or storms such as those I had seen at Mont St. Michel were unlikely.

Here, unimpeded by nature, men loaded and unloaded ships along the arched breakwater that stretched into the Schlei Fjord. They shouted at each other — in three Southern and three Northern dialects — from broad-bottomed merchant ships, lying still in a calm sea.

Garrad pointed out the few Northerners with short hair and bangs down to their eyes. "How do you suppose they see through that mass of hair when they work?"

Most men's hair hung long over their necks, pulled back from their faces by ornamented headbands. Except for the headbands and an odd painting of colors around their eyes, the men looked like us.

I realized for the first time that Garrad had always worn his hair in a style more Northern than Norman, long over his ears and the back of his head, sometimes long enough to hang on his shoulders.

I returned to studying the workers and merchants. Most had mustaches and rounded or pointed beards so neatly trimmed that both Garrad and I would need to shape ours to look truly Danish.

I stroked my beard and felt its fuzziness. I did not relish seeing a barber, so I decided that monks should be unkempt. We would look holier that way.

Most men wore knee-length tunics not unlike Norman ones, flaring at the hips below colored belts bearing combs and single-edged knives. Few of their leggings fit as tightly as ours did, and most puffed out in peculiar shapes, stopping just above or just below the wearer's knees. From there dyed stockings or leather leggings ran down to their shoes, which were tied at the ankles.

Their most elegant articles of clothing, though, were their cloaks. Though they resembled Norman cloaks in being pinned at the right shoulder to keep the sword arm free, and though some resembled the shaggy cloaks worn by the common people in Falaise, most were of a finer wool or linen. These smaller cloaks ended in two points, the points either hanging down the back or — what I thought looked warrior-like—one point in front, one in back. I wished I had such a cloak.

Garrad leaned over to nudge me and point at a band of wealthy-looking Danes not far from the pier. "Look around their necks."

All sorts of things dangled from their neck-cords: pendants, figurines, bells, glass beads, even small knives.

As we retraced the route into the town's center, I noticed that the women, too, had objects dangling on them, suspended from decorated brooches, as big as my palm, just off each shoulder. From the right-hand brooches hung silver chains, beads, and jewels. From the left-hand ones hung keys, knives, combs, scissors, purses, and bone needle cases, all elaborately decorated. They too wore necklaces, mostly of glass beads and silver.

The cloaks on the better-dressed women, though, were pulled back, exposing not only strapped dresses but also bare arms; the chemises on the wealthier women were sleeveless. I could see from the way the men stared at them that they found bare, white arms attractive. So did I.

Like the men, the women wore intricately designed finger-rings but far more arm-rings of braided silver and some elaborate earrings. Like the men also, most women painted stripes of yellow, blue, or red around their eyes, a style I had never seen at home.

The dresses and cloaks of the women on the walkways were more brightly colored than those I had seen inside the houses. Outside, too, more women adorned their hair with flowers and ribbons or ornamented headdresses. Normans seemed drab and undecorated by comparison.

Garrad tried, as usual, to teach me, but I was distracted by the Danes. I finally focused on him as he said, "... the largest market town in the North. Look, those decorated swords were probably made by the Franks, while the basalt millstones over there come from the Rhineland. There's glassware from Rouen itself. Those soapstone pots and dishes are from Norway."

His mentioning Norway made my stomach queasy, so I changed the subject. "Are there more craftsmen here than in Arras or Rouen?"

"Hedeby is known for good potters, weavers, jewelers, and such. They turn out products for commoners as well as for nobles."

"Don't all craftsmen?"

"You don't see what I mean. The goods they make for the richer families they then reproduce more cheaply for the common people. That's why people here look so colorful."

I had noticed that even the wooden saddles and collar harnesses on the horses were painted and decorated.

"To find a more brightly colored group," Garrad said, "you would have to go to Baghdad. We'll take advantage of the lower costs, too. I want a smith to convert William's and Tostig's gifts into gold pieces. It will be easier to bargain for slaves. And I can give you some gold pieces to take north with you."

I heard the comment with dismay. "Aren't you going with me?"

We dismounted and pulled our horses to an empty part of the street.

Garrad leaned toward me, speaking softly in Norman French, "I don't think I can. There's a rebellion forming in Rouen that will come as an especially hard blow to William. The leader of the rebels is, as I suspected, his cousin, Guy. I'll need to be back in Normandy by autumn."

My disappointment over losing Garrad was overcome by my surprise about the rebellion. "Guy leading a rebellion? He can't lead his horse out of a stable."

"That's why I must go back. Guy is being manipulated. His pride and his pliable nature are, as always, his worst enemies. I need to stop him before his ambition leads him too far astray."

"Perhaps I should return with you." My appetite for adventure and foreign lands had long since been sated.

"I would be happy to have you accompany me, but your task will not be finished soon enough for me to stay. I should leave as soon as I find an escort for you, but you are unlikely to find Hardraada or Magnus for many days. Perhaps weeks."

"Yes … I suppose you're right."

We led our horses back up the center street, stopping to trade for blackberries and plums, which cheered me somewhat, and new shoes to replace my worn ones.

The Danish merchants did not regard gold as highly as had the Arras traders. They valued silver more. Their comments about Garrad's pieces concerned only the beauty of the designs.

At the goldsmith's shop, Garrad laid Tostig's arm-rings and one of William's gilded helmets on the table, keeping the other helmets back. The smith, a broad man in a scarlet tunic with red stripes painted over his eyes, expressed his surprise at seeing monks with such fine goldwork.

Garrad thanked him for the compliment. "Gifts from our Norman lord. Duke William is a rich and powerful man. This is only a trifle compared to what he showers on monasteries and the poor."

Though William was indeed generous, I realized that Garrad intended this bit of boasting to build Normandy's reputation in the North.

He continued, "We hear that the Danish King has no less wealth, but he spends it on wars."

"Costly wars," the goldsmith muttered. He pushed the sleeves of his tunic up to his elbows.

Garrad kept speaking as if he had not heard the man, "Of course, now that King Sweyn is allied to Prince Harald Hardraada, there will be more battles. And more wealth."

The goldsmith laid down his hammer and wiped his brow. "More wealth?"

"Hasn't word reached here? Prince Harald brings with him all his booty … from Byzantium."

"I didn't know that," the goldsmith replied. "That may explain the new fleet."

Garrad looked surprised, and I was not sure whether he was or not. "King Sweyn has a new fleet? That's good. With new ships, the next battle in Danish territory may reverse past losses to King Magnus in Norway."

"Well," the goldsmith said slowly, "you haven't heard the latest tales, I see."

"We've been traveling a long time," I said.

"King Sweyn and Prince Harald have recaptured Zealand and Fyn islands from the Norwegians."

"Then King Magnus has already suffered his first defeat," Garrad said.

"Perhaps Prince Harald has improved your King's fighting skills," I said.

The goldsmith glowered at me. "You're a Southerner and a monk, so I don't expect you to know this. But no one needs to teach a Danish king how to fight."

Garrad collected the gold pieces and took my arm, leading me from the shop.

"He meant no offense," he said, as we bent through the door. "Not all Southern monks have heard of the prowess of Danish warriors. And he's young." With that, we were in the street.

"I'm sorry —"

"Don't be. The Danes are overly sensitive about their King. He hasn't won a battle in years. He's a poor strategist. Retaking the islands, Zealand and Fyn, will only remind the Danes of Denmark's past dominance of the North when Canute was their King. Besides, we learned much from him, while all he'll remember is that we're stupid Southerners."

At the slave market, Garrad chatted with a trader as he had with the goldsmith. The trader, though, was an Icelander. Icelanders remained free of alliances with Norwegian or Danish lords. With this reputation, they often heard more news and more secrets than anyone else.

Garrad offered the trader a gilded helmet for information.

"King Magnus," the trader whispered to us, pulling the brim of his leather hat down, "doesn't want to fight his uncle, Prince Harald. King Magnus hasn't even built a large enough fleet to attack Denmark."

"I wouldn't think King Magnus's earls would be happy about such an excursion, anyway," Garrad said.

"They're not. Many have refused to help, saying they owe the King no more war service this year." He shrugged. "They're loyal to the King, though, and will fight if he fights. After all, a battle is something a Norwegian lord cannot resist."

Garrad nodded knowingly and then asked, "Will King Magnus make a joint alliance with Prince Harald and King Sweyn?"

"Never with King Sweyn. King Magnus considers King Sweyn a usurper." The man leaned closer to us. "I hear that King Magnus wants to win Prince Harald back to the Norwegians."

Garrad raised his eyebrows. "How?"

"I'm not sure, but King Magnus does have half of Norway to offer."

Garrad thanked the man and handed him the gilded helmet. The trader pushed it into a leather sack behind him.

I took a deep breath and said to Garrad just loud enough for the man to hear, "It's too bad for such a fine merchant that these slaves are diseased."

The trader's jaw dropped at the word "diseased."

"Yes," Garrad replied, "perhaps we could do something to help him save his business …"

We liberated almost twenty slaves, most of them Christians, with the gold that would normally have freed only five.

Garrad spoke with the freed slaves a long time. They were Irish and had been seized by Norwegians raiding from the Orkneys.

Since I did not understand their language, I wandered away, looking over merchants' goods and asking questions. The Danes smiled and spoke slowly to me, as if I were stupid. I supposed my Danish sounded foreign to them.

I drifted toward the edges of the town.

Near the northernmost edge, I spotted an oddly shaped wooden building with a multi-layered roof, looking like several longships piled on top of each other, at the peak of which was a cross.

I stopped a passing townsman, one of the few dressed in an undyed tunic, and he replied to my question, "That's the church of St. Ansgar."

Garrad had once mentioned this famous Dane. "Was he a monk?"

"Yes." The townsman looked appropriately reverent. "Two hundred years ago, St. Ansgar braved bandits and pirates to carry Christianity to the heathen Swedes. He was as courageous as he was saintly."

I thanked the man and strolled toward the church, studying its intricately carved wood. I peeked through the door and noticed the crucifix. It was impossible not to notice it. A single beam of light fell on it, the result of the design of the surrounding windows.

I studied the architecture of the roof. It was built so that, as the sun moved across the sky, its rays would fall through one of twelve angled window slits, keeping the crucifix in light the entire day.

The Healer on the cross struck me as odd somehow. I had seen the triumphant figure mounting the cross before. This figure emphasized triumph differently. Missing was the calm carved on Norman saviors. This face resembled a warrior returning from battle. The eyes showed ferocity, while the mouth was almost arrogant. I imagined that Odin and Thor looked little different.

I drifted away from the church and, lost in thought, almost bumped into a standing stone, its black background covered with red-and-white winding script. Though my spoken Danish was improving rapidly, I could not read Northern runes.

I asked several passers-by, eventually finding one, a young man in a long, blue robe, who could.

"Few people can read runes as well as I, Brother," he said, proudly.

"I'm sure you're well trained. What do these say?"

"Let's see. They say: 'Thorolf, a houseguard of the King of Denmark, raised this stone in memory of his comrade Eirik, who met his death when warriors besieged Hedeby. He was a captain, a man of noble birth.'"

"Do you know of this battle or of Eirik and Thorolf?"

He shook his head. "All I can see is that the rune style is recent. The battle cannot have been long ago. Hedeby soldiers did repel an attack within this month. It's likely that Thorolf's friend Eirik died in that attack."

I thanked him, complimenting him on his skill, and he strode away, beaming.

Picturing the noble Eirik dying in battle, I wondered about his fate. Had his time come prematurely? Or had he died after years of service to the Danish King and after a lifelong friendship with the maker of this memorial stone, Thorolf?

Was Eirik survived by noble sons and daughters, or had he been cut down before he had any family?

I glanced back at Ansgar's church. Where did Thorolf imagine his noble friend to be spending eternity? Did he think that Eirik now feasted in the Hall of Warriors, Valhalla, with gods of thunder? Or did Thorolf picture Eirik sailing his longship in a Christian heaven?

My musings were interrupted by shouting. I turned to see a tall man arguing with a shorter one. They stood in front of a shop, over which hung a sign with an arrow on it — a bow maker's shop.

The shorter man wore a brown tunic with tight sleeves decorated by yellow and green bands. Tan leggings stretched down to his shoes. He had painted yellow stripes over his eyes. With his hands on his hips and his body thrust forward, he resembled many of the merchants that inhabited Hedeby.

The taller man wore a red-and-blue striped tunic held by a leather belt with snakelike patterns on it. His white trousers billowed to his ankles, drawn in by high leather leggings. His hair hung long over his shoulders, falling onto a gold-trimmed cloak. Around his forehead ran a white silk headband. He had no eye decoration, though, and he spoke Norwegian.

In fact, the cause of the argument, I thought, might be the difference in dialects.

I stepped forward, saying to the shorter man, in my most solemn voice, "Good day, brother merchant. May I be of assistance here? I am familiar with all the Northern variations of Danish. Perhaps I can help."

The tall man stepped back to face me, drawing his cloak around him and giving me a stiff, short bow. His long face was further lengthened by a forked beard, which his mustache drooped to meet. He watched me through half-closed eyes.

"Brother monk, this ... gentleman," the merchant said, his teeth clenched, "apparently wants me to craft a bow for him, but he will accept none of the designs I show him." He waved toward his shop.

I bent through the door to see variously shaped bows hanging against the back wall. None was as long as mine, but few archers in the world could boast bows as long. Nonetheless, the workmanship appeared sound.

"Do not misunderstand me," the bow maker said as I reemerged. "I want to help this man. He is a Norwegian noble, and I want his patronage. I make every kind of bow that can be made, but he seems to want something else. I cannot make a bow like an axe!"

Adopting the Norwegian dialect, I asked the taller man what he wanted.

He stared at me for a moment, his eyelids remaining half closed. "I want this dull-witted merchant to craft a new bow, which he seems unwilling to do."

"What kind of bow?"

"It is called a crossbow. I saw one in the South."

I had never heard of such a weapon, but I was willing to describe it to the bow maker.

The Norwegian noble, though, drew away, gesturing in frustration. "I have dealt with Hedeby craftsmen before, and they have always done fine work. This man seems to be either lazy or an idiot. I have been speaking perfectly clearly to him."

As he gestured, his cloak fell open, revealing an unsheathed knife thrust in his belt. On the white, bone handle, red markings crawled down to a double-edged blade, curving three times to its point. Along the blade, a narrow, red line snaked.

It was identical to the knife Voldred had used to stab me.

CHAPTER 11

A QUESTION OF KILLING

A.D. 1046

At first I wanted to run. The man obviously did not want to kill me, though. Of course, an accomplice of Voldred would not recognize me. I carried no crutch and did not appear to be Norman.

The Norwegian noble was speaking. "Brother monk, what is wrong? Do you understand me?"

"Uh, yes, please forgive me. I was … um …seeking help from God. A silent prayer for guidance. I believe … yes, the Lord has spoken to me."

The noble's eyelids opened all the way.

"Yes," I continued, "you must teach this man how to make a crossbow. He will learn. The Lord has touched his heart."

To the merchant, I said quietly and hurriedly, "The noble wants you to make a new kind of bow, something called a crossbow, which lays a bow at right angles to a firing mechanism. He will sketch it for you and explain what you need to know. You simply have to make allowances for his Norwegian dialect. Are you willing?"

"Of course."

I turned to the noble. "You see, my lord. God has opened his mind. You need only draw the design of the bow for him and speak slowly. Are you willing?"

The noble seemed surprised but answered, "Of course."

"Good. I must take my leave."

"A moment." The noble grabbed my arm.

I had almost escaped.

"Are you from a Flemish monastery?" he asked, mistaking my accent.

"Yes, my lord, from St. Vaast in Arras." It was only half a lie.

"You are a fine solver of problems, and you are instructed by God. We need more monks like you in Norway. If you are traveling north, I will be pleased to escort you."

All I wanted was to run.

Seeing my hesitation, he added, "I am not without position in the court of the King. I am Thorir, half-brother of King Magnus of Norway. Even now, I am on the King's errand."

I opened my mouth, but nothing came out.

Thorir continued speaking. "I remain in Hedeby until this bow maker finishes my weapon." He did not volunteer where he was lodging. "If you wish to accompany me north, leave word with the bow maker, and I will meet you."

I thanked him, muttered a Latin blessing, and backed away. Then I spun and strode down the street as if I had never limped in my life.

I found Garrad at the slave-trader's booth, the Irish men and women crowded around him, jabbering.

I wrenched him away from them and told him what had happened. His face turned serious, and he remained silent a long time.

Then he bade farewell to the freed slaves and led the horses and me through the crowds on the main street of Hedeby.

We mounted and rode along the Connecting Rampart to the Army Road. Trotting the horses through the break in the Danework, we turned north, the way we had come that morning.

Not far up the Army Road, Garrad pulled his horse to a stop. He waited for a wagon behind us to rattle past and disappear into the distance. Searching in all directions, he turned his horse's head east into the forest. I followed him.

We halted at a tightly clustered grove of birches, tying the horses there. Gesturing me to join him, he sank onto the soft earth.

He began, "We must consider our next step carefully. If both of us return to Falaise because of a false perception —"

"I saw the knife."

"Yes, but what if it doesn't mean anything?"

"It means something to me."

"Listen to this. The Irish slaves were brought to Hedeby by way of Norway, and no one bought them in Norway."

"So? What does that have to do with — ?"

"Norwegian farmers usually buy slaves to work their farms, especially as summer draws to a close. The farmers need the help. They even pay the slaves. When I lived in the Irish kingdoms, I met monks who had bought their freedom by herding Norwegian livestock."

I failed to see how this related to the knife. I said distractedly, "Perhaps the farmers don't need help this year. Maybe it was a bad farming year."

"It was the best year of the new millennium. One Irish slave who speaks the Norwegian dialect overheard farmers saying that they were desperate for help. The crops were better than they had been for decades. What do you make of that?"

"The farmers must not be prospering as much as their crops."

"That's right. They lack extra wealth for trading. What makes farmers poor in a good farming year?"

"I don't know." I was becoming impatient. "Taxes and tolls for war?"

"Yes. King Magnus must have consumed the country's wealth with his wars. That means that Magnus must bargain with Prince Harald — Hardraada — for Hardraada's silver and gold."

"What does this have to do with Thorir and the knife?"

"Nothing, directly. It does mean, though, that Magnus is open to negotiation. Now. At this moment. He needs wealth, and William has wealth. If you can get to Magnus before Hardraada does and win his friendship for Normandy ... well, you may not have to deal with Hardraada at all. Thorir will take you to Magnus." He tilted his head and raised an eyebrow. "Oddly, he's the best escort you could have. Meeting him is a stroke of good fortune."

"Good fortune! What about his knife? He may be in league with Voldred. There may be others, other assassins." I tried to sound as miserable as possible. "I don't know how many people want me dead."

He put his good hand on my shoulder. "Thorir did not try to kill you today, and he let you go, even though he knew he may never see you again. As for Voldred, we don't know whether he's alive or dead. Besides, even Voldred couldn't recognize you now."

I looked down at myself.

"If your life were in peril," he continued, "I would take you back with me, of course. If you maintain your disguise, though, you're safe. And an alliance with Magnus could save Normandy. Remember, if Hardraada seizes power with Magnus, they could be on the coast of Normandy by next summer. We would be helpless. Worse, if Guy leads a rebellion against William, Normandy will be easy prey. Magnus and Hardraada could not resist striking us."

I said nothing.

"Cuin, an alliance with Magnus is critical now. All our lives may depend on it."

I remained silent.

He took some gold pieces from the bag hanging at his side and smiled at me. "This is a bribe. Your first bribe as an emissary. It is, however, the only honest bribe you'll ever be offered, so you should take it. I'll even add the other two gold helmets I have."

I sighed. I knew I had no choice. "I'll take it. And the helmets."

The next morning, I rode with Garrad to the opening in the Danework, amid a caravan of wagons, two-wheeled carts, donkeys, and horses.

Eventually, we reached the divide in the road.

His last instruction was, "Be wary when you negotiate with Magnus. Or Hardraada, should it come to that. They're warriors. They'll want to emerge victorious even over emissaries. You'll need to impress them when you speak."

I nodded.

"God be with you, Cuin. I will see you again as soon as I can."

"Good. God be with you, Garrad."

I watched him and the black horse disappear into the crowd of merchants, knights, and pilgrims traveling south on the Army Road.

I stared after him until I could see him no more.

True to his word, Thorir appeared at the bow maker's shop to meet me. He spoke curtly to the bow maker and to me as well, apparently forgetting that God guided me.

I decided that this was merely his manner of speaking. I had met courtiers in Normandy with similar traits — habitually but unintentionally rude.

The knife was nowhere to be seen.

The bow maker had finished the crossbow, and it indeed resembled an axe. The bow itself had been shortened and attached to a wooden handle with an arrow groove where normally a man's arm would be. The bowstring could be pulled taut and fixed to a metal trigger. The archer squeezed the trigger to release the arrow.

I watched Thorir draw the string back and hook it, bracing the bow with his foot. He put a short, unfeathered arrow in the groove and fitted it to the string. The loading was slow. But the arrow, once released, flew with remarkable speed. It thumped into a nearby gate, and Thorir had to struggle to pull it out. He carried the arrow back to us, his eyes opened wide, staring at the crossbow.

This was a weapon William would love, I thought. Even the bow maker was impressed. I spied a copy of the crossbow hanging at the back of his shop.

Thorir and I rode from town accompanied by two men, King Magnus's guards, he said. I wanted to engage him in conversation, hoping the subject of the knife would come up, so that I could discover its origin, but he spoke first.

"What's your name, Brother?" He regarded me through half-closed eyes.

"I'm called after the saints of Africa and England, my lord. My name is Augustine."

"I have a house guard from Africa. You might have much to talk about."

The logic of this eluded me.

He continued, "A member of my household journeyed to Spain to buy him. He's black. All black. That's why I wanted him. He looks like a demon and terrifies my enemies."

"A black man? His skin is black?"

"Brownish black, yes."

"Are his eyes black? And his teeth?"

He snorted at me. "No, not his teeth, but his hair is black, and his eyes are black."

"Is there no white in his eyes at all?"

"None." His voice sounded mocking.

"Does he speak?"

"Certainly he speaks. He's a man, not an animal. He's a valuable guard, too. The most valuable I have. He was a child when I acquired him, and I taught him the Northern languages as well as how to dress and to fight. He bought his freedom after he came of age. He never returned to Africa, though."

"What's his name? Is it African?"

"He has taken the name of one of their gods — Onyame."

Here was an opportunity to speak as a monk, so I asked, with all the zeal I could summon, "He's named after a pagan god? Is he a Christian?"

"Of course he's a Christian. All the court is Christian, after the work of Saint Olaf."

"Saint Olaf?"

"You are ignorant for a Flemish monk. The father of King Magnus is a saint."

I knew that King Olaf, even with his aggressive conversions, as Lanfranc had called them, was now considered a saint. My fear had clouded my mind.

He continued, "The sick from all over the North have been healed by praying to Saint Olaf or touching his relics. He even rescued Prince Harald in Byzantium."

I wanted to show him that I did know Northern history. "King Olaf died when he and Prince Harald fought together at Stiklestad. Isn't that so? How could Olaf rescue Harald in Byzantium years later?"

"A stupid question for a monk. Saint Olaf came to him in a vision. He led Prince Harald from prison in the same way the angel freed Saint Peter."

"Ah, yes, of course," I said, slowly, trying to sound monkish again.

"Many Flemish people pray to Saint Olaf. How do you not know that he is a saint?"

I had an opening to reveal my background. "I am not Flemish, my lord. I was protecting my identity from strangers. I am sorry for deceiving you, but I too am on an errand — not for a king but for a duke."

His eyes widened. "Who are you?"

"I am a monk, and my name is Augustine, but I'm from Rouen, where William, Duke of Normandy, holds court. I have been sent to present this gift to King Magnus" — I indicated the blanket which held the bow — "and to negotiate a treaty with him. Duke William knows that King Magnus has no animosity toward Normandy. He feels an alliance would benefit everyone — in friendship and in trade."

Thorir looked chagrined, probably because he had treated me as an inferior. He might have offended not only a ducal emissary but also a Norman noble. "Are you Duke William's man?"

"Not the way you mean it. I'm not a noble, but I am the Duke's emissary in the North."

He appeared relieved, but his voice became more respectful. "Of course, King Magnus has no animosity toward Normandy. He will smile on your proposal, Brother Augustine, especially for greater trade."

I knew this was a standard diplomatic answer.

He continued, "What is the gift, if I may know?"

"A mere token of gifts to follow, my lord, a long bow. I'll show it to you when we stop."

"I am certain that the King will be gratified." He paused. "I too have a gift."

He swept his cloak away and jerked the curved knife from his belt.

I gasped and leaned backward, almost tumbling from my mount.

"What's wrong?" He displayed the knife in the palm of his hand.

My heart pounded, and I stammered, "I'm sorry. It just startled me. I've never seen a knife like that."

He raised his chin. "You never will. There are only two in the world, and King Magnus has the other one. The cutting of this red stone is unique. Byzantine designers use this twisting pattern but not in this stone."

I took a deep breath to calm myself. "Then … it's not Byzantine?"

"Of course not. This knife and its companion were a gift to King Magnus from a visiting lord many years ago."

"Do you know which lord?"

"The King never told me."

"Where is the other knife?"

"I just told you. King Magnus has it in his treasury."

"Oh, yes. I'm sorry."

He apparently did not know that Magnus had given the other knife to Voldred, which led me to hope that Thorir had no role in trying to kill me. Nonetheless, the question remained: why would the King of Norway send an assassin to kill a crippled Norman villager?

I wondered whether Thorir knew Voldred. I could not risk asking him, though.

He raised the knife higher. "This knife I'm to offer to — "

He stopped himself. He hesitated to be too open with me, I guessed.

I needed to learn as much as I could, especially now, since my life was tied to Magnus and these knives. So I finished his thought, "To Prince Harald Hardraada in return for an alliance with King Magnus."

He blinked at me. "How did you know that?"

"Duke William follows the affairs of the North, even secret ones."

"How?"

"I cannot say. I don't even know myself."

He lowered his eyelids again to half-closed and let his head drift back, surveying the treetops.

Then he leaned forward in his saddle and spoke. "I am relieved that your Duke and you know my objective. Because we must approach Prince Harald with caution. Presently he stays in the camp of the Danish King."

"Do you know where the camp is?"

"One of the Danish King's own men is our spy. He brought us word. They have pitched a secret camp just off the first landfall from Fyn Island. King Sweyn, the usurper, headquarters in his tents. Prince Harald remains on his ships. Together, they have been raiding northern Denmark. Many towns have submitted to them."

"On what terms will you negotiate? Prince Harald could use the Danish fleet to attack Norway, and King Magnus could not stop him. He lacks the ships."

He looked at me sharply. "Who told you that?"

"Duke William."

He frowned. "Your Duke has good sources. We have sent spies south with the rumor that King Magnus has built a large fleet, but he has not. He has only the few ships left from earlier battles. We hope the rumor will encourage Prince Harald to negotiate."

"Why should he negotiate at all?"

He hesitated. "Because King Magnus offers him half of Norway."

Garrad and the Icelandic slave-trader had guessed correctly.

I decided to try a diplomatic ploy. I had seen Garrad use them in Hedeby.

"Perhaps Prince Harald will negotiate simply because he doesn't like the Danish King. Duke William has heard that they quarrel."

This was plausible. Even if Thorir denied it, I would learn something.

Instead, he exclaimed, "Is your Duke a wizard? How does he know these things? Our spy just told us that a week ago. Duke William would have to be a bird to have heard that and dispatched you here so quickly."

"Again, I cannot say how he knows., but I assure you he's no wizard, my lord." I was solemn. "He's a Christian."

Thorir shook his head. "Well, he must have the best messengers in the world."

He does, I thought.

We pressed north. Though Thorir and the two guards knew the countryside well, they chose a winding, inland route through the local oak and beech forests to lose any followers. That night, we found a clearing in a broad valley beside an inlet.

As we dismounted, Thorir stared at the water, commenting that he would prefer a broad-bottomed river barge to his ache-producing saddle. At that moment, feeling the tenderness in my posterior parts, I agreed with him.

After bathing in the inlet and downing a hearty dinner, we rested before a low, nearly smokeless fire, carefully controlled by one of the guards.

Thorir admired my bow, commenting on its length and beauty.

When I offered to let him try it, he strung it eagerly. He pulled it with effort and sent an arrow whistling into a nearby spruce.

He ran his hand along its length. "A fine gift for King Magnus." He turned to face me, the half-closed eyelids opening for a moment. "It would be even more appropriate for Prince Harald. He has the arms to pull it."

I tucked my hands inside my sleeves, monk-fashion, and asked, "Why would I give King Magnus' gift to Prince Harald?"

He handed the bow to one of his guards. "I must win Prince Harald from King Sweyn. It will be easier if my offer includes an alliance with the Duke of Normandy." This sounded like a command. "If we persuade Prince Harald to leave the Danish King and join us, Magnus will be grateful enough to overlook not receiving a gift." This softened the command.

I dropped my head in thought for a moment. Perhaps encountering Thorir was the good fortune Garrad had thought it was. If Thorir could help me win an alliance with both Hardraada and Magnus, my mission would be a greater success than any of us had imagined. Far from attacking us, whoever ruled Norway would be our ally.

William's only remaining problems would be the Pope and the Holy Roman Empire.

Thorir asked, "Has God enlightened your mind about my proposal?"

So that was why he had softened his commanding tone and waited patiently for my reply.

I nodded. "It's an excellent suggestion, my lord."

He gave me a rare smile. "Fine, Brother Augustine. Now let us examine more closely how this crossbow works."

The next evening, we located the Danish camp, where we hoped Sweyn and Hardraada would be camped. Thorir had taken care that we arrive at night.

His guards located the Danish lookouts, and we skirted their positions easily. Apparently, no one feared an attack on the secret camp.

Thorir and his guards, though, muttered among themselves about the dangers of approaching the camp openly.

"We can't just walk down there," one of the guards said.

"The Danes will take us as attackers or spies," another said.

As we knelt on the top of a low hill, scanning the tents and ships, I realized that I was the only person who could walk safely into the camp, and Thorir and his men knew it.

If I volunteered before they asked, I would appear courageous. At this moment, however, I wished William had sent someone else in my place.

I whispered to Thorir, "I can go down there. A monk can move easily anywhere. I may learn whether Prince Harald and King Sweyn have quarreled again."

He agreed. "Especially if you locate the King's tent. Do you know what King Sweyn looks like?"

"No."

"He's easy to identify. He walks with a limp."

"What if he's sitting down?"

He looked disgusted. "If you get that close, you will hear him called 'my lord King'." He regained his respect and concern. "You must take a weapon to protect yourself. Even if God protects you."

"Won't that make me suspicious?"

"Perhaps in Normandy it would, but here monks are warriors. To be safe, though, take the bow you brought for King Magnus. You can say it's a gift for the King or Prince Harald, depending on who stops you."

"That's a good idea."

"Now go. We will wait here for you."

I strung the bow, hooked it over my shoulder, placed several arrows in my quiver, and crept down the hill.

Though the moon was half full, I slipped from shadow to shadow, reaching the tents without being seen.

Hearing voices in the center of the encampment, I edged toward them. The voices led me to the largest tent.

From the smell of the food, I guessed that a dinner was being held inside. Obviously, King Sweyn and perhaps Hardraada fed the Danish army inside, at least those soldiers who were not away raiding.

My stomach growled, and I silently reprimanded it. I had no choice but to wait until the King emerged and follow him to his tent, even though it meant remaining in scenting distance of what could be described as a mouth-watering meal.

Seeing no guard nearby, I crouched down to wait.

Time crawled by. My stomach continued to complain, while my courage — what little of it had accompanied me down the hill — slipped away like sand in Garrad's hourglass. I wished I were sitting inside his hut.

At that moment, angry shouting rose above the din inside the tent. There was a shuffling and clattering of weapons and more shouting.

Then, two groups of men issued from the entrance and wheeled in opposite directions. All of them were dressed in long, patterned tunics with puffed leggings. Their hair, parted in the middle, flowed from under their headbands. Most carried spears or axes.

The man leading one group was young, dark-haired, and dark-bearded, muttering angrily at his men. As he walked, he limped. King Sweyn of Denmark.

At the head of the other group paced a fair-haired, light-bearded giant, who remained imperiously silent. Prince Harald, called Hardraada. I watched him stride to a pier and turn onto it, reaching its end in a few steps.

He lowered his huge frame into a boat. I marveled that the boat did not sink.

His men joined him and rowed toward a longship moored some distance out to sea.

Oddly, the rowboat seemed to veer to the left just as it reached the longship. This peculiar maneuver would be invisible to anyone on shore whose vision had not been trained as mine had. What did it mean? Did Hardraada intend to enter his longship by some roundabout route?

I turned in time to glimpse the Danish troop winding through the tents. I would soon lose sight of them. To follow, though, I would have to stop watching Hardraada's boat and worse, surrender my hiding-place.

I had to follow. I could not swim to Hardraada's longship to discover anything, so Sweyn's tent remained my best source of information.

I took a breath, pulled my hood over my head, put my hand on the taut bowstring, and stepped from the shadows. If God really did protect me, then —

"You, monk!" a voice rang out. "What are you doing here?"

I spun around to see a long-haired, mustached man moving toward me. On his head rested a rounded helmet, a nose-piece stretching down from it. He carried a spear and sword. Was he a guard? A royal house guard perhaps?

Why did he call to me? Were there no monks in camp? Did the unusually long bow make me appear more than a common warrior-monk? Or was he afraid that I might be one of Hardraada's men?

He reached my side and seized my arm.

I struggled to keep my voice calm. "Blessings on you, brother."

"Who are you, and what are you doing here?"

I went blank for a moment. Then I recalled the memorial stone at Hedeby that the young rune-reader had translated for me.

"I'm of the household of the King's guard Thorolf. I'm sent to tell him of a death."

"Thorolf's with a raiding party. I can —"

I interrupted him. "Take me to the King then. The death is of an old comrade, Eirik. His ghost, accompanied by St. Ansgar, has visited Thorolf's household while I was in attendance."

The man took a step backward. I realized with relief that he was a typical Northerner, who, as the Goliards had told me back in St. Vaast, treated ghostly visitations as seriously as diplomatic visits.

I repeated my request, adding, "Such a vision is not to be kept from one risking battle."

"No, no, certainly not. Come with me."

I followed him, keeping my face hidden and my hands folded inside my sleeves, which prevented his noticing that I was drenched with sweat and trembling all over.

We halted before a tent entrance. Loud voices drifted from it. The guard disappeared inside. A voice barked a command.

The guard reappeared, his face drawn.

"The King speaks with his men. He will see you when he finishes." He bent toward me and whispered, "He's very angry, brother. Even a ghost and a saint didn't break his rage. You do well to wait."

"Thank you. You may leave me now. I wish to pray quietly. Blessings on you."

He murmured his thanks and marched away.

I peered from side to side, spotting no one. Then I stepped into the shadow at the side of the tent. I sneaked along it until I could hear what the voices were saying.

One of them mumbled something, to which the other bellowed, "Chop that Land-Waster to bits! Then slice its owner up and throw the pieces to the fish!"

The fury in the voice withered what was left of my courage. My knees weakened.

When the next words rang out, "Fetch that monk!" I tiptoed from the tent, slipped through the shadows, and fled into the woods.

I hobbled up the hill to Thorir.

"What did you discover?" he asked.

I paused to regain my breath. I had discovered little, and I felt foolish. I had, though, heard one thing.

After I summarized my encounter with the guard, I asked, "What's the Land-Waster?"

"Prince Harald's war banner, the one with the black raven on it," one of the guards replied.

"What did you hear about it?" Thorir asked.

"I heard King Sweyn order his men to cut it and its owner to pieces."

"They must not!"

"Why? Wouldn't that eliminate a threat to Norway? You would have to deal only with King Sweyn. Magnus has beaten him before."

"You do not understand. King Magnus does not want another battle. His treasure stores are empty. Prince Harald has a fortune in booty. If King Sweyn slays Prince Harald and seizes it, the Danes will have the means to create a huge fleet. They will defeat us easily." He pushed his face closer to mine. "And they will have an invasion fleet to sail south to Normandy."

My mouth fell open. "We must warn Prince Harald then. I saw where his ship was moored. I'll lead you."

"An alien band would be seized immediately. You can move freely in the camp. You have to do it."

"Me? Won't the guards wonder why I fled? Won't they think I'm a spy?"

"Why would they? All you did was fail to appear. Was a guard nearby when you fled?"

"No, I was left alone — at my own request."

"Wisely done. No one saw where you went or when you went there. So, King Sweyn may simply believe that you wandered off. By now he may be eager to meet the monk who saw a ghost. The story will still work for you."

I hesitated.

He pushed at my arm. "Go quickly. You will be in no danger, but keep the bow with you, just in case. You will not fail. God protects you."

I wished that he would forget that.

Reluctantly, I stole back down the hill, skirting the main body of the camp. I paused in the tent shadow closest to the pier. No soldier was in sight. I crept toward a deserted dinghy.

On the far side of the pier was only a narrow beach and forest — nowhere to hide, but no tents or guards, either.

A movement on the water caught my eye, and I focused on it. Two rowers pulled a boat toward Hardraada's longship. Few waves rose in resistance, so they closed the distance between the pier and the ship rapidly.

Assassins?

A band of men burst from the tent nearest me. I stumbled back into the shadow, stifling a gasp. One man glanced in my direction but strode on. They pushed into another tent not far away.

When I searched the sea again, the boat bobbed beside Hardraada's longship. The rowers had vanished.

I scrambled toward the pier. Crouching as I ran, I slid two arrows from my quiver.

I focused on the longship. The moon silhouetted two figures. They bent from sight and then straightened. They ripped some covering away and pulled their weapons. Axes.

I had guessed correctly: assassins. They were the killers King Sweyn had sent to slay Hardraada.

I recalled Thorir's words: Prince Harald must not die. Garrad's words pounded in my head, too: "Get an alliance with a Northern leader. It could save all our lives."

I stared at the killers. No normal archer could shoot such a distance with any accuracy.

But I could.

I had already notched one arrow and taken aim. I let it fly just over one assassin's head.

An instant later, as he raised his axe, my arrow drove into its handle. The axe clattered to the ship. The assassin dropped from sight.

I heard a gasp from the shore behind me. I fell to the pier, searching over my shoulder for its source. I could see no one.

I turned back to the ship. Too late. The second axe-wielder drove his weapon down toward his victim. I shuddered.

A crack rang out, as if the axe had fallen on ... wood.

At first, I was stunned. Then I realized why Hardraada's boat had veered away and why his longship had been left unguarded. He had abandoned it. He had suspected the assassination attempt and had put a log in his bed on the deck.

Now, though, I had to act. The assassins would return to King Sweyn to report both their failure and the mysterious bowman. The King would alert the camp to find me and to pursue Hardraada.

I quickly shot three arrows over the assassins' heads, hoping they would flee. They ducked and scrambled into their boat, but they rowed toward the pier. Toward me.

I began to sweat. Would I have to kill them? How could I?

I silently cursed everyone for forcing me to make such a decision: Sweyn, Hardraada, Thorir, even William.

I realized that I could not kill anyone.

I would not just lie here and die, though. I could make the assassins believe they faced more than one archer. I quickly drew three more arrows and shot at the boat's bow. Then three more.

My hand fell on my last two arrows. I groaned. If the assassins kept coming —
Another sound behind me. In the forest. Again it sounded like a gasp.

I dropped from the pier and squeezed myself behind a piling. On my knees, I seized another arrow from the quiver and notched it immediately. I could see nothing in the darkness but the woods.

I heard a splash. I glanced back out to sea and could see the assassins' boat. My six arrows were buried in its bow, and one assassin had jumped into the water. The second threw himself in behind his partner, and they swam for the shore on the far side of the inlet.

I breathed a sigh of relief before I heard a sound from behind me again. I whirled around.

From the forest emerged a form that was not a tree but was as large as a tree. Stooped over, it swung its body along the fringe of the woods. Toward me.

If it was another assassin … I felt panic in my chest. I pulled my bowstring back.

The form now straightened, rising to an enormous height. It lumbered in my direction, bearing a round, wooden shield and a sword the size of a tree limb. I almost believed that some oak had sprung to life and now strode toward me.

Two other figures crawled from the woods behind it. More assassins?

I pressed against the wooden piling. It offered little protection, and its dampness reminded me of blood.

Perhaps I could deceive this group, too. I sprang from behind the piling and let the arrow fly.

The walking tree swept its shield upward with incredible speed. The arrow smacked into the shield, splitting it. The shield lowered, and a face appeared.

I had already drawn my last arrow and let it fly — just over the head. As it whistled by, the eyes in the huge face widened.

"Friend archer," the face hissed in the Norwegian dialect, "why do you seek to kill me when you just tried to save me? I come to extend friendship for so brave a deed, but I nearly lose my head."

I mustered as commanding a voice as I could. "Who are you?"

"Harald, Sigurd's son, Prince of Norway."

It was Hardraada.

CHAPTER 12

KINGS AND DIPLOMATS

A.D. 1046

"I've never seen archery like that," Hardraada said. "Never seen arrows shot so far with such force and with such accuracy, especially with the intent not to kill anyone."

He raised his left eyebrow, creating a bizarre effect, since the eyebrow was already higher than the right.

Sitting behind him in the open field, his men repeated what he said. The murmur ran through all sixty of them. They stared at me.

Thorir, sitting beside Hardraada and swatting at late-afternoon insects, lifted his eyelids and added, "This one is guided by God."

"Does that mean you could not have missed if you had wanted to hit me, Brother Augustine?"

Hardraada's chest, still covered in chain mail, heaved as he spoke. Even sitting, he seemed like some bearded oak, related to the trees surrounding the clearing where we camped. His green tunic and leggings added to the effect.

As Garrad had predicted, Hardraada aimed at defeating me. His question forced me to answer either that God could not guide my aim or that I could have killed him. One reply would force me to speak as less than a monk. The other would imply that he was a lesser warrior, insulting him and infuriating his men.

"Surely God guided us both, my lord. With the blessing of Saint Benedict, my arrow flew toward heaven instead of toward you. With your protection by Saint Olaf, no arrow could have penetrated your shield defense."

He smiled. "What was left of my shield."

I had survived the first skirmish.

I needed to continue to survive. Now that my archery skills had aided Hardraada in his quarrel with King Sweyn — and Hardraada had returned the favor by letting me accompany him north as he escaped from Sweyn's camp — we were within two day's travel of King Magnus. Magnus too was encamped in Denmark, just north of where we now rested.

Nonetheless, I had to confront Hardraada's cunning every time we spoke, and the day after tomorrow I would face a second danger: Magnus, the man who may have sent Voldred to kill me.

Hardraada continued to stare at me.

I had to direct the conversation away from my bowmanship and toward something that would distract him. "If it's not an impolite question, my lord, why did King Sweyn dispatch men to murder you?"

"It is a question that should be answered for the man who strove to protect my life." He leaned forward in his carved wooden chair. "For your ears and for those of your Duke."

"Duke William will hear of King Sweyn's treachery."

He nodded and leaned back, assuming a storyteller's air. "We had a feast last evening, adequate, though not meeting Byzantine standards."

To me the feast had smelled more than adequate.

Hardraada continued, "After we ate, Sweyn goaded me. Why he did I do not know. He failed at first. Then he asked me which of my treasures I valued most highly. I have many treasures — my sword, my axe, my spear, my ships, and my men — but I replied, my war banner, the Land-Waster. I have never lost a battle when it waved above me and my men."

Thorir said, "It was Sweyn's cursing of the Land-Waster that led to Brother Augustine's saving your life."

I silently thanked him for the phrase "saving your life" and decided to include him in my prayers.

Hardraada smiled at me. "Yes. Most fortunate. Guided by God, you say?"

Thorir nodded.

"Well, Sweyn is now accursed of God. Sweyn said to me, 'I will believe in the banner's power only when you have fought three battles against your nephew King Magnus' — the very number he himself had lost to Magnus

— 'and won all of them.' Of course, he intended to belittle me. Before his men and mine." He looked around, allowing the silence to settle everywhere.

I knew that Hardraada's making war on a kinsman without provocation violated the Northern warrior code. I could not imagine myself ever taunting Hardraada, though, so I wondered what sort of man Sweyn was.

Hardraada was speaking again. "I decided that Sweyn's insolence deserved a threat. I replied, 'I am well aware of my kinship with Magnus. I do not need you to remind me of it. It is true that my nephew and I are now at war with one another. But there is no reason why he and I could not have a more amicable meeting.'"

An approving murmur ran through his men. I noticed two of the courtiers nearest Hardraada whisper to each other and glance at me.

"Sweyn's insolence only grew. He said, 'Some people complain, Harald, that the only pledges you honor are those you think will profit yourself.' Think of it! This from him! The man Magnus had made regent in Denmark. The man who then stole the Danish crown from Magnus!"

He rose and strode up and down. His voice rose and fell in a martial cadence.

His men sat open-mouthed, staring at him, as if they had never heard any of this, as if they themselves had not been present the night before.

He continued, "So I said, 'I have violated my pledges a few times. Far fewer, though, than the times you have broken faith with King Magnus.' At that, he was the one goaded. His soldiers began to stir, and my men and I were outnumbered. So we made a strategic retreat." He turned to smile at me.

"That was when I saw you row toward your ship," I said, "but you veered off before reaching it."

His smile faded. "You saw that? From the shore?"

Had I given away a skill I should have kept hidden? "Well, I wasn't certain, but it seemed so —"

"Your eyesight is as unusual as your bowmanship." He studied me. "Yes, we approached the ship from the rear. We warned those on board that Sweyn might send men. Assassins. I know him to be treacherous in calm but more treacherous in anger."

"He had been treacherous toward Magnus," Thorir said.

Hardraada nodded his agreement. "We rowed a roundabout route to the shore. We stopped at the edge of the camp to watch Sweyn. What we found instead was a monk with a huge bow and arms like Thor."

As his men stirred, scrutinizing me, I tried to shrug modestly. I could think of nothing to say.

Hardraada stopped pacing to stare at me. "You are an unusual monk. I knew Norman monks in Sicily. Ones who followed the Norman lords there. You are unlike any of them." He was silent for a moment. "Would you join Thorir and my men for poems and stories in my tent? And more ale, of course."

After what Garrad had said, I knew I could not trust Hardraada until he made some public statement of alliance with Normandy, and his comments about my being unusual worried me. He may suspect that I was a spy, and my life could be threatened every moment I spent with him.

"I am grateful for the appealing offer, my lord. For the present, though I would like permission to study your longship. I've never seen such a beautiful vessel at close range."

He smiled. "I appreciate that. Southerners would be fascinated by the fastest ships in the world. You have my permission."

I thanked him and excused myself. I was shaking and needed to walk.

As I strode toward the ship, I realized that my foot felt sore, but I made sure that there was no hint of a limp.

I was, of course, less than fascinated by Hardraada's ship — by any ship, for that matter — but it had given me an escape. Anyway, I could perhaps learn something for shipbuilders back home in Rouen. William would expect that.

At my feet, I noticed pieces of the amber that decorated Danish shores. I knelt to pick one up, so that I could sneak a backward glance at the camp. Hardraada and his men still watched me. I would have to make my interest in the ship convincing.

I rose, flipped the amber in the air, and wandered toward the water.

I found a black-bearded workman, clad in a brown tunic and tan leggings, inspecting the boats. I noticed earlier that he had remained with the ships, while the other men constructed tent-frames for Hardraada, Thorir, and themselves. This workman, then, must be a shipbuilder and repairer.

Though I intended only to discuss the weather and retreat to my tent, I noticed one of Hardraada's men strolling toward me with the same studied casualness that I had used myself. So I marched up to the shipbuilder and asked about Hardraada's longship — loudly.

The shipbuilder gave me a short bow. "It's an honor to offer knowledge to a God-guided monk." He had obviously been talking to Thorir.

I had to make an equally dignified response. "It's my honor to learn about so worthy a craft from so obviously worthy a craftsman."

He beamed at me. "My father built ships before me, and his father before him. This one" — he waved his hand — "I built myself."

With almost too much enthusiasm, he seized my arm and led me up a wooden plank over the side of Hardraada's longship, its yellow, brown, and blue stripes gleaming in the late afternoon sun. I admired the intricate carving along the top plank, its dragon patterns highlighted in white and black at the rowers' holes.

He noticed my glance. "Since Prince Harald and his men have removed their shields from the sides, you can see the fine carving on the top strake. It extends all the way from the forestem to the afterstem."

My eyes followed the sweep of his arm. Mounting the forestem and carved from the same piece of wood, the rounded head of a mysterious beast snarled at the sea.

The builder grinned. "My son did the carving."

I said, again loudly, "Your son does beautiful work. We have nothing like this in Normandy."

I spotted Hardraada's man out of the corner of my eye. His strolling had taken him along the plank leading to the ship.

I directed my focus to the white-and-blue-striped sail wrapped around the mast. "When we pulled into the harbor today, I saw two men lower this by a network of ropes. How did they manage it? This sail is huge."

The builder lifted the ropes, tracing their patterns. "These must be tied in the proper way, so that pulling at two points are enough to draw the sail in and fold it around the mast. You see, our sails are larger than any in the world — at least, larger than any I've seen."

"Were you with Prince Harald in Byzantium?"

"Yes, and in many other lands in the South. Most ships there are like our barges, knorrs we call them, shallow harbor craft, river crossers, and the like. The sails of Byzantine ships are small compared to ours and so need rowers to propel them. That ship —" he pointed to a broad-hulled craft, anchored about thirty feet away — "That's a cargo ship. It needs no holes for rowers, because its sail is large and the network of ropes efficient at catching any wind. The hull is designed so that the ship moves with the slightest breeze. Because it's not used in war —"

"Warriors can't be dependent on the whims of the wind?"

He smiled at me. "That's right. A cargo ship can rely on the whims of the wind, as you say, so it doesn't need rowers. It can be sailed with a crew of five. One man to steer" — he pointed to the right rear side of the ship, where the tiller hovered over the steerboard — "one man to bail" — he pointed to the opposite side — "a lookout on the mast or watching from the ship's shoulder, and two men to manage the sail."

I sneaked a backward glance while the builder spoke. Hardraada's man still stared down at the water, but now he knelt on the plank, obviously trying to catch our every word.

I turned back to the builder. "Have you worked in battle ships?"

"I'm not permitted to fight, but I've built ships for war. And I've seen battles from the shore."

Hardraada's man straightened and took a step back toward the shore.

"Did you ever see Prince Harald lose a battle at sea?"

Hardraada's man paused.

The builder shook his head, grinning. "Prince Harald has never lost a battle anywhere. Not since he was wounded at Stiklestad in his youth." He leaned toward me and said under his breath, "In the South, warriors call him Hardraada, the Ruthless. Please don't tell him I told you that."

Hardraada's man smiled and moved toward the shore again.

"I won't." Then I made a loud comment about the hull's overlapping planks, which had been shaped into wedges at their ends. "This is fine workmanship. Is it oak under the paint?"

"Yes. I prefer oak, though I've built ships with ash and beech. Other shipbuilders use alder, birch, even willow. The lashings that hold the planks together — under the sea-line, where we can't use nails — can be done with willow. These lashings, though, happen to be spruce-roots. What do you build ships with in Normandy?"

"I haven't seen many ships. In the harbor at Rouen, I think they're oak. I've been on the Seine a few times in river dinghies. They were built with pine."

Hardraada's man reached the shore and paced back to his lord. I breathed deeply with relief.

Not noticing, the builder stroked his pointed beard and said. "Hmm, yes, pine would work. We use pine for knorrs and river ferries. Oak and ash can be hard to find, and we have to travel far for it."

My relief was giving way to drowsiness, I thanked the shipbuilder and strolled back toward the camp.

I passed Hardraada's man, who had now found a more exciting pastime than following monks. He was betting on a wrestling match between two of his comrades.

One of Thorir's guards found me and escorted me to my tent. The guard stayed in the same tent, though whether to protect me or to prevent my escape, I could not decide.

Thorir began negotiating with Hardraada immediately. The next morning, I watched him enter Hardraada's tent alone, presumably to discuss the offers sent from Magnus.

While I rested on a stump outside my tent and tried to calm my fears, two courtiers strode toward me. I recognized them as the men sitting close to Hardraada on the previous afternoon, staring at me and whispering.

Reminding myself to be cautious, I rose and greeted them.

Unlike Thorir, their manners were excellent. The taller of the two, a brown-bearded man wearing a blue cloak over a yellow shirt and leggings, inquired how I had slept and whether I had enjoyed my late-morning breakfast.

His shorter companion, wearing a green tunic that stretched comically below his knees, complimented me on my role in helping Hardraada escape from King Sweyn.

I paused before speaking. Comments made to Hardraada's men had to be carefully crafted. "I'm pleased to be of service to your lord."

"Oh, he is not our lord," the taller one said. "I am Ulf, one of King Magnus's emissaries." The name meant 'wolf', and Ulf's pointed nose and slitted eyes did remind me of a wolf.

I formally introduced myself to him and turned to the shorter one, doing the same.

"I am Vandrad." The shorter one bowed slightly.

His name surprised me. In the Northern tongue it meant "one who is in trouble." It was almost a code for someone in disguise.

I was trying so hard not to look at the scar that stretched from above his left eye to the middle of his forehead that the meaning of the name immediately left my mind.

"Why weren't you traveling with Earl Thorir?" I asked.

They exchanged glances. "Our mission, like his, is secret. King Magnus couldn't be certain that every emissary would succeed, so he sent several. I'm certain that Earl Thorir doesn't even know who we are."

I needed to be as wary of Magnus's as Hardraada's men, so I hesitated to say more. I was saved from having to reply, though, by one of Hardraada's personal guards, who strode toward us.

He bowed to Ulf and Vandrad — which seemed odd, since they were Magnus's men — and invited me to join Hardraada and Thorir.

As I reached inside the tent to get the long bow, Ulf stepped toward me. "Would you join us at dinner later this evening? We would be honored to have a distinguished emissary seated with us."

Vandrad nodded eagerly.

"Certainly," I said. "It's a gracious offer, and I accept."

Ulf smiled. "We look forward to seeing you this evening."

Handing the bow to the guard outside Hardraada's tent, I leaned through the entrance to see Hardraada resting in his carved chair and Thorir perched on a wooden bench, looking less sleepy than usual.

Hardraada did not wear his armor, so his green silk tunic hung over tan linen leggings and brown shoes, laced far over his knees. The style, I thought, must be Byzantine. His red silk headband, though, was a fashion that I had come to expect from Northern warriors.

Thorir provided the diplomatic introduction. "The monk Augustine has been sent from Duke William of Normandy with an offer of friendship." He leaned toward Hardraada. "He is the Duke's principal emissary."

Hardraada raised his left eyebrow, and again it created a bizarre effect. "So young."

"Somewhat young, my lord," I said, trying to keep my voice steady. "I'm twenty, and I've known Duke William all my life."

"I would have guessed younger," Hardraada said. "I am surprised that a commoner monk — Thorir has told me you are not a noble — would be a lifelong companion of the young Duke. You were raised in both Falaise and Rouen then?"

He would have taken pains to learn all he could about William's life. Now he also knew my age and that I was either from Falaise or Rouen. I wanted to keep my boyhood in Falaise a secret as long as I was in the North, where Voldred might be lurking.

"As I told Earl Thorir, I'm from Rouen, and I've known the Duke a long time, though I haven't been one of his noble companions. Many of his companions are commoners, though. His mother was a villager in Falaise, as you no doubt know."

Hardraada nodded but said nothing. Regarding me silently, he gave me time to wonder whether my reply had been adequate.

Thorir, apparently feeling the silence, said, "I will check on my guards and rejoin you for our meal."

He rose, made a half-bow in Hardraada's direction, nodded to me, and slipped through the tent door. I wished that he would have stayed.

Hardraada continued to stare at me. Eventually he asked, "Is silence a rule in Normandy?"

"I don't understand your question, my lord."

"There is an ancient verse in Norway. It runs something like this:

Modest a man should be
But talk well if he intends to be wise
And expects praise from men:
Fimbul-fambi the fool is called,
Unable to open his mouth.

Do you have some teaching like this where you come from?"

"The priests and monks who trained me expected us to be articulate, but —"

"Then you know how to speak with men?"

"Of course, my lord."

"What is your real name?"

I was so determined to maintain my disguise that the question rendered me speechless.

"I know you would not reveal it in travel," he added. "So the name you gave Thorir would be false. Who are you really?"

I cleared my throat. "My name is Augustine, my lord, a monk of St. Ouen. I'm Duke William's emissary to the North."

He was silent for a time. "As you wish, Brother ... Augustine. Does the Duke have other Northern emissaries?"

"Not at present."

"He has spies though. He does spy on us."

"Not that I know of, my lord."

"How then does he come by his uncanny knowledge of events here? Thorir told me how much he knows."

Thorir certainly talked a great deal for an emissary of Magnus. "I don't know all of the Duke's devices."

"Probably a chain of hidden riders to carry news quickly. Do you know about them?"

"No, my lord."

"Of course. Thorir said that you did not. You do agree he has them, though?"

I had to slow the pace of the exchange. "Duke William has uncounted wealth, weapons, and men. I don't doubt that he has everything you say and more. He'll probably hear of our movements before King Magnus does."

He sat back and smiled. "Your Duke is undoubtedly formidable. An ally to value."

This gave me a diplomatic opening. I took a deep breath. "Yes, and he feels likewise that Prince Harald would be a valuable ally. He hopes he can form a lasting friendship with so experienced and so respected a leader."

He gave me a sidelong look. "And so rich? Thorir says Duke William knows of my wealth."

"Thorir has informed you thoroughly."

"He is my kinsman."

This had not occurred to me, though it should have. If Thorir was Magnus's half-brother and Hardraada was Magnus's uncle, Thorir would be a cousin to Hardraada.

"The Duke has heard of your wealth," I said, "as has the whole world. Of course, he has no interest in it. He lacks nothing. In fact, he had sent a gift — though it's a mere token of what will follow if you accept his friendship …"

He raised his left eyebrow again and reached inside his tunic. He paused, then swept a weapon out, brandishing it high in the air.

It was the snakelike knife.

My head jerked up and back involuntarily. Thorir would have given him the knife as the gift from King Magnus. Nonetheless, its sudden appearance startled me.

"Is your gift as elegant as this?"

I took another breath and kept my voice as even as I could. "With respect to King Magnus and Earl Thorir, the Duke's gift is more useful and more suited to the talents of a great warrior."

He nodded approval, placing the knife in his lap. "What is this gift?"

"If I may step outside?"

He nodded again. I rose and returned with the bow.

Before I could speak, he said, "So the weapon used to save my life was intended for me?"

"Yes, my lord."

"As a gift."

"Yes, of course."

"A bow may be used as other than a gift, you know."

"I know, my lord."

He smiled broadly and said in a pleasant tone, "It is beautifully crafted. And longer than any I have seen. It has also done me service even before I have pulled it once." He leaned around me to call outside. "Halldor!"

A bearded head appeared in the entrance. "My lord?"

"Take this bow. It is my gift from the Norman Duke. See what you can do with it. I will join you soon."

The man called Halldor cradled the bow in his arms and left the tent.

Hardraada leaned back, still smiling. "You and I can be friends. We have a bond through that bow. It saved my life." His hand fell, apparently unconsciously, on the curved knife. Was he serious about friendship?

"My lord, I'm gratified to have been of any service in Duke William's stead. You had, though, already saved your own life."

"Yes, but you drove the assassins away. They might have aroused the camp. My men and I could have been captured and killed. I am in your debt."

Before I could offer my response, he thrust the knife toward me. "Where have you seen this knife before?"

Again, my body jerked. I regained my composure as quickly as I could. "It's from King Magnus, isn't it?"

"Thorir told me it frightened you, even the first time you saw it. Why? You are a formidable archer. A mere knife, Byzantine or not, would hold no terror for you."

"Is it Byzantine?"

"Of course, and you have seen it before. Where? In Magnus's court? Do you know Magnus? Is your accent feigned? Are you one of his spies?"

I needed time. I put on what felt like a weak smile. "I was not aware that I spoke with an accent, my lord. I thought my Northern speech was flawless." Nonetheless, he had trapped me. I either had to admit that I was afraid of the knife or claim to be a spy for his recent enemy. Or explain the knife's background.

"Are you one of Magnus's men?" he demanded again.

"My lord, I'm a Norman monk —"

"Are you? A beard and no tonsure?"

"I haven't had the opportunity to keep up my appearance."

"You had the opportunity this morning. You did nothing as a monk would, so far as I could see."

I swallowed. "Meditation doesn't show outwardly, my lord. And I needed to be prepared to speak with you at an instant's notice."

He stared at me. "You are at court at Rouen? Thorir said so. You were raised elsewhere?"

I hesitated, then said, "No, my lord, at Rouen."

"And the knife?"

"The sort of design we've never seen in Normandy."

"Do you mean that with all Duke William's wealth and weapons, he has never seen a common Byzantine knife?"

Fortunately, I knew from Thorir that the knife was uncommon. "Of course, the Duke has seen Byzantine designs, my lord, but none such as this. As for me, well, I'm easily startled — from years in seclusion. In addition, I'm younger than you. There's much I have yet to see."

"Duke William is younger than you are, is he not?"

"Yes." I should not have drawn attention to age. It could suggest inexperience to Hardraada.

"Certainly," he said. "A young Duke has much to learn."

I mentally kicked myself.

He rose, putting a hand on my shoulder. "Let us have a closer look at this bow." He sounded friendly again.

I followed him through the tent door, breathing easily — briefly. Again, I had survived the diplomatic battles, but I had accomplished nothing. He had formally agreed to nothing, unless his acceptance of the gift meant something more than it would have in Normandy.

We joined Halldor and the other men, who were muttering over the bow's length. They had trouble pulling it, so that their shots were poorly aimed and weak.

Hardraada took the bow, fitted an arrow to it, and stretched it until it seemed about to break. The arrow he released drove into a distant spruce, and one of Halldor's men had to struggle to free it.

Hardraada grinned. "A wonderful weapon!" Eyeing his warriors, he handed the bow to me. "The monk Augustine has many talents. Emissary and archer, among others I have yet to discover. Can he match my shot?"

I took the bow. The frustration I felt over bumbling the negotiations channeled into my arms. I bent the bow deeply and let the arrow fly, hitting a mark almost twice the distance of Hardraada's.

His men gasped.

Hardraada clapped my shoulder, winking at me. "There is more than one way to win a battle, is there not?"

I stared up at his triumphant face. With him, I was not sure there was.

Ulf and Vandrad turned out to be as friendly as they were polite. They cheered me at dinner that evening, which I appreciated, and accompanied me to my tent afterward, telling stories of Norway and making jests about the royal court.

Vandrad still looked comical in his too-long tunic, and his face twisted humorously at each of Ulf's stories. He laughed out loud at them, though he must have heard them before.

I replied with tales of Normandy, the most humorous I could recall, and they laughed at every one.

The jug of mead we carried away from dinner was soon empty, but Vandrad disappeared for a few moments to return with a second one.

As we traded toasts of friendship, I said, "This is more healing than the herbed brandywine I used to have as a child."

Ulf laughed. "You must have been raised with a healer. Our healers here have the same remedies against the winter cold. They simply consume more of it, since we have more cold!"

Vandrad found this hilarious. "You've now found a remedy to match herbed brandywine," he said, lifting his tankard. "If you heal in Norway with mead, you'll be more popular than the King himself!"

I joined him. "Perhaps I should return to healing and give up being an emissary!"

Ulf fell on my shoulder, laughing. "As either, you'd fare better with King Magnus. All you get from Harald is hard counsel!" He punned on the meaning of "Hardraada"— both "ruthless" and "hard counsel"— so he must have heard the nickname.

"That's all I got today," I said.

"Then you deserve more healing!" Ulf said, pouring me more mead.

We drank and laughed for many hours. I slept remarkably well that night.

The next morning, all of us crowded into Hardraada's few ships and sailed north. Escaping the crush and smell of the warriors — they smeared themselves with some revolting oil — I found an isolated corner in the cargo ship. I wanted to be near my pony when we landed, and, as the shipbuilder had said, the cargo ship was broader and flatter than the warships. It pitched less.

No storms troubled the sea, though, and the day remained clear. The voyage was more comfortable than I deserved for my night of indulgence.

My anxiety, however, increased as we neared the camp of King Magnus.

If Voldred had survived, would he be with Magnus? Would he recognize me?

Soon we reached a long inlet lying near the tip of the Danish Jutland. King Magnus's fleet — modest, as we'd heard — rocked in the harbor, while red and yellow tents dotted the woods nearby. A crowd of warriors began to gather on the shore.

I tried to imagine Magnus's appearance. I had trouble shaking the image of Voldred with a crown on his head.

"Magnus the Good and the Kind, he's called," Ulf had said, "and though he's a fierce warrior in battle, it's a reputation he deserves."

I stared at the shore. As the ships were pulled toward him, Magnus stood there to greet us as if he were a house guard, though his purple tunic, white-and-blue-striped leggings, and jeweled fur cloak confirmed his station.

Voldred was nowhere to be seen.

Magnus's face was the opposite of what I had imagined. Instead of being long and drawn, it was square and full, trimmed by a neat brown beard. His eyes wrinkled in a squint, which made him look as if he were about to laugh. His voice was pleasant, and he smiled as he spoke.

What surprised me most was his age. This feared king appeared to be only a few years older than I was.

After formal introductions, he hugged Hardraada, grinning at his size. "It has been sixteen years since you and I fought together at the Battle of Stiklestad. You were tall then, but you have become a giant, just as I heard you had. The poets will be singing songs about your head touching the clouds!"

Hardraada laughed at this and returned the friendly greeting. "My nephew has the stature of a king. No height can overreach that."

Behind Magnus, his men whispered to each other, apparently approving Hardraada's response.

Magnus then welcomed Thorir, offering gifts for Thorir's successful negotiations. I wondered whether he would greet Ulf and Vandrad as warmly, but they were nowhere to be seen.

Thorir introduced me. "This is Brother Augustine, one of the few Southerners who understands the Northern tongue. He helped me in Hedeby, and I asked him to come north. He is guided by God."

Magnus smiled at me. "A holy monk is always welcome here, Brother Augustine. We are delighted to have you visit us."

I murmured my thanks, adding a Latin blessing.

He moved to greet Hardraada's men, talking and jesting with each one.

I stared at him, confused. Why would such a nice man want to kill me? Was it possible that he knew nothing about Voldred? I began to entertain this possibility, especially when I saw the enormous feast he had ordered. King Magnus was indeed kind, as Ulf had said.

He seated me between himself and Thorir and asked me to bless the food. I gave a blessing in Latin, which I then translated into the Northern speech.

Magnus praised the prayer and even praised my translation. I made a mental note to boast about this to Garrad.

A serving-man then brought all of us towels and a bowl of water to wash our hands before eating, a custom I had encountered in Western Normandy when I was young. My only objection to it was that it delayed getting to the food.

When not talking with Hardraada, who towered over him on the other side, Magnus conversed with me about my trip from Denmark, always offering me more food. When I admired the drinking-horn Thorir passed in my direction, Magnus overheard and presented it to me as a gift — full of ale.

I almost choked while quaffing the wave that poured from it when I lifted it, but Magnus politely looked the other way until I coughed my way to recovery. Garrad had warned me about Northern drinking horns, and now I knew why.

After the feast, Thorir's two guards accompanied me to my tent, where they again stayed. "To insure that you have the opportunity to complete your mission," one said.

They lit two oil lamps on the table in the center of the tent and took out a wooden board and playing pieces.

"What are those pieces made of, if you don't mind telling me?" I asked.

"Whalebone," they both replied, apparently eager to sound knowledgeable.

"The game is called …?"

"Hnefatafl." Both of them spoke together again, and the result sounded like a sneeze. "It's like chess. Do you play chess?"

I said yes, and they began to teach me hnefatafl, made easier by the berry wine delivered by one of King Magnus's guards.

A few hours later, I stretched out on my cot. The berry wine and friendly games of hnefatafl having eased my anxieties, I felt less anxious and soon drifted off to sleep.

A trumpet awakened me, and I rolled over to find Thorir sitting on the next cot, dressed in a gold tunic and green leggings and watching me through heavy eyelids.

"God gives his protected ones sound sleep. I wondered if it would take an angel's trumpet to rouse you."

I felt disoriented. "I'm sorry, my lord. Have I missed some event? Have I detained you from anything?"

"You have not detained me, but you have missed something. Get up and bathe. I will relate everything."

As I washed at the shore — in water cold enough to awaken me completely — Thorir recounted the previous night's events.

After the feast and after I had left with my two hnefatafl-playing guards, King Magnus had appeared at Hardraada's tent, offering clothing, weapons, and gold to Hardraada's men. Then Magnus had held out two reed-straws, one of which Hardraada took.

Magnus had said, "With this reed-straw, I give you half of Norway, together with all its dues and duties and all the estates within it. Though I request precedence in greetings, rank, and harbor berths, I offer equality in every other way."

Harald had thanked him, and they had spent the rest of the evening drinking toasts of friendship and making boasts about how loyal they would be to each other.

I pulled my robe over my tunic and laced my shoes around my ankles. "Then Magnus and Hardraada are to be joint kings?"

"The crowning ceremony is this morning, at which your prayers will be welcome."

The outcome must have pleased Thorir. He had forgotten to be rude.

Later that morning, Magnus's army and Hardraada's men assembled in a circle near the feasting table, the two kings seated on carved wooden chairs in the middle of the circle.

Magnus wore a red silk tunic with a white belt and white leggings, while Hardraada still wore his green silk tunic and yellow leggings. Both had red silk headbands holding their hair back.

Magnus rose and spoke. "I announce to all assembled that I have given half of Norway to my uncle, Harald, Sigurd's son. He will not only rule half the land. He will be King as lawfully as I over all the land, giving me precedence only when diplomacy and judgment demand it."

I spotted Ulf and Vandrad at the edge of the crowd behind Magnus and Hardraada. Their eyes met mine, and they frowned. Joint kingship was not uncommon, so that could not be the reason for the frowns. Probably, I guessed, they resented their King giving so much away to Hardraada.

"Henceforth," Magnus continued, "Harald, Sigurd's son, will be King Harald of Norway."

He signaled to four men standing near him, dressed in yellow cloaks and holding narrow-necked, round trumpets with flaring bells. At his sign, the men lifted the trumpets to their lips and blew, a drum thudding behind them.

Magnus and Hardraada both lifted their heads higher, but the noise sounded to me like geese being strangled with the drummer pounding their execution. I struggled not to grimace.

Amid the din, Thorir stepped forward and presented Hardraada with what I assumed to be the Norwegian badges of office. Fortunately, the completion of this ritual silenced the trumpeters and the drummer.

Hardraada thanked Magnus for his generosity. "We shall rule Norway peacefully together. We shall together vanquish all our enemies in the North and the South."

He glanced, I thought, in my direction. I hoped that William did not count as one of those enemies and silently rebuked myself for not yet confirming an alliance between Norway and Normandy.

After the ceremony, Hardraada and his men returned to their ships but were soon back on land to set up their own tent camp. As they had at our earlier campsite, most of the men erected tents from the poles and oiled cloth they had brought with them. A few others dragged the ships onto the shore on rollers. They then raised tilts, the peaked cloth coverings I had seen the assassins rip away, under which they would sleep.

Ulf and Vandrad found me watching this construction from my tent. I was also awaiting a reply to my request for a meeting with Magnus and Hardraada.

"Two kings to deal with is an unexpected turn of events," Ulf said.

"Certainly not as easy as one," I replied.

Vandrad stared at the sky. "It's unfortunate there's not only one." He tried to sound casual.

"That's certain," Ulf added.

I agreed.

Vandrad looked at Ulf and then me. "You're a healer, aren't you?" Before I could answer, he continued, "What would you recommend for the itching on my head and falling hair?"

His hair did not appear thin, but I said, "I've seen Northmen bathing with dried nettles in the water around them."

"Yes," Vandrad said, "it makes the body smell sweet."

Until you smear the body with oil, I thought. Out loud I said, "Simply wash your hair with the nettle water, taking care to scrub your head, and it will relieve the itching and help your hair grow."

"What if I swallow it accidentally?" Vandrad surely knew the effects of an herb he had bathed in all his life, so he apparently wanted to determine whether I knew.

I had already revealed that I was a healer, so I replied, "It's a purifier. It will remove poisons from your body. And it's a good antidote to poison in general." I stared at him for a moment. "You two already know that."

Vandrad smiled. "Yes, we do, but we wanted to discover ... We suspected from your knowledge that you're a well trained healer." He looked at Ulf, who stepped closer to me.

"We want to ask you something," Ulf began.

At that moment one of Thorir's guards turned the corner of the tent and spoke my name. He frowned at Ulf and Vandrad. "The King will see you now, Brother Augustine."

"Excuse me," I said to them. "I'm supposed to meet with King Magnus, and I hope the result of the meeting will please both of you."

"Good," Ulf said. "We'll speak with you later."

Vandrad smiled. "Yes. Later."

The guard, still frowning, led me away.

I found Thorir just outside Magnus's tent.

He snapped at the guard and me in his normal tone — annoyed: "You took too long to get here. King Magnus was just about to see you when one of Hardraada's men intruded. He is in there now. You will have to wait."

I thanked him for what he had done and lowered myself onto a log bench.

After a few minutes, Magnus himself stepped through the tent entrance, dressed in his red silk tunic and gold leggings. "I am sorry not to be able to talk with you, Brother Augustine. King Harald has invited me to a feast at his tents. May we postpone our conversation?"

I had no choice, so I replied, "Certainly, your majesty. I'm only pleased that you're willing to grant me an audience at all."

Magnus smiled. "After the feast then."

"After the feast, your majesty."

He patted my shoulder. "You are a good-tempered emissary. It speaks well for your Duke."

I was less good-tempered inwardly, however. The near-misses on the alliances were making me more and more frustrated.

Then I smelled the spices and herbs cooking in Hardraada's camp. Perhaps one more feast would not delay my mission too much.

Polite as ever, Magnus took only sixty of his own men with him to match exactly the number that Hardraada had. Thorir was among the sixty. I accompanied Thorir, but he informed me that I did not count as one of the sixty on either side.

Inside Hardraada's tent, the largest one, the feast table was stuffed with food. With little patience, I waited for the two kings to seat themselves ceremoniously beside each other on the high seat atop a platform with its own table. They gave an unnecessarily formal toast.

A priest near Magnus offered a prayer in praise of bounty, we washed our hands with towels, and — finally — began to eat.

My eating was interrupted often by toasts, jests, pledges, songs, and boasts. Apparently, everyone in the tent was determined to be loyal to everyone else to the death. The name of Olaf, former King now saint, was mentioned often.

Seeming more serious, the court-poets, all Icelandic, offered heroic poems. Their structure was as complex as the Latin poetry I knew, perhaps more so.

Some of Hardraada's own poems were recited, and Thorir leaned over to tell me that almost every warrior, especially the chieftains, composed poetry.

At the end of the recitals, Hardraada asked one of his poets to summarize the recent past. The man, dressed like the other warriors, rose and spoke to the assembled men:

> *Once the seafaring warriors*
> *Had little hope of peace.*
> *Fear stirred in men's hearts,*
> *Warships lay off the beaches.*
> *Death-dealing King Magnus*
> *Would sail his vessels southwards,*
> *While Harald's ocean-dragons*
> *Were pointing to the North.*

Addressing Hardraada directly, he continued:

> *You split the ocean with your keels,*
> *Far-traveled King of men,*
> *When sailing west from Denmark.*
> *Fine ships ploughed the flood-tide.*
> *King Magnus offered to share*
> *Half his lands and men with you.;*
> *When royal kinsmen met,*
> *The reunion was a joyful one.*

Both kings praised the poet, and I marveled at his grand, rhythmic recitation, reflecting how clumsy my own speech must sound.

After more eating, punctuated by more toasts, I began to feel drowsy. So, when Magnus's and Hardraada's men turned to singing, I wandered outside. Even if I did know the songs, my voice would not be a welcome addition.

I eased my back against the smooth bark of a nearby beech, its branches and leaves shading me from the afternoon sun. With the songs and smells lulling me into rest, I dozed until a general clamor awoke me. It was still afternoon.

I blinked at Hardraada's tent. His men bustled in and out of it, carrying chests, bundles of clothing, weapons, and armor. It appeared to be gift-giving time, and I should be present with my gifts.

I pulled myself to my feet and hurried to my tent. I found the sack with Tostig's arm-rings as well as the gilded helmets and gold-pieces that Garrad had given me.

By the time I returned to the feast-tent, a ceremony was in progress. I slipped inside, craning my neck to see over Hardraada's men. Noticing my sack, they stepped aside, allowing me to edge closer to the platform where the two Kings stood, the feasting table having been removed.

As I approached, Hardraada was speaking, his hand indicating a pile of gold and silver pieces, ornaments, and jewelry. The pile, larger than any I had ever seen, rested on a huge ox-hide spread before the kings.

"Yesterday, Magnus, you gave me a great kingdom, which you had wrested from your enemies and mine. You made a partnership with me. This was generously done, because you had fought hard for it. For my own part, I have spent much time in foreign lands. I had to undergo many hazards to amass the treasure you see before you. I want to share this wealth with you. We shall own all this equally, just as we share the kingdom of Norway jointly."

He ordered his men to take scales and weights and divide the treasure into two equal parts. Magnus's men looked pleased. Most carried gifts of clothing and weapons that they had already received individually, and their smiles showed that they felt their King well treated.

I looked around for Ulf and Vandrad but could not locate them in the crowd.

Magnus's face registered both amazement and delight, while Hardraada seemed almost playful, picking up a gold ingot the size of a man's head. "Where is your gold, nephew, that can match this lump?"

Magnus shook his head, smiling. "My wars have so reduced my resources that all the gold and silver I have left is what I have on my own person. After the gifts I gave your men yesterday, I have no more gold in my possession than this." From his arm, he took a thick bracelet, decorated with geometric patterns, and handed it to Hardraada.

Garrad had guessed correctly Magnus's lack of wealth, but he had not guessed the extent. As Thorir said, another war would have been impossible for Magnus.

Hardraada studied the bracelet. "This is a small piece of gold, nephew, for a King who owns two kingdoms." He drew his face into seriousness. "Yet there are some who would doubt your claim even to this bracelet."

Hardraada, the aggressive negotiator, had some advantage in mind. I shook my head and decided that he would be angling for an advantage at his own funeral.

Magnus's response surprised me, though. A seasoned warrior should be accustomed to hard dealing.

Instead, his face reddened, and he replied gravely, almost haltingly, "If I am not the rightful owner of that bracelet, then I do not know what I can rightly call my own. My father, King Olaf, gave me that bracelet when we parted for the last time."

Hardraada replied through a chuckle, "That is true, nephew. Your father gave you this bracelet … after he had taken it from my father for some trifling reason. It is also true that it was not an easy time for minor kings in Norway when your father stood at the height of his power."

Magnus did not reply. Hardraada had won another victory, and I felt sorry for Magnus, the man who might want me dead.

I decided to rescue him. Before I lost my nerve, I forced myself forward.

"Noble Kings," I said, hoping to have used the proper address, "and noble lords and warriors, may I speak?"

Magnus nodded. Hardraada gave me a half smile.

"My lords, your majesties, though I have no gift to equal either a kingdom or a fortune in gold, I do have gifts. From my own lord, Duke William of Normandy."

Magnus's face, on which I had hoped to see appreciation, went from blank to alarmed.

I kept speaking. "These are mere tokens of what will follow, especially in sealing the friendship the Duke feels for the Kings of Norway."

I drew the gold helmets from the sack and laid one at the feet of each King. They seemed tiny next to the piles of gold, silver, and jewels, but their patterns and jewels made them as elegant as any piece in the piles on either side of me.

Magnus and Hardraada both thanked me, picking up the helmets and admiring them.

"This is remarkable craftsmanship," Hardraada said. "It matches the beauty and craftsmanship of the bow I have already received from the Norman Duke."

This was intended to be another victory over Magnus. By now, though, Thorir would have told Magnus that the bow had been meant for him rather than for Hardraada.

I replied, "You do me honor, my lord, for I carved the bow myself."

Hardraada smiled. "Yet another talent of our archer-monk, healer, and emissary. What else will we learn of him?"

How did he know I was a healer? I had taken care not to mention that to him.

I lost no time in wondering, though. I had an opportunity to win a victory of my own with Magnus. I had given Thorir an arm-ring earlier. Now I drew the last arm-ring from the sack and laid it at Magnus's feet.

"I present this to King Magnus of Norway with wishes of friendship from Duke William. I hope this will be some compensation for the King's last bracelet, which in his generosity he has recently parted with."

Magnus looked serious for a moment and then smiled. "My deepest thanks to your Duke. And to you. The friendship is established, and I hope it will be long and deep."

I breathed a sigh of relief. One alliance was won.

Hardraada, a half-smile intact, said nothing.

I bowed and stepped back into the crowd of men, but Hardraada called to me.

"Brother Augustine, we cannot seem ungenerous when your Duke has been so kind to us." He turned to Thorir. "Cousin, give our young monk a helmet, shield, knife, and fine clothing." He looked at me. "I would offer a bow, but none here suits your talents, and I am certain that you will soon craft your own. There is a Byzantine cross on the edge of the pile that I especially want you to have."

One of Thorir's guards brought me the armor and clothing, which included a blue tunic and white leggings, soft black leather shoes, a two-pointed white cloak resembling those I had admired in Hedeby, a brooch of twisting dragons, a leather belt, and blue linen headband.

The other guard handed me the Byzantine cross. On the front of it was the same snakelike pattern as on Voldred's knife. This one, though, was carved from some white stone that I did not recognize.

I gazed at Hardraada, controlling my face and voice. "Thank you, my lord King. You have been more than generous with an undeserving messenger."

"Indeed, no," he replied. "Your service has already made you more deserving than I can repay. You may ask any boon as long as you live, and I will grant it."

I thanked him and bowed again. I had gained a personal boon but not yet an alliance with Normandy.

After Thorir placed one last gift in front of me — a gold chain for the cross — Hardraada called him back to the platform.

"Thorir, you have reunited me with my kinsman and my country. Yours should be the most valuable gifts of all."

He gave Thorir a silver-handled maple bowl hooped with gilded silver, which he filled with new-minted silver coins and two gold bracelets. He then took off his own cloak, a purple one lined with white fur, and presented it to Thorir, promising him high honors and friendship.

I hoped to use this moment to slip away and calm my nerves, but I heard Hardraada's voice call my name. "Brother Augustine! Come! Let us hear what a monk has to offer the new Kings."

Was this Northern courtesy? Or was he testing me again to determine whether I was really a monk?

I trod slowly toward the platform, and the crowd quieted, the eyes of the Northern warriors on me.

I opened my mouth, hoping that something, anything, holy would come out. "My lords, any monk could only wish that the two great Kings of Norway would follow the greatest King, who, by the will of God, appeared in Southern lands, but whose example has been repeated here in the North."

I hoped the Kings would think of Saint Olaf, and I saw Magnus nod. The warriors continued staring at me.

Hardraada leaned toward me in a gesture that meant privacy while he said loudly, "A song or a poem, Brother Augustine!"

"My lord, I can assure you that you do not want a song from me."

"A poem, then!"

Recitation. This was worse than the priests' school in Rouen. I licked my lips, which had become suddenly dry. The warriors blinked and glanced at each other.

I began, "Long ago, when I was a child in the monastery, I learned a Latin verse of an ancient thinker, a philosopher named Proclus, who though not a Christian, was a wise man, I'm told. He addressed his verse to the nine Muses, the daughters of Jove, his highest God. Here in the North, you might call them the Norns, the Fates, though the Norns are three in number. The poem lacks the grandeur of those I've heard here, and my poor translation will only make it worse, but I'll recite it as best I can:

> *Glory and praise to those sweet lamps of earth,*
> *The nine fair daughters of Almighty Jove*
> *Who all the passage dark to death from birth*
> *Lead wandering souls with their bright beams of Love.*
> *Through cares of mortal life, through pain and woe,*
> *The tender solace of their counsel saves,*
> *The healing secrets of their songs forego*
> *Despair, and when we tremble at the waves*
> *Of life's wild sea of murk incertitude,*
> *Their gentle touch upon the helm is pressed,*
> *Their hand points to the beacon-star of Good,*
> *Where we shall make our harbor, and have rest,*
> *The heaven of our home wherefrom we fell,*
> *Allured by this poor show of lower things,*
> *Tempted among earth's dull deceits to dwell:*
> *But oh, great Sisters, hear his prayer who sings,*
> *And calm the restless flutter of his breast,*
> *And fill him with the thirst for Wisdom's stream,*

> *Nor ever suffer thoughts or men unblessed*
> *To turn his vision from the Eternal Beam.*
> *Ever and ever higher from the throng*
> *Lawless and witless, lead his feet aright*
> *Life's perils and perplexities among,*
> *To the white center of the sacred Light.*
> *Feed him with food of that rich fruit which grows*
> *On stems of splendid learning — dower him still*
> *With gifts of eloquence to vanquish those*
> *Who err — let soft persuasion change their will.*
> *Hear, heavenly Sisters, hear! oh, you who know*
> *The winds of Wisdom's sea, the course to steer,*
> *Who light the Flame that lightens all below,*
> *And bring the spirits of the perfect there*
> *Where the immortals are, when this life's fever*
> *Is left behind as a dread gulf o'erpassed;*
> *And souls like mariners, escaped forever,*
> *Throng on the happy homeland, saved at last."*

The faces of the warriors turned up toward me, their mouths half open, and there was silence, until Hardraada said, "This, little Brother, was worthy of a true monk."

I bowed toward him, but what did his words mean? Did he now believe that I was a monk, or that I had delivered the poem the way a true monk would, even though I was not one myself?

I straightened to find his eyes still on me, expectantly.

I was rescued by Thorir, who appeared at my side me, smiling. I had seen him smile so seldom that his face surprised me. "That was excellently done. Excellently. Come with me now. My longship has arrived from home. I have something for you, and there is someone I want you to meet." He looked up at Hardraada and Magnus. "My Kings, may I take Brother Augustine away?"

They nodded their consent, and he thanked them.

He led me through the soldiers, who praised the poem and clapped me on the back. We passed the Kings' platform, edged around a stand of spears, and bent through the back entrance of the tent. As I emerged from the entrance, Thorir stepped abruptly aside, and I almost fell backward.

Before me loomed a gigantic, black-haired, black-bearded, brown-skinned demon, dressed in a black tunic, leggings, and cloak, all trimmed with white fur. A mammoth sword hung from his side, its scabbard silver, the sword hilt and pommel black. In one hand he gripped a black-handled axe with a silver-edged blade, silver patterns snaking over it.

"This," said Thorir, "is Onyame, the finest of my house guards." To the demon he said, "This is the monk I mentioned, Brother Augustine. He is in your keeping until his departure."

Onyame half-bowed. In a voice that issued from the center of the earth, he said, "I'm pleased to be of service to a monk, especially one guided by God. Thorir has told me about you, Brother Augustine. Guarding you is an honor for me, one of the highest Thorir has bestowed on me."

This was more gracious than I expected from a demon, so I blurted out, "It's my honor. That is, it's an honor to be guarded by someone so highly esteemed by Earl Thorir."

Thorir wheeled back toward the tent. "I must not leave the Kings for long, and I am free to go now that you are well protected, Brother Augustine."

"Thank you," I said, even though I was not sure how protected I felt, being guarded by my own personal demon.

Onyame spoke again, and again I marveled at his voice. It was deeper than any in Normandy, excepting Ralph of Tosny's, which William and I called "the Voice of God."

He smiled as he spoke, and I noted that his teeth were white, as Thorir had insisted back in Hedeby. "I suppose you'd rather be in Normandy than be well guarded in Denmark."

The comment and smile surprised me. "Yes, I would. Does it show?"

"Northerners have a saying, 'Far from home is far from joy.' I've been a traveler in strange lands myself. I know how it feels. God must have plans for you here, though."

"Even if God does not, Duke William does."

Onyame stepped toward the tent, so that we both stood beside an open tent flap, the Kings' table just visible inside.

He inclined his head toward the tent. "Earl Thorir has told me of your mission to negotiate with the two Kings. It sounds as difficult as his."

"His has been remarkably successful. I hope mine will be the same."

I saw the white teeth again. "You think his has been successful?"

"The Kings seem to be getting along."

"Do they?" He motioned me closer to the tent. "Listen."

Through the tent flap, the voices of Magnus's courtiers drifted:

"… and, my lord Magnus, King Harald saved himself at the Battle of Stiklestad rather than your father."

"His scheming in Byzantium is well known. He's not to be trusted."

"With his wealth and your men, he could seize Norway from you."

Onyame turned to me. "Now, listen down here."

I strode behind him a few steps and leaned near an open tent flap where I heard Hardraada's courtiers:

"... but not your father, King Harald. King Olaf treated him badly, even though your father had offered his support. Will King Magnus the son do the same as his father?"

"When King Magnus would not meet you upon your return, you were forced to go to King Sweyn, who nearly killed you."

"Why does King Magnus insist on precedence over you in harbor? That is humiliation."

Onyame motioned me away. "The marriage of King Magnus and King Harald is not a love-match. Their different personalities and experiences would, under the best circumstances, give them trouble. As you have heard, their men will work hard to increase the ill will. Unhappily, this won't make Earl Thorir's or your work easier."

"I see that now. Thank you for the warning." I began to like this demon. He understood the workings of the Northern courts and seemed interested in my mission. "I've had one success. King Magnus publicly accepted friendship with Normandy, and I have an audience with him after the feast."

"You're not seeking a treaty?"

"No, only friendship. That's enough for Duke William's purposes."

"Then King Magnus will probably meet with you tomorrow morning."

I glanced at the feasting. "Yes, of course."

"May I be of some service to you until then?"

"There is one task … Do you think Thorir could arrange another audience with King Harald for me? Thorir is a kinsman of Harald's, and he has been generous enough to offer his help before. Harald hasn't committed to friendship with Normandy yet, though I believe he will."

"If you deal with him cleverly enough. I know that Earl Thorir himself had difficulty negotiating with King Harald, even though Thorir's handled many diplomatic missions for Magnus. And Earl Thorir is, as you say, a kinsman of King Harald's."

I nodded. "Harald is … a demanding negotiator."

"As his reputation has it. You're an emissary of a noble lord yourself, though. You need not give in to demands."

"He's avoided demands, though not wiles."

He laughed. "Northerners have another saying, 'The tongue is the head's bane,' and that's the bane Harald uses against his adversaries in his battles of words."

"I'm afraid he's used it against me already."

He lowered his head in thought and raised it again. "I shall speak with Earl Thorir tonight. He's cheerful already, but his mood will be even better after more gifts and ale. I'm sure he'll be willing to arrange a meeting with King Harald."

"Thank you."

Tomorrow could bring, finally, an end to my work in the North. I thought of Garrad and William and even Anette and wondered how soon I might be back in the South.

I knew the end of July must be near, but I was not certain. "If I may ask, Onyame, do you know what day it is?"

He smiled. "Of course. It's almost the last day of July, Saint Olaf's death day."

As the celebration of the alliance and of Saint Olaf continued, I returned to my tent, alone this time.

That night, I dreamed that a white-haired warrior, wearing a red silk tunic like Magnus's, strode into my tent, which had been opened by the dragon. The old warrior whispered something in my ear, but I could not understand his words. He waved his right arm toward the tent entrance, where two men stood, and then he held up a sword in the position of warning. The two men glanced at each other and hurried away, though not before I recognized their faces: Ulf and Vandrad.

I awoke, and the inside of the tent was still dark. As I drifted back to sleep, I wondered whether I was being warned away from Ulf and Vandrad or they were being warned away from me.

The next morning, I perched on the log bench outside the largest of Magnus's tents, where I had sat with Thorir the day before. No guards stood watch, so I waited for them to rise.

My enthusiasm to finish my mission had awakened me early. The feast kept the rest of the camp asleep.

I worried about my dream. Should I avoid Ulf and Vandrad? Were they somehow connected to Voldred? They did not seem dangerous, however. If anything, they seemed dull-witted.

I realized that I needed to concentrate, but on different matters. I needed to focus on what to say to Magnus.

Now that friendship had been established, I could perhaps consider a binding alliance with Norway, though William had given me no instructions about trade or court visits, the sorts of things alliances included. Should I ask Magnus if he desired a treaty?

What I wanted to ask him was whether he had sent an assassin, a Berserker warrior, to Normandy to kill a lame villager. I knew that was an impossible question. Here, face to face with the man who may know why Voldred wanted to kill me, I could not ask it without risking my life and my mission.

Possibly, Magnus knew nothing of Voldred's knife. Perhaps Voldred had stolen it from Magnus's treasury, and the King had not missed it yet.

Clearly, Hardraada knew nothing. He had revealed his own ignorance when he gave me the cross, which now hung from its gold chain around my neck. He obviously believed the knife to be a common Byzantine one. So he had found a cross with a similar pattern to see whether I would react to it or even wear it. Thorir, though, had emphasized that the knife was not Byzantine and that its stone was what made it unique, not its design.

I stood to straighten my new blue tunic and smooth the white leggings under my robe. Though I wanted to maintain my disguise as a monk, I hoped for an opportunity to wear the warrior's cloak as well. My new jeweled knife hung in its silver sheath at my waist, and I traced its twisting patterns with my fingers.

The head of a Norwegian soldier poked from the entrance of a smaller tent nearby. It disappeared, and I heard a voice say, "Yes, my lord, he's standing next to the large tent."

The head reappeared, followed by a body. "King Magnus regrets that you've been waiting, Brother Augustine. He'll see you now."

I began to step through the tent, but the guard stopped me.

"I'm sorry, but I must have the knife you're wearing. I trust that you understand."

"Of course." I relinquished the only means of self-defense I had.

He nodded at me, and I pushed through the tent door.

CHAPTER 13

POISON AND A BEAR

A.D. 1046

King Magnus slouched in an undecorated wooden chair in a corner of the tent, a plain brown cloak wrapped around him. His eyes were fixed on the ground, but they stared at nothing.

I waited.

Eventually, he stirred and turned to me. For a moment, he searched my face as if looking for something. Then he offered me a bench near his chair and spoke slowly. "I did not realize at first that you were from Normandy. Please tell me about your Duke."

It was not an unexpected question, so I boasted about William's wise leadership, his strength as a ruler, and his skill in arms.

Magnus listened attentively. "Has his reign been … a difficult one? Has he had troubles?"

"Troubles, my lord?"

"Yes. You know that my own father was killed in a rebellion. He was a great king, the greatest Norway has ever seen, but he had difficulties. Every king does."

I wondered if Magnus sought a diplomatic victory, as Hardraada had, but he seemed to be groping for some information.

I answered as carefully as I could. "As you say, my lord, every ruler has difficulties. Duke William has had his and will have more, I'm sure. He's been blessed with so few troubles, though, that I can't recall any worthy of recounting."

He shifted on his chair. "Has he been … popular? Do the other nobles and the people respect him?"

"Of course, my lord. He may not be as loved as you and your father are here. Duke William's not a saint. Not yet, at least."

He smiled. "Well spoken. Loyally spoken. You know, Brother Augustine, my father was not always loved. He imposed the religion of the cross" — he glanced at mine, hanging outside my robe — "with a determination not welcome in a country that tolerated many religions. His own nobles and farmers killed him at the Battle of Stiklestad. They almost killed Harald and me as well. As a saint, however, he is loved. As a King, I am … respected."

I hesitated and then said, "I shall inform Duke William that you've accepted his gifts. He'll be pleased. Was there something about the friendship between Normandy and Norway that we should discuss further?"

"Not now. There will be time for that later. Thorir tells me you are coming north with us, and I want to discuss Normandy with you at length. There is much I wish to know."

This took me by surprise. "In truth, my lord, if I could speak with King Harald and guarantee Normandy's friendship with him, I could carry the good news back to Duke William immediately."

He called for the guard. "Of course, I will be delighted if Harald shares my goodwill toward Normandy, but I do wish you to come north with us. I would like to learn more about Duke William. It will … ground my affection for him and his land."

"As you wish, my lord. Thank you for seeing me."

"It has been my pleasure. I look forward to our future talks." To the guard he said, "Please escort Brother Augustine to King Harald's tent."

As I rounded the last tent before Hardraada's, my head sagging, Ulf and Vandrad pulled me away from the guard.

"Where are you going?" Ulf whispered.

I leaned away from him. "Why are you whispering?"

He glanced at Vandrad, who nodded back at him. With Vandrad guarding our retreat, he led me into the woods behind an oak.

"Have you had trouble negotiating with King Harald?"

"I haven't seen him yet."

Vandrad drew beside us. "He won't agree to anything, will he?"

"You heard him at the feast. He remains uncommitted."

"King Magnus, on the other hand, has declared friendship with your Duke," Ulf said.

"Publicly. At the feast. You heard that as well."

They glanced at each other again.

Ulf began to whisper again. "How would you feel if we could eliminate the threat of King Harald's refusal?"

"How?"

Ulf leaned toward me. "Do you know of a poison that admits of no antidote?"

I frowned at him.

"You are a healer," Vandrad said, "and you know about poisons."

"I'm a healer, not a poisoner."

"You do know about poisons, though," Vandrad said.

"Yes, but I don't administer them."

They glanced at each other yet again. It was becoming annoying.

Ulf whispered, "What if someone else administered the poison? All you would have to do is provide the knowledge."

"You're suggesting that a Norman emissary show you how to poison a Norwegian King, with whom he's supposed to be discussing friendship."

"If that Norwegian King," Ulf said, "were to die because of ... let us say, rotten food, then your mission would be finished." He paused. "Unless you wish to risk your work on the whims of King Harald."

I felt like Eve talking to the serpent. I hesitated. "I know of no poison that cannot be treated."

"There's a kind of mushroom —" Vandrad said.

A noise from the forest interrupted him. I thought I saw a black bear slip through the tree shadows not far from us.

Ulf and Vandrad, however, twisted their heads toward the camp. I began to point in the direction of the bear, but Vandrad whispered, "I see the guard. I'll draw him off."

I did not see the guard, but Ulf took my arm and drew me deeper into the forest.

I resisted. "I saw a bear —"

"No bear would come this close to camp in daylight." He pointed at the trunks of the nearby trees. "Somewhere in this forest grows a poisonous mushroom, I've heard. You know where it grows, what it looks like."

I took a breath. "I learned about something like that as a child, but I've developed an antidote, especially if I can administer it soon enough."

"Are you certain? What antidote?"

I had to be cautious. "It's a mixture of goldenseal, masterwort ... and other plants. I won't fail to administer it, if I'm called for."

"What if you're not called for?" When I hesitated, he asked, "Would you agree to show me where the mushroom is? That's all you need to do."

I studied his face. "Why do you want to poison King Harald?"

He snorted. "That should be obvious. He'll own all of Norway before King Magnus can stop him."

Vandrad reappeared. "The guard won't be put off any longer. He has orders to take you to King Harald."

I was rescued.

"Remember," Ulf said, "one meal, and you could go home."

"You could have this year's Christmas feast in Normandy," Vandrad said.

That was a tempting thought. I excused myself and joined the guard.

As I covered the short distance to Hardraada's tent, I reviewed the conversation with them. Going home ... a Norman Christmas feast ...

Did they think, though, that they could poison Hardraada and not have his men examine — strenuously — every disgruntled follower of Magnus who had been near Hardraada's food? Did they think that a healer from Normandy would not be suspect?

I shook my head. How could grown men be so stupid?

As the guard ushered me through the tent door, Hardraada rose, glowering. His face looked red under his light beard, redder for the contrast with his white tunic and headband.

Before I could say anything, he roared, "So, you're plotting against me, are you?"

I was stunned but blurted out, "No, my lord, of course not."

"Do you deny that you met with two men to discuss poisoning me?"

The guard must have overheard. I swallowed. "Well, I —"

He took a step toward me. "Do you deny it?"

"This is not what it seems. Two men approached me with an offer —"

"An offer? An offer! You call poisoning a king an offer! Is that the way things are done in Normandy?"

"My lord, I've done nothing —"

"And nothing will be done, until I hold court on this murderous plot. Guard!"

"If I may just explain —"

He seized his axe and shook it at me. "You'll explain before the Kings of Norway and the Assembly, if I haven't killed you first."

The guard reappeared.

"Strip him of his knife and then take him to his tent. See that he remains there."

Thorir was the first person to visit me. He bent through the tent door, revealing the growing dusk behind him.

I assumed that the entire camp had buzzed all day with news of the poisoning plot, but he only regarded me through half-closed eyes and asked, "Have you been meeting secretly with two of King Harald's men?"

"King Harald's men? Of course not. Who told you that?"

"I heard a rumor. It is nothing."

"Harald believes I've plotted with Magnus's men," I began.

He ignored me and glanced around the tent. "In the morning we sail north."

"I suppose my fate will be decided then."

He frowned at me. "They need to gain support for next year's campaign in Denmark. They will lay plans to carry the war-arrow through the Uplands, calling their nobles to war service as they travel. Then King Magnus will visit the shrine of Saint Olaf to pray for aid and to trim the hair and nails on his father's body. He does it every year. Collect your belongings and be ready to leave early."

"What about—?"

He was already gone.

A few minutes later, I heard scratching on the tent sides. The bottom of the tent raised, and Vandrad's head peered up from under it. The oil lamps deepened the shadows on his face.

I paced toward him. "I could happily step on you. King Harald has learned of your plans and blames me. I may be executed tomorrow."

Vandrad whispered, "Not if you join us."

"I did that earlier, and now I'm imprisoned."

"If you help us, all will be well. With Hardraada dead, you'll be free. Since King Magnus has already declared his friendship with Normandy, you'll have completed your mission."

"Oh? Magnus will consider negotiations with a poisoner binding? I think not. He won't trust me or any other Norman."

"You're mistaken. There was little love between King Magnus and Hardraada when they met, and their courtiers are quenching that."

I recalled the whisperings at the feast.

"I can assure you," he added, "that King Magnus will say nothing against you or Normandy. All you need to do is show us the mushroom. We'll do the rest."

I glared at him, fighting the impulse to squash him.

He was right, though. I either joined them or faced Hardraada's death-sentence at the court in Kaupang.

I silently cursed the whole situation, including Hardraada, Ulf, and Vandrad. I should have heeded the dream-warning from Saint Olaf. Instead, I was trapped.

"All right."

"Come. Ulf has drawn the guard away."

I found my monk's robe lying next to the armor and the two-pointed white cloak Hardraada had given me. I pulled my robe over my tunic and leggings and drew the hood over my head. I pushed my old knife into my belt. Hardraada was once again the owner of my new jeweled one.

I glanced through the tent door flap. In the growing darkness, no guard was visible. Indeed, no guards seemed to be anywhere around the tent, which seemed odd. All I could see were two of the ginger cats who seemed to be everywhere in the North.

I had no time to wonder what the absence of guards meant. Ulf crouched at the side of the tent and waved me toward him. Vandrad crept from behind the tent, motioning to me with equal urgency.

They both wore dark gray cloaks over black tunics. Without a word, they crept into the forest. I followed.

As soon as the trees shielded us, Ulf lit a torch under a soapstone jar. The light silhouetted their tunics and cloaks, and for the first time, I could see that they wore not only knives but also swords at their belts.

"Where is it?" Ulf hissed at me.

In the uneven light, I studied the trees, searching for the elms that would support the mushroom. As they crept behind me, Ulf and Vandrad slung cloths on branches to mark our path.

Not far into the forest I located an elm, its wrinkled bark unmistakable even in the darkness. I bent down. A few feet from my face were the deadly plants.

At that instant, though, I realized that I could not reveal them to Ulf or Vandrad or anyone. I did not trust them, nor could I play a part in a poisoning, even to save my life.

"No, these aren't the ones ..." I began.

"He's lying!" Vandrad cried out.

The torch Ulf carried hit the earth beside me. I twisted to see both of their swords raised high in the air.

At the same moment, a roar filled the forest. A black form leaped toward us, bellowing.

Ulf and Vandrad froze. The black form swatted their swords away.

"Bear!" they screamed and stumbled backward.

The bear slashed at them. Ulf spun and tripped over the tree's roots. Vandrad fell over him.

The bear leaped at them. Regaining their feet, they dashed toward the camp.

Pausing, the bear stiffened. And swung around toward me.

I tried to rise, but my weaker leg buckled under me. I snatched at the elm to pull myself up.

Before I reached a standing position, though, the bear seized me. One of its paws closed around my body, another around my mouth, holding me fast.

The paws were hands.

From deeper in the forest, I heard running. Then many hands pinned my arms and legs and forced a gag into my mouth.

I recognized the bitter taste. The cloth had been soaked in an infusion of mandrake root. Before long, I would be unconscious.

The hands lifted me into the air, face upward. The tops of the trees, darkly silhouetted against a darker sky, sped by. I was being borne into the forest away from the camp. Long minutes later, the trees gave way to star masses, and I heard water, waves splashing against a shore. My eyelids drooped.

I recognized footfalls on wood, and I was lifted higher then abruptly lower. My back came to rest on a hard surface. Had I been carried onto a longship?

The hands released me.

My head and body became heavy. I struggled to keep my eyes open. They closed. I forced them open again.

The bear's head appeared before me, and it turned into Onyame. His voice rumbled something, but I could not make out the words.

When I awoke, I was sprawled on a straw mat on the ground. My body still felt heavy. I rolled my head to examine my surroundings.

Behind me pine trees stretched into a cloud-filled sky. They mounted a steep hill, perhaps a mountain, until they disappeared from sight. On either side of me stretched a white sandy coast, dotted with black rocks.

I tried to raise myself, and my body responded, though sluggishly. I pushed myself into a sitting position. I saw, some distance out to sea, Onyame and three other men working on a longship anchored in the water. Black and white stripes decorated the ship, its white sail showing a black circle in the middle. Two black shields hung on either side of the ship. Standing in the ship's center were a horse, a goat, and my pony.

I felt disoriented. All around me were mountains, their sides as sharp as cliffs, plunging from cloudy heights into the sea. They slanted enough for the pines to cling to them perilously. Narrow beaches, like the one I lay on, edged the mountains.

This was not Denmark.

I gazed back at the longship. Onyame's head swung in my direction. He said something to the men and lowered himself into a dinghy. With a few strokes of its oars, he reached the shore.

Still dressed in black, he lumbered toward me, smiling.

I returned the smile, though mine must have been weaker than his. "You wouldn't be the bear who saved my life last night, would you?"

His laugh sounded like thunder in the mountains. "Yes. I thought I identified myself before you fell asleep. I apologize that I didn't explain my motives to you, but I couldn't allow you to be killed."

"I thought the bear intended to kill me."

"No, only carry you away quickly."

"And put me to sleep. I tasted the mandrake root. Thank you for saving me." I looked around. "Where am I, and why am I here?"

He spread his arms. "This is Norway, of course. We're a few miles south of Kaupang. The rest you'll have to explain to me."

Mead was warming over a fire nearby, and he knelt to pour a mug of it. He handed it to me.

As I sipped it, my stomach and head calmed. "What do you wish to have explained?"

He stretched his legs out and sat facing me. "I saw you twice in the forest with those two men. What were you doing?"

"So I did see a bear hidden among the trees."

"It's a useful disguise in a land where people can turn into bears."

I let the rising steam from the mug warm my face. "Well, since King Harald misunderstood those meetings, someone should know the truth." I looked up at him. "Those two men wanted me to show them a mushroom that would poison King Harald — to prevent his taking half of Norway from King Magnus. In the end, though, I couldn't."

He glanced at the sky and then back at me. "Yes, that's what I heard, but if I hadn't heard it myself, I wouldn't have believed you. I'd have thought you were plotting against King Magnus."

"King Magnus? Ulf and Vandrad want to kill Harald."

"Ulf and Vandrad? Who are they?"

"The two men, of course."

"Those men are not named Ulf and Vandrad, and they wouldn't kill their own lord."

"Their own lord? They're Magnus's men, and they intend to kill Harald."

He leaned back on his elbows. "Ah, I see. They told you they were in the service of King Magnus. That's how they convinced you to cooperate with them." He shook his head. "You've been deceived. Those two, by whatever names you know them, are King Harald Hardraada's men."

"Hardraada's? How can that be? Are you certain?"

"Didn't Earl Thorir ask you if you'd been meeting with King Harald's men?"

"I thought he'd been confused by the camp gossip about my plotting."

"There was no gossip. I overheard you talking with those two — what did you call them?"

"Ulf and Vandrad."

"I saw you with them in the forest and suspected a plot. I told Earl Thorir. When you denied the meeting, he wanted to let the matter rest. He said that a monk guided by God couldn't lie, but I knew you'd met with King Harald's men."

"Is this true? Didn't Hardraada raise the cry that he'd discovered a plot?"

"No. Why would he, when his own men were involved?"

"Ulf and Vandrad said —"

"Did you ever see Ulf and Vandrad, as you call them, talking with King Magnus? Did any of King Magnus's men ever recognize them?"

I tried to recall all of our meetings. As I replayed them in my mind, I groaned. "In fact, one of Harald's men bowed to them, while Magnus's men were hostile to them. And they never seemed to be around when Magnus and Harald were together."

"They deceived you, Brother Augustine."

I put my head in my hands. "I've been tricked. I should have seen the signs all around me. That's how Hardraada knew I was a healer. They told him. And they must have told him about the plot. Of course. When I first spotted you disguised as a bear, Vandrad left us. He claimed to be keeping the guard away, but he must have gone to Hardraada."

"Those two were going to kill you. That's why I attacked them as I did."

"They would have poisoned Magnus, blamed it on me, and then produced my body to show they had taken revenge for Magnus's death — in King Harald's name, of course."

Onyame nodded slowly. "Harald would then be sole King of Norway and have an excuse for raiding Normandy. In fact, if he could convince the Norwegian Assembly — even now — that you had plotted against either of the two Kings, they would give their blessing for an invasion of your home."

I shook my head. "I've been a fool. I thought Ulf and Vandrad were being stupid. I was the stupid one." I looked up at Onyame. "Is Magnus in danger?"

"I told Earl Thorir to have someone watch King Magnus's food in the event that my suspicions proved valid. King Magnus has been careful with eating anyway. He doesn't trust King Harald." He stirred the fire. "Did you give them the poison?"

"No, but they may have it. I located the plant then denied that it was the one. As you approached, they were accusing me of lying."

"That's unfortunate."

"I've failed miserably. Magnus, if he lives, will believe I was sent to kill him rather than win his friendship. Hardraada has agreed to nothing. And Normandy is in greater danger than when I left it."

"Is there an antidote to the poison?"

"I have one."

"Do King Harald's men know you have it?"

"I told Ulf and Vandrad that I do."

He ran his hand over his beard. "They wanted to kill you anyway. Knowing that you have an antidote gives them one more reason to want you dead. You're not safe here. Are you willing to go home, to return to Normandy? You could warn your Duke about the raids that may follow."

I hung my head. I would like nothing better than to return to quiet Falaise.

I would return in failure, though. And Normandy would face a new danger, one that I had brought on it.

"I can't go back. I must find a way to stop Hardraada. Or get to Magnus. I don't know how, but I can't let Hardraada use my stupidity as a weapon against my home."

Onyame nodded slowly. "I understand." He gazed at the men working on the ship. "Well, you can't challenge King Harald to single combat. Or build a fleet against him. You need a plan. And for that, you need refuge from the men you call Ulf and Vandrad."

"Won't they believe I'm dead? Killed by a bear?"

He turned his gaze back to me. "Many people know my bear disguise. They'll soon realize what's happened. There's no body, no bear tracks. And because their scheme can't work until you're dead, they'll come after you." He glanced at his ship again. "If I send someone back to warn King Magnus about poisoning, which I must, I'm one man short for a sea voyage." He looked at me. "I need five men to cross to the edge of the world."

That did not sound like a better prospect than facing Ulf and Vandrad. "I know nothing about sailing, especially to the edge of the world."

"Can you bail?"

"I don't see what sailing away will accomplish —"

"King Harald can't move against Normandy until the two plotters execute their scheme: killing you and King Magnus. If Earl Thorir protects King Magnus and I protect you, King Harald can do nothing. Except fight Danes. That gives us time to plan. And there's a person on my route who may aid us."

"I don't understand. What route? Where are we going?"

"First to Kaupang, the first trading town north of us. We must hurry, though. King Harald has probably sent a longship after you already, and we're only a day ahead of them." He pulled himself up, looking almost the height of the mountains, and held out a hand to help me rise. "The rest will become clear as we travel. With good fortune and the grace of the God who watches over you, I can take you to the only person I know who can defeat as mighty a warrior as Harald."

CHAPTER 14

A CHASE AROUND THE WORLD

A.D. 1046

Because the wind was strong and in our favor, we sped toward Kaupang. Rowing contributed little to our progress. Though the ship had four oarholes, only one of the crewmen, named Vagn, and I were free. The other two worked the sails, while Onyame stood at the tiller.

Vagn and I pulled oars on either side of the ship, but rowing was not among my talents. Vagn wanted to abandon the effort, but I insisted that we use every device to press closer to Kaupang.

By late afternoon, though, we heard Onyame's voice, booming over the rush of the wind and water, "Vagn! Brother Augustine! You can rest now. Look!"

In the distance a town lay behind a flat, sheltered harbor, surrounded by groves of trees. Kaupang. In the Northern tongue, the name meant "marketplace," so I anticipated a village such as Hedeby.

I was right. Men loaded ships at two wharves, beyond which lay wooden houses and shops, decorated with painted strips of carved wood. Unlike Hedeby, though, Kaupang was not surrounded by palisade-walls. I could see colorfully clad townspeople calling to each other and striding from the wharves to the village and back again.

As our ship drew near, a crowd grew at the wharf, adding to the mass of workers near the ships. Over their heads, sea gulls cried, echoing the shouts of the townspeople.

"They're expecting news about the King," Onyame called to me. "I don't see the nobles yet. Runners must be summoning them."

Our ship bumped against the pier, and at that moment, we spotted about thirty nobles and knights spurring horses along the road that led to the harbor. Children and dogs ran alongside, greeting the riders. The nobles, though, gazed straight ahead, lifting their heads even higher into the air.

Like the Danish nobles, the Norwegian ones wore brightly colored clothes, their tunics and leggings displaying multi-hued designs. Their ankle-laced goatskin or calfskin shoes — I could not tell which — had been dyed, and gems seemed to sparkle in them. Fur-lined robes sailed out behind the nobles: purple, blue, white, and scarlet, laced with silver. Some robes had shoulder-braids sewn with gold thread that glinted in the late-day sun.

Huge-pommeled swords in carved scabbards inlaid with jewels hung from the warriors' waists. Axes were slung over their shoulders or thrust in their belts, while spears protruded from their saddles. Over stern faces, their hair flowed from patterned headbands. Their mustaches and beards were as neatly trimmed as the Danes, and many wore the eye make-up I had seen in Denmark.

As they rode, a shrill rattle rose from their horses' manes. I spied a metal-and-wood grate attached to the horses' collar-harnesses. The chilling sound it produced was intended either to terrify opponents in battle or to annoy visitors from Normandy.

The nobles reined in not far from the ship, and the infernal rattling stopped, replaced by the snorting of the horses. Each noble sat proudly in his wooden saddle, his legs jutting forward, showing copper-inlaid, iron stirrups and silver-decorated spurs. The leather reins, passing through the bronze collar-harnesses, had geometric designs pressed into them, some etched in gold.

King Magnus may have lacked the goods to fight another war, but his nobles showed no signs of poverty.

Onyame and his men tied the longship's ropes to the bollards and stepped onto the pier.

The nobles dismounted, and Onyame strode forward to confer with them. I remained behind, pretending to work on the ship, so that no one would recognize me as a foreigner.

My monk's robe was gone, too identified with me to be a good disguise, Onyame had said. As a result, I was left with the blue tunic, white leggings, leather belt, and shoes that had been my gifts from Hardraada. Around my neck hung the gold cross on its gold chain.

I must have appeared almost as wealthy as the nobles. Gazing at their robes, though, I lamented having left my pointed warrior-cloak in Denmark.

Taking a break from my pretended tasks, I straightened to stretch my back and to study Kaupang. It bore the painted signs that indicated a market town. Here, though, were far more banners than I had ever seen. I deduced from their symbols — shields, swords, axes, and the like — that they represented not Kaupang's merchants but its warrior families. The nobles participated in more than fighting.

The decorated planks on the sides of the houses were carved like the planks of the better longships I had seen. The graceful, twisting patterns made the wood seem alive, and I hoped to get closer to see what creatures were represented.

Having finished his conference, Onyame returned to the ship.

He followed my gaze. "How do you like Kaupang?"

"It's charming."

He nodded. "I've spent much of my time here, when I'm in Norway, that is."

"It seems to be a wealthier town than where I was raised."

"It's near the Westfold, where the nobles live. The town supplies them with luxuries, which in turn makes the town rich. Wealthier than Hedeby certainly. The Kaupang merchants trade with Hedeby, though in convoys to discourage the pirates that frequent eastern Jutland." He lifted me onto the pier as if I were a barrel of wine and motioned me to follow him. "Come, I'll show you the town. I've told the nobles of the arrival of the Kings, and we've been invited to a meal. We're a full day ahead of any pursuers, I'm certain, and we can leave early tomorrow morning." He turned to face me. "Please, though, Brother Augustine, let me do the talking."

I scowled at him. "My Northern speech has served me well up to now."

He looked surprised. "Has it?"

As we strolled through Kaupang's market, I slowly regained my land legs. At first, the ground seemed to pitch like the sea. We had seen most of Kaupang by the time the land felt normal again.

In spite of the evidence of my legs, Kaupang stood fairly still, like most of the larger market towns I had seen — Rouen, Arras, and Hedeby. I spotted the familiar local goods: cows, goats, chickens, iron pots, wooden benches, cloth, tunics, shoes, and food of all kinds.

Here, of course, the edibles included seal and whale meat. Among the imported goods, I recognized Rhenish pottery and Frankish glassware. The ornaments from England and Ireland reminded me that the Norwegians had colonies there.

The merchants mostly bartered, but they also used Arab and Byzantine money. I spotted coins from Mercia and London as well, some with Edward's head on them, though the head bore no resemblance to Edward himself, only a crown to suggest that he was King of England.

Like Hedeby, Kaupang was full of craftsmen. I especially noticed weavers, metalworkers, and, as Garrad had predicted, soapstone dish-makers.

We strolled by several warehouses full of white bundles.

"Norway," I said to Onyame, "must have massive numbers of ducks and geese. I've never seen so much down."

"Actually, no," he said, his voice rising. "We have only one duck, about two leagues high and twice that wide." He laughed at his own jest.

As we continued our walk, I spotted horseshoes hanging over many doorways for good luck, something I had seen in Hedeby but barely noticed, since the same feature was common in Western Normandy, where the old religion still lingered. I was surprised to find them here, though, in a country so famous for its Christian Saint-King, Olaf. Perhaps the Church had less impact here than it had in southern lands.

The clothing of the local people caught my attention. Unlike Hedeby, where most townspeople looked like nobles, here the wealthy dressed in high style, while the common people wore shaggy wool. Though scarlet, yellow, and green shades appeared everywhere, I noticed more undyed cloth being worn than I had seen in Hedeby — not on many people, but it was noticeable.

"Those people with the plain clothes —"

"Slaves," Onyame said, his voice dropping its mischievous tone. "They can't wear colors until they work themselves out of slavery."

"There seem to be only a few, though."

"Yes. We have so many people to do the work that we need fewer slaves than in previous years. The bishops, of course, would like to abolish slavery, but the nobles want slaves. More for status than function, I think." He smiled at me. "Nobles can't help being that way. They're reared badly."

That evening, we dined with one of the badly reared nobles, who turned out to be remarkably polite. I feasted as I never had before, which calmed lingering fears I had about pursuers.

Arranged around a rectangular wooden table, we sat in a huge hall with carved pillars arrayed on either side of us in long rows. Behind the hall's fireplace-end were two small rooms, serving a larger kitchen beyond them. From this end emerged dishes full of food. Many dishes.

At the opposite end, to which I paid less and less attention, a carved wooden divider hid what I supposed were the bedchambers of the lord and lady. From the longer walls protruded the benches where children, guests, and servants would sleep, as they did in the noble homes in Normandy.

Just above and behind our heads were narrow embroideries, thin tapestries suspended either from beams or the wall. I guessed that the ones opposite me related events from the family in whose house we dined.

The embroideries reminded me of the wall-hangings in Norman halls and churches. These Northern ones, though, displayed simple panels with large enough designs that everyone could see them.

And they were ideally situated. If they had hung lower, the heads of the diners would have blocked them. If they had hung higher, they would have been lost in smoke. As it was, their messages would be visible to every diner at every meal. Because of the longer northern summer days, light still streamed through the door and smoke holes, allowing the patterns to be seen clearly.

Interrupting my musings, one of the diners rose and began to speak. Though the wine had made my head fuzzy, I understood his speech and recognized his accent as Icelandic. He was delivering a lay, so I realized that he must be a trained skaldic poet, similar to the ones I had heard in Magnus's camp.

The lay concerned Odin, the All-Father, the High God of the old religion. Odin had heard that a King of earth had become so parsimonious that he would kill his guests if he thought he had too many.

In the North, I knew, calling anyone inhospitable is a great slander, so Odin determined to visit the King to discover the truth.

Disguised in a blue cloak — "Odin always disguises himself in a blue cloak that can turn gray," Onyame whispered to me — Odin visited the King's hall, but he revealed nothing about himself, even when questioned. This angered the King, who was as cruel as he was parsimonious. To force his guest to speak, the King had Odin bound between two fires for eight nights.

The King's son Agnar, a generous youth, visited Odin and gave him a horn from which to drink. The poet recited Odin's words:

> *You are fierce, fire, too fierce for comfort,*
> *Recede from me, savage flame:*
> *My cloak is beginning to catch fire,*
> *Its fur is singed and smolders.*
> *Hail, Agnar! The Highest One*
> *Bids you a grateful greeting:*
> *For one drink your reward shall be*
> *Greater than any man has got.*

From the wisdom he had gained by hanging on the Tree of Life and surrendering one of his own eyes, Odin named all the many worlds for young Agnar, including his own names:

> *I am now Odin, I was Ygg before,*
> *Thud my name before that,*
> *Wakeful and Heavens-Roar, Hanged and Skilfing,*
> *Goth and Jalk among gods,*
> *Unraveler, Sleep-bringer: they are really one:*
> *Many names for me.*

The evil King, though, paid the price for not seeing God in the changing forms of men, the poet said: he stumbled on his own sword.

Odin vanished, and Agnar, the good son, ruled for many years.

Sitting not far from me was a priest who leaned toward Onyame and slurred a pronouncement, "The old gods are dead, dead, though. Odin, too."

Apparently, he had drunk more wine than his profession prepared him for, though that would have been a considerable amount.

"Do you know," he continued, "that Saint Olaf once destroyed an altar to Thor? He smashed it, smashed it to the heavens. All the snakes and toads and rats who'd been living on the offerings — demons in disguise — fled!"

I was glad I had finished eating before learning about that particular Christian triumph.

After more story-telling, singing, poetry, and toasting, we returned to the ship to spend the night on our uncomfortable straw mats. I wondered out loud whether we should borrow some of Kaupang's down for our beds and pillows.

Onyame commented that the hard bed should have penance-value for a monk.

"I have no sins as severe as this," I said and fell asleep.

The next morning, I awoke to both a sore back from the penance-bed and aching shoulders. I recalled my poor attempts at rowing. At least my arms thought I had done work.

I squinted through the sunlight at the longship's interior. The other benches were empty. I had slept longer than my companions. I splashed water onto my face and scrambled over tent frames and dinghies that must have been loaded onto the ship before I awoke.

I overheard Onyame on the pier and glanced up to see him negotiating with a merchant.

"... three families," Onyame was saying. "I can carry no more than that. I want to return with more lumber than usual."

"We do need more oak," the merchant said, "but this family has paid a high fee, and they wish to go only as far as the Faeroe Islands. They don't even wish to return, at least not within the next few years."

"All right. I'll take them."

The merchant nodded. "Now I must be going. I shouldn't be seen doing business on the Sabbath. I did load your ships exactly as you requested, my friend."

"Thank you. I appreciate your helping me today. We must leave immediately, or I wouldn't have asked."

They were discussing two other longships anchored nearby, jammed with barrels, skins, boxes, a wooden bed, and tent frames, surrounding several horses, goats, dogs, and a group of people.

I approached Onyame. "Good morning. I'm sorry I slept so long."

He grinned at me. "Thorir told me that the sleep of angels seizes you at night, and even the long days of sunlight don't keep you awake. I had work to do, anyway, before we could sail."

"Are we taking all these goods and people somewhere?"

"Yes. The Shetland Islands, the Faeroe Islands, Iceland, Greenland, and ultimately Vineland, where we'll stay until spring. I don't enjoy winters in Kaupang, seldom seeing daylight."

"Is that where we're going? Vineland?"

"Yes. It has more trees than anywhere in the North, more than I've ever seen, except in Africa. Every summer, I deliver goods to the islands and then collect Vineland wood to bring back here for ships and houses. Greenland has no wood at all, and Iceland and the islands very little. I can even find the kinds of oak and ash that are becoming scarce here in Norway."

"We'll be collecting wood all winter?"

"We'll have help, but yes."

As I had begun to fear, I would not return to Normandy by autumn. I wondered whether the rumor of my being killed by a bear would reach William. Or Anette.

"Look." Onyame pointed behind me.

For a moment, I feared a pursuing ship from Denmark. I twisted to see two boat-processions sailing in a stately fashion from the west. Dozens of longships, striped in green, brown, yellow, and orange, glided toward Kaupang, bearing colorfully dressed men, women, and children.

"They're coming for the Sunday services."

"A beautiful sight," I said, relieved.

"Especially for a monk, I'm sure."

I turned back toward him. "Yes. In Rouen, the people will be walking in crowds to the castle church."

He put a huge hand on my shoulder. "I'm sorry you won't see Normandy before next summer. We need to stay ahead of your pursuers, though. Hardraada and his men do not give up easily."

I decided not to sound homesick. "It's my own fault. How long will it take us to get to Vineland?"

"We'll be there within a month. Unless there are storms, or you bail too slowly. Then it may take a week more."

Though the trip to Kaupang had been beautiful, sailing around the coast was even more so, and the scenery took my mind off Normandy, Hardraada, Ulf, and Vandrad. Fjords plunged into the landscape, while forested mountains rose into snowcaps. Onyame pointed out carved cliffs along the route — massive men and animals painted hundreds of years before the memory of any Norwegian.

At intervals waterfalls escaped from the gray mountain rock and poured themselves elegantly into the ocean below. Sea birds flew across the face of the mountains, while whales and dolphins occasionally broke though the ocean's surface.

Rounding the western tip of Norway, we headed north. The winds had carried us from Kaupang toward Bergen on the west coast. Just south of Bergen at Hernar, one of the places King Olaf had held councils, we struck out to sea.

Toward the Shetland Islands.

Fortunately, the waves washed by us harmlessly, so on the first day, I did little bailing. Despite short sessions with the bucket, though, my muscles felt strained, and I feared the soreness to come, which, if I had kept my healing pouch, I could have prevented.

As we lost sight of land — the wind was brisk — I found myself staring at the sea as it stretched from blue to green in the distance. I thought I spied something on the horizon, but I could not be certain. I felt anxious, recalling that I could neither swim well nor far.

Late that night, I leaned over the side of the ship and watched the water's rippling. The night remained light — there was almost no darkness now — but enough of dusk settled around the ship that the water was dark.

All that separated me from this black depth were thin pieces of wood.

Behind me, Onyame leaned against the after-stem of the ship, holding the tiller, which was carved in the shape of a wolf's head below the grip. He stood like a rock silhouetted against the sky. I imagined that the following ships navigated by his form.

I climbed onto the deck not far from him.

"The sea's too rhythmic for bailing," he said, his voice sounding like the depths of the ocean itself.

"Yes, as my arms are pleased to discover."

I sat down against the ship's side planks. Dropping my head back to stare at the sky, I breathed deeply. Since Onyame and his crew did not smear themselves with the stinking oil that Hardraada's men used, I could smell the animals and the salt air.

I remained silent, thinking for a few moments and then said, "Onyame, should I have faced Hardraada? Was leaving the right choice?"

He did not answer for a long time. "I don't think you had a choice. Do you?"

"I'm not sure. Running is scarcely a maneuver that a warrior will respect, though. I'll have to face him sooner or later, and he's likely to think me a coward."

"King Harald knows the value of a strategic withdrawal. Like all good warriors, he never goes into battle without knowing where his retreat corridor lies."

"I'm a bad warrior then. Without you, I'd have had no retreat corridor."

"God protects you and supplied me."

I nodded. "I'm grateful to both of you." The sea darkened around us. "Where does this corridor lead, anyway? What did you say about the edge of the world?"

He smiled. "We'll be there soon enough. Are you eager to see it?"

"Well, no. I'm accustomed to lake and river crossings. Going over the edge of the world sounds harrowing."

He looked me up and down. "I think you're tall enough to survive the passage."

"Tall enough?"

"Yes, tall enough."

He wouldn't say anymore, and from his look, I suspected that I may be the object of a jest.

So I returned to my bench, spread my straw mat, and fell into an uneasy sleep.

The next morning I awoke later than everyone else again. The sea and sky reflected each other in a calm blue, and the ship rocked less than most carts I had traveled in. Our speed seemed slower but steady.

Onyame stood at the wolf's-head tiller, looking relaxed.

"Good morning, Brother Augustine!" he called to me as I crawled up on his deck. "Why don't you rest on the bench next to me until we need you as a bailer?"

I thanked him. "Have you been here all night?"

"No. Thorkel and Sigvald took their turns. I've had some sleep. Not as much as you've had, though."

I glanced behind him. "Have you seen anyone pursuing us?"

"Not yet, but it will take them a day or so to catch us."

I stared toward the ship's forestem. In the distance, wedges of land rose from the water's surface.

"The Shetland Islands," Onyame said. "The ones to the north are the three largest."

"The Faeroe Islands lie beyond that?"

"Yes, you'll be able to see them from the largest Shetland isle if the day is clear. It's easy sailing, unless we run into a storm. There shouldn't be many this time of year, though. Even near Greenland."

"Vineland? Is it easy sailing as well?"

He shrugged. "It's not difficult."

I wanted to know more about the edge of the world, but I hesitated to say so. "How will we get there?"

He smiled. "We'll sail. In the ship."

"I mean, how will you navigate?"

"Very easily. The course we're taking allows each next landfall to be in sight. Or nearly so. If the day is cloudy, we can follow the swimming patterns of whales or the flightlines of birds."

"What about at night?"

"The same as on land. The Pole Star makes navigation especially easy, though there's not much night left now, as you'd have noticed if you'd been awake."

"What about storms? Could we be driven off course? Could we sail off the edge by mistake?"

"Hmm. That's a good question."

I could see that he was struggling to look serious, but the end of the world was no light matter to me.

His face drew into mock-concern. "If we're driven into the frozen North, we could resort to the tables made in Iceland. I do have those. Perhaps I should take them out, in preparation."

"Tables? What tables?"

"Well, because Iceland is so close to the edge of the world, the Icelanders have constructed sophisticated tables that give the sun's midday height for every week through the year, as observed in northern Iceland, of course. So, if we happen to be blown too close to the edge, I can hold up a stick like this" — he held up his knife at arm's length — "marking the half-width of the sun, and then use that to measure the sun's height. The table will then tell me on what line of sail I happen to be."

I heard Vagn's voice behind me.

"I also have a bearing-dial that operates the same way," Onyame was saying. "Ah, you're needed for bailing."

It was late evening when I returned, exhausted, to Onyame's deck. This time I lay flat on the warm boards, breathing heavily.

He gazed down at me. "Your bailing is improving."

"Thank you," I said, panting. "I've been thinking while I bailed."

"A good strategy. Keeps the mind off tired arms."

"What happens if there's no sun, and we're lost in a storm —"

His laugh cut me off. "Can't you think about anything else?" He pointed. "Have you looked at the sky recently? Have you seen that before?"

I rolled over and raised myself on my elbow so that I could peer over the loading side of the ship. I drew in a sharp breath.

Swirling up from the horizon into the sky were massive swaths of white, blue, and green clouds, looking like unearthly smoke. Some shifted to a violet hue and then back to blue and green, rippling across the sky.

"They've been building for some time now," Onyame said.

I pulled myself into a sitting position. "What are they?"

"The Great Lights."

"What causes them?"

"The Gods who live inside the earth, I've been told."

I continued to gape. "How often does this happen?"

"Fairly often. I've never made a trip north that I didn't see them at least once."

As he spoke, the green and blue bands curled slowly and blended into each other. A scarlet band, like a huge wall-hanging, surged up from beneath them. In a few moments, the entire sky was deep red.

"How do you like that?" he asked.

"I'm not sure I do. It's beautiful. But it looks like blood."

"It looks like a sunset."

"Perhaps it's a bad omen."

He sighed. "Then say a prayer. A silent one, please."

Within a few days, we reached the southern tip of the largest of the Shetland Islands. We were escorted all the way into land by flocks of sea gulls. In front of us, a town of six longhouses and three large barns perched on a rocky beach. Behind them, the cliffs seemed intent on pushing the town into the sea.

No wharf existed, so we soaked our feet dragging the ships onto the beach where rocky fingers did not prohibit a landing. The bay was flat, though, so our task was easy, and the passengers helped.

My muscles had grown accustomed to ship work — bailing, rowing, and lifting. So pulling the ship seemed less demanding than I would have thought. The Northern longships were, as the builder had said back in Denmark, as light as they were sleek.

I noticed some boathouses nearby, but Onyame told us to leave the ships on the beach for the night. The boathouses, I guessed, were for storing vessels in bad weather.

The town's houses, looking like grassy barrows, were in fact wooden frames covered with turf. Like the farmhouses that sprawled along the island's coast, they were surrounded by bathhouses, smithies, outhouses, and tool sheds.

The townspeople ran to meet us, shouting and clapping. As they greeted us, I noted that they dressed more plainly than the Kaupang Norwegians. Nonetheless, the men milling around me wore colorfully dyed headbands and belts. Geometric designs edged their tunics.

The women's scarves and aprons had green and blue patterns. Their cloaks and shawls were pinned with bronze or gilded brooches at each shoulder, decorated with the same writhing patterns I had seen in Hedeby and Kaupang. The scarves and headbands did hard duty, since the ocean winds constantly disheveled everyone's hair.

While the women's dresses blew around their legs, requiring some holding down, the younger girls solved the wind problem with short, tight woolen skirts, under which ran long leggings down to a high boot. I had not noticed this style of dress before, and I found it attractive.

One of the girls with particularly shapely legs smiled at me. I thought that I should behave in a monklike fashion, until I recalled that I no longer wore monk's robes and my tonsure had grown over. So I smiled back politely.

Onyame spotted my smile and stepped aside to ask whether I was renouncing my vows.

"If I lived in a village full of such young women," I said in a tone to match his, "I'm afraid I'd have to."

The townspeople had the same friendly greetings for the families who had arrived with us. They were openly pleased as Onyame and his men unpacked the goods they had ordered the previous summer.

Their broad, open faces wore equally broad smiles, and I could see that no haggling went on in the islands. Everyone was delighted with every new bolt of cloth, pair of shoes, cask of wine, or box of soapstone dishes, regardless of color or condition.

Onyame could write, I noticed, and busily scratched new orders on pieces of leather. Vagn delivered the letters we had brought and received others to take on to the Faeroes, Iceland, and Greenland.

We spent the night as guests in one of the cozy turf houses, and I felt safe. As I slept on a well-cushioned bench, I dreamed about a young woman in a short woolen skirt, graceful leggings, and high boots.

We spent one more day depositing goods and people in tiny towns set only a short distance back from the fjords. Then we sailed for the Faeroe Islands.

The sea cooperated by remaining so still that I was relieved of bailing altogether. Assured that we were still ahead of any pursuers, I used the opportunity to practice hnefatafl with Sigvald and Vagn and to talk with Onyame.

"Have you ever sailed back to Africa?"

He shook his head slowly, still staring at the sea.

"Do you ever wish to? To see your home?"

"Often."

This surprised me. "Why don't you return? Thorir said you're free."

"It's not exactly what you think. You see, I have visions of home, of the African forests. When I was a boy, I used to lie on my back in the tops of the trees and stare at the sky. It may sound strange to you, but the sky would speak to me." He gave me a sidelong glance. "It was probably a Christian saint speaking of course, but my people called the sky by the name of God, Onyame. I thought Onyame spoke to me, which is how I was named."

"Was it common to give children the name of God?"

"Very uncommon. I'd heard something from the sky, though, and the people believed I was special. Those visions — not quite visions, more like forgotten conversations — are what I remember of Africa. If I returned, it would be to try to hear them again. I'm sure I couldn't, though."

"Do you have visions now?"

"I ... had some training years ago — but no, not very often." He raised his eyebrows at me. "I suppose that seems odd to a monk with whom God speaks on even small matters."

"No, not odd at all."

Within a few days, we sailed into an inlet of one of the larger Faeroe Islands. Here the turf houses blended into the steep, grassy hills behind them. The farms scattered along the coast were almost invisible from a distance.

I could discern people running, though, and herds of sheep clinging to the slopes.

The wind died down for a moment, a rare occurrence, and I could make my voice heard at the back of the ship. "Faeroe," I called to Onyame, seeing a chance to stop bailing. "It means 'sheep', doesn't it?"

"Yes."

I could have guessed the reason, but I asked, "Why?"

He laughed. "All right, you may rest."

I gratefully dropped the bucket, which now weighed as much as the world itself, and dragged myself to the bench beside the wolf's-head tiller.

"Don't you see any sheep on the hills?" he asked.

I pretended to peer at the island. "Are there sheep?"

"It's a shame your eyesight is deteriorating. I intended to let you take the watch and have Vagn bail, but apparently your eyes are not up to the task."

I glanced at him and then at the island again. "Oh, yes, I see sheep everywhere. On the hills, near the houses. They're swimming in the ocean, and a few have taken up ship-building. Now, why is this place called the Sheep Islands?"

He smiled. "The younger sons of the Norwegian nobles, those who weren't raiding the Shetlands or the Orkneys, first came here for pastureland. For their sheep. Of course, they fished here, too. And still do. A few weeks from now they'll have their most important fishing event. They trap whales in the fjords. With nets. Then they have enough whale meat to last all winter. It's bloody, though."

Blood not being my favorite subject, I guided the conversation elsewhere. "The sheep must be willing to climb to eat. The mountains here are steep."

"Very steep."

I stared at the sheep in the distance. "Willing to walk for a meal. I can appreciate that."

As we unloaded the goods for the farmers and shepherds living along the narrow coast in front of the mountains, the last of the four families we had brought with us scurried to shore. Their friends and relatives raced down to greet them noisily. Onyame took more orders and letters.

The crew and I were fed in one of the turf houses by a man who seemed to be the town's leader. Onyame, though, did not join us.

After the meal, I found him near his ship.

"Ah, here you are," he said. "I want to show you something. Do you mind a little climb?" He pointed at a steep slope, the top of which represented more than a little climb.

"If you're going up to graze, I just ate."

He was already several paces away, though, and my words drowned in the wind. I hurried to follow him, but his legs quickly outdistanced mine. I noted how little I had walked on the ship and how much my legs complained, especially the weaker one.

Finally I caught up with him as he rested on a flat stone. He was studying the sea. I panted, but the wind seemed to drive the breath out of me. I struggled for air.

"There," he said, "do you see?"

I followed his hand and spotted a longship in the distance.

I pushed my hair into my headband and turned to him. "A pirate ship? You mentioned pirates in Kaupang. Perhaps they saw your goods."

He gave me a frowning glance. "Don't you recognize those colors?"

I squinted at the ship's sides. They were striped in yellow, brown, and blue. I sighed. "Yes, they look familiar."

"Those are the colors of King Harald's longship, the one he brought back from Constantinople. He'll be in Norway, wooing the nobles, so he's not likely to be on board. That means it's been turned over to his men. I think we can guess to whom and for what purpose."

I nodded. "I'm afraid I can." Then I noticed a mass of dark clouds in the distance. "What's that?"

"A storm. We're pursued by more than King Harald's men." He gazed down at our ships. "We should leave as soon as we're unloaded."

"Are we safe with a storm approaching?"

"With Harald's ship that close, we're not safe if we stay. I've found the sea to be less terrible than warriors."

Before long, we had pulled the ships back into the water and headed for the open sea and Iceland.

We slipped around the most northerly of the Faeroes without seeing the yellow, brown, and blue ship behind us. With every screech of a gull, though, I glanced backward, expecting to see a warrior shrieking for my death.

Onyame, steering while talking with Vagn, noticed my nervousness. "Rowing, Brother Augustine, will keep your mind off your pursuers and help us outdistance the storm."

I saw Vagn grimace as I replied, "That's a good idea."

I seized my oar, while Vagn lowered himself reluctantly onto his seat and seized the opposite oar. "Please ask God to give you both strength and consistency."

I assured him that I would.

Not far from land, though, the storm caught us. Within minutes, the sky was swallowed by a gray mist, at the center of which rode black clouds. The wind, always high, now drove at us from several directions, and Onyame shouted orders that I barely heard.

The crew and I collapsed the sail, dragged in the oars, and closed the oarholes with the round, swiveling shutters the master shipbuilder had showed me in Denmark. Vagn, Thorkel, and Sigvald hauled in their own colored shields, along with Onyame's two black ones, to store with the barrels. We tightened the lashings around the supplies.

Rain began to fall, first lightly then more heavily.

From the ships behind us, I heard the cries of the animals and saw the crewmen bind them. My pony complained even more loudly than the goats.

The waves at first chopped irregularly, slapping against the ship's sides, but the prow cut through them easily. Then the waves began to grow.

Onyame lashed himself to the steersman's position and swung the prow diagonally, allowing the ship to glide over the waves' crests. I clung to the side at first, feeling queasy. I was not permitted to be sick, though. Water splashed onto my face, and Vagn shouted at me to bail. He had already seized a bucket himself.

I wedged my legs between the mast and some boxes and grabbed my bucket.

As I bailed, I could see Onyame pull the tiller up and down along the block of wood that fastened it to the side of the ship. The wolf's head rose and fell with the water.

Two massive waves drove at us in quick succession.

Onyame leaned against the tiller, twisting us out of the way. At each crest, using the leather strap and a rope attached to the bottom of the rudder, Onyame lifted the rudder clear of the water, so that we eased over both waves.

I shifted with rolling of the ship to keep my balance. At the second wave, I fell against Vagn. He pushed me back into place, lashed my waist and hips to the mast, and resumed bailing.

One wave arched over us before Onyame could avoid it. It hit with such force that most of the water pounded along the inner arc of the longship and washed out. As it passed, the crewmen and I grabbed the mast. The water drove at us, and our hands were wrenched away from the slick wood. Our lashings held. I felt the straps cut into my waist and hips.

Then we bailed again, hurling black water back into a blacker sea.

My eye caught the other two ships, pitching with the waves. The misty forms of the men on them, barely visible, contorted in the act of bailing, too.

The animals, almost ghosts, jerked against the ropes and leather straps that bound them to the ship. With the ocean roaring in my ears, I could no longer hear their cries. Then the rain became a blowing downpour. Ships, men, and animals vanished behind a wall of water.

As the rain drenched us, we bailed even faster, and I felt my feet and legs ache as I twisted to hurl water into the sea. My hips felt bruised, and my arms leaden. But I bailed.

After what seemed hours, the waves began to diminish, though the rain continued.

Vagn signaled me to rest. I sank against the mast. Before long, Thorkel, Sigvald, and Vagn stopped bailing and dropped onto the ship's deck. In front of us, a shaft of light, seeming like an arm of God, brightened the sea. Sea birds circled inside it.

The rain stopped. The ships reappeared behind us, the men waving and the animals trumpeting our successful passage.

When we reached the sunny patch, Thorkel and Sigvald lifted the floorboards of the deck. With the little remaining strength in my arms, I helped Vagn bail the water that had been trapped under them. Then, Thorkel and Sigvald raised the sail again.

I crawled up on the rear deck and lay near Onyame as he unbound himself.

He looked down at me. "Your first storm."

My arms, shoulders, hips, and waist felt as if I had fallen down stone steps. I was certain every muscle in my body would ache for a month, and that I would have cuts and bruises everywhere.

Nonetheless, I tried to sound courageous. "It wasn't as bad as I thought it might be."

"No," he said, more coolly than I would have wished, "we were never in any danger." He glanced at me. "Except from exhaustion."

"Yes," I said, breathing heavily, "my arms have been ruined. I'll never bail again."

He smiled. "This is a fine ship. We had it better than our comrades." He nodded toward the other longships.

"What do you mean? How could it have been worse?"

"We maneuvered better. They took in more water and had more bailing to do. You see, when this ship was being planned, I asked the builder to move the rudder farther back, closer to the stern. I also asked him to broaden the rudder's end. As a result, we responded to the waves more quickly than the other two ships could. All in all, though, the storm dealt us only a glancing blow, and we came through it easily."

I nodded and mumbled, "Yes, easily," and fell asleep.

What may have been hours later, Onyame's voice awakened me. "Brother Augustine, look."

I barely had the strength in my arms to raise myself. As I did, the wind struck my back, which was still damp.

I spotted a sprawling land mass in the distance. "Is that Iceland?"

"Yes. I've checked the tables and bearing-dial just for you. That land is, in fact, Iceland. You may also be pleased to learn that King Harald's ship is nowhere to be seen."

I swung my head around. "Has the storm driven it away?"

"No, I suspect that my asking a few of the Faeroes' residents to detain it accounts for its absence. We'll have our day's lead back now, I think."

After another night's sleep, I awoke to the calls of gulls. Peering into the distance, I spied a gray and green coastline, illumined by the morning sun.

I pulled myself from my bed and rubbed some salve that Vagn had given me onto the bruises and burns that now appeared on my hips and legs. Then I joined Onyame in the stern. He greeted me cheerfully.

"The land looks friendly enough," I said.

"It is."

"The name makes it sound bleak, though."

"It is bleak in places, but it wasn't named for that. As poets tell the tale, the island was named by the explorer Floki. He saw ice floating everywhere, and when he sailed north just one day, he found a frozen sea. So he called it the Land of Ice. Iceland itself, though, is pleasant enough. A little barren here and there, since the settlers have cut trees for building. And strange lava rocks crop up everywhere. It's nothing like Greenland, however, that great rock. And we'll see the sun all day and all night."

The first inlet we pulled into resembled many we had seen before, except for the occasional ice floes and the black sand. Inland, the turfed farmhouses were joined to the outer buildings, creating one sprawling house, like a monastery complex. These many-winged homes nestled in the ocean-end of a tree-lined river valley. The valley stretched away from us to the north, its floor broken with black lava rocks covered by moss. On its western side green hills gave way to ice-peaked mountains.

While the crew unloaded the few boxes marked for the shepherds and farmers, I gingerly placed my aching body against a black rock and slid down into a sitting position. Onyame and a teen-aged boy, the son of one of the local shepherds, joined me.

"This is a local boy who enjoys talking to any traveler," Onyame said after he introduced us. Apparently to protect my identity, he told the boy that my name was Brother Ambrose.

"I like to get all the news of the South that I can, Brother Ambrose," the boy said.

Following Onyame's lead, I answered his many questions without giving away my Norman identity.

In turn I asked him about his life in Iceland. He boasted of his family's fishing prowess and their sheep. He loved the river, he told me, gesturing toward it, and intended to move farther inland when he was older.

"My brothers have already moved into the valley farther north. They fish the river. Salmon and trout. They've built strong turf houses on fine stone bases. It's the kind of house I'm going to have when I'm older."

As he spoke, I let my head rest against the rock and took a deep breath. I stared up the river.

"Near their homestead is a great fire-mountain," the boy was saying, "always steaming and bubbling ..."

Suddenly he faded. The dragon appeared and lifted me beyond the inlet and up the valley to the fire-mountain. Just as the boy described, turf houses on rock foundations huddled at the fire-mountain's foot not far from the river.

In my vision, though, the mountain did more than steam and bubble. As I watched, it exploded in a shaft of fiery steam, spewing ash all over the valley. A river of molten rock scarred its face.

The boy himself, older, screamed and herded sheep away from the red-hot showers. In vain.

The dragon hissed, "Warn them."

I jerked back to the present.

The boy broke off his description. "Are you all right, Brother Ambrose?"

"The mountain will explode," I said, without thinking. "Sometime in the future. I don't know when. You and your brothers and your families and flocks will be killed. So will your friends. All of you. All who live in that valley."

The boy jumped up, staring at me, and backed away.

Onyame leaned toward me. "Brother Ambrose?"

"Onyame, this valley, the entire settlement along it, will be wiped out. The people must be warned." I turned to the boy. "Do you understand? You must warn your brothers and their friends. They must leave the valley."

The boy glanced at Onyame. "Is he mad?"

"Brother Ambrose is guided by God. He's a Southerner, but he's not mad."

"I'm telling you the truth," I said. "I've had a vision. Just now. I often have visions, some about the future. I've seen the destruction of this valley."

The boy tilted his head at me. "How many of your visions have come true?"

I frowned. "One."

He glanced at Onyame. "Not a large number. Not large enough for my brothers and their friends to abandon their homes, even if they do believe me." He looked back at me. "Will you speak with them?"

"Will they believe me?"

"They respect the visions of seers. But monks from the South?"

Onyame touched my arm. "Icelanders have only recently stopped worshipping Thor and Odin. Just after the Great Assembly at the turn of the millennium." He glanced at the boy. "Is that correct?"

The boy nodded. "Though we respect Christian monks, the visions we're accustomed to hearing come from the old seers."

"Will you leave us alone for a moment, please?"

The boy hurried away — gratefully, I thought.

Onyame faced me. "Are you certain of this vision?"

"Yes, but it happened quickly." I twisted to study the rock I sat on. "It must be this stone." I leaned back. "Will you sit with your back against it?"

He gave me a stare but then did as I requested.

"Now look up the valley and think of nothing else. Perhaps this will help." I lifted my arm from the elbow, so that it ran parallel with his forearm. I gripped his hand.

For a long while nothing happened.

Then the river valley melted away, and the river drifted beneath me. Though the dragon did not appear, I was flying again.

There was the burning mountain, its flaming rock, ash spewing into the air. The smoldering turf houses. The shrieks of sheep and dogs and human beings, drowned in the mountain's roar. The boy's face disappeared with a scream beneath flowing rock.

Then I flew back down the valley, the rock burning below me.

Onyame bolted upright. He blinked and stared at me.

"Did you see it?" I asked.

"Yes."

"This large rock must be a gate to other times. God has used it to give us a vision of the future. To warn these people."

"The rock?"

"I know of one like it in Normandy. Will the people here believe the vision now that both of us have seen it?"

"I don't know. We don't have any authority here. Besides, even if the people believed us now, our words would be forgotten in a few years. Unless they were put into a legal decree."

"We can't let the village be destroyed. I haven't been given a vision just to ignore it."

He paused. "Our plan of sail takes us around the southwestern tip of Iceland into the Bay of Smoke. There's a town there. Inland from the town, about a day's ride, the Iceland Assembly meets every summer. All the head men of Iceland attend. They'll be there even now, disputing matters of law. If we can persuade them that we've had a warning vision from God, they could make a decree. Icelanders have a high regard for law."

"Can we do that?"

"For a decree, we'll need more than our own vision. We'll need support and some sign. Perhaps God will provide that, too."

I hesitated and then said, "Surely He will."

"I hope so. But, Brother Augustine — or Ambrose, as I think I should call you while we're in Iceland — if we take the extra time to travel inland, King Harald's men may overtake us." He glanced out to sea.

"Yes, I see." I hung my head for a moment.

Then I looked up at him. "You know I'm not courageous. I'd rather run from Hardraada's ship, even if it meant running over the edge of the world. I'd rather flee than meddle in the affairs of a country I know nothing about. The man who trained me, though, taught me that I can't flee visions." I breathed a resigned sigh. "I may not escape Hardraada's men, but I surely cannot escape a destiny given to me by God."

We reached the Bay of Smoke within a day.

CHAPTER 15

HERVOR

A.D. 1046

"The story is that a son of Arnar named Ingolfur was fleeing Norway in his longship. He threw a pair of high seat pillars into the sea and swore that he would make his home wherever they washed ashore. His men eventually found them in this bay."

As we sat near Onyame in the steersman's end of the ship, Vagn was instructing me.

My chin in my hands, I sat staring at the mountain-ringed coast of southwestern Iceland and listening to the cries of the seabirds. My body still ached as I leaned forward on the bench near him, hoping that this land would not be the site of my death, where Ulf and Vandrad caught me.

"Look." Vagn was pointing. "Even now you can see the smoke filling the fjord and drifting toward the sea from those two hot springs. Iceland is covered with springs such as those."

Shaking off my fears, I focused my eyes on Reykjavik, "the Bay of Smoke," and the town at the bay's edge.

As in the Faeroes and the Shetlands, the town's dwellings were long-roofed turf-buildings, the turf resting on stone foundations. From many of the buildings, the smoke of cooking fires escaped to mingle with the mist, in which everything, including the townspeople and animals, seemed to float.

"Beautiful, isn't it?" Onyame stood beside me.

I nodded half-heartedly and rubbed a sore shoulder.

As we rocked into the harbor, the people and their houses emerged sharply from the mist, especially the brightly colored tunics and cloaks of the townspeople, their brooches and necklaces adding flashes of gold and bronze. Everyone seemed to have postponed the day's business to march toward the harbor, shouting greetings over the barking of their dogs and the shrieks of the gulls. In a few minutes the houses stood deserted.

I noticed that none of the doors had horseshoes over them. I recalled that, in Hedeby and Kaupang, as in Western Normandy, this remnant of Thor-worship continued to serve as both decoration and protection. Here, however, where Christianity had peacefully triumphed at the turn of the millennium, the horseshoes had disappeared. The people shouting blessings at us were thoroughgoing Christians.

They greeted Onyame warmly but called him Bjorn, the Northern word for bear. Perhaps they knew of his disguise.

Onyame introduced me as Brother Ambrose, explaining that I had lost my robe in a storm. Several of the Icelandic men, all bearded and long-haired, gave me reverent half-bows and shook my hand heartily.

Subdued smiles appeared briefly on their faces when I greeted them in my best Norse dialect. So, when some of the women stepped forward to greet me, I gave them a Latin blessing.

One woman, her waist-length hair pulled down through a silver belt, offered me some beautifully woven blue cloth. "There are twelve ells here. A gift. If you would please pray for my brother, Thorvald. He sailed to the edge of the world three years ago and has never returned."

I said I would and gave Onyame my most alarmed look. He ignored me.

As soon as we delivered our goods — wheat, barley, linen cloth, and a few swords and arm-rings — we unloaded the horses. Sigvald, Vagn, and Thorkel volunteered to stay with the ship and hide it from our pursuers.

We spent the night in the home of an assistant to one of the local headmen, one who would be part of the Assembly I would have to address about the volcano. The assistant, Thorgill, was a cheerful, broad-faced man with brown hair and a brown beard with gray streaks running through both.

When we talked, he listened carefully, concentrating on every word. When he spoke, his speech was deliberate, his words carefully chosen. Thorgill, I thought, was a thoughtful and wise advisor.

His home was one of the larger turf-roofed houses, built on a wooden frame, its slim wooden pillars running at intervals the length of the house. Wooden partitions divided the main room, where we gathered around an oblong fire pit to eat, from the sections where the animals and humans slept — at opposite ends of the house.

Sleep was late in coming, though. We sat outside after the evening meal and talked for a long time before I began to feel tired. I had adapted to the longer days, letting my body inform me when, sunny sky or not, I needed to sleep.

Thorgill talked at length about the summer Assembly, his pride obvious even when he spoke slowly and simply, probably to allow me to understand the Icelandic version of the Norse language.

"There have been Law Assemblies in the Northern countries since before the Romans had their empire," he said. "Norway, Denmark, Sweden, the islands, they all have them."

Onyame smiled at him. "Iceland's is the most impressive, is it not, my friend?"

Thorgill returned the smile. "The most impressive because everyone comes to it at least once every few years. Because the entire law is recited once every three years, a third being recited each summer by the Lawspeaker. Because all of us know that we live according to law. And because the Assembly ensures that our courts give us justice. As soon as the Assembly first convenes each summer —"

"On a Thursday evening," Onyame said.

"Yes," Thorgill said, "on the eve of Thor's Day, judges are chosen to handle law cases that have been brought from the four quarters of the land. The judges deliberate carefully, and the entire process is open. Everyone may attend."

"In addition," Onyame said, "the Assembly courts offer individuals many responses to grievances. It's a sophisticated process."

Thorgill became more enthusiastic. "Yes, for instance, an offender may offer 'self-judgment,' admitting his wrong and allowing the aggrieved person to set terms. Because we value moderation and temperance, compromises are easily reached, and cases resolved to the satisfaction of everyone involved."

"It does sound impressive," I said. I turned toward Onyame. "It sounds as if Icelanders love law the way Normans do."

Thorgill was suddenly interested in Normandy. "Please tell me how law is administered where you live. What is your sense of justice?"

So we had a long exchange about law, even comparing it to the way Lanfranc talked about law south of the Alps. "The expansion of law through the Church," I said, "has made Southern countries even more conscious that justice and peace must coexist."

Thorgill nodded. "When the Christians began to devise their own laws here, about half a century ago, we realized that the two sources of law would become a problem, dividing us. So, at the end of the Old Millennium, a respected Lawspeaker was asked to decide between the old religion and Christianity."

I nodded. "I recall that when King Olaf's … less than gentle ways of conversion were directed at Iceland, the people here resisted."

Thorgill frowned, "The early missionaries King Olaf sent destroyed so many sanctuaries and images of Thor and Odin and Freyr, even killing those who spoke against them, that they were ignored, even outlawed."

"When King Olaf seized Icelanders living in Norway," Onyame added, "threatening to kill or maim them if the country did not convert, Icelanders realized they had to address the issue."

"At first," Thorgill said, "The Christians and traditionalists tried to separate their courts and laws. During the first Assembly of the New Millennium, however, the Lawspeaker, Thorgirr Thorkelsson, reminded us that if we divided the law, we would also divide the peace."

"A phrase that has become both famed and familiar in Iceland," Onyame said, and I recalled that Lanfranc had repeated it when Garrad and I first visited him.

"Thorgirr Thorkelsson was chosen to resolve the matter," Thorgill continued. "Though he was a traditionalist, devoted to the old gods, both sides admired him. He had also been constitutionally chosen for the highest task in the land, that of Lawspeaker. He retired to his tent, lying under a cloak for part of a day and the following night. When he emerged, he declared that all people would convert to Christianity, though the traditionalists could practice their religion in private."

"So," Onyame said, "Iceland became an example of what a Law Assembly could do, even threatened with divisive forces."

Thorgill nodded. "It is our dedication to law that keeps us free, peaceful, and one people."

The next morning, Onyame and I purchased ale and what he described as "the well known Icelandic dried fish" and set out toward the Assembly Plain. Some of the town's leaders, who would be part of the Assembly, escorted us.

In spite of my soreness, I felt oddly happy to be back on a pony, this time one of the careful-footed Icelandic ponies. He neither pitched nor required bailing. He just picked his way slowly over the strange Icelandic terrain.

And it was strange. All around us the land angled as if it had been drinking too much ale. Sharply sloping black rock, sometimes covered with green moss, created an almost impassable terrain. But simple roads allowed the ponies to make their deliberate headway.

Here and there the sharply sloping rock was broken by pine stands, heaths, and scrub grasses. They made little impact on the jagged lava fields, and I was not surprised that most trees had retreated to the brown, flat-topped mountains surrounding us.

Some of the lava rock had rounded to humps that rose like bodies from the earth. I thought about the stories of trolls that Vagn and Sigvald had recounted. I almost expected the largest of lava humps, freed from their enchantments, to leap at us and seize us for their next meal, especially since, as we rode, vapor issued from the earth, as if some devil of the depths were fuming over the peaceful Christian conversion above.

When I mentioned my image to Thorgill, he smiled at me. "I have heard a less Christian explanation, Brother Ambrose. My grandfather used to say that deep in middle-earth caverns, dwarves work over their forges and the elf-smith Volund pounds his golden rings."

"Well, whether it issues from a devil or elf-smith, I would welcome the steam's warmth. Your summer feels like a Norman autumn."

Always the polite and generous host, Thorgill took a blanket from the back of his saddle and threw it over me. I thanked him heartily.

The night we arrived at the Assembly Plain, I also welcomed the extra blanket Onyame offered me. My mat lay on a bench in a small, low-walled turf farmhouse, and I was shivering.

We were the guests of the wealthiest of the local headman's tenants. The tenant was pleased to have company, since his wife had died and both his sons had recently fled the district, or the "Quarter," as he called it.

He explained to me, as if I were not very intelligent, that Iceland was divided into quarters, with each quarter having three sections, making Iceland a sacred twelvefold space, like all ancient lands.

"My sons had to leave," he said, repeating something he had just told Onyame in my presence, "because they stole another tenant's cow for a feast. They also abused one of the headman's sons." He shrugged. "They're high-spirited boys. I paid compensation for the cow, twelve silver ounces, while the Assembly court sentenced my sons to lesser outlawry." He gave me a patronizing look. "That means they'll be out of Iceland for three years."

Onyame leaned toward me. "From the way you speak, he thinks you have trouble understanding the language."

I replied, in my best Icelandic, that I understood everything perfectly, even if I needed some minor practice with the dialect.

To both of them, this seemed amusing.

The next morning we arose earlier than I would have wished, but the local officials were already awake. Apparently, the Icelandic day began as if it were a monastery observing Prime, at six o'clock in the morning. It reminded me of over-zealous Falaise farmers. For his part, Onyame made a comment about my sleeping late, which I ignored.

We ate dried fish as we walked toward the Assembly Plain.

"How do you like the fish?" Onyame asked.

"If Iceland has become famous for this stuff, the fame is unlikely to spread."

Other travelers joined us, mostly robed in red, green, or light brown wool. Some were cloaked in blue linen. Most wore beautifully designed woolen or leather hats, except for one tall blonde man, who held his hair with a leather headband studded with gold.

When he saw me staring at his headband, the blonde-bearded man joined me and greeted me, realizing — from my speech, I supposed — that I was a foreigner. He commented on the huge farms in the valley, most of which sprawled over huge tracts of land.

"When the original settlers arrived here two hundred years ago," he said, "they created farms that remain vast to this day."

"Where the land allows," I said.

He smiled. "Yes, where the lava fields relent. Even a woman in those days could claim as much land as she could walk around from dawn to sunset on a spring day while leading a two-year-old heifer."

"A generous practice."

As we rounded a corner created by massive lava cliffs, a wide plain stretched before us — the Assembly Plain.

In the middle of the Plain spread a lake, no doubt trying to warm itself in the sun. There were no hot springs here, and the sky was a chilled blue. A river fed the lake, and in the river's center a sandy islet drifted.

"The dueling place," the blonde-bearded man said, pointing. "Not very long ago two men might settle a dispute by arms on that islet in the Oxar River, if they weren't satisfied with arbitration." He smiled. "These days we tend to trust the laws and the advocates more."

The plain itself was covered with gray rocks, some breaking down into small clefts or large, water-filled ravines, others disappearing beneath lava heaps. Between them, small birches twisted toward the sun. In the distance the nearest mountains almost hid the snow crests behind them.

In front of me, a wooden church, resembling Saint Ansgar's in Hedeby, pointed up at the mountains like some tiny worshipper before its gods. Off to my left sprawled a farmhouse, its outer buildings attached to it in the now familiar Icelandic fashion.

The Plain also hosted brightly dressed Icelanders. A few grouped around tents or the many turf-and-stone enclosures spread across the valley — "booths," my traveling companion called them, though some were larger than Falaise huts.

The bulk of the men and women, however, reclined on long, grass-covered slopes to my right. This group sparkled in the sun, displaying finger-rings, arm-rings, bracelets, and necklaces.

Most of them wore no more than I did — light wool tunics, cotton or linen leggings, and calfskin shoes — but they seemed warmer, chatting with their neighbors or gazing down at the level opening.

Behind this group, a winding path led up to the Assembly Place, situated on a moss-covered plateau created by flattened lava rocks, which nonetheless revealed, here and there, black-rock clefts that could trip the unwary. I decided that a broken leg would be the least consequence if someone fell into one of these.

As we neared the Assembly Place, Onyame questioned one of the guards. The Assembly would soon adjourn, the guard told us.

Earlier in the day, the headmen had joined the people in the valley at the Law Rock, bordering one side of the Assembly Plain and sloping down into it, to hear the Lawspeaker's recitation of the Christian Laws: rules governing the use of churches, priests' functions, holy-day feasts, and punishments for sorcery.

Now, up here on the Assembly Place, the headmen and their advisors were considering new Christian decrees and hearing law cases.

When Onyame replied that we had an urgent mission and that I was a God-guided monk, the guard raised his eyebrows and hurried us though a low stone gate toward the open space that served as the Assembly Place.

We paused at the outer edge of three concentric circles of benches, on which the Assemblymen sat. The headmen from all four quarters occupied the middle circle. A quick count told me that there were about fifty of them.

Like our traveling companions, they were draped in rich clothes, mostly of blue, green, or russet, many cloaks embroidered with gold or silver thread. The shoulder-length hair was held either by leather hats or linen headbands.

Many finger-rings and arm-rings glinted in the sun, poised next to jeweled swords and gilded axes.

"Each headman," the guard replied to my whispered question, "has two advisers, surrounding each headman on the inner and outer benches."

Whether this was for ease of discussion or for protection, the guard did not say.

The speaker, to whom the Assemblymen listened attentively, was recommending that slavery be abolished. It was, he argued, a practice frowned upon by the Church, hated by God, and unworthy of a Christian republic. I nodded, thinking that this was an auspicious moment to arrive with our request for a decree.

"... already being the custom to use outlawry rather than slavery," the man was concluding. "Even fines are not only preferable but more useful to the leaders of this Assembly and local Assemblies. Finally, as most landowners now realize, tenants are a superior alternative. In keeping with Christian ideals, we have already ended the exposure of children and the eating of horseflesh. Shall not slavery, which has neither honor nor practical value, follow?"

The man gave a short bow, and a few cries of approval flew up from the three circles of benches. Most of the faces remained grim, however. The decree would not soon pass, and I wondered whether the Assemblymen resented being reminded that they could no longer eat horses, the delicacy, as in Western Normandy, of the old religion.

My heart pounded as the speaker left the circle and Onyame strode forward, moving inside the circle.

Only the Lawspeaker was permitted to stand in the middle, I guessed as I watched Onyame step just inside the three circles of benches, his black tunic and leggings contrasting with their brightly colored clothes around him.

He gave a short bow to the Lawspeaker, who returned a solemn nod, and he smiled at several of the headmen, who nodded to him.

Onyame was obviously known and respected, and the Lawspeaker, a gray-bearded, gray-cloaked man, granted him permission to speak immediately. Like the people near the Bay of Smoke, the Lawspeaker called him "Bjorn" — "Bear."

Onyame thanked him and faced east, turning slowly as he spoke. "My lords and friends, against my regular custom, I stand here on a mission from God rather than from the merchants of Norway, though I hope you will receive my words as graciously as you receive my goods."

The Lawspeaker, on whose face I focused, smiled.

"I come to you," Onyame continued, "with an unusual request and a monk from the South, Brother Ambrose." He motioned me to join him. "He lost his monk's robe in a storm, but we have supplied him with clothes appropriate for a God-guided monk."

My heart and head pounded as I slipped through the circles of benches.

"Brother Ambrose has had a vision, a vision concerning Mount Hekla. God has allowed me to share this vision. I am grateful to have had it, but it is alarming." He paused. "The mountain of fire will spill its contents over the adjoining town sometime in the future. The villagers live unaware of the danger."

The Assemblymen and their advisers exchanged frowns, while the people sitting outside the circles — apparently the public could observe Assembly matters — murmured and shook their heads at each other.

The Lawspeaker took a step forward. "This is no small matter, Bjorn. For years, you have brought us only good, and no doubt you intend to help us now. Can you be certain of this vision?"

"I will take an oath on the Cross."

From the western sector, a voice almost as deep as Onyame's asked, "Can you determine the time?"

"It seemed a long time, perhaps a generation, but some alive now will see it happen."

From the southern sector another voice came, "Does the monk speak with you?"

"Will the monk address the Assembly," asked the Lawspeaker, "so that we can judge whether he speaks the truth or not?"

My mouth had dried and my head hummed, but I stepped closer to Onyame.

Trying not to notice the intense stares from the encircling benches, I forced out some words, "My lords, I would not bring this matter before you except to save the lives of the townspeople at the foot of the fire-mountain you call Hekla. I come from the South and have no other reason to interfere in your affairs." My voice shook, and the speech was anything but impressive.

The Lawspeaker strode toward me. "Brother ..."

"Ambrose," Onyame reminded him.

"Brother Ambrose, how can we be certain that your vision is a true one? Our friend Bjorn offered to take a sacred oath. No doubt you will as well."

My mouth failed to produce any sound, so I nodded.

The Lawspeaker continued, "What sign can you show us?"

Onyame glanced at me. I had hoped that some sign would come, but nothing happened.

The Assemblymen and their advisers leaned forward, some thrusting their heads toward me to hear my reply.

I tried to keep my gaze from retreating to the mossy ground, but it did. My shoulders sagged. "I have no sign for you."

The Lawspeaker asked, "Did you say 'no sign'?"

I lifted my head again. "That is what I said."

The headmen of the Assembly studied me, unspeaking. The onlookers stared down from the grassy slope. The air, which had felt cool earlier, seemed to become dense.

"I am the sign."

I lifted my head and turned to locate the owner of the commanding female voice. Onyame twisted, too, and I thought he smiled slightly.

Behind us stood an old woman, white-haired and deeply lined. She wore a blue strapped cloak, covered in gems down to its hem. A string of glass beads hung around her neck, and her head was covered by a black hood with a white lining, both made of what appeared to be animal skin, perhaps lambskin.

Her right hand held a wooden staff with a brass-mounted knob on it, stones set around the base of the knob. Her belt was made of twisted, dried wood, and from it dangled a skin pouch. Hairy shoes covered her feet, probably made from calfskin. The shoe's laces had tin knobs on their ends. Her hands were covered with white gloves, matching the lining of her hood.

One of the headmen called out, "Volva, you have not requested permission to speak."

"I need no permission when Odin summons me." She lifted her staff and turned slowly in a circle, gazing at the headmen and advisers. "Nonetheless, I do not sacrifice propriety. I will accept permission to speak."

She gazed at the Lawspeaker, and he nodded.

She turned back toward us, her eyebrows pressed together. Drawing a long breath, she said, "What this monk and our friend Bear say is true. Mount Hekla has doomed your kinsmen. It doomed those who lived under it in ages past. Now it will again. The settlement there will be destroyed just over fifty summers from now. This is a vision I had two days ago, given to me by Odin. Now this monk's God confirms what Odin has told me."

There was silence for a moment. The Lawspeaker strode to a nearby bench to lean toward a man wearing the robes of a Christian priest. They spoke in low tones.

The Lawspeaker then walked around the circle, bending to hear what the Assemblymen said.

Returning to the Stone, the Lawspeaker said, "We have heard your visions in the past, Volva, and they have always proven true. Since what the old God and the new God have shown are in agreement, we shall hear this request for a decree when we meet in the morning."

The woman nodded, spun on her heel, and marched through the benches, the headmen and their advisers leaning away from her.

Onyame thanked the Lawspeaker. I made a short bow, and we followed the woman.

When we were out of earshot of the Assemblymen, I pulled in a breath of relief and whispered to Onyame. "Who is this Volva? Do you know her?"

"Very well. And the headmen won't take her words lightly. We've received our help from God."

A few feet ahead, the woman halted and turned to us. Expressionless, she nodded at Onyame, who returned the nod.

"I wish to speak to this one," she said, pointing her staff at me.

I backed away from the staff, but Onyame pushed me forward. The woman turned again and strode across the lava plains.

"Go with her," he said.

"But —"

"You must go. It's God's will."

I glanced after her and back at him again.

He waved a hand. "It's all right. I'll take care of your pony."

"I'm not concerned about my pony."

He pushed at my arm. "She won't harm you. Go."

Though the sun remained high in the Icelandic sky, it was evening when the old woman and I reached a bluff of lava rocks. I had discovered that walking on Iceland's moss-covered lava terrain was as demanding as climbing rocky slopes. My feet and legs ached as I stared at pine and spruce trees at the foot of the bluff.

A mist had settled around the trees, but I could see the old woman kneel, muttering over some chickweed. She tugged at some of the leaves, avoiding the tiny white flowers.

Then, abruptly, she turned as if she was going to walk into the bluff itself, pushed aside some tall bushes and leaned through a low wooden door hidden behind the trees and bushes.

The knob on her staff glowed, offering the only light inside. The entrance, it turned out, was not a simple doorway but a dark, winding tunnel, which got lower and darker as we pressed through it.

Three times other tunnels joined it, creating a kind of crossroads, and the woman turned first one way and then another, as if even she was not certain of the right direction. Then I realized that she used this strategy to disorient me, so that I could not repeat the pattern on my own.

Gradually the tunnel's roof pushed so far down that I was bent nearly to the ground. At that point, the woman disappeared through a hole.

I thrust myself through the hole and emerged into a rather average hut, not unlike Garrad's. A torch sputtered in its holder, casting an uneven light on the stone walls, against which stood shelves laden with pots and jars. From pegs hung linen pouches, and I smelled the herbs I had become familiar with in Falaise, especially rue, fennel, and sweet woodruff.

The woman threw back her hood and seized the sputtering torch, lighting three others around the hut. She then knelt and lit already prepared kindling in the fireplace.

Like the walls of the hut, the fireplace bent in toward the center of the room as it extended upward. The walls eventually formed a narrow chute that substituted for the hut's ceiling. The chute disappeared in a smokehole far above my head.

The old woman faced me. The stern look had vanished, though. She greeted me with a smile not unlike what I might expect from my Falaise mothers.

"Welcome to my home."

"Thank you," I said, trying to be as polite as possible. "I'm pleased to be invited, though I don't know to what I owe this honor."

She waved me toward the fire, which had sprung to life almost instantly. "I recognized you. As soon as you spoke of your vision. That's why I invited you." She put the chickweed down on a low table. "You needn't be so formal. I'm not a headman, you know. I'm not formidable."

"I beg your pardon. I don't mean to offend. From your presence at the Assembly, though, I took you to be unusually formidable."

She took off her gloves and busied herself over bowls of herbs. "Yes, well, you saw the Volva."

"Isn't that your name?"

"Ah, a Northern word your teacher didn't tell you about. Well, 'Volva' is a word that means, when people here are being polite, a seer or prophetess of the old religion. My name is Hervor, which is what I hope you will call me. And you are?"

"Ambrose. Brother Ambrose."

"Yes, well, Brother Ambrose, outside here, outside this hut, my position and my life depend on people treating me as a Volva."

"Your life depends on being a priestess of Thor and Odin?"

"And of the old Goddesses, especially Freya of the Ancient Magic. Does that surprise you?"

"Well, yes."

She stared at me for a moment. "I see. The monks and priests of the South, that's your experience, isn't it? They get their respect from the Church and from their patrons. It's not like that here, not for what's left of the old religion, the traditional religion. People here respect the Christian priests. The headmen are their patrons, their protectors. I have no patrons, no protectors." She waved a wooden spoon in the air. "You see?"

"The Christian teachings are obviously much respected here."

She smiled. "Yes, they are, while I have only myself and the old Gods. So the people must fear me. Otherwise, they would kill me, especially if they suspected that I had bewitched them or their lands. That's always been the way. With all the Volvas before me."

"Kill you?"

She spun, scowling, and tapped me lightly on the head with her forefinger. "My mother was burned in her own house by a crowd who believed she hadn't given them a true vision." She waved her hand toward the walls of her hut. "That's why I don't live in a house anyone can find. Not a wooden one, either."

I was stunned. "Did that really happen?"

"Of course it did."

"I'm very sorry."

She shrugged. "It was many years ago. I was young, and now I'm old." She returned to her bowls. "I'll join her, of course — though that's many years in the future, Odin tells me — but I want to go peacefully, not murdered by a mob." She paused a moment. "Her vision was true, you know. They just couldn't see it." She began mixing again. "That's to be expected, though. There are many fools in the world."

"I'm sorry," I repeated. I could think of nothing else to say, especially to a non-Christian.

She nodded at me and then removed her hood, cloak, and the string of glass beads and draped them carefully over a pegged, wooden pole in a corner. Over her undyed tunic, she wore a brown, sleeveless wool dress, a surprising contrast to the jeweled, fur-lined cloak.

"So you're curious. You wish to know why I've asked you here."

"If it's not impolite. I hope, of course, that it has to do with the decree and that you have a strategy for making the Assembly pass it ... to save those people at the foot of the volcano. I'm pleased, however, to have your hospitality, whatever the reason."

She smiled broadly. "What manners! What a fine emissary you must be."

Did she know I was an emissary?

"You needn't worry about the decree or those people, though. The Assembly will pass it. They've never ignored a vision of mine, so even less will they ignore two visions. And you, Brother — what was your name again?"

"Ambrose."

"Yes, Ambrose." She drew her head back. "Ambrose. Ambrose. No, that's not it. That's not your name, is it?"

Having already played this game with Hardraada, I was prepared to insist that it was.

She muttered, "No, I can't see the name, but it's not Ambrose. No, something harder-sounding. Given to you a long time ago, but not at birth and not by parents. By a little boy, a little Duke-to-be, in fact. Yes, I have him. Duke William the Norman, and you're now his emissary. Of course. You're fleeing someone who's trying to kill you, though. My, my, several people are trying to kill you." She raised an eyebrow at me. "You were courageous to come here with your vision. You're pursued."

I gaped at her. "How do you know all that?"

"You needn't be impressed. It's not difficult. I have the second sight, you see. I've trained it all my life, all my life trained the few skills I have. So I can see your thoughts, some of them, at least. As Odin gives me leave, and Odin has given me leave in your case. You're special to me. In danger, too. I'll help you."

"Special?"

"Yes, of course. You're to be my last student, Brother ... oh, what is your name?"

I rose, causing a twinge of pain to shoot through my bad foot. "I'm sorry, but I can't be anyone's student. I'm a Christian, I have a job to do, and I'm on my way —" I stopped myself. I shouldn't reveal anymore — unless she already knew it. "Do you also know where I'm going?"

"That's simple enough. If you're traveling with Bear, you're headed for Vineland. So I shall accompany you. Though I detest sea voyages. Please sit down. Standing pains your foot, and your pain distresses me. And don't be concerned. I shall not interfere with your mission, Brother ... Brother ... hmm, there's part of the problem — you're not a monk at all. In fact, you have no position, no title. You're a hermit of some sort, and you're not even called by the name of your village, only by your name. What is it?"

Obviously she would discover it sooner or later. "Cuin."

"Ah, yes. Cuin. Cuin. After Alcuin, the Sage of York, of course. Duke William wants to be for the Normans what Charlemagne was for the Franks, a great unifier. Appropriate." She smiled at me. "You needn't fear that your study with me will endanger anything. Especially your dedication to the Christian teachings."

"You are a practitioner of the old religion."

Her eyes crinkled. They reminded me of Onyame's look just before he made some mischievous remark. "Why, yes, it's true that I'm a practitioner of the old religion. How clever of you to notice. In fact, I'm the last prophetess of the old religions in this land. There will be no more. Do you know why?"

I shook my head.

"Come, come, come. You're not dull-witted. The teachings of the Christians have supplanted our work. We are dying out. Slowly, though. The Volva still has some wisdom to pass on, some events to shepherd. Nothing to conflict with your Christian teachings, though, I assure you. Not at all. Shall I tell you something?"

There seemed no stopping her.

"All of my students, except one, have been Christians. Now, what do you say to that?"

I wasn't sure what to say. "I'm relieved to hear it."

"You're my sixth Christian, my seventh student. Each Volva has seven students, and you're my seventh. That won't surprise you, of course. Didn't you spend your childhood with King Edward the Saxon? Edward's a seventh son. And Duke William too? Duke William is the seventh Duke of Normandy, as you know. So you're my seventh student. For the seventh age."

"I'm not sure what you mean."

She waved her spoon again. "Don't Christians say that this is the beginning of the sixth age? Six thousand years after creation?"

"Yes, the priests where I grew up taught me that."

"Falaise!" she said.

"Yes. And Rouen."

"Ah, yes. Rouen, too. Falaise and Rouen. Falaise. That reminds me of something, but what I can't recall. Well, anyway, I've had a student for each age. A symbol for each age, you might say. My fifth was a warrior. My sixth was a traveler, a communicator. And you'll be my seventh, a hermit." She shook her head. "What will the seventh age will look like if you're a hermit?"

"I'm also a healer."

"Are you? Why, yes, of course. An emissary, too. I'd forgotten. Well, that's good for the seventh age then, isn't it? Healing and diplomacy."

I could think of nothing to reply. I should have been feeling afraid of pursuit and feeling stupid for rushing here with a vision that would not apply for over fifty years. With Hervor, though, I felt oddly safe, as if nothing could harm me. I hoped the feeling was not some spell she had cast on me.

"I do not cast spells."

"Do you hear everything I'm thinking?"

"Only what I need to hear." She bent to stir the fire and shifted a pot over the flame. "Enough of that now. Supper. Will you put more wood on here?"

I slipped a few logs under the pot, and soon we had a meal of herbs, leaves, and flowers, accompanied by a drink that I had already sampled in Denmark, a mixture of cranberries, bog myrtle, and honey, all of which seemed to me as delicious as any feast set by the Kings of Norway.

The next morning, I awoke even earlier than when I was staying at St. Vaast. I sat up, blinking, to find Hervor squatting near me and poking me with a stick. Behind her the fire glowed in the fireplace.

"Who's that man I see?"

I rubbed my eyes. "What man?"

"The man who was your teacher, a warrior himself, now turned to healing. What's his name?"

I yawned. "Garrad."

"Yes, that's it. " She stopped poking me. "A fine teacher you've had. He's taught you the best of the Christian teachings — by example, too, I can see — and much about healing. More than Christian teachings as well. That's good. You need to know about the new teachings and the old. The old will die, though. Even Odin will die. All the war-gods will die. Not for a while, though. The time is not yet."

I knew nothing at this hour of the morning. "You don't have any warm cider, do you?"

To my amazement, she reached behind her and produced a cup of cider, warmed by the fire. "Here. Though I don't understand why you drink that wretched liquid. It tastes foul."

"I didn't think that people drank this in the North."

"Well, most people do not, of course, but Odin and Freya both said that you would want it. So over the night, they made some for you. Why, I do not know. How can you drink it?" She shook her head. "Men are more mysterious than the Gods."

I washed in a not sufficiently warmed bucket of water and devoured a piece of coarse bread. I could taste the pine bark in it, and the grit ground against my teeth.

Then Hervor led me back through her maze of an entrance. We emerged into what I assumed was a morning fog, which clung to the pines and rocks around her door.

A few feet away, to my surprise, we stepped into a sunny morning. I peered backward at the fog bank. Hervor strode ahead of me in silence, and I hurried to follow.

Every time I opened my mouth to ask her about the fog, she shook her head sharply. Then I remembered that, outside her hut, she was the Volva. I should do nothing to endanger that status.

Near the Assembly Plain, a crowd had already gathered around the Assembly Place. The Assemblymen and their advisers sat on their benches. A man's voice, not the Lawspeaker's, drifted toward us.

Onyame stood just outside the circle and nodded as we approached. He said in a low voice, "They're trying to determine whether there's enough evidence to bring a case to the Assembly next week."

A man standing just inside the circle was introducing nine witnesses, his "jury," to attest to the fact that he had been wronged. He spoke of their character and of his own in high-toned, almost poetic terms. During this oration, I discerned that his name was Hoskuld.

"I name these witnesses," Hoskuld said, "to testify that I give notice of an action against Kol Thorsteinson for unlawful assault, inasmuch as he attacked Atli Sigurdson, my servant. I request both compensation and that Kol be sentenced to full outlawry on this charge, not to be fed or forwarded or helped or harbored."

When the Lawspeaker asked Hoskuld why he wanted a sentence of outlawry in addition to compensation, Hoskuld replied, "Because he came with intent to harm."

The Lawspeaker nodded. "To consider him an outlaw for that reason is in accord with the law."

When the Lawspeaker noted that Hoskuld was himself the target of a suit, Hoskuld replied, "My local Quarter Assembly gave me immunity to prosecute this case."

The Lawspeaker nodded again. "In this also you have the law on your side, though even legality will not please Kol's supporters."

Hoskuld concluded, "Because the case involves my property, and because Kol was legally an outlaw at the time of the crime, I request the right to assess my own compensation."

I saw many Assemblymen nod, and two rose to support him. Apparently, Hoskuld had a strong case.

I leaned toward Onyame, "What is his complaint?"

"In a fit of temper, Kol buried his ax in Atli's head."

My mouth fell open, but Onyame showed no emotion.

So I shrugged and said, "It is surprising what people will take offense at."

Onyame turned to say something, but at that moment, the Lawspeaker summoned him. He strode into the circle.

After a preliminary comment from the Lawspeaker, a formality of reintroducing our case, Onyame began to speak. "I appear this morning at the request of the Lawspeaker and with the permission of the Assembled headmen. I thank all of you for this opportunity."

The Assemblymen murmured approvingly and nodded.

"I remind you of the vision that Brother Ambrose and I had of the eruption of Mount Hekla fifty summers from now, and that Hervor, the Volva, has had the same vision, even to the agreement of the time. I can add that since we spoke here last evening, I have encountered three Assemblymen who have had dreams about danger to the same village. These visions and dreams can only be interpreted as benevolent warnings from both the warrior Gods and the Christian God."

The Lawspeaker stepped toward him. "Will you take the oath?" He lifted a jeweled silver cross and a book that had to be a Bible. "Brother Ambrose and the Volva?"

Onyame nodded. "I will."

Hervor stepped into the circle beside him. I hurried to follow. Onyame and I swore on the Bible that our accounts of our visions were true and that we believed them to be from God.

Hervor took the same oath on a large gold ring with red stones set in it.

Then one of the headmen stood and requested permission to speak. "I too have had a dream," the Assemblyman said, "in which I saw Bjorn and this monk striding down from the sky. I'm certain their vision comes from God."

A second Assemblyman rose. "A few weeks before the Assembly, one of my shepherds saw the dead hero Gunnar sitting in his burial mound, surrounded by four lights and singing. He sang that the fire-mountain would consume as many men as his own spear had while he was alive. I thought little of it at the time, but I see now that it confirms the vision that has been given here."

A third Assemblyman, smiling at Onyame, rose. "It seems that we have our confirmation."

A dozen other men rose and echoed the confirmation.

The Lawspeaker held up his hand. "The visions of Bjorn, Brother Ambrose, and the Volva have the public support of more than twelve men. Shall there be a decree?"

The Assemblymen called out their agreement.

"Is there opposition?"

No one spoke.

"Then, this Assembly decrees that the village at the foot of Mount Hekla will be abandoned just under fifty summers from now. I shall appoint messengers to carry the decree to the village, where it will be heard at the local autumn Assembly. I shall also request two poets to render the vision in verse. The decree itself will be repeated every third summer at this Assembly, in accordance with custom, until the vision becomes reality."

The Lawspeaker then turned and thanked us. "The custom of the Assembly is to present gifts to all bringing messages of aid. Accordingly, I offer our friends arm-rings and bracelets of gold and ivory."

"Thank you," Onyame said, accepting the arm-ring and bracelet. "I am grateful to the Assembly."

Hervor gave her head a short bow. "A Volva always recognizes generosity."

"I am ... grateful, too," I said, stammering, "but is there the possibility of —?"

The Lawspeaker smiled, almost as if he knew what I wanted. "Do you wish some other gift, Brother Ambrose?"

Encouraged, I said, "I understand that Icelanders make beautiful wool blankets and gloves, and I wondered whether —"

The Lawspeaker held up his hand. "You need say no more. A Southerner must surely be accustomed to warmer weather." He motioned to two young men seated behind him who disappeared briefly into a nearby enclosure and reappeared, carrying a large, carved wooden chest.

The Lawspeaker returned my arm-ring and bracelet to the chest. Searching for a few seconds, he drew out a wool blanket, blue with swirling scarlet patterns. He also located a pair of gloves, which, as he carried them toward me, appeared to be of white wool, embroidered with gold thread.

"May these gifts reflect this Assembly's appreciation of your concern for the people living near Mount Hekla."

"Thank you. I am grateful to the Assembly for its patience with a stranger and for its kindness."

After the three of us had wound our way through the Assembly benches and found a private spot on the edge of the Assemblymen's booths, Hervor drew Onyame aside. While she spoke to him in hushed tones, I studied my new blanket and gloves, which were only slightly large. I was still admiring the gold embroidery on the gloves when they strode back to me.

Hervor smiled. "I apologize for leaving you standing here. Bear and I are in agreement. I shall be going with you."

I eyed him. "How fortunate."

"I must leave you two for a short time," she said. "But I will return quickly." She strode back toward the Assembly circle.

Onyame put his hand on my shoulder. "So you had an interesting talk with Hervor."

"Strange at least. She apparently thinks I am some sort of student of hers. She seems harmless, though, as you said."

"She has already been a help to us."

"It seems so." I recalled my manners. "How have you spent the night? That was a remarkable amount of support you generated. It must have taken no small effort."

"Less than you might think. I have many friends here. Besides, most of the headmen know my reputation as a placer of bets."

"You placed bets for support?"

"Not exactly. I bet on the horse-fights and the matches at the Wrestling Slope to the gain of those who know me best. I made good my reputation for choosing losers, thus making my old acquaintances even richer and more disposed to help me. That reminds me. I must report that I lost the two ells of cloth the woman gave you to pray for her brother, Thorvald, the one she thinks sailed off the edge of the world."

I opened my mouth, first in surprise and then to complain about his betting with my property.

He interrupted me. "It was used for a good purpose. Besides, you need not pray for Thorvald. I know exactly where he is, and he is beyond all Christian prayers."

Before I could say anything, Hervor returned, and Onyame excused himself to join a man who had been shouting "Bjorn!" at him from some distance away.

She took my arm and led me back to her hut.

As we reached the edge of the mist that seemed a permanent part of her entrance, Hervor paused to speak to me. "You must start training. Are you ready?"

"Training?" I felt that Garrad had already over-trained me. "What exactly am I to learn?"

"One art and another. Visions of the future, certainly. Perhaps of the past. You are a receiver of visions. You have a dragon with you for that. That is what we must develop. Are you willing?"

"To do what?"

"Follow me."

She strode behind the pines and spruce clustered at the hut's entrance until she reached a stand of ash trees. The trees were huge, at least the height of twelve men, and stretched massive limbs out into the mist. Seven of them stood in a row, their bark looking grayer than usual.

The tree in the center had been stripped of its lower limbs, though the scars had grown over. A well had been sunk a few feet away from its trunk, so I assumed the limbs had been stripped to allow for the well's stone sides and wooden frame.

Hervor walked past this center ash to the tree just to its right. Seizing a branch, she began to climb. I grabbed the branch and pulled myself up behind her. Even in the dampness created by the mist, the diamond-shaped fissures on the bark offered sure grips. The spacing of the branches made the climb easy, even with my weak foot.

We soon reached a height at which I no longer wished to look down. Not long after that, Hervor crawled out along one of the wide branches. Brushing aside the leaves, I crawled behind her.

Abruptly she straightened and stepped from our branch onto one growing from the center ash. It was a short step, but my heart pounded in fear as she took it.

"Stand up."

I obeyed, clinging to branches around me.

"Come along."

"I would rather stay here."

"We must be on the center tree. Come. You will be safe."

I took a deep breath and eased my foot off the branch. It pulled back, almost by itself. "I cannot get it to move."

"All right. How many leaves are there at the end of that twig next to you?"

I counted. "Seven."

"Of course. An ash may have more, though, may it not?"

"Sometimes. What's —?"

"How many on this limb?"

I counted again. "Seven."

"On this one next to my head?"

"Seven again."

"On this one on the far side of my head?"

"I cannot see all of it. One, two, three, four, five —"

"Now step."

Almost against my will, one of my feet lifted from the branch and stepped across. Then the other did the same. My heart and head pounded so much that I thought I might pass out.

I found myself standing beside her.

"Well done."

"I did not do it. My feet just —"

"Follow me."

She picked her way slowly toward the center ash's trunk, and I shuffled my feet behind her.

"One small step at a time." Her voice was reassuring.

We reached the trunk. It gave off a musty scent, almost like some ancient castle library, something I had never smelled on an ash.

Hervor sat down, her feet resting on a branch below, her back supported by several limbs behind her. She motioned me to do the same, and I eased myself into a sitting position. Cautiously. I breathed heavily as I secured my back and legs.

"Look down," she said.

"Must I?"

"Look down."

I let my gaze slip through the leaves until I located the base of the ash. Where I had earlier noticed the absence of lower branches there now coiled a huge, green serpent. It lifted its head toward me, its tongue darting in and out.

"Where did that come from?"

Without taking her eyes from me, Hervor said, "Never fear. It will be gone before we go down."

"If it's not, I'm not going down."

"Hush now." She closed her eyes and began chanting in a low voice.

I watched her until she whispered, "Sleep. Sleep."

"In a tree? This far off the ground?"

A cry from above startled me. I grabbed the branch I was sitting on.

"Everything is all right," Hervor said.

I glanced up to see an eagle circling the tree. Then it settled onto one of the topmost branches.

"I cannot sleep with that perched up there."

Unmoving, her eyes still closed, she said, "It will not harm you. Be quiet. Relax. Close your eyes."

A squirrel raced passed me, chattering, and I seized the branch again.

"Pay no attention. That is Ratatosk. He will not harm you either. Relax. Close your eyes."

"I may get dizzy and —"

She put her hand over mine. "Be still. Close your eyes, and let your mind drift."

Reluctantly I closed my eyes.

I heard her voice. "Let your mind go. Let it sink. Let it sink deeply into the past. Let it go from yesterday to the day before yesterday to the day before that. And keep going. To the year before that day and the year before that ..."

As she spoke, almost chanting, my body went slack. Despite the branches that bit into my back and legs, I felt warm and relaxed.

At first I could see only the blackness of my own eyelids. Soon, however, colors and shapes began to swim in the blackness. Then figures and landscapes appeared, blurred at first then clear.

These became scenes, and I recognized the events of my own life, running from the vision in Iceland back to my travels in Norway, Denmark and Flanders, working with Garrad and William in my childhood.

Hervor's voice played underneath the scenes. "You sit on a child of Yggdrasil, the Tree of Life. All things that live or ever have lived can come to you. Let them come. Everything that has ever happened in the world is here. You can see all of it. Whatever you wish to see. Let it all come. Let this life come. Let the last life you lived come. Let the one before that and the one before that and the one before that ..."

Her voice seemed to drown in a bright light, almost blinding, that flashed before my closed eyes. I winced. Then I opened my eyes.

I squinted and turned my eyes away from the blinding sun. I blinked and saw forms lying near me. Soldiers, sprawled in death-poses, covered with leather and blood.

I lay on a battlefield. I was a soldier. And I was dying. I could feel the life slipping away from some wound in my body.

Pain shot up and down my left leg, and my chest ached almost unbearably. I gasped. I had to do something to stop the pain.

Almost without thinking, I raised myself onto one elbow. For a moment, the ache in my chest eased. I drew in a breath.

Not far from me, a group of men, dressed in mail and short, red tunics resembling mine, searched among the dead. In the center of the group stooped a tall form, draped in a long scarlet cloak. My arm gave way, and I fell back to the damp earth, exhausted.

"Here is one!" someone cried. "Come, see, my lord. One of our own." Footsteps pounded around me. "But, oh God, he is dying."

A shadow fell over my face. Someone touched my chest, neck and wrists. Then the shadow disappeared. "Yes, he is dying."

Another shadow fell over me, and I could make out the tall man kneeling next to me. His voice was quiet. "Is there anything I can do for you, my valiant friend?"

I squinted up at him. His face blocked the sun, creating an aura of light around his head. As my eyes focused on the face, I recognized it.

It belonged to the Emperor. To Charlemagne. He had survived the battle and was the victor.

I tried to make my voice work, but nothing came. So I just shook my head.

A nearby voice said, "He fought bravely. See, my lord, these corpses are Catalonians. Two, no, three of them. Here, the one who got closest to him has run a spear through his chest where the chain was faulty. And into his foot. But our man killed him, too."

At that moment, the pain seared through my chest and foot again. I tried to control my face, but I could feel my jaw tighten.

The Emperor turned his head. "Is there anything you can do for the pain?"

The man who must have been a healer replied, "I have some mandrake, my lord. It will help a little."

I tasted the mandrake and brandy mixture as it slipped, a few drops at a time, into my mouth. I barely had the strength to swallow it.

The Emperor's voice came again. "Does that help, my friend?"

Again my voice would not work, so I smiled as best I could.

An attendant spoke from behind the haloed head, "See the insignia, my lord. He led this company. Many dead over by that knoll. He must have fought alone at the end."

The Emperor bent closer to me. "My friend, did you fight unaided against these Catalonians?"

I forced my head into a nod.

He closed his eyes for a moment and then reopened them. "Listen to me. From this day forward, you are no longer a common soldier. From this moment, you are my brother. You will be honored in all my prayers and all the prayers said for my family."

I smiled again and raised my hand in a salute. He reached out and clasped it. Suddenly his face was William's. He was Charlemagne, but he was also William.

A voice behind him said, "The fiend who killed him, shall we chop off his head?" The attendant grabbed the helmet of the dead assailant and jerked it upward.

The Emperor gazed at me. I shook my head.

"No," the Emperor said. "Our friend does not wish it. Nor do I."

I rolled my head to the side and saw the attendant shrug and tug at the helmet. "At least we shall claim this prize."

As he pulled the helmet upward, the dead face, its eyes staring at nothing, was visible for a moment. With a shock I recognized the face: Voldred's.

I awoke abruptly to find myself on the branch with Hervor beside me, holding my chest to keep me from falling.

"So, you are bound to only two men."

I gulped in air. "Did you see that? Those men? What was that?"

"I saw the shadows, not the forms. It was not my life to see. It was yours, one of the earlier lives you lived in this world."

"It cannot be. According to the priests, we live only one life and move to another world."

"Understand it anyway you must. All that is important is that you are bound to only two men. A good thing for a disciple. Do you know them?"

"Yes. Yes, I do."

"Good."

I thought of the stone in Garrad's hut. "That seemed to be a real vision. What is this place?"

"A tree of vision. It can become the Tree of Life. It is a child of the Tree of Life, Yggdrasil, the World Tree, whose three roots stretch into all three realms of the world. At its base lies the Well of Fate, the source of all wisdom and the spring of the destiny of all living creatures. The Gods sit in council in such a tree every day. So, here is where I learn what I need to know, as we did today."

I glanced down. The snake was gone. I looked up, and the eagle, too, had vanished.

Catching my glances, she said, "The eagle and the serpent live at either end of Yggdrasil, and the squirrel, Ratatosk, carries insults between them. When this ash returns to being just another tree, all three vanish. That is all you need to know of them. Come, now we go down."

In a near-daze, I climbed down behind her.

The next morning she roused me from sleep. She was already dressed in her blue cloak with its black hood. "I have no cider for you this morning."

I thought it might be an apology. "That is all right."

She snorted. "It certainly is. I am delighted not to have the stuff stinking up my hut. Come along now. We must be meeting Bear."

As I washed and munched on a dried apple, she poured tea she had prepared into a bladder — I could smell sweet woodruff, raspberry and liverwort, I thought — and folded what appeared to be a length of blue-gray cloth and tucked it under her arm.

After I pulled my tunic and leggings over my underclothes, she grabbed my arm and pulled me into a standing position. "We shall make it easy on your foot this morning. While we walk, you can tell me how you injured it."

"I did not injure it. I was born —"

She pushed me toward the entrance. "Come. Talk while we walk. And make certain you have all your possessions, even your blanket. We shall not return."

"I have it."

I crawled through the entrance tunnel. Lit only by her staff behind me, the ceiling to the entrance-tunnel finally lifted, and I could walk erect.

Then she passed in front of me, leading through the winding, crisscrossing tunnels. "Talk now."

"My foot was deformed at birth, turned inward even worse than it is now. So my parents abandoned me at a wayside cross outside Falaise. Some passing hermit discovered me and delivered me to the village, where I was adopted."

"By whom?"

"The entire village. The families took turns having me stay with them."

"How did you meet Duke William?"

"When he was a child, his mother often hid him in the village. From assassins. We became friends, and his mother allowed me to come to the castle often. Even to be trained by the priests and archery-masters."

We reached the entrance, the mist masking everything except the green-black blurs that would be pines and spruce trees.

Among the shadows a deeper shadow stirred, and before I had time to determine what it was, a voice startled me. "Good morning."

Onyame stood before us. A hooded gray cloak, which I had not seen him wear before, had hidden him in the mist.

I returned the greeting. "You surprised me. That cloak —"

He laughed and brushed his hands over it. A layer of dust drifted away from it, and the robe shone bright blue.

Hervor brushed her blue-gray robe, and it too seemed to shine with some inner blue light. I stared at one, then the other.

Hervor spoke to my confusion. "These are the robes of Volvas. And their students."

I gaped at Onyame. "You?"

Hervor stepped toward him and took his arm. "Bear is my sixth student."

"Why didn't you tell me?" I asked him.

"What sense would it have made before you met Hervor? Besides, how was I to know that you would be the seventh student? I'm as surprised as you must have been, though I think you're a fine choice."

"Thank you."

"The robes turn gray," Hervor said, "when covered with even a bit of dust, rendering any wearer nearly invisible. He can go where he pleases. When brushed, the robe shines like a sunlit sky. Even in my mist here."

"How is that possible? What is the material?"

"The secret is not in the material. It's in the weaving. And that is a Volva's secret, given to me by Freya, one that I cannot pass on to a Christian student."

I studied the blue cloth shimmering on Onyame's shoulders. "Can you pass it on to a non-Christian student?"

"I have, yes, but I fear he will neither use nor pass on the knowledge."

"Why not?"

She shook her head. "He is a prisoner, bound by an oath to the King of Norway. Some mission that consumes him." She sighed. "A disappointment to me, of course. But every Volva knows that one of her students might fail."

I looked back at Onyame, still surprised. "Then you must have been able to see the vision at Mount Hekla because of your training here."

"Yes," he replied, "though Hervor has not trained me much in visions. She has mostly taught me about carrying people and goods from one place to another."

"Did you need training for that?"

He smiled. "To locate just those people and just those goods that will change the places they are taken to, yes, for that I needed training. The training helped me to identify you."

"How?"

"I could sense that you needed to be taken somewhere. I would like to explain further, but we should be going. The bell has already rung for the Assembly to convene, and this is a good time for us to escape. We need to slip by unnoticed, if we can."

"Then let's be on our way," Hervor said. She glanced at me. "You need something against the weather besides your blanket." She stepped back and unfolded the blue-gray cloth, shaking it. It was another hooded blue cloak. "Here. This is yours."

I stared as it hung, shining, from her hands. "Mine?"

"Every student has one."

"Thank you. It's very beautiful."

Onyame smiled. "Also warm by day and night. I can tell you that from experience." He watched me put the robe on. "We want to roll them in dust before we go, though."

"Why?" Hervor asked.

"Two of King Harald's men seek the life of Brother Ambrose, unjustly, of course. They have followed us, as we suspected, since we left Norway. Now they have reached the Assembly Plain."

"Ulf and Vandrad? Here?" I heard my voice shake.

"The two you call Ulf and Vandrad, yes."

Hervor bent to roll her cloak in the dust. "Then we all need to be gray before we step into the morning sun."

As we reached a lava rise near the Assembly Plain, Onyame directed our gaze to where he had spotted Ulf and Vandrad. They had wandered only a few feet away, so I picked them out easily.

Behind them stood a taller form, its head hanging forward. When the Lawspeaker rose near the Law Rock to address the Assembly, the head lifted, its angular features outlined by the sun. Across the forehead ran a scar that dipped toward the left eye.

I gasped and took a step backward.

Hervor did not move, but Onyame turned to me. "What is it?"

"The man with Ulf and Vandrad. He's … I mean, he seemed … I thought I knew him."

Onyame squinted at Voldred. "It's not likely that you've seen that one before. He's a Norwegian in the service of King Magnus. His name is Voldred."

"Is Voldred here?" Hervor asked.

"Yes, and he's our obstacle to slipping away. He wants to speak with you."

"No," she said.

"You must see him."

She gave a disgusted groan. "Yes, of course."

"First, I'll have to get him away from those other two."

I stared at both of them. "Do you know that man?"

Onyame nodded. "All of Hervor's students know Voldred. He's the example for the rest of us. He's the one who failed."

CHAPTER 16

THE END OF THE WORLD

A.D. 1046

Hervor swung her hooded head in my direction. "Voldred's the student I spoke of earlier, you see. The one who's not a Christian. The one, as Bear reminds me, who's done nothing with what I taught him. "

I could hardly believe what I was hearing. "Voldred is one of your disciples?"

"Student, yes. I don't have disciples."

"You once called me a disciple …" I began.

She cut me off. "Don't take things dogmatically. Don't listen for truth or fact or certainty. That's your first lesson. Statements should be treated like breezes passing by you."

"I'm not sure I understand."

"Have you not studied the teachings of the Awakened One, the one called, in his own land, the Buddha? His teachings came to the North long ago. He is the source of that insight I just offered you."

My attention had returned to Voldred.

Hervor watched my face. "You know him." It was more of a statement than a question.

My mind raced. Could Onyame and Hervor be involved in trying to kill me, having failed to do so only because they did not know who I was? Onyame had carried me here without my knowing why.

I recalled the sacrifice I had witnessed in Denmark: the horned head-dresses and the horned goat, just like the one Voldred had demanded from the farmer. Could Hervor and Onyame could be part of an ancient religion that sought my life?

Even if they were not, Hervor knew my name. If she told Voldred, he would recognize me as the Falaise cripple he had been trying to kill.

"No," I replied.

Hervor continued to study me, while Onyame spoke, "Voldred is not Hervor's failure. In fact, it's hard to know what caused the failure, his Berserker training or King Magnus."

"King Magnus," Hervor said.

"As you know, I'm not certain," Onyame replied. To me he said, "Hervor and I have debated this before. You see, Voldred belonged to one of the few families that resisted King Olaf's conversions efforts."

Hervor tilted her head toward me. "The sainted father of King Magnus lacked gentleness when he converted others to the Christian faith. The families that resisted had to do so with either deception or force."

"In Voldred's case," Onyame continued, "his family — a fine one, almost a noble one — secretly gave him to a band of Berserkers to be trained. That's the cause of his failure, I believe. The Berserker training that once created terrifying warriors now twists men into killers. Anyway, when the band happened to be raiding in Iceland, Voldred met Hervor, and learning that she knew more about the old religions than his Berserker masters, he asked to be trained by her."

"I knew it was wrong. Taking a student at his own request." She shook her head. "Especially a Berserker. But he was eager and curious. And intelligent. He grasped teachings so quickly that I just … well, I did. Then King Magnus undid my work. If he hadn't sworn Voldred to some infernal mission in the South, I'd have been able to teach him more. His character wouldn't have turned."

I watched her face. Perhaps she and Onyame knew nothing of Voldred's mission, and killing me had been Magnus's idea alone.

"What did you train him in?" I asked, though I thought my voice sounded weak.

Hervor replied, "The power of rituals."

"Not weapons?"

"Weapons? Weapons? A Volva knows nothing of weapons," she said.

Onyame had been examining me. "You do know Voldred, don't you? How? He's a mysterious character and, I'd have thought, a dangerous friend if you're not a Berserker."

I considered whether or how I should answer.

Before I did, though, Hervor said to Onyame,. "Of course he knows Voldred. Falaise. That's what I recalled when I heard the name. Voldred has been there, but Voldred is not a friend of his, Bear. Can't you see that? He wants to avoid Voldred." She eyed me. "Isn't that right?"

"Yes."

"So let's do that," she said. "Shall we skirt the Assembly Plain and make for the ships?"

Onyame put up his hand. "As I said, Voldred wants to speak with you. A Volva cannot refuse —"

"I'd forgotten. He spoke with you." She paused. "Well, he need not see the face of my last student. We can at least keep Cuin from him."

Onyame frowned at her. "Cuin?"

"That's Brother Ambrose's real name. He's a hermit, not a monk. I assume we should hide all of that from Voldred as well." She looked at me.

"I'd be grateful if you did."

"Well, Bear, draw Voldred away from King Harald's men. Bring him here. I'll speak with him, put him off, and we can escape to your ships." She put her hand on my arm. "Do not fear. He'll get nowhere near you."

As Voldred approached with Onyame, I felt my legs become weak and unsettled, as if I wanted to run but lacked the strength. I pulled the hood of the now-grayed cloak over my eyes, so all that showed were my nose and beard.

I could just see Voldred's face with its hawkish nose and long scar. I now realized that the white hair had deceived me, as Garrad's white hair had done. This man was not that much older than Garrad. Dressed in an undyed tunic and leggings, partially covered with a gray cloak, he appeared to be a middle-aged peasant.

There was no sign of the terrible knife.

Voldred greeted Hervor, and she returned the greeting, adding an introduction for me. "He's in special training," she said, "and his face must not be seen by anyone until it's completed."

Voldred nodded. His growling voice startled me. It still seemed a thing of nightmares. "I understand the restrictions of rites."

I prayed he would obey them as well as he understood them.

Hervor asked, "What does the Volva's student wish to consult her about?"

He snorted and again startled me.

Hervor said, "You know you may speak in front of my other students."

Voldred hesitated and then said, "My mission for King Magnus. I need guidance."

She replied, "That's not a subject I'm happy to discuss."

"There is no one else I can talk to about it."

"Why don't you talk to King Magnus? Have him release you? Free you from whatever it is that's consumed most of your manhood?"

"I'm bound by an oath!" His voice rose. "You know that! The most solemn of oaths that can be taken."

"A binding oath? To a Christian king?"

"You know the answer to that. I'm bound whether he's a Christian or not. He made me swear by Mjolnir, the hammer of Thor. I no longer wish to be bound, but he will not release me."

She pushed her head toward him. "Will you break the oath?"

He snorted again. "Break an oath? I'm a Norwegian and a Berserker. How can I break an oath? What will be left of my honor if I begin breaking oaths? What will the gods to whom I swore do to me then?"

Onyame said, "The Icelanders have a saying, 'One oath abused does not make all oaths worthless.'"

Voldred scowled at him. "Let the Icelanders try to live by that. Let them tell it to their Gods."

Hervor straightened. "What will you do then?"

The scowl vanished. "Is there nothing you can do?"

"Voldred, if I could do anything to free you from King Magnus, I'd have done it years ago."

He seemed to freeze. "Then I must flee him. I have no choice. I cannot disobey him."

"Flee? Flee? Isn't that breaking the oath?"

Voldred's voice began to sound desperate, which startled me as much as his harshness had. "Only for a time. It may be enough. The men I've come with tell me that King Magnus will not live long."

Onyame broke in. "What did they tell you?"

"King Magnus is marked for death. If he dies, I shall be released."

"Will you?" Hervor said. "I didn't realize that death released a Berserker from a vow. What of the Gods?"

He frowned and shook his head. "I need time to think. I need to get away. I just need … This vow, this damnable curse, has forced me to travel incessantly. Perhaps all I need do is not go south."

"Is it so easy? Why haven't you done it before?"

He threw his hands into the air. "I'm cursed! You know that the vow binds me to go south. I must fulfill it. I must go. I thought that you would do something or know something though. If Magnus dies, surely there's a way —"

"I didn't bind you to this vow, and I cannot unbind you, even if Magnus dies. Either you must free yourself, or he must release you. Why don't you talk to him?"

Voldred almost shouted, "I've just done that. He bound me further. I should be in the South at this moment. But I had to get away. To think. That's why I came here. If you can't help me, I'll go further, over the edge of the world." He turned to Onyame. "You're going to Vineland. Take me with you."

I froze.

"I can't —" Onyame said.

"You cannot refuse a fellow student," Voldred said.

Onyame was silent for a moment. "You're right. Of course, I'll take you."

I was stunned.

"However," Onyame said, "you may travel in the ships behind mine, but you must not come on mine."

"It matters not at all. I'll travel wherever I can."

"You must also swear not to speak to or approach Hervor's new student."

"Of course, I shall ignore him. You have my word. I have no interest in him, anyway." His head swung toward me. "Who is he?"

"He's the seventh," Hervor said.

"Ah, yes," Voldred said.

"Finally," Onyame said, "you must get rid of those two men with you. Do you know that they're searching for me?"

"You and some monk, though they wouldn't say why."

"There's no need for you to know. Just send them away, across the country. Then meet us back here, and we'll go."

Voldred nodded and strode away.

When he was completely out of sight, I threw back my hood and glared at Onyame. "The man I've tried to avoid all my life will now accompany me to the end of the earth."

"I'm sorry. I had no choice. But he won't set foot on my ship. Of that you may be assured."

"Perhaps I should visit him on his ship."

"Why do you wish to avoid him so much? He seems too preoccupied with this mission of Magnus's to be any present danger to anyone."

Hervor's hood turned toward Onyame. "Think, Bear. Voldred's mission. It has something to do with Cuin." She turned to me. "Doesn't it? He's been sent by King Magnus to find you. Hmm. To kill you. That's it, isn't it?"

Onyame stared at me. "Is this true?"

I could not hide the truth from Hervor, and it seemed clear that neither she nor Onyame desired my death. "Yes. He's been chasing me since I was a child. I don't know why. I don't know why King Magnus wants me dead." I gritted my teeth. "Of course, now I'll have an opportunity to ask Voldred about it, if I wish."

Onyame put his hand on my shoulder. "Have no fear. We'll keep him from you. I already have a plan. Come. You'll spend a safer winter than you ever have."

We rode to the ships without incident, except that Voldred always seemed closer to me than I wished. Whenever steam hissed from the ground, I jumped and startled the pony.

Voldred remained in his saddle, apparently oblivious to his surroundings, his head drooped forward.

At the harbor, Onyame hurried me aboard his ship, and we set out in front of the other two. Voldred was assigned to the third ship, the farthest from us.

With no immediate bailing to do, I slouched on the bench next to Onyame, my hood over my head. Hervor leaned over the ship's prow, frowning at the sea.

The ocean chopped lightly as we sailed toward the southeastern coast of Greenland. The sky was clear, though it felt cold.

"Well," Onyame said, his hand resting on the tiller, "not only can Voldred not get near you, but he can't see you. He's looking backward at Iceland."

I glanced back at the third ship.

Onyame continued, "No doubt recalling his training, trying to think of anything that will free him from his vow to kill you."

"I hope he's successful."

"He won't be. Once Magnus had him swear on Thor's hammer, he was lost. Rituals were his training, and Magnus used that against him. To bind him." He turned his head. "Our pace will keep us well ahead of King Harald's men, too. Ulf and Vandrad. You will remain safe."

"Until we reach land."

"You need have no fear in Greenland. We won't be staying long. There's little there. A few small settlements. Rocky hills and mountains and an ice sheet behind them that stretches to the north as far as one can see. Nothing else, unless you become friendly with the seals and walruses, which I don't advise."

"What about the evenings? How shall I avoid Voldred in the evenings?"

"I'll simply refuse the hospitality of the settlers, and we'll sleep on the ships. You'll be safe. And you'll feel better than Hervor."

I looked toward the ship's prow. "What's she doing up there? Searching for dolphins?"

"She's trying not to be sick. Sea voyages have a bad effect on her."

"Perhaps some herbs —"

"Nothing helps. It's the curse of the Volvas. They can't travel over the sea. She'll sip the tea she makes from Icelandic liverwort and woodruff. She'll chew the ginger root I've gotten for her from Southern traders. Those only allow her to survive the ocean, though, not enjoy it."

I recalled how I had felt during the storm. "I sympathize with her."

"Yes, even with Voldred behind you, I'm sure you feel better than she does."

With the winds and currents driving us, we soon reached and rounded the southern tip of Greenland. I studied the snow-topped mountains, wondering whether I was seeing any part of the ice sheet that Onyame had mentioned.

I caught glimpses of bears and foxes, winding their way among the rocks, dwarf birch and scrub alder that clung to the shore. Some of the willows that had been used in shipbuilding survived, but they seemed oddly out of place in the rocky terrain.

Within a few days, we rounded a cliff-finger and rowed the three ships into a long fjord, farms dotting its shores.

Sigvald took the oar opposite Vagn, so I remained with Onyame.

"Eiriksfjord," Onyame was saying, "the largest of the fjords of the Eastern Settlement. It's where Eirik Thorvaldson himself farmed."

"Should I know who that is?"

"He's the Norwegian who named this great rock 'the Green Land.'"

"A jest?"

"He intended to attract settlers, since his personality would not. He had been exiled from both Norway and Iceland for being too quick to settle arguments with his axe."

"The man who settled this was a murderer?"

"More than once. His enemies called him Eirik the Red and not just because of the color of his hair and beard. A fine explorer, though. He sailed all around Greenland, laying out the Eastern Settlement. During Iceland's worst famine, he convinced several hundred Icelanders to join him here. Probably saved them from starvation. Then with his son Leif, he investigated the Western lands where we're headed: Flatstoneland, Forestland, and Vineland.

As far as I know, he and Leif were among the first to sail off the edge of the world."

I glanced at him. "They lived to tell about those places, didn't they?"

"Well, Leif the Lucky —" he began but was interrupted by the cries of wool-draped farmers from the shore, waving their arms as they ran toward us. Onyame leaned against the tiller.

After we unloaded the goods the Greenlanders had ordered — during which time Voldred sat alone on the third ship, brooding — Onyame pointed out Eirik's own farm, now occupied by his family, its great hall surrounded by a turfed fire-house, sleeping-chamber, well-house, and various storehouses and barns.

"Do you know what that is?" he asked, pointing.

I studied the small stone-and-turf structure with the cross jutting from its roof. "It appears to be a church."

"Yes, Eirik's wife Thjohild built it. Against his wishes. Though Eirik belonged to the old religion, his wife, converted by her son Leif, was a Christian." He laughed lightly. "I've heard that this chapel infuriated Eirik all his life, but Thjohild wouldn't let him touch it."

Hervor appeared beside us, her face slightly less pale.

"Are you feeling better?" I asked.

"Somewhat, thank you. The land feels good, though it sways. We may have a greater problem than my stomach, though. Is the ship of your friends striped with yellow, blue, and brown?"

"Ulf and Vandrad are hardly my friends."

Onyame frowned at her. "That's their ship, yes. Have you seen it?"

"It's sailing just to the southeast of the fjord. One of the Greenlander's children spotted it from the cliff."

Onyame muttered something under his breath.

I turned to him. "Could Voldred have told them where we were going?"

He strode past Hervor, glancing toward the sea. "The more pressing question is, can we get away in time?" He turned to her. "How close was the ship to the mouth of the fjord?"

"They're sailing sharply from the southeast, perhaps half an hour away, the child said."

Breaking into a run, Onyame called to us, "We must leave. Now."

We raced behind him. Hervor moved remarkably quickly for an old woman recovering from seasickness.

I did not even notice whether my leg and foot ached.

When we reached the shoreline, Onyame shouted at the crewmen. They bade quick farewells to the Greenlanders and pushed the three ships into the sea.

Thorkel and Sigvald tightened the sail. Vagn and I grabbed our oars. The crewmen on the other ships, including Voldred, did the same. Soon the three ships were cutting through the fjord's choppy waves toward the sea, pulling forward more quickly than I had ever seen them.

I strained every muscle trying to make ours move even faster, and for the first time Vagn did not complain about my rowing.

In a few minutes, we reached the entrance to the fjord. I was afraid even to glance toward the southeast as we rounded the cliff to the north.

As hard as I rowed, though, the rocks seemed to slip by more and more slowly.

Thorkel stood watch in the stern, calling out, "All clear. All clear."

For how long, though?

We approached an inlet on the northern side of the cliff. If we could slip into it, we would be hidden from any vessel entering the fjord's mouth.

Thorkel fell silent. Then he cried, "A ship's prow!"

Onyame twisted the tiller. We spun toward the inlet.

"One last pull and then silence!" Onyame shouted.

I wrenched my oar through the water and felt the ship spurt into the inlet. We glided toward the shore, and then Onyame swung us parallel with it. I stared at the cliff we had just rounded and held my breath.

At a sign from Onyame, Thorkel threw himself into the water and splashed ashore. He leaped over the rocks on the beach and began to climb, using his hands to speed himself along. Soon he reached the cliff's top and disappeared.

I glanced at Vagn. "We'll know soon," he said.

What seemed like half a day later, Thorkel reappeared, smiling and waving.

Vagn called to Onyame, "A fine piece of maneuvering. They didn't see us."

I heaved a sigh of relief. We had eluded Ulf and Vandrad once more.

For the next two days, we sped north along Greenland's west coast, again pushed by ocean currents and prevailing winds. Vagn kept watch when he was not rowing, but he saw no sign of Ulf and Vandrad's ship.

He did point out dolphins, leaping as they swam not far from us. He also spotted three black and two blue-gray whales, their huge backs rising in the water like great waves. How they tolerated the ice-strewn sea, though, I could not understand.

I had trouble just tolerating the rains we encountered. Here, unlike the milder, southeastern side of Greenland, the sun would often yield to a bank of clouds, wrap us in fog and pelt us with icy, stinging rain. The ship would pitch, and I would hear Hervor groaning. Then the clouds would move off, and the sun would reappear.

In spite of these abrupt weather shifts and the drenching of our cloaks and shoes, we soon reached our second destination, a wide, arching fjord with a string of farms clinging to its southern tip.

"The Western Settlement," Onyame said, "the last group of houses and fishing huts we'll see before reaching Vineland."

I stared at the turf buildings and wondered who would live in such a place, cold and desolate even in the summer. But the farmers seemed normal enough — tall, smiling, and hearty — and grateful to have the supplies we had brought them.

Again, Onyame did not stay long, and we were soon back on the ships, rowing for the sea.

For a time, Hervor seemed less ill. One afternoon, she picked her way toward the center of the ship, where I had stationed myself for bailing.

I hurled two buckets of water into the sea and greeted her. "I'm happy you're feeling better."

"Thank you. It's the colder, northern air. It gives me temporary relief."

"I'm sorry the sea voyage is difficult for you. Onyame said it was a problem for Volvas."

"That is so. And a worse problem for me. My father never traveled, either. I've been told that he too hated sea voyages."

"Didn't you know your father?"

She shook her head. "No. He had a secret alliance with my mother. No one ever knew. He was a Christian. Later married to a Christian woman. A fine man, I was told. He had the second sight, too."

"What happened to him?"

"He was burned alive with his sons and his Christian wife by his enemies, led by Flosi Thordarson."

"I'm very sorry." I wished there was something else I could say, but I could think of nothing.

"He knew about it, though. He was warned."

"The second sight?"

"That and a vision of the witch-ride."

"The witch-ride?"

"Ah, yes. You don't have that in Christian Normandy."

"Not that I've ever heard," I said. "Perhaps in Western Normandy, where they still worship Thor and Odin, they'd know of it."

She stared at the gray land in the distance. "Well, not long before my father was burned alive, a neighbor of his saw the witch-ride. The neighbor, a man called Hildiglum, Runolf's son, was standing outside his house. He heard a great roar. The earth and sky seemed to quiver, he said. He looked to the west and spied a ring of fire. In its center rode a man on what Hildiglum thought must be a gray horse, but it didn't look exactly like a horse. Whatever it was, the rider galloped past Hildiglum at a great speed, bearing above his head a blazing firebrand. Hildiglum could see and hear him distinctly. The rider shouted, 'I ride a horse with icy mane, forelock dripping, evil-bringing, fire at each end, and poison in the middle! Flosi's plans are like this flying firebrand — Flosi's plans are like this flying firebrand!'

"The rider hurled the firebrand east towards the mountains. A vast fire erupted, blotting the mountains from sight. The rider galloped east towards the flames and vanished into them."

I gaped at her.

"That was the witch-ride. A few weeks later, Flosi and his men burned my father and his family inside their own home."

We were sat, silent, for a long time. Then I said, "I'm sorry that your parents met such terrible fates."

"Yes, there are many terrible fates in the North. Many." She nodded toward me. "As there are in the South."

We pressed north until we reached a series of narrow fjords, barely wide enough for two longships. Onyame steered us into one of these, its steep sides allowing only little flat land for farms or pasture.

Here winter approached already. Even in the sun, snow encroached on the lower hills, and the wind felt thoroughly chilled. Ice floes speckled the ocean, making it resemble the black and gray seals that rolled on the rocky beaches.

My shoulders ached as I watched the seals, but they apparently had the good sense to be born without bones or muscles, so they could flop all over the rocks without injury.

We delivered wood to the lone farm and its wool-draped inhabitants. As we pulled back into the sea, avoiding the larger ice floes, the farmer, his wife and children waved gloved farewells.

Onyame and the crew also pulled on woolen hats and gloves. To keep the wind from penetrating their skin, Sigvald, Vagn and Thorkel smeared themselves with the foul-smelling oil I had first encountered in Denmark.

Onyame and I pulled our blue-gray cloaks more tightly around us, so we remained warm. I thought about expressing my gratitude to Hervor again. As I watched her groan at the ice floes, though, I decided to postpone the conversation.

At the mouth of the fjord, Onyame did not steer north but pointed the ship west toward the open sea. We had so seldom been out of sight of land that I was anxious at first, especially since the ice floes now seemed to grow into arching, blue-white hills, barriers to any northern passage.

Onyame skirted the floes easily, though, and assured me that land was not far away.

"It will appear on the horizon before long. Even now you can see some of the birds that make their home on Flatstoneland."

He was right. Long-necked geese and ducks flew overhead, and by the following morning, a rocky, ice-seized land stretched along the horizon, looking even more gray and barren than Greenland.

Within a few days, we had pulled the longship parallel to Flatstoneland and headed south. The gray and white coastland sailed by under an unusually dark blue sky. The ocean all around us looked black, and I was not surprised that settlers had not been inspired to land here.

Several times I glanced back at the two ships behind us and spotted Voldred's form. Once I prayed that the Lord might move Voldred's mind to strand himself here away from King Magnus, but the two ships, like ours, did not put in at any harbor on Flatstoneland.

As we plunged southward, the air warmed markedly, and the crew pulled off their woolen clothes and stopped using the foul-smelling oil, much to my relief

Evenings began to have some dusk in them, and by the time we reached Forestland, night had regained much of its darkness.

We put in at two white-sand beaches along the coast to search for food and fresh water. During the second stop, I joined Vagn and Thorkel to forage for roots, berries and bark far away from the hunting party of which Voldred was a member.

That night, as we sat around a blaze situated far from the fires of the other two ships, I placed myself between Hervor and Onyame.

"How did King Magnus come to bind Voldred to his vow?"

Hervor blew out a breath. "He tricked him."

"It hardly seems possible to trick a person into taking a vow to kill someone."

"You must recall," Onyame said, "that Voldred trained in rituals. They're his passion."

"And his undoing, which was why I trained him in the first place." Hervor shook her head. "He was tricked in spite of my training."

They fell silent again, so I asked, "What did Magnus do?"

Hervor let Onyame answer. "He asked Voldred to perform one of the old rites."

"Magnus is a Christian. Why would he —?"

"He claimed that he wanted to test the dedication of his non-Christian men," Onyame replied. "Voldred was, in spite of being a Berserker, the King's man."

I craned my neck forward. "So Voldred performed a sacrifice for Magnus?"

Onyame nodded. "Apparently in a private place behind one of Magnus's great halls. Voldred built the altar and slew a horned goat, burning its entrails on the altar and spilling its blood —"

I held up my hand. "Please, nothing about blood."

"I thought you wanted to know how Magnus bound Voldred."

"I do, but I don't want to know about the demise of an unfortunate goat. Besides, I don't see how that would bind Voldred."

Onyame continued. "Voldred thought that the ritual was merely the King's way of assuring a Berserker's allegiance."

Hervor snorted. "Voldred is nothing if not loyal."

Onyame hunched closer to the fire. "Then Magnus began to talk about how the Northern kingdoms could be undone by a Southerner, how the Northern Kings could come to naught, just because a single boy was allowed to live, how he himself, the King of Norway, would be left without a kingdom because of this boy, as had been prophesied by a famous Icelandic seer."

"The Prophecy of the Four Crowns, we call it here," Hervor said. "A Southern boy is supposed to be the rightful heir to the thrones of Denmark, Norway, England, and some Southern land, perhaps France, though the boy named in the prophecy is Norman. The fulfillment of the prophecy will precede the Death of the North. A thousand years later will come Ragnarok, the final battle. All the war gods will die. As I told you. So the Prophecy of the Four Crowns burns in Magnus's mind."

Onyame continued, "When Magnus asked whether a King's man, a Berserker warrior, could allow the death of the North, Voldred of course said no."

Hervor huffed. "What else could he say?"

"The King wanted to know whether Voldred would be bound by an oath to undo the prophecy. Assuming the oath meant remaining a warrior,

Voldred saw no harm in it. It would only prove his loyalty. At Magnus's urging, he swore an oath at the altar. The King then asked whether he would be bound to anything the King asked to undo the prophecy. Again Voldred swore he would. On Mjolnir, Thor's hammer."

"The fool," Hervor muttered.

"Voldred realized too late that he was trapped. The King had already bound him to killing the Southern boy mentioned in the Four Crowns' Prophecy."

"The Norman cripple who will undo Northern power," Hervor added.

Onyame glanced down at me. "Odd. You're not a cripple, and you don't look formidable."

I threw a stone at the fire, and sparks flew from it. "I was born with a deformed foot. I was in fact a Norman cripple, so that part fits, but many children in many Norman villages are cripples. The Prophecy must be about William, and I happened to be the only cripple he had as a friend. People are always trying to kill William. He is formidable and will become more so, if he lives."

"Can the seer have meant Duke William?" Onyame asked. "Not only is the Duke not a cripple, but there's another, more significant part of the Prophecy that doesn't fit him."

"What part?"

"The instrument of the Four Crowns uniting is to be a nephew of King Canute. Duke William is not a nephew of Canute."

"Perhaps it's a confusion," I said. "Lady Emma, the sister of William's grandfather, married King Canute, so that would make Canute William's ... great-uncle by marriage, wouldn't it?"

"We know that William's notorious great-aunt Emma married King Canute," Onyame replied. "That's well known in the North. It seems unlikely, though, that a seer would get both the physical description and the family relations wrong. Certainly Magnus and Voldred aren't convinced of that, or they'd have been trying to kill Duke William instead of you."

I almost wailed, "If only I could convince them!" I glanced at Hervor. "Could you?"

She hesitated a moment. "No. No. Voldred claimed that his whole life had been ruined by some cripple from Falaise. This boy was the cause of all the battles he never fought, all the lives he never lived, all the time he never spent with his family. Now I see what he meant."

"If you could convince him that there's been a confusion —"

She raised an eyebrow at me. "Could I convince him that he's wasted his life on a confusion? Why would he believe me? As Onyame says, Duke William is neither a cripple nor a nephew of King Canute."

"I don't understand, though. How can Voldred believe that I am this person? I couldn't be the King of anything. I'm a commoner. I told you that —"

She raised a hand. "Voldred will take the Icelandic seer at his word, as King Magnus has done. Besides, even if Voldred believed the seer had made a mistake, it wouldn't release him from his vow to King Magnus. Or to the Gods, which he fears more than anything. He swore at an altar on the hammer of Thor and on the name of Odin, the God who hung on a tree, that he would kill you. After that vow, he's determined to do just that. If I convinced him that William was the boy in the Four Crowns Prophecy, he'd be determined to kill Duke William. Is that a better alternative?"

My body sagged. "Then you must not speak to him. William's life is in enough danger. I've already put the whole of Normandy at risk, and undoing that may cost me my life."

Hervor frowned at Onyame.

"He often carries on like that," Onyame said, "though he has indeed blundered in an affair with King Harald. And he does need a solution."

"I'm afraid," Hervor said, "that the solution won't include talking Voldred out of killing you. There might be a way to release him from his vow." She nodded at Onyame, who nodded back. "My talking to him can't be the way, however. I'm sorry."

I jerked my hood farther down over my eyes. "So am I."

As we pushed south of Forestland, daylight and darkness returned to normal.

The currents stayed with us, but the wind did not, so Onyame steered a zigzag course to gain what wind we could. As a result, we had to row more, but I did not complain. Vineland, I was told, was not far away.

We had no idea how close behind us Ulf and Vandrad might be.

Then one cloudy morning, Onyame nudged one of my sore shoulders and pointed to the left side of the channel opening before us. "Vineland."

In front of the longship, a brown, sandy coast gave way to reddish brown rock shelves. Beyond the rocks stood grass-covered turf houses like the ones in Iceland and Greenland.

Here, though, the houses were surrounded by wooden buildings of many sizes and hemmed in by trees — not just the few pine, spruce, and birch we had seen scattered around Iceland and Greenland but also rows of oak, beech, and maple.

As we pulled the ships ashore, the Vinelanders ran to greet us with smiles and friendly cries. They jabbered at us in a dialect that seemed to combine Icelandic and Norwegian.

They also dressed like Icelanders or Greenlanders but with subtle differences. Their cloaks, belts and shoes were decorated with colored pins and a strange fur. Their hair was uniformly long and held by headbands, but they wore longer braids, tied in knots I had not previously seen in the North.

"We won't stay long," Onyame bent to say.

He must have seen me looking first at Voldred, whose ship had landed not far from us, and then out to sea for any sign of Ulf and Vandrad.

Nor did we stay long. That same afternoon, Onyame gathered the crews of the three ships onto an open stretch of the beach. The sun had burned away the morning clouds, and the day was warm.

Nonetheless, I huddled myself against the rock that was farthest from Voldred. Hervor stationed herself not far from me, breathing deeply and pressing her heels against a rock.

"As is my custom," Onyame told the crews, "I'm leaving two of the ships here to gather wood for the spring trip back to Norway, and I'm pressing farther south myself. I need more of the oaks that grow there, and I have a passenger in special training under Hervor. We'll need the winter to accomplish what we must. So we're sailing on immediately. I want to reach another landfall before dark. As usual, I'll return as soon as I can after the last snowfall. I hope you fare well during the winter. And gather as much wood as the ships will hold."

The other crews said their farewells, and we returned to Onyame's ship, pushing it back into the sea.

I had seen Voldred say something to Onyame as we parted, which Onyame told me was an assurance that Voldred would return to Norway with us in the spring.

For now the distance between us was widening with every gust of wind and stroke of the oar. It was the first time I enjoyed rowing.

We sailed along the west coast of Vineland, though Onyame soon began calling it "the People's Land." When I asked him what that meant, he said that I would discover soon enough. Hervor still hung over the ship's side, so I could not ask her.

Contradicting what Onyame had told the Vinelanders and the crews of the other two ships, we sailed even at night and slept on the ship.

"If Ulf and Vandrad put in at Vineland," Onyame said, "they'll think we're spending the night on some beach to the south." He stood at the tiller, a light night wind in his face. "Our sailing on should keep them at a fair distance until we determine what to do about them."

I heartily approved of the deception and began to believe Onyame's promise to keep me safe through the winter.

Nonetheless, I asked, "Is there an edge of the earth? I heard once that the earth is like a ball and has no edges."

"The earth may be like a ball. There are holes in it, though, and some of the holes have edges."

"Holes in the earth?"

"Yes, leading to the lands where the dwarves and trolls live. Don't Southerners talk about them?"

"Yes, but I didn't think that they lived inside the earth."

"Where do Norman trolls live? Do you assign them their own villages?"

"No, of course we don't. There just aren't that many trolls in Normandy, and I hadn't thought about them very much." I fell silent for a moment. "Where is this edge? Will we be approaching it soon?"

"Yes, but I'm afraid you won't see much of it. There's a mist ahead, and we may arrive at the edge in a full fog. Fog is common here, so there's nothing we can do. But we'll have to ... frighten the trolls away. And the demons, of course."

"Demons?"

"We can't go over the edge of the earth and not encounter a demon. That's a normal hazard."

Before I could determine whether he was serious, he shouted, "Vagn! The shields! We're close by, and there's a fog ahead."

"I see it," Vagn shouted back, and he, Thorkel and Sigvald hauled their shields from the sides of the ship. Using their fists, they began to pound the shields.

Hervor gave a loud groan and crawled back toward us. She gripped the side of the ship near my bench.

"Hervor?" I turned toward her, but she clung to the side, looking as gray as the fog, which closed in more and more.

Nothing else was visible. All that was left to my senses was the smell of salt air and the accursed pounding on the shields.

Soon, though, I thought I heard cries of seabirds and then voices. Onyame shouted at the crew for silence.

"What was that?" I asked.

Vagn and Thorkel cried out together, "The edge of the world!"

Abruptly a monstrous black shape loomed before us, and cries rang out around it in a gibberish language — the tongue of the demons.

Onyame leaned against the tiller, and Thorkel and Sigvald, dropping their shields, jerked the sail-ropes. Vagn grabbed his oar and pulled hard on it. The longship groaned and heaved to the left.

The devilish cries grew, and the black shape slipped by us.

I wrapped my arms around my bench. Hervor hung on the side next to me.

Black shapes formed in front of us, and the howls continued. Sigvald pounded on his shield again, to which the demons replied with shrieks and whistles.

We struck something, and the longship lurched to a stop. I tightened my grip. Surely now we would tip forward and plunge down eternally, demons flying at our heads. The back of the ship shifted in the water, but the front remained wedged on the edge of the earth.

To my amazement, Onyame abandoned the tiller and stepped toward me. Hervor took a deep breath and straightened.

"What are you doing?" I shouted at them over the demon's cries.

Hervor stepped in behind him and seized my arm. "Come."

"No!" I grabbed my bench more tightly.

They pried me off and dragged me to the steersman's side of the ship.

The howls of the demons rose, accompanied by a thudding of devilish drums. And an ominous scraping sound — the ship was slipping off the edge.

I looked wildly from Onyame's face to Hervor's. They betrayed nothing, but I suddenly realized the evil intent: to hurl me into oblivion.

So Onyame and Hervor had been in on the plot to kill me after all. This was how they would free Voldred from his vow.

Here, at the end of all life, I finally learned the truth.

"Throw him over," commanded Hervor, the Volva-edge on her voice.

Struggling, I stared into the faces of the demons, now emerging from the misty depths, their heads carved into hideous shapes, their eyes slanted with anger and hate, their skin red with hellfire.

"No!" I screamed again.

Onyame and Hervor lifted me and flung me into the demons' outstretched arms.

CHAPTER 17

RED ANGELS

A.D. 1046

Dark arms caught me. Dark red mouths shrieked. I struggled and cried out, but my cries drowned in the din.

Then I stopped struggling and stared from form to form.

What had appeared as carved demon heads were colored designs painted on reddish-brown faces. Human faces. Around the faces hung long black hair, held in headbands. The faces belonged to human bodies, tall and draped with bead-strings, blankets and animal skins. And grinning.

Beneath my feet were no flames. Only sand.

Hervor and Onyame jumped down behind me, laughing with the men and women and calling to them in the same gibberish that had greeted me. The reddish-brown people hugged Onyame and Hervor, beaming at them and chattering. I heard them repeat one word again and again that sounded like "nikmak."

Vagn, Thorkel and Sigvald splashed from the ship and pulled it onto what I now recognized as a fog-drenched beach.

Onyame shouted, "I'm sorry, Cuin, but this is the tradition for everyone's first trip over the edge of the world. You were so very convinced about demons!"

I sputtered at him, "I could have died of fright!"

"No one has yet."

Hervor edged toward me, her arms entwined with two of the reddish-brown people. "At least we're finally off that accursed water. Be thankful you have land under your feet. Besides, in time, you'll laugh over this."

"No, I won't."

Onyame translated this to the red people, who howled with laughter, pounded me on the back and rubbed my head and called out "nikmak" again.

It was annoying. "What are they doing?'

"They're greeting you as a friend."

"It's charming." I grimaced as they continued their pounding and rubbing.

"Who are these people?"

"The People," Onyame replied, stepping closer to me.

"I can see that they're people, but what people?"

"They call themselves Lnu'k, the People. Or the Human Beings. That's all. This is the Land of the People."

"I see. Can you persuade them to stop beating me?"

"They're just being friendly. They're very friendly. And they're calling you a 'kin-friend,'—'ni'kmaq' — because you are allied with Hervor and me. You'll like them."

"Perhaps. If they stop pounding on me."

After the "People" released me, Onyame and Hervor pointed to the ship, still speaking the People's language. With Onyame leading, a group of them joined the crew and began unloading what was left of our supplies.

Though I felt only partially recovered, I helped them and added, for Onyame to hear, a few grumbles about terrifying people to death. He paid no attention.

The People then herded us back to where Hervor conversed with the main group.

In the distance behind Hervor, I could discern shadows in the fog. As we walked toward the shadows, they sharpened into odd-looking enclosures, some round, some conical. Wooden racks stood around them. I heard the barking of dogs and saw the movement of small, brown forms.

Deciding to forgive Onyame for the moment, I asked him, "Is this a village?"

The People still surrounded him, and two woman in particular had attached themselves to his arms as he walked. "A kind of village and certainly one of the largest gatherings of the People. Several related families live here, enlarged by the group that came just to meet us. There are other groups scattered back into the forest, especially at this time of year. This is where this group spends the summer."

"They have separate huts for other seasons?"

"These are birchbark strips tied with black birch roots over spruce frames. They're easily moved. We won't winter here. We'll join the other groups farther up on the lake."

"That's good." Then I realized what he meant. "Will we be spending a whole year with these … these 'People'?"

"Not quite a year. Until spring. This is one place no assassin will find you. Only a handful of Northerners have ever come here, and all have traveled with me and my crew."

"What about Hardraada and Magnus?"

"They'll have time to forget you and begin squabbling with each other. That can't hurt your mission."

I began to reply, but the smell of roasting meat reached my nostrils. My fears about the Norwegian Kings and the year ahead vanished. "Is that for us?"

"What?"

"The food."

He took a deep breath and smiled. "Yes, the People always have food prepared. They've known about our coming for some time."

"They have? How?"

Before he could answer, we reached the largest of the rounded birchbark-and-spruce structures, and several of the People urged him into it.

Hervor appeared beside me.

I directed my question to her. "Did the People know we were coming?"

"Yes. We pounded on the shields."

"That was a sign?"

She nodded. "The second sight is here, too. They have long known that we were near. Come. Let's go in and eat."

I needed no second invitation. We bent through the entrance.

In the center of the round enclosure stood a wooden spit with meat suspended from it on leather thongs. The thongs had been twisted, so that as they untwisted and retwisted, the meat turned. Under the meat, burning logs, encased in a circle of wooden stones, glowed as if they had been lit hours earlier. On either side of the spit were small grills of green wood placed directly on the coals, on which smaller pieces of meat were cooking. Lying just inside the stone circle were pockets of leaves.

Hervor nodded toward the spit. "Bear meat. Inside those leaves will be clams and mussels, I hope."

She directed me to kneel on the rushes covering the dirt floor. As I did, I spied a second fire at the far end of the enclosure. It, too, was cooking meat suspended on thongs, but I could not identify its smell.

"Walrus," she said in reply to my glance. "Next to it are seeds and roots. Some we don't even have in the North. I'm sure you'll enjoy their taste. Especially since you can swallow that wretched cider."

I would have given her a haughty look, but my attention had already shifted to several of the People, men and women, carrying woven baskets of blueberries and raspberries.

Two other women bore skins filled with a liquid that smelled of cranberries. They deposited the skins near the walrus, where three other women, holding wooden tongs, knelt over hardwood logs. Then I realized that the logs served as kettles.

"What are the tongs for?" I asked Hervor.

"Boiling meat."

"They boil meat with tongs?"

"Don't be dull-witted. They use the tongs to handle the hot stones. Stones from the fire. To heat the water. That boils the meat." She sniffed the air. "Geese or ducks in this log, I think. Probably fish stew in the that one. Groundnuts, maybe wild rice or maize, green corn, in the third."

"What's that sweet smell, like berries cooking?"

"Ah, that smells good, doesn't it? Elderberry bread. You deserve that, after all you've been through."

"I look forward to it," I said, just in time to be served a slab of meat, which Hervor identified as bear, on a wooden plate. Its arrival ended the conversation.

During the feast, I remained next to Hervor. Onyame sat not far away, still surrounded by the two women who had become a semi-permanent part of his upper body. As he ate, he spoke, and the People listened attentively.

I assumed he was describing our journey from Denmark. I heard my name several times, along with my aliases, Augustine and Ambrose. The People did not stare at me, though. They merely nodded at intervals. Occasionally they laughed, and I gave Onyame a sharp look to warn him that I did not want to be the object of some jest. Once again he ignored me.

Since the People were polite enough not to stare at me, I did not stare at them. But corner-of-the-eye glances served just as well. The People had separated themselves into groups. The women sat on one side of the enclosure, the men on the other. Thus I could alternate my glances, seeming to be looking back and forth at random.

The first thing I noticed was that the separation of the men from the women did little to discourage interaction, if that was what it was intended to do. Indeed, the men and women appeared to be exchanging both friendly and flirtatious looks.

"Yes, they're flirting with each other," Hervor said in a low voice, apparently reading my thoughts.

The children had been moved farther away. The distance prevented their learning flirting prematurely, I thought — fortunate, since the younger ones were naked — and they remained separated from the adult conversation. This was especially useful, because the children sat little and were seldom quiet, though I noticed that they were not loud.

A few men and women, fully dressed, sat near the children but did nothing except pat or stroke them throughout the meal.

I finished the meat, vegetables, and tubers I had been given and was enjoying the cranberry liquid when Hervor leaned toward me again and whispered, "Do you want some of the sweet elderberry bread?"

"Yes, please."

Between bites, I returned to studying the People, who sat straight and tall all around me. In fact, their height was what I had noticed immediately. Even seated, most of them towered over everyone except Onyame. Even the older people sat very straight, making their height seem even greater.

When I asked Hervor about it, she whispered, "This particular group is related to some of the Tall People."

Both men and women had the slightly slanted eyes that I had seen from the ship. Only now they did not resemble the eyes of demons, though I realized that I had never seen a demon face to face. Whatever demons' eyes looked like, the People's eyes seemed cheerful and friendly. They were set in reddish-brown faces, reddened further by the fire's glow. Each face was smooth, except for weathered wrinkles on the older faces.

Unlike Northerners, the men wore no beards. In fact I could not even discern the stubbled chins common in Normandy, where men shaved every three or four days. Here, the men seemed to have no beards at all. This feature made the men seem younger than they probably were.

Both men's and women's faces had the multi-colored designs painted on them that had made me mistake them for demons. Patches and stripes of black, yellow and green covered the foreheads, noses, cheeks and chins. I could not discern any common patterns, though. The designs seemed individual to each man or woman.

As the People ate or smiled, I noticed their teeth. They were unusually straight and white. As in Normandy and the North, the teeth of the elders were ground down from eating coarse bread. Here, though, everyone seemed to have all of his or her teeth — and healthy teeth.

The hair of both men and women was black and hung long over the shoulders, sometimes plaited in the strange braids I had noticed at the Vineland settlement. Apparently the settlers there had been influenced by these braids, so I deduced that groups of the People lived near Vineland as well.

The loincloths and leather leggings that I had noticed earlier were painted with geometric patterns — red, violet, green, and different shades of yellow. The blankets and furred robes hanging over the shoulders of both men and women were similarly decorated and tied in front with thongs. Some women also wore leather tunics, decorated with the long pins I had seen at Vineland.

Around the necks of both men and women hung necklaces from which dangled shells, stones, or the feet of animals and seabirds. Some sort of crooked knife also hung from the necks of men and women.

The People began replying to Onyame and reciting what sounded like long, poetic stories. Their speech had marked cadences, repetitions, and even rhyming sounds.

"They sound as if they're reciting poetry," I whispered to Hervor.

"The People's language sounds that way, yes. It lends itself to rhyming. And the People speak rhythmically. They use many images. Like the ones in Icelandic poetry. About mountains, trees, rivers, animals, clouds."

I reached for another hunk of elderberry bread.

Hervor leaned toward me again. "How do you like them?"

"Very tasty."

"Not the hunks of bread. The People."

"Well, anyone who can make bread as good as this must be admirable."

"They're beautiful, too, don't you think?"

"The hunks of bread?"

"The People. Can you stop thinking about the bread?"

I took another mouthful. "I don't think so."

"A young woman has been glancing at you. With some interest."

I wiped crumbs off my mouth and sat up straight. "She has? Which one?"

"Keep your eyes open. You'll notice."

In a few moments, I spotted a young woman to my right, sitting against the side of the enclosure. She was shorter than most of the People and had a fuller figure. She may have been a few years younger than I, with a roundish, pretty face, braided hair with more waves in it than the other women, and a red and white blanket over her shoulders, hanging down to her waist.

As Hervor had said, she gave me a sidelong glance, smiled at me, and nodded.

"She may get to know you, to like you," Hervor said quietly. "She may even invite you to her bed."

I widened my eyes at Hervor, who just smiled.

"I've had a hard day," I said. "I think I'd better just stay in my own bed tonight, wherever it happens to be."

My bed happened to be in the center of a conical-shaped enclosure, which was constructed, like the round enclosures, of birchbark sheets tied with roots to tall poles. The poles leaned together at the top, creating a smokehole.

Furs had been strewn invitingly over a rush-covered floor.

Onyame was my escort and was talking as I sank onto the furs. "The People call this a wikuom. The round ones are called wikuoms, too. It will keep you comfortable even in the fog."

I felt drowsy. "Wikuoms? What does it mean?"

"A dwelling or shelter."

"Not a home?"

"The People consider the entire world home. A wikuom is merely a covering, like a blanket to us."

I blinked to keep my eyes from closing. "The whole world? Well, they might feel at home in Falaise, but I doubt they'd be comfortable at court in Rouen."

"Does anyone feel at home at court? This wikuom will feel much more like home than any court."

"It's inviting, this 'shelter.' The feast and the trials of the day"— I gave him another sharp look, which he again ignored — "will at least mean a good night's sleep."

"If you can sleep on the ship, you'll have no trouble sleeping on these furs." He rose. "I've never seen you have trouble sleeping anywhere, though."

I lay down and looked up at him. My eyes felt heavy, but I managed to ask, "Aren't you sleeping here?"

"No, I have a wikuom of my own ..."

I heard no more.

The following morning dawned bright, and the sun slanted through the top of the wikuom. I yawned and glanced around at the other furs. I had slept alone.

As I stretched and smoothed my hair and beard into place, Onyame crouched through the doorway.

I straightened and stood up. "Good morning."

He grinned at me. "A fine morning. Did you sleep well?"

"Very well, thank you. Especially since I needed to recover from both a feast and the shock of being thrown off the edge of the world. In spite of that cruel treatment, I'm ready to face a sunny day." I stepped toward the entrance.

"Good. I think I should warn you —"

I had already pushed through the rounded doorway, which someone had covered with skins to keep out the chill of the previous night's fog.

I glanced backward at the skins and the birchbark strips that had protected me all night. They were decorated with geometric red and yellow patterns. Like the patterns on the faces of the People, they were pleasing, and I smiled at them.

When I turned to face the village, though, I stopped short. My mouth fell open.

All around me were the things I might have expected to see: a few round and several conical wikuoms, external cooking fires, drying racks, baskets, clay pots, brown dogs lying near the fires or engaged in play, a white-sand beach spreading out toward a calm ocean. On either side of the beach stretched long fingers of stone, the northern one being the black, pine-covered cliff we had barely missed as we sailed into the harbor. Of course, the People worked on the beach, no longer wearing the robes that had protected them from the chilly fog.

What I did not expect to see, however, was the female dress. Or lack of it. The women, young and old, had abandoned their tunics and wore only the soft-leather skirts or leggings I had seen the night before.

Nothing else.

Onyame stepped beside me. "I wanted to warn you about their mode of dress. I see you've already noticed. Try not to stare."

"How can I not stare?"

"It's true that they have beautiful bodies, but they have a strict etiquette about respecting each other's privacy."

I arched my eyebrows at him. "Privacy?"

"Their notion of privacy, which includes not staring."

"Well, respecting their privacy is going to take some discipline."

He put a hand on my shoulder. "Did you have any training as a monk?"

"No. Though just now, I wish I had."

He smiled. "Perhaps later you'll be happy you did not."

He accompanied me to the edge of a small stream just north of the beach, where I washed, keeping my eyes fixed on the water. The stream branched off from a wide, rapid river just to the south of the cliff-finger.

Then we joined one of three large groups of the People on the beach, where Hervor already sat next to an older man.

I tried to keep my eyes on faces, especially the women's, while Onyame translated my greetings and thanks to the People for all they had done for me.

They smiled and nodded in return. One of the dogs settled down next to me, apparently adopting me for the moment. I scratched behind his ears and stroked his back.

A person sat down next to me, and I saw with relief that he was a man. Though he was dressed like the People — with a loincloth, leggings and a painted skin tunic pulled over against the morning breeze — he was not one of them. He had a full brown beard and a light-skinned face, tanned only by the summer's sun. The reddish brown tints of the People's skin were missing.

He greeted me in the Icelandic dialect. "Good morning. I understand your name is Cuin and that you're a Southerner. I'm an Icelander myself. My name is Thorvald."

"I'm pleased to meet you, Thorvald," I replied, extending my hand. "Oddly, your name seems familiar, though I'm not sure why."

"Didn't Bear tell you about me?"

Onyame spoke up, "This is the man whose sister you met near the Bay of Smoke — the one who gave you the cloth to pray for her brother."

"Now I remember. The cloth you bet unsuccessfully on horses and wrestlers."

"The same." Onyame said, smiling broadly. "Thorvald fled Iceland to escape that sister and her husband."

Thorvald smiled at me. "They were too strong-willed for me. Living here with the People, though, is my ideal life. Quiet and peaceful."

"I see. No one from Iceland ever comes here?"

"Not this far south."

Onyame passed me a wooden plate, holding what I identified as smoked fish, groundnuts, green corn, raspberries, and some elderberry bread. I thanked him and began to eat.

"That brings us back to Ulf and Vandrad," Onyame said. "Unlike most Northerners, they will journey this far south. With the help of some of the People, Hervor and I have formulated a plan to deal to deal with them. Though it may be risky."

"You're not planning to kill them, are you?" I asked between bites.

"The People would never agree to killing anyone," Thorvald said.

"Not kill," Onyame said, "but they will help us push Ulf and Vandrad off the edge of the world. In one of Hervor's fogs."

After I had eaten, Onyame, Hervor and I, accompanied by ten of the People carrying digging tools, left the village. We strode toward the river not far from where I had washed before breakfast.

We crossed a rope bridge suspended between two trees, and I could look down at the water and watch it rush into the bay. Having crossed the river and toiled up a massive stone, we trod single file along a pine-enclosed path that edged the cliff-finger.

Soon, through the trees to my right, the ocean appeared, glinting in the morning sun. I squinted at its brightness and then swung my head to my left, where the pines pointed toward the mountains behind them.

I caught the shapes of several women out of the corner of my eye and quickly jerked my head forward again. Finding Onyame just ahead of me, I concentrated on his back as if he were a poem I was copying back in the St. Vaast monastery.

Hervor and he led us along the winding path, packed earth broken here and there by stretches of stones, which had been rounded by the ocean's waves. I took my eyes off Onyame only to focus on the stones, taking care that my shoes did not slip on them. A few hundred feet north of the People's village, we reached another bay.

Onyame shielded his eyes with his hand and glanced at the sky. "Good. It's sunny, but we have a cool morning for digging."

I stepped beside him, breathing heavily. "Digging what?"

"A path wide enough for a longship."

Since concentrating on not staring had consumed my mental energy, I began to work without questioning him. Following his lead, I borrowed a digging tool from one of the People — a man — and began scraping around a bush.

By morning's end, we had dug bushes and and small trees all they way from the bay to a stream several hundred feet behind the bay. The People had followed us, replanting the bushes and trees farther back in the forest.

"What about this stream?" I asked Hervor as we paused for a rest. I rubbed my lower back.

"Don't bother about it. A person can wade through it. And the longship will have no trouble with it."

Behind us, the People were cutting down the last of three tall trees that had blocked the beginning of the path. I turned to watch them. Fortunately, they were all men.

The ax-wielders hesitated before chopping, though. They stepped close to the trees and spoke.

"What are they doing?" I asked Hervor.

She squinted at them. "Telling the trees that they're sorry. That they'll use all of the tree. That it will become part of the People's lives. The tree likes to know. It's willing to give itself, but it wants to know what for. It feels relieved, I would say."

If that was true, by week's end there were ten relieved trees between the bay and the place where our work finally ended.

I leaned on my digging tool and stared at a lake large large enough for a fleet of longships. We had cleared steadily uphill, so the lake stood high above the bay, stretching between two bowl-shaped mountains that joined at its western end.

At the eastern end, a river rushed down the hill, aiming, I supposed, at the ocean.

"This is the head of the People's river," Hervor told me, "The one we cross every morning. Near the village."

"Ah, yes. The one that creates the small sloping waterfall near where I wash."

"Wide enough for a longship."

I looked at it with new interest. "Is it?"

"Yes. First, we get the longship onto this lake. Then the river carries it back toward the ocean."

I rubbed my lower back, which had by now become an hourly habit. "I think I see what your plan is. Finally."

She patted my arm. "Good. Good boy. Clever."

I frowned at her. "More clever than you may think. It apparently hasn't occurred to you that a longship can't walk. The path is wide enough, certainly, but how will we ever get a longship up it? We'd have to mount the ship on rollers and pull it with ropes, all the while hoping that Ulf and Vandrad wouldn't bother to leave the ship to kill me."

She grinned and patted me again, as if I were a dog. "Leave that to me. And the People."

That night, I spent my leisure time with Hervor, as I had all week.

Onyame had worked near us during the day, but he spent his evenings with the two women who had clung to him since the first night. Occasionally, they were joined by an earnest-looking young man.

I did not have an opportunity to ask Onyame who these People were, especially since I had distractions of my own — the women's attire and the food. I was happy for the meals, because there was constant cooking going on in the village, and whenever we returned from our clearing work, I could smell the food. The women baked bread or cooked groundnuts or smoked meat and fish on racks built over smoldering fires, while glazed pottery with geometric designs held steaming liquids, local teas or berry drinks.

Most of the People seemed curious about me and took pains to converse with me through Hervor. They seemed very polite, at least in translation, and they often laughed, teasing me and each other.

They were also eager to teach me their language, and I was eager to learn.

The small, brown dog who had adopted me the first night became a constant companion in the evenings. He brought another dog with him each night, until I had often had five dogs lying around me, vying for ear-scratching. Apparently my technique was good, and word had spread among the Canine People that the newcomer had talent.

The night we finished the path was no different. Three dogs lay near me.

About ten of the People, talking and laughing, grouped around the firepit just outside my dwelling. Hervor and I would not be alone. The night was clear and cool, so the women who sat cross-legged near me wore robes, to my relief.

Sitting behind us, away from the firepit, were another three men. I had learned by this time that anyone who did not wish to speak only had to move away from the firepit, so no conversation would be directed to these three until they returned to the circle.

One of the People commented on the dogs, saying that I had attracted "Star Persons."

"What does that mean?" I asked Hervor.

"To the People, the stars are Shape-Changers. They take many forms. As stars, they hunt through the sky. Stars are also singers. And birds of fire. And animals. Animals on the Earth World were once Star Persons. Dogs are Star Persons from what we in the North would call the Dog Star, Sirius."

The same man who had noticed the dogs said something, and Hervor translated it. "He says that he wonders something. That's the same as asking a question here, though you need not answer it. He wonders what kind of child attracts Star Persons."

"What does he mean by that? What kind of childhood did I have that I attract dogs?"

"Just that, yes."

In our early conversations, the People had chuckled whenever I mentioned a Norman name. Now, when I replied to the man that I had spent my childhood in a castle with Duke William, general hilarity broke out. They repeated "Duke William" over and over, exaggerating the sounds by contorting their mouths, and I realized that my language must sound as odd to them as theirs sounded to me.

After the laughter settled down, I told them about my life in the castle and how the dogs there often followed me around, so they seemed like friends.

In return, I wanted to ask the People about their land and how they prepared their food. I was certain that Garrad would be curious about the land, while the Falaise castle cooks could benefit from detailed descriptions of the food-preparation.

Hervor helped me express my desire in a way that was not a direct question, something considered intrusive to the People.

"Part of respecting privacy," she said, "is not asking direct questions, which forces an answer. This the People consider overly aggressive."

"How do I make my desire for knowledge known to them then?"

"You shape your question in the form of a desire to know something. Then you let them respond. I'll help you shape the requests."

Which she did. I stated my desire to know about their lives. And their food.

The People readily volunteered details of food gathering and cooking. They also explained how they made many of their tools as well, especially the crooked knives that all of them wore around their necks — a long, sharpened beaver's tooth hafted to a carved wooden handle, painted with several colors.

They referred to the beaver as "a Beaver Person," and I noticed that they referred to all animals, plants and even rocks as Persons: "Sturgeon Persons" or "Clay Persons" or "Tobacco Persons."

Tobacco Persons appeared often, since all the men, women and children owned their own stone, shell or wooden pipes, in which they smoked the plant called "Tobacco Person," often mixed with the leaves, bark, and what I recognized as stems of bearberry and lobelia.

In a lull in the story-telling, I turned to Hervor. "They call themselves 'People,' but they also call everything else a 'Person.' Is everything a person to them? A living being? Ensouled?"

She nodded. "The animals are Persons. The plants are Persons. The stones are Persons. And they can change their shapes, as you've heard. Animals were once stars. Boulders are Persons resting or contemplating."

"They're all alive then?"

"Alive and powerful. All Persons have Power, a Power unique to that Person. Not all choose to use it, though. Not all know how to use it."

"You mean that even rocks and trees have Power?"

"Yes. They use it more quietly than human Persons. In turn, human Persons use their Power less than the Mn'tu'k, the Spirit Persons."

"Like angels?"

"Perhaps. They may take form. Or not. They live in all the six worlds. Each world shimmers in their presence."

I looked at her blankly.

She thought for a moment. "What would that mean to you? Hmm. They're sacred, your priests might say. Don't ask about religion, though. No word in their language means religion, so I suppose you couldn't ask them, if you wished to. But don't wish to, since it will be considered both unanswerable and impolite."

After I volunteered stories about the lives of Abraham, Moses, Jesus, the apostles, martyrs, and saints, several of the People replied with stories about how their world had been created and how they received certain plants and animals from "the Land Above the Earth." They spoke of people who could change their shapes, of ghosts and guardians, of animal-spirit-helpers and men and women with great powers.

The person I had talked with most — and did again this evening — was the young woman Hervor had noticed watching me the first night. Every time I sat somewhere, she seemed to be sitting near me.

Her name was Young Moons, and speaking with her was more an ordeal than clearing a path for a longship. She was friendly enough. Her speech, as rhythmic and image-laden as others, Hervor could easily translate.

She seemed, though, to wear less than most of the women around me. Her loin cloth was as brief as it could be and still fulfill its intended task, while her leggings seemed tighter and more revealing than those of the other women. Her only other articles of clothing, except for the robe she wore this evening and other cool evenings, were her shoes, called "mocassins" by the People.

She was pretty, I thought, and her hair had black curls in it, different from the straight hair of most of the People, to which I found myself drawn. Her figure, which I could not avoid noticing, had all of the grace of the People and nothing to discourage staring, being fuller in her hips and much fuller in her chest.

I tried not to stare, though, and to keep my mind on our discussions. Young Moons, though, seemed intent on keeping her mind on me, so my concentration lapsed more than once.

This night, however, my conversations with Young Moons broke off when Hervor, accompanied by an old man she often spoke with, disappeared from the firepit.

The rest of us sat in silence. Even the dogs lay quietly but kept their eyes open. I knew by now that if the people fell silent, there was a good reason, so I did as well.

We sat for a long time. The People seemed to have patience that I did not. Where had Hervor gone, and when would she return? After what felt like half the night, I noticed a mist drifting around us. One of the now-familiar summer fogs began to enshroud the village.

The dogs stood and began to pace.

A women rose and fetched some berry bread and offered it to us. Everyone sitting around the firepit tore off a piece of it.

Hervor returned as I was finishing my piece.

"The longship is arriving," she said, translating for the People.

My stomach turned queasy, but I forced the bread down.

Young Moons leaned toward me and smiled, her face looking like an angel.

Onyame, having apparently separated himself from his two women companions, appeared, towering over me. "How soon?" he asked Hervor.

"Not long now."

"It's a good fog," he said.

Hervor nodded. "Thank you."

I rose and faced Hervor. "Did you make this fog?"

"Of course."

"How? Could you teach me?"

"It's not part of your training."

Onyame took me by the arm. "Come. I want to hide you where you can watch the spectacle."

Accompanied by twenty-four of the people, he led me along the same path we walked everyday to and from our work, but with the fog pressing around us, I had to stay close behind him to follow the path. The rounded rocks seemed more slippery and demanded more concentration.

We reached the northern bay before I realized we had left the cliff-finger.

Onyame concealed me between Sigvald and Vagn in a copse of bushes and oak trees. Thorkel had remained in the village.

The People, looking like spirits in the distance, crowded on the beach near the cleared path. Onyame, Hervor, and the old man stood at their head.

I shivered near Sigvald, whether from the chilly fog or the thought of facing Ulf and Vandrad, I could not tell.

"Probably both," Vagn replied as I thought out loud.

Sigvald silenced us. "Listen!"

We turned our ears toward the bay, and I could soon hear — though I could see nothing but mist — the cries of a Norwegian crew and the creaking of a longship.

Sigvald pointed. "Look. The People are setting out in their canoes."

The word "canoes," I had learned, referred to craft made from birchbark with their sides curved up in the center to keep out waves. These were what we could barely discern, their now-grayed forms gliding into the bay.

The plan was that, hidden by mist, the canoes would slip unseen behind the longship. Three of the men, strong swimmers, would drop into the water near the longship's stern and guide it toward the shore. In the fog, all this would be invisible to us.

"I still don't know what this is supposed to accomplish," I said to Vagn.

"I do," he replied, "but I I'm not sure I believe it."

"What?"

"Just listen. That's what I was told. To listen."

We listened. In a few minutes, a cry drifted toward us through the fog. Then a second. And a third. Then a host of cries. They were not Northern cries, though. They issued from the People.

We heard pounding, as if many sticks were striking hollow logs. The rhythmic beats increased in volume, joining the cries. I winced at the noise. The shouts and pounding seemed to be beating directly on my head.

Then Sigvald pointed. "Look! There!"

Through the fog we could see the longship as it entered the bay. I thought I could see forms moving on it. Any sound they might have been making, though, was drowned by the pounding and the cries.

The longship beached itself.

The cries and pounding rose to an almost unbearable level. I put my hands over my ears.

The longship shuddered. Then it lifted out of the water and began to sail through the air. I blinked. The fog blurred my vision, but I could not see anything holding the ship.

The People ran beside it, chanting and waving their arms — but they did not touch it.

I glanced at Vagn, who muttered, "I don't know what I'm seeing."

The ship sailed along the path we had cleared for it and floated into the forest beyond our sight.

I stared at Vagn again. "Did that ship —? Did you see it —?"

He looked dazed. "I saw it," he repeated, "but I don't understand what I saw."

"Did it ... float? In the air? Was that some sort of miracle?"

"If it were a miracle, I might understand it," Vagn said, "but this is Hervor's doing. And the old man, the Man with the Power."

I gaped at him. "Hervor and that man made a longship fly?"

"Yes!" shouted Sigvald, who seemed eager to seize the impossible. "Come on! Let's get back to the river's mouth."

Falling in behind Sigvald, Vagn and I trotted as quickly as we could in the fog. We traced the narrow path back toward the People's village.

I stubbed my toes on exposed roots and wrenched my ankles on the slippery stones, but I cursed in Norman French, so that Sigvald and Vagn would not hear me. Of course, Sigvald and Vagn had taught me Northern curses, which they never hesitated to use in bad weather or crises.

We reached the cliff overlooking the river and threw our bodies onto the massive rock, hiding behind one of its ledges. We crouched there, trying to hear over the river's rapids and our own panting.

The cries and pounding, far away, abruptly stopped.

We waited for long minutes, but nothing happened.

Then, as we listened more than watched, the longship approached, lurching through the river. We could hear the crew, cursing and praying — and doing both loudly.

Piercing hoots and howls accompanied them. The People still trotted beside the ship, doing their best to sound like demons. Sigvald let out a few shrieks, and when my ears recovered, I joined him. Vagn just stared at us.

Driven by the river, the longship swept by us like some ghostly sea-monster, rushing down the sloping rapids toward the bay.

The People shrieked more loudly. In the village the dogs barked.

The Norwegian crew replied with cries of terror. I even thought I heard Ulf's voice howling about "the edge of the world" and warning everyone to prepare to battle monsters. A voice I did not recognize cried out, "We're going over the edge! We're going over! We'll be killed!"

Sigvald, Vagn, and I abandoned our hiding-place.

We stumbled to the bottom of the rapid to see the longship shoot into the bay, twist seaward with the current, and with the aid of four strong swimmers provided by the People, push into the ocean.

We heard the crew crying for the open sea, and soon the longship vanished in the mist.

CHAPTER 18

VISIONS

A.D. 1046

The next morning dawned sunny again, and I rose earlier than I ever had, even for the fairs and festivals back in Falaise.

The People, apparently exhausted, had returned to their wikuoms immediately after the disappearance of Ulf and Vandrad's longship. Even Hervor and Onyame had retired. Young Moons alone had seemed eager to talk, but I could not understand most of what she said. So I had postponed my questions.

Now, however, I was eager for answers.

I found Hervor and Onyame at the firepit near my wikuom, and I squatted between them. Onyame's two female companions apparently had morning tasks, so, except for two dogs, the three of us sat alone.

"Good morning," he said. "You're a surprising sight."

"Good morning," I said to both of them. "I had a surprise of my own last night, and I want to know what happened, if you don't mind telling me."

Hervor grinned. "We sent your friends away. Over the edge of the world."

"They're not my friends."

"Whoever they are, they won't sail this way again."

I gazed at Onyame. "How did Ulf and Vandrad's longship get from the bay to the lake?"

He smiled at me as if I were a not-very-bright child. "We cleared a path. Don't you recall? Or were you too busy trying not to notice Young Moons?"

"How did the ship move along that path? It looked as if it was sailing in the air."

"It was sailing in the air," Hervor said.

I frowned at her. "Longships can't fly."

"Some ships," Hervor said slowly, "can sail on things other than water."

"What things?"

Onyame poked at the fire. "The voices of the People."

I watched him for the trace of a smile, but I could find none. So I said, "Ships don't sail on voices."

Hervor looked at Onyame. "He's young," she said.

"Not that young," he replied.

"Very certain," she said. "The young can be very certain."

They both looked at me.

"Do you mean," I asked, "that a ship can sail on voices? On sound? All that shouting and pounding had something to do with —? No. The People lifted it onto logs and rolled it." I stared at each of them in turn. "Didn't they?"

"Did you see any rollers?" Hervor asked.

I paused before answering.

Onyame smiled at me and dropped his voice into its deeper, more serious tone. "You see, there's an ancient knowledge about voices and drums, about what sounds can do when they're used properly. One of the People has that knowledge."

"The old man who's always with Hervor?"

Onyame nodded. "He's a healer and a man of Great Power, a puoin. With his instructions, the People lifted the longship into the air. Not far, but far enough to float it along the path we made."

I looked at him blankly. This did not seem to be one of his jests. I looked at Hervor. "Is that true?"

"It's a knowledge I have myself. Many of the Volvas and Wise Men had it. But it's closely guarded knowledge. Here, there's no danger of its being discovered."

"I would suppose," Onyame said, "that the crew of that ship are convinced that demons lifted them into the air and sailed them off the world, but that they managed to get back to the ocean and escape, though only barely."

I did not know what to think. I pondered what they had said, while one of the dogs pressed himself against me, nudging my hand, and I absent-mindedly scratched his ears.

Hervor eventually ended the silence. "Young Moons wants to speak with you. This morning. She wants you to join her. In her wikuom tonight."

"What?"

Onyame stretched his huge hands over the fire. "She's reached the marrying age, and her parents have been dead a long time. No one has suggested a match to her, so it's her choice. She may ask whom she wishes to join her."

"To marry her?"

"The People's version of marriage, yes," he said. "It may be worth considering. You wouldn't be the first traveler from the North — or the South in your case — to marry one of the People." He paused. "You've noticed the women accompanying me."

"How could I not?"

"One of them is my wife."

"Your wife?"

"Yes. That's one of the reasons that Sigvald, Vagn, Thorkel, and I come here every summer and spend the winter. Haven't you guessed? Our wives are here, and this way we can spend most of the year with them. Even Thorvald has a wife here."

"So that's why ... I see now. I don't know what to say. Except that your wife is beautiful."

He nodded. "She'll appreciate the compliment. Thank you."

"What's her name?"

"In the language of the People, her name means 'the Woman Who Sings to the Dawn,' so I call her 'Dawn Woman'."

"It's a pleasing name." I hesitated before speaking again. "Did the ship really fly?"

Hervor leaned toward me. "Are you curious?"

"Yes."

"You don't want to join Young Moons?" Onyame asked.

"She's very pretty, but I barely know her."

Hervor nodded. "You're undecided. Very well. Young Moons can wait. And your friends no longer chase you. For awhile at least. You want to know more. So there's work to be done. That will keep you occupied."

"What work? Will you teach me how to float ships?"

"No. I'll teach you about visions," she said. "That's what you're destined to learn."

The day's training, though, had nothing to do with visions. First, Hervor led me some distance along a rocky path south of the village. Then she instructed me to sit down, facing the ocean.

"What for?" I asked, though I obeyed.

"To focus on that stone in front of you."

"I can see it."

"I know you can see it. But I want you to see only it. For as long as you can."

After a few minutes, during which time my back and legs began to ache, I said, "This is not very interesting."

"It's not meant to be interesting. You must learn to concentrate."

"I can concentrate. On whatever job happens to be at hand."

She shook her head. "Not long enough. Focus on the stone again."

I focused.

Hervor was more determined to teach me to concentrate than I would ever have guessed. For the next ten days, every morning and afternoon I walked along that southern path, stopped wherever Hervor told me, and stared at some stone or leaf or piece of driftwood.

Occasionally a flock of pigeons would darken the sky, or some harbor seals would call to us. When I glanced up, Hervor returned me to my work.

"Concentrate."

"I'm trying."

"Don't try. You've seen that you can't force your mind. Just let it settle onto what you see. Be interested in what you see. And only that. If your mind wanders away, bring it back to what interests you. Gently."

She sounded like Garrad.

"Breathe calmly, too," she said. "Don't let your breath disturb you."

"Breathing doesn't disturb me. It never has."

She scowled. "There's a saying in the North, 'a glib tongue that goes on chattering sings to its own harm'."

I could not think of a reply, so I refocused on an abandoned feather lying in front of me.

During the evenings back in the village, I had a more enjoyable time, sitting at the fire circle and watching the People sing and dance, including Young Moons, who seemed more beautiful every time I saw her.

The People imitated animals and acted out events, while their dangles of bone clicked with their movements. Some of the men pounded birch bark slabs with sticks, while others shook rattles made of fish-skin pulled over wooden frames, probably filled with pebbles. A few played bone whistles, creating — along with the singing — a rousing and, it seemed to me, joyful accompaniment.

The People's music reminded me of what I had heard back in Normandy, but the joy in the People's music alternating with a calm, far-away quality was striking. Often, as I walked along the southern path in the mornings or afternoons to practice concentration, I would hear a single flutelike tone somewhere in the distance, which I almost mistook for the wind. It had that calm quality.

Hervor told me that it was one of the People, playing "being alone" music. Its sound relaxed me but made me long for something else, some other world perhaps, which I could not name.

When the evening's singing and dancing ended, the People encouraged me to join them in their games, especially one in which I used a wooden bowl to toss six dice, or what appeared to be dice, made from the shin-bones of some large animal. I was lucky at this game, and the People encouraged me all the more.

As a result, I began to learn more words of their language, and I could even form simple questions — with Young Moons' help. And she was always eager to help, which I began to enjoy.

One evening, when I was playing the dice-game with Onyame and two of the People, I asked them about their unusually long bows and well-fletched arrows. When they did not reply, I assumed I was not making myself clear.

"No, your question is clear enough," Onyame said, "but a thing like that is never approached directly. Remember? I'll speak to them."

He said a few words, after which there was a brief silence. One of the men then replied, and Onyame paused and then spoke again. The man replied again. This exchange continued for several minutes.

"What did you say?" I asked Onyame, when he turned back to me.

"I said that bows and arrows such as those of the People are not known to the Normans. He replied that such knowledge could be useful when a person needed to hunt. I said that was true. He said that such things as making long bows and arrows could be learned. I said that learning such things could be valuable. He said that there might be teachers of that skill here. I said that there might be people, especially Norman people, who would be willing to be taught by such teachers. And there might be one of those Normans here. He said that if a Norman wanted to be taught, he was sure that it would be possible for that Norman to learn."

"What does all of that mean?"

"It means that he's willing to teach you."

So, for the next few weeks, whenever Hervor released me from concentration-practice, I worked with the bow-maker. Most of my unoccupied time occurred in the afternoons and evenings, and I noted that he was available whenever I was.

Like most of the People, his daily tasks took little time, so that he could spend his day talking with other People, engaging in creative projects, playing, or teaching.

He was a skilled and patient teacher, so that by the end of his instruction, I had crafted a new long bow, even longer than the one I had given Hardraada.

The bow-maker admired it, and I thanked him as best I could in his own language. He seemed pleased when I said it deserved to have some of the People's designs on it.

"You'll need permission, though," Hervor said, as she admired the bow.

"Permission to use some designs? Are they like the family or shield symbols used in Normandy?"

"The designs you see around you are sacred to the People. The designs have Power. The People won't stop you from using them, but you may offend someone. You may bring harm to yourself. Or others."

"I see. How do I get permission?"

"I'll ask. Perhaps they'll tell you stories. Among the People, those who know you like you. They think you're simple but nice. So it shouldn't be difficult."

Nor was it. For the next three evenings, I sat in a wikuom with four elders, two men and two women, including Young Moons, and listened to the tales they told, translated by Hervor.

For the first two nights, the elders recounted stories about "the World Beneath the Earth" and "the World Beneath the Water." These two worlds seemed filled with monsters, shape-changing children, and starving adults who dreamed of eating meat until the fat dripped down their chins, which reminded me of the less careful lords who dined with Duke Robert at Rouen Castle.

On the third night, the elders spoke about visions. One of the men and one of the women nodded. Their faces illumined by the fire, they joined to tell a story that "came from the west," the story of a mouse who, granted visions of life in the worlds beyond his, willingly gave up his eyes to help his fellow creatures and was transformed into an eagle.

"Like Odin," Hervor added at the end of the tale. "Odin gave up one of his eyes. To gain wisdom."

"All things give away by nature," the female elder said. "Only human people must learn giving away. They are given so much that giving away becomes natural and easy."

I knew that I did not understand completely what this meant. Nonetheless, it appealed to me, and I asked permission to use the symbols of the eye, the mouse, and the eagle on my bow.

The elders sat quietly for a long time. Then one of them spoke to Hervor.

"They have granted you permission."

The next morning Hervor stopped my concentration-sessions. For three days she did not approach me for training.

So, on the third morning I took one of the dogs with me along the southern path and continued my concentration work, which I did for another week. I had come to enjoy it. I used the remainder each day to carve and paint my bow and make some clothes for the cooler weather that was now arriving.

With the help of Young Moons, I had learned how to make the fur-lined leather shoes, the moccasins, that promised to be warmer during the winter months than my worn Norman shoes. She had showed me how to pierce the leather with a bone awl and use a bone needle to sew the leather in close stitches with strands of dried animal sinew.

Of course, my moccasins did not have the skill of those made by the People. But they would keep my feet warm and comfortable. Young Moons also made me heavy leggings and sleeves and a furred tunic.

I had gradually become accustomed to her dressing habits, and on the second evening, I found myself thanking her in her own language without ever thinking of lowering my eyes from hers.

Until she turned her bare back to me to walk away.

For a moment, I just stared at her back. Seeing the homes of the People around her, the trees towering in the background, and the blue sky, I thought that this was the most beautiful sight I had ever seen. And Young Moons was in the center of it.

She paused and cocked her head, as if listening to something.

I kept staring, thinking that the whole scene was so appealing that I could just fall into it — the trees, the sky, and Young Moons.

She turned and walked back toward me. She reached out her hand. "Come with me, please. Come to my wikuom this night."

I took her hand and let her lead me.

On the seventh morning that Hervor had not engaged me in concentration training, I strode along the southern path again, feeling elated, the brown dog trailing behind me.

I felt new, somehow. I hummed a Norman love-song to myself and then fell silent.

I had heard something. Normally the only sounds that accompanied me were the ocean and the wind in the trees. This morning, however, I heard music in the distance, a flutelike sound.

At first, I assumed that one of the People was playing "being alone" music.

This sounded different. The music had the calm, far-away quality, but it also seemed more joyous, as if two or three flutes had joined, creating overtones and undertones that I had never heard.

I did not wish to intrude, but I was curious. I strode into the forest toward the music.

The dog refused to follow me and remained on the path. I walked on alone.

The music did not seem to get closer, so I pressed on. And on. I walked almost in a daze, and before I knew it, I was deep in the forest, the pines and spruce and maple and beech trees thick around me.

Then the music stopped.

I looked around and realized that I had not paid attention to my path. I could see the sun directly overhead through the trees, but it would be little help until much later in the day.

Suddenly, I heard a sound behind me and turned to see a huge form, almost twice my size, standing only a few arm's lengths away from me.

It was one of the Tall People.

A man. He had light-colored hair and light skin, and his eyes seemed to be a deep blue. He wore a long robe, made from a material that could have been a skin, but I knew of no animal large enough to produce such a skin. Around his waist was a cord of some kind. He wore shoes that resembled the moccasins of the People.

He said something in a language I did not understand.

So I replied in the language of the People, "I do not know what you are saying. Who are you?"

He replied in the same language, "Who are you?" He moved his gaze over me. "Your skin is light. Are you from the stars?"

"No, not the stars. I'm from a world on the other side of the ocean."

He raised his head and turned it to his left. "Oh, the ocean. I see." He pointed. "Well, you had better return there. You are lost in the deep forest. If you do not leave now, you will not be able to return."

With that, he turned and walked away with huge strides. Soon he was gone, almost as if he had taken a few steps and then vanished.

Without thinking, I turned and walked in the direction he had indicated.

I heard the music again and moved toward it. This time, I seemed to be closing on it, so I walked more quickly.

I realized that I must be walking toward the ocean and away from the deep forest. After a long time — I could not determine how long — I spied the ocean through the trees.

In a few more steps, I saw the brown dog, sitting and staring at a small tree near the path. The music seemed to be coming from the tree.

As I picked my way around the last large pine and reached the small tree, the music stopped.

The dog turned to yap at me, wagging his tail.

I looked around at the ground for traces of a Music Person, but there were no marks, except for my own footprints.

I lifted the dog into my arms and almost ran back to the village.

Hervor waited at its edge, watching me. "There you are. I thought you might still be lost."

I gave her a questioning look. "Did you read my thoughts?"

She shook her head. "I heard the music."

"You did? How could you?"

"It wasn't ordinary music. You heard Mi'kmwesu'k, a flute-player. They always play when someone is lost."

I lowered the dog. "That's what got me lost. Was it one of the People playing a prank?"

"Flute-players were once People. But no more. They're more than People. They live in the deep forest. They help anyone who's lost."

"Well, they did me no good with their playing. I was afraid I'd have to spend the whole day there. Then I saw one of the Tall People, who pointed me toward the ocean. As I came out of the deep forest, I could see where the sun was setting."

"One of the Tall People found you? You must have been deep in the forest."

"I'd have been lost the whole of the day if not for him."

She tilted her head at me. "You were lost the whole of the day."

I glanced at the sun. "No, it was noon when I realized I was lost. That must not have been very long ago."

She smiled oddly. "You've been gone all night."

I thought she must be jesting with me, as Onyame often did. I grinned. "I wasn't gone more than a third of the day. The dog was with me all the time."

"The dog returned here yesterday afternoon and went out again this morning."

"No, that can't be what happened."

She still smiled. "You don't see, do you? You heard a flute-player. In the deep forest. There's no time there. The Tall Person realized that you were traveling loosely in time and returned you."

"What? Are you saying that I spent less than a day in the forest, but more than a day passed here?"

She nodded.

"How?"

"It does happen."

I paused. "I've heard of saints doing something like that, but I'm not a saint."

"The flute-player's music can't be heard by all. You heard them before they knew you were there. Your Inner Power heard them. Your training has brought it out. And very few people meet a Tall Person." She was quiet for awhile. "That means it's time. Come to my wikuom this evening."

I still did not know whether I was the object of a jest or not, so I asked Onyame about flute-players.

"Mi'kmwesu'k?" he said. "They're what a Person here may become, a Master of the Deep Forest. That's where they live, where everything is fluid, and time and even places move oddly. Why do you ask?"

"I think I heard one."

"Ah, so that's why you were gone overnight." He smiled. "That's a good thing. Your training must be going well. What does Hervor say?"

"She wants to see me tonight in her wikuom."

That night, as I bent into her dwelling, I found Hervor sitting by the fire pit with the old man, the one who knew the secret of sailing longships on voices. I recalled that Onyame had also called him a healer.

"Good evening," I said.

Hervor nodded.

"Will this man be training me now?" I asked.

"That's why he's here. I wish to ask him to train you."

I sat down beside them. "Thank you."

"Be silent now."

I dropped into silence, and they sat unspeaking, gazing at the fire. I expected Hervor to convey my request, but she continued to sit in silence, as did the old man.

The night passed by. I waited as patiently as I could, but neither of them appeared to have any interest in anything but the fire, which had long since died and left only glowing coals.

Able to contain myself no longer, I cleared my throat. I had noticed that this was a sign among the People that someone wished to speak. Permission to speak was not always granted, and those making the request remained silent.

I was less patient, though, and cleared my throat a second time. When I got no response, I cleared it a third time.

Hervor swung her head toward me. "What do you want?"

"I'm sorry to disturb you, but when do you intend to ask him about my request?"

She shook her head. "Must you be dull-witted, or do you choose to be?"

"It must be necessary. I'm sure I didn't choose it. When will you ask him?"

"I have been asking him. I've told him all I know about you. He's just granted the request."

"You haven't said a word to each other."

She gave me an annoyed look. "The old man is a puoin. He's respected and feared among the People. A master of healing and ritual. I'm a Volva. We don't need words."

The puoin then spoke for the first time, and Hervor translated, "It is my Power to move through all the Six Worlds: the World Beneath the Earth, the World Beneath the Water, the Earth World, the Ghost World, the World Above the Earth and the World Above the Sky. I use the Power given to Persons."

He fell silent.

"What Power?" I asked Hervor.

"Kinap, the Power in the world. The Power that flows through the world and allows the world to flow."

"God?"

"The People call Power "Kinap." God to them would be "Kji-kinap," the Great Power, the Holding-Together Power, the Power that Makes Everything Move Together."

The puoin spoke again. "All Persons — Wind Persons and Tree-Persons and Stone Persons — participate in Power, though many choose not to use it." He shrugged. "The choice is theirs. The puoinaq use Power to heal, to cure, and to guide. They choose to use Power, just as some choose not to use it."

"He doesn't mean that they use God, does he?"

"Certainly not," Hervor said. "People who use Power are kinapaq. That means they grow. They learn."

"This elder, too?"

"Yes, he is kinapaq. His name now is the Man Who Walks with Power. He has listened and learned. As Odin learned when he hung on the Tree of Life. As your teacher learned when he was wounded and recovered. They expand themselves to use Power. Learning is the route for the kinapaq."

"Can he use this Power to do anything?"

"To do many things, yes. They cannot abuse Power, though. If they do, it turns on them. It's controlled by Kji-kinap, the Great Power. It cannot be abused. At least not for long."

"Do you mean that the Power that makes all things flow together cannot be used to destroy, which would mean separating or tearing apart?"

She paused and then nodded. "That's one way of thinking about it."

The puoin repeated the word "kinapaq" and spoke again. Hervor translated, "Kinapaq can outrun a Wind Person, dive deep into Sea Person, lift whole Tree Persons, and carry many Caribou Persons on their backs. They dance, and their feet sink deep."

He paused and began to sing:

> *"One of them was a boy*
> *He was blind from his birth,*
> *But he frightened his mother by his sight.*
> *He could tell her what was coming,*
> *What was coming from far off.*
> *What was near he could not see.*
> *He could see Bear Person and Moose Person*
> *Far away beyond the mountains;*
> *He could see through everything."*

The puoin fell silent.

I leaned toward Hervor. "Is this the kind of Power you intend to teach me? To see through everything?"

"The Power of visions is yours. That's clear. A special Power. Your visions are of events and dangers far off in time and place. Such as your vision of Mount Hekla. You can also see what keeps dangers away."

The puoin spoke again, "The Power to warn others before terrible things happen is the Power of the nikani-kjijitekewinu, the 'One Who Knows in Advance.' A Person can learn to be open to this Power. But only Kji-kinap"—

"The Greatest Power," Hervor translated.

— "can give this Power."

He let his head drop onto his chest.

Hervor motioned toward the entrance. I rose on stiff legs, thanked them, and hobbled out.

Young Moons was waiting for me, looking even more beautiful, and took my hand. She looked long and seriously at my face, and we spent much of the night talking about Power.

The next morning, I scrambled to keep up with Hervor and the Man Who Walks with Power as they led me along a rocky path. Heading north rather than south this time, we reached a distant cliff-finger that stretched out into the sea. A narrow path, lined with tree roots, rimmed it.

We pressed along the path toward the end of the cliff-finger, the ocean far below us, so deep blue that it looked almost black, except where it curled around the rocks. I could not see the ocean on the far side of the cliff, though, because thick stands of pine, spruce, and maple trees hid it.

At the cliff-finger's point, we halted. Several small, rocky islands just to the north of us held seals and birds, shrieking at each other about seal and bird matters, I imagined. When the birds leaped into the sky, they massed in wave upon wave, hiding the sun, as if they were clouds.

There were no real clouds in the sky, though, as Hervor pointed out. "That is your task. What the puoin wants you to do."

"What?"

"Form clouds in the sky."

"How does he expect me to do that? That's God's work."

"Who told you that?"

"The priests of Falaise."

She shook her head. "Sit down. Put your back against this rock. You're going to help God."

I had no objection to helping God with anything, but I was skeptical that this was a useful exercise. Nevertheless, I obeyed.

The Man Who Walks with Power began to lead me through concentration exercises, similar to the ones Hervor had taught me. I expected them to do no more than improve my alertness, though. I did not think that clouds would appear.

"Ask the Cloud Persons where they are, whether they will allow themselves to be seen by you. Ask their permission to see them. Then let the Cloud Persons form from the air," Hervor was translating.

Nothing happened for a long time.

"Ask the Cloud People to play with you. Ask them to let you shape the air," Hervor said. "Catch it and shape it into clouds. Do you see what is forming?"

The only thing forming was a doze. My eyes felt heavy, and blinking them took longer and longer.

"Larger!" the puoin said, smiling.

I opened my eyes wide and saw a whisp of cloud in the sky.

"Larger!" Hervor repeated.

"I heard him."

She frowned at me. "Don't talk. Concentrate. Be with the Cloud People."

I had tried to be respectful before. From the outside. So now I turned inward. My mind seemed to form ideas by itself.

I found myself inwardly reaching toward the Cloud People. My mind pictured their beauty and recalled their astonishing shapes, how they had inspired me since I was a child. I asked them to allow me to be with them, to play with them.

To my amazement, the whisp began to grow. It spread itself into a string of whisps.

"Clump them," Hervor said. "Make them one." She nudged me. "Keep talking with them."

It was as if the Cloud People and I had entered into a dance, some creative movement together. As they shaped themselves inside me, I saw within my mind one large cloud. Exactly then, the whisps in the sky drifted toward each other, forming a larger and larger cloud, its shape both familiar, as if a friend, and yet large and far beyond me.

"Now solid," Hervor translated the puoin's command. "Invite in the whole Cloud Person."

The whispy mass in the sky and I seemed to move together, and it became more and more solid, both inside me and in the sky itself.

"Good!" Hervor translated the puoin's compliment. "Now invite in another and another until there are six Cloud Persons together, side by side, like the Six Worlds."

So I did, and in time — I didn't really know how much time passed — six elegant, other-worldly clouds stood in the sky.

The Man Who Walks with Power was full of praise and smiles.

He soon began to wave his arms, however, and shout something. Hervor translated, "Ask them to fade and vanish. Ask them to return to their ancient home."

I began to return to my normal perception. I felt fatigued, and I thought that it surely must be past mealtime.

Hervor repeated her request. "Ask them to return. The Man Who Walks with Power wants you to ask them to return to their ancient homes."

Now I did feel hungry.

"You may eat when the Cloud Persons are gone," the puoin said through Hervor, and I wondered whether he had heard my thoughts or was just offering me my favorite reward.

I concentrated harder and returned to the Cloud People. They gently lost whisps on one edge after another. I found my hunger intruding.

In the distance, the birds' cries led my thoughts away from the cliff and my stomach. I watched the birds soar into the air and drift there, their white and black wings catching the sun.

I decided to let my concentration follow their flight. I could let the beating of the birds' wings send the Cloud Persons home. At least, that is what I told myself, hoping that my mind would follow the wings.

The birds, though, after mounting the clouds, just hung in the sky, flapping their wings occasionally. Their lazy flight seemed so restful that I almost dozed again — probably from lack of food.

Beyond the birds' wings, however, the clouds began to swirl into whisps. I sharpened my focus. The swirling increased. Blue spaces began to peek through the clouds. I let my mind invite each whisp back into air.

One after another, at a deliberate pace, they vanished.

"Wonderful!" the Man Who Walks with Power said and rose and strode away, smiling and humming to himself.

I glanced at Hervor.

"The next lesson is tomorrow," she said. "Now, let's eat."

The next morning, though a few clouds already occupied the sky, the Man Who Walks with Power asked for six more, grouped in a small circle.

I talked with the Cloud People again, this time in a less focused, more relaxed way. Again, six Cloud Persons appeared.

"Now," he said with Hervor translating, "walk up to them."

"I can't walk on clouds. I've barely learned to walk on the ground without limping."

He smiled as Hervor translated. "We work on that next," he said. "For now, forget your feet, and fly to the Cloud Persons."

"I didn't mean that I couldn't walk but flying was fine," I said. "I can't fly either."

Before Hervor could translate, the puoin added, "Go with your second body. Not this heavy one. Your light one."

"I don't have a second body, unless he means my soul, and only God can move that."

"That may seem so," Hervor said. "Nonetheless, you have a second body. It will fly. You usually see a dragon, don't you? Well, go to it and fly."

"Your second body flies in your dreams," the puoin added, with Hervor translating. "Remember your dreams, and you will know how your second body flies."

Protesting would do no good, and it could lengthen the time to my next meal. So I tried to imagine the body that flew in my dreams.

For a long time, though, nothing happened. No walking or flying. No dragon appeared. The clouds stayed in the sky above me, and I felt my legs pressed firmly onto the grassy ground. In a short time, the clouds even began to drift apart.

The Man Who Walks with Power rose and threw back a word as he walked away. "Tomorrow."

Watching him walk away, I said to Hervor, "I tried, but I can't do what he wants."

She put her hand on my shoulder. "You're an archer. You learned to aim arrows. It took practice. Walking with clouds takes practice."

"What is this training for, anyway, if I may ask? What's the point of these clouds?"

"For having visions. To give you a method. He's teaching you the surest way. Traveling the clouds."

I did not travel the clouds the next day, though, or the day after that or for many days. I invited clouds and wished them away. But I did no flying.

Until the beginning of the third week. I was making the last cloud, letting my thoughts fly into the sky with the birds when I suddenly found myself on top of the clouds. I heard a hiss and turned to see the dragon's head next to mine.

I was so startled that I cried out. My body jerked, and I was back on the ground.

The puoin grinned, rose, and said, "Tomorrow you fly."

He was right. The next morning, after forming six clouds, I found myself again on top of them. I still felt frightened, but I did not cry out. The dragon appeared beside me.

"Stay there," the puoin instructed through Hervor. I could hear both of them as if they were standing behind me. "Stay on the Cloud Persons and ask for a vision."

"Ask for a vision? I can barely stand here."

"Ask the Great Power," Hervor translated. "Ask only the Great Power. Ask no lesser powers. If you do, you'll fall. And never fly again."

"I don't feel as if I'm flying. I seem to be walking."

The Man Who Walks with Power said, "Because of your foot. It binds you to walking. All right. You may walk on the Cloud Persons. They allow it. Now ask for a vision."

I ran through the exercises Hervor had taught me. As my mind cleared and focused, I slipped into the center of the clouds. For a long time only a white haze drifted before my eyes.

Then I stopped walking on the clouds and just floated. I heard the dragon hissing from what seemed to be a great distance.

In front of me shapes began to form. Some scene opened below me. I saw shadowed houses and shops clustered around the juncture of two rivers.

The buildings and the rivers sharpened. I recognized the Orne and the Odon Rivers in Normandy. The town was Caen. A group of men sat together outside in a large square. I recognized William and many of the nobles and prelates from Rouen, Falaise, and other Norman towns.

William spoke, making a declaration of some sort.

I heard a voice from outside the vision, Hervor's voice: "Concentrate. Hear the words."

I leaned toward the vision. The dragon supported me somehow, so I could lean far over.

I heard William say, "The Truce of God will exempt only my own men, who will police it. All other forces, unless summoned by ducal command, will remain inactive, completely inactive"— he paused to look from face to face —"from Vespers on Wednesday evening to Matins the following Monday."

The Truce of God. William had finally succeeded in instituting it among the Norman lords.

I found myself on the ground again. Hervor and the puoin were gazing at me.

Dazed from the cloud-walking, I said, "The Truce of God. The fighting must be severe in Normandy." Then I blinked and focused on their faces. "Was that a true vision? Did I see a real event happening?"

"Yes," the Man Who Walks with Power said. "Tomorrow rest from this. But come to see me."

The next morning dawned cool, and the sky remained clear. In fact it was so deep blue that it startled me. The ocean seemed pale by comparison.

I donned my blue-gray robe and pulled on my moccasins. Young Moons brought me some berry bread, and we sat in silence, eating and gazing at the ocean.

Eventually, I said to her, "I haven't thought to ask you. What is the meaning of your name? The longer meaning, I mean?"

She smiled, seeming pleased. "I had a vision when I was young about living past the moon, on worlds beyond the moon. Beyond all moons everywhere. In that vision, I was always young. I knew that was my true home, where I was always a young woman. So I was named the Woman Who Stays Young in the Worlds Beyond the Moons, or Young Moons." She moved close to me and kissed me. "I am happy that you wanted to know. Now you must go to seek more of your own visions."

The puoin sat inside his wikuom with Hervor. A fire glowed inside his circle of stones. I took off my robe and joined them.

The puoin smiled at me. Through Hervor, he said, "Your foot is misshapen, and it gives you pain."

I nodded.

He continued, "There are ways that things can change and give less pain."

"Are there?"

"Of course," Hervor said and translated something longer to the puoin.

"I would be happy," he said, "to teach some of the ways of reducing pain and changing things."

"Whatever he wants to do," I said to Hervor, "he may do." I removed my moccasin.

The puoin leaned toward me and studied my foot. Then he touched it lightly, running his fingers along it as if he were drawing a line. "I can change its shape."

"Can he? How?"

Hervor spoke to the puoin again.

"It can be created new," he replied. "We soak it morning and evening. We give your moccasin a different shape by putting Moss Persons inside it. We paint on the moccasin the whirling cross of creation and take you back there. Then your foot is recreated. A new shape."

I did not notice any change in my foot, though, until a week later.

For several near-autumn days, I had helped two men hunt small game: squirrel, beaver, and even pigeons swarming overhead. Imitating the hunters, I apologized to whatever I had killed for its violent death and thanked it for sacrificing its life so that the People and I could remain alive. I promised to place its bones in trees or rivers where dogs would not gnaw on them.

I also offered a prayer to the Great Power for providing me with sustenance.

Though I felt I should contribute to the food supply, especially with winter approaching, the hunters thanked me repeatedly for my help, as if I had done them a great favor. They praised my bow-work until I felt embarrassed.

Onyame, serving as my translator, whispered in my ear that I needed to reciprocate.

"How?"

He shrugged. "These two are good fishermen. Perhaps you can join them the next time they go out. Shall I ask them for you?"

"Yes, thank you."

Even with my rudimentary grasp of their language I realized before Onyame translated that their next outing was that night, several hours after complete darkness.

I groaned inwardly but smiled at them. "I will be pleased to come with you," I said in their language.

Out of the corner of my eye, I caught Onyame grinning.

Abandoning my fir-bough bed in the middle of a chilly night was a sacrifice, but I had no choice. It was a double sacrifice, because this had also been a night when Young Moons wanted me to join her in her wikuom.

As I stumbled from my own wikuom, yawning, I grumbled to myself about Onyame and the customs of the People. Not far away, I saw the two fishermen, laughing and waving to me to join them.

I fell in behind them as they carried a canoe far into the forest. The moon and stars provided sufficient light for walking but not for missing the occasional rock or root with my toes, so I had occasion to mutter Norman and Icelandic curses. I wondered about curses in the People's language, but no one had offered to teach me any.

The two men stopped near a lake. I recognized it as the source of the river that had carried Ulf and Vandrad's longship out to sea. They lowered the canoe onto the river.

Lifting me into the canoe, they positioned themselves at either end. The man in the bow sat with a forked spear poised, while the man at the rear became a steersman, dipping a paddle in the water. I lifted the birchbark torch that would attract the fish.

After what seemed half the night, we did attract a fish — a huge sturgeon, almost as long as the canoe.

The spearsman waited until he could see a spot below the bony plates on the sturgeon's back and then struck. His cry told us he had succeeded. As did the abrupt jerk we felt. While it remained alive, the sturgeon obviously had no intention of joining us in the canoe. It thrashed, almost capsizing us, and then sped downstream.

The canoe rocked and raced forward.

The spearsman clutched the spear tightly. I threw the torch into the river and jammed my feet against the canoe, gripping its sides. The steersman struggled with his paddle.

I thought I heard the two fishermen laugh. I stared at the spearman in disbelief as he cried out that "the Sturgeon Person" had great spirit. The steersman shouted his agreement.

In my turn, I loudly cursed the fact that fish were so big here — in Norman French.

Then I realized that the sturgeon was pulling us toward the rapids. I could hear the roar of water rushing over rocks. I pressed my feet even more tightly against the canoe.

We approached the rapids. I gritted my teeth. Surely the rocks would tear the canoe into birchbark strips.

The spearman's body went limp. He relaxed his grip. Was he letting the sturgeon go?

Abruptly he jerked the spear in the direction of the shore, and the sturgeon swerved. The canoe lurched toward the right bank. He jerked the spear again, and the sturgeon flopped against the bank.

A few moments later, the canoe rested on the shore, and the sturgeon lay dead. The fishermen were apologizing to it, and I was offering a prayer of thanks to whatever saint or angel happened to be responsible for rescuing us from the rapids.

Remembering the point of this life-threatening exercise, I then praised the fishing skill of the two men, as best I could in their language. I expressed my amazement at their handling of the sturgeon and the canoe. I thanked them for keeping me from going over the rapids, while apologizing that I had done nothing but cling to the canoe's sides.

That was when I realized that my foot did not hurt. I glanced down at it. Pressing it against the side of the canoe should have caused me pain. Great pain. But I had felt none.

I leaned down and pulled the moccasin off. In the darkness my foot seemed to look different. I ran my hand along it. Its shape was different, just as Hervor and the Man Who Walks with Power had said it would be.

I straightened, wondering whether such a thing was possible. I bent and checked the foot again. Where muscles had clumped painfully together, there was now a smooth line. I ran my hand over it several times. I stood up again.

The two fishermen stared at me, and I said the People's word for foot. They continued to stare. I repeated the word and waved the foot. They gazed down at it, and I could see their teeth as they smiled in the darkness.

I took several steps and felt no pain at all. I brought my weight down hard on the foot. Again no pain.

I jumped up and down several times. The fishermen laughed at my gyrations, and I laughed with them.

The next morning, I could not find the Man Who Walks with Power to thank him, but I did find Hervor in her wikuom.

"It's good," she said. "Now you see. Power changes things."

I began to speak, but she held up her hand. "It's time. To ask for another vision. Come."

She led me along the northern cliff path. Below us the white peaks of the ocean's waves matched the color of the clouds, and there were many clouds in the sky to match. A circle of them, six, already stood above the cliff's edge.

When we reached the edge, I saw movement among the pine trees just in front of me.

The puoin's head appeared from around one of the trees. "Your foot has changed."

"Yes, and I want to thank you. What you've done is a miracle."

He shook his head. "It's Power. Come. Use it yourself."

I lowered myself next to him, placing my back against the stone on which I always rested.

I gazed into the sky at the six clouds. Soon a seventh, larger one floated in their middle.

"Fly up to the Cloud Persons now," he said. "Walk if you wish." He smiled.

I calmed myself, breathed deeply and cleared my mind. Soon I found myself among the clouds with the dragon. As usual I was startled for a moment, but I caught my breath and stopped myself from crying out.

"Safe," the dragon hissed.

"Now"— the puoin's voice seemed behind me again —"let any vision come, if it will."

For a long time, nothing happened. Then I relaxed and floated in the center cloud, the dragon supporting me again. Eventually, the cloud's whiteness began to recede, replaced by a slightly darker haze. The haze swirled into a shape, and before long the shape became a head.

As I focused on it, the head became the face of a white-haired, white-bearded man. It was Garrad.

"Cuin?" His voice startled me. I heard it as if he were sitting next to me.

"Garrad?"

"Yes. Cuin, are you there? Are you alive?"

"Alive? Of course, I'm alive."

He smiled. "As I suspected. We received a message that Duke William's emissary, a Brother Augustine, had been killed by a bear. We couldn't believe that you were dead. I'm happy to have you confirm it, though."

"Are you really here?"

He looked around. "I'm not sure what you mean. I'm in my hut, leaning against the great stone. Where are you?"

"In the Land of the People."

"Cuin, be serious. Where are you?"

"I'm just south of what the Northerners call Vineland, on the other side of the world, beyond Iceland and Greenland."

"How did you get there?"

"I sailed with a Norwegian houseguard."

"Who's that woman with you?"

"Can you see Hervor?"

"Hervor? Is that her name? Who is she?"

"She's an Icelander, the last prophetess of the old Northern religion. She's training me here."

He frowned. "Training you? In what?"

"In visions. The Man Who Walks with Power, too. He's a healer. Can you see him?"

"Only the woman." He paused. "Is it wise to have all these people teach you?"

"It's all right. They're teaching me good things."

"Are you certain?"

"I'm not as young as I used to be, you know."

"You're not as old as you could be, either. We'll discuss it when you return to Normandy. Why are you in that place, anyway?"

"To escape danger. I was brought here by the houseguard of Earl Thorir. Do you remember Thorir from Hedeby?"

"He turned out to be a friend, after all?"

"The best I've had so far, excepting his houseguard, Onyame, who saved my life. Garrad, my missions haven't been … successful. It seems that Hardraada — who now shares the Norwegian kingship with Magnus —"

"Yes, the Goliards brought me word of the dual kingship in Norway."

"Well, Hardraada and Magnus want me dead. They're both harboring mistaken notions about me."

"I'm sorry to hear that." He shook his head. "Things are not much better here. The nobles have stirred up trouble for William."

"I thought so. I saw him institute the Truce of God at Caen."

"Did you have a vision? Is there a great stone there?"

"There are stones here. The People here call them the bones of the earth, but they're not responsible for the visions. The clouds are. I've learned to walk on the clouds."

He shook his head. "I never know when you're serious. Is that why the Norwegian Kings want you dead? Did you frustrate them beyond endurance?"

"I wish that were the cause. Hardraada thinks I've plotted against him, which I haven't. Magnus didn't want to let me leave for some reason I couldn't determine, but by now he must distrust me."

The vision began to fade. Some words formed in Garrad's mouth, but his image was gone before I could understand him.

I was back on the ground, sitting next to the Man Who Walks with Power. Hervor was watching me, while the puoin seemed to be asleep.

I sat up. "Can I get him back? He may have been saying something important. I also wanted to tell him about my foot and about Voldred and the flying ship."

"He slipped away from you," Hervor said. "He ended the vision."

"Why?"

"I have no idea."

"I'm sorry he spoke slightingly of you and the Man Who Walks with Power."

She shrugged. "It matters not at all. He doesn't know us."

"Was that a vision from God? It wasn't like the vision of Mount Hekla."

"What you call "God" allowed you to see the future of Mount Hekla, and that God allowed you to speak with your teacher."

I pondered this a moment. "Do all of my visions come from God then? The Great Power?"

"Certainly not. You may have silly visions. People often do."

"How can I tell the difference?"

"The same way you judge any message. Does it create things? Or does it bring destruction? Does it help you? Of does it not?"

"Sometimes that's not easy to determine."

She huffed. "Of course not. Do you want ease? It takes time and work. As do all things worth doing."

The Man Who Walks with Power seemed to wake up. He shielded his eyes and gazed at the sky. "Come. A rain will fall soon. Thunder Persons will soon beat their wings."

He stared at me. "You must learn to cast your visions, so that others can see them. You have done it once."

As I wondered how much training I would need, he smiled and whispered something to Hervor.

She laughed. "The Man Who Walks with Power says that it's the last thing you will need to learn from him, and that it's easy."

I smiled and said that I could tolerate something easy now.

The three of us wound our way back along the cliff path.

By the time the autumn chill had settled in, I had learned to cast my visions. And it had been easy, as the Man Who Walks with Power promised — so easy that the summer sped by.

Now, one group of the People, including the Man Who Walks with Power, moved into the forest. Onyame, Sigvald, Vagn, and I accompanied them, helping them form stones into fire-circles and rebuild their wikuoms near a river where they could trap salmon and eels.

Young Moons stayed behind, telling me that she needed to seek some visions of her own. "I do not think I will need much time," she said. "I think I will be within another moon cycle."

"Trapping fish isn't going to be difficult here," I mentioned to Onyame as we lashed spruce poles together for drying racks. "Have you glanced at the river? It has more fish than water in it."

"I know, and the People have an easy method for catching them."

"They could just walk in and scoop them up."

"Easier than that. They build small dams along the river and place nets on the opposite side of the dam. When salmon or eels jump the dam, they fall into the nets. They're trapped there until the People come to get them." He grinned. "Everything the People do is easy."

"Except for fishing in the middle of the night."

"They're like monks."

"They don't seem monkish to me," I said.

"I mean that the People prefer to spend their time exchanging and discussing stories or seeking and contemplating visions."

"As well as making beautiful things and making love."

He nodded, smiling. "You're right. That is a better life than monks have."

We returned to those People still encamped on the seacoast, but even this group was planning to move up to the salmon-filled river.

Young Moons was nowhere to be seen, and I was told that she still slept in the forest, seeking visions.

When I asked Hervor whether she knew what Young Moons was seeking, she shook her head at me. "The People will not respond to you incessant questioning, so you've come to me, I see." She turned serious. "I think you should know this. Since Young Moons is, like all the People, private, she has probably never told you that she was born with a deformity. Unlike yours, hers was internal, something the elder healers discovered as she became a young woman."

"Is she ill? She seems healthy."

Hervor stepped closer. "She is healthy, but she cannot have children. She's probably seeking a vision about whether the two of you should be together, since you will be childless."

I breathed a deep sigh. "Hervor, with the life I've had, I've never even thought about having children. Of course, it crossed my mind when I met Young Moons, but my only real desire is to be with her. If we do not have children, we shall still have a life together."

She gave me a quick nod. "Then that is what Young Moons will learn in her visions."

A few days later, I untied the birch bark strips of my wikuom and warmed and soaked them, so that I could roll them up for carrying. With Onyame's help, I lashed the spruce poles together.

Onyame had showed me how to use a tumpline, the carrying strap that the People wore across their foreheads or chests for bearing heavy loads, but I had not had an opportunity to carry anything with it. Now, carrying my own supplies and wikuom, I found it satisfactory.

Which was fortunate, because we stayed on the salmon river only a few weeks. Then we dismantled all the wikuoms and prepared to carry our loads even farther into the forest. The permanent winter camp was a day's walk inland.

When we reached the camp, Onyame, his wife, and their other young female companion helped me reconstruct my wikuom. The young man who sometimes accompanied them had already gone into the forest to hunt.

Now that I knew some of the People's language, I tried conversing with Onyame's wife. I also said a few words to the young woman. She smiled pleasantly at me.

I drew Onyame aside. "I'm afraid I've never learned the young woman's name. I never had an opportunity to ask her, and I was trying to respect her privacy."

"Her name is Onyama."

"Onyama? That sounds African and remarkably like your name."

"Not here. My name here, as in Iceland, is Bear, but yes, her name is like my name. She's my daughter."

My mouth fell open. "Your daughter? Why didn't you tell me? I thought she must be a friend of your wife. Or perhaps her sister. You certainly have a casual way of regarding your family."

He laughed. "As you just noted, privacy is highly valued here. You would call it, I think, a spiritual matter. The People consider privacy their spiritual privilege. For that reason, asking direct questions and trading family information, so common in Norway and Normandy, are not done here. The People don't inquire into each other's lives unless they're invited or there's a compelling reason."

"I see. Was I being rude?"

"No. I am a Northerner, after all."

"I'm relieved." I took a breath. "Your daughter is as beautiful as your wife."

"It's gracious of you to say so. She's charming, stronger in will than either her mother or I, an interesting quality for us to observe. A fine young woman. She's to be married. You may have seen the young man, too. He's living with us for a year, so that he and my daughter can make all they need for their own wikuom — tools, clothing, a sled, and so on. You'll be able to see their wedding this summer. It's a fine ceremony."

"I'll enjoy that." I paused. "Then we're not leaving in the spring?"

"In the first place, after we return from the winter village, it will take us time to get the wood we need and to load it. In the second place, we can't have the wedding until my daughter's husband-to-be hunts and forages for all the food needed for the wedding."

"Can't we help him?"

"He must do it himself. He must kill his first moose. He's a gentle boy and has never felt moved to kill anything, certainly not anything very large. Among the People, though, a boy is not a man until he kills a moose."

"The big deer with the rounded antlers. We've eaten it before."

"Yes, it's even better during a winter feast."

If it was to delay our journey, I certainly hoped so.

The winter camp sat on the sandy beach of a small lake, situated not far from the bend of a river. Its ice-flecked banks provided beautiful scenery during the day, while its rushing sound soothed me to sleep even during the coldest nights.

And it was a cold winter.

Most of my time was spent inside wikuoms, doing concentration exercises or listening to stories. Young Moons had rejoined the People but withdrew from me, saying only that she needed to contemplate her visions.

The Man Who Walks with Power spent more time with me, recounting the stories of the People, and in particular one that he wanted me to hear. On the day that I calculated was near Christmas, he invited me to his wikuom to tell it.

"Two old ones of the People," he began, "are living deep in the forest with their two daughters, and these daughters are shy and beautiful. The chief of this band of the People has a son, a handsome son, who wishes a wife. But the two daughters do not wish to marry.

"Living in this same camp of the People is another young man. He is not handsome. He does not work hard. He is a great jester. This young man says to his friends, 'I could get one of those girls, one of those beautiful shy girls, to marry me, if I wanted to.' His friends are all laughing at this, and they decide to take him to the home of the young girls to try his luck. The girls pay no attention to him, and he says nothing to them. His friends laugh.

"Much later this young man is walking in the forest, and he sees an old woman. Her face is all wrinkled. But her hair is fastened up with many wonderful ornamented hair-strings, which trail their ends down over her shoulders, all the way down to her feet.

"'Where are you going?' this old woman asks the young man.

"'Nowhere in particular,' he answers. 'And you? Where have you come from, my grandmother?'

"'I have not come far,' says this old woman all draped with beautiful hair-strings. 'But you, grandchild: it is said that you wish to marry, to marry one of those beautiful shy women, those daughters of the old ones living out on the edge of your camp.'

"'No,' he says, 'I do not wish this.' He is sorry he ever made that jest.

"'But I can help you,' says this old woman, peering up at him through all those hair-strings. She reaches up and removes one of her many hair-strings. 'Carry this in your pouch, your medicine pouch. Carry it for a while, then watch out for a time to get close to the younger of those beautiful girls, and throw this hair-string upon her back. But do not let her see you do this. Do not let her feel you do this.'

"'I shall do as you say, my grandmother,' says the young man.

"He calls his friends together once again to visit the old ones. They arrive right at dinner time, so the two shy girls are sitting with their parents around the fire, eating, and there is no time for them to hide. As they are all playing games after supper, the young man drops the hair-string on the back of the younger of those beautiful girls.

"Now it is morning. The sun has come from beneath the earth. That young man is out walking in the forest, and he sees a strange thing to see deep within the forest. It is that young girl, that shy and beautiful young girl. The Power of the hair-string has brought her to him.

"'Where are you going?' she says to him.

"'I am going hunting,' he tells her. 'But why do I find you out here alone in the forest? Where have you come from? Are you lost?'

"'Oh, no,' she says to him. 'I am not lost.'

"'I will take you back to your parents and tell them I found you out wandering in the woods. I will tell them you did not know the way home.'

"'Yes,' this girl says to him. 'Yes.'

"And so the young man takes home the beautiful shy girl and speaks with her parents. 'I found your daughter wandering in the forest, and I have brought her home to you.'

"'Then she is your wife, if you wish,' says the father, 'for it is what she wishes.'

"So a feast is celebrated where all the People recognize the marriage.

"Now the young man is going to visit the chief's son. He wants to help him catch a wife, the other beautiful shy daughter, so that he and the chief's son will be as close as brothers.

"'My wife's sister is alone now,' the not-handsome young man says, looking at nothing in particular. 'Now that her sister is living apart from their family. My wife's sister is left behind, with no one next to her to talk with in the night.'

"'It is not good to be alone,' says the chief's son, looking at nothing in particular. 'I have felt that way myself.'

"'My wife,' says the young man, 'has a beautiful hair-string. It came out of the forest. I have been thinking that her sister would like a hair-string such as that.'

"'When next you go into the forest,' says the chief's son, 'perhaps I will accompany you.'

"Now it is morning. The sun has come from beneath the earth, and these two young men are walking deeper into the forest, walking out to hunt, walking out to hunt hair-strings.

"And then the chief's son is seeing something. It is an old woman, all wrinkled. She is sitting on a tree trunk, looking at him. And many beautiful hair-strings are tied from the roll of hair at the back of her head. There are so many of them that they almost cover her shoulders like a robe. They are hanging down almost to her feet.

"The chief's son greets her very politely. 'My grandmother,' he says, 'where have you come from?'

"'From not very far away,' she replies. 'And you, grandchild: are your eyes still following after the old ones' older daughter?'

"'My eyes have sometimes been looking in that direction,' says the chief's son.

"'Then take this hair-string,' says the old woman. 'Your brother here will tell you how to use it. Do not speak of anything you have seen.'

"And the not-handsome young man instructs the chief's son. It is done, and when so many moons have passed, the chief's son goes into the forest again. He is going hunting. This time he is hunting a wife.

"He walks deeper into the forest, and he sees the older daughter of the old ones; she is following him.

"'Where are you going?' she asks.

"'I am going hunting. But you, what are you doing here? Are you lost?'

"'No,' she says, gazing and gazing at him. 'No, I am not lost.'

"'I will take you home to your parents,' he says. 'You cannot stay out here alone. I will tell them you were lost, and I have found you. For I have found you, have I not?'

"'Yes,' she says, 'you have found me.'

"It is a big marriage feast they are having, with much meat to eat, with games and dancing to celebrate. The chief's son looks at his new wife. She is wearing the hair-string which he dropped on her back. Its Power has called her to him. He smiles.

"Now after this, that not-hard-working, not-handsome young man and the chief's son are as close as brothers. They are often together, and they hunt together as well.

"One day they are sitting together. 'If a man wanted to learn how to run very swiftly,' says the chief's son to no one in particular, 'there is a thing that could help him do this.'

"'A man who runs fast would be a better hunter,' says the not-hard-working, not-handsome young man, 'and he could run away from his enemies so fast that he would end up chasing them.' He is still making jests.

"'Not many of the People know how to teach this,' says the chief's son, looking up at the sky. 'And perhaps not many can learn such a thing, either.'

"'Perhaps if someone would teach, someone would learn,' says the not-handsome young man to his friend.

"And so the chief's son is showing him how to do it. 'You must gather feathers,' he says. 'You must wait for a day when the wind is blowing very fast. Let the feathers fly out into the wind; let them run before the wind. Then let yourself run after them. Soon you will be able to run fast. The feathers will pull you. The wind blowing will push you. Soon you will run faster. Soon you will be running right past those feathers. And at last you will find yourself running faster than the wind. And once you learn this, it will never go away from you.'

"The not-handsome young man does as he is told, and little by little, Power comes up in him, stronger and stronger, until he is running faster than a man can run, faster than feathers fly. He is running faster than the wind.

"This time the chief's son and the not-handsome young man are having a smoke out in the forest. The chief's son leans back against a tree and half-closes his eyes. 'Many things are living in this forest,' he says to no one in particular. 'Some of them are dangerous.'

"'Yes,' says his wife's sister's husband, to no one in particular. 'Some of them are very dangerous.'

"'Some things cannot be killed,' says the chief's son, 'and some things a man cannot escape from by running away, even if he can run very fast.' He is watching his friend out of the corner of his eye. 'If a man should meet one of those things ...'

"'... he can turn white and die of fright,' says the not-handsome young man, still making jests. He is lying on the ground, looking up at the sky. 'But perhaps there might be something else he could do?'

"'Not many of the People could teach something like this,' says the chief's son. 'And perhaps not many could learn it, either.'

"'If someone would teach, perhaps someone would learn.'

"And so the chief's son begins to teach Escaping to his friend. They are brothers.

"'Find some old ragged clothes,' he says, 'the ugliest you can get, and put them on over your own clothes. Then you must go out looking for a fight. Provoke someone until he attacks you, and when he has seized you, slip out of your rags and run away. If you can do this, then you will be able to escape from any man who may take hold of you. You will be able to escape from any animal who may leap upon you. You will be able to escape from anything that lives in this forest. And once you have learned this, it will never leave you.'

"So, the not-handsome young man gets himself some really ugly clothes and goes looking for a fight. He yells 'Ya, ya, ya' at a man until the man is crazy with anger and attacks him to shut up his mouth, to stop all that ya ya.

"As soon as the other man's hands grab him, that not-handsome young man begins to wriggle out of his ugly clothes. Power comes up in him, and he slips out of them just like an eel. He leaves them there, lying on the ground, and the man stomps up and down on them. He beats up those clothes. All this time the not-handsome young man is laughing at him from a safe distance away.

"One day the chief's son and the friend who helped him catch a wife are out paddling on the river. They are letting the canoe drift downstream, and the chief's son says, 'If someone were to take a handful of moose hair and roll it up between their thumb and first finger, they would learn something useful. If they were to take this hair and hold it into the wind and let it loose to blow where it will, they would see something useful. They would be able to see any moose that is anywhere around, for a great distance. But perhaps this is not of any interest.'

"'If someone were to take the hair of other animals,' says his friend, 'and do likewise, perhaps he would see those kinds of animals?'

"'Perhaps,' says the chief's son. 'But there are not many of the People who can learn such a thing.'

"'When someone teaches, someone listens,' says the not-handsome young man, and he soon learns this lesson.

"Now he is asking a question one day while they are spearing salmon. 'Fish,' he says to the chief's son, 'have no hair.'

"'That is true,' says his friend as they thrust and jab their spears into the water. After a while he speaks again to no one in particular. 'Fish have bones,' he says, looking off into the distance. 'If someone were to powder up their bones, and let their dust blow in the wind, who knows what he might see?'

"'Ah,' says his friend, spearing a big salmon. 'Here is a big one. I shall ask it if I may have its bones.'

"He takes the salmon bones, grinds them to a powder and when the wind blows, stands upon a rock by the river and lets the dust fly where it will. Now he has learned another lesson. Now he can see fish and call them to him.

"Moons go by, and this not-handsome young man is thinking and dreaming all the time. He goes to the chief's son. They are brothers. 'All the time I am Dreaming of whales and of whale-songs.'

"'Whales,' says the other, 'live forever, unless they are killed.' Then he smiles to himself, remembering. But that is all he says.

"And so the not-handsome young man goes away to learn this lesson. He is going to do something. He is going to take whalebone and burn it.

So he burns whalebone, crushes it up fine, until it is powder and then waits for the wind to change. He waits for the wind to blow out to sea. There is a rock-place, a point where rock runs way out into the sea. He waits there, out at the very end.

"Now the wind is changing, blowing out to sea. He lifts his hand and lets some of the whale dust blow out on the wind. And at once he sees something. He sees a great number of whales, swimming far out on the ocean. So he blows dust toward them a second time to call them in to him, and they come closer.

"Seven times this not-handsome young man blows that whale-bone dust, and then he sees the Person he has called, the Person who has come to him. It is an enormous whale. It is Whale Person.

"Whale Person comes alongside the rock on which that not-handsome young man is standing and speaks to him. 'What is it that you want?' asks Whale Person.

"'I have Dreamed you,' says the man. 'I want Power.'

"'Put your hand into my mouth,' says Whale Person, 'under my tongue and take it.'

"There is medicine under Whale Person's tongue, and now the man holds it.

"'You have Power,' says Whale Person. 'You may accomplish whatever it is that you desire. This medicine defends you against sickness. It defends you against wild beasts and attacks of your enemies. This medicine makes you invulnerable.'

"Whale Person dives into the sea, and that not-handsome young man goes home again. And now in the camp of the People, life is very good. There are many animals in the forest, and they can be called right up to the doors of the wikuoms, where they give themselves to be killed and eaten. No enemies attack the People, and they all have many children.

"And when the old chief grows feeble, his son comes to the not-handsome young man. 'Can he be made well and young again?'

"'Let what is to come to him,' says his friend, 'come to him.'

"And when death takes the old man, the chief's son speaks again. 'Perhaps a Powerful man should be chief,' he says to his wife's sister's husband. 'Perhaps you should do this, and not I.'

"'A Powerful man is chief,' the not-handsome man replies. 'And he has a brother to help him.'"

The winter passed quickly. Warm inside the People's furs and wikuoms, I scarcely noticed the severe cold. I even learned winter skills, including how to fish through the ice-sheet covering the lake and how to walk on snowshoes, bent ash frames strung with the uncured skin of a moose.

The snowshoes were particularly useful during hunts, allowing the hunters to walk on top of the snow, and with my foot feeling normal and strong, I joined in many hunts. They gave me an opportunity to increase the winter food supply, which I had a talent for reducing, several women had told me, and to practice with my new longbow.

The small brown dog, the one that had apparently been a Star Person previously, ran along beside me. He often sank in the snow, and I had to pull him out of deep snow banks several times. Undeterred, he shook itself and dashed forward, only to sink again.

While the dog was light enough to sink shallowly, our most common prey on the hunts, the moose, sank deeply. The hunters and I could close on it and kill it, though the task took many arrows.

During my last hunt, however, I single-handedly brought down a moose as it struggled through the deep snow. I needed a dozen arrows to do so but no other hunters. I apologized to the moose, and then the women butchered it, though as usual, I could not look at the bloody body. We hauled it back on two of the People's sleds.

I found myself speaking to the dead moose during the entire trip home and asking for his help and blessing.

I felt sad about killing such a great being, but I heard again and again in my mind: "I am fine, little brother. You needed me, and I have left easily. I will return, as do all beings."

That evening, the People sang about my kill. The women offered me enough food to make me feel like a hero, and I did my best to eat all of it.

They also hung the moose's intestines, stuffed with fat, meat and berries, in my wikuom for smoking. This was considered a valuable gift, Onyame told me, as was the large box of the moose's fat that accompanied it.

The People considered fat more of a delicacy than I did, so I in turn offered it to Onyame's daughter and husband-to-be. They thanked me as if I had given them gold.

I had an ulterior motive, though, because I hoped to inspire the boy to go after his own moose, which he as yet seemed unwilling to do.

With the moose, though, Young Moons, who had been keeping her distance from me, now reappeared at my side. She asked to accompany me to my wikuom, and I agreed.

As we walked, she put her arm around my waist and leaned her head against me, and I felt as if I could fly, even without clouds. We pushed through the opening to my wikuom and rekindled the fire. Young Moons began to tell me about her visions.

They had been so long and so disturbing that she had consulted the Man Who Walks with Power many times. Eventually, she arrived at some meaning, but she was not clear about them yet.

Pulling off her robe, she pressed her body next to me and urged me down onto my furs, which we pulled over us. I felt a surge of passion run through my body such as I had never experienced, even in the nights we had spent together. I kissed her, and she began to whisper to me.

"In my visions, we are in love, and we live together. You return to your homeland for a time, come back to me, and then I accompany you to your home. In the end, your world is threatened, but you and your friends end the threat and then bring a dead man back to life. Then we return here. Do you understand this?"

All I understood was that I loved this woman and wanted to live with her. Though we talked about what the future may bring, we focused our winter energies on being together as often as possible.

A. D. 1047

When spring arrived, we moved our wikuoms back to the salmon-river and then to the summer camp. The spring weather was unusually mild.

Hervor and the Man Who Walks with Power returned me to the cliff's edge and my training in visions.

I had one more vision of Garrad. He said nothing but looked over his shoulder, where I could just see the face of a woman. I recognized Marie, who had helped Garrad with healing sometimes. I wondered what she was doing in his hut.

I also had one other vision of William. As I floated in the clouds with the dragon, I saw an open field, patched here and there with snow. There was a battle taking place on it. I leaned toward the vision and saw William.

He was covered in chain mail. His conical helmet was dented and his shield battered, but his greatsword cut huge swaths in the enemy's forces, knocking down many men. People thronged around him, and I recognized the lesser Norman nobles and common people fighting on William's side, shouting with frosted breath the Norman battle cry: "God aid us!"

The French king, Henry, fought at William's side, and his French soldiers hurled the French battle cry into the air: "Mountjoye-Saint Denys!"

Arrayed against William's and Henry's forces were some of the greater nobles, especially the West Norman ones. At their head, as Garrad had feared, rode William's cousin Guy. The West Normans rushed into battle with their cry: "Thor aid us!"

The scene changed, and William was hunting. I recognized the forest and the Roman ruins near Valognes on the Cotentin peninsula. The hunting party left the forest, and William strode into a house in Valognes and lay down to sleep.

A group of nobles seemed to hover over his head. They spoke in low, West Norman voices, and I heard them plotting William's death.

Behind them in hiding, craning his head forward and straining to hear their plans was William's fool, Gollet. He inched backward and raced from the building.

Apparently the plotting had not taken place in Valognes, because Gollet ran for a long time. Arriving in Valognes on foot, panting and gasping, he gaped wildly around, trying to determine in which house William slept.

Frustrated, he stood in the middle of the street and cried out, "Up, up, my lord! Your enemies are astir and seek your life. They come even now, all armed! To horse, my lord, to horse!"

William ran from one of the houses, still pulling on his tunic and leggings. He spoke in low but alarmed tones to Gollet and then leaped onto his horse.

Galloping southeast toward the estuary formed by the Rivers Douve and Vire, he found an ebbing tide and easily forded the Vire, reaching the Bayeux side of the river near the church of Saint Clement.

He dismounted and went inside. I heard him thank God for Gollet's warning and for the ebb tide and ask for aid in escaping the nobles.

"You're more of a fool than Gollet, your fool!" I thought to myself. "This is not the time for prayer!"

Just beyond the church, out of William's sight, the rebel nobles and their henchmen swung into their saddles. The plotting had been taking place in Bayeux, just beyond Saint Clement's church.

William stepped from the church. If he mounted his horse and took to the road at that moment, the nobles would be upon him.

I watched in terror. Then I heard the dragon's voice: "Warn him."

Almost without intending to, I yelled out loud, "Stop! Don't move!"

As if he had heard me, William froze in the shadows of the church's entrance. Hearing the horses, he pressed himself against the darkened door and watched as the nobles rode down the road leading from Bayeux to Valognes.

He glanced around and then sprang onto his horse. Turning from Bayeux, he took the road that followed the coast toward Falaise. He arrived much later, exhausted, in a small town almost fifty miles from Bayeux. Standing at the gate of one of the houses was an elderly man.

William paused. He leaned from his saddle toward the man. "Good morning, good sir. Could you please show me the fastest route to Falaise?"

"My lord," the man said, respectfully, "you are Duke William, are you not? Why do you ride unaccompanied so early in the morning on so fatigued an animal? Are you fleeing someone?"

"Who are you, since you know me?"

"My lord, I'm a knight of the Count of Bayeux, and I hold this town, Ryes, for you. You may tell me your trouble frankly and openly, because I will save your life as if it were my own."

"Do not trust strangers!" I thought to myself.

Instead William said, "I flee a band of nobles, mostly the lords of the lands west of the River Dives, who are intent on my death."

"Then come into my house. I will give you food and drink, a fresh horse, and a bodyguard of my three sons to escort you to Falaise."

I shuddered as William accompanied the old knight into his house.

The knight, though, was as good as his word. Soon William and the knight's three sons were riding the remaining twenty miles to Falaise, while the knight himself continued to stand in front of his gate.

The vision widened, so that I could see William and his escort and still watch the old knight.

The rebel lords arrived at the knight's gate. Apparently, they had reached Valognes and searched for William. Finding that he had escaped, they had followed him along the coast road to Ryes.

One of the nobles shouted at the old knight, "Have you seen a rider come along this road? A young man?"

"Yes," the knight replied, "but he will not have gotten far on the lame horse he was riding. He should be just down that road." He pointed away from Falaise.

The nobles galloped in the exactly the opposite direction that William had ridden.

The last thing I saw was William riding through the gate of Falaise Castle with the knight's three sons.

Onyame, Sigvald, Vagn, Thorkel, and I spent the remainder of the spring cutting and bundling the wood to take North. The People helped us, and I worked alongside them, singing with them, even when I did not understand the words. As Onyame had predicted, gathering and loading the wood occupied us until midsummer. We worked at a slow pace, though, to match the pace of Onyama's future husband.

"It would be rude," Onyame said, "to make him feel that he was delaying our departure."

Before long, though, he was. He had collected the food that was required for the feast, and the women in the two families had cooked, smoked, and dried what could not be kept fresh until the marriage ceremony. But the young man apparently had no ability to kill a moose.

I had conflicting feelings about his incompetence, because I wanted to stay with Young Moons, but I had a task to complete in Norway.

When August arrived, I began to fear sailing conditions. "Shouldn't we help him?" I asked Onyame one night as he visited me at the fire in front of my wikuom.

He gazed up at the stars. "The time is not right."

"What do you mean?"

"If the time were right for the marriage and for our leaving, a moose would surrender itself to him. The Masters of the Forest would see to it."

"In a few more weeks, though, it will be autumn in Greenland with winter conditions. How will we make the passage to the Western Settlement?"

"We will make it. When the time is right."

Eventually, the time was right. The young man killed his moose and thanked its spirit for delivering it. The wedding feast began soon after.

Onyame's daughter had cut her hair, as had her future husband, though it still hung over her shoulders from a decorated headband, long enough for yellow-dyed braids. She wore a white robe painted with red and black designs and had mussel shells and copper dangles sewn on the front of her strapped dress. Her face had been painted in swirling designs, red and brown.

The young man's face was also painted in red and brown, and he wore a headband covered with bone beads, copper tubes, shells, with a blue-jay's wing on either side of the band. His robe was also of white fur, and his leggings and sleeves were painted with blue, yellow, and black geometric designs.

All around both of them in the beautifully decorated and woven reed and ash baskets were the goods necessary for their new life in their new wikuom, which stood, freshly painted, not far from Onyame and his wife's.

That night I joined the People and Young Moons in a celebration that seemed more festive than anything I had experienced back in Normandy.

The next morning, just after I had finished replacing the moss in my moccasins, Hervor poked her head through my entrance and summoned me to the wikuom of the Man Who Walks with Power.

When we arrived, he sat silently at the far end, smoking his stone pipe, his eyes closed. We sat down and waited.

After a long time of silence, he spoke, "I have worked with you as long as our time has allowed. You have learned much. You still live in danger. None of your visions has helped you find a way to end that danger. The time is now right. We must seek a helping vision."

We did not follow the northern cliff path, though. Instead, the three of us plunged into the forest in the direction of the winter camp. We walked in silence for a long time, and it was noon before we halted.

Around us birches, maples, beeches, pines, and spruce stretched far into the sky. Immediately in front of us was a massive ash, easily as large as the one Hervor and I had climbed in Iceland.

To my dismay, Hervor and the Man Who Walks with Power began to climb it.

"Must I follow?" I asked.

The puoin looked down at me. "The Tree that goes through the Six Worlds has its roots in the World Beneath the Earth. Its branches extend into the World Above the Earth. It is on this Tree that you can see far enough to get the help you need."

I sighed and pulled myself onto the closest limb.

We climbed for a long time. I kept my eyes on the next branch above me, taking care not to look down. I told myself over and over that the tree was as solid as the ground. And a friend.

Eventually Hervor and the Man Who Walks with Power stopped. He lowered himself onto a branch just above her head, while she chose one on the opposite side of the trunk at the same height.

"Come sit beside me," he said. "I will keep you from falling."

This was a better offer than Hervor had made back in Iceland, so I climbed up to him. He made a place for me on his branch next to the trunk. I wrapped one arm as far around it as I could, though the trunk was huge.

The other arm the puoin entwined with his own. "Now fly to the Cloud Persons."

"They're closer from here. Perhaps I can just walk."

Hervor translated what I said, and the Man Who Walks with Power laughed.

Neither of them gave any other instructions, though, so I calmed my mind and focused on what clouds I could see through the tree's great limbs.

Soon I felt myself on top of the clouds next to the dragon.

As I floated in them, a scene opened onto a tent, in the middle of which sat a huge figure, hunched over, its head in its hands. A person appeared behind the figure, said something, and the figure turned and straightened.

It had the face of King Harald of Norway. "Send them in."

With a shock, I recognized Ulf and Vandrad. They entered and sat before Hardraada.

He stared at them for a long time and then said, "So you involve me in your plot and then let your prey escape. Is that the end to which all your planning comes?"

"My lord," said Vandrad, "we never expected him to be rescued by the Bear or to sail off the edge of the world."

"Bah! There is no edge of the world. You were deceived."

Ulf spoke up, croaking until he got control of his voice, "We saw it, my lord! We almost plunged over it. Demons assailed us, and only by the grace of God and the saints to whom we prayed did we survive to return to you."

Hardraada rose and stared down at them. "You two are fools. It was folly to ask you to watch the Norman but even greater folly to agree to your plan. As soon as the Norman discovers who you are, he'll realize everything."

"He must have been seized by the demons and pulled off the edge of the world," Vandrad repeated.

"Silence! One more word about the edge of the world, and I'll throw you off it myself."

"At least," Ulf croaked, "there's been no sign of him. He could have been killed."

Hardraada glowered at them. "If he's not killed, you two will be. King Magnus must discover nothing of your idiotic plot."

"He knows nothing," Vandrad said.

I breathed a sigh of relief when I heard this and said out loud to myself, "Praise the saints for that."

Hardraada froze and turned his head slowly, as if he was searching for something. His frown made his uneven eyes draw into a straight line.

I was afraid that he might see me, so I pulled away.

I was on the tree branch again, then on the ground, and a light rain was falling.

A few days later, we bid the People good-bye on a sunny morning. I bid a long, tearful farewell to Young Moons.

"We will see each other again soon, and then we will be together for longer than you can imagine," she said. "I shall see your world, too, though we will live here."

"I'll hold that in my heart. Nothing would delight me more than to see you again soon and spend all of my life with you!"

The Man Who Walks with Power came to the ship to give me a skin bag full of herbs and plants.

"You have much you wish to do," he said to me.

I nodded. "You have helped me more than you know. I am grateful."

He grinned. "I have driven you. As Hervor instructed me. I have one last teaching for you, most important."

I leaned toward him. "I'm eager to hear it."

"You need do nothing. What I have taught you, all that I have taught you, is not necessary." He waved his arms and looked around. "All this, all life, is with you. Now and in all seasons. You need do nothing to have it. It is yours. Let it be. Nothing needs to be done."

I stared at him. "I'm not sure I understand. I have a great deal to do."

"Yes. You will do it. It is your life. It is your dance, like the trees dancing when they wed the wind. After a wedding, what happens? Lovers play. That is what to do with life. It is always there, waiting, like a lover." He gave me a smile which, for a moment, looked like Onyame's mischievous one. "Is love work?" He smiled again. "As you walk through the world as a speaker-to-warriors, walk as a lover. Your life with Young Moons has taught you."

He grasped my hands for a moment. "You work with men. Men who lead. Stand with these men. That is all you need. You know what to say and do. Stand. Stand on the earth. You have wisdom and power, all you need for these men, these men you call …" he paused and then said, in Norman French, "formidable." He smiled again. "Now, you also are 'formidable'."

He turned and walked away. I watched him until a crowd of the People closed around me again.

One of the elders gave me a crooked knife with a beautifully carved maple handle. I thanked him and thanked all of the People standing near him for all of their help. Many of them came forward to wrap their arms around me and clap me on the back.

Young Moons came forward to embrace me once more.

Looking at Young Moons and the People, I thought that if I did not leave now, I never would. I understood why Onyame came back year after year. And I would join him.

CHAPTER 19

THE DEATH OF A KING

A.D. 1047

As we approached Vineland, I slouched in my bailer's seat, missing Young Moons and dreading my meeting with Voldred.

Onyame sang to himself as he steered, while the rest of the crew went silently about their handling of the sails. Hervor leaned over the bow, groaning.

When we reached Vineland, though, I was relieved. Voldred was gone. Early in the summer, a ship had arrived from King Magnus, and Voldred had taken it back to Norway. The King wanted to see him immediately.

Within a few days, we had loaded the other two ships and were pulling into the ocean away from the shore, the grass-covered homes of the Vinelanders disappearing into the distance.

We encountered another cold winter, and storms impeded our passage to Greenland's Western and Eastern Settlements. I remembered how much I disliked bailing and being chilled and soaked. Nonetheless, we delivered wood to the grateful inhabitants all along both settlements and were headed for Iceland before a few weeks had passed.

Several times, the green curtain of the Great Lights appeared in the late-night sky, and I tried flying on top of them to lose my earlier dread of them. I was successful only once, but it was enough. They shimmered under me like sheets of water, their white, green, and red bands filling the sky for as far as I could see.

While I floated above them, I seemed to be in a different world, where the dragon also floated, whispering about other worlds. I listened and watched in awe, and suddenly everything was gone. I was disappointed to find myself back on the hard wood of the longship.

Fighting her seasickness, Hervor began talking to me more as we approached Iceland. She reminded me of all she had taught me and tried to crowd in as many instructions as she could.

Soon, though, she was standing on the shore at the Bay of Smoke, and we were exchanging farewells.

"I don't know how to thank you for all your help and training," I said. "I can't even remember myself before I met you. I seem to have been changed completely."

"The Gods and the People did that. Not I."

"Will I see you again?"

"Yes. There are events that we must share. Until then, farewell."

"Farewell and be careful among the Icelanders."

The crew and I pulled the ship into a cold sea and were gone.

We passed through the islands quickly, but storm-plagued seas made it late September before we reached Kaupang.

There we discovered that the Norwegian Kings had spent the summer raiding in Denmark, intent on winning land back from King Sweyn, now universally regarded as a usurper.

Nonetheless, Hardraada and Magnus had already fallen out publicly, even over trivial matters. A Kaupang merchant related an incident about the royal berths, when the ships of the Kings arrived at nearly the same time.

"I heard it from the poets," the merchant said, "so I trust it. It seems that King Harald arrived ahead of King Magnus and should have given way to King Magnus's ship."

"The agreement was," Onyame noted, "that King Magnus would have precedence in the harbor berths."

"Yes, but King Harald had pulled his ships in first."

I smiled. "Hardraaada, testing and maneuvering, as always."

"King Magnus," the merchant continued, "told his men to arm themselves for fighting, if King Harald's men would not move off. King Harald, seeing King Magnus's anger, shouted to him men, 'Cut the moorings and get the ships out of this berth. Nephew Magnus is angry.'"

"I don't think such a comment was intended to please Magnus," Onyame said, "even though the yielding of the berth would have."

"Later," the merchant said, "when King Harald and several of his men visited King Magnus on Magnus's ship, Harald said, 'I had thought we were among friends, but I begin to doubt whether you want it to be so. It's true, however, that youth is always hasty, so I shall regard your conduct as no more than a mark of youth.' 'It was a mark of my birth, not my youth,' King Magnus replied. 'If this trivial matter had been allowed to go by default, there would soon have been another. I want to honor our agreement in every respect, and I expect you to observe my rights in the same way.' To which King Harald said, as he returned to his ships, 'It's also an old custom that it's the wiser man who must always give way.' King Harald cannot bear to lose a battle, even the small ones."

We remained at Kaupang only long enough to unload our goods, bid farewell to the other two ships, and have a new monk's robe sewn for me to re-establish my Northern disguise.

By putting in at almost every landfall in Denmark and asking for information, we eventually discovered that King Sweyn had fled to Skaane, a Danish province in the southern part of the land of the Swedes.

Magnus and Hardraada, still raiding, were in the middle of Jutland somewhere.

Unfortunately, the inquiries cost us time. The end of October was only a few days away. We had seen threats of snow, though it had as yet held off, at least along the coast.

Sailing still south, we put in at a harbor near a small Danish town called Suderup. Onyame had spotted several Norwegian ships and recognized the colors of one of them. "Earl Thorir."

"That would be fortunate. He would surely be with the kings."

As soon as we pulled the ship ashore, Thorir did indeed appear with a crowd of men and greeted us. He was dressed less formally than when I had last seen him, and he was armored for battle.

He seemed happy to see us — for Thorir — but he was bothered by something. So we cut our greetings short and recounted none of the stories we could have told him.

"Your coming is a godsend," Thorir said. "The word has gone around that you are a healer, Brother Augustine."

"Has it also gone around that I am a poisoner, as Hardraada's men would have everyone believe?"

"Yes, but we knew that a God-guided monk could not be a common assassin. I did not believe it, and the King does not believe it. He is the one who needs you. He has been poisoned. He is dying."

"Poisoned? How?"

I heard Onyame groan behind me.

"No one knows." Thorir replied. "No healer here has been able to do anything. The King remains calm, believing he is doomed, but surely, you, a Brother to whom God speaks —"

"Will you take me to him?"

"Yes. We hoped you would agree to see him."

We were led through a forested area to a meadow, at the far end of which was a tent camp. I recognized the large meeting tent of the Kings and the small, modest one in which I had met with Magnus just before my flight.

"Where's King Harald?" I asked Thorir as we neared the tent.

"He is on his ships, swearing to bring to justice the Danish King, Sweyn, whom he claims must have had King Magnus poisoned, since Magnus had defeated him in battle so many times."

"When might he return?"

"We are not certain," Thorir said, "but he cannot be more than a few sailing days away. King Sweyn is at Skaane."

"Yes, we received that message."

We reached the tent door, and Thorir pushed his head in, whispering until he discovered that Magnus was awake.

He pulled his head back out. "The King wishes to see you immediately."

I bent through the tent door. Magnus was at the back of the tent.

As he lay on his sick-bed, I scarcely recognized him. His face had paled to almost corpse-color, his lips bluish-purple. His hair fell here and there, reminding me of an unruly bush. His arms, emaciated, lay limp at his side over the blanket that covered the rest of him.

How did Thorir think that this dying shell could recover?

I slowly straightened, threw back the hood of the blue robe and cleared my throat. It struck me that here lay the man who had sought my death for over ten years, and now he himself had been killed by the mushroom I had found for his assassins.

I should have been relieved, I thought, but how could any man's death be a relief?

He opened his eyes with what seemed to be terrible pain. He recognized me and smiled. He paused as if gathering strength to speak, then said with a strain, "I am pleased to see you again, Brother Augustine."

"Your majesty, I can try to cure you. I've prepared some antidotes for what I think has poisoned you. Even at this late time, they may work. Of course, I can also offer prayers."

He slowly shook his head, though it seemed to take great effort.

"There is no cure for me, even prayer."

I began to protest, but he lifted his hand from the wrist, motioning me to wait. I watched as he took a deep breath.

His breathing became more regular, and his words came with less difficulty. "Two nights ago, my father, Saint Olaf, came to me in a dream."

"You don't have to speak, you majesty, if it pains you."

He raised his hand again. "I must tell you. I need your help."

He seemed far beyond my help.

He spoke again. "In the dream, my father said to me, 'You have a choice, my son: you may come with me now, or you may live to be the most powerful of kings and grow very old. But if you live, you will commit a crime so heinous that you could scarcely, if ever, be able to expiate it.'"

I heard myself say, "Your majesty, no. You could never —"

He had continued speaking, slowly. "I said to my father, 'I want you to choose for me.'" He smiled wanly. "I am young, you know."

I nodded. I recalled that this dying king was not yet twenty-five years old.

"My father said, 'You are to come with me.' So I am destined to die now and join him." He smiled again. "What a feast we shall have with the warriors and kings of the past." He swallowed, slowly. "But, Brother Augustine, I am afraid ... afraid I may have already committed the terrible crime. You must help me stop it."

"How? What crime, your majesty?"

"When I was a boy, I heard of a vision from an Icelandic seer. It predicted that the power of the North and even my own life would be ended by the nephew of King Canute. The nephew would also be a lame, bastard son of Duke Robert of Normandy, thus heir to both Canute's Danish empire, including Denmark, Norway, and England and perhaps even Normandy."

He paused and groaned. Then he continued, "I was young, foolish, and ambitious. I sought out one of the families that resisted my father, followers of the old religion. I knew they would have no Christian qualms about killing a man. I tricked one of their sons into killing this crippled, illegitimate Norman boy."

I had guessed correctly. Because of a garbled version of the Four Crowns Prophecy, Magnus had mistaken me for William. Ironically, William had indeed caused Magnus's death — through the gullibility of his emissary.

He continued, "I could try to excuse my crime by saying that I was a boy and frightened by predictions of my own death. The assassin even returned a few years after, saying that he had located the crippled child and barely missed killing him. I should have stopped him then, but I was still afraid."

"Your majesty —" I began.

"Listen, this is my greatest sin. The assassin returned just last year. He had found the boy again, now a young man, and had been badly wounded trying to carry out my orders. He had wounded the young man but had not killed him." He closed his eyes. "He wanted permission to end his quest. I refused it."

The pain on his face made me anxious. I tried to calm him. "Your majesty, can you believe the dream about your father?"

"My father has come to me in dreams before. A few years ago, my brother-in-law and I led an expedition against the Wends, who were attacking Denmark. You may have heard of it. It was a great battle, just north of Hedeby. The night before the battle, Michaelmas Eve, my father appeared to me and told me that if I carried his battle-axe, Hel, against the Wends, I would not even need armor. I would slaughter them. I fought in a red silk kirtle, and the Wends passed out of the world."

"Your majesty, if you believed that a young Norman was coming to kill you, of course you would keep your man searching for him."

He opened his eyes. "You are an emissary. Do you see what I may cause? As my father said in the dream, it is a crime for which I could never atone. Your Duke is a great man. He has links to many territories, alliances with them. Around Normandy, even England. You are giving him more here."

At least with Magnus, I had been successful in building William's reputation.

He now spoke with greater effort. "Our power is fading. Duke William and his allies could be the instruments for bringing a less violent way of living in our world, fulfilling the promise of the new Christian Millennium."

I sat back. Magnus was not just worried about his own guilt. He was not even worried about the death of a single man. Men had died around him all his life. As he approached his own death, he was concerned for the whole world.

"Your majesty, may I speak?"

He nodded.

"I know about the assassin you sent. His name is Voldred, isn't it?"

He opened his eyes wide. "How did you know? Had Duke William discovered his identity?"

"No, your majesty. I have. You see, the Icelander's vision was wrong in several details. Duke William is a bastard, that's true, but he's not lame. I am. I've also been a companion of Duke William's almost since his birth, so the mistake was easy to make. You see, I was a village bastard, or so the local villagers believed, since I was abandoned. They always assumed some peasant or cleric had regretted fathering a lame child and exposed me to die. So my name became 'Lod,' the Norman nickname for a bastard child. When Voldred came looking for a lame bastard, he found me.

"The second mistake." I continued, "is that Duke William is not the nephew of King Canute. Rather, his grandfather's sister, his great-aunt, was Canute's wife. It was Duke William whom Voldred should have sought. Instead he's spent his life seeking me, while Duke William lives. Do you see that God has allowed this error, so that you could not commit the terrible crime your father mentioned? Your soul remains free of it."

"Voldred will not stop now, though" he said, his voice more strained. "I called him back here ... to stop him. Misunderstanding the call, he went directly to the South. Without ever stopping to speak with me. He must believe that I would have pressed him to finish his task, and he went south to do it. He will stop. He is bound by a vow. The old religion."

"I know."

"Your life is not safe until I release him, but I will not live to release him. So you must do it for me."

"How?"

He pulled at his blanket. "I have something. Something that will make Voldred believe you are my messenger." He pulled again, and now a bone handle emerged from the blanket, now a long curved blade with a red streak on it.

I gaped at it. It was identical to Voldred's.

"I see that you are familiar with it." He smiled weakly. "Now I know that you have seen not only the knife Thorir gave to my uncle, King Harald. You have also seen the one I gave to Voldred when I was a youth. Thorir believes that there were only two. I kept this third one secret from everyone, except Voldred. It is my link to him, and it will be your link, too. When he sees it, he will know you can have received it only from me."

I hesitated to take anything resembling the weapon I had feared for so many years.

"Take it," he said, his breath coming in slow gasps. "What could have brought your death will now save your life."

I picked it up by the handle gingerly and held it, afraid to put it in my belt. It might accidentally accomplish the task I had always feared it would.

"Thank you, your majesty." I watched his face, which now appeared more peaceful, almost serene. I genuinely wanted to help him, but I also wanted to complete my mission.

Only Hardraada, as King of Norway and Denmark, could prevent that now — by refusing an alliance or by pursuing me as an assassin.

"Your majesty, though I shudder to even think it, this must be said, now: there's one other … possibility … of a great crime."

He nodded. "I have thought of it as well. Letting my uncle have the thrones of both Norway and Denmark."

"Yes, your majesty. The Danish Assembly will place great value on whatever decision you make. If you choose King Harald, he will control the entire North."

"As an emissary from the South, you recall the raids of the past and invasions by weaker lords than Harald, which were nonetheless terrible."

"Your majesty, I —"

"It is what I would recall if I were an emissary." His eyes took on a faraway cast. "It is what I should think of as a true king. Harald must not be allowed to dominate the North and the world. It would mean an age of blood, and that would be a far greater crime than a single death."

"I understand, your majesty, but who can stop him?"

"Ironically, a usurper who has wronged me at every turn. His ambition is as great as Harald's."

"Sweyn?"

"No one else."

"But —"

"Yes, I know he has trouble winning a battle." He smiled grimly. "In spite of Harald's experience and reputation, though, he may be unable to seize a whole country. He may be better at raiding and besieging the castles of the Holy Land than he is at winning a kingdom. And many Norwegian lords will refuse to aid him. He is not popular in Norway."

"You'll give the Danish throne to Sweyn then?"

He nodded once. "You can deliver the message. I will send Thorir with you. Call him for me."

I called, and Thorir appeared, frowning at Magnus's drawn face.

"Thorir, you and Brother Augustine must find King Sweyn. You know Sweyn's temper, and Brother Augustine's presence will guarantee that you are escorted safely to his camp. Tell him that I bequeath him the kingship of Denmark."

Thorir looked stunned.

"To hold, at all costs, against my uncle," Magnus continued. "Harald will become King of Norway, but he must not become King of Denmark, too."

Thorir looked at me, and I nodded.

Magnus smiled weakly. "I know that Sweyn is a miserable fighter. How long can he stand against Harald? Brother Augustine and I agree, though, that this is what my father wants me to do. This is the meaning of the dream, which both you and Brother Augustine know about. This will atone for sins I have committed and prevent a greater sin that I might have committed."

He leaned, in agony it seemed, over the far side of the bed, reached something leather and handed it to Thorir. "In case I have misinterpreted my father's wishes and in case Sweyn cannot repel Harald, this may help."

"What is it?"

"Directions to where I have concealed the wealth that Harald brought back from Byzantium and gave to me. It will build fleets for many years to come. Even if Sweyn fights poorly, Harald will have difficulty defeating the armies that this will supply."

He breathed a long sigh. "I want a few more words with you, Thorir. You, Brother Augustine, must prepare to sail. You and Thorir must leave before I die, because news of my death will spur Harald to some action, and you must reach Sweyn before that. God go with you, as I know He does."

"And with you, your majesty."

I backed toward the tent door. Magnus raised his hand toward me. "Brother Augustine, I am sorry for the fear I must have caused you."

"It has been forgotten, your majesty, after I have been in the presence of so great a King."

Before the fact of Magnus's death could sink in, a rider arrived at the camp with news that King Harald Hardraada was marching with his men toward us. He had summoned all of King Magnus's men to assemble in the open meadow, so that he could address them.

Thorir drew me toward the rear of the crowding warriors — Hardraada's own men and Magnus' men, all of them uncertain as to what would happen next.

"We are too late to get to Sweyn," Thorir whispered, "and we may be sure, as Magnus had suspected, that Hardraada intends to seize Denmark immediately. Nonetheless, we need to be certain of his next move."

So, we waited for Hardraada's arrival, and he was not long in coming.

Standing in front of the wooden throne on a platform in front of the combined Norwegian forces, Hardraada looked gigantic and sounded the same.

"Brave warriors of Norway," he thundered, "I intend to complete the work of the noble King who lies here asleep in God and whom we all mourn. I will go to the Viborg Assembly to have the surviving King of Norway —" he was careful not to refer to himself directly —"named King of Denmark, to reclaim the land that was taken from Norway, from King Magnus, by the usurper Sweyn. This is the right of Norway, and when the right has been recognized, we Norwegians will rule the Danes forever."

I groaned quietly to Thorir. Hardraada intended to attack Sweyn immediately.

"Fear not," Thorir said softly. "We shall complete the mission we were given." He rose from the seated band. "Your majesty King, may I have permission to speak?"

Hardraada knew better than to refuse Magnus's chief emissary and friend.

"Of course, Earl Thorir. You wish to speak from your grief and sorrow, and we will grieve with you." He sat down.

Cleverly said, I thought. If Thorir disagreed with Hardraada, his disagreement could be dismissed as the ravings of grief.

"Your majesty King and my fellow warriors," Thorir said, "when King Olaf fell on the battlefield at Stiklestad — where our noble King Harald was himself wounded and almost killed — all Norwegians, those on both sides of the battle, felt the loss as keenly as we feel the loss of King Magnus. Perhaps we even feel it more. For while King Olaf would later become Saint Olaf, King Magnus has been to us, for all his life, Magnus the Good. His works of justice and generosity have brightened our lives for many years, and we mourn that they have died with him."

I glanced around the crowd of armored warriors, their faces gone slack, tears in many eyes.

Thorir continued. "After Stiklestad, the Norwegians who opposed King Olaf and those who fought with him, like our King Harald, stopped to mourn and to take his body to his final resting place. In Christian propriety. They felt the shock of grief as we now feel it, and their feet felt so leaden that all they could do was walk mindlessly to a sacred grave, later to become a shrine. Will it be different for our good King Magnus?"

Taking Magnus's body home rather than attacking Sweyn would have been the only suggestion that Hardraada did not want to hear. Yet Thorir had just suggested this.

Nonetheless Hardraada's face showed no emotion.

Thorir had been clever enough not to suggest it openly, but he must have been appealing to something in the men. Somewhere, there must have been opposition to Hardraada.

Einar Paunch-Shaker, the most powerful of the powerful lord in the north of Norway, rose and requested permission to speak. A huge, rotund, fur-draped man, he seemed almost as impressive as Hardraada, and again Hardraada could not refuse.

"My lords and friends," Einar said, facing the men of northern Norway, "we have a duty, a Christian duty, to bring the body of our friend and king, Magnus the Good, home to rest beside his father. This is an obligation urged on us both by God and by the love we felt for this man, this kindest of all the Kings of Norway." His voice rose. "Can it be that this duty is to be set aside to go plundering? To covet the possessions of another ruler in a foreign land? Can it be that the right we have to claim Denmark is greater than our duty to bring our lord home?" He turned to Hardraada. "I can tell you, your majesty King, with all respect, that we of the North will leave today to return the body of King Magnus to his home and his father."

Thorir, still standing, said, his voice heavy with sorrow, "My men and I have heart for nothing else, friend Einar. We shall accompany you."

Hardraada had lost. He rose slowly. "My good friends and noble lords. You have reminded me of my Christian duty, a duty which, in my zeal for the quest begun by King Magnus, I had almost forgotten. We shall, of course, bear his body home. The dignity of Norway in the face of the indignity of the Danish usurper can be regained at another time, when we have ceased mourning."

That night, while the camp slept, Thorir and I slipped away toward Onyame's longship, where Onyame already stood at the tiller.

Crouching along the makeshift wharf, we avoided the dozing guard. With a single push, the ship glided soundlessly into the water, and only the oars disturbed the night's silence.

I did not even notice the passage from Jutland to Skaane, where Sweyn was encamped. I only half noticed when Thorir explained to me how his men would delay Hardraada's departure until we returned.

Without intending it, I had slipped into the world "above the clouds" as I had done under the training of Hervor and the Man Who Walks with Power. It seemed as if the dragon had come to get me and had carried me somewhere.

For a time, except for the dragon's face, I saw only blackness. Then I saw the face of Magnus and next to it the stern face that I seemed to know was Saint Olaf, his father. It was the face of the old warrior who had warned me about Ulf and Vandrad originally.

Magnus and his father were now together, as Magnus' dream had promised.

Magnus's eyes seemed to be gazing at something with concern, though, and I followed the gaze. It fell first on the scene of a siege, many wooden towers surrounding a castle in the middle of a river.

I recognized William, giving orders to the besieging army, and I recognized the castle. It had belonged to Count Gilbert before he was murdered in front of Edward and me. Now it belonged to William's cousin, Guy.

Then I saw Edward, sitting on a throne, his head in his hands. Over him hovered, threateningly it seemed, several faces, among which I recognized Tostig's. The other faces could only be Tostig's brothers and his father, Earl Godwin. Edward was being pressed by Godwin's family.

Then the vision faded, though I still was only partially aware of my surroundings.

I realized that Edward and William, oppressed by troubles at home, might despair of ever seeing an alliance with the Northern crowns or help from anyone within their own territories.

Only being urged by Onyame to don my monk's habit again and being escorted down a winding forest path toward King Sweyn's tent returned me to full alertness.

I glanced around. Onyame, Thorir and I stood in a small clearing, its wild grasses crushed by folded tents, saddled horses, and shouting Danish warriors.

"Someone is planning to flee even farther from Norway," Thorir whispered.

Covered in a plain, undyed riding cloak, King Sweyn strode from the largest tent, his limp noticeable, his beard untrimmed and his hair unkempt.

"What do these men want?" he demanded of the guard.

"They bring a message from King Magnus. This is Earl Thorir of Steig, King Magnus's half-brother, with his house guard. This is a God-guided monk, Brother Augustine of Normandy."

I heard myself say, almost as if it had just occurred, "The King has died, your majesty."

Sweyn's eyes widened. "King Magnus? Dead?"

Thorir paused to let the news have its impact. "Poisoned. Killed, I suspect, by partisans of King Harald."

"That I can believe. Magnus dead, though ..." Sweyn motioned for his chair to be brought and slumped into it. "There was little love lost between us at the end, but he was a fine man. A good King." He made the sign of the cross and sighed. "A great King."

Thorir spoke again. "Your majesty, King Magnus's dying wish was that you hold the throne of Denmark against King Harald."

Sweyn looked up. "He wished what?"

"That you hold Denmark against King Harald's onslaughts."

"Did he say that?"

A monk's touch was required. "I was his advisor at the last moments of life. Along with Earl Thorir. In the name of God, he desired this with all his heart."

"Why?"

"Surely you know the character of King Harald," Thorir said, "and knew the character of King Magnus well enough to answer that." Thorir did not commit himself.

"Yes, of course. Yes."

"King Magnus has also sent these directions." Thorir handed him the piece of leather he had received from Magnus. "They show where he stored the wealth necessary for you to build a fleet to withstand King Harald."

Sweyn took the leather from him, shaking his head. A long silence followed. "All of this is hard to take in. I thank you heartily, of course." He looked up at us, frowning. "Will not Harald seize Denmark immediately — before I can even return — and then press my own nobles into service to defeat me? I will have no opportunity to fulfill Magnus's last wish, even with the aid of his wealth."

"King Harald prepares at this moment to return to Norway to bury King Magnus," Thorir said. "He cannot possibly return with a fleet before next summer."

Sweyn squinted at him. "Can this be possible? Harald abandoning such an advantage?"

"I can assure you, your majesty," I said, "that it is true. If I may say so, Earl Thorir has seen to it himself."

"Ah." He studied Thorir's face. "I see." He looked at me again. "What did you say your name was, Brother?"

"Augustine, your majesty."

"What is your role in this, Brother Augustine? You are not a Northerner, are you?"

"I'm a Norman, your majesty. On a mission from William, Duke of Normandy, to forge alliances with the Northern kings. The Duke is prepared to offer you friendship." I caught Thorir's glance at me. "He is not equipped to join any Northern forces at present, including Denmark's. He must be cautious, but he will not aid any enemy of yours. On that you have my solemn word, sworn on the Holy Book and holy relics, if you wish."

Sweyn considered me for a moment. "Thank you, Brother Augustine. Earl Thorir is well known to us. Even if he were not, your word itself would be sufficient. You are both a monk and the emissary of a noble lord. Duke William's reputation is growing here. I am grateful for his friendship."

I decided to try to extend the diplomacy. "King Edward of England also will smile on your kingship and not threaten it in any way, if you will accept his friendship."

Sweyn looked surprised. "Gladly! More than gladly!" He took a deep breath and stood up. "Well. Hmm. God has reversed my fortunes with a stroke, through King Magnus and his emissaries. I thank both of you and offer you my hospitality, rough though it may be here."

"Thank you, your majesty," Thorir said, "but we must return to King Harald's camp to join the party bearing King Magnus's body north."

"I understand. I can promise you that I shall gather my forces and be waiting in Denmark in the spring for any attack of King Harald's. I shall never flee from Denmark again as long as I live."

Thorir gave him a short bow. "I'm certain King Magnus could have wished for no more, your majesty."

"That was well done, Brother Augustine," Thorir said, as we sailed back toward Jutland.

"Yes, we convinced him easily, and he sounds determined."

"I meant your offer of friendship with Duke William. That was surely an inspiration of the moment."

"Yes. Things seem to have taken a positive turn, even for my overlord. I thought of the Icelandic prophecy, and, well, the Four Crowns may yet come together. Though at the price of Magnus's life. That I regret."

"He was a good King. I shall be sorry to live under King Harald."

"Will you be safe?"

He paused. "I have been considering that. If we return to the camp and my men have heard of any hostility, I shall accept King Sweyn's offer of hospitality, even if it means not accompanying King Magnus's body home. I would rather visit Magnus' grave later than be buried alongside him now."

Hardraada was more than hostile, we learned on the morning of our return. His men actively sought Thorir, which meant a direct threat to Thorir's life.

"I cannot stay here," Thorir said. "I shall instead spend a quiet winter in Skaane with King Sweyn. Then I shall go with him to Denmark. It seems that I shall be changing countries now."

Thorir ordered Onyame to prepare ships to sail back to Skaane.

As Onyame plunged into the forest toward the harbor, I asked him, "How long before you sail?"

He stopped to look at me. "Are you planning to visit King Harald?"

"I must try once more to win the alliance for Normandy. Magnus is dead. Sweyn has unexpectedly fallen into a friendship with Normandy. So only Hardraada remains."

"What will you do?"

When I told him my strategy, he said, "That is a risk. Do you want me to join you?"

"I appreciate your offer of support, but no. The risk must be mine alone. Besides, if it fails, Ulf and Vandrad will have my life soon, anyway, and my mission would have ended in failure. If I am not at the harbor soon, perhaps Thorir and you should sail on to Skaane without me."

"I will ask some of Thorir's men to watch for you. They will bring me word of any threat to you, and if I can help, I will."

"Thank you. You have been a fine and good friend."

"God go with you."

As far as I knew, Hardraada had not detected my presence in camp. The blue-robed hermit who traveled with Onyame bore no resemblance to the monk whose life Ulf and Vandrad had sought.

Since Hardraada's plans of conquest had been delayed, he had time to see visitors. So, I was granted an audience with him immediately.

As I slipped through the tent door, I noticed the bow I had given him, a quiver of arrows next to it — where I had expected to find it. Good fortune had given me the weapon I now needed.

Because the guard had searched me thoroughly before I entered and because a hermit did not seem threatening, Hardraada had his back to me for a moment, pouring himself a horn of some liquid.

"I do not imagine you wish anything to drink," he began as he turned around, but his eyes widened as he faced an arrow, drawn in the bow I held.

"If you make a single sound, I may be startled and release this arrow, so please sit down quietly, your majesty."

He smiled. "Why, Brother Augustine. Back from the dead? Surely you and I have no quarrel."

"Quarrel, your majesty? Certainly not. I was just trying the bow again while you poured your wine, and now it is … caught … in a most embarrassing position. I trust it will ease as we speak."

"About what?"

"Saving you a defeat, your majesty."

"A defeat? I know of no defeats facing me. None that I cannot handle, that is."

The bow tightened, and his face became serious.

"My apologies, your majesty. My nerves. You see, I came north on a mission of friendship. After risking my life and my soul to save you, I offered you my friendship and Duke William's. You graciously replied with an offer of gifts and a boon for me. Before our friendship could be consummated, however, two of your men contrived to undo it. Now they present you with a defeat. A defeat I can transform into victory. With your help, of course."

"I am willing to help you, Brother Augustine. Will you lower your bow now?"

"First, I ask the boon you offered."

"Anything, as I promised."

"My life and your oath of friendship with me and all of my friends, including Duke William."

"I never intended anything but friendship for you and your lord."

"Your men did, and you believed their lies about me."

"I do not know what you mean."

"You did accuse me of plotting against you."

"I learned later that it was untrue."

The bow's tension relaxed slightly.

Encouraged, Hardraada said, "Two of my overzealous men tried to draw you into a nefarious plot, yes. When I confronted them, they denied it but soon after set out to destroy the only evidence against them — you."

I wondered whether he expected me to believe this tale. "Well, your majesty, they almost lost my friendship and the friendship of my Duke for you. More, they have cost you an easy victory over Denmark. In fact, you may never be able to seize Denmark from Sweyn now. Though if any warrior can, you would be that warrior."

"I do not understand you."

"First, is the boon of friendship granted?"

"It is granted."

"You swear it?"

"Yes."

"Even on the holy relics of a nearby church?"

"Yes."

For a Northern warrior, that was good enough. I lowered the bow. "Then, your majesty, I bear sad news. The men that I know as Ulf and Vandrad did not seek my help to poison you but to poison King Magnus. Which they have done, as you know."

"I did not know how the good King died. I would be grieved to learn that any of my men had a hand in it."

"You just learned it. They poisoned him, and he knew he had been poisoned. So, as you may have discovered by now or soon will, he sent Earl Thorir to King Sweyn with the promise of the throne of Denmark. Thorir and I delivered the message in front of Sweyn's men. We also delivered much of the wealth you gave King Magnus, so that Sweyn can rebuild his fleet and feed his army."

Hardraada's jaw tightened.

I continued, "You see, your majesty, your two men lost an easy victory for you. I would have supported your claim to Denmark and presented it to Duke William if your two men had not driven me off and if you had not believed them and accused me. Further, since you yourself were saved by Saint Olaf in Byzantium, you will appreciate this: King Magnus was told by Saint Olaf in a dream that he was destined to die this autumn. You would have had the throne to yourself even if your men had not poisoned King Magnus. You would, however, have been loved rather than hated, because your complicity in the poisoning has made you hated by the men of northern Norway." He stirred, so I added, "The poisoners were your men."

He spoke through his clenched jaw, "Not for long."

"So you see the defeat they have given you. Not merely denying you a victory over Denmark this autumn but also earning for you the hatred of many of the Norwegians."

He paused a long time. "I see. You can transform this, Brother Augustine?"

"I can once again offer the friendship of Duke William, which you have so graciously accepted. I can also offer the friendship of King Edward of England."

"I did not know you were an emissary for Normandy and England, though I am happy to accept the friendship of both, especially considering my present circumstances — though the friendships seem worth little just now. Your Duke faces troubles at home and King Edward ... as you may know, his throne might have been mine."

I recalled that Hardraada and Hardecanute had made a mutual vow about their thrones. "I am not convinced that you would want the English throne now, would you, your majesty?"

He smiled grimly. "If you mean would I want to be married to Edith of Wessex and consult her father and brothers on every decision I make, no. About that you are correct."

His spies had been unusually efficient, but I was not shaken. "Duke William's troubles will soon pass, and if you accept his friendship formally, you will have a powerful ally in the South, who is also allied to King Henry of

France and Count Baldwin of Flanders." I trusted my vision that Henry had aided William, and I hoped that my brief conversations with Baldwin at St. Vaast would remain in the Count's memory.

"Has Duke William so many friends? They do not aid him in battle." He was testing my information.

"King Henry does, your majesty."

He paused. "Yes, that's true. For now."

"Even more, I can tell you that King Sweyn cannot rebuild his fleet or army before next summer."

"I already knew that."

"If you seize the two men who poisoned King Magnus, denounce them, and publicly grieve for King Magnus, you will regain the respect of the Norwegians. I am not one of your advisors, so I do not offer this counsel impudently. I offer it as a friend and the emissary of Duke William and King Edward, whose support for you I will now make public, especially to the northern Norwegian lords. You will once again be seen to be a leader respected by other leaders."

He stared at me, stroking his blonde beard. It was the first time I had ever seen him do something from habit.

He studied me for a long time, and the silence settled around me almost threateningly.

When he spoke, his voice was deeper. "What, Brother Augustine, did you think was to stop me from seizing my sword and killing you?"

He was admitting defeat. He knew as well as I that I could put several arrows through him before he even reached his sword.

I smiled at him. "I never supposed that you would be so inhospitable as to slice up a guest as you would the meat you serve at your table."

He returned the smile. "It would not be considered inhospitable in Byzantium."

"This is not Byzantium, your majesty, and you are not a mercenary here. You are the King of Norway."

He let his head nod several times, with studied unintentionality. "You know, Brother Augustine, or whatever your name is"— he paused, but I said nothing —"if you were not Duke William's and King Edwards' emissary, I would make you mine."

"You are too gracious, your majesty."

"Would you accept?"

I hesitated. "If I were not born and bred a Norman, I certainly would."

He breathed deeply and then laughed. "That is a clever answer."

"To a clever offer."

His face became serious, and for a moment he looked tired. "No, Brother Augustine, the offer was genuine."

I bowed my head. "Thank you, your majesty. It is an offer I shall remember all my life."

"I hope you do."

"Now, your majesty, with your indulgence, I request a last word."

He nodded. "You may have it."

"An apology. That the two poisoners, whom I mistakenly believed had been sent by you, forced me to resort to … a weapon. To draw a bow on a king is a grave matter, on a friend an even more grave matter, and on a fellow child of God a thrice grave matter, for which I beg your forgiveness, as the last part of my boon. I shall do penance for it upon my return to Normandy." I shook my head in regret. "As you see, the poisoners have almost defeated our friendship and yours with Normandy and England."

"That is so."

"If you accept my apology, your majesty, you restore those friendships."

He cocked his head, watching me for a time. "I believe you are sincere."

"I am, your majesty."

"Well, Brother Augustine, I accept your apology as readily as I accept your friendship."

"And the friendship of my Duke and King Edward."

He smiled. "Most heartily. You see, Brother Augustine, contrary to what you may believe, I had nothing to do with the plotting of the men who ensnared you. They came to me with the story of your complicity in their plan, and I expressed my disapproval, but they assured me I had nothing to lose by going along with them."

"They said the same to me, your majesty."

"No doubt they did. So I took advantage of the situation: a tactic common to any warrior. When I realized that you had been taken, probably by Thorir's bear, I insisted that they find you and make amends with you anyway they could. I am not one to be at odds with a God-guided monk"— he paused —"especially one who draws a bow the way you do. You may not know this, but they returned with the story that they had made peace with you and that you had returned to the South."

"An astonishing tale."

"I hope you believe me, Brother Augustine. I have no desire to be your enemy, and I can assure you that when I find these two, they will be dealt with as severely as they wanted me to deal with you."

"I am grateful, your majesty, for both your frankness and your fairness."

He grinned. "Well, as you promised, Brother Augustine, I may not have won Denmark today, but I have won two alliances and regained a friend. This is a day of victory, after all."

After I left the tent, I lost Hardraada's guard in the forest. He had undoubtedly received orders to follow me, probably to locate Thorir.

I did not begrudge Hardraada his stratagems now. I had his promise, and I knew the devotion of Northern lords to sworn obligations.

Now, if William could hold Normandy and if Edward could keep the Earl Godwin at bay, an alliance of the Four Crowns would be won, and the Prophecy that Magnus so feared would be fulfilled.

Nonetheless, the vision Magnus had given me revealed that William and Edward faced challenges and perhaps despair. They would need to know as soon as possible that I had succeeded in the North.

Even though going South meant encountering Voldred again.

CHAPTER 20

RAPID RETURNS

A.D. 1047

When I reached Onyame's longship, Thorir had already sailed.
"He didn't wish to wait," Onyame explained after he had given orders for the crewmen to push the ship into the water, "and I'd rather spend the winter with you in Flanders and Normandy than with King Sweyn in Skaane. I assume that we'll stop first in Flanders."

"It's good that Thorir didn't wait. Hardraada's men followed me for a time, but after losing me, they would probably come here. Yes, we'll be headed to Flanders, and I'm delighted to have you and your crew accompany me."

He smiled and handed me my bucket. "You'll be accompanying us. You're still our bailer."

Winter followed us all the way south and had arrived in Arras by the time Onyame and I did. Christmas was not far behind.

I needed to reach William and Edward as soon as possible, but I had to confirm the alliance with Count Baldwin, and I wanted to see Anette.

Count Baldwin was at St. Vaast, so we were able to visit both him and the monks who had helped me.

The Count was delighted to be part of an alliance that included Normandy, England, Denmark, and Norway. Any ally that strengthened his position against the Holy Roman Emperor would have been to his liking.

I did not find Anette immediately, so I left messages for her. The St. Vaast Abbot told us that she had been often in the company of a young merchant's son, a long-time friend of hers. He was a nice man, the Abbot reported, and had consoled her through the winter. After that, the young man and she had left, and he had heard nothing more about her.

We had been in Arras only a day, mostly warming ourselves by the fire of our inn and recalling the year with the People, when the young man found us.

Brushing the snow from his robe, he said, "I'm Thiebaut, son of the merchant Bernard. What is it you want with my wife?"

I pulled back the hood of my robe. "I'm not sure who you mean, sir. We're looking for a young healer named Anette. My name is Cuin. I'm from Falaise —"

"You! It can't be! We heard that you were dead! By heaven, I'm pleased to see you! We've prayed for something like this! Anette will be delighted!"

"Is she all right?"

"I hope so. She's my wife."

I must have looked surprised, but he guessed the wrong reason.

"I'm sorry if you had other intentions," he said, "but when you didn't return by early autumn, Anette and I sent messengers to Normandy and Hedeby. I knew Anette was worried about you. The Hedeby messenger could discover nothing about a Cuin, but he did hear of one Brother Augustine, who matched your description. Knowing that you had used that same name here, Anette was certain you were that particular Augustine. The messenger said that this monk had been killed in the deep forest by a bear. Then a Norman messenger reported that Duke William's emissary had been killed in Denmark. At first Anette was inconsolable. Within a few months, though, she told me that it must be God's will that she and I marry."

He hung his head. "If you did have other intentions, I'm sorry to report that we're happy together."

I smiled. "I'm certain that you are, and I'm delighted that you are." I rose. "I had only intentions of friendship for Anette, and I see that marrying you is a great good — a happy life with a fine man."

"You may see her if you wait. She's been doing healing work with Lady Matilda."

"I would love to, and I will upon my return. For now, my companion and I must return to Normandy. Thank you for coming, and it's been my pleasure to meet you. Please give my fondest regards to Anette. And best wishes to both of you."

Early the next morning, Onyame and I mounted our horses and headed south as quickly as we could ride.

A. D. 1048

We had planned to visit Rouen first, and I hoped to find William there. Interrupted by a snowstorm, we stopped at a farmhouse a league northeast of the city to ask where the nearest inn might be.

The farmer blinked at us through the snow falling onto his eyelashes. "It is late in the day," he observed, tilting his head.

I muttered to Onyame in Danish, "After traveling all day, I hadn't noticed that it was late."

"What?" the farmer asked.

In Norman French, I said, loudly, "Yes, it is, and we're on our way to Rouen, but we shall not arrive there tonight if the storm worsens."

"That's true." He paused. "Rouen?"

"Yes, to see Duke William. He's a friend."

The farmer's head straightened. "You're friends of the Duke? Well, that's a different matter." He leaned forward, glancing around furtively. "You'd be well advised to come inside and spend the night with us. No inn nearby is safe, even if you could find it in the snow."

"Safe?"

The farmer would say no more until we sat in front of his fire, our feet propped toward it, behind his bolted door. The farmer's wife, as smiling as he was straight-faced, served us hot cider.

When the woman's back was turned, Onyame grimaced at his mug and asked in Danish, "What is this?"

"Cider. Don't complain. It's good for you. I'm a healer. I know."

When I turned back to him, the farmer was staring at me.

"My friend is a Northern warrior," I said. "He's famous there and has come to be of service to Duke William. As you can see, He's from the Far South, Africa."

The man had probably never heard of any place south of Anjou.

He leaned forward in his chair, and his voice fell almost to a whisper. "I remain loyal to the young Duke, God preserve him, but not all people here are."

"Here?"

"Around Rouen. Apparently you've not heard. Rouen has been taken by rebels. A terrible thing, with the young Duke's problems and all."

I translated for Onyame and then said to the farmer, "Problems?"

"You do know about the murder attempt and the battle near Caen? And King Henry?"

"We know nothing. We've been in the North for over a year."

"Then there's much to tell. Let me begin again. There was a revolt. A serious one. There's been fighting here for years, but this year it got worse. Well, it didn't really begin with fighting. It began with a plot against the Duke's life. I know that's hard to believe, even of nobles, but Duke William had to flee all the way from Valognes to Falaise. If not for his fool, Gollet, and a noble knight from Ryes, he would have been killed."

My vision of William's midnight flight from assassins had been accurate.

"A despicable business," the farmer said, "but it got worse. The Western nobles and some others from around Brionne joined — for a reason you'll soon know but never guess — to raise an army against the Duke, but Duke William, in spite of his youth, went straight to King Henry in Paris, was his own emissary, and the King agreed to help. Well, just southeast of Caen. Do you know Serqueville, Begrenville and Airan, those little villages with a plain lying between them? I have a brother living in Airan. Val-es-Dunes, that's the place. The two armies met there in February. It was a terrible battle, but the Duke slaughtered seven hundred of the traitors!"

There was at least some exaggeration in that number.

The farmer continued, "Ralph of Tesson, do you know him, the one men call the Badger? Well, he abandoned his own side to join the young

Duke, because he feared the Duke's fury. The way the story reached me is that Ralph kept his knights out of the fighting — he had over one hundred — until he saw the way the battle was going. In a short time, the Duke had killed another thousand men or more. Ralph had made a vow that he would be the first man to strike the Duke in battle, and you know what a vow means to a Norman." He glanced at Onyame, and I translated.

"It means the same to us in the North," Onyame said, and I repeated his statement for the farmer in Norman French.

The farmer looked satisfied. "That's good to hear. Well, Ralph took his horse toward Duke William at a slow trot, waving his hand to show that he had no weapon and that he wanted to talk. The Duke's men said to Duke William, 'My lord, Ralph of Tesson approaches, the Badger himself. There is no knowing what mischief he may be up to.' Ralph just rode up to Duke, grinning and relaxed, struck the Duke lightly on the shoulder, and said, 'I swore that I'd be the first to strike you, my lord, and now I have fulfilled my vow. My knights and I are at your command. We shall charge the enemy together.' Duke William and his knights laughed and joined the Badger in a charge, and they killed four thousand men."

By my count, William had now killed more knights than lived in the whole of Normandy.

"As you might guess, before long the King and his men and the Duke and his men were driving the rebels back across the Orne." He grimaced slightly, but he no doubt enjoyed the grisly detail he was about to give us. "You know, the rebels, cowards, were afraid and just ran. They feared crossing the Orne because of the early spring floods and tried to ford it at that narrow place between Allemagne and Fontenay. But most were driven into the river, where they drowned. Like the Pharaoh's men chasing Moses. Their bodies clogged the mills of Borbillon." He sat back in his chair. "That's the fate they deserved."

I translated quickly for Onyame and then asked, "Was Duke William harmed?"

"Not a mark on him."

"The King?"

"Not a scratch. Good news for your friends in Flanders, where Count Baldwin will be happy that his brother-in-law survived another battle."

I stared at him. "King Henry is the Count's brother-in-law?"

The farmer nodded. "King Henry's sister has been married to Count Baldwin for years. They have a fine daughter, Matilda. Your friends in Flanders would know that."

"Yes," I said, "and they probably told me, but it didn't sink in. So, Matilda is the King Henry's niece."

The farmer nodded, looking wise.

That made Matilda more than a match for William, and I saw why Garrad had been thinking about the two of them.

The farmer continued. "That's not the end of the story, you know. Once the rebels had been beaten, the Duke called one of those meetings with all the lords and the bishops and priests."

"An ecclesiastical council?"

"Thats it. At Caen. He declared the Truce of God. All fighting had to stop from Wednesday evening to Monday morning and during the high holy seasons."

That vision had been accurate as well.

"Do you think that stopped the rebels? No, sir. Taking advantage of poor Duke William's being tied down at Brionne, they seized Rouen. That's why you dare not go there if you're friends of the Duke."

"Why is Duke William tied down at Brionne?" I asked.

"This is the part you won't believe. Do you know who the leader of the rebels was?" He waited for our response.

I knew it was Guy of Burgundy, but I just shrugged. "I have no idea."

"The Duke's own cousin and best boyhood friend, Guy of Burgundy."

I feigned astonishment. "That's hardly to be believed."

"I told you that you would be shocked. Well, the Duke chased that weasel Guy back to the castle at Brionne."

"The one that stands on the island in the River Risle? Near Bec Abbey?"

"That's the one. The Duke had given Guy that castle as a gift after poor Count Gilbert was killed."

I thought of the day Edward and I witnessed Gilbert's death outside Brionne Castle. The castle had seen murder, and now it witnessed a siege.

The farmer said, "The Duke has had his siege towers on the banks of the Risle for months now, but Guy won't come out. Who knows when that will end?"

Two days later, having avoided Rouen, we arrived in the valley leading to Bec Abbey. With the stream ice-rimmed and trees sparkling in the afternoon sun, Bec Forest looked more peaceful than I had ever seen it.

Many of the abbey's wooden structures had been rebuilt with stone, though some were still of wood and still not well built. All of them sat farther up the hillside, though, away from the stream. I even detected drainage ditches, filled with stones, just visible beneath the light snow. Smoke trailed from each building, though no one was visible anywhere.

"It is time for Nones, so the brothers will be occupied. This is also a significant saint's day, St. Anastasius, I think, so they'll be celebrating that, as well."

Just as we dismounted, Abbot Herluin himself, followed by Lanfranc, emerged from one of the buildings, followed by a crowd of the brothers.

"Abbot Herluin?"

"Yes, my son?"

I smiled at him. "I'm —"

Before I could get my name out, Lanfranc leaned toward the Abbot and said, smiling, "Cuin of Falaise in his Northern disguise."

"Cuin!" Herluin said, "Bless you! I'm delighted to see you again! We had heard that you were killed, but then Garrad said that you were alive."

I introduced Onyame, who received more stares than I would have thought Herluin had in him.

Herluin turned to introduce Lanfranc to Onyame. "This is my prior, Lanfranc, whom you know already, Cuin."

My mouth dropped open. "Prior?"

Lanfranc's face, mischievous as ever, broadened into a grin. "Yes. The Abbot has graciously given me certain responsibilities —"

Herluin interrupted, smiling, "He runs the entire abbey. We would have all frozen to death, died of fever, or slipped into the lax habits of Fecamp if not for Prior Lanfranc. Not to mention his teaching —"

It was Lanfranc's turn to interrupt, "Father, you over-praise me. You are the light of Bec, and without that, none of us would be able to see the way forward."

Herluin replied, "It was God's goodness that sent Prior Lanfranc to us, and we have been blessed as a result."

"Excuse me," I said. "As much as I'm enjoying this dialectic of praise and counter-praise, I wonder whether the abbey still has a fine bakehouse and kitchen with a fireplace?"

Lanfranc laughed, "Yes, we must remember Cuin's prowess in the kitchen. Please forgive us for not showing you to a warm room and food immediately."

After we had been fed, we settled into the too drafty stone-and-wood building that served as the abbey guesthouse. Lanfranc freed himself from his late-day duties to serve as our host until Vespers.

Onyame and I pressed around a newly built fire, while Lanfranc sat on a nearby bench, his back against a stone wall.

"Tell me where you've been and where you met your impressive friend," Lanfranc said.

I gave him a summary of my travels, at which he expressed the enthusiasm that living at Bec had not diminished.

"I'm eager to see William and talk to him about some matters … concerning Flanders," I concluded.

Lanfranc smiled. "Then you've heard about the romance between Duke William and Lady Matilda?"

"William and Matilda? That's the match I wanted to discuss with you."

"It may not be a perfect match," Lanfranc said. "At this present moment, she loathes him, by her own account, and has asked every bishop she knows to condemn the marriage on the grounds of consanguinity."

"Why? What has he done? Consanguinity? William isn't related to Matilda, is he?"

"You may not know that Count Baldwin's family and thus Matilda are descended from Charlemagne, England's Alfred the Great, and Rollo, the first Duke of Normandy. So, that puts her within the seven degrees of relation to Duke William."

I found the explanation unsatisfactory, but I was not focused on the consanguinity issue. "I don't understand why Matilda dislikes William."

"You'll have to ask Duke William about that. Count Baldwin, by contrast, is delighted about the prospect, according to what Garrad tells me — he's my source for all of this — and has been pressing Lady Matilda to look more favorably on Duke William's suit."

He fell silent as he stroked one of the many abbey cats that seemed drawn to him. "To keep down the rats and mice," he said, so apparently our conversation about William had temporarily ended.

"You have nice cells here for hardened sinners," I said. "If you sit on these benches long enough, even the devil will take pity on you."

"My bed is worse." He chuckled. "I shall be sainted if anyone ever discovers how hard it is. I console myself with the thought that Saint Antony had a harder bed in his cave in Egypt and was thus able to defeat the powers of darkness."

I pulled my blue cloak around me, folding my arms across my chest inside it. "If I may ask, how did you come to this? You never reminded me of Saint Antony."

"Do you mean that I seem too young not to want a wife? I'm forty-six years old, you know."

"No, I mean that you always seemed jovial and ... worldly."

"Too superficial to be concerned about God and death and prayer?" he said, smiling.

"No, though you seemed very much in the world."

"Perhaps too much. Do you know that I had a wife?"

I raised my eyebrows. "No. Is having a wife excessively worldly?"

He smiled. "I've always enjoyed your questions. To answer this one, let me recall some of my personal history following our first meeting. When I left Avranches, I taught at several cathedral schools, and while teaching at one, Bayeux, I met a young woman, a sweet soul, and we fell in love. We were married within a year, but she died of the fever the following summer."

"I am sorry."

"She was too pure not to be with God, I suppose. I was disconsolate. Not that I lacked experience of death. While in Pavia, I witnessed many rebellions and struggles over who would rule Lombardy, as you know. My father was killed in one of these battles, brutally. Though I grieved for him, my mind was all for Roman law, Lombard statutes, the canons of the church, and disputing with other jurists and students."

"I'm sorry to hear that, too. As you say, I knew about the political difficulties of your family, but I didn't know your father had been killed. You have my condolences, and your father will have my prayers."

"Thank you. Of course, I was teaching at the time. Then the struggles between the Holy Roman Emperor and the cities in Lombardy became so severe that many of my students were imprisoned or killed."

I translated for Onyame and added, "That was when Lanfranc decided to come north and eventually settled in Normandy."

Lanfranc was saying the same thing for Onyame's benefit, knowing that I already knew his personal history: "I decided to come north, where many Lombards had already made places for themselves in Burgundy, Paris, and especially Normandy. We knew that the ducal family, from Duke William's grandfather on, supported cathedral schools. I was still young and shallow, though. Then I faced the death of the person dearest to me in all the world."

He hung his head for a moment, and I saw the lines on his forehead and around his eyes.

He looked up at me. "Do you know that I didn't know how to pray for her? I knew the law, history, political movements, but nothing of any importance."

"Those don't seem unimportant."

"Not in their own realms, no. They have their own seriousness, mostly derived from their consequences. I had witnessed that in Lombardy. Men may lose all their worldly goods, as I did, be imprisoned and tortured, as my friends were, or even die, as my father did. They have then lost their goods, their freedom of movement, their bodies. What of their souls, though? I knew nothing about that."

"You wouldn't say that their goods, their freedom, or their bodies were of no consequence, would you?"

He smiled. "No, I'm no Stoic, though I admire Epictetus and Marcus Aurelius. The soul, though, is of first importance. It's what matters most, above all else. Why else would so many great men and women be willing to lose all for their souls?"

"I confess that has been a mystery to me, even when Garrad explained it."

"Well, do you see that, after my wife died, I had to know? I had to grasp it, really make it part of my life."

"I do see that."

He sighed. "So, I wandered from one monastery to another. While teaching at the cathedral schools, I had seen the cathedrals and their priests. I knew that their concerns were largely with local church rites and local people. I needed more. So I went to the abbeys at Mont Saint Michel, Jumieges, Saint Ouen, Fecamp and others, intending to join each one, all of them seemed more worldly than the law."

I thought of Herluin, who had experienced the same.

"Then one day, I was walking alone in the forest of Ouche, just outside Rouen. It was foolish to be alone in a forest near dark, but I wasn't thinking clearly. I couldn't have appeared to be wealthy, but neither did I look like a peasant. Robbers attacked me, tied me to a tree, and left me. They pushed the hood of my cap over my eyes, so that I could see nothing. Again I came face to face with my inability to pray. I said out loud to God that if I were delivered from this forest, I would devote my life to learning how to pray. I would work in the humblest house of God, building its holiness until only praise for divine goodness could be heard coming from it. I said this over and over again, all night."

"You were there the entire night?"

"Yes, and oddly, it seemed a short time. In the morning, some travelers heard me. After they had freed me, I asked them where to find the poorest, most humble abbey in the world. They said, 'We know no poorer monastery than one which a certain man of God built very near here.' I took it as a sign that I'd been guided, even by robbers, to Bec, so I presented myself to Abbot Herluin."

"Poor Herluin must have been surprised to see a renowned Southern scholar turn up at his small monastery."

"He told me he thought it a miracle, and I agreed that I'd been guided by God. Since my first work was to learn to pray, I went into seclusion until I did."

"Yes, Garrad told me. The seclusion lasted three years, is that right?"

"Yes. I was troubled. Even here the discipline of the brothers seemed lax. They were untrained and jealous of each other. I had seen too many schools and courts with the same problems, and I did not want to live among them in a monastery. So I decided to become a hermit."

His choice had paralleled Herluin's. "Apparently without success."

"I did not want to disturb Abbot Herluin. He's a fine man, a peaceful man, and he disapproved of the brothers' behavior as much as I did, but he didn't know how to handle them. So I made plans to slip away unnoticed. I asked the gardener to bring me the roots of a certain wild thistle, claiming I had a stomach ailment. What I wanted, though, was to orient myself to a hermit's diet."

"As hermits, Garrad and I eat better than that, I assure you."

He smiled. "Well, as I was about to leave, Herluin called for me." He paused. "I have told no one about this."

"I'll tell no one, and Onyame always respects privacy."

"Herluin had been given a vision. His own nephew, who had recently died, had appeared to him. The boy wore a white robe. When Herluin asked if he was all right, the nephew said, 'Yes, good Father, I am well, since through the mercy of God and your intercession, I am freed from all torment. I bring you a message: you must keep Master Lanfranc near you, because he yearns for the solitary life. His work, though, is here. Take stock therefore of what you do, since you will gain no advantage if he should desert you.' The boy then disappeared. When Herluin related this to me, and he was in tears, I promised that I would stay and build the abbey as a place to praise God, as I had vowed in the forest of Ouche."

I remained silent for a time. "Then you're bound here?"

"Yes."

"Well, I wish you could help me with Duke William, but I won't ask that now."

"I appreciate that. From what you've recounted, though, your mission for the Duke was successful."

"Yes, but you must know about the battle at Val-es-Dunes, the siege of Brionne, and the seizing of Rouen by rebels. William needs sound advisors around him just now. If not, the alliance of the Four Crowns could slip away from us in the South and East, even though the North is won."

He nodded. "I'm not certain that the entire North is won. In England, Earl Godwin is still a threat to Edward."

"William's need is greater now."

"I agree. So you must get word to the Duke as quickly as possible about your work in the North and your presence here. Shall I send a messenger?"

"William can't read, and I wouldn't want any of his courtiers reading for him. These matters are too ... delicate."

"Then I shall pray for good traveling weather tomorrow."

CHAPTER 21

THE DUKE, THE KING, AND THE KILLER

A. D. 1048

Lanfranc's prayers were answered, so we journeyed easily to Brionne. Not far from the castle, we encountered two guards posted on the outskirts of a sprawling military encampment.

One guard stepped in front of us, holding a spear across the front of a heavy woolen robe, under which was the chain-loop armor that Norman enemies ridiculed as "fish scales" or "fish mail." Over his conical helmet with its long nosepiece he had pulled the cloak of his hood against the cold.

"We've come to see Duke William," I said after he greeted us and asked our business. "Please tell him that a hermit has returned from the North with a longer bow than he set out with."

He grunted something to his companion and strode toward the camp. The other guard continued to stare at Onyame.

Within a few moments, William appeared on the road, outpacing the guard and several of his knights, who scrambled to keep up with him. He wore no helmet, and his hair seemed blacker than I remembered it. He looked taller than he had been, if that was possible.

As he shouted something back to his knights, who then returned to the camp, I saw that he still shaved the back of his head in the Norman style and marveled that his head did not freeze.

A work-stained robe, once bright scarlet, flowed around him as he ran. He wore no armor, so his green tunic and brown leggings were visible, as was the greatsword that I always expected to find wherever William was.

As he approached, his stern look broke into a grin. "Cuin! Is that you inside that robe? Where in this world of ours have you been?"

I jumped down from the pony, and he seized me in a wrenching hug. "You've given me some sleepless nights! We heard that you had been killed by a bear!"

I extricated myself. "As you can see, I survived the bear. In fact, I brought the bear with me."

William followed the motion of my hand. "He looks like a human being to me, Cuin, though a darker one than most I have seen."

"My lord Duke, this is Onyame, house guard to Earl Thorir of Steig and warrior, traveler, student of the old and new religions, seaman, and friend. Onyame, this is —"

William stepped forward and seized Onyame's hand, to the surprise of both of us. "A friend of Cuin's is my friend, and I welcome you to Normandy."

I translated, and Onyame replied, "I have never had so gracious a welcome from any lord. I can see why Cuin boasts about you so readily."

Before I could translate, William replied in Norwegian, "Cuin exaggerates because he must. I order him to. Without him and my advisors and knights, I could not govern my stables!"

Onyame laughed heartily.

I gaped at him. "Where did you learn the Northern languages?"

"In Rouen, of course. A Duke has to be able to do something. I can't seem to master writing, so I had better learn to speak. Besides, I can't be less trained than my nobles, many of whom have Norwegian ancestry. Some of them are determined to trick me out of my lands if they can't beat me out of them."

"I'm sorry about the rebellion," I began, but he interrupted me.

"Come to my tent." He repeated the invitation in Norwegian for Onyame. "It may not be elegant, but it is warm."

As we settled ourselves onto wooden chairs near an open fire in William's huge tent, one of his soldiers appeared inside the entrance. "No reply, my lord."

William's face looked unusually serious. "No refusal?"

"No reply at all, my lord."

"Thank you, Roger. Try again tomorrow."

"Yes, my lord."

William turned to us, his face relaxing. "Everyday I send a message to Guy, offering him surrender terms. None of his men will be killed, and he won't be harmed, if he yields the castle and publicly recognizes my right to the entire duchy and swears loyalty to me. So far he has ignored the messages." This time I translated for Onyame.

"I saw the siege-towers," Onyame said. "How long do you think he can remain inside?"

"My spies tell me that he has provisions for perhaps two years. He sits on a river, so water is no problem."

William then translated for Onyame, who replied, "Two years is a long time."

"Yes, but if I defeat Guy, the other Western nobles will fall into line."

"What about Rouen?" I asked.

"Guy's work, too, which is why I must wait him out here. Defeating him is the key to my power in the west. I'm weak to the south, where Maine and Anjou boil up trouble for me. As long as King Henry supports me, though, the lords of Maine and Anjou are less of a threat. Since the battle at Val-es-Dunes ... Have you heard about that?"

"One of your loyal farmers outside Rouen told us. A noble victory."

"Always the common people and the lesser nobles and knights support me. These ambitious lords, though —" He stopped himself. "After the battle, no one from the western regions has dared confront me openly. Seizing Rouen is an angry child's reaction. As soon as good weather returns, I shall retake it and force the invaders back into the countryside. So I need to retain Henry's support and to gain other support, perhaps someone like Count Baldwin of Flanders."

"At least," I said, "you won't have to worry about the North."

"You were successful, then. Thank God! Garrad said you would be."

"I'm glad he was so confident, but the task was not an easy one. Is Garrad well, by the way?"

"Well and happy."

"How is Arlette?"

"Well, but showing her age more than she should. Her husband is kind to her, as you know, but she's never recovered from her ... well, from the hardness of her early life."

"Your father's death."

"Yes." He paused. "Do you know that Garrad is married?"

"Is he? I can scarcely believe, it, but I thought I saw ... Is he married to Marie?"

"Yes. If you've not seen Garrad, how did you know?"

I hesitated, though there was no need. William's devotion for religion included taking visions seriously. "I saw it in a vision."

"So, what Garrad told me is true. He said that he had seen you in some far away land on the other side of the world."

"Yes, I spoke with him and saw Marie in his hut. I saw you, too, fighting at Val-es-Dunes and fleeing Valognes from the rebel assassins."

William narrowed his eyes. "Did you shout at me?"

"Did you hear that?"

"That shout was what kept me from walking into the path of the assassins. It saved my life."

"Why did you stop in the church? That was an unnecessary risk, was it not?"

"God did preserve me and did enable me to hear your warning cry all the way from the other side of the world. Where were you, anyway?"

"That's a long tale."

"I shall call for cider then. We have time."

By the time I finished the story, aided by Onyame, several hours had passed. William concentrated on every word, even the translations for Onyame.

When we finished, he said, "It was quite a journey. You've done well. Not only for Normandy. Your vision of Edward was accurate. He's been more and more cornered by Godwin and his sons. Godwin has forced Edward to remove many Normans from positions of influence."

"I have been concerned about that, which is why I tried to strengthen Edward's position with the Northern rulers."

"That was good work. Edward would like to move against Godwin's family, to establish his authority over Godwin, but he fears an invasion from the North. He assumed, as I did when I heard of King Magnus's death, that Harald Hardraada was in control of both Norway and Denmark and would soon turn his eyes south."

"I see. Edward would need Godwin's support if Hardraada invaded."

"Yes. This news, that Sweyn has been given the Danish throne, will relieve Edward as well as give him an opening to confront Godwin. I think you should go to England as soon as possible."

I leaned toward him. "William, eager as I'm to be on the road again, there is the matter of Flanders. The Prior of Bec, Lanfranc —"

"The jurist and teacher?"

"Yes, a famous one, perhaps the best in the world."

"I've met him only once, but Abbot Herluin did all the talking." He shrugged his shoulders. "The famous Lanfranc seemed just pleasant."

"His pleasantness fooled me at first. I thought he was a fool. He just happens to be remarkably cheerful. He said that Count Baldwin —."

William's face went stern again. "The Count and I are on good terms just now. We seek the same end to … a matter of mutual concern."

"Your marriage to Matilda?"

"How did you hear about that?"

"Lanfranc knew. He had heard it from Garrad. Lanfranc's an ally to have, if you challenge the threat of consanguinity."

He huffed at me. "If you mean that Matilda and I are too closely related, just say so without the Latin. You sound like a priest. We're more than fifth cousins, Matilda and I."

"The relation, however, must be beyond the seventh —"

"It matters not at all what it is, seventh or hundredth. The powers behind the Pope are using this to further their ambitions in southern Italy. The Pope wants the Norman rulers in Sicily, Cuin. I'm the leverage to get at them, even though I have no power over them."

"I don't understand. Just now, from what the southern Goliards have told me, the papacy is mass of confusion about which faction will rule. I suspect, though, that the German faction will have their own Pope by year's end. Surely, in that time, the marriage could be approved ... somehow."

He stared at his feet for a long time. "The lady won't have me, under any circumstances. I have not behaved ... properly ... I think."

I groaned inwardly. "What happened, William?"

He glanced at Onyame. "It's an embarrassment to me."

"You had better let us help you then. Both Onyame and I are married."

He stared at both of us. "You are? How did that come to pass? Where is she? Who is she? Tell me everything."

"In time. I'd prefer to address the matter of Matilda now."

He paused again. "All right, but you're both sworn to secrecy." He translated this for Onyame, who nodded earnestly.

William began, "I'm not a polished courtier, you know."

"I'd never noticed that."

"Don't be impertinent to your Duke," he replied, managing a half-smile. "I know hunting and fighting. I don't know anything about women or wooing. Worse, I've never felt like this before. I don't know how to act."

I turned to Onyame. "Most of our village friends were married before William and I were in our late teens. William's own father had been married to some Danish girl, I heard, at age sixteen or so and met Arlette when he was about eighteen. William and I, on the other hand, well, we'd been busy just trying to stay alive, so ..."

William had been watching me closely and now interrupted. "Where did you hear that?"

"What?"

"About my father and the young Danish woman."

"In the North. Someone mentioned it to me in passing, someone in Hedeby or Kaupang perhaps. I think it was an Icelandic merchant. That's odd. How would he know about your family's personal history? Is it important?"

"No," he said, hesitating. "I was just curious."

"Matilda?" I reminded him.

"Yes, well, I negotiated with Count Baldwin, and he was delighted at the prospect of a marriage between Normandy and Flanders, a wedding of such forces as to keep the Holy Roman Emperor and the Pope at bay. It would help me as well."

"I heard that the Count's been wedding himself to the French side of the world."

William sighed. "Matilda sees things differently. She smiles on this Brihtic from somewhere in England. The Severn valley, I've been told."

"Who is he?"

"I've been able to discover only that he came here at the recommendation of Earl Tostig of Wessex. I think Earl Godwin, Tostig's father, may have heard of my proposal to Count Baldwin in Flanders — Godwin and he are on good terms — and sent a rival."

"Yes, Tostig was courting Baldwin's half-sister Judith when I was in Flanders, recovering at the St. Vaast monastery."

When I translated for Onyame, he smiled and said, "Earl Godwin certainly does not want a Norman ally of King Edward to ally himself to Count Baldwin."

William nodded at him. "I think that this Brihtic has been sent to capture Matilda from me. It will cost me more than a marriage if he succeeds. I need the Count's support."

"Brihtic surely can't be much of an obstacle," I said. "I know Matilda somewhat. You and she are so much alike that I at first thought she was the Duke of Normandy in some clever disguise. A short, beautiful disguise, of course."

William did not laugh, so I knew his embarrassment was growing. "Yes. Well, I sent a messenger to Matilda, demanding to know why she looked askance at my proposal."

"Demanding?"

"I am a Duke, you know."

"I have no doubt that she was aware of your title, but she is the daughter of a Count and the granddaughter of a King. Did she reply?"

He paused. "She said that she'd rather be a nun than married to a bastard Duke whose talents included incivility and a knack for attracting rebellions."

"Oh, that was undiplomatic."

"So I sent word that I'd show her the difference between a bastard and a Duke, if she cared to see me in person."

I groaned. "You replied with a threat?"

"What did she say?" Onyame asked in Norwegian.

"She didn't say anything. She hid in one of Count Baldwin's palaces. At Bruges."

I tried a jest. "Did you storm the palace?"

"Yes."

"What?"

William grimaced at me. "I didn't storm it. It's just ... well, she wouldn't receive any messages, wouldn't see anyone I sent."

"So you went yourself?"

"Of course."

"Mounted, armed, and at the head of an army?"

"Alone, but ..." His dropped his head. "I humiliated myself and mistreated her."

"William, what did you do?"

He looked pained. "When I arrived at the palace, no one seemed to be guarding it. Almost no one. I encountered only a few soldiers, but I didn't hurt them. Well, I had to break the arm of one."

"No, that wouldn't hurt, I agree."

"That's not the worst of it. I think I hurt Matilda."

I could not hide my alarm. "Physically? Did you strike her?"

"Of course not, but ... I did ... push her. Perhaps I grabbed her shoulders too roughly." He swallowed. "And I threw her on the bed."

"You were in her bedchamber? You didn't ...?"

He looked at me in disgust. "Of course not. I'm not a barbarian. As I said, no one was around, so I just followed the voices and found her in her bedchamber. I threw her attendants out."

"Physically?"

"Certainly not. They're women."

"So is Matilda."

"She wouldn't listen to anything I said." His voice rose, sounding harsh. "She accused me of being improper, even common."

"You were in her bedchamber."

"She had no right to call me common! I'm a Duke, whether my grandfather was a tanner or a King!" He paused a long time and then groaned. "I did behave improperly."

I sighed and watched him for a time. Then I said, "Matilda is an intelligent woman, determined, even stubborn, her friends tell me. She is also fair-minded, and she's a good judge of character. If you speak with her, approach her as a friend rather than as … an invading Duke, I think that she will be drawn to you."

He shook his head, dropping it into his hands. "What about this Brithic?"

"If it helps, Count Baldwin's court healer told me that Matilda is not usually drawn to courtiers. She finds the superficial lords that surround her father disgusting."

He looked up at me.

"Of course, neither does she like rough, dim-witted knights," I said, "which she probably believes you are."

He groaned again.

"However," I said, "if you give her the opportunity to know you, I'm certain that she would find you just the sort of character she admires."

He gazed at me for a time. "Brihtic?"

I thought for a moment. "I have a solution, one that will serve all of us well."

"I'll give you a castle if you do."

"I don't want a castle." I leaned toward William. "Listen: King Edward needs to know that he has a free hand to move against Earl Godwin, and I can tell him that. You need to get rid of an Englishman who's roaming around

Flanders romancing Matilda. Onyame needs to sail north again, so that this spring he can rejoin his family. And I may just join him."

William translated for Onyame this time, apparently eager to hear my solution.

"How does this plan sound to you?" I asked. "Onyame and I return to Flanders and convey your apology to Matilda, along with a glowing description of your character and an invitation for a dinner, at which you two can become properly acquainted. I also ask Count Baldwin to renew his friendship with King Edward. Then Onyame delivers me to England, where I both inform Edward of his renewed friendship with Baldwin and ask him to force this Brihtic back to England. Onyame and I then sail north, while you court Matilda and confer with Baldwin about the wedding."

William stared at me for awhile and then smiled slowly. "A fine solution." He rubbed his hands together. "This is the best news I've had since these damned rebellions began. When can you leave?"

"After the Christmas feast."

A sumptuous Christmas feast came and went, and we were supplied with warm clothing and provisions. As we finished packing, William brought me a message.

"I sent word to Garrad that you were here. I was sure he'd want to know."

"Thank you. I'll be delighted to see him."

William shook his head. "He's not free to join us, unfortunately. This is what I received back today."

In Garrad's hand, a Latin message read: "I look forward to seeing you, but the rebellion demands my attention. A Northern warrior has been looking for you in Falaise. His description matches Voldred, so I advise you to avoid Falaise this winter. I will let you know when it is safe, using Duke William's messenger. Farewell."

I showed it to William, and he put his hand on my shoulder. It was the first time I realized how huge his hands and arms were.

"Cuin, I want to tell you something, but I don't want you to ask me any questions about what I say. Will you promise me not to?"

"Certainly."

"With the knife that King Magnus gave you, you may be able to convince Voldred to abandon his quest. I know that's your intention. If you find him in Normandy, you may be able to approach him. However, and this is what I hope you'll hear without your usual questions, if he goes to England, don't assume that he'll be receptive to anything you have to say. He may want to kill you in spite of Magnus's knife."

"I don't understand. What difference would a trip to England make?"

"I'm sworn not to say. Just please avoid Voldred if he's in England. Will you?"

"If you say so, my lord."

"I'm not asking as your Duke. I'm asking as … a friend."

The diplomatic work in Flanders went more easily than I could have hoped. The key was Anette.

Our reunion was delightful. As Anette greeted me, I felt as if we had never parted, as if our friendship had traveled easily through time. Putting aside her usual formality, she hugged me, weeping, and then recovered to look carefully at me, ask about my health, and wonder about my foot.

"I'll tell you everything," I said, smiling at her.

She and her husband listened intently as I recounted the events that had taken me to the end of the world and back.

Anette was particularly fascinated by the shape of my foot and even asked to look at it. I had long since given up hoping not to be embarrassed by Anette and her openness, so I allowed her to study it briefly.

Then I came to William's problem with Matilda, and Thiebaut and she listened especially carefully.

"Matilda is drawn to Brihtic," Anette said, "but for all his charm, his position is below Matilda's. She does not intend to marry him, but she does enjoy his company. And his attention."

I translated for Onyame and said, "Brihtic's presence, though —"

"Excludes William," Anette finished my thought, as she had done during our theological discussions back in St. Vaast.

"If I can arrange to force Brihtic back to England," I said, "then perhaps Matilda would feel more open to William?"

Anette smiled. "Though he's charming and Matilda does enjoy those charms, Brihtic is a courtier's courtier, and he does not seem …"

"You don't like him."

"Not for Matilda."

I thought for a moment. "So, if we can make it seem as if Brihtic left Flanders of his own accord, if I can get Edward to pull him back to England suddenly …"

"Yes, if you can make it seem that Brihtic chose to leave, Matilda has just enough pride for it to be wounded."

I laughed. "If you didn't have such a fine husband, I'd engage you as my diplomatic assistant."

Anette smiled and put her hand on her husband's. "Thank you for the compliment. I'll set the stage here for romantic disappointment. You do your part in England, and Duke William and Matilda may yet be together."

After bidding Anette and Thiebaut farewell, we made for the coast, interrupted only once by snow.

As we were about to put out to sea, a messenger from William caught us. He carried a message from Garrad, in Latin again: "Duke William tells me that you're visiting King Edward. I personally followed Voldred when he left Falaise last week. He made his way to the coast and for reasons I can't fathom, is looking for a ship to England. He may be there before you. Be careful in your movements. God be with you."

Knowing Voldred as he did, Onyame advised that we travel down the coast from Flanders toward Normandy to see if we could discover anything about Voldred's movements.

We hired horses — and I found as close a mount to my old pony as I could — and headed south.

As we arrived near the mouth of the River Somme just beyond the town of Eu, the early evening was turning cold. The weather had been mild for winter, but the winter nights had been chilled.

We rode to the top of a steep hill to survey the channel that led to England. Gradually, the sea came into view, the moon reflecting in it, brightening the land around us. Strips of cloud, though, hid it now and then as they raced ahead of a strong westerly wind. Below, the waves mimicked the whipping clouds. Storms often hit Ponthieu's coast in winter, and one appeared to be mounting now.

We dismounted, and I stared hard at the land jutting out into the ocean. It was a common mooring place for ships skirting the coast or pressing south from England. It hooked like a shepherd's crook, offering a small but protected harbor.

Now lights flickered along the strip — but they sat too far out to sea.

Getting Onyame's attention, I pointed to the lights. "Do you see how close those bonfires are positioned?"

He stared for a moment. "Yes, dangerously close. Any ship's captain, mistaking those as harbor lights, will run his ship onto these rocks." He pointed to the outer edge of the hook.

"Who would light bonfires to draw ships onto the rocks?"

"This is an all too common practice on seacoasts."

As he spoke, I noticed a dark figure darting between the fires. He stirred one, then ran to the other, stirred it, and ran to the next. When he reached the farthest one, he stared out to sea. Then he dashed back down the line of fires, building each to a blaze.

Onyame saw the same figure. "There's the saboteur." He turned to look out to sea. "There's the ship."

I studied the sea where he was pointing. There it was, a ship struggling against the wind, aiming for the jutting strip. Its captain probably hoped to land before the storm rose. But the ship was headed too far inland too fast.

"What's going on here?" I asked Onyame.

"The man lighting the fires has companions hidden somewhere nearby. After the ship is lured onto the rocks, they'll seize what treasures they can from the ship and its crew. Then, if any crew members or passengers have wealth or position, the raiders will hold them for ransom."

I watched the scene unfold with a growing sense of dread. "Could we light a warning fire from here?"

"That would only confuse the ship's captain further. Besides, these raiders will be determined. They're usually poor villagers, and a shipwreck or two a year may be the difference between a good life and a miserable one. Even between survival and starvation."

"There's nothing we can do?"

"Unfortunately not. Even the laws of the sea favor raiding. Wreckage belongs to anyone who finds it, especially the local lord. If other inhabitants benefit along with the lord, he doesn't complain. If they find a noble to be ransomed, the lord negotiates it, and both he and his people benefit."

"So, in a bad fishing and farming year, these people become desperate. Desperate enough to do this."

He nodded. "You and I know that local lords also engage in war or put on extravagant events that drain local resources."

"So sabotaging ships becomes a logical occupation."

"Not ethical but logical, yes."

Both of us fell silent for a moment, and then he said, "If you watch the skill with which these people lure ships, it's remarkable."

"I see what you mean."

"Look!" He pointed.

The dark figure suddenly paused to crouch down. His form seemed to disappear beneath the waves, the rocks, and the rolling ship.

Suddenly he stood straight up, watching as the ship loomed over the boulders, then shrieked as the rocks rent its sides.

He waved his arms, probably signaling his companions, and raced down the line of bonfires, kicking sand on them. Meanwhile, the ship twisted, wrenched onto its side by the wind and waves.

I heard the cries of men and the shrieks of horses. Our horses whinnied in response, startling me.

For a moment, the dark figure dropped to the ground, searching the coast in our direction. Onyame and I dropped down together, hoping not to be seen.

The saboteur turned his head slowly, and as the last bonfire smoldered not far from him, I could make out an odd-shaped cap, angling across his face, probably to hide his features from the surviving sailors. Then he disappeared.

Onyame turned to me and then rose. "We need to go down there."

"Yes, if anyone's hurt, we can help."

We hobbled the horses and scrambled toward the wreck.

As we rounded the entrance to the strip of land, I caught, out of the corner of my eye, a shadow flitting among the rocks. Ignoring it, I quickened my run to keep up with Onyame, who was now far ahead of me, and soon arrived where men and animals were crawling from the wreckage.

One large seaman, obviously not one of the injured, seized me.

To my amazement and dismay, he cried to the others, "Here's one of them! Let's kill him before his fellow-thieves arrive!"

He spoke Saxon English, and I tried to shout in the same language that I was a healer, coming to help. But the howl of the winds, the crashing of the waves, the cries of the men and the din of the animals buried my voice. From being so roughly pinioned, I had trouble getting my breath.

I shouted again, "I'm a healer! I can help!"

"Healer!" the man spat at the word. "Raider, more likely!" He tightened his grip, so that my throat would soon be crushed.

Three other seamen shook free of the wreck and clambered over broken timbers and rocks toward me.

Then I heard a voice above and behind me. "He's telling the truth! He and I were putting out the fires some brigands had set, but we were too late."

The seaman loosened his grip and swung toward the voice. A bearded man in a leather tunic, a hat angled over his forehead, hiding his eyes and nose stood there. The odd-shaped hat — it was the raider himself.

"He's Eu's physician," the raider shouted. "Let him go. He can help you."

By now, a seaman who seemed to be the ship's captain climbed up the rocks. "Release him," he ordered loudly. "If he's a physician, we need him. If not, we'll soon know. And look around. There are no raiders anywhere. These two are probably telling the truth."

Apparently, the raider had signaled his fellow villagers to keep their distance, noticing, I supposed, that much of the crew was unharmed, armed, and angry.

The seaman grunted an apology and freed me. I took a grateful breath of salt air.

The raider grabbed my arm and led me down the rocks, saying, "Let's get to work…"

"Thiry," I said in a low voice, choosing a Norman name that was also common in Flanders.

"Greetings, Thiry." He lowered his voice. "I'm Fier. If you know nothing about healing, just do as I do."

I saw Onyame in the distance, shouting at the captain and his men, who were nodding.

"That," I said pointing, "is Onyame." There was no hiding that Onyame was African.

"What's he doing?" Fier asked.

"Probably convincing the captain and his men that we were innocent bystanders."

Fier stared at him for a moment. "Let's hope that our stories coincide in some points."

By that time, Onyame was running toward us. I quickly introduced him to Fier and whispered the name I had taken for myself.

Onyame indeed had been assuring the captain that we were not raiders, and his appearance alone was enough to convince the crew.

He shouted over the wind, "Most of the crew seem fine, but we need to help the few who are injured."

I nodded and said quietly to Fier, "I am a healer. Choosing to identify me as a doctor was providential."

The three of us stepped carefully over the wet rocks and splintered sides of the ship to reach the men inside. Onyame lifted them out easily. Only six had demanding gashes and bruises, though one's arm had to be set, as did the leg of another.

I worked as quickly as I could, first stopping the bleeding, as much for my comfort as for the men's, and then binding the wounds. These men had seen many years at sea and so bore pain stoically.

Fier turned out to be an excellent assistant. Whenever I turned to look for wrappings or fresh water, he already had them. He even seemed to anticipate the ship's lurchings, making sure the injured men were secure while I worked on them. He cheerily told them, in Saxon English, that they would be fine, making complimentary comments about the condition of the ship and the skill of its captain.

Onyame glanced at me occasionally, nodding in Fier's direction. I nodded back. This was indeed a skilled saboteur.

When we finished, we helped the injured to shore as best we could, and eventually all were lying comfortably on the sand.

Or sitting. Some of the older seaman refused to lie down. Two even joined in the work of unloading the ship, which had not sunk.

Morning was dawning by the time the supplies and animals were collected on the beach.

The captain approached us. "We owe you three our lives, driving those raiders off. You patched up the men, too. I'm grateful." He extended his hand.

As he took it, Fier replied, "We'll go into the village to find some place for you and your men to stay. And some food and dry clothes."

"I'm grateful again. I'll see you get some kind of reward. The richest of these goods are headed for the Count of Ponthieu himself, and he'll be glad to hear they're not drowned or stolen."

Onyame stayed to speak with the captain, as Fier and I walked back toward the horses.

When we were out of hearing range, I said, "I appreciate that you saved my life —"

"Give it not a thought," he interrupted me. He had dropped into a recognizable dialect of Norman French. "I could see you needed help. And your large friend had disappeared."

"I needed it because of you. You set those fires."

"Yes, I did." He grinned. "A fine piece of work it was, too. The ship hit just where I aimed it."

"Who are you?"

"It takes skill to guide ships like that."

"Who are you?" I repeated.

"I told you. Fier. Who are you? You're Norman, not Flemish. So, a Norman healer."

"I'm the physician of Eu, remember? You told the ship's captain that yourself."

He nodded. "I know you're not the physician of Eu, because I am. It's a good thing those Saxons didn't take a good look at your clothes."

"You're Eu's physician? Why do you behave like a common raider —?"

"There's nothing common about my work. You saw it. That ship hit at the perfect place and speed. Any harder, the men would have been killed. Any farther down the coast, and the supplies would have scattered."

By this time, Onyame had returned.

Fier was still talking. "It takes years to learn to judge the wind and ocean like that."

I translated for Onyame, who added, "That's true. No one was killed tonight."

"No one ever has been killed," Fier said, returning to Saxon English, which Onyame understood.

Fier turned to me. "You're a healer. You know a man can't live on tending a few peasants and their animals. It can be a short life, too. Some of the sicknesses these Saxons bring over can kill even a physician. So I add to my income."

"Surely, wrecking a few ships alone ... do you have accomplices?"

"A few villagers help me, though all the villagers know what I'm up to, and they know that they'll benefit from my efforts. You see, most raiders just smash a ship and collect what men and booty they can. Here, I run the ships on the ground gently. Not all the supplies can be immediately retrieved, so as things wash up over the next few days, the villagers collect them. As for me, I tell the wrecked crew the same story I gave tonight. Then I help the injured and collect my reward."

We had reached the horses. "How do you know there will be a reward?"

"Most of the ships that come here bring goods for the Count. I know there'll be some gold in it for me, maybe some cloth, spices, whatever he's trading for."

"How can you tell? This one looked like a Saxon merchant ship."

"I make a guess from the Count's expectation of a shipment. You see, he tells me. I'm his physician, too."

He switched back to Norman French. "I have other resources for receiving rewards. I'm a healer with access to many body parts."

"What does that mean?"

"I make relics."

When I translated, Onyame laughed out loud.

I recalled all the pilgrims who visited Duke Robert in Falaise and Rouen, realizing over the years how easily they were deceived by forged relics.

Fier must have read my look as disapproval, because he said, "Don't you believe that the saints could have many bodies? Wouldn't they want all their worshippers to feel satisfied? I've heard that one saint created additional bodies to keep his followers from fighting."

"You're creating relics from other, non-saintly bodies," I said.

He nodded at me solemnly. "Yes, in that way I'm helping the saints in their acts of celestial diplomacy. They're busy, after all, and have other things to do."

After the translation, Onyame laughed again.

"Listen," Fier said, "the captain and his crew will discover in the village that you're not the local physician, so I need to get there in time to offer a story, that you're my Norman cousin come to visit perhaps."

"They won't think I'm Flemish?"

"Not with that accent."

"I don't have an accent."

Onyame and Fier looked at each other and smiled.

"All right. For you, my real name: it's Cuin, and I'm from the Norman village of Falaise. I'm an emissary for Duke William, and I'm a healer."

"Wonderful! Why don't you and your friend spend the night in my home? We can discuss healing and whatever else you want to tell me about your lives and journeys."

I looked at Onyame, who said, "We do need a place to stay the night. My men are settled on the ships." To Fier he said, "We're on our way to England tomorrow."

"Splendid! I'll show you my home."

So we had a comfortable night in a large wooden hut, discussing healing and politics. And winds and waves. And how to make relics from recent bones.

In the morning, Fier made me promise to visit him in the future, if only, as he put it, "to have another healer to exchange ideas with."

He walked us back to the shore, said his farewells, and made his way back to his village.

Onyame and I led our horses toward the ships.

"I know Hervor can make a fog, but can she make a storm?" I asked Onyame.

"If there's a need."

"There may be a need. This experience has given me some ideas." I looked back at Fier, striding toward his village. "I think we've just made a valuable friend."

Having traded often in London, Onyame knew the passage from Flanders to London well. His crew had been fretting over being stranded on the Flemish coast. When we finally arrived, they let us know that they were delighted to be making for somewhere "more civilized."

London was more than civilized, though, as I discovered. It was huge. The morning we arrived, people seemed packed into the streets, stacked on the bridges, and hanging from the upper windows of the wooden and stone houses that lined the River Thames.

The fresh snowfall the night before had kept no one inside, and the crowds bridged the mile-long gap that Edward hoped to maintain between London and Westminster, where he preferred to live and where he was rebuilding a huge abbey.

Onyame had seen the rebuilding project and pointed it out to me. "The place it sits on is called Thornley Isle." He leaned against the tiller, staring at the number of people swarming over this small island in the river. "Do you know why King Edward dislikes London?"

"We hear some stories in Normandy, but I suppose that he associates it with all the problems he's had with the lords and merchants. On the other hand, I've also heard that, with the exception of Earl Godwin, he's well liked now."

Edward's court at Westminster gave the impression that he was indeed well liked. The great hall thronged with lords draped in jeweled, furred, and feathered robes, merchants in striped and dotted tunics, and clerics in long robes and gowns, some stitched with gold or silver thread.

Onyame and I in our blue-gray cloaks seemed plain.

By the time I caught the attention of an official-looking courtier, probably Edward's seneschal or chamberlain, my eyes had almost become accustomed to the smoky room, but my nose could not get used to the smells of the people. Over the din of the hall, I said to Onyame, "These people stink."

"I don't think they bathe as much as you do, certainly not as much as we do in the North, and even less than the People."

"The Normans sometimes smell bad to me, which I've always attributed to the fact that both William's mother and Garrad insisted that I bathe a great deal. These noble, though, smell at least as bad as the Norman lords."

The courtier appeared at my elbow. "The King wishes to see you in a private chamber. I'll show you."

I began to translate for Onyame, when he said, "I speak the Saxon tongues, as you may recall from our recent conversation with Fier."

"Oh, yes. I had forgotten."

"Saxon English is not all that distant from the Danish or Norwegian dialects."

"That's true, but Edward may speak Norman French to me. If he does, I'll translate for you."

Edward, however, gave me no time to translate anything at first. As we entered the room and bowed, he sprang from his wooden chair by a small fireplace and grasped me by the hand. He looked as pale as ever, the lines of his forty-five years apparent, but his grip showed that he was healthy.

Onyame looked surprised by the enthusiastic familiarity showed me by a King, but Edward was equally cordial when I introduced Onyame as a good friend and fellow emissary.

"He's a Northerner," I said.

Switching to the West Saxon dialect, Edward said to him, "You don't look Northern, my friend."

"I'm originally African, your majesty, but I've spent most of my life in Norway."

"You and I have something in common, then," Edward said. "Though I was born here, I spent most of my life in Normandy. I'm not sure where I feel at home, but here I must stay."

He motioned us toward the chairs grouped around the fire and glanced at me as I walked toward them. "So, you've lost your crutch at last. You must have found a fine healer. Was it through prayer or more tangible means?"

"Both, your majesty, but many means have gone into freeing me from my crutch. I've had the good fortune to meet fine healers."

"Good. Now, I was told you have something to tell me."

He studied me through the same large eyes that I remembered from my youth, though now more lined. Unlike most of his courtiers, he maintained his beard, though it seemed less full than mine and showed streaks of gray among the white that I always associated with Edward.

"I have spent the last two years in the North, your majesty."

"Then you know of the death of King Magnus."

"I was with the King when he died."

Edward raised his eyebrows. "Did he know of your parentage?"

Was Edward still concerned with my having had an "unfortunate" birth?

"No, your majesty. He knew that I was a bastard, village child, but I was speaking with him in the capacity of an advisor. I had made the acquaintance of his half-brother, Earl Thorir of Steig, for whom Onyame is a house guard."

Edward stared at me for a moment. "Oh, I see. Yes, of course. An advisor, though?"

"I was disguised as a monk, and Thorir believed that I was guided by God. What may not have reached you yet, your majesty, is that King Magnus did not give Denmark to King Harald but to King Sweyn."

Edward straightened. "That had not been confirmed yet. So, it's true. That's useful."

"There's more, your majesty. I ... induced both King Harald and King Sweyn to swear that they would never attack Normandy. With the Danish throne going to Sweyn and Harald now king of Norway, the two are likely to be occupied fighting each other, and thus not you, for several years to come."

Edward smiled. "That is what I hope."

"There is more. Both have agreed to friendship with King Edward of England, though not a formal alliance, as has Count Baldwin of Flanders, who has agreed not to support any invasion of England. So you've won three Northern friendships."

He looked startled. "How did you come to perform such a service?"

I briefly described the events of the year before, omitting my early blunders and the flight to the Land of the People. Onyame filled in details that I missed.

When we finished, Edward smiled broadly, something I had seen him do few times in his youth. "This is good fortune unlooked for! I've had minor dealings with King Sweyn of Denmark and have little to fear from him, I think. He's not a great warrior."

"I know."

"I've always feared an attack from Norway. Over the years, King Magnus' threats forced me to stand many nights on the main ship of the fleet at Sandwich. Now, to know that, with Magnus gone, both the Kings of Norway and Denmark have pledged friendship, well … hmm. Even if they honor those pledges for a short time, that offers me more than you know. This is a sign from God! It frees me to deal with some problems closer to home: Godwin and his family, never an easy matter. Thank you, Cuin!"

"On the matter of Earl Godwin, your majesty …"

"You have something to offer?"

"If I may be somewhat bold, your majesty, I have a question that may lead to diplomatic advice."

"Yes?"

"How are your relations with Tostig of Wessex?"

"Earl Tostig seems to be the best of them, brash but congenial. He also enjoys being at court."

"Good. My suggestion is that you court him at court."

Edward smiled. "I've benefited from your diplomacy, so, I'll do as you advise, but to what end?"

"Tostig is likely to connect himself to Count Baldwin's family. By marriage. In addition, while he admires his older brother, he also envies him."

"Hmm. The link to Baldwin will always help. As for Tostig's relation to his brother, that envy could be useful. So, if I want a friendly connection with Godwin's family, I can see that Tostig is my best choice."

"If there is a division in the family, you may want allies on at least one side."

He smiled again. "Well advised. And well done! I now have friends in Norway, Denmark, and Normandy. You'll be richly rewarded."

"I'll be much rewarded, your majesty, if you can help me with a small matter in Flanders."

He paused and stared at me for a moment, as if his mind had wandered and he was seeing me for the first time. "An alliance between Normandy and the three crowns of the North."

"That's what I hope I have accomplished, at least for some time to come."

"An alliance of four crowns, Cuin, on your initiative."

I was becoming concerned that the matter of Baldwin and Brithic would slip away. "Yes, your majesty, but I need to press you on a matter dealing with Count Baldwin."

He frowned. "Count Baldwin? Well, I'll help anyway I can. Of course. As you know, my ties to Flanders just now are not strong. Count Baldwin has remained inimical to the Emperor and the Pope, while I need the help of both of them. So, the Count and I have been on opposite sides of several rebellions in the Empire. Indeed, King Sweyn and I have found ourselves thrown together, needing the help of both the Emperor and the Pope." He looked at me a moment. "And you suggest that Tostig, once linked to Count Baldwin's family by marriage, may mean better relations with Baldwin in the future, since Tostig would be both mutual friend and family member?"

Though I was thinking about the power of the Pope and the Empire, I must have looked confused.

"I'm married to Tostig's sister," he reminded me. "Tostig is my brother-in-law."

"Of course. My thoughts wandered. Yes, Tostig would be a friend of both you and Baldwin, and you have the family relation to strengthen the friendship." I leaned toward him. "Your ties to Baldwin may be strengthened further if you help me, your majesty. Because it's not a Flemish matter I need help with. It's an English matter. You see, Duke William would like to wed Lady Matilda, Count Baldwin's daughter."

He raised his eyebrows. "Would he? Well, now, that would be a helpful match. Through William, I'd have an even stronger relation to Count Baldwin."

"The difficulty, your majesty, is that Duke William has a rival in Flanders, a Saxon. From the Severn valley, I've been told. His name is Brihtic."

"I'm not sure I know him, but He's probably from some land around Shrewsbury. Is he a knight or a noble?"

"For Lady Matilda to cast friendly eyes on him, he would have to be a lord of some sort, but only a minor one, I've been told."

"Then I'll have him called to England for service. If he doesn't happen to owe me service, I'll find someone to whom he does owe service."

"My deepest thanks, your majesty. This would be a great help for Duke William and me."

"Are you always rewarded by Duke William's gain?" Before I could reply, he added, "Well, I'll see that you're rewarded personally. You shall return to Normandy a richer man than you came!"

"I need no reward, your majesty. I was more than happy to be of help to William and you. I thank you for your generosity, though."

It was generosity indeed. Edward had two new tunics and pairs of leggings, a short jacket, a long cloak, and a new pair of shoes made for me and gave me a jeweled dagger and sheath, three gold arm-rings, and a dozen silver coins with his likeness on them.

He gave Onyame a new black robe with silver-threaded designs around its edges, two arm-rings, silver ones to match Onyame's black tunic and gray leggings, and silver pieces for Onyame's part in helping me with my Northern mission.

While we waited for our clothes to finish being sewed, Onyame and I strolled around Westminster and London, and we visited Edward for supper every night, at his request.

I wanted to visit the nuns Edith, Agnes, and their sisters in Chester. I recalled their invitation after I had freed them from slavery in Arras.

They were far to the north, though, and within a few days we were ready to leave.

As we bid farewell to Edward that last morning, again in his private chamber, he said, "Cuin, if all goes well, I could be in a position to invite Duke William here for an Easter or Christmas court. I know that he has troubles in Normandy, though. When do you think he might be able to come?"

"I don't know, your majesty. I know that he hopes to have the rebellions in hand by the end of this year or next. His strategy is siege rather than battle, if he can avoid the latter. So, it may take some time."

He held up his hand. "He's welcome here any time, and I hope you will convey that message."

"I'll inform Duke William, and I'm sure he will be grateful."

He smiled. "Good. And since you've brought me good news, I have good news for you. A friend of yours is in London."

"A friend?"

"I don't know him myself. He's a Northerner, I believe. He said he was a friend and wished to learn everything about you that he could."

Onyame glanced at me, and I must have looked dismayed, because Edward immediately asked, "He's a friend, isn't he? He showed us an old crutch that you'd given him, and I recognized the way you used to carve them."

"Why did he come looking for me here, your majesty?"

"Now that I recall our conversation, he wasn't looking for you exactly. He was looking for information about your birth and background."

"Why? I wasn't born anywhere near England."

Edward hesitated. "Yes. Why, indeed? I told him you were here yourself, accompanied by your large, dark-skinned friend, and that you no longer used such a crutch as he showed us. I thought that would make a friend of yours happy, and he seemed happy indeed. I told him you were leaving tomorrow, though, and that he needed to remain close to the palace if he wanted to find you." He looked at my face closely, frowning. "Have I blundered?"

"No, your majesty. I have blundered. I neglected to tell you that I eventually discovered the identity of the assassin who sought my life all those years ago in Normandy. He's a Berserker warrior from Norway, and his name is Voldred."

He shook his head. "I had forgotten those old episodes, assuming they were in the past. This man told us his name was Valgard of Voll, an Icelandic poet, and that he would sing poems for us tonight at supper."

Onyame replied, "You may be assured that this man will offer no poems at supper, your majesty. He will simply wait for Cuin to be vulnerable."

Edward frowned. "Have no fear, Cuin. I'll allow no harm to come to you." For a moment, I wondered if Edward recalled the harm done to his own brother so many years before. "I'll send an escort of knights to see you safely to your longship, and we'll seize this Voldred, if he comes to supper. We'll hide you tonight and hope he makes an appearance. If not, tomorrow is Sunday, and we'll get you out of Westminster and London before either place stirs."

Early the next morning, Onyame and I returned to the palace, but Voldred had been neither seen nor taken.

Edward was awake already, having said an early Mass for us in his chapel. We thanked him and slipped from the palace with a company of his knights.

As Edward had predicted, Westminster was still asleep. The morning was cold, but streaks of dawn promised a sunny day. I saw no one near the river. We pushed away from the dock, and the longship creaked into the blue-black water. The knights waved us away and watched us drift toward London. Then they marched back to the palace.

Just after we passed London, I spotted a solitary figure sitting on a stone bluff on the closest shore. As we approached, it rose, draped in a blue-gray cloak, shining under the early-morning sun.

It was Voldred. A huge sword hung at his side, a shield resting under his arm.

Onyame saw him at the same time and leaned over from the tiller to pick up his spear and sword. He gave orders to the crewmen, and they momentarily abandoned their oars to lift their shields from the side of the longship and surround me with them.

"He can't reach you from here, even with a bow," Onyame said, "though you may be able to reach him."

"He has a shield. Besides, I don't want to kill him. I want to convince him to go home."

Voldred called to us, "So, fellow disciples! You deceived me all through the North."

I pulled Magnus's knife from my robe and held it up, crying out, "This is the knife of the man who swore you to your mission. He's dead, but before he died, he released you!"

I could still see his stern face as we pulled farther away from him. "A stolen knife won't deceive me, Cuin of Falaise. You can't hide from me forever in Normandy. You've escaped for the last time."

We were almost out of hearing range. "No! It's a mistake, a confusion! I'm not the man in the Prophecy!"

I could barely hear his last words: "I would have believed that in Iceland, but now I know. Do you think I'm a fool? Or have you been the fool? You're the nephew of King Canute and the son of Duke Robert of Normandy, and for the life of the North, you're going to die!"

CHAPTER 22

THE SECRET

A. D. 1048

"The assassin said that?" Lanfranc leaned back in his chair.

"He shouted it. I had to tell the crewmen to ignore him, that he was mad, but even Onyame thought that visiting you to discover the truth was more important than our trip back to the People. Only something of this magnitude would keep me from my new wife or Onyame from his."

Yellow spring flowers already pushed through the snow in Bec forest outside Lanfranc's window, but I only glanced at them. "Is it true?"

He shrugged. "There's been a rumor around Normandy for years, which I've since discovered to be plausible. It begins with King Canute. Apparently, at some time in his life, Canute heard the Icelandic prophecy about England, Denmark, Norway, and a southern territory — the Four Crowns Prophecy that I discussed with you and Garrad back in Avranches. Canute could easily have assumed that the southern territory was Normandy. As you know well by now, the prophecy said that a lame, illegitimate son of a Norman Duke would turn the three Northern crowns to his own ends."

His statement reminded me of my meeting with Edward. "That's why King Edward kept repeating that comment about my getting an alliance for Normandy with the three kingdoms of Norway, Denmark, and England."

Lanfranc nodded. "Yes, he must have thought it remarkable that the Four Crowns Prophecy seemed to be coming true. The original prophecy, though, mentioned only three crowns — the Duke of Normandy doesn't wear a crown — but suggested that a fourth crown might be involved because of what the Norman Duke would achieve."

"Such as the crown of France perhaps?"

"Perhaps. As far as I could determine, the original prophecy said nothing about Canute. Apparently, Canute himself added that. Somehow, he altered the prophecy, so that this son of a Norman Duke would be from Canute's line and unite the entire North under one rule. He even had four knives made for the relevant rulers: one for the Duke of Normandy, and three for the Kings of Denmark, Norway, and England, so that these rulers would understand their destinies. Of course, Canute himself held three of the knives during his life, since by … what? … 1027, I think, he was King of Denmark, Norway, and England."

"Even some Swedish territory fell under Canute's rule, I learned in my Northern travels. Could that have been a fourth crown?"

"I don't know. Of course, Cuin, all of this was secret. King Canute never talked about it. He made none of this public. Apparently, Canute's role in the prophecy was known only to a few people close to him." He shrugged. "Of course, some of them whispered the secret around, which is how I heard about it when I visited my Northern students."

"So, my forging this alliance makes Voldred think that I am the person described in the prophecy."

"Yes, and the four knives could come together in ways —" he began.

I reached inside my robe and drew out the snakelike knife. I felt a tremor of fear as it glinted in the firelight. "Knives like this one?"

His eyes opened wide. "Where did you get that?"

"King Magnus gave it to me, and Voldred tried to kill me with another one."

"Hmm. So it was Magnus who had the knives. No one knew what happened to them. After Canute's death, they vanished."

"I'm fairly certain that Magnus had Voldred steal them after Canute died. Magnus told me that in his youth he had ordered Voldred to do foolish things."

"So you have one, and Voldred has one," he said. "Do you know who has the other two?"

"I know that Magnus gave one to King Harald as a gift. Magnus must have guessed that Hardraada or Hardraada's men would kill him, so the gift of the knife would remind Hardraada that he would be one of the Kings subdued by the Southern ruler." I shook my head. "In the end, Magnus was a good man. He knew Hardraada's character and did not want to subject the North to it. Yet …" I paused and sighed.

"He was responsible for the peril in which you continuously find yourself —yes. Strange, isn't it?" He paused. "Do you know where the fourth knife is?"

"I assumed that Magnus had it, but I don't know that. I'm fairly certain that Edward does not, from the way he talked and acted."

Lanfranc thought for a moment. "I wonder whether it's in England. Well, that's a matter for later. Now, where was I?"

"Canute heard the prophecy and had the knives made," I reminded him.

"Yes, that's right. Canute, unlike Magnus, had learned not to resist prophecies, which is why he decided to use this one. If Normandy were to produce a dynamic ruler who would unite the South and the North, the ruler would be of Canute's own blood. The northern war culture would survive and dominate the South."

"The old war gods would still rule."

"Yes. Canute's strategy appeared to be flawless. He was astute enough to see that Richard, then Duke of Normandy, would not be a strong ruler. So while Richard's brother Robert was merely lord of the Hiesmes, Canute proposed that his own sister Estrith marry Robert."

"Duke Robert allied himself to the North?"

"Keep in mind, Cuin, that Robert was not a duke in those days. He realized that if he never became Duke of Normandy — if his brother Richard lived to be old, which we know he did not — then he, Robert, would always be a lesser noble, scrambling for land."

I nodded. "I see. If Robert agreed to Canute's proposal, he might have a noble position in England."

"And in Norway and Denmark. You recall that Canute controlled all three regions — and part of Sweden, as you just reminded me. So, for Robert, Canute's sister was a stroke of wonderful fortune. And she was willing."

An abbey cat jumped into Lanfranc's lap, utter a lightly trilled greeting, and then leaped back down to resume some feline business elsewhere.

"So," he continued, "they contracted a marriage. Robert and Estrith must both have been about sixteen years old. Robert was wary, so he delayed having the marriage legally consummated while consummating it physically."

I raised my eyebrows but realized that Robert had taken the same tack with Arlette. "Robert seemed wary of marriage all his life."

He smiled. "Normans, like their Northern ancestors, do not easily submit to marriage. In any event, Estrith had a baby within a year. A celebration was planned, but nothing happened. Everything went quiet in all the towns of the Hiesmes. Then the word leaked out from the villages that the baby had been a boy, deformed in some way. Taking this as a sign from God, Robert sent Estrith back to England, where she retreated to a monastery."

"What about the child?"

"The servants said they exposed him, knowing that, as with most exposed children, he would be rescued. They said that they had been ordered not to reveal the child's identity, so that Norman nobles could neither kill the child nor draw him into a rebellion." He paused. "The sort of rebellion that Guy of Burgundy now leads."

"You think that I may be that child?"

"Your assassin thinks so."

"What happened to Estrith?"

"Canute married her off to Earl Ulf of Orkney, whose sister, by the way, is married to Earl Godwin of Wessex."

"So, that's Godwin's connection to Canute and the Danes in England."

Lanfranc nodded. "Yes, but Godwin later fell out with Ulf, fatally. Rumor has it that Godwin had Ulf killed. Before he did, Estrith gave birth to the man who is now King Sweyn of Denmark."

"What? King Sweyn? The one who walks with a limp?"

"Yes, strange, isn't it? Both of you ..."

My head seemed unable to settle into thought, but I heard myself ask, "What does all of this mean?"

"If it's all true, and Garrad can confirm it or not, you are the son of the late Duke Robert and Estrith, sister of King Canute. Therefore, you are half Norman and half Danish, noble from your father's line and royal from your mother's."

"I'm a commoner."

"If this is true, you are a commoner in upbringing only. You would be Duke William's half-brother, King Sweyn's half-brother, nephew to the now deceased King Canute, and even great-nephew of Queen Emma, through her marriage to Canute, and so related by that marriage to King Edward of England. In addition to all that, Estrith, Sweyn's mother, is now Queen Estrith of Denmark, since Sweyn is presently unmarried — and thus his mother becomes queen. So, you would also be the son of a Queen."

The cat decided to return to Lanfranc's lap just then. Lanfranc smiled at the cat while saying to me to me, "For an orphan, you may have a large number of relations."

I stared at the cat, my mind having gone blank. "It's not possible." I paused. "Is it?"

"You should draw no firm conclusions until you speak to Garrad. I can tell you, though, that when I mentioned these rumors to him, he asked me not to repeat them in your presence."

I was silent for a long time. Lanfranc waited patiently.

Eventually, he said, "At least, you'll be able to ask Garrad about all of this soon. I sent him word of your arrival, and he and his wife will be traveling here in about a week."

I sat thinking for a long time, barely taking in that Garrad and Marie were coming. Then I heard myself ask, "Is William still at Brionne? I promised to take him word of my meeting with Edward."

"Yes, he's still trying to get Guy out of Brionne Castle."

"The roads are clear? Would I have time to get to him and back before Garrad arrives here?"

"Probably. The roads may be somewhat muddy, and you must be careful about fording even the small streams, but they're passable."

I rejoined Onyame, and we made for William's camp.

Arriving at Brionne, Onyame and I found William standing near one of the siege towers, facing the stone castle rising in the middle of the Risle. The river rushed with early spring melting, setting the castle farther from William's reach.

William had his hands on his hips, staring wordlessly ahead, ignoring the occasional suggestions from the knights surrounding him.

Mud and water had invaded their shoes and leggings, staining the bottoms of their cloaks. They shifted from foot to foot, miserably. William stared at the castle, unmoving, and said nothing.

The guard who escorted me shrugged his shoulders after William ignored a second announcement of a visitor.

"Don't be concerned," I said to him, loudly. "I'm accustomed to this. When our Duke was a child, I often mistook him for deaf."

William jerked his head around. "Cuin! Why didn't you say you were here?"

"I was trying to give this guard the privilege."

"How did your trip to England go?"

"Well, but strange. Onyame is back in your tent, trying to stay dry. Do you mind if we join him?"

"I'm not accomplishing anything here."

As soon as we pushed through his tent door and he greeted Onyame, I faced William.

"Voldred found me in England, though he was too far away to do me any harm. Nonetheless, he told me something. Do you know what?"

He watched me while he sat down. "I probably do, but I'm sworn not to say."

Onyame sank into a chair as well.

I remained standing, facing William. "I thought Voldred had made the same mistake Magnus made, but then Lanfranc told me about a rumor. Can this possibly be true?"

"I cannot say. I've sworn an oath not to speak about it."

"Can you nod or shake your head?"

He thought for a moment. "That wouldn't break the oath, would it?"

"Did Duke Robert have a child by Estrith, King Canute's sister?"

He nodded.

"The child was deformed and for that reason exposed?"

He nodded again, showing no expression.

"Did the child survive?"

He nodded.

I took a deep breath. "Is the child alive today — in Normandy?"

He nodded.

"Is that child in this tent at this moment?"

He smiled and nodded.

I slumped into a chair. "How can this be, William? You know, better than anyone, that I've always thought of myself as a commoner, a villager. Given the way the nobles treated you, I was proud to be common. Now, this other self emerges —"

Onyame said to William, "Cuin is your half-brother, then, and that's why Lady Arlette took him in at the castle."

He nodded again.

"How —?" I began.

He interrupted me. "I can say nothing. I have an oath. Garrad is the only one not bound. You'll have to learn the rest from him. I'm very relieved, though, that you know."

"Are you? With that traitor Guy sitting over in Brionne Castle? I'd think that you'd dread having another relation who could be used in rebellions."

"I do, but the nobles never discovered your identity. And they never will. That's for the safety of both of us, though I'm willing to give you anything you want, any title, any lands."

"I've never wanted titles or lands."

He frowned, seeming to ignore what I had said. "Of course, at present I'm in no position to give much away. I'm barely holding on to my own lands, as the nobles eat away at them and fail to pay me dues or service or both." He raised his hands. "I have known you most of your life, Cuin. I know your character. You're not a threat."

"You do know that for certain." I thought for a moment, realizing that whoever else was a relation of mine, William had always seemed like a brother. "Getting used to you as a half-brother is likely to be the easiest adjustment I'll have to make."

He smiled. "Probably."

I thought for a moment. "This does mean, though, that I'm you're older brother. You've never treated your older brother with the respect that he deserves, have you? I hope you feel chagrined about all that archery practice. And forcing me to ride. You're a demanding younger brother." I paused. "That's why you can be a Duke, and I never could."

He laughed. "I'm very relieved that you know now. It has been hard on me not being able to let you know why you were special to all of us."

"With the ill treatment I've received, I wonder how I'd have been treated if I were not special." I gave him a moment to appreciate the slight humor and then said, "I'm sorry I can't help you with the nobles here, but I do have a good word from King Edward."

He leaned forward in his chair. "What?"

"He's ordering Brihtic to leave Flanders immediately. He also wants to strengthen his hand against Godwin, so he's delighted to know of the friendship pledges I extracted from Sweyn and especially Hardraada. He's pleased with the prospect of your marriage to Matilda, which gives him a link he needs to Count Baldwin."

William clenched his fists. "Good. Now if I can just hang on to Rouen, get these Western lords and Guy under control ... What did Matilda say?"

"I almost forgot. She's willing to meet with you, provided I get her father's approval and that ... the meeting begin with an apology."

He stiffened. "Will she apologize for calling me a commoner and a bastard?"

"She already has." I lied, and when I translated for Onyame, he gave me a glance that might have been disapproval. Since he had ignored my reproving glances in the past, I felt free to ignore his.

"Well, then I'll apologize, too." William hesitated, and his body relaxed. "God knows I'm not proud of what I did, and I'd welcome the opportunity to ask her forgiveness. How soon can you arrange a meeting?"

"I'll attend to it as soon as I finish my meeting with Garrad, who is probably at Bec Abbey by now."

Garrad had arrived at Bec Abbey by the time we returned, and we found him with Marie and Lanfranc in the guesthouse.

Lanfranc greeted us and excused himself, his duties as Prior drawing him away.

I greeted Garrad and Marie. Marie seemed as pleasant as ever, and Garrad seemed not to have aged at all.

Then I recalled what the Goliard leader had told me. Garrad was just past his middle thirties. Only the snow-white hair and beard had deceived me.

He looked much happier with Marie at his side, which I commented on.

For his part, Garrad grinned at me and thumped on my back with his good hand, which he then extended to Onyame, addressing him in Norwegian.

Onyame smiled broadly. "Flawless! Where did you learn to speak so well?"

"In the North," Garrad replied. "There's no better place."

We settled into chairs in front of the fire, and Garrad put on more logs and poked at the dwindling flame. As he did, he asked us to recount all our travels, saying that he had no secrets from Marie, and that the two of them needed to know everything, since they were already involved.

"You see," he concluded, "Voldred followed us from Falaise."

I leaped to my feet.

"Don't fear," he said, motioning me back down, "though that leap tells me more about your foot than I knew in Hedeby. When Marie and I realized we were being followed and who was following us, we detoured to Preaux, to the abbey of Saint Pierre. Do you remember, Cuin, when William took the ducal role in dedicating the church there — the year Duke Robert went on his pilgrimage? Well, as far as Voldred knows, Marie and I are at this moment restricted to the abbey guesthouse of Saint Pierre with fever. By the time he gets tired of waiting for us to recover, weeks will have gone by, and you'll be back on the other side of the world, if what Lanfranc tells me is true."

"How did you escape?" Onyame asked.

"With the help of the Abbot, we slipped out in the middle of the night," Marie said, shivering.

Garrad smiled at her. "It was as cold as the Northern Hel, but the coldness guaranteed that Voldred wouldn't follow us. So, you two, talk. If it's not in Norman French, I'll translate for Marie." He looked at me seriously. "I know there's a lot that you've learned in your travels that will demand explanations from me as well."

When we finished our tales a few hours later, I mentioned our visit to William.

Garrad chuckled. "So you got around the oath William took. That's not easy. I admire your ingenuity."

"Is it true?" I asked.

"Do you think William would lie to you?" Garrad replied.

"No, but it seems incredible."

"You've been reared to believe it was incredible. That was always our plan."

Onyame leaned forward. "Does this mean that Cuin could have been Duke of Normandy and King of Denmark and England?"

Garrad nodded. "And Norway, at present. Recall that King Canute would have been happy to have one of his nephews become King of the entire North after his sons died, and all have been dead about five years now." He said to me, "Would you want to have been a Duke and a King?"

"No self-respecting villager wants to be a noble. We know the fear Kings live in, and I saw how William was hounded by assassins."

"So were you," Marie said.

"Yes, but I always assumed that to be the result of some mistake. Besides, I've lived with the fear of one person trying to kill me. If I were royal, I'd have to live with the fear of … how many assassins? I couldn't tolerate what William has suffered. I don't have his constitution."

"That's exactly what Robert and I thought all those years ago, though we had only our wits and astrology to aid us. We always kept one thing in mind: as the heir to so many thrones, you'd be the most dangerous child in the world. And the most in jeopardy. There were attempts on your life immediately."

"Even before Voldred?"

"Yes. We had to smuggle you out of Normandy. We took you first to be with your mother at the monastery in England where she'd been taken. In Chester, but she'd already left."

"Estrith was a nun at Chester?"

"She took refuge in the abbey there briefly, yes. Why?"

"The nuns I freed in Arras were from Chester. It's just strange to contemplate …"

"Yes. As I said, we smuggled you to England. We realized that we had to deceive Canute — who would have named you successor to every throne he had, since you would have been a Duke and brought Normandy into his empire. So we staged your death. For the Normans, we returned you here as an orphan."

He stared at me for a moment and then gazed into the fire. "Perhaps Robert and I were wrong. You could have been the immediate fulfillment of the Four Crowns' Prophecy, but you probably wouldn't have lived. If you had, you could have set off succession wars in England, Denmark, and Norway. That's why Magnus was so afraid of you, even when he was a child."

"He thought I would take over the North, or that it would tear itself apart, trying to use me?"

He nodded. "Robert and I thought there could be another way to fulfill the prophecy, though. We wanted to have a hand in the North's destiny. We wanted the war gods to be stopped. Especially after Arlette had her dream about William."

I sighed. "You did change destiny. The war gods are fading, as Hervor often says. Further, I can do as an emissary what I may have failed to do as a ruler."

"That's what Robert and I hoped. Though the task may not be as complete as you think, especially in England, if Godwin's family takes control."

Onyame interjected, "What was this dream of Lady Arlette's?"

"I need to lead up to that," Garrad replied. "Let's see … what's the beginning of it all? I think the beginning of my life as a hermit, probably. My travels around the North and through the lands south of the Alps had just ended. I had returned to Falaise and lived with my father for a time. I didn't fit in with people easily, however. So I built myself the hut where you were trained and where Marie and I now live. When I was not traveling and studying in the North or the South, I stayed there."

"Your father?" I interrupted him. "I know all the people in the village. Who —?"

"Fulbert the tanner."

"Arlette's father? You're her brother?" I shook my head. "I feel as if I must have been asleep all these years! I thought she had only two brothers."

"So did many villagers after I changed my name, lost the use of my arm, and turned white." He used his good hand to point at his hair and beard. "Nonetheless, I was sought out for advice, especially after I'd spent a few years studying. I was the one Fulbert, our father, came to when Duke Robert first met Arlette. You know that story, don't you? About Robert meeting Arlette?"

"The villagers never told me."

Garrad smiled. "That's unduly cautious of them. There's no hint of your birth in it. Well, Arlette was washing linen in the Ante one day, while Robert was returning from hunting, a falcon on his wrist, the story goes. He was eighteen, I think — she may have been sixteen — and they were immediately drawn to each other. Robert told me later that he'd never met a girl so beautiful and so intelligent. He sent a discreet knight to Arlette to invite her to the castle the same evening. Our father, Fulbert, came to me in a confused fury. I went to Arlette and asked her what she wanted. She replied — you know Arlette, Cuin — that she wanted to go in the daylight, riding on a palfrey, with the drawbridge of Falaise Castle lowered in her honor and an apartment prepared for her reception."

I laughed. "Yes, that sounds like Arlette."

He smiled. "Our father became more furious, but I advised him to let her go, if that was what she wanted. I had received a vision about Arlette's being the mother of rulers. That settled Father. He allowed her to go. Robert consented to her terms. So she went."

"That's why William kept consulting you. Duke Robert was your brother-in-law, and you're William's uncle."

He nodded.

"Arlette had a dream?" Onyame reminded him.

"Yes, when Arlette discovered she was expecting a child, she had a dream that a great tree grew from her body, its branches spreading over Normandy and England. Green leaves grew from the branches, putting out some ancient fire. She brought the dream to me for interpretation. I told her that her son, my nephew, would be a great ruler who would unite the North and the South, as King David had done in ancient times. The war gods of the North would give way to a peace from the South. Her dream paralleled my vision."

All of us were silent for a time, and then I asked, "Do the villagers know?"

"Over time, they discovered everything."

"Everyone knows about this, then, except me."

"I'm afraid so." He gestured with his good hand. "You see, everyone knew a lame ruler could never survive in Normandy, and I didn't think that an Aquarian would ever want to rule most of the world. Besides, the local people weren't entirely happy about Robert's alliance with Estrith, Canute's sister. When you were born, your foot was considered God's judgment on Robert for having entered into such a bond and even on his brother, Duke Richard, for having allowed it."

"As far as the Normans were concerned then," I said, "Robert had no choice but to abandon Estrith and her illegitimate son. No one would have accepted me."

"That's the way it seemed to us. So, we smuggled you to Chester, to the monastery nearby, to be with Estrith, though we missed her. Nonetheless, we had the opportunity to spread the story in England that you had died. Of fever. When Estrith married the Earl of Orkney, a clever Chester nun named Edyth, who now runs the part of the monastery where the nuns reside, helped us return you to Normandy, where Robert planned to have you adopted first by the villagers, later by Arlette, and then by me."

"A nun named Edyth? From the monastery near Chester? Edyth is one of the nuns I freed in Flanders. She now directs the nuns near Chester."

He shook his head and smiled. "I didn't realize that. That's something close to a miracle, I'd say."

"It's —" I began.

"Yes, good people have been involved in your life. And now, I see, some of them have been repaid, in this case, by you yourself." He fell silent. "Robert was a good man."

"It seems that he didn't get any reward for saving me."

"There were other factors involved in his end. Powers and events far beyond your help." He stared out the window for a moment and then added, "He didn't poison his brother, though. That's what the villagers think, and in their eyes, that's the cause of his untimely death. Does Onyame know about that?"

I told Onyame about the dinner at which Robert's brother, Duke Richard, had been poisoned and about the villagers' suspicions.

"What you don't know," Garrad said, "is that, days before that dinner, Robert and I had heard rumors that Richard might be poisoned. Robert did nothing. His ambition ruled him then. He told himself that he did not believe the rumors, but he didn't want to believe them, as he later realized. After Richard died, Robert couldn't forgive himself. That's why he went on the pilgrimage at such a young age. He was only twenty-four, as you know."

"What happened to him?" Onyame asked.

"I know only what I've heard from those of his men who came back," Garrad said. "Travelers sometimes embellish the truth. Sometimes they invent it. What these travelers said sounds like Robert, though. First, before he left, he asked me to contact Herlwin of Conteville."

"Count Herlwin is Arlette's husband now," I said to Onyame.

"It was Robert who saw to their marriage in case he died on the pilgrimage. He knew they'd be suited to each other, though not in the way he and Arlette were suited. I've never seen such passion." Garrad sighed. "Of course, he didn't survive the pilgrimage." He turned to me. "Did you know he went barefoot the entire way?"

"He told me that himself. I was young, so I didn't think much of it."

"Thought it's not uncommon, not every Duke would humble himself like that. You may also recall that he and his small band of knights carried with them a treasure-chest full of gold, precious stones, and jewelry."

"I saw them pack it."

"Robert gave gifts to every traveler, to every poor family, to every orphan and widow he could find along the way."

I thought of William, having already developed a reputation for the same generosity to the poor.

Garrad was still speaking, "... not only kindness, but also forbearance. One night in Burgundy, he and the knights approached a gatekeeper at a castle where they hoped to spend the night. By this time, Robert limped and was covered with road-dust. Mistaking him for a beggar, the gatekeeper struck him across the shoulders with his staff. The knights dashed up to punish the man, but Robert stopped them. He said, 'Let him be. I'd rather take the blow than have it fall on my good city of Rouen.'

"In Rome, he delighted the citizens with a typical response. Seeing the statues of unclothed Greeks and Romans, he expressed mock horror. Taking the richest clothes he had, and knowing full well that the people would take them when he departed, he draped the statues. He said that someone had to take pity on the nakedness of such noble personages." Garrad laughed lightly.

"In Byzantium, he shod his mules with gold but told the smiths to forge the nails too short. As the mules clopped into the city, attracting much attention in the poor section they chose to enter, the glittering shoes fell off, Robert's gifts to the poor. When he and the knights met the Emperor and were given leave to sit, they followed the Norman fashion of sitting on their cloaks, their richest, fur-lined cloaks. When they rose, they left them behind, and the court attendants claimed them." He fell silent for a moment. "That was your father."

"Did you hear any more of him?" Onyame asked.

"I received word that on Robert's return from southern France to the Holy Land, he met a Norman knight on the road. By this time, he couldn't walk and was being carried by sixteen black servants in relays of four, with whom, the knight told me, Robert jested, as he would. He rewarded them richly and thanked them often for bearing him, but he also told them that his deteriorating body would become thinner every day, so that their load would become lighter.

"He told the knight to tell me that Robert, once Duke of Normandy, now fortunate pilgrim, was being carried off to Paradise by four black demons, who had turned out to be angels, at which the slaves laughed heartily." Garrad paused. "Later, he died of what was taken for fever and was buried in St. Mary's Church in Nicea. The knight's message, though, was his last direct one to me."

"When did you learn about my birth?"

"As soon as you were born. When your foot showed its deformity, Robert came to me. We had already worried that you'd be small. Canute's whole family was, as you know. We also knew that you were a Water Bearer, and Aquarian children are often small. The deformity just made things worse. If you were healthy, it would be too easy for rebellious lords to control you. If you were frail in addition to being small and lame, it would be too easy to kill you, which nobles were already trying to do."

"If they got to Guy," I said, "they'd have gotten to me. I have no special character for resisting wealth and power. I just happened to have been raised a commoner who, in the end, cannot imagine having to live the life of a noble."

"Which is as we intended. Of course, your character resembles Guy's in no way, I have to say. When you were returned from Chester, we arranged to expose you in the forest. I found you — a remarkable coincidence, which would prove to the villagers that you were not cursed. Not only were they convinced, but they thought you were positively blessed. They quarreled about who should have a child certain to bring good fortune. I made peace by working out the arrangement of sharing you among several families. You can judge how successfully this worked by recalling your childhood. I couldn't see at first whether you would have a hard childhood or an easy one. I knew that most of the families would be kind to you. In fact, I checked now and then. I made certain you worked hard but were punished as little as possible, though I've no doubt you were a troublesome child."

"I was angelic, and no one ever had to punish me."

He smiled. "Robert and I agreed that I'd eventually meet you again, another remarkable coincidence designed to increase your local status. Then I'd teach you whatever I could. Above all, you were not to be raised a warrior or have anything to do with ruling. We wanted you to be an emissary, a diplomat."

He paused for a moment. "You had a good father, after all, but you had no contact with your mother. That's where Arlette came in. When Robert told her about you, she wanted you in the castle whenever she was in Falaise. This, by the way, increased your reputation in the village, and after the miracle of the wine barrels, you were on the path to becoming a local saint. If

Voldred had succeeded in murdering you, the villagers would have made your bones the chief relics in the local church."

"An honor I'm happy to have forgone." I glanced at Onyame. "Now that Voldred has been mentioned again, I believe Onyame and I should be headed for Flanders. I have orders from Duke William to press Count Baldwin on the matter of Lady Matilda and to invite her back here when the weather improves."

"Cuin," Marie said, "now that Voldred is back in Normandy, why don't you just have the Duke seize him? He is an assassin, isn't he?"

"He's not really an assassin. He's a warrior who was deceived by King Magnus. I appreciate your suggestion, but I would rather talk to him. If the Duke's men try to seize him, I'm afraid someone might be harmed. Voldred's a fierce warrior, and he's not as old as we thought. Besides, I have an obligation to him. He's a fellow-student of mine."

Garrad frowned. "In that old Northern religion? I'm not sure how bound you should be to that."

I did not translate his comment for Onyame. "I know you're unsure about its value, but my training is not tied to the war gods."

"Has Voldred not been a warrior?"

"Yes, but Voldred has also been a victim, as much as I am, of the mistaken interpretation of a prophecy. Since I wasn't trained to be a ruler, I can't possibly conquer the North. I can only wed it to the South through friendship. Voldred has wasted much of his life on this error. I want to correct that."

"What if he's equally determined," Marie asked, "to kill you?"

"I won't know that unless I talk to him, and if the Duke's men kill him, I won't have that opportunity. I am also convinced that this is what Magnus wanted me to do. It was his dying wish."

CHAPTER 23

ENGAGEMENTS

A. D. 1049

Back in Flanders, Count Baldwin was entrenched in his castle at Lille. Before other business carried him away, I begged a private interview. We met in a large room behind the great hall, one in which special guests could sleep after a feast.

The Count, though wrapped in a fine red cloak, ordered a fire made against the chill. Pulling my blue-gray cloak around me, I held my silence until the attendants brought it to a roar and then retired.

"My lord," I began, "Duke William asks your permission to visit the Lady Matilda here privately, to try to mend the rift between them that occurred as a result of his hastiness and bad temper, for which he sincerely apologizes and has done much penance. Then he hopes that she will visit Normandy to experience its beauty for herself."

"I have been told about the peace-offerings you bear. I'm agreeable if Matilda is. Will it succeed, do you think? All this talking? My daughter, and from what I hear, your Duke, can be intransigent when they wish. Will talking bring the two of them together?"

"I think so, my lord. I even feel that wedding announcements could be made soon."

He smiled. "I hope you're right, but, my boy, a word in confidence: there will be other obstacles, other objections."

"Whose, my lord?"

"The Pope's."

"Surely the issue of consanguinity can be overlooked."

"That's not the issue, though it will be pressed into service, no doubt."

"Pope Benedict has no interest in William, though. All his heart and mind are fixed on Italy, on Tuscany, I've been told."

"You've been away, Cuin. Benedict is no longer Pope. He's been replaced by one of the Holy Roman Emperor's favorites, a Pope calling himself Leo IX. This Leo cares very much about a marriage between Flanders and Normandy. Let us recall that the Holy Roman Emperor wasn't happy about my marriage to King Henry's sister all those years ago. This wedding will please the present Emperor even less."

"So, the Emperor will move Heaven and earth — in this case, Heaven, threatening excommunication — to see that you are not allied to Normandy?"

"Yes, so I urge you to build the love nest as quickly as possible." He leaned over and smiled. "Though I appreciate that, with these two, doing so will be far from easy."

It was far from easy. By the time William arrived at Lille, Matilda had traveled with her father to Arras, so William, Onyame, and I set out on horseback to find her. My pony was as slow as always, which gave William time to express his anger.

"I have all of Normandy to govern, Rouen occupied by my enemies, that damnable Guy refusing to yield Brionne castle, and she decides to take a trip with her father!"

"You need a rest from governing," I told him as we rode. "As for Rouen, it will fall as soon as you ride into it, I'm sure. And surely Guy will surrender this year, won't he?"

"That's what I thought two years ago. He hasn't moved, and here I am trailing an over-indulged, dull-witted girl all over Flanders!"

"She's scarcely dull-witted. Matilda is one of the most intelligent people I've ever met, male or female. From her character, I discern that if she was over-indulged, she's recovered from the over-indulgence."

"She's ignoring that I have too many demands on me to chase her all over the countryside. She thinks I'm a commoner. I call that dull-witted."

He still smarted from Matilda's early comment.

Onyame repeated my lie, "She has apologized for that, my lord."

I glanced at him and nodded at his complicity. He returned the nod.

William remained oblivious to this exchange, still fuming. "I suppose you both think that this shows her nobility."

I knew I should not reply to that thorny comment, so I said, "I have a proposition, my lord Duke. If you greet Lady Matilda cheerfully and with equanimity, I promise to extract Guy from Brionne Castle." After a two-year siege, Guy had to be running out of supplies, and he did not realize, as I did, that William would not kill him.

William eyed me. "How can you get him out?"

"I'll use some emissary tricks I've learned. Do you accept my proposition?"

"On the condition that you have that vermin out of Brionne by Christmas, I shall be on my best behavior. She'll think I'm an emissary myself."

Unfortunately, Matilda was not on her best behavior. Since William wanted no one to know that he had left Normandy, we stayed in disguise at the abbey guesthouse at St. Vaast.

When we sent word to Matilda, she insisted that we visit her at the castle in Arras.

William fumed and then agreed, on the condition that we could return early enough to maintain our St. Vaast quarters and thus William's disguise.

Matilda replied by inviting us to a feast, which would undoubtedly last far into the night, and St. Vaast would be locked before we returned. Worse, William would have little time to see Matilda privately.

To prevent William's ripping the guesthouse apart with his own hands, I offered to visit Matilda and explain our situation to her.

"Explain?" William shouted, pacing up and down in the guesthouse. "She understands very well! She needs manners, not explanations!"

He threw open the door and stalked out.

Onyame strode over to me. "I wonder whether you'll ever get them together. Are you certain they're as much a match as you originally thought?"

"More now than ever."

"I suppose I see what you mean, but this kind of match could be fatal for both of them."

I laughed at him. "You may be right, but I think that once she learns to love him, their determination will turn to devotion."

"He'll need to love her, too."

"He already does. That's why he's so angry. William is seldom angry like this. His usual anger is cold. And dangerous, as his foes can relate." I turned to watch William walking away. "Let's keep in mind what Lanfranc and Garrad said; for William to be the instrument of a North-South alliance, he needs a link to the Saxons, and Matilda is related to King Alfred the Great."

Onyame produced an open smile. "I don't think diplomatic concerns will have much impact on these two just now. I may be able to help, though, since I know something of love. Let's join your Duke outside. His lady is being careful rather than rude, and that's a good sign."

We slipped out the door into a cloudy afternoon and found William pounding his hand steadily on a tree, but only half conscious of it, as if he had begun doing it earlier and now was doing it simply from habit. His eyes stared at nothing.

I tried to give Onyame an opening. "You know," I said, "Lady Matilda hasn't actually acted improperly." William turned his deepening frown on me. "Keep in mind," I added, "that I'm your half-brother. God is just and will not forgive your murdering me. Also, I can get Guy out of Brionne Castle."

Onyame saved me. "Duke William, if Matilda really didn't want to see you, she wouldn't have invited you here. So, Cuin and I will beg an audience with her. This very afternoon. Accompanied by a single, tall, bodyguard — a hooded, Norman bodyguard. When we see Matilda, so will he."

He pondered for a moment and then, to my surprise, grinned. "A fine plan. I'll be delighted to guard both of you."

As he walked away, I asked Onyame, "How did you know that strategy would succeed?"

"Because you insisted that he loves her."

When we were shown into the room adjoining the great hall that afternoon, Matilda was sitting in front of the fire reading.

Even smaller and more delicate-looking than I remembered, she seemed almost like a graceful child. I reminded myself that she was fully nineteen years old, a young woman.

I wore my black shoes, blue tunic and white leggings, my silver cross hanging on my chest. The once-frayed sleeves of my tunic had been mended with silver thread.

William wore a scarlet tunic with black leggings and red shoes. At his gold belt rested a gold-handled knife in a jeweled sheath.

I had sprinkled his clothes with all-heal to perfume them and had dusted basil powder on him to stimulate love in Matilda.

Unfortunately, Matilda, dressed all in white, smelled of lavender, obviously to offset the effects of basil. I recalled with chagrin that the Lady Matilda had a vast knowledge of herbs.

I opened my mission with formal greetings and gratitude for her healing me at our last visit. She received both with dignity and with what seemed genuine warmth.

That gave me the opening to introduce Onyame, whose huge presence and powerful voice would have impressed anyone and did not fail with Matilda.

Onyame bowed. "It is an honor to meet you, my lady." He turned slightly aside and added, "I know that you have not had the formal pleasure of meeting a noble lord, William, Duke of Normandy."

Matilda's face, gazing up at the near-giant standing next to Onyame, fell into seriousness. Before it could fall into anything worse, though, William acted.

He threw back the hood of his cloak, bowed, and knelt before Matilda. "I am and hope to ever be your servant, my lady."

"Please rise, Duke William," Matilda said, more icily than I had hoped.

Drawing himself from his kneeling position, William rose, towering over her.

He apparently realized how intimidating he must be and immediately said, "Would you allow me to escort you back to your chair before the fire and place myself on the stool next to it? It would be my honor."

She nodded wordlessly and allowed herself to be escorted.

I had planned a speech about their apologies having been exchanged and accepted, but I rejected it. They needed no reminders of the past.

They desperately needed conversation, though. I said, "My lady, Duke William has just accompanied us from Lille, where he was visiting. He's been occupied —"

"Besieging his own cousin at Brionne, I have been informed," she said. Her tone made besieging a rebellious cousin sound like a mortal sin.

"To end a rebellion," I began to explain.

William cut me off. "My lady, if you will permit me, I would rather discuss matters closer to you. Cuin tells me that you are a fine healer and know more about healing than even our friend Garrad. I also know that you're actively involved in your father's interactions with the Holy Roman Emperor, a subject that interests me very much. Would you permit me to ask you about these and other matters?"

I looked at him, astonished. Where had William developed such skills? How had he come by the art of flattery? Normans generally were known for flattery, but William was not.

Then I saw the truth in his face. William had never been able to flatter, never able to disarm an opponent except in battle. He sincerely wanted to know about this tiny woman. He wanted to ask about her life, her ideas, her activities. She might soon be his wife, and more importantly, he was in love with her.

So they discussed her life and her interests far into the evening, ignoring any party we all might have attended.

The next day went the same way. William refused to talk about anything or with anyone but Matilda, so that by the time we wound our way back to the guesthouse, we had spent several hours listening to her. By the end of the week, he had remained an attentive audience for five afternoons.

On the fifth afternoon, as we rose to leave, Matilda asked me to remain behind for a few moments.

William and Onyame returned to the horses.

It was over an hour before I joined them.

William watched my face. Eventually he said, "She's a remarkable woman. I doubt that a man could have a more capable wife, friend, and fellow-ruler." Then he added, "I'll admit my curiosity about your conversation with Lady Matilda, though it may be inappropriate to ask what it was about."

"It's entirely appropriate," I said. "She wanted to know about you. She asked me to tell her everything I knew about you, everything I'd learned growing up with you and living in the Normandy governed by you. So I told her."

"And?"

"I told her that you were a fine lord, a brilliant governor of men and lands, a noble character, and someone so like her that you could have one of the finest marriages in history. In other words, I lied."

William raised his eyebrows. "What did she say?"

"She would like to know whether you have any proposal for her to consider."

Only a few days passed before William turned from lover to Duke again.

On a cloudless summer morning, he marched into the guesthouse at St. Vaast, shouting, "To the devil with both of them!"

"You haven't quarreled with Matilda, have you?" I asked.

" Of course not! Why aren't you packing?"

I began packing. "Both of whom?"

"That Emperor's Pope, Leo. And the Emperor himself. He's sent Leo, or maybe it was Leo's idea to gain some respect in the French and Italian states, I don't know. But he's been traveling all over the Holy Roman Empire since last summer."

"Pope Leo traveling? Wouldn't that be normal for a new Pope?"

"Does this sound normal?" William's voice raised, sounding harsher than usual. "He's announced that he'll hold a council this autumn to discuss the issue of —" he paused to pronounce the word distinctly and with disgust —"consanguinity."

"Oh, this is bad. Consanguinity is his excuse to —"

"Denounce my marriage to Matilda, yes. How did he hear about the announcement so soon?"

"You know that the Pope and the Emperor have spies."

"Well, they'll not have the best of me. I'll have my marriage, regardless of any Pope's ecclesiastical pronouncements." He paused and began to pace. "But excommunication, he can't threaten that." He spun toward me. "Can he?" He paced again. "He could threaten, but he may not follow through. Cuin, I want you to take this consanguinity problem to your friend Lanfranc when we return. Bec Abbey is now under Guy's sway, but if Lanfranc is loyal to neither Guy nor the Pope, I could use his help."

"Yes, of course. But — return? Where are we going?"

He frowned at me. "Hasn't the infirmarian told you?"

"I haven't seen him in days. I've been planning your wedding."

"There's a plague of fever. It began in Falaise and has reached to Grandmesnil and Conteville. My mother has it, and her husband has called for me. He thinks that she may not live long."

CHAPTER 24

DEATH OF A LADY

A. D. 1049

By the time we arrived in Conteville, I saw that the Count had good reason to send for us. Not only was the fever raging everywhere, but Lady Arlette was more than ill. She was, as he suspected, dying.

She seemed to be asleep, so I slipped quietly beside the bed and studied her face. Having not seen forty years yet, it nonetheless looked sunken and aged.

I took her hand to check her palm, and her eyes opened.

She smiled weakly. "I'm happy to see you, Cuin. Garrad is here, looking after me, but I don't feel very well."

"We'll heal you, my lady. William is here with me."

William knelt beside me, and I placed Arlette's hand in his. She studied him. Then she smiled again, this time almost cheerfully, and for a moment, I believed she could recover.

"It's been too long, son. Too long, always. And for too brief a time. Don't you always say so?"

"Yes, but I'll stay a longer time now."

She lifted his hand to her face. Then the smile faded, and the color drained away again. She whispered to him, "This time, I shall not stay long."

I heard a step behind me, and a hand touched my shoulder. I looked around to see Garrad, dressed in a gray robe, his bad arm tucked in a front pouch, his face serious. With his head, he motioned me away. I slipped through the great hall and out into the sunlight.

I took a deep breath. "She looks terribly ill to me."

"To me, as well." He summarized his treatment.

"I'd have done nothing different," I said, "so I have nothing to offer, I'm afraid."

He nodded, looking grim. "She's not the only sick person. The fever seems to be everywhere. Again, it's aggravated by the heat and the crowding in the villages and towns."

"Where's Marie? Is she well?"

"Yes. She's in Falaise. Will you return with me? I've seen nothing of Voldred."

"I'm not sure."

He smiled. "Marie and I would be pleased to see you. And there's fever in Falaise, too. I could use your help."

"I may want to stay with William. This illness of Arlette's along with the news about Pope Leo …"

"Yes, I'm sorry about that. Lanfranc's already heard about the Pope's intention to condemn William's marriage."

"Matilda's determined, nonetheless. So is William."

"So should we be, for purposes of unity. Matilda is the link William needs to Count Baldwin and to her uncle, King Henry. She has the added prestige of being descended from the Saxon King, Alfred the Great."

"She's also capable of ruling a territory herself. Even William is impressed with her in that capacity."

He sighed. "I'm glad for him, then. He may soon need a wife to console him."

Arlette died two days later.

Her husband had just founded an abbey at Grestain, an easy two days' ride from Conteville. He wanted to be buried there when he died, and now he wanted Arlette's body to rest there.

We held a small funeral service at Conteville, where the priest asked me to pray over the body. Unlike the children I had prayed over when I was young, this body represented more than a lost companion.

"However," I said in my Latin prayer, "God is most merciful to his most merciful children, and none had more mercy than Lady Arlette. She may be parted from us for now, but she cannot ever be parted from the kingdom of Heaven."

William showed no emotion, as I expected. but he spent many hours alone while the rest of us prepared for the trip to Grestain.

When we reached the abbey, a young monk stood out in front, the dust of the building visible behind him through the trees. His hands were folded into his robe, and his hood hung over his face.

"Greetings," he said. "I've been expecting you."

Garrad greeted him for all of us and then asked, "Has a messenger preceded us?"

The monk replied, "God has preceded you. I've been given a vision, and I believe it's for you. Are you the funeral party for a lady named Arlette, and is her son among you?"

"We bear the body of the Lady Arlette," Garrad replied. "Duke William is her son. How did you know he would be among us?"

"I was working on one of the buildings a few days ago when I stumbled," the monk replied, "striking my head on a tree limb as I fell. By the time I hit the ground, I was not breathing, and my brothers thought I had died. I, however, saw myself lying on the ground. I saw my own body, as if I were outside it. Then a young man with a shining countenance and a bright garment guided me away to the northeast."

I sensed that the young monk had been given a genuine vision, and I swung down from my pony to hear everything he had to say.

"We came to a valley of great depth and infinite length," he continued. "On its left flames rose, while on the right hail and snow poured down violently, and men's souls fled from one side to the other, enduring the heat or cold as long as they could. My guide said, 'This is not Hell.'"

"It sounds like Hell to me," I whispered to Garrad, who had dismounted to join me.

The young monk went on, "My guide told me that this was the vale where souls are punished, those souls who, delaying to confess their crimes, repent at the point of death. From that vale, we passed through shades of night, until there appeared before us globes of black flames, rising out of and falling back into what seemed a great pit. I heard a voice say, 'This is the mouth of Hell.'

"Then my guide led me to the southeast. There we discovered a beautiful light and heard voices singing more harmoniously than I have ever heard, and a wonderful fragrance proceeded from the place, sweeter than all the fields of flowers in the world. 'Here,' my guide said, 'reside those not so perfect as to deserve to be immediately admitted into the kingdom of Heaven. Yet shall they all, at the Day of Judgment, see God, and partake of the joys of His kingdom.'

"Just beyond that I could see a more beautiful light, heard even more harmonious music, and detected an even more fragrant odor, all far surpassing what I had just seen. 'There,' my guide said, 'is the entrance to the kingdom of Heaven.' And I saw walking toward it, smiling, a beautiful young woman in a radiant gown. She turned and smiled at me and said, 'Tell my son when he comes in three days' time that Arlette has passed into Paradise and walks, through the grace of God, toward Heaven itself. When he joins me, though it will be many years from now, he must strive toward the pure light. There he will find me.' Then I awoke, and my brothers were astonished that I was uninjured. I told them my vision, and I have been posted here to meet you. You are all welcome."

After the burial service, William excused me from service long enough for me to return to Falaise with Garrad to help cure the fever. We rode with him along the Risle River south to Brionne, and then we sped west to Falaise.

Within two days, I could smell the tanners' works and see the castle in the distance. Seeing the castle made me smile, despite the sad news we bore and the fever victims we would undoubtedly find in the village.

Falaise had grown in my absence. The village boasted new wooden houses, a church rebuilt in stone and a new village water clock in the town center. Several new mills and stone houses dotted the lakes at the foot of the castle, and most of the castle had now been converted from wood to stone.

The villagers were even friendlier than I remembered, especially when we began to heal fever victims.

The news of Arlette's death was met with mourning, but at a High Mass on the Sabbath, I repeated the vision the young monk had recited. This stilled much of the weeping, and the atmosphere turned to a reverent rejoicing.

That I was the person to repeat the vision added to its impact in the minds of the villagers. That I had returned without my crutch seemed to them to be another miracle. I realized that my status as 'guided by God' was increasing, in spite of my efforts to seem normal.

As we went about our healing work, though, Garrad and I said nothing about my having discovered my parentage.

I visited Garrad and Marie in their hut but slept in the village in spite of their offers for me to join them. I was being shared from home to home again, and the villagers insisted that I repeat my childhood pattern.

Each evening, as I set out toward the village, Garrad called to me. "Do you have your bow?"

"Yes, thank you, but I won't need it."

One evening, after Garrad and I had worked a full day on a new hut for me and were feeling exhausted, he suggested that I join Marie and him for a quiet evening.

"Thank you, no. The villagers will think I've been harmed. Or ascended. I'll be one of the local saints by morning."

He smiled. "All right. String your bow before you go. It is Friday."

I obeyed but said, "I'm sure Voldred has returned to the North in frustration by now." And I set out toward the road to the village.

As I left the forest and reached the road, the sky over Falaise caught my attention. A ring of orange-red clouds, looking almost like fire, surrounded a grayish-purple cloud, which, as I watched, seemed to shape itself into a horse and then a horse and rider. It invaded one of the orange-red clouds, and for a moment, it seemed to catch fire at its tip, where the rider's arm would be.

For a moment, I thought of the witch-ride Hervor had told me about, and a chill ran down my back. Then the clouds closed into a red lump, tinted with purple, and I laughed at my own fear.

At that moment, though, I heard footsteps behind me. I remembered the night Voldred had chased me, a night not very different from this one.

These footsteps, though, would surely belong to a villager, wanting once again to remind me of the "miracle of the wine barrels" or comment on the healing of my foot.

I gripped my bow more tightly in my right hand, but I turned to greet what I was sure would be a friend.

I saw instead a huge, dark figure pacing quickly behind me, only a few feet away. Its hand slipped into its robe and jerked out a knife, which flashed into the air.

The last rays of the fading sun glinted on its serpentine curves. The figure leaped toward me with a Berserker cry.

It was Voldred.

CHAPTER 25

THE LAST ASSASSIN

A. D. 1049

I had no time to run. The knife plunged toward me.

Without thinking, I grabbed the bow with both hands and swung it desperately at the knife hand, spinning to my right as I did.

Voldred's blow missed, but its force carried him just beyond my body, which was still turning and so now faced him directly.

Though moving past me with great speed, he stumbled slightly, caught himself, pivoted on his right foot and aimed another blow at my chest.

Though he was falling away from me and the blow had less force than the first, the knife found its mark. I felt a dull pain shoot through my chest, and I staggered backward.

I heard a scraping noise as the knife hit me — and felt only a dull ache.

As Voldred took an additional step away from me to regain his balance and as I staggered away from him, I had just enough time to jerk an arrow from my quiver and fit it to the bow. And aim it at his head.

He had stopped moving and was gaping at my chest, the setting sun behind me turning his face grotesquely red.

Keeping the bow as taut as I could, I gasped, "Don't move."

He continued to stare, unmoving.

I took a long step back from him and glanced down at where his gaze was focused, where I felt the dull ache in my chest.

Where the knife had ripped my tunic open, the cross with the snakelike pattern hung, a gash running across the pattern where the knife had struck it.

The cross that Hardraada had given me, intending to intimidate me, had caught the knife's thrust.

"It's true," he whispered. "Your God, that terrible God of yours, protects you. Even now, when my cause is just."

I stepped one step further back, breathing heavily.

"Kill me," he said. "I've lost. Your God wields more power than the warrior-gods I serve, though that power is evil."

I panted, trying to think. I recalled the vision in Hervor's hut about Charlemagne. "I should kill you. But I won't."

He stared at me and looked startled and then frowned.

"You believe your cause is just," I went on, "but it's a mistake. You've been deceived."

"You're the son of Duke Robert, the nephew of King Canute, the murderer of King Magnus, and someday the destroyer of the North."

"I am the son of the Duke Robert and Canute's nephew, yes. I did not murder King Magnus, however, and I have no power to destroy the North. You may travel back to Norway, if you wish, and confirm that two rebellious servants of King Harald Hardraada killed Magnus. I swear that as a student of Hervor. King Harald himself will tell you so. He will tell you that I am his friend and a friend of Norway. King Sweyn, though Harald's enemy, will also tell you that I am his friend. Indeed, though he doesn't know it, I'm his half-brother, which you know already."

He stared at me as if he had frozen.

I continued, "I'm an emissary, not a warrior. I was raised to speak different languages, to speak with kings and clerics, and to heal. I have training in no weapon but a bow, and I live as a commoner. I have no lands, no armies, no knights, not even a single bodyguard. I can do nothing to the North but unite it to the South: emissary's work. That work will not destroy the North but strengthen it."

He remained unmoving for a long time and then slumped to the ground. "Why should I believe that? That evil God of yours... I failed to prevent Magnus's death. I failed. A lifetime of trying, and I failed. He's dead, after all."

I relaxed the bow but kept the arrow notched.

"I swear to you that I didn't kill him," I repeated. "Two of King Harald's men did, against the wishes of Harald and without my knowledge."

He glowered at me, and I retightened the arrow.

He finally spoke, "They told me that it was you who prepared the poison and urged them to administer it."

"That's a lie, and King Harald himself can assure you on that point."

"King Harald! One of your accomplices in this murder! How has he fared as a result of the death? King of all Norway."

"It was to be, whether you believe so or not. King Magnus chose to die. His father appeared to him in a dream, and gave him a choice —"

"No warrior chooses to die by poison! He was a great warrior and should have died in battle!"

"He was a follower of the Christian teachings first. His father, a Christian saint, came to him in a dream and predicted Magnus' death, a death that would save Magnus from committing terrible sins."

He spat at the ground. "You Christians! Sins and evil! Like your God, you're consumed by darkness. King Magnus was a warrior in his heart, and he sits now in Valhalla with Odin and Thor and —"

"If so, you did fail him. He did not die a warrior. He did not die in battle, fighting to the end. In truth, though, he chose to die, fighting a greater foe. He died the way he wished, as a good man with a pure soul. I know. I was with him when he died."

"He would never have tolerated his own assassin —"

I lowered the bow and pulled the knife from inside my tunic. "He gave me this. You know that King Harald has one. Yours lies there. There's a fourth in England" — I was guessing from what Lanfranc had told me — "which by now you probably know as well. This is the one that belonged to King Magnus. I swear it by all the saints and by Heaven. And I swear it to a fellow student of Hervor."

The anger drained from his face. "I've seen the fourth knife in England." His eyes narrowed. "Did you steal this one after King Magnus died?"

"Do you believe that he would leave it lying around for an assassin to steal? If I had been his assassin, do you believe while he was dying, he would have told me the story of how he tricked you to swear loyalty to him? How he made you build an altar to the old gods and swear on them, and while you were swearing, he added the oath that you had to protect him, to protect him by killing me?"

His mouth hung half open, as if he was about to say something, but no words came out.

"From the time I met him," I said, "I was King Magnus's friend. I was his friend at his death, and he asked me to release you from your vow."

He stared at me a long time. "He did not release me himself. You could be lying. And the ritual still binds me —"

The image of a god hanging on a tree flashed through my mind. "Does it? Are you certain? As a fellow-student of Hervor, tell me: what binds you?"

He paused, as if struggling within himself. "Since you ask as a fellow-student, I'm bound to reply. King Magnus made me swear by Odin on the hammer of Thor."

"Tell me, again as a fellow-student: what gives power to rites?"

"If Hervor taught you, you know. The rite itself, the actions and words."

"Then if I now went through the motions and repeated the words of some ritual of the old religion, it would be effective?"

He snorted. "You're a poor student if you believe that. For the ritual to be effective, you'd have to understand what you were doing, know the meaning of the ritual. As Hervor trained me to know. You, it seems —."

I interrupted him. "That's right. Hervor taught you what makes a ritual powerful enough to bind you to another. She also taught you what does not bind you. If you went through the ritual with Magnus, and he did not mean what you meant, you would not be bound to him."

He hesitated. "Of course not, but he did mean Odin and Thor. I was there —"

"No, he did not. You failed to realize the one thing that was missing from the ritual. King Magnus was a Christian. He made you swear by 'the God who hung on the tree,' didn't he? You repeated the phrase when we were in the North."

He nodded. "Yes, the God Odin."

I took a deep breath. "He never said Odin, did he? He only said, 'the God who hung on the tree,' didn't he?"

He paused, shaking his head. "No, something is wrong here. King Magnus said, 'the God who died on the tree.' I originally said, 'the God who hung on a tree,' and he made me change it and repeat it."

"Change it to 'the God who died on the tree.' Don't you see? Odin did not die on a tree. Magnus meant Jesus, not Odin." I seized my cross, covering the top with my hand. "He made you swear on an image like this, didn't he? An image you took to be Thor's hammer."

His face went blank. "No. It can't … I can't have …"

"That's right. It's a cross. You were doubly deceived. Magnus did not bind you. As a Christian, he could not. You've been free all along. You're free now."

He stared at my cross for a long time. Then he groaned. "No."

"Yes. Magnus deceived you and then wanted to free you. He told me himself to free you. You've never been bound."

"It can't be." He slumped. "First my family. Then Magnus. Now my life. All gone."

"Your family?"

He turned angry again. "Yes! My wife and daughters, both killed in a raid. By you Normans. A retaliatory raid for what the Viking warriors had done to you. My wife and daughters never harmed a Norman!"

"Retaliatory raids? There were no retaliatory raids." I tried to collect my thoughts. "For your family to have been killed in a raid by Normans, it would had to have happened while I was a youth in Normandy. There were no raids. William's father barely maintained his authority while alive, and as a young Duke, William struggled even more. We had no armies or weapons for raids."

"That's a lie! My family died in a raid!"

"On my honor as a student of Hervor, especially speaking to a fellow-student, there were no raids." I thought for a moment. "Who told you this?"

"King Magnus, of course."

I stepped back a few steps, reset the bow in my hands, and tried to think.

Then I heard the dragon-whisper in my mind: "Search the North with your vision skills."

Voldred seemed frozen, unmoving. I took another step back and cast my mind into the vision realm.

A mist came and cleared. I saw a tall woman with blonde hair, going gray. Near her stood a young woman probably in her early twenties, tall and blonde. Some distance away — was it in a neighboring village? — a shorter, darker young woman held a young child, and a young man stood in the background.

"Your wife," I said out loud, "is tall and blonde with a strong profile, almost stern but still beautiful. She has unusually blue eyes. Very blue. She parts her hair in the middle and wears a headband, colorful, lots of color in the headband, even though the rest of her clothes have plain colors."

He stared at me. "What deception is this?"

"You know I have the power of visions. You have two daughters. One is blonde like her mother, while the other has dark, slightly wavy hair, like yours."

He stared at me. "What is this? Are you seeing them as they were, when I last saw them? Fifteen years ago? Are you seeing them as they are in the Otherworld?"

"I'm seeing them as they are now." I brought my vision fully back to the present and looked straight at him. "You were lied to. Your family is still alive, and you have a grandchild."

He straightened. "It can't be ... you're ..."

"I can cast the vision to you. You know that. As a fellow-student, you may see even more easily than others. Sit. Clear your mind. The vision will form in it."

He hesitated but finally took a deep breath and sat down, staring ahead. I kept my distance and kept an arrow fixed in the bow.

I could not determine whether he was convinced, but I knew he would take my vision skills seriously.

I cast my mind into the vision realm again, sharpening my focus on the three women. I could feel the image float in the air between us.

"Focus!" the dragon-voice hissed. I focused even more on the three of them.

I heard him gasp loudly.

I said out loud, "See that your wife's hair is graying naturally. See that your daughters have now grown. How long has it been since you have been away from them? Fifteen years perhaps? See how old they are now. See that the older stays near your wife, while the younger has married and has a child. Your grandchild."

"It can't be. They must be …"

"I can tell you that your wife still waits for you. I can see in her heart that she believes you still to be alive somewhere and that you will return to her. That is why your older daughter stays with her. She too believes that you will return."

The vision faded. I breathed deeply and turned to him.

He crumpled to the earth. He sat silently, bowed, for a long time.

Eventually I said, "You were not bound by Magnus, and the grief that fueled your fury is now swept away. Your family is alive, and your life belongs to you again."

He raised his eyes, staring ahead, for another long period of time. I heard him mutter quietly again and again, "What have I been doing? What have I been doing? Where are they? What have they been doing all this time?"

Eventually, I lowered the bow and knelt down, facing him, though still several steps away. "Listen to me, Voldred, please. As a fellow-student. Your life is not what you thought. Mine is not, either. Everything has just changed."

He focused on my face and said — without malice, "Has that God of yours changed?"

"I know how the Christian God must sound to you. For all the killing that King Olaf did, for all of King Magnus's fears, however, the Christian God is not a God of war. Heaven knows I've hoped myself that He was, when I felt weak and vulnerable, but the war to save me never came. It never would. The Christian Savior never carried a weapon. He was a healer."

He took a deep breath. "Is it so? And you stand there with a bow?"

"To defend myself, I do. Would you do less?"

"I thought a Christian would do more."

I straightened and studied him.

I took a deep breath. "Yes. Very well. Let us be clear, though. Not only a Christian must do more. Everyone must do more, even the followers of the old religion. Even the followers of Thor must have honor and finally, peace."

I dropped the bow and the knife. "If you truly believe that the Christian God is evil and that I killed Magnus, if you believe that I stole this knife and that you have not been released from your oath, if you want to devote the rest of your life to killing rather than being a husband to your wife, a father to your daughters, and a grandfather to your grandchild, then kill, and begin with me now, your fellow-student."

I watched his face for a time and then added, "But this killing will be a ritual from which you cannot be released. Rather than living and eventually dying as a warrior, you will have become, irrevocably, a murderer."

My head was pounding. I felt the strain of the vision and casting the vision to Voldred. I felt the ache in my chest and the tenderness of every part of my body, as if my skin would hurt if anyone merely touched it.

He watched me for a long time, a small eternity it seemed. Then he stretched his hand toward his curved knife. He slowly rose and stepped over the bow and the other knife. He took one more step and faced me. He stood so close that I could no longer see the knife in his hand.

The hand suddenly jerked up and thrust toward my chest, just below the cross.

But it was the handle of the knife that struck me.

"Here," he cried. "Take this accursed thing. Take this, this weapon of my doom. I never want to see it again as long as I live."

I began to breathe again and almost fainted from lightheadedness and then dizziness. My chest ached so much that I felt it would cave in.

I stepped back and looked down at the weapon. "No. King Magnus … It was his wish that you keep the knife. He made me keep his, too, though I wanted nothing but to be rid of it."

He dropped the knife.

I knelt and picked it up. "These knives can mean something else now, to both of us. You're free. I'm free." I held the knife in my open hand. "Take it home with you, and if you wish, bury it on your land. Or let it remind you of what you lost and what you gained in these years. Didn't Hervor teach us that all living is a balance of loss and gain, death and rebirth?"

He stared at me.

"We both want the same thing," I said. "The knives can now represent that. Not the destruction of the North, as you've feared at my hands. Not the destruction of the South, as I've always feared at the hands of Northmen. But the strengthening of both of them, so that everyone who lives in either realm can be safe. My friends can be safe, and your wife and daughters can be safe."

His jaw worked for a moment. Then he was silent for a long time again. He slumped back onto the ground and stared straight ahead. Eventually he repeated my words quietly, "The strength of both of them. So that everyone can be safe." He nodded slowly, heavily. "Can that ever be true?"

"We want the same thing, you and I. You've dedicated your life to saving the North, but by means of assassination, a means forced on you by Magnus, which he regretted. How many years have you done this? Fifteen, did you say?"

He stared at the ground for a long time, then spoke as if the words caused him pain. "I'm forty. King Magnus's oath and the belief that my family had been murdered made me lose the last fifteen years of my life."

"You have more than fifteen more years to live. Far more. How do you wish to spend them?"

A short time later, I pounded on Garrad's door. I heard him call something to Marie, and the door swung open, lighting the now-dark forest around me.

"Cuin! I thought you were headed for the village."

"I was. I need some help with a bad bruise, though. And I'd like you to meet someone who needs help finding his family … and his life."

We stayed in Falaise another few weeks, curing the remaining fever victims and finishing the hut I had begun building.

And healing.

Voldred stayed with us to help, insisting that he owed me a debt for the years of trying to kill me.

I urged him to go north to find his family, but he said that he was not ready to face them yet. He needed to create a life that he could present to them with honor. He could not present them with the life of an assassin, he said.

So he helped me build my hut, and I allowed him time and silence to consider what his life might be in the future. He spent many hours sitting and staring at the sky or the trees.

When he was in their home, Garrad and Marie treated him as a member of the family and told him everything about my early life that they knew, which I appreciated more than I could tell them.

Garrad also taught him how to prepare a few ointments and tinctures and, with a stream of poor jests, had him sample different herbed wines.

For their part, the townspeople considered the conversion of an assassin yet another act of God, the third of my "miracles," and they treated Voldred like a saint. Women wanted pieces of his hair and beard, and little children tried to cut off pieces of clothing with their small knives.

"If this keeps up," one of my village mothers told him, "you'll be as naked as Our Lord on the cross, and we can't have you competing with the Savior in that way."

So she made him a new blue tunic and leggings, which combined with his gray-blue robe to produce an elegant effect.

The healing time eventually came to an end. During the fourth week, Garrad received a message from William.

"One of my Goliard friends delivered it last night," Garrad said. "They're staying at the castle. It's the same group that accompanied you north, Cuin."

For Voldred, I said, "They're not just any group of wandering monks."

Garrad nodded. "Cuin already knows that these particular Goliards have worked with me for years. They're the group I fought with in England."

I was surprised at this detail. "Even Rolf, the leader? He said that he'd only met you after the battle in which you lost the use of your arm."

"They would all say that. These days, Goliards are supposed to be monks who have soured on the church. They're not supposed to be warriors. That would make them suspect, but this group is … how shall I say it? … more versatile. I will note that Rolf would be pleased to work with you as well as with me. He told me that after he visited you at St. Vaast."

"That I would very much value."

Voldred cleared his throat. He was participating more and more in conversations. "What does Duke William's message say?"

"He wants Cuin to make good on his promise to get Guy out of Brionne Castle. To end the siege."

Voldred raised his eyebrows at me. "You promised that?"

"I did."

"Since I have sworn an oath to aid you," Voldred said, "I will help you before I return North. I will guard you and help you fulfill your promise."

"Thank you. I do not feel that your oath is necessary, but I appreciate your help. Indeed, it's the best help I could hope for."

Garrad interrupted our exchange. "There's more. I need you to talk to Lanfranc about William's marriage. William is still in a rage about the Pope's threats of excommunication."

"I can do that."

"Good. And be sure to ask Lanfranc about this council of the Pope's and make sure William does nothing that will bar later reconciliation."

"Aren't you coming with us?"

He shook his head. "I'm still the healer here, you know. The fever has not been completely defeated. Autumn is only a week away. I have preparations, both for my herbs and for the winter."

"I'll be sorry not to have your company and Marie's," Voldred said, somewhat formally but warmly.

"Is there anything else you'd like us to do?" I intentionally included Voldred in the question.

"Yes. Get Guy out of Brionne Castle, if you really have some plan. If not, promise him anything. Tell him he can be Duke of something or King of France or Pope. Just get him out. The lords who have taken Rouen have avoided opposing William, but if Guy continues to resist, they will surely march against William."

Voldred and I decided to go first to Bec Abbey to see Lanfranc.

We rode along the same path that I had taken a few years earlier. I sat on the same fat pony, and the same Goliards rode as our escort.

With Voldred next to me, his knife in his belt, a new bow I had made for him slung over his shoulder, and a sword Garrad had given him hanging from his other shoulder, I scarcely needed the Goliards to protect me.

Indeed, they made a comical bodyguard, singing the same irreverent songs they had sung before.

They stayed well ahead of and behind us, though, so I had time to speak with Voldred privately.

Early in our journey, I said to him, "I hesitate to ask, but how did you come to Magnus' attention originally? Didn't he have his own soldiers?"

"I happened to be traveling in Denmark, taking time away from my farm, and I met some mercenaries at Hedeby. When they discovered that I was a Berserker, they said that I might be able to serve King Magnus, for whom they worked. In those days, I was still struggling with whether to be a farmer or a mercenary. My fighting skills were better than my farming skills."

"So you were looking for work?"

"Yes. And King Magnus offered significant rewards. Then came the oath, and I realized too late that I had been trapped. I sent messages to my neighbors, asking them to help my wife with the farm and headed south. Of course, I could not kill a boy, but I fell in with some assassins who'd been hired by Norman nobles to kill young William. Since I had no stomach for killing a child, and I told them that, they agreed to do it for me. For which I had to pay them, of course."

"That produced 'the miracle of the wine barrels' for me."

"Yes, as the villagers told me repeatedly these past weeks. I returned north, thinking the job was done and I was free of Magnus. Before I reached my family, though, King Magnus discovered that you and young William were still alive. Only Odin in his wisdom knows how he discovered that." He paused and looked at me. "Would you prefer that I not refer to the old gods?"

"You may say what you wish. I'm not so much of a Christian that I don't recognize the power of Odin. He managed to produce cider in Iceland."

Voldred smiled and continued, "Magnus was in a rage. Of course, he was just a boy himself, focused only on his fear of being killed and having his country destroyed. So I returned to the South. That was when I began to learn more Norman French. I had learned a little of the language on my first trip, but now I needed to master it. I found that in Falaise a lame boy was moving to and from the village, training in something secret. In the forest. From listening to the gossip in Falaise village, I learned your identity — enough to know that you were my victim. I assumed that your training in the forest must be of a particularly terrible kind, that you were being trained to be some fearsome, evil warrior. Indeed, the rumor was that your mentor was a former warrior so fierce that even Berserkers admired him. So I determined to end your life quickly."

"You almost did. You now know, of course, what that training was. And you've met my teacher." I laughed. "I wish you could have seen me trying to handle weapons. The only people afraid were my teachers. They were afraid I'd accidentally kill myself. Or them. But you were already gone."

"Yes, Some villager sent me all over Normandy, hunting for you."

He became quiet for a moment. "It was during that time that Magnus sent messengers, informing me that my wife and children had been killed by Normans. I was in despair. Magnus insisted I stay in the South, so I dragged myself, almost unthinking, from one Norman monastery or cathedral to another."

I shook my head. "I'm sorry that Magnus and I cost you so much."

He stared at me. "We cost you no less."

"Odd as it may sound, I was only the victim. I did not have to wrestle with that terrible oath and the terrible deed associated with it."

He was quiet again and then sighed. "The strange turn is that I found the Norman teachers and monks consoling. I used my family's death as the reason for my being there, and they tried to help me. And learning Norman French and Latin kept my mind occupied. By the time I arrived in Avranches, where Lanfranc was teaching, I knew both languages fairly well. I was still grieving, but I found Lanfranc helpful. He wasn't as serious as the monks."

"He seems at first glance something of a fool, I'd say."

A smile slowly appeared. "At first I thought he was mad, but he made me laugh several times. Then I saw you."

"You attacked us that night."

"Yes, as you've told me. You may be surprised to learn that I only overheard your discussing King Magnus, and what was said — I forget it now — threw me into a Berserker rage, and I attacked. I didn't realize who you were until you were leaving. Lanfranc had asked me to get some supplies for his friends who were returning to Falaise. When I asked whether the supplies were to be put on horses, he said no, that one of you had a limp, and that in spite of that, you had walked all the way from Falaise. I tried to follow you but lost you in the forest."

"Garrad heard you and hid us behind a small rise."

"Ah, that's what happened. Well, after that, I thought I might never find you. I was tired and wanted to see the North again."

"Is that when you met Hervor?"

"Yes. I'd trained with her earlier, but only briefly — before Magnus had me take the vow. That's how I began to learn about oaths and rituals. So I headed north to study further with her, hoping for some way to free myself. Then Magnus sent for me and ordered me back to Normandy." He groaned and shook his head. "I dreaded the mission. By the time I reached here, I was angry, furious that my life had been reduced to this one task."

"You did seem that way to those who met you. There was a farmer near Arras …"

"I recall that. I stopped to get a goat from him. I'd found a local group worshipping the elder religion, and I wanted help from the oldest gods." He shook his head. "I was unkind to the farmer and felt bad about it afterwards. I owe him a goat."

"I met the farmer. He thought you were the only monk he'd ever met that came from the devil!"

"So he might. I threatened him with the knife. You know what happened after that. I was wounded during my attack on you by the mysterious rider you've now identified as Earl Tostig of Wessex."

"I saw that he gave you a serious wound."

"It kept me nearly immobile for a year,. The healers of the elder religion nursed me, but I wasn't completely recovered until the following spring."

"When I was traveling to Hedeby."

"Yes. I discovered from one of the St. Vaast monks, a cheerful infirmarian who lacked all caution, that you had recovered and headed north. By that time, though, I was beginning to accept what the Falaise villagers had said — that you were protected by God. So I returned to Magnus, begging release again. He refused and tricked me into a second oath, nearly the same as the first, so I fled north again, hoping to get some relief from Hervor. I found King Harald's two men, who I now know were Ulf and Vandrad. They said they were following someone headed for Iceland. I joined them."

"If you'd have remained in Vineland, Hervor and I would have tried to release you from your vow. Could we have succeeded?"

"I don't know. I don't think so. I was so wary of vows and their power that I probably would have seen your efforts as another trap."

"Why did you return to the South?"

"Word arrived in Vineland that Magnus wanted to see me. I thought that he wanted to upbraid me for failing in my mission. So I went South again without seeing him."

"If you'd only seen him, you'd have discovered that he wanted to release you from the oaths."

He sighed deeply. "That would have changed many things. I heard about his death when I passed through Hedeby again, where I found King Harald's two men, Ulf and Vandrad. They were hiding. They said some demons had flung them off the end of the earth and that they had escaped only with the help of God. Of course, I believed them when they said that you had killed King Magnus."

"The People, Onyame, and I were the demons who threw them off the edge of the world, which in reality was a small, gradual waterfall leading to a foggy bay, the fog being the work of Hervor. If Ulf and Vandrad had turned back, they would have found sand and us. Instead, they set out to sea."

He smiled. "That must have been amusing to Onyame. He enjoys that sort of adventure. They were terrified, though. I was certain that they'd never sail again. They said they would never leave Hedeby as long as they lived. It was as close to the sea as they needed to be."

I paused. "How did you end up in England?"

"When I returned to Falaise, I pressed the villagers, who had long forgotten who I was, about your birth. Eventually, I got most of the story. Then I journeyed to England to discover where Canute had hidden your mother. He had hidden her in some monastery to keep the story of her Norman attachment from getting out."

"No one in England knew about me, though."

"King Edward did, and he thought he was telling a friend who knew your secret. So I rode to the monastery near Chester, where I had doubly good fortune. I learned more about your birth. I met a nun named Edyth, who had known you in Arras. She described enough about you to enable me to find you. With King Edward's complicity, though, you slipped away again — one last time."

"You said you'd seen the fourth knife in England. Does Edward have it?"

"I'm sorry to say that he doesn't. If he did, our work would be easier."

"What do you mean? Who has the knife?"

"King Edward wants the North and South to unite peacefully. He told me so himself. He was, in fact, the first person to insist that you were an emissary and not a warrior. That's why I believed you later in Falaise. No, the man who has the knife doesn't want peaceful unity, as far as I can see. He wants to rule both the North and the South. And he is formidable."

"Who is he?"

"Harold, son of Earl Godwin, Edward's arch-enemy."

We met Lanfranc in his newly built but rough quarters. He listened closely as I told him about Voldred's oath and our reconciliation, and he even made a jest about the conversion of the Berserker North.

When we finished, though, he leaned toward us, his face serious.

"I know that for you, Cuin, the Prophecy of the Four Crowns means friendly relations between Normandy and the Northern kingdoms. And your friendship with Voldred is a good omen for that. However, the consanguinity issue represents a major threat to Normandy. If William marries Matilda and the Pope excommunicates them, Normandy becomes fair game for any ambitious ruler in the North or the South."

"Would the Pope go so far?"

"I'm sure he will. It's his best weapon … after the Emperor's armies, of course."

"Is excommunication such a terrible threat for a ruler such as Duke William?" Voldred asked.

"No Christian king will openly ally himself to an excommunicate," Lanfranc replied, "nor will any enterprise of William's be blessed by the Church. On the contrary, anyone who invades Normandy and overthrows the Duke will have papal blessing."

Voldred shook his head. "Would that Odin had such power over Kings."

"I have a plan," Lanfranc said. "I've been summoned to the Pope's council at Rheims, and I leave tomorrow. Though I have no doubt that the marriage will be forbidden, I can speak with some bishops. I'm not without friends. We may be able to delay the excommunication threat until efforts have been made to dissuade William and Matilda."

"We don't want to dissuade them," I said.

"Of course not, but the Pope doesn't know that. We must be seen to agree with him at first and work on reconciliation later. Otherwise, there's no hope of avoiding William's excommunication."

"So, for this to work," I said, "you must agree publicly with the Pope on consanguinity, risking William's wrath. Because William will discover your position. You're not an average prior in some shabby monastery, although the building skills here remain uneven."

"Even I have heard of the brilliant prior who teaches at Bec," Voldred said.

Lanfranc nodded his gratitude for the praise. "So I will avoid our good Duke until the matter is resolved."

"Then you will have our prayers while you're at the council," I said, "because you will need them both there and when you return."

CHAPTER 26

GIDEON'S ARMY

A. D. 1049

Though Lanfranc left the next day, I stayed at Bec to help fight a fever, which claimed, among those who were in bed for a week or more, Voldred. By the time my work was done and Voldred was fit to ride again, almost two weeks had passed.

When we arrived in Brionne two days later, we found William in a fury. He was at the siege camp, pacing in his tent.

After he recovered from Voldred's presence, which seemed to fascinate him, he began raging about the Pope and Guy and the rebellious barons.

Our queries about Matilda and his positive responses calmed him only temporarily. "Between the Pope and Guy, I may never get to marry her!" he shouted to no one in particular.

"You knew that the Pope was opposed —" I began.

"I never believed he'd condemn the marriage formally, but he's done just that. At a council in Rheims. An ecclesiastical council!"

"Did he threaten excommunication?"

"Isn't that what's implied?"

"The lack of a stated threat may give us some time."

He ignored me.

"What will you do, Duke William?" Voldred asked.

William sat in a chair, and we followed suit.

"I've already held my own council," he said, "here in Brionne."

"On what?" I asked. "You didn't get the clerics here to discuss your marriage, did you? That would offend the Pope, and Garrad said —"

"I'd be willing to do more than offend the Pope!" He jumped up and began pacing again. "No, I'm no fool. We discussed transubstantiation."

"Was Lanfranc there?" I asked.

"Yes, but I didn't talk much to him. He was silent on the issue of consanguinity. In fact, everyone said that he'd argued the transubstantiation debate brilliantly, but he kept quiet about consanguinity. I expected more."

"Garrad said Lanfranc would be cautious. He can't help you with the Pope if he's branded as an opponent to papal councils. He said so himself."

"That's true. Caution is his best tactic then." He paced more vigorously. "I still would have appreciated some sign from him about his loyalty. Bec Abbey does remain under Guy's rule as long as he holds Brionne Castle. So, formally, Lanfranc is his man."

"William —" I began.

He spun toward me. "You said you could get him out of the castle. I need you to do that. As soon as possible."

I had a plan, but I wondered whether he was just speaking from anger or some other urgency. "You've besieged Guy here for a long time. Why must I get him out now?"

"You know that King Henry no longer looks with a protective eye upon Normandy."

"I'd heard that he might withdraw support from you."

"Henry is worried that I'm too powerful and might threaten him in the future. He's looking for some weakness or some … event that might allow him to march into Normandy and once here, take it over, take it away from me."

"And Guy?"

"I have recent information that Guy's supporters in Rouen will hold the city against me until I abandon the siege — to force me to abandon the siege. If I lost both Brionne Castle and Rouen, Henry would have his reason to enter Normandy again. He would use the division between Upper and Lower Normandy to his advantage. This is what invaders always do, divide to make conquest easier. I have no doubt that Henry would do the same."

"I see."

"Cuin, I need Guy out of that castle. I've had the siege in place for almost three years. I've even led minor campaigns against the surrounding territory, hoping that would bring him out."

I shook my head. "He controls the region, but he has no loyalty to it, nor would he protect it. So threatening it will have no effect on him. He's so terrified of you that nothing but your absence will make him leave the castle."

He stared at me. "I need a resolution."

"I think that I can get him out. Before that, though, I need to free Rouen, and I can do so within two days. Then half of your concern would disappear, and Guy would know that he cannot depend upon the nobles who took Rouen."

"Can you do that? It may be dangerous."

"I have a plan. And my own Berserker bodyguard."

That night, I slipped outside of the camp and into the forest. I left Voldred sleeping in the tent William had prepared for us.

I summoned the dragon and called for a vision of Hervor. I found her inside her home, preparing for sleep. She recognized me immediately.

"What do you want, you Norman scoundrel? I'm preparing to sleep here … Odin's beard! Who's that with you? Do you have Voldred there?"

"How did you see him? He's not here with me."

"Dear, dear, teaching you is always hard work. I can see him next to you whether he's there physically or not. I do not need to see him physically, and your vision power does not require his presence. What has transpired there? Why is he with you?"

I explained briefly what had happened. At the end, she said, "Well done. Now why are you invading my sleep?"

"I need a favor, but I'm not sure whether you are willing to grant it or even can."

I saw her frown, which she always did when someone challenged her abilities. "What do you want me to do?"

"I would like a dense fog around Rouen tomorrow night. Is that possible?"

"Of course, it's possible. What do you want it for? Oh, I see — to win it back for your Duke. All right. All right. For him, I will do it. He's a ruler with an unusual future."

"Thank you. I'm very grateful. When will I see you again —?"

"I have to sleep now. You'll see me soon enough. Fare well there."

And she was gone.

Getting into Rouen was not easy, even though merchants and local inhabitants came and went in large numbers.

The rebel barons had stationed guards everywhere, at every gate, near every store, at every inn, listening to conversations, asking people where they had come from and what their business was, all the while demanding some show of loyalty to Guy of Burgundy and the "true Norman lords."

Voldred and I outfitted ourselves in monks' robes, noting with amusement how much of our lives we had spent as monks, and claimed to be passing through the city on the way to the abbey of St. Wandrille, ignorant of the events of the recent past.

I recalled the madman's vision from when I was a boy. He had said that I would save Rouen, and when I shared his vision, I had heard the name Gideon from the Old Testament.

Gideon was the seed of my plan.

As Voldred and I talked with merchants, I whispered to them, "Have you heard that Duke William plans to attack Rouen? With a massive force that he's collected from the North, Viking warriors, Berserkers, and slaughter all those who remain loyal to the rebel barons."

We were met each time with wide eyes, open mouths, and most importantly, credulity. The news would be all over Rouen within the day.

Then we made our way silently, almost invisibly, to the outer courtyard.

I drew Voldred aside. "You heard me talking to Duke William about a plan I have."

He nodded.

"If all goes well," I continued, "we will have these soldiers out of Rouen by tomorrow."

He produced a rare smile. "The two of us?"

"Yes, though perhaps we'll need some of William's army to deal with stragglers."

"I am eager to hear this plan."

"It's taken from the Christian Bible, and it may help us greatly. If you would be willing, may I direct you?"

"I don't know what in the Christian writings would help us here, but I'm willing, especially if you show me how two men can empty an entire city."

I smiled at him. "First, all you must do is take off your monk's habit and stroll around the camp. Then return here. Be sure to bump into soldiers, though. If they become hostile, ignore them and move on quickly. Will you do that and meet me back here? I'll return myself as soon as I can."

"I'll do as you ask and then wait for you here."

He strode away, and I pressed into the center of the tents and found any soldiers who seemed to be posted at guard duty.

I drifted close to each one and said, "I've just returned from the town. Have you heard about Duke William's attack?" When the guard said no, I said, "He's commanding an army of Northern Berserkers and intends to attack the castle at any moment. I've even seen some Berserkers in the town, perhaps spying. A merchant told me there were some here in the castle itself. They're brash, you know, and fearless. Like animals. They become animals when they fight. And they can kill ten men at a blow."

I moved to the next guard. I repeated my story and added, "Many are disguised as Western Normans."

His eyes opened wide. "Treachery as well as assault?"

"That Duke William can be a devil," I said.

After I had spread rumors among thirty of the guards, I returned to the town's center to purchase clay pots and knives.

Then I returned to the meeting-place. Voldred already waited there, hidden in a shadow. He had put his monk's robe on again.

"Did you have any trouble?" I asked.

"None at all. What shall we do now?"

"Wait for dark and a fog."

The fog, a heavy one, began to descend on the city just after dark. When I was sure that most guards in the camp and city were asleep, Voldred and I wrapped our blue-gray cloaks around us.

We crept to a corner where two of the city's walls met. I directed him to a darkened place close to one wall with his share of the clay pots and knives. I moved not far away, in range of the other wall.

I called out softly. "It's time."

We hurled the clay pots into the air as fast as we could, screaming, "The Vikings! Berserkers! They're upon us!" The pots shattered against storefronts and street stones.

We flung the knives at the castle walls, still shrieking as the knives clattered against the stone — and found anything we could on the streets and hurled it where it would make the most noise as we raced around the town.

Then we dashed through the courtyard gate. We could already see the soldiers springing from their tents. As the dense fog obscured their vision, they waved their weapons and began to slash at each other.

We ran toward a nearby hiding place in the forest and slipped behind a tree.

As we ran, I said, panting, "The story of Gideon in our Old Testament. This is what he did to take a city."

"I should have studied the Christian writings more closely."

We reached the trees and slipped behind a large one.

I leaned around the tree. I could see light flickering through the fog as if from out-of-control fires, and I could hear cries of soldiers, accompanied by the clang of swords and the shrieks of townspeople.

As the sounds grew louder, I heard Voldred begin to breathe heavily. Then more heavily. Then more.

Apparently, the fighting stirred something in him. His breathing became harsh. Suddenly, he drew his breath in sharply and let out a Berserker cry. It seemed to shatter the air around me. And was met by even louder cries of fear in the town.

The cry hit my ears and spine, and my body jerked and shuddered.

I took a deep breath and turned to look at him over my shoulder. "Do you have to do that?"

For a moment, he stared at me, stunned.

Then he began to laugh — a deep laugh, first soft and then louder and harder until he had to sit down.

He kept laughing for a long time, sometimes sounding almost as if he was crying, and then he was laughing again.

Eventually he said, "No."

The next day, as I was returning from a scouting mission in a now unmanned Rouen, William and Voldred waited for me with the siege-camp guard. Standing in front of the soldiers, the two of them looked like two huge oaks standing before a forest.

William swept me past the soldiers, while Voldred, displaying more enthusiasm than I had ever seen, excluding his attacks on me, thumped me on the back.

"It worked," Voldred said.

William grinned at me. "Most of the soldiers whom the rebel lords had called to service have been recalled."

"Yes," I said, "I found almost no fighters in Rouen."

"Returned to their homes," William said.

"Apparently," Voldred said, smiling, "Berserker warriors entered the castle unheeded, like wild animals stealing into a camp in the night, wounded many of the soldiers, even killed a few and then fled, without anyone seeing them go."

"I'm sorry some men were killed." I said. "I didn't think —"

William grabbed my shoulders. "Cuin! It was a success. The strategy worked. I can ride into Rouen whenever I wish."

Voldred's face became serious. "A warrior becomes accustomed to men dying," he said to me.

"I'm not a warrior."

"I would have lost more men," William said, "if I had stormed the city, and so would the rebel lords, far more than killed each other in the confusion you created."

"That's true," Voldred said.

"There were a few deaths," William said, "but the retaking of Rouen, thanks to you — and Gideon — was easy."

Getting Guy out of Brionne castle proved more difficult.

I managed to get close enough to the castle to shout my propositions to Guy's men, but no reply came to my entreaties. I tried promises of leniency, even rewards. I resorted to threats, but those also produced nothing.

"It's no surprise," Voldred said. "You threaten like an child. If you wish, I can teach you how to threaten."

We stamped in the cold, trying to find places to stand where the mud would not invade our shoes.

"I never believed that threats would work," I said. "I have a better idea."

The siege-tower guards, standing nearby, called to us. "It's the Duke!"

"Well?" William demanded, as he strode up to us, his breath frosting in the air as he panted from his ride. "Has he agreed to move? You've been at this all day."

I took a breath, and the chilled air hurt my lungs. "No. He won't listen. Or if he is listening, he won't reply. Of course, I didn't expect him to."

"Would it help if you could talk to him face to face?" Voldred asked.

"I'd like to do that myself," William said.

"So would I," I added. "Have you tried tunneling under the castle?"

William scowled at me. "That's a river, not a moat."

Voldred glanced at the river and then at us. "Does it freeze in the winter?"

"No, it's too deep and rapid," William said.

"If it were to freeze," Voldred asked, "would there be a way you could get inside? Is there some entrance we could use?"

"Yes," I said, "and I have been pondering that possibility." I looked at William. "Can you divert the river upstream, so that it is more placid here?"

"A frozen lake would support two men on bone skates," Voldred added, "if you know how to enter the castle once we get there."

"I know how to get into the castle," I said. "Edward showed me secret passages when I was a boy. And William and I found more when we played there."

William was watching both of us. "My men are doing nothing here. If they go upstream and dig canals away from the river, divert most of the water around the castle and bring it back in below the castle ... "

I continued his thought, " The result would be that the castle would have a lake around it."

"A lake," Voldred added, "getting shallower the more Guy and his men drink from it. A lake that would freeze quickly in this weather."

Voldred and I joined in the digging of the canals. Over the next week, we scraped at the ground with freezing hands and muddied shoes and leggings. We hauled stones and mud to the river's edge and began dumping them into the icy water. In the end, it took us nearly a month to create the canals and dam the river, but not two days after we finished, we had hard freezes.

Within a few days, we had a cloud-darkened night, and the assault began.

Voldred and I put on our robes, grayed with dust created from the dried mud that had clung to us for weeks, and armed ourselves with our knives, bows, and the two pairs of bone skates he had made. We crept to the edge of the ice.

From my first attempt, I realized that I had little talent for skating. Voldred almost laughed out loud at my first steps onto the ice. I frowned at him, and he took my arm.

With his help, I half-slid, half-stumbled across the lake until we reached the darkest part of the wall, just inside one of the corner towers.

Crouching, we crept toward one of the secret entrances. I hoped it was still there and unguarded.

It was there, but it was not unguarded. A lone soldier stood in the shadows, wrapped in furs and flapping his arms around himself. He did not notice us, but the last thing he would have expected were two attackers on skates.

Voldred began to creep forward.

"Don't kill him," I whispered.

At that, the guard spun toward us, and Voldred leaped on him. Almost instantly, the man fell limply onto the frozen ground.

"We'd better drag him inside," Voldred said. "If we leave him here, he'll freeze to death, and then there would have been little point in not killing him."

Voldred slung the man over his shoulder, and I found the door stone and pushed it. It yielded, swinging aside and showing a narrow opening.

We slipped inside, and Voldred placed the guard quietly on the ground. He pointed toward the end of the passageway just above us, and I understood that he wanted to scout for more guards.

I began tying and gagging the unconscious guard with strips from his own clothing when Voldred returned with two more, one over each shoulder.

"There aren't any more," he whispered.

I began tearing strips from their tunics. "Good. I don't want this tying to become an all-night task."

When the guards were secure, we crawled toward the entrance, and Voldred pushed it open, looking cautiously around the doorway. He motioned me forward, and I followed him through it.

Assuming that Guy would be sleeping off the great hall just above us, I led Voldred to the winding steps that led from the ground level to the great hall. The stone floor felt as icy as the river, and I shivered as we walked.

Men and even women snored on the benches along each side of the hall, and a crowd of children slept before a fire, now fading to embers. The fire-keeper himself had fallen asleep. The chilled room still smelled of ale, herbs, and people who had bathed too seldom, and I grimaced through my shivering.

I spotted two guards dozing at the far end of the hall in front of the bedchamber usually reserved for the lord and his lady. I pointed toward it and then into the air.

We slipped just inside the hall and mounted one of the massive beams that led up to the wooden framework supporting the roof. We climbed into the framework and crawled along it, crouching under our robes whenever it creaked loudly.

No one stirred. Invaders were not expected.

Before long we were pushing through the passageway leading to the lord's bedchamber.

Guy's bed was covered with heavy woolen blankets, draped over the heavy-beamed frame that supported a canopy. A sputtering fire in the fireplace dimly revealed the patterns on the blankets, matching the wall-hangings that prevented the cold air from seeping too easily through the walls.

The windows that looked onto the castle yard below had been shuttered, but the chill air forced through them anywhere a crack remained untarred.

Voldred bolted the door and then lifted several logs onto the fire.

I fitted an arrow to my bow and pulled back the blanket closest to the fire.

Guy lay there alone, and I was relieved. Any lady he might have shared the bed with had apparently decided to spend the night in the women's chamber at the opposite end of the hall.

I nodded to Voldred. He rose and pulling back the blanket on the opposite side of the bed, positioned himself next to Guy. In one move, he put one hand across Guy's body, another at his mouth.

I pulled my bow taut and aimed the arrow at Guy's widened eyes. "If you remain completely silent, we'll have a pleasant conversation. Your door is bolted and your guards are asleep."

"If you cry out," Voldred added, "we'll kill you and escape through the secret passage near here."

"We'd rather talk, though," I said, "and we won't harm you if you're willing to discuss ending the siege."

He nodded. Voldred released him and he sat up, pulling his blankets around him. As he did, Voldred jerked the blankets away, revealing a sword and knife. Guy did not move, and Voldred lifted them out of the bed.

"Come sit by the fire," I said, my bow still trained on him. "It will be warmer."

He nodded and pulled a woolen blanket off the bed to wrap around him. He looked smaller than I remembered him.

He settled into a chair next to Voldred, who now sat near the fire, his knife pointed in Guy's direction. I remained standing, relaxing my arrow but keeping it on the bowstring.

"How did you get in here?"

"Perhaps you don't remember me. I'm Cuin. From Falaise. A friend of Duke William's. We played here as children, and I'm familiar with all the passageways."

His face pulled into a sneer. "I remember you. The village bastard, weren't you?"

Voldred raised his knife. "I call it unwise to insult a man who holds a bow on you. And he is considerably more than the village bastard."

"The point of our visit," I said, "is to end the siege. You know that you can't stay here forever, but you also know that William will."

Guy snorted. "The barons loyal to me hold Rouen, and they will soon —"

I cut him off. "The barons have fled Rouen, their armies having returned to their homes under the threat of Duke William's attack. The ducal ranks, however, have been swelled by Northern warriors."

"I don't believe you."

"It's difficult to get current reports inside a besieged castle," Voldred said, "but I'm not a Norman, as you can tell. I'm a Berserker, and I'm here in the service of Duke William. If you wish more proof, I can take you to the tower and show you the tents of my countrymen. However, they would probably shoot you from the banks of the river. They're frustrated by inactivity. So perhaps that's not a good strategy for you."

"The rebellion has collapsed," I said, "and Duke William is so much at his leisure that he's planning his wedding. Your head would be a nice wedding present, and I'm sure we'd be richly rewarded for presenting it."

Guy glanced at both of us.

Voldred looked at his knife reflectively and muttered to himself about "cutting off a head as good use of a blade."

"If the truth be told," I said, "I'd rather have your hand in an agreement than your head. First, a severed head bleeds a great deal, and I'm uneasy around blood. Second, Duke William will reward me more for your living body. Believe it or not, he wants to show you mercy. He'll exile you, of course."

"I'd rather have his head," Voldred said.

Guy shrank away from Voldred and spoke almost desperately to me. "William doesn't want to kill me? How can I believe that?"

"You should know William's character well enough to know that he does not want you dead. He'll tell you that himself, if you give him the opportunity."

"When? Is he here?"

"No, but we can escort you to him this very night, and he will assure you."

"He will kill me!"

"If you don't come with us," Voldred said, with appropriate menace, "I will kill you. You have a better chance with Duke William."

"All we want," I said, "is your word that you will order your men to end the siege. We'll take you to the Duke for all the assurances you may wish. You have my word that you will be unharmed."

"Will you swear on that cross you're wearing?"

"Yes. You will be unharmed during your meeting with William. Then you may return here to pack for your journey ... south, perhaps?"

He thought for a time, keeping his haughty look. Then his shoulders fell, and his body's rigidity seemed to collapse. "All right. I will accompany you, and I will order my men to leave the castle. You have my word."

"And you have ours," I said. "Shall we dress for an evening's walk?"

At the Christmas feast in Brionne, William held court long enough to pardon everyone inside the castle, except Guy, whom he ordered into exile.

Then he ordered the dam and the siege towers dismantled and the army to group itself for a march at the beginning of the new year.

A month later, Voldred and I followed the army into Rouen.

A. D. 1050

Among William's first official acts back in Rouen Castle was to recognize my marriage to a foreign woman. After I refused titles and estates, he granted me land near Garrad's hut, exactly where I had already built my own hut, with Voldred's help.

Later that week, the three of us, William, Voldred and I, sat in the great hall, warming ourselves by a large fire.

"You and your wife may use the land whenever you're on this side of the sea," William said. "That is the least you deserve."

I thanked him, but he waved my thanks aside.

"By the way," he added, "I've put that friend of yours, Lanfranc, to work in Rome."

"I'm not sure what you mean."

"Well, I'd ordered him out of the country for failing to help me with Pope Leo."

"You did what —?"

He held up his hand. "I was angry that he seemed to side with the Pope about my marriage, so I ordered him to leave Normandy. The day after he received the order, I happened to be riding — with some purpose, I confess — just on the outskirts of Bec. There I saw Prior Lanfranc riding a lame horse toward the border. I told him loudly that he had been ordered out of the country a day earlier and asked why he was not yet gone. Do you know what he said to me?"

I was too disturbed to reply.

William grinned. "He said to me, 'Well, my lord Duke, if you had ordered a healthy horse for me along with your order me to leave, I would be gone by now and not struggling toward your border on this lame one.' A healthy horse! I laughed so hard I almost fell off my own horse. A man with that character needs to be working for me! So I told him he was indeed ordered to leave Normandy but only to go to Rome to plead my case. When he finished with that, he was welcome back in Normandy as my legal and ecclesiastical advisor."

William then turned to Voldred, who apparently enjoyed the story more than I did. "I would employ Northerners, too, if I had them. Would you be willing to journey north to gather a group of Berserker warriors for me? To serve as guards whenever I have need of them?"

"I long to see the North," Voldred said. "I have regained my honor, and I can now face my family." He thought for a moment. "Yes, I know many Berserkers who would be honored to be in your service."

William nodded. "Good. Then I shall see that you're well supplied for a journey north."

CHAPTER 27

A MARRIAGE

A. D. 1051

Ringed by Garrad, Marie, me, and Young Moons — who had returned with me to Normandy after my trip back to the People's Land — Voldred warmed himself in front of a fire in Garrad and Marie's hut, recounting his trip north, almost animatedly.

He had reconnected with his wife and daughters and had spent much of the year establishing himself as a successful farmer, "most of which I owe to the skills of my wife."

He had also found Berserkers who were being treated like common brigands and so were delighted to have an opportunity to serve Duke William, whose name was becoming known in the North. Some had accompanied him back to Normandy, wishing to enter William's service as soon as possible.

"We came south just ahead of an army led by King Harald of Norway," he concluded.

"Had you seen Hardraada before that?" I asked.

"Yes, I had spoken with him about the death of King Magnus, and he confirmed everything you told me. As I expected. He also told me of his intention to attack King Sweyn of Denmark again, as he has done every summer. He was aiming for Hedeby, so I went there first. I found his two men, Ulf and Vandrad, still hiding from him. I suggested that they flee south, where they might be of use to some other lord."

"Did you suggest any particular lord?" Garrad asked.

"Count Baldwin of Flanders is the wealthiest and most powerful lord in that area," I said.

Voldred smiled. "I recommended Count Baldwin, and they seemed interested."

"Did Hardraada attack Hedeby?" I asked. "Did the town resist? Was Sweyn there?"

"King Sweyn was not there, no. Fortunately. As we watched from a distance, Hedeby burned to the ground. Only the men, women, and children who had earlier thrown themselves on Hardraada's mercy survived."

"I'm sorry to hear that," Garrad said. "Hedeby was a fine town."

"I'm sorry, too," I said. I paused and then asked, "What of Ulf and Vandrad?"

"I don't know whether they escaped or not," Voldred said.

I shook my head. "They caused me great trouble, but I would not wish them harm."

"Did you hear anything more of King Sweyn?" Garrad asked.

"Only that he's determined to keep fighting King Harald — Hardraada — until Hardraada stops raiding Denmark."

"I hope Sweyn succeeds," I said, "and I believe from Magnus's deathbed vision that he will."

"I also have word from Duke William," Voldred said.

"You went to Rouen before coming here?" I asked, grinning at him. "What kind of loyalty is that?"

He smiled. "First, our Duke is determined to marry this year, and Lady Matilda is more determined. So, the wedding will be held this summer or autumn, as soon as King Edward vanquishes Earl Godwin of Wessex."

"Vanquishes?" I said. "Is Edward in open conflict with Godwin?"

"Yes, since some cleric in England died late last year. An important one. Duke William told us about it."

"That will be the Archbishop of Canterbury," Garrad said. "You may or may not know, Voldred, that Canterbury's Archbishop is the most important church official in England, perhaps even in the entire North."

"Well," Voldred continued, "he died. Godwin wanted to put his own man in, but Edward is determined that the Bishop of London should have the office."

"The present Bishop of London is Robert of Jumieges," Garrad said. "He's a Norman who risked his life to cross the Channel with Edward originally, when Edward first returned to England. Robert wouldn't be a choice that Godwin and his sons would like."

"King Edward also intends to accuse both his mother and Earl Godwin of the murder of his brother," Voldred said, "which will give him the grounds, as Duke William put it, to call Godwin to task for the way he's dominated England since King Canute died."

"Edward doesn't have to worry about any other threat just now," I said. "Even though Tostig has recently married Judith, Count Baldwin's half-sister — he was courting her back when I was recovering in St. Vaast, as you may recall — that does not ally Baldwin with Godwin against Edward. Quite the opposite: Tostig and King Edward like each other, and Tostig sees himself as an under-appreciated younger brother in Godwin's family."

"Yes," Voldred said, "King Edward knows that Count Baldwin won't attack him and that he's safe from any Northern attack, thanks to Cuin, so he feels free to move against Godwin in England."

"If Edward can free himself from Godwin's domination," Garrad said, "he'll know a security in his reign that has for the present eluded him."

I nodded at him. "I agree, and that's a boon for us. As you've always said, Edward's security is Normandy's security."

For a time, as Rolf and his Goliard spies later told us, Edward's security seemed assured. In March, he announced that Robert of Jumieges would become Archbishop of Canterbury.

Rolf recounted the events that followed.

"One of Robert's first act was to accuse Lady Emma, Edward's mother, of complicity in the death of her son, Alfred."

Garrad said, "As we know all too well, Edward has never forgiven his mother for Alfred's death."

Rolf nodded. "The Lady Emma replied by requesting the ordeal by hot iron."

Young Moons looked alarmed when I translated. "What is that?"

"In accordance with common-law custom," Rolf replied, "Lady Emma carried a red-hot iron bar in her hands for three paces and then had her hands bound with a cloth blessed by a priest."

Young Moons and I grimaced together.

"After three days," Rolf continued, "her hands showed no signs of burns. She was declared innocent."

Young Moons volunteered that applying certain herbs to the hands before the ordeal could help prevent burning, and I nodded at her, having thought the same.

Garrad breathed in sharply. "So, that leaves Godwin as the remaining accomplice in the death of Alfred."

"Yes," Rolf said, "and King Edward was determined to deal with him as well. Using an incident involving one of his kinsmen, the King exiled Godwin and his sons, including Edward's own wife, Godwin's daughter, whom he sent to a nunnery."

"What incident?" Garrad asked.

"Last month," Rolf replied, "King Edward's brother-in-law — you know him, Eustace, the Count of Boulogne — was returning from visiting the King in London and had an altercation with the people of Dover. It seems that Count Eustace wanted to quarter his men in the town, as he has a right to do. The Dover burgesses, however, refused."

"Dover," I said. "That's in Godwin's domain. Godwin himself may have ordered the burgesses to refuse."

"Perhaps," Rolf said, "but Godwin was celebrating the marriage of his son at the time and so appeared to have nothing to do with the refusal."

"That's right," I said. "Tostig's marriage to Judith would have happened last month."

"Yes. Well, Count Eustace wasn't happy about the reply of the burgesses. So his men began destroying parts of the town. Oddly, the burgesses had a town militia already summoned and armed, which is why I suspect Godwin's complicity, and seven of the Count's men were killed."

"The militia?" Marie asked.

"One killed. So, Count Eustace returned to King Edward with his story."

"Edward would be furious," Garrad said.

"He was. Since Dover is in Godwin's domain, as Cuin just reminded us, King Edward ordered Earl Godwin to punish the burgesses. Godwin refused, so the King called him to court for punishment. Earl Godwin and his sons appeared with an army instead."

Young Moons was alarmed again. "Did they fight?"

Rolf smiled. "No. The King was prepared. He had already summoned many leaders, including the Earls of northern England, to court."

"Why would the northern Earls aid Edward?" I asked. "Do they trust him?"

Garrad nodded at me. "What you may have forgotten is that the rise of Godwin's family in the south and midlands of England threatens the northern Earls. They've become jealous of Godwin's power."

"Yes, and that is how the King delivered his master-stroke," Rolf said. "He had also summoned all those who owed him service in the south, which included the knights serving under Godwin and his sons."

"Brilliant," Garrad said.

"So, Godwin had to flee to Flanders. He had no choice."

"A few elements of Edward's situation bother me," I said. "First, Edward is still treated as a foreigner by many of the Saxon lords. He doesn't yet have their full support. Second, he has Normans in powerful positions in England — Robert of Jumieges is one among many — and the Saxon lords cannot look kindly on that. Third, he just put his own wife, the Queen of England, in a nunnery. He cannot have an heir of his own body, as will now be apparent to all. So, every claimant to the throne can feel that he is now a step closer to it."

"Those are good points," Garrad said.

Rolf added, "King Edward has another looming threat. While most of Godwin's family went to Flanders, Harold, Godwin's most powerful son, fled to Ireland with several other Earls. What we hear is that he is angry about his treatment at Edward's hands. He plans to return in strength. One of my men heard him swear, after a certain volume of ale, that he would return England to Saxon rule and perhaps even to the old religion."

"Harold is not a threat to be taken lightly," Garrad said.

"I agree," Rolf said. "We should watch his movements carefully."

"That also means," Garrad said, "that if Godwin and Harold or either of them returns in force, Edward may be made to yield his crown to someone else. That would pose a threat to Normandy's security. If Earl Harold took the crown, he could draw on both his Saxon and Danish roots. I've heard that

Harold is ambitious. A new Saxon empire to rival Canute's old Danish one might please him. And threaten us."

"Could William be of any help to Edward?" I asked.

"Edward needs to consolidate his strength," Garrad said, "and any friends will help."

"I could visit Edward in England when Young Moons and I return to the People later this summer. I might encourage Edward to invite William to England before the year's end, something Edward himself mentioned to me when I last saw him. Even the presence of an ally may be useful."

"That's an excellent idea," Garrad said. "I may even push you to go earlier, and" — he glanced at Young Moons — "with my apologies to your wife, I'm hoping you will remain in Normandy through the winter. I think next year may be a dangerous one, and I do not want Edward to be left unattended or William to be without his best emissary."

When I translated for Young Moons, she replied, "The needs here are greater than our need to winter with our people."

So, within a few weeks, while summer was still in full bloom, Young Moons and I traveled to England, where Edward received us graciously.

Edward seemed happy, almost carefree, a mood that I had seldom seen on him. He talked freely about hunting and hawking, both of which he enjoyed but seemed to savor more now.

He also talked happily about giving the Godwin family earldoms to "more worthy lords."

I asked about how his nobles now felt, and he seemed confident that the Earls supported him in exiling Godwin's family.

I remained concerned about the northern lords. "I hear that that the north is less amenable to the 'Norman King,' as they insist on calling you."

"In spite of my Saxon father." He smiled. "You remain well-informed, I see."

"Many of us in Normandy follow your reign with interest, your majesty."

"Yes, the northern nobles remain a problem. In truth, I've never ventured farther north than Gloucester." He paused. "I would appreciate Duke William's advice on that. I admire how he has handled his neighbors."

I was relieved to hear this, and I smiled. "How he has managed to survive, perhaps?"

"Yes, and I would enjoy having him at the Christmas court. If you will mention this to him, I'll send a formal invitation later in the year."

"I will be happy to, your majesty, and I know he'll be delighted to see you again."

That summer, Edward did indeed send a formal invitation to William by way of the new Archbishop of Canterbury, Robert of Jumieges himself.

Archbishop Robert had to travel to Rome to receive the pallium — the official mantle that symbolized Robert's new ecclesiastical jurisdiction — from the Pope. On his way, he stopped in Rouen to invite William to the Christmas court at Westminster.

Garrad and I appreciated Edward's grand gesture in sending a high official to Normandy, as if he must have some serious message, even though we knew it was merely an invitation to the Christmas court.

Edward was allowing his Norman favorites to interact publicly, and he was letting the rest of the world know it.

We supposed that part of his intention was to alarm Godwin and his sons, making them believe that something important was happening behind their backs.

Garrad said, "It's as if Edward is poking the exiles with a stick."

"I agree," I said. "So, now we watch how Godwin's family responds to that stick."

It was the morning of Saint Luke's Day, a cool but pleasant autumn day.

Garrad's head appeared at one of my open windows. "Are you ready to receive visitors? No, I see. Are you always this messy?"

"Young Moons and I have been working on herbs for the winter," I began, indicating where she sat making infusions. "I don't have time for —"

"You and your wife will have to cease working then," he said, coming in through the door. "We need to plan for a wedding."

Young Moons stood and without waiting for the translation asked in Norman French, "Who is getting married?"

"William?" I asked hopefully.

He smiled. "Rolf and the Goliards have returned with accounts of events from both England and Rome. The Roman event is the relevant one: Lanfranc has convinced the Pope that Duke William will be an ally to Christianity, especially when it comes to winning Northerners away from the old war gods. There will be no official sanction of the wedding but no threat of excommunication, either. Lanfranc has also convinced William that the consanguinity issue can be settled in the future, especially if William and Matilda are willing to build the appropriate monasteries."

"So, the new bride and groom will be —" Young Moons began.

"Lady Matilda of Flanders and Duke William of Normandy."

Bundled into our brightest-colored cotton leggings, wool tunics, and robes, Garrad, Marie, Young Moons, and I rode from Falaise under a sunny but cool sky. Since we journeyed leisurely and stopped often, we took three full days to get to Bec.

We visited Lanfranc and congratulated him on his success in Rome. He was cheerful as usual and cheerfully modest about his role.

Abbot Herluin seemed unusually happy, and I wondered whether Lanfranc was affecting him. I asked Herluin if the lightheartedness of his Prior was undermining his usual reverence, and he appreciated the humor.

He also expressed his joy at the upcoming marriage and said he would offer prayers for the happiness of Duke William and Lady Matilda.

The next day, we rode hastily to Rouen in a cold rain, joining William's party there. William added a note of impatience to the pomp, so we left almost immediately for the northernmost corner of Normandy: Eu on the River Bresle.

As we approached the church the next day, we saw in the distance the old Norse castle built by Rolf, the first Duke of Normandy.

Rolf the Goliard winked at me and whispered, "You see, had I not developed into a great coward, I could have been a great warrior like my namesake." His gaze suddenly swung away from me, and his eyes widened. "Now there is a costume!"

The rest of the Norman party had arrived, led by William, almost aglow in a tunic sewn with crosses and fleurons of gold, the golden-threaded hem embroidered with many images from the Bible, embellished with golden clasps, enamels, cameos, and precious stones. Over it he had hung a red robe, draping down to his purple boots. His crowned helmet was decorated with three jewels and golden oak leaves.

Matilda appeared, as tiny and slender as ever, her cheeks flushed and looking all the more pink against her blond hair and her Flemish mantle of white wool and fur. Behind her walked her attendants, carrying gilded sprigs of rosemary.

She smiled at William. He stared at her.

Count Baldwin stood beside her, ready to join the Normans in the procession to the church.

William, though, did not move.

The other members of the party stood still, too. They seemed not to know how to respond. Nor would they engage with William.

Like most people, William's family and friends were in awe of him and knew to leave him alone when he was in a formal setting. So apparently, they were prepared to treat his immobility as a part of the ceremony.

I, however, knew William's movements. The man whom I had seen confront warriors and Archbishops, when faced with the tiny woman who was to be his wife, had frozen.

After pausing to be amused, I nudged Odo, William's half-brother, who nudged Robert, William's other half-brother, who nudged William. William recovered from his stupor and nodded to Matilda.

All of us then marched in procession to the church.

After the service, we rode in another celebrative procession, this one returning us to Rouen. William kept his black horse close to the white mule of his new wife.

Garrad, Marie, Young Moons, and I rode near the rear, where my pony felt the pace was right for him. Behind us rode William's Berserker guard, led on this occasion by Voldred.

After several days of celebrating at Rouen Castle, Voldred, Garrad, Marie, Young Moons, and I returned home with the Falaise villagers who had journeyed to Rouen to pay their respects to the Duke and his new wife.

As we rode, Garrad urged me to fall back some distance, which was no strain for my pony, so that we could talk. Voldred joined us.

Garrad began, "I want to talk with both of you about Godwin's son, Harold. I know that you, Voldred, have been following his movements since the exile of his family."

"He's still in Ireland?" I asked.

"Yes," Voldred replied, "and the Irish king is happy that Harold intends to raid England."

My mouth fell open. "Harold is going to raid his own country?"

"As early as this winter," Voldred said. "He's not only angry at King Edward for exiling him, but — "

"— he's also using the raids to make agreements with leaders in the north of England," Garrad said.

I looked back and forth at both of them. "Do you mean that he hopes to forge private alliances with the Danes who live in the north of the country?"

"It appears that way to the Berserkers that I sent to join him," Voldred said.

"Spy on him, you mean."

Voldred nodded.

"If Harold joins his family's forces with the Danes …" I paused. "Could he persuade other nobles to join him?"

"Just now, his star is not in the ascendant," Garrad replied, "but he is popular and likeable."

I shook my head. "If Harold allies his father and brothers with Danes in the north, that represents a force that could swamp Edward."

"Could he take the crown from Edward?" Voldred asked.

"Not without the agreement of the Council, but he might force their hand." I turned back to Garrad. "So we need some strategy that prevents Harold from allying the Danes in the north of England to the Danes in Denmark, where his cousin Sweyn rules."

Garrad smiled. "King Sweyn is also your half-brother, in case that had slipped your mind."

"I do recall that. And I appreciate your friendly reminder, but I'm trying to formulate a strategy that will prevent Harold's creating a new Danish

Empire, which would threaten us just as much as King Canute's did. Being Sweyn's half-brother will not help me." I frowned at him. "You seem to be less concerned about Edward than I am. Do you have some strategy in mind?"

Garrad smiled again. "Consider: how has your half-brother survived, even when he has no military skill and is pitted against a foe as formidable as Hardraada?"

I tilted my head and stared into the sky for a moment. "Sweyn became King because of divisions in the North, not because he won battles. So you are suggesting that we find a similar divisive strategy relative to Harold."

Garrad seemed pleased with this. "Can you construct one?"

"I need to strategize from the basic situation, and you two can help me with that."

Voldred almost laughed. "I shall enjoy being a party to any strategy that does not involve Berserker warfare, if only for the novelty of the exercise."

I nodded at him, appreciating the humor. "All right then. Let's examine what is happening now. First, though Edward controls England and has placed many Normans in powerful positions around him, the major threats to his control — and thus our safety here in Normandy — are Godwin and his sons, including Harold and Tostig. Edward already courts the favor of Tostig —"

"— who envies his brother, Harold," Garrad said.

"Cuin and I heard the same when we were in England," Voldred said.

I nodded. "So, if Edward continues to establish a friendship with Tostig, he is one son we need not worry about. Indeed, if Edward keeps Tostig close to him at court, then Tostig will remain estranged from those in his earldom. We cannot let Tostig have any real influence in England. If he does need allies, he must be forced to look outside the country."

"I don't understand why," Voldred said.

"My apologies for not being clearer," I replied. "From a diplomatic view, Harold and Tostig may be friendly brothers, but their personalities are opposites. So for our purposes, they are enemies. Tostig is rough, direct, unpolished, and sometimes slow-witted, even though well meaning. In any fight, whether diplomatic or military, he will respond to the most obvious threat, which can be presented to him by anyone he trusts."

Voldred continued to stare at me blankly.

"Tostig can be manipulated to believe that his interests are what his friends tell him they are," Garrad explained.

I nodded. "Harold, by contrast, is charming, brilliant, not easily fooled, and apparently brutal when he needs to be."

"How do you know that he is brutal?" Voldred asked.

"As we know, Harold is prepared to attack his own country to get back in power. He will use the same device that brutal commanders, including William, have used throughout history — raiding the countryside until the ruler responds to him. And he will use his intelligence and charisma to win alliances in the north of England, as we just discussed."

"So," Voldred said, "if Tostig has no real power in England, the differences of the two brothers work in our favor if any real conflict arises between the two of them."

"Yes," I said, amused that he had said "in our favor," identifying himself with Norman concerns. "Tostig's link to Flanders may be used to push him even further away from his brother, Harold. It is possible that he could be allied in the future to one of the Northern Kings, either Sweyn or Hardraada, against his own family."

Voldred nodded. "Diplomats think like war leaders, I see."

"War leaders think like diplomats," I said, smiling.

"That leaves Harold as our greatest threat," Garrad said.

I nodded my agreement. "Harold also gives us our best diplomatic strategy. In the long run, we must ally him to William."

The three of us fell silent, letting our horses take their heads and move us toward Falaise.

"For now,' Garrad said, "we need you two back in England."

"Why?" Voldred asked.

"Harold will attack from Ireland, while his father Godwin will attack from Flanders."

"Do you believe that Godwin will attack?" Voldred asked.

"He's been a major power in England for thirty years or more," Garrad replied. "He won't surrender that power easily. You two need to be with Edward to prepare him."

"It's true that Edward continues to ignore the threat," I said. "His elation at getting rid of Godwin's domination has blinded him to the consequences of exiling such a powerful family."

"I would feel as he does, were I King and finally given the opportunity to be King," Garrad said. "So you two must watch over Edward and be prepared to respond when Godwin's family retaliates. It could be dangerous. Indeed, I suspect that it will be."

CHAPTER 28

STATECRAFT

A. D. 1051

Voldred, Young Moons, and I returned to Edward's court, from which Voldred pushed north to spend the winter with his family.

We greeted William when he arrived for Christmas in England, surrounded by his half-brothers and several nobles. He had been careful to present the visit as festive rather than official. He even ensured that his conversations with Edward happened in social situations.

Edward continued to appear jubilant, glorying in his victory over Earl Godwin and his family, stripping the Earls of any power they might have had, while at the same time surrounding himself with Norman advisors.

I looked upon this with some concern, as I mentioned to William in a private talk in his chambers. "Earl Godwin and his sons will almost certainly return in force. And soon."

William nodded. "I have mentioned that to Edward. but he seems to ignore the possibility. Unlike you, he is neither perceptive nor a diplomat."

"Nor is he a foresighted military strategist such as you, and I return the compliment intentionally: can you mention a few defensive strategies to him?"

"I have mentioned that Earl Harold will probably attack from Ireland next spring."

"And Godwin will likely attack from Flanders. I don't see how Edward can defeat the family a second time. Godwin and Harold will be determined not to repeat the mistakes that led to their exile."

"Edward seems determined to ignore the threat, though, since nothing I say has had any effect on him."

"Then we must make plans of our own, must we not?"

"Yes." He stepped close to me and took my arm. "Cuin, I want you to stay close to events unfolding here. Even if Edward must allow Godwin's family to return, I want you to ensure that he does not lose the throne as well. Normandy cannot stand another threat now."

"I'll do all I can to assure that Edward remains King of England, even if his power must be diminished." I paused. "You do recall your mother's vision, do you not? She thought that you might be a ruler in England."

For a moment he looked startled. "What have you heard?"

"Nothing. Why?"

He walked to the hearth and back to me. "Just before I came to the Christmas court, two messengers found me in Rouen and told me that King Edward wanted to see me, particularly to talk about ruling in England after he's gone."

I raised my eyebrows. "Did Edward want to discuss that?"

"I don't think so, but the two messengers, after accompanying me to England, disappeared. When I approached Edward, he said that he hadn't sent any messengers, though he would not object to discussing England's future with me. He knows about my mother's dream, too."

"What did you say?"

"What do you suppose I said? No, of course. I'm just beginning to feel safe in my own skin."

"No assassin has found his way to you recently?"

"Not for many years, thank God, but Normandy isn't secure yet. There's much to do just to secure its borders. We've just resolved much of our internal strife, a large part of which came from your resourcefulness."

"Thank you. I agree about Normandy's security. Except for your father-in-law in Flanders, our neighbors do not sit easily on our borders."

"Without Baldwin and the fact that Flanders is so influential, and without the work you've done with Hardraada and Sweyn, I would be surrounded on all sides by … ambition."

"Who sent the two men, if Edward did not?"

"I would like to know that myself, but being unable to find them, I can't ask them."

"Could you describe them to me? I have an odd suspicion, but it may be nothing."

He thought for a moment. "One was tall with a brown beard and brown hair, a long face with narrow eyes and a pointed nose. The other was noticeably shorter, just about your size, black beard and hair and an odd scar that ran across his forehead."

I groaned. "I don't know how this can be, but the men you describe are the two who caused my troubles with the Northern kings. They're the ones who chased me around the world, trying to kill me. The names they gave me were Ulf and Vandrad."

"In whose service are they?"

"They were in Hardraada's, but his last intention regarding them was to have them executed."

"Apparently, he didn't realize that intention."

"I don't see why they would carry such a message from Hardraada, though. Hardraada likes Edward well enough to leave him alone and has enough trouble with his own nobles and with Sweyn."

William turned back to the fire. "Then who sent this message? And why?"

"We have to find Ulf and Vandrad."

He stared at me for a moment. "Will they have remained here in England to see what happens as a result of my thinking that Edward may promise his throne to me?"

"What else would be probable?"

"Hmm. So, they want to see how I respond. Or how Edward responds."

"Or how both of you respond. Which means that they'll be lurking in the shadows, as they did when Hardraada and Magnus met. And the shadows are where I can move easily."

I asked Edward for permission to roam the castle and quietly linger in the background of court sessions, which he granted.

The next day, I searched among the nobles and their attendants, but Ulf and Vandrad were not to be found. As I moved from chamber to chamber, hall to hall, I realized that they were likely to hide where no one would look for a royal emissary.

That evening, as dusk was settling, I took a small bow that I had made a few months earlier and hid it under my dusted blue-gray cloak. I made my way to the large hall set aside for the commoner staff of visiting nobles and clerics.

On my way, I noticed an unoccupied side room. If Ulf and Vandrad were in the common hall, I would have a private place to take them.

As I entered the common hall with its fraying tapestries and random piles of blankets, I saw that many servants had settled in for the cold night near one fire or another, while others remained busy, darting in and out of the room.

Fresh straw was on the floor, so the room smelled fairly good, a boon for my nose, especially if I had to be there much of the night. I slipped in unnoticed and stationed myself in a dark corner.

For some time, I saw no one that resembled Ulf or Vandrad, and I wondered whether they had left the castle.

As I was pondering that possibility, two figures entered the far end of the room, moving cautiously from one servant group to the next, as if searching for something. They wore plain brown cloaks with hoods, and their shoes were caked with mud. They had been outside the castle earlier in the evening.

As they approached the corner where I hid, they paused, looking around.

Then one hissed to the other, "Here's a place we can sleep. No one will know us."

The other nodded. "I think you're right."

Ulf and Vandrad.

I shook my cloak so that it would appear more blue than gray, stepped from the shadows, and in two large strides stood next to them, the hood of my cloak concealing my face.

"One of the King's servants would like a word with you two," I said, "about a place to sleep."

They looked startled, and Vandrad smiled. "That's good fortune then."

Ulf looked suspicious.

I continued, "The King's servants do not like to see anyone without a sleeping place. King Edward insists on this hospitality."

"That's gracious of the King," Vandrad said.

"Who are you?" Ulf asked.

"Just a messenger. If you would follow me, we shall find more comfortable accommodations for you."

I turned to go, and Vandrad followed me. Ulf hesitated, hanging back.

"Come on," Vandrad said. "What have we to fear from the King's servants? Besides, this one is offering us a place to sleep."

"I'm not sure …" Ulf began, but we were already out of the common hall.

I quickly stepped a few paces away, pulled my bow from under my robe, and strung an arrow in it before either of them could do anything but look alarmed.

"Now, gentlemen, you will accompany me to a side chamber just down this corridor. If you are quiet and agreeable, both of you will live."

They paused for a moment, so I pulled back on the arrow and aimed it at Ulf's head. "Now."

They moved quickly, and I directed them into the empty side room. Both of them put their backs against the far wall, getting as far away from the arrow point as possible.

Ulf repeated his earlier challenge, but now in a hushed tone, "Who are you?"

I shook the hood from my face and said, "You know me as Brother Augustine of Normandy."

Ulf groaned.

"It can't be," Vandrad said. "You cannot appear again! You've been the bane of our lives!"

"I've been a bane to you? You tried to kill me."

"Unsuccessfully," Vandrad said, "and King Harald nearly killed us for conspiring to kill King Magnus and letting you escape. Then we had to chase you to the end of the world."

"Which we nearly fell over," Ulf said. "Upon our return, King Magnus died, and King Harald nearly killed us for that, too."

"Then you returned," Vandrad concluded, "only to become King Harald's best friend, so we were forced to flee again."

I tightened the bow. "Trying to kill someone does, after all, have destructive consequences."

They pressed themselves more tightly against the wall. "What do you want from us?" Ulf asked.

"I want to know who sent you to Duke William with the message that King Edward wanted William to succeed him as England's King."

They glanced at each other.

"When you left the service of King Harald of Norway," I said, "you became spies for hire. You offered yourselves to Count Baldwin of Flanders, who sent you on to someone else." I was guessing, but I knew that Baldwin would not send the false message. "Who was that?"

They glanced at each other again but remained silent.

"If you are spies for hire," I said, "I can hire you. I'll pay far more than whoever hired you, if you tell me the source of the false message."

Ulf huffed. "You would hire us? After we tried to kill you?"

"I represent both King Edward and Duke William, who pay much better than … who was it that gave you the false message?"

Vandrad shrugged. "King Henry."

For a moment I almost lost my composure. Why would the King in Paris, who had been a supporter of William, send such a message? "Why?"

"We don't know," Vandrad said.

"That's the truth," Ulf said. "He paid us to deliver the message and then watch the reactions of your Duke and King Edward. That's all."

I hesitated. "Then let us join the King and the Duke and see their reactions at a close distance. This way."

Marching two men through the castle with a bow aimed at them eventually attracted the attention of some castle guards, whom I asked to escort us to King Edward. Fortunately, the guards recognized me, and they agreed to summon William as well.

It was not long before the three of us stood in a side chamber where Edward heard private appeals.

Though a large fire burned nearby, Ulf and Vandrad shivered. Edward sat in front of them, and William sat not far from Edward, studying their faces.

"Please tell the King and the Duke what you told me," I said.

Vandrad began, addressing William, "We're sorry, my lord Duke, but we were paid to tell you that King Edward was offering you the throne. We did not mean you any ill."

Ulf made a small bow to Edward. "Nor did we intend any harm to you, your majesty."

"Who paid you to do this?" Edward asked.

"King Henry in Paris, your majesty," Vandrad said.

I saw William twitch, which was as much reaction as he would allow himself to have.

"I find that hard to believe," Edward said. "Why would King Henry send a message that would only make matters difficult here, especially for Duke William?"

"We don't know," Vandrad said.

William leaned forward and stared at the two men. "You have no idea why King Henry would want me to believe a falsehood? You cannot make a guess?"

Vandrad swallowed. "We have heard rumors, my lord, that King Henry worries about your ... growing power."

William stared hard at him. "You mean he wants to see how ambitious I am."

"That may be behind his actions," Ulf said.

William leaned back. "So, if I were to press King Edward for the throne of England, King Henry would see me as ambitious ... and do what?"

"We have no idea, my lord," Vandrad said.

William pulled out his knife and stared at it for a time. "You cannot think of anything you've seen or heard?"

"You're spies for hire," I said, "so either you have heard something, or you're not very good at what you do."

Vandrad licked his lips nervously. "We may have heard that King Henry is making plans to take Normandy away from you, my lord."

William straightened in his chair. "To invade Normandy, you mean."

Both of them replied, "Yes, my lord."

William nodded at them. "Thank you for that information. You'll be rewarded."

They looked surprised.

"I do not kill spies or messengers," William said. "If you help me, I will help you."

"Thank you, my lord," they both said.

William nodded to me. "Cuin, see that arrangements are made to pay these two men. And let's explore what service they may offer us in the future."

"You may go now," Edward said.

Ulf and Vandrad backed away, turning to me for the next move. As I led them into the hallway, William rose and caught my arm.

"When you've finished with these two, rejoin us. Apparently, we need to plan for an invasion."

When I returned, Edward and William were deep in conversation. They waved me into a chair near them.

"What do you make of King Henry's plot?" Edward asked.

"I was surprised, your majesty, that King Henry has moved so far away from supporting Duke William that he is contacting nobles within Normandy to aid in an invasion."

"Is that what Ulf and Vandrad told you?" William asked.

"Yes."

"That is disquieting," Edward said.

"He may also enlist the aid of nobles in border counties," William said, "especially Geoffrey Martel in Maine. He's had eyes on Normandy for some time."

Edward turned to William. "What will you do?"

"I cannot fight my overlord."

"He plans to invade your territory."

"I will not fight someone I am sworn to serve."

Edward smiled. "Nor would I expect that of you."

"Shall I visit King Henry's court in Paris?" I asked.

"To what end?" William replied. "Henry plots against me and assumes I know nothing about it. If we march into his court, he knows that we know."

"Further," Edward said, "Henry expects one of two reactions: either I'm angry with you for wanting my throne, or I alienate my own people by promising the throne to an outsider. Either way he gains." He looked at me. "Diplomacy cannot alter Henry's plans when he has such expectations. Your best efforts will not work, Cuin."

I looked at the fire for a moment. "Then perhaps we give King Henry neither reaction. Perhaps we give him what he gave us: a rumor. We let it be spread about that Duke William may have been promised the throne, but the Council, as our good King Edward knows, would never allow a Norman to take the throne, so it's a mere rumor. While Henry's trying to discover what really happened, we've returned to Normandy to plan for his invasion."

William nodded. "I do need time to plan a response, especially one that avoids open conflict with my overlord."

"I agree," Edward said to William. Then to me he said, "Can you trust the two spies to carry this message?"

I smiled. "Yes, certainly. I will send Rolf and his Goliards as an escort, of course, so that Ulf and Vandrad appreciate my trust."

Edward smiled. "A precaution I would take as well."

"So, now, my lords," I said, "your duty and my interest in the Christmas feast require that you present yourselves to the court as if nothing has happened."

The next morning, William drew me into one of the side rooms, its fire just lit and its narrow windows covered against the cold.

"I don't want you to return to Normandy with me," he said. "I can plan for Henry's attack on Normandy. He can't move this winter, and that gives me time."

"I agree. Nor is he likely to muster enough troops before summer."

He nodded. "If I can dissuade some nobles from joining him, I may slow his plans." He stared at the fire. "His attack is a danger, but it may be further away than he imagines. In any event, it's not one that requires your skills. I would rather you remain here with Edward."

"Because of his struggle with Godwin's family?"

"Yes. We know Godwin and his sons, especially Harold. They're as much a threat to Edward as Henry is to me, but I am alerted to my danger, while Edward remains ignorant of his."

"I'll keep you informed."

"Good. So, you and your wife will remain here at court?"

"Of course."

A.D. 1052

Young Moons and I were still in England in late winter when the Lady Emma, Edward's mother, died in Winchester. At age seventy, she died alone, without any signs of wealth or power around her.

When Young Moons asked me about the reduced conditions surrounding her death, I replied, "Edward became King about ten years ago, and he immediately confiscated Lady Emma's lands and treasures. The story at the time was that she had plotted with young King Magnus of Norway to seize the English throne from Edward."

"Was that true? Plotting against her own son?"

"I don't know. As you may have noticed, the people on this side of the world do not have the close relations to their children that the People do. Emma never favored Edward in any way. In his turn, he always blamed her for his brother Alfred's death. That she should plot against him or that he should reduce her to poverty is not surprising."

She shook her head. "I do not really understand that."

"Often, I don't either."

We were also in England when stories of Harold's raids in the western parts of the country reached Edward.

By now I was convinced that Godwin and Harold would join forces to descend on England by summer. In the messages I exchanged with William, he agreed with me. Both of us continued to hope that, even if Godwin and his sons forced their way back into power, they would leave Edward on the throne.

Though I wanted a peaceful resolution, Harold had already demonstrated through his raids that he was angry enough to kill his countrymen. An appeal to him to be peaceful seemed futile.

That left Godwin and Harold's brother Tostig, both now in Flanders. I decided to focus on Godwin.

My first step was to eliminate as many of Godwin's potential allies as possible.

I sent a message, by way of the Goliards, to Thorir, who was still with King Sweyn in Denmark, asking him to keep Sweyn and Hardraada focused on their war with each other, Denmark against Norway, so that neither would aid Godwin against Edward.

I also asked the Goliards to pass a letter through Thorir to Onyame. A plan was forming in my mind that required Hervor's help. I hoped that Onyame, during his journey back from the People, would convince her to join us in England.

Finally, I sent the Goliards to Voldred with a message to meet me at Edward's court in early summer with as many Berserkers as he could find. William and I did not know whether Edward would be prepared for Godwin's and Harold's forces later in the year, but we hoped to be.

I received a message from William not long after he returned to Normandy: "It seems that Edward did listen to my appeals. In a letter I just received from him, he reports that he plans to have the naval fleet ready for an attack by the summer. He has enjoyed his triumph over Godwin, but he knows he will have to defend that triumph."

I sent a message back to William: "As I ponder the situation here, I feel that Edward has no choice but to let Godwin and his sons return. He should not resist it. The alternative is civil war."

William's reply was: "I agree. Godwin and his sons will not stop fighting until they are allowed to return. Neither would I, if I had been exiled from my home."

"So," I said to Young Moons after reading the last message, "we must ensure that the return of Godwin and his sons happens as peacefully as possible."

She nodded seriously. "What this means is that you and your friends must make this return happen with no killing."

"With as little violence as possible, yes. Now, while his triumph is fresh, Edward vehemently opposes bringing the exiles home. He's taking William's advice about activating the royal navy, but he's not doing it to ease the return of Godwin, as I would prefer."

"He's doing it to keep this family out of this country."

"Yes."

She thought for a moment. "So, you must find another way to convince King Edward to allow the return while keeping the exiled family from fighting. And that means that you must talk with the family elder."

"Yes, I must negotiate with Godwin. From what I know of Godwin over the years, I'll need all my skills."

As spring arrived, I traveled once again to Flanders in disguise as Brother Augustine, leaving Young Moons at Edward's court, where she wanted to learn more about England.

Once again I sought out Count Baldwin, and once again, Anette and her husband aided me. They discovered when the Count would pay one of his regular visits to the monastery of St. Vaast, so that I could be there to meet him.

Count Baldwin was as friendly as ever, as were the monks and the infirmarian who had helped me all those years ago, and he arranged to have me meet Godwin in Bruges, the busy, wealthy trading town where the aging Earl of Wessex was staying with some supporters, including his son Tostig and Tostig's new wife Judith.

I smiled to myself as I thought about Tostig, the gruff earl who had saved my life years earlier and whom I had mistaken for a mere courtier, as I had also mistaken his interactions with Judith. Looking back, I now had no doubt that Godwin himself had been involved in Tostig's courting of Judith. The political advantages were obvious.

So, on a sunny spring morning in an old villa just inside the city's stone walls, I came face to face for the first time with the formidable Earl Godwin of Wessex, the father of Earls Tostig and Harold.

He was different from what I had envisioned. I did see part of what I expected physically. The father of the Wessex family was tall with long white hair and a white beard, both worn in the Saxon style.

His face, though, was more lined and weathered than many nobles his age, and I knew the Earl to be just over sixty years old, indicating that he had participated in many campaigns and was actively, physically involved in ruling Wessex and the other lands given to his sons.

He looked almost tired and more pale than someone who clearly preferred being out in the world, so I wondered about his health.

What surprised me most, though, was the thoughtful, contemplative look he seemed to have, combined with an ability to concentrate that made me feel uncomfortable when that concentration was fixed on me.

As soon as introductions were completed and we were sitting comfortably in a large side room with high-backed, carved wooden chairs, he spoke — before I could get out my thanks at his willingness to meet with me.

"You are the young man whom my son Tostig saved here, are you not ... what was it? seven years ago? Duke William's man? This disguise of yours is the same that you used then, I believe, to make your travels easier."

I was astonished at his memory and information, though I should not have been, considering how many reigns and Kings he had survived.

I did not want to hesitate, though, and thus seem discomfited by his knowledge. "Yes, my lord, and my gratitude toward your family is now compounded by your willingness to speak with me."

He moved his head forward, concentrating his stare. "You are a noble, are you not? Your position with Duke William, your manner of speaking. ... I have heard stories about a hidden identity, and I am certain that you were the subject of them."

I drew my breath in sharply, not knowing how to respond.

He nodded, looking solemn. "I see that there is some secrecy involved here, and I shall respect your privacy." He paused. "You know, my own past includes much that I have ... sheltered, and I have moved among men who held positions of power that I could not hold. Might your life be something like that?"

"Your insight is remarkable, my lord, and I thank you for maintaining discretion about my past. I shall do the same with yours." I wanted him to wonder what I might know about his past, but I was not doing so defensively. He seemed non-threatening, despite his reputation.

"Thank you."

Before he could speak again, I said, "This gives me yet another reason for wanting to help you and your family, my lord."

He raised his eyebrows. "You grew up in Normandy during the time our present King Edward was there, did you not? You are a friend of the King, is that not true?"

"We did share some time together, my lord, and I am familiar with the King, though whether he would call me a friend, I do not know. To be clear, my acquaintance with him puts me in a position to be of help to your family. I know the King's nature, if not his present intentions."

"You would like to help him avoid civil war."

Again, his directness startled me. "Yes, my lord, and I would like to see your family avoid it as well."

He nodded and looked out the window. "I want to return to my own land, of course, but I want it to be a peaceful place when I return. I want to avoid a war there not cause one." He turned back to me. "You must realize that, or you would not be talking with me."

"Yes, I was told that you refused to resort to arms last autumn, even to your own disadvantage, angering some of your followers. It was clear that you do not want war."

"I was angry with the King, but I would not shed blood over that anger … which is not true of my son, as you no doubt know."

I nodded. "Yes, I do know about Earl Harold's raiding."

"Harold is angry, as we all are, but his raiding is more than just anger. I do not think that King Edward will let us return without …" He hesitated a long time, and I gave him time to choose his words. "Without some real threat from my family. I am sure that Harold thinks the same."

"I think that you are right. Earl Harold's movements are strategic."

He looked surprised.

I continued, "If I may, my lord, please allow me to consider your past in England: you have had to navigate between Saxon lords and an unsteady Saxon King, Ethelred, which you did successfully. Then you had to navigate between the Saxon lords and the Danish Empire. You also did that successfully. You have now been navigating between the Saxons, the remaining Danes, and the Normans who arrived with King Edward. And you have done so successfully."

"In light of what I know of you, I consider that praise."

"As you should, my lord. You have many skills for dealing with difficult situations and shifting circumstances." I paused for a moment. "At present, King Edward is trying to navigate between the Saxons and the Normans, since he is both. However, as much as I might admire the King, he does not have your experience in working with diverse interests."

He watched me closely. "You are suggesting that the King has limited responses, relative to mine."

"Yes, my lord, especially when he feels bested by your skills. He might feel, even as King, oppressed by you."

He was quiet for a time.

I waited and then spoke again. "A powerful Earl, especially one related to Saxon and Danish lords in England, would want a King to feel this way. It would be a desirable goal, a goal any powerful lord would want to achieve in a land where yet another foreign element has been introduced, possibly to his detriment. Especially if that element — in this instance, the Norman influence — were introduced by a new King."

He raised his eyebrows at my comments but remained quiet.

"In short, my lord, you would hope that the King, who favors his Norman friends, would regard you as intimidatingly powerful. Otherwise, your power and even your existence would be at risk."

He stared at me for a time and then looked out the window. When he turned back to me, he said, slowly, "I am surprised by your insight into my position."

"Positively surprised, I hope, my lord."

"Yes." He paused for a moment. "I think we can have a sound discussion about my family's return to England, you and I."

"I think so, too, my lord."

"I suspect that you are in a position to help me return with a minimum of violence."

"I am ... especially if, as I surmise, you want neither the King's crown nor civil war."

"I want neither." He paused. "Though my son may."

"Earl Harold? Your son is a natural leader, from what I hear, and much loved in England, except in the southwest, which is why he feels free to raid there."

He paused again. "Yes."

"Fortunately, his long-term strategy is a factor that we need not consider at present."

"No. We can focus on the immediate situation and leave Harold's future to him. He would have it no other way."

"Other forces will have to deal with Earl Harold, which is beyond my concern at this moment."

He stared at me while I spoke and added, "Though not beyond your overall plans, I would suppose."

"You would suppose correctly, my lord, but fortunately those matters need not enter our discussion."

"With the exception that, when my forces meet Harold's, we must not be in a position to attack England openly, though Harold may be interested in doing so. Harold and I will have to join forces. He expects that."

"Eventually, yes, You would need to meet somewhere near London, I suppose."

"Yes, I know many of London's leaders, and they would have the most to gain in urging the King to negotiate."

"First, though, you might want to appear to be the kind of threat that Earl Harold now poses — without being an actual threat. Is that possible?"

He nodded. "I can raid the coast in a way that is mere appearance. I can land on the south coast near the lands where I was lord and request that the local leaders report extensive raiding to the King, though I shall not harm any people or property, since they are, after all, mine."

"A good plan, my lord."

"I will not openly engage the King, either, even if Harold does."

"As he very well may."

He sounded weary. "Yes, I'm afraid that our greatest problem is Harold's wrath combined with his ambition. I can choose and guide my allies carefully, so that none wants war with King Edward. If Harold joins me, however, he may rally all present to the opposite of my wishes."

I leaned toward him. "I can prevent that, my lord, if you delay your raiding tactic for a time and instead arrange to meet Earl Harold in the English Channel near, let's say, Sandwich."

"Where the royal fleet is usually stationed?"

"Yes, and it will be there again, I assure you."

"Ah, so the royal fleet is to keep us apart."

"Yes and no, my lord. Yes, you must allow the royal fleet to block your advance, but no, neither you nor Harold will have to engage the fleet. You must simply be willing to sail back to Flanders. If you do this, I can make certain that Harold will not meet you, and there will be no fighting."

He raised his eyebrows. "You can? How?"

"If you don't mind, I would prefer that to be a private matter for now. The method will be obvious when it is applied. It will do no harm to either side. You have my word on that."

"I will not press you on your strategy then," he said and smiled for the first time. "But I will be interested in seeing its realization."

"Thank you. So, if we are successful in the plans we have outlined, you and Earl Harold will arrange to meet at sea but will be prevented from doing so. I will see to that. We hope, do we not, that this gives your son time to consider the consequences of bloodshed. Then, if you can convince Earl Harold to join you in sailing to London later in the year, everyone, including the King, will want to negotiate to avoid a bloody altercation."

He sat back in his chair and nodded. "I agree, and I am certain that, if we do succeed, my son will agree. Most of the local leaders in London would rather negotiate with me than support the King, if such support meant violence."

"Then, my lord, we have a plan for two separate attacks, the first of which, failing, gives both King Edward and Earl Harold time to consider the ravages of war."

"And the second returns my family peacefully home."

"Let us hope so, my lord."

As I was leaving Count Baldwin's rooms in Bruges, I encountered Tostig. I had hoped to find him before I left.

He was standing in a hallway, admiring weapons. He was not surprised to see me, so I supposed that he had been informed of my visit.

"It's good to see you healthy and not in an infirmary," he said cheerfully, "but you're still wearing this dull robe. Can't you find a more colorful disguise?"

I glanced at his blue leggings flowing into red boots and a green tunic with gold thread running through it. "I think that you have enough color for both of us."

He laughed. "Ah, I recall the wit. As you see, my life has become, as has my brother's, lavish in recent years." He became serious. "You've spoken with my father?"

"Yes."

"To the end of returning us to our positions in England?"

I began to reply, but he interrupted me, his voice rising. "You do know that we never should have been exiled."

I wanted to discover how our strategy of Edward befriending Tostig had affected Tostig's attitude toward the King, so I said, "I recall that you were less than happy with King Edward's policies when we first met seven years ago. Your exile must not have endeared you to him further."

He made a huffing noise. "I like King Edward. Indeed, I've spent a great amount of time with him and my sister, the Queen. He is a good man. As I said when you and I first met, though, his Norman advisors lead him astray."

"All the more reason for you to return to England to offer your counsel?"

"I can't tell whether you mean that as a witticism or not, but yes."

"I was serious. I hope to see your family peacefully restored to your lands and possessions and you in a position to advise the King. I am certain that you are a good friend to him and will be a good advisor in the future."

He looked surprised. "I thought that you and your Duke would be relieved to see my family's influence lessened in England."

"Why? Duke William wants good people in positions of strength. He has his reports of your family from me, for the most part, and except for your wardrobe, I have nothing but good to say."

He laughed.

I continued, "I personally have nothing but goodwill for the man who saved my life. I have no doubt that your friendship with King Edward will be as much a boon to him as it was to me. A King surrounded by Normans will need your friendship."

"I appreciate that sentiment, Cuin. I hope that soon it will be a reality. Without bloodshed."

"I hope so, too, for both of you. To that end, would you mind if I ask you about how your father and your brother handle military campaigns? You've accompanied both of them, I think."

"Yes, I have. Both are clever in battle and in working with soldiers and militia, but Harold is brilliant."

"Harold's tactics are those which interest me most."

So we continued talking for several hours more, Tostig enjoying recounting what he knew, and, I suspected, expanding his own battle feats beyond what might have actually happened. I knew him to be a good fighter, though, so I did not doubt his general prowess.

As we parted, he said to me, "My father and my brother are my family, but I also have my wife here. King Edward is a good man, a friend. I will not participate in any battles this summer. Not against the King. My heart would not be in them."

On my return to England, I received a message from Onyame that he was bringing Hervor with him and that they would arrive by early summer. Hervor had been told by Odin that I needed her help, and she was coming to give it in person.

That same night, as I was falling asleep, the dragon voice sounded in my head: "Remain awake," it hissed. "There is one with whom you must speak."

Hervor appeared in a vision.

She was dressed exactly as she had been in Iceland, looking very much the formal Volva and sounding like her: "You're not just sleeping there, are you?"

"Only when it gets dark."

She snorted and said, "There is work to be done, and you must remain vigilant."

"So I suppose my long rest is over."

"Don't be impertinent. Listen: your King is amassing a fleet on his south coast."

"Yes, we didn't want him to be unprotected, and he seemed to be somewhat casual about defending his borders."

"Fine, fine, but his enemies are also amassing fleets."

"That's true, but Earl Godwin wants that to be just a gesture. I spoke with him."

"Yes, I saw the conversation you had with him. Excellent work."

"You did? I didn't suppose that you would be so interested in the affairs of the South."

"I'm not. Odin showed the event to me."

"Why —?"

She cut me off, "None of your incessant questioning now. Earl Godwin is not the problem. His son Harold is. He is not just — what did you say? — making gestures. He sees this as an opportunity to seize the country himself."

"Do you mean that he intends to become King?"

"Yes. Odin has seen into his soul. It is an ambitious one, more than you may realize. Listen: Harold's older brother will die on his present pilgrimage to the Holy Land, and his younger brother, Tostig, has no strength to lead a country. The father, Godwin, is dying. That leaves Harold as head of the family and in control, directly or indirectly, of most of England."

"Godwin is dying? He seemed weary, but —"

"Godwin will return to his lands in England, but he will die within the year of his return, on the festival that the Christians have named after the goddess Eoster. Odin has seen that as well."

"Does Harold know this?"

"He knows that his father is ill, though he does not know when death will take him."

"So we must stop Harold somehow, deal him some defeat, and keep him from joining forces with Godwin at a critical moment. As you know, that's what Godwin and I discussed."

"Yes, and I suppose that your plans involve my storms. With those, I can keep Harold away from his father, especially if they are both at sea. But you must see to the defeat. That's why I agreed to come to you in person."

In late spring, Edward did order the royal fleet to the south and east of London to prepare for an assault from Flanders.

Since the Goliards had assured me that Godwin continued to restrain his belligerent supporters, I knew that Godwin's assault would be to demonstrate his power rather than to shed blood. He was following the plans we had made in Bruges.

Harold's reactions remained the real threat.

Shortly after Edward's order to the fleet, Voldred arrived with twenty Berserkers. I was delighted, since twenty such warriors would be a match for an force twice that size.

The same week, Onyame arrived with Hervor.

As Hervor looked Voldred up and down, she said to him, "With Odin's help, I have watched your new life unfold, the one given to you by Cuin."

Voldred smiled. "I am a new person, and I do owe that to your seventh student. I am even becoming a farmer."

She smiled in return. "Not a good one, so I hope that you continue to train in rituals and move your Berserkers into positions that can help the seventh student."

I interrupted them. "I am standing here, you know."

Hervor turned to me. "Yes, we know you're here. We're just not talking with you presently."

Onyame laughed, giving Young Moons and I an opening to ask him about his winter with the People. When he finished his account, I asked everyone to join me in a side courtyard not far from Edward's personal quarters.

"We must now strategize about the coming summer and autumn."

I began by summarizing what I knew of Godwin's intentions: to appear threatening but to avoid bloodshed. Hervor repeated Odin's warning that Harold wanted to seize the throne of England.

"So," I concluded, "we must consider how to convince Harold that England is not his to rule."

"At least not yet," Onyame said.

I nodded at him and continued, "To our immediate advantage is the fact that Godwin does not intend to join forces with Harold for that purpose."

"As you realized in your recent conversation in Flanders," Hervor said, "Godwin cannot prevent Harold from taking command of all Godwin's forces and more."

"Yes, that is a threat," I said. "So, we need to keep them apart, which is why I asked Onyame to contact you. I hoped that you could create a fog or a storm to keep Harold from Godwin's men."

"Odin suggested the same. That is why I came here and tolerated that … sea voyage. At a distance, I cannot work a storm or a fog, but in person, I can work with Odin's forces to create both, if need be."

I saw Onyame smile, so I knew that she was not overstating her abilities.

"You have seen her do this?" I asked him.

"Heavy rain, high winds, fogs, and more," he said, the smile broadening. "You may have snow and sea monsters, if you need them."

"Not snow or sea monsters," she said to him. "This is not their season."

I could not determine whether they were being serious or not, but I was certain that we had the method for keeping Harold separated from Godwin.

"Where will you need to be, physically?" I asked Hervor.

"I will take a position near the Channel. Not on it, mind you. Just near it. Being even briefly on the Channel is worse than the entire trip from Iceland."

"So, now that we know how to keep Harold away from Godwin's forces," I said, "we need to reduce Harold's confidence in his own forces."

"Can you do this without bloodshed?" Young Moons asked.

The rest of us glanced at each other.

Voldred finally spoke. "This will involve battle, and men will be wounded. Whether any men will be killed depends on how determined Harold is to press further into England."

She looked at him with concern.

"I know England and Ireland well enough," he added, "to anticipate Harold's attack."

"So that all of us know," I said, "I've told Voldred that Harold has little support in the south and west of England. He will not be picking up supporters as he goes. Instead, he will be picking up provisions."

"In other words," Onyame said, "he'll be raiding."

Voldred nodded. "As he has done all winter from Ireland."

"When I was in Flanders," I said, "I talked at length with his brother, Tostig, about Harold's tactics. Harold does not amass provisions. He gets them by raiding and then raids again when he needs them. Since he lacks support in the southwest of England, he cannot build his forces there."

"He will be seen as a raider only," Onyame said. "So, whatever force he enters with will be all the force he has."

"My Berserkers and I will intercept him," Voldred said. "Harold will have to sail up the Bay of Bristol. With the aid of the Goliards, we can track his movements. Wherever he lands, we will join the local militia and whatever force King Edward has sent."

"Harold will believe that he is encountering local resistance to his raiding, the kind he has experienced all winter," Onyame said, "but behind that local force will be twenty Berserkers."

"That should provide the defeat we need to undermine Harold's drive to seize King Edward's crown."

"I'll relate our plans to Edward," I said. "He intends to keep Godwin's family out of England. I think that the summer's events, however, will prove to him that the exile must end."

The plans worked as we thought they would — with one terrible exception. Harold and his men sailed in nine ships up the Bristol Channel to the Severn River and landed at Porlock, wading ashore to raid for provisions.

Voldred and his Berserkers joined soldiers drawn from two local shires to meet the threat. The combined forces eventually drove Harold back to his ships.

Harold, however, was more of a threat than we imagined. He was a formidable soldier, a brilliant strategist, as Tostig had claimed, and a leader for whom men would risk their lives.

By the time he was driven back to his ships, Harold had burned homes and crops, taken captives, and killed more than thirty nobles and soldiers. The Berserkers struggled to match his onslaught.

Young Moons gasped when she heard the numbers of the dead. I too felt a deep sadness, thinking of the men whose lives would no longer enrich their families and their communities.

Back in his ships, Harold had rounded Land's End and sailed up the Channel, hoping to join Godwin's forces near Sandwich. And take command of them.

The forces never arrived.

Godwin had sailed from the River Yser and landed at Dungeness in Kent. As we had planned, the royal navy, now forty ships strong, forced him back to Pevensey in East Sussex.

Then the the storm hit.

First, a fog settled between the royal navy and Godwin's ships, slowly enveloping both fleets. Then a storm, driving strong westerly winds before it, blew both fleets up the Channel.

The royal navy returned to Sandwich, while Godwin's ships were blown almost all the way back up the Yser. He and his supporters returned to Flanders.

Harold was left alone in a foggy channel. He sailed back to Ireland.

Though Harold's plan to seize the throne had been thwarted, Edward realized how dangerous Godwin's family was when they plotted revenge.

When a combined force of Godwin's and Harold's sailed up the Thames later in the summer and two armies faced each other on different sides of the river, threatening civil war again, Edward reluctantly reinstated the family. Peacefully.

Our plans had worked as we hoped they would.

Godwin was once again Earl of Wessex.

Harold was again Earl of East Anglia.

Tostig was promised the earldom of Northumbria.

Queen Edith was returned to her station with all her lands and possessions.

The Normans at court, with a few exceptions, fled to Normandy.

Edward continued to be King of England.

A. D. 1053

Remaining in England to guarantee that Edward's position was not threatened, I determined to stay through the winter.

Onyame returned to the People, and I asked Young Moons to return with him, fearing that if events turned against Edward, the court might become a dangerous place to be. She agreed. In the event of trouble, I could disguise myself and escape more easily without her. So she sailed with Onyame.

William remained in Normandy, where he had threats to deal with, but he encouraged me to remain in England to observe what was happening between Edward and Godwin's family.

I kept Voldred and his Berserkers near me, along with Rolf and some of the Goliards. In my mind, the Berserkers had become the King's guard, while the Goliards were my eyes and ears beyond Edward's court.

I spent time with all of them, but I also frequented the royal library, especially to study the methods of England's royal physicians, adding these to my own skills.

By spring, when Edward returned from the last of his winter travels, I could report that there had been no movements against him. He was relieved. When I told him about Earl Godwin, he was even more relieved.

Having been cleared of all charges, Godwin was now an open supporter of Edward. He was, in fact, the most vocal Saxon supporter of the King. I received regular reports that his efforts had unified the other nobles behind Edward. Most of these nobles were members of Godwin's family, but that did not diminish his efforts.

Appreciating the support, Edward invited Godwin and his family to the Easter court at Winchester.

From the moment Godwin arrived, though, we could see that he was unwell. Edward was concerned and asked me to advise Godwin on his health.

Fortunately, Godwin was willing to meet with me. For several days, I examined him as often and as closely as I could, making recommendations about his diet, offering some herbs, and advising rest, but he resisted my suggestions.

"I appreciate your efforts, my young friend," he said at my last session with him. "You certainly have more skill than the healers around me. I recall from last summer's events that even the weather responds to you."

I smiled and assured him that I had no influence on the weather.

He continued, "My time in this world is coming to an end. I know you have powerful methods and medicines, but when that time comes, I trust that you will let me go."

"I will honor your wishes, my lord."

"Thank you." He turned and strode from the healing chamber.

A few days later, as I walked down a hall not far from the King's chambers, the dragon's voice hissed in my head: "Turn left at the next corridor and listen."

"Is there a vision there?" I asked inwardly.

"No," the dragon said. "A conversation. One that could change the world. Go now."

I turned down the next corridor and did hear loud voices coming from a side room. I recognized Godwin's voice but not that of the other man.

Godwin was speaking.: "… genuinely believe that this King can be good for relations with the Welsh and the Irish."

"I cannot believe that this King can be effective … need a stronger hand … I have friends in both Wales and Ireland."

"You have a stronger hand," Godwin said, more emphatically than I had heard him speak when he and I conversed. "Offer your services."

The other man's voice became sharp, so that I could hear him better. "I do not intend to save this King from his own lack of ability."

Godwin's voice tempered. "Listen to me, Harold. I have had to adapt to the Saxon Kingship of Ethelred —" but he was cut off.

By the other man: Godwin's son, Earl Harold of East Anglia.

Harold was speaking. "You have told me this before."

"Not in this way. Listen to me. You know that I do not have long to live. I know that you need to make important decisions about your position as soon as I am gone. You will be the Earl of Wessex, the second most powerful man in the country. Let me advise you."

A pause. "Very well, father."

"You know that I had to tolerate King Ethelred, and he was incompetent. I had to let him believe himself to be a competent king, while I revealed to the other lords my own abilities. The strategy worked."

"How can I make it appear that I believe King Edward, a Norman, to be competent to rule Saxons?"

"He is half-Saxon, but that is not what I am advising. You cannot pretend. You simply need to build your competence on his lack of ability."

Another pause. "What exactly do you mean?"

"After King Ethelred, I had to ally myself with King Canute, who was competent but intended merely to make England a part of his larger empire. I had to deal with his Norman wife, Emma, and his Danish sons. In all that time —"

Harold interrupted him again. "You always preserved your power and extended it. King Edward, however, wants to curtail my power. As he hoped to curtail yours."

"Listen carefully, Harold. What I am advising is that you ally yourself to Edward and step into every role where his abilities end and yours begin. He will have no choice but to think of you as a supporter, since that is what you will be."

Harold paused again. "I see. I support him, and in so doing, demonstrate my abilities to the other lords."

"And to the people."

"I remind all of them that the house of Wessex was, before Canute, the house of the Kings of this land."

"Further," Godwin said, "to the lesser nobles, to the Church, and to the people, you demonstrate that the old house of Wessex still lives in England. That it remains as powerful as it was before Canute. When Edward is gone, you will be the obvious choice to be King."

There was silence for a moment.

Godwin continued, "You have abilities that I did not have: leadership skills, battle skills, even the ability to win over the people. I've watched you. You can fight or charm your way through any crisis. You know how to gain support in war and in peace. I was a powerful Earl. You can be King."

Another pause, then Harold's voice again. "Edward and my sister have no children, and we both know that they never will. There are a few heirs outside the country, but the Council would not seriously consider them."

"Yes, unlike me, you need not trust to hope. You may claim the royal position yourself. You have the character and the skills."

"Thank you, father."

"I am simply telling you what I see and what is obvious to anyone in England who is not a Norman. Even to some Normans."

Harold paused, and when he replied, his voice was harsh. "I will never see England controlled by a Norman again. I will see the reverse: Normandy controlled by a Saxon."

Godwin's voice was lower. "Initially, you must be measured in your aims: the kingship."

"I can achieve greater aims. I can recreate the Canute's Empire and rule it from London. The Saxons can ally with the old Danish Empire or defeat it. I have connections throughout the South, and I will make more friends there. I can negotiate with the Pope and the Holy Roman Empire. Eventually, I may even drive the Pope and the Empire back into Rome."

"That is not measured ambition, Harold, even if it is possible. The King of France and other leaders stand in your way."

There was silence then Harold's voice again. "There are few leaders who stand in my way, and I can wait." Another pause. "A Saxon King will be the sole power in the North, though. As it was in the days of King Alfred. That power may even extend to the South, as it did in King Canute's day."

I heard the dragon whisper, "Leave now, before you are discovered."

I slipped away quickly.

As I entered my quarters, I was repeating inwardly what Harold had said. While I had taken steps to prevent both Hardraada and Sweyn from establishing a unified Northern empire, Harold in England had been planning his own empire, one that included Normandy.

Harold's empire-building enterprise began almost immediately, but not through his own action. Through the action of fate.

At dinner the following evening, Earl Godwin, pale and ill, was seated next to the King.

I sat farther down in the great hall but close enough to notice when one of the serving boys nearly tripped over some obstacle and caught himself and the food he was carrying.

The King turned and congratulated him on his physical skill. One of the nobles, seeing an opening to engage the King's pleasure, commented, "The young lad regained his balance by using one foot to help the other, which was in need."

There was general mirth over the light jest, so another lord offered what was apparently a note of wisdom: "Thus should a man support a friend in need and one brother help another."

As the word "brother" was uttered, I saw Edward's face fall, and my mind returned to his many diatribes about Alfred's death. I held my breath. Would he —?

I did not finish the thought before he spoke, "So would my brother have helped me if he had been allowed to live."

The room became silent, and everyone stared at Godwin. Though he had been legally exonerated of Alfred's death, he must have felt the stares as accusations.

He had been eating a piece of bread, which now seemed to stick in his throat. He opened his mouth to say something, but only guttural sounds came out. He turned completely white, choked for a moment, and fell to the ground.

Edward sprang up and shouted, "Lords, be quick. Raise him up and take him to my personal chamber." He looked at me and nodded, and I rose to follow the men carrying the body.

They placed Godwin on a long couch opposite the King's bed. By the time he was positioned and covered with blankets, he seemed to be sleeping, and his body was relaxed.

Edward then appeared and ordered the men out. He turned to me. "I do not know whether this man murdered my brother or not. I do not know whether this is divine judgment or a dying man's weakness, but he is a child of God, and I would have you care for him with all the skill that you have."

"I will do my best, your majesty. As you can see, he is very weak. I don't know how much longer he will be in this world."

"I trust that you will do your best and that it will be better than any physician I have here."

At that moment, a tall man with a blonde mustache and long blonde hair, worn in the Saxon style, almost ran into the room. His face, open and well balanced, appeared to be in pain.

Behind him was Tostig.

King Edward moved toward me and touched my shoulder. "Tend to him with your best skills, Cuin. I will send my physicians to offer you any aid you may need."

"Yes, your majesty."

Edward paused long enough to smile at me. "A God-guided healer and a man of your birth need not call me that, but I appreciate that you always do."

I smiled back at him.

He turned to the two nobles. "Your father could not be in better hands," he said strode from the room.

The tall blonde man stared at me, unmoving.

Tostig leaned down. "How is he, Cuin?"

"I have yet to determine that, but you know that his health has been failing for many months." I recalled Hervor's vision that Godwin would die at Easter, "the festival the Christians named after the goddess Eoster," she had said. Easter was three days away. "I do not think he will live past Easter."

Tostig sighed and stared at his father for a long time. I gave him a more detailed analysis of his father's health, based on my sessions with him, and he listened carefully.

"I didn't expect him to live long," he eventually said, "but somehow I didn't think he would die this soon." He fell silent again, watching his father's still face.

The movement of the tall man behind him finally stirred him. He rose and stepped aside. "Cuin, this is my older brother, Harold."

I turned to face the threat to Edward's throne, Earl Harold of East Anglia and soon to be, at Godwin's passing, the Earl of Wessex.

"Harold," Tostig continued, "this is the man whose life I saved eight years ago in Flanders, an emissary of Duke William of Normandy and for our purposes now, a knowledgeable healer. His name, oddly, is simply Cuin."

I rose to give a short bow to Harold and got out the words, "It is my pleasure to meet such a distinguished lord," before Tostig interrupted me.

"Don't be deceived by either his size or his manners," he said to Harold. "He is not only a formidable healer and, I later discovered, an equally formidable archer, but he is also the secret child we've heard about since we were young, the unacknowledged son of Duke Robert of Normandy and Estrith, King Canute's niece, who is also the mother of King Sweyn of Denmark and the present Queen of Denmark."

Harold raised his eyebrows.

Tostig continued, "This man has claim to more thrones than anyone alive, but he wants none of them. I've never known what to make of him."

I had to say something. "In my turn, I'm not sure what to make of such an introduction, my lord, but I am pleased to meet you, Earl Harold, though I wish the circumstances of our meeting were more auspicious."

Harold stirred and offered a polite smile. "It is my pleasure to meet you, Cuin of Normandy and England and Denmark."

In an instant, Harold had shifted from astonishment to charm. I felt a power from him, some great force, that captured my attention and, without my intending it, my admiration. I had occasionally felt this in William's presence.

He turned serious and asked, "Do you sincerely believe that our father will not live beyond Easter?"

"You may consider his aspect yourself, my lord. He is pale, barely breathes, and has little interest in this world anymore."

Inwardly, I thought, "With the power you have, Harold, you could heal him." I did not know why the thought came to me, though.

"So," he said, "it may be more astonishing if he lives until Easter."

"I would not wish to be insensitive, my lord, but yes, your appraisal seems accurate."

Tostig interrupted. "Is there anything that you can do for him, Cuin?"

"I attended him several times over the past few weeks, and he would follow none of the regimens I suggested. At this point, all I can do is watch and try to get some herbs into him through teas." I hesitated. "And breathe with him as he goes over to the other world."

"Thank you," Tostig said.

Harold echoed the statement, and the two of them left me to their father.

Earl Godwin of Wessex died three days later.

Earl Harold of East Anglia became the new Earl of Wessex and the new head of the family that Godwin had spread all over England.

During Godwin's last illness, I saw the brothers seldom and had few exchanges with Edward, but I kept Voldred and the Berserkers especially close to the court. Harold was about to become the most powerful landholder in England, and I wanted to ensure that, for the moment, his ambition ended there.

Through the Goliards, I sent carefully worded messages to Garrad and Onyame, urging a meeting about Harold's aims. For my own immediate purposes, I wanted to return to Young Moons, but I knew that I had to stay close to Edward until we could be certain about Harold's immediate ambitions.

Onyame sailed down to meet me at Sandwich, and Garrad joined us a few days later, bringing a surprise guest, Osbern.

Since the death of his father — the first poisoning I had witnessed as a child on a snowy night twenty years earlier — Osbern had matured into an enthusiastic supporter of William and everything Norman.

Osbern and I had remained friends, and I had gained his admiration by the successful completion of my mission to gain Northern support for William.

I was glad to see him, and he returned my enthusiasm.

"You have achieved a great deal for our good Duke while remaining almost completely hidden from public view." He shook his head several times and kept repeating, "Remarkable!"

I thanked him and returned the compliment. "I know that William values your advice on every important issue and counts you as a loyal supporter. And," I added, "it is good to see my old friend again."

The five of us, Garrad, Onyame, Osbern, Voldred, and I, met in the same room where we had planned the peaceful return of Godwin's exiled family a year earlier.

I began by repeating what I had overheard Harold claim and finished by saying, "Harold, the new Earl of Wessex, controls most of England directly and, through the earldoms of his brothers, the rest of the country. At this time, only one earldom, Mercia, is controlled by someone who is not a member of Harold's family."

Osbern drew his breath in sharply. "That much land!"

"More land than that," Voldred added. "Rolf and his Goliards told me that Harold, while Earl of East Anglia, began a policy of seizing local lands from the Church, sometimes by force. Since his local patronage is more valued than that of a distant Pope in Rome, he gains both the land and the support of local clergy, and most of those clergymen are warriors as well as clerics."

"Yes," Onyame said, "Cuin and I had discussed this policy of Harold's: gaining land at the expense of the Church, which he uses to expand his local support."

"He also has support in Ireland and friends in Scotland and Wales," I said, "especially Wales, where Edward is challenged by King Gruffydd, who once again defeated the King's forces last year."

"We can't forget," Garrad added, "that Harold's brother, Earl Tostig, is married to Judith, Count Baldwin's half-sister, so Harold has ties to Flanders. As he said in the conversation that Cuin overheard, he could also force negotiations with the Holy Roman Empire. Right now, there are few limits to his reach."

"He is willing to build his connections patiently," I said. "He can win most of the world by either force or diplomacy."

"Let us also remember," Garrad said, "that before Canute divided England into the four earldoms — Mercia, East Anglia, Northumbria, and Wessex — it was dominated solely by the house of Wessex. England's Kings came from that house, and Wessex was the unifying power in the country. At least, that is how the Saxons remember the history."

"What is he like, this Earl of Wessex?" Osbern asked.

I replied, "He is as formidable a warrior as any Berserker, as strong a leader as William, and as intelligent as any diplomat I've ever met."

Osbern frowned. "As good a leader as William? That cannot be."

Garrad handled the answer. "That's what all of us hope."

"Do we need to consider that the Pope has refused to bless Duke William's marriage?" Onyame asked.

Garrad nodded. "I see where this line of thought leads. In addition to Harold, we need to keep in mind that William could be threatened from other quarters. The Pope could demand that he yield more land and treasure to the Church, in return for the Pope's blessing his marriage."

Onyame nodded. "I've learned from Cuin that the clergy in Normandy are more loyal to Duke William than they are to the Pope, something the Pope would like to change."

"I agree," Garrad said. "The Pope's definition of 'unity' — that everyone should obey the Pope — is not William's definition."

Voldred stirred. "Is Duke William safe from both the Kings of Norway and Denmark, Hardraada and Sweyn?"

"Cuin has already gained the friendship of Hardraada and Sweyn," Osbern replied.

"Yes," I said, "and that friendship holds as long as the two Kings remain alive and at war with each other. This may not always be so. Recently, for example, one of Hardraada's sons raided England."

Voldred smiled. "I do not mean to seem disrespectful of a threat, but Hardraada has seven sons, and raiding another country is the way young warriors pass their time."

I smiled at Voldred's attempt at light-heartedness. "I hope that's all it is."

Garrad interrupted me. "Nonetheless, your point is well made. Harold is a far greater threat than either the King of Denmark or the King of Norway and his sons."

"Then," Onyame concluded, "something must be done to ally Earl Harold to Duke William. For now, they are equal. A Duke in the South is the same rank as an Earl in the North. We could perhaps bring them together. And should, before Harold becomes King of England."

"Or we need to block Harold's access to Normandy," Voldred said.

Everyone became silent.

Eventually I spoke, "For my part, I need to consult one of the People."

"The Man Who Walks with Power?" Onyame asked.

"Yes."

Garrad smiled, "You're not just needing this so that you can see your young wife again, are you?"

I returned the smile. "Of course, but I also need to talk with the puoin and expand my skills if I'm going to deal with an adversary such as Harold. Given the power alliances in the North now, I don't see how William can resist Harold's invasion. Or how Harold's empire-building can be stopped. So, as Onyame and Voldred have suggested, we must find an alternative to defeat."

Garrad nodded. "I agree. William will be occupied with threats from King Henry and from his neighbors, but he can handle those, even if they are immediate. We, however, must find a strategy for the long term that keeps Normandy out of a Saxon empire."

Onyame and I reached the People early in the summer, arriving on a sunny morning. We were greeted enthusiastically, especially by Onyame's wife and Young Moons.

I sought out the Man Who Walks with Power. He was playing with some children outside his home. I waited for him to finish and asked permission to speak with him. He waved me inside to sit down.

I sat silently for awhile and then asked permission to tell him about the events in England and Normandy that troubled me. He nodded.

When I finished, he remained silent. I waited, remembering that on this side of the world, I had to practice patience. I watched the late-afternoon warmth turn into early evening.

Eventually he smiled. "Go to your home and be with your wife. Do not spend your first day home with an old man." He laughed. "Come to see me tomorrow morning. Then we visit the beings that can help you." As I rose to leave, he added, "Bring Bear with you."

The next morning Onyame and I found the Man Who Walks with Power standing not far from the opening of his home, staring into the sky.

We approached and waited.

Soon he turned and greeted Onyame, who returned a greeting of respect. Then he did the same with me and invited us to follow him into the forest.

We walked through many old tree people and eventually found a grassy opening, where we sat, facing each other.

After a long silence, the puoin turned toward me and said, "There is much work that you must do. You face a great challenge in your land."

I nodded.

He continued, "This work, this training, will take" — he stretched his arms out from his sides — "many seasons. You will not leave here for several years."

I was surprised, but I knew that the Man Who Walks with Power could see into the future and could determine what skills I might need and when.

He was speaking again. "You have a Serpent-Person who gives you visions."

I nodded. "As you noticed during my original training, when I have a vision, a dragon guides me. He has begun to direct some of my diplomatic work, as I mentioned yesterday, when I said that an inner voice had led me to listen to Harold's plans to build an empire."

"This Serpent-Person comes from another world, one that helps our world." He paused and spread his hands open. "From one tree trunk, many branches go out. From each path you choose, many paths branch."

"I see."

"The Serpent-Person, the dragon as you call him, sees many branches. He points to the one that helps you. For this reason, you have him as a guide, and he works with you. This is why." He used his left index finger to trace lines along his open right hand. "He sees the paths." He then ran his finger along his right thumb. "He shows you this path, the good path for you."

I nodded again.

He waved his hand in Onyame's direction. "Bear is a traveler. He travels many paths and has many guides, human people, star people, water people. This is how he finds his way."

Onyame nodded.

"The dragon is from another world, one far from here. There." He pointed to the sky. "Other dragons live in the sky, many who have come here. They are not like your dragon, Cuin. They do this." He placed some dirt in his hand and held it out. Then he closed his hand on the dirt, and it slipped out of his hand, falling onto the earth.

He glanced at Onyame to help me understand.

"They grasp," Onyame said. "They try to control, to own, to dominate whatever they touch, but their grasping always fails. Whatever they try to grasp slips away, because the method of grasping cannot work."

The Man Who Walks with Power nodded. "Because grasping cannot work, as Bear says, they grasp harder. It is all they know." He squeezed his hand tightly. "It begins to hurt. It hurts everyone. The dirt. Them. Everyone. It is a path of hurting." He suddenly laughed. "They are grasping dragons."

When I opened my mouth to ask what he meant, he waved his hand to silence me. "This is all you need to know: that your dragon, your Serpent-Person, is not a grasping dragon."

He got up and walked around from one tree to the next. He then sat and looked at me. "You ask questions. Some are straight. Like trees."

Then he got up and ran in a circle within the trees. He stopped to look at me. "Some are like this. Because they run from here to here, they run in a circle."

He stopped and walked to one tree. "The straight questions look at one tree at a time. One tree."

"Are you overly concerned with trees today?" I asked.

He stared at me, and Onyame rendered my joke more clearly in the People's language.

The puoin began to laugh and then laughed harder.

I glanced at Onyame. "I didn't think it was that funny."

"Neither did I, but the puoin is like that, you know."

Eventually, the puoin stopped laughing and looked at me. "Now we visit your Serpent-Person dragon, your guide and helper."

He looked behind himself. "Here." He pointed to a large rock that I had not noticed. It resembled the rock in Garrad's hut.

I moved to the rock and sat with my back against it.

"Bear, too," the puoin said. "He accompanies you."

Onyame sat down beside me. The Man Who Walks with Power nodded.

I closed my eyes, and immediately the dragon appeared. I could hear it dimly hissing, and then it began to twist and circle.

It said: "For the work you must do, over the next span of years, first you need to see everything you have done in the past. You must live within your own history, your own lineage, to be able to stand. For the next few months, I will lead you back through your life, so that you relive everything from where you are now. This is the beginning of what you need to keep the 'grasping ones' from throwing the world out of balance."

So, for the remainder of the summer and into the autumn, I relived my life.

I saw myself being born and taken up by Garrad and Duke Robert, delivered to Chester, and then later to the Falaise villagers and being raised there, often joining my half-brother William and his mother in Falaise and Rouen Castles.

I saw my father, Duke Robert, and Arlette planning my early training and William urging them that I should learn to use weapons.

I saw the travels around Normandy with Garrad, the ocean at Mont St. Michel, and the brothers at Bec Abbey led by Herluin. I saw Lanfranc and his gray cat, moving from Avranches to Bec Abbey.

I saw the assassination attempts, the death of Duke Robert on his pilgrimage, the death of Edward's brother, Alfred, the death of Osbern's father and the killing of Count Gilbert of Brionne, which Edward and I witnessed.

I saw Edward take the throne of England and agree to marry Edith, Godwin's daughter and Harold and Tostig's sister.

I watched myself ride away with Rolf and the Goliards, Voldred's attack and Tostig's rescue, meeting Anette, Matilda, Count Baldwin, and the monks at St. Vaast, buying the nun Edyth and her sisters out of slavery, losing my crutch, my trip north, the interrupted sacrifice of a goat, Garrad's ride with me to Hedeby, meeting Thorir and Onyame and eventually Hardraada.

I watched Ulf and Vandrad deceive me, Onyame come to my rescue, and the trip through the islands and Iceland, where I saw the Law Assembly and Hervor's hut. And Voldred, Ulf, and Vandrad.

I saw myself bailing during my first storm and gazing at the Great Lights in the Northern sky. I saw myself thrown off Onyame's ship into the arms of the People. I saw myself meeting Young Moons and the Man Who Walks with Power.

I saw my return, the death of Magnus, and my confrontation with Hardraada. I recalled King Sweyn's face as I told him that Magnus had given him the throne of Denmark, and now I knew that this King of Denmark was my half-brother, and that his mother, the Queen of Denmark, was my mother.

I saw Voldred shouting my true identity and Lanfranc confirming it, the last assassination attempt by Voldred, and our joining to help William retake Rouen and Brionne Castle from Guy — and the death of Arlette.

I saw Tostig marry Judith, Count Baldwin's half-sister. I saw Young Moons and I walk through the marriage ceremony of the People. I saw a tall William marry a tiny Matilda, in whose presence he was unable to move.

I saw Edward expel Godwin's family, the return of the family helped by Hervor's storm, the death of Godwin, and the reach of Harold of Wessex stretching all over the world.

By mid-autumn, the visions had ended, and I had spent many day in deep contemplation about the meaning of all I had seen.

I also spent delightful nights with Young Moons, and we talked at length about what I was being shown. As I relived my life in conversation with her, she told me about her childhood and life with the People. She commented that her life sounded quiet and graceful compared to mine.

As winter approached, I began to have long conversations with the Man Who Walks with Power. We talked for long days, which became weeks and months.

A.D. 1054

One midwinter day, the Man Who Walks with Power mentioned to me that I should seek a vision, but that for safety, we should stay inside his home.

I was happy to do this, because while staying inside his home may have meant safety to him, it meant warmth to me. I lay down on a pile of blankets and skins, closed my eyes, and the dragon appeared.

Only now, the Man Who Walks with Power stood beside the dragon.

'Your Duke is in danger," the dragon hissed. "He needs help."

"I'm far away," I replied. "The most I can do is watch and say something that he may or may not hear."

"I am here," the Man Who Walks with Power said. "I can make certain that the bridge to your brother is strong."

There was a pause, and the dragon spoke again. "Duke William has been drawn into a war with his own King, as all of you feared. A King he is sworn to serve. He cannot break an oath to serve this King, because no one would ever have an oath-breaker as a leader and because your brother would never break an oath. Now, observe."

As I watched, Garrad and King Edward emerged, sitting in Edward's private chamber. Apparently Garrad has taken over my function of helping Edward remain on the throne.

Edward had a fur robe around his shoulders, and his stained boots suggested that he had been outside earlier in the day, probably hunting and hawking. Garrad wore a brown tunic and leggings that I had seen before, and he was wearing shoes that suggested that he was spending the day in the castle, avoiding the damp winter weather outside.

Edward was speaking. "I know that my messenger must have told you about the threat in Normandy."

"Yes, sire," Garrad said, "but as yet, I have few details."

Edward sighed. "From what I've heard, William asked his uncle, the Count of Talou, to hold the fortified hill castle at Arques for him."

Garrad nodded. "You may recall that the northern region between Eu and Mortemer is a good location for protecting upper Normandy. I recall that William thought having his uncle protect it for him would be a good idea."

"Yes," Edward said, "I visited the castle at Arques while I was in Rouen, and I would value such a fortress myself."

"I would not have chosen the Count of Talou to guard Arques, however. I had overheard him openly envy William's power in Normandy. I said so to William, but you know how loyal William is to his family."

"You're right in your assessment," Edward said. "The Count seized the castle for himself while William was at the other end of Normandy, putting down a threat from Anjou."

"That's Geoffrey Martel's county. Was William successful?"

"He was, but that brought King Henry's attention to William's growing power."

Garrad shook his head. "Growing power? William is barely able to defend his own borders from the likes of Geoffrey."

"I agree, but King Henry saw an opportunity to support William's uncle in seizing Arques. He marched toward Arques, determined to reduce William's hold on Normandy."

"William would never attack his own lord, as we both know" Garrad said, "and King Henry knows that."

"Henry must have thought that he could take Arques before William could make a move. Then the deed would be done. William would never attack his overlord, so King Henry would have a stronghold inside Normandy from which to extend his own power."

Garrad frowned.

Edward smiled. "Let me at least allay some fears. William, our determined young Duke, did what only he can do. He took a small force, including a captain of his, Walter Giffard, and rode at top speed for Arques."

"I know Walter Giffard. He's a fearless fighter, like William, and a determined leader."

"William arrived a half day ahead of his men, with Walter the only person near him, still far behind. As William approached the castle at Arques, a force of thirty men saw him coming. Thirty armed soldiers. William alone. Seeing William in a rage, they fled into the castle, locked the gates, and refused to come out, even though William was thundering for them and his uncle."

Garrad smiled and shook his head. "So, William's reputation for ferocity has spread all over Normandy at last."

"It saved his life, I suspect. When Walter Giffard and his soldiers arrived, William instructed them to lay siege to the castle. You and I know that when William besieges a castle, it falls."

"William's siege skills are unequalled, as far as I know, though Cuin says that Harald Hardraada of Norway has similar skills."

Edward continued, "William returned south, taking care to avoid King Henry. Henry was less than careful with his advance on Arques, though, and Walter Giffard ambushed the King's force. Henry returned to Paris with his life, but barely."

Garrad leaned toward Edward. "William thought that was the end of the King's ambition, I suppose. Apparently it was not, or we would not be having this conversation."

Edward nodded. "These events occurred last autumn, and by December, King Henry had returned with two larger forces and a better strategy. The King himself led one force up the west bank of the Seine toward Rouen, while one of his half-brothers led the other north and east of the Seine."

"They intended to crush William from two sides then. Probably with the help of Geoffrey 'the Hammer' Martel or at least Geoffrey's friends in southern Normandy, who've always been a threat to William's southern border, as you know."

"Yes, many southern lords joined the King and were raiding along the Seine, while the King's brother established himself near Mortemer, from which his army could plunder the countryside. William had tried to warn villagers there and along the Seine to flee, to hide themselves and their livestock in the forests. Some ignored him, unfortunately, and paid a heavy price for doing so."

Garrad shook his head. "William hates undisciplined marauding like that. Did he attack?"

"No. I would have attacked, and so would most leaders. William, however, kept calling up those lords who owed him service and building his forces. He also sent men and instructions to the local lords at Mortemer, under Roger, their chief."

"Thus avoiding any direct involvement in an attack on the King's brother," Garrad said.

"That's right. Roger followed William's instructions exactly. Like William himself, he waited for an opening. A few nights later, when the French soldiers had celebrated their marauding with more than usual enthusiasm and were sleeping soundly, Roger rallied the local lords and surrounded the camp. At dawn, Roger and the lords attacked. Though the battle lasted well into the afternoon, the defeat was so complete that the messenger who reached William told him that each Norman 'had two horses and one French soldier, and ransoming all these was going to put a hole in the King Henry's purse!'"

"One half of the threat has been eliminated," Garrad was saying, "but the threat from the King remains …"

At that moment, I felt myself being pulled from the land of the People to William's camp not far from Evreux, the town outside of which King Henry and his troops slept.

William was pacing in front of his tent, muttering to himself.

The dragon hissed to me, "He can hear you, and he needs your help. His best strategies have just reached their end. His own King …"

As the dragon's voice faded, I could hear William muttering, "My own King attacking me, and I can do nothing. I have an oath. An oath."

"And no one would follow a Duke who's an oath-breaker," I said out loud.

William stopped and stepped back, startled. For a moment, his hand went to his knife. "Who's there? Who is that? Where are you?"

"I'm here, William, standing next to you, though I'm on the other side of the world."

"Cuin? Is that you? Where are you? Are you hiding somewhere?"

"I told you, William. I'm on the other side of the world, and I'm visiting you in a vision. It has happened before, you recall, just before the battle of Val-es-Dunes."

"This is not some jest of yours?"

"I will wait while you search the area, but no, this is no jest. I'm on the other side of the world, and I'm visiting you because you need advice."

William walked around his tent, looked inside, and then drew a sharp breath. "Are you alive, Cuin, or a ghost?"

"If I were a ghost, you could see me, but all you can do is hear me. I'm alive, with my teachers, my friends, and my wife, in the land where they live, where Onyame and I often sail. You know of the place."

He sighed and stood still. "You came to advise me? To do what? To break my oath to my overlord? Or to negotiate with him, when his men are poised to destroy me?"

"Let's concentrate on the situation before us, William. Your overlord has come to seize Normandy, and you've managed to defeat half of his forces."

"The other half remains, Cuin. Very near where I'm standing. My oath is making me defenseless, and your strength, negotiation, will not work with this King. Our individual and combined skills are useless now." He began pacing again. "Do you recall that this King would not even have his throne if it were not for the Dukes of Normandy?"

"I recall that your father, our father, Duke Robert, once regained Henry's throne for him. As Henry once helped you keep Normandy."

His voice was unusually harsh. "I do recall that as well."

"I know that Henry will not negotiate, William. He's here to conquer not talk. We simply need a device that is neither attack nor negotiation. We need something that will frighten the French troops into giving up their attack."

He stopped pacing. "Frighten? Yes, I see."

There was a long pause. "Who has the most impressive voice in all Normandy?" I asked.

"Ralph of Tosny,. You remember that as boys, we used to call him 'the voice of God.'"

"Yes, because of the depth and power with which he could project whatever he wanted to say. And Ralph's family?"

He began to nod. "I see what you're suggesting. Ralph's father — what did they call him in the Southern lands? — 'the terror of the Saracens'. His reputation would have reached Paris long ago."

"And would have had time to ripen into respect, even awe. If Ralph's voice were to reach them now …"

"This might just work." He smiled. "Cuin, you're brilliant, and I'm going to give you … something … when you return."

I was already back in the land of the People, though, watching the events in Normandy unfold.

I saw Ralph climb an ancient oak tree at the edge of the French camp in the middle of the night. I watched him cup his hands and cry at the top of his voice: "This is Ralph of Tosny, son of Roger of Tosny, the terror of the Saracens! Awake, Frenchmen! Up! You have slept too long! Go and bury your friends who lie dead at Mortemer, all destroyed by the invincible forces of Normandy!"

I saw the soldiers stumble from their tents, listening to Ralph repeat his threat again and again. I saw them grab what belongings they could, leaving their tents and most of their plunder.

I watched them sweep past King Henry, who soon mounted and joined them, fleeing all the way back to Paris — without a single pursuer behind them.

The dragon hissed and twisted and returned me to the home of the Man Who Walks with Power.

I could feel the stone at my back, and I could hear Onyame and the puoin laughing.

The next morning, I awoke to find the Man Who Walks with Power sitting near the fire with Young Moons, both of them speaking softly in the language of the People. I rose and put on warm clothes.

As I did, the puoin motioned for me to join them and sit between them.

I thanked him, the three of us exchanged greetings, and I sat down near the fire, Young Moons seated to my left and the puoin to my right.

"In the night," the puoin said, "I had a vision of your Duke. He is safe for now. He faces one last battle with his own King. In how you measure time, that would be two, maybe three years. You must be there to help him. But not yet. There is a greater task beyond this one for you and your Duke. For that you need more training."

"What kind of training?"

"You need to talk with your wife."

I looked at Young Moons, who smiled at me.

The puoin rose and left.

"What is it that I am supposed to talk with you about?"

She smiled at me and touched my hand. "I have listened to the people in your world. I have heard you and the others make plans to keep your lands … safe. You have this interest. Safety?"

"Yes."

"You think about this safety with weapons. With battle." She raised her arms, crossed them, and thrust them out. "You defend yourselves. You attack. For safety."

I nodded. "Yes, that's how we think."

"You have a threat to your safety now: your Duke's King, Henry. The Man Who Walks with Power has said that this threat will arise one more time. And it will be put down. Then you have another threat, a greater one: the man to your north, the light-haired man, Harold."

I nodded again. "Harold, Earl of Wessex, wants to build a formidable empire in the North and conquer as much of my world as he can. I came here to discover some strategy to deal with him."

"Your Duke is his greatest threat."

"I imagine that Harold regards William as an obstacle to his empire-building, yes."

"Among the People, when we have foes, we exchange gifts with them. We talk with each other. We hunt together. We fish together. We are enemies one day. The next day we are friends. I have listened to you and your friends, Garrad, Voldred, and Bear, speak of your foes, their strengths, and their weaknesses. You compare them with your strengths and weaknesses."

"Yes, we strategize that way."

"So, Duke William is compared with Earl Harold, and the threat to your safety becomes a great cloud in the sky to you. Harold is a coming storm."

"That would be a good description."

"You must have your Duke talk with this Earl, hunt with him, fish with him."

I smiled. "That's a good idea, but it would take almost a miracle to bring the two of them together to talk and hunt. I don't know whether either of them fishes."

Knowing that I was making a joke, she laughed. "Instead of fishing, perhaps they could swim. They must swim, because you have rivers in your land."

"Yes, they do swim. Of that I'm sure."

"You must make the miracle."

"What miracle?"

"You said that it would take a miracle to bring them together. You have friends to make the miracle."

"Do I?"

"Hervor makes storms. Bear brings people together and moves things from one place to another. You and your dragon have visions. You talk to many people, many leaders in your world. So, you and your friends can make the miracle." She paused. "Then this Harold Earl of Wessex and William Duke of Normandy will talk and hunt and be foes no longer."

CHAPTER 29

STRATEGIES

A. D. 1055

I remained with the People through most of the next six seasons, training and seeking visions. Onyame continued to carry goods from the land of the People to the islands, which helped the Icelanders end a devastating famine, bringing in goods offered by our old friend, King Harald Hardraada of Norway.

During the second year that I remained with the People, Onyame informed me that Tostig had officially become Earl of Northumbria, a position he had been promised after his family returned from exile.

"So now," Onyame said, "even the old northern Danish stronghold is under the control of one of Earl Harold's brothers."

We sat in front of his home on a sunny morning, listening to the quiet hum that was the People going about their daily lives.

"Will the north of England accept Tostig, do you think?" I eventually asked him.

"Earl Tostig is half Danish. It may work, but Northumbria is a strange land for a Saxon to rule, and Tostig will have to respect the local lords. That reminds me. Tostig has become a favorite at court, and he spends most of his days with his sister Queen Edith and with King Edward."

"He said as much when I last spoke with him in Flanders. So, our plan to have Tostig and Edward become friends is still working."

"Yes, aided by Queen Edith's delight at having her brother at court."

"Well, let's hope that this growing friendship helps us with Harold in the future."

"In the meantime," Onyame said, "an additional earldom has been created for Leofwine, another of Earl Harold's younger brothers."

I shook my head. "Now only one of England's five earldoms is not held by someone in Harold's family."

"Earl Harold continues to expand his personal empire, so there's no doubt what he's planning."

I paused to listen to some laughter in the background. Then I said, "Harold publicly maintains a lavish lifestyle, does he not?"

Onyame nodded. "He wants to be seen as wealthy, and he rewards his followers with land and gifts. As Voldred and I discovered earlier, he continues to seize Church property to enrich himself and his supporters. I've now found twenty-four cases brought against him by Church officials, and I doubt I've found every case."

"Harold has never cared for the Church, from what I hear. One of the Goliards called him a pagan."

Onyame dropped his head to stare at his moccasins. "I've discovered even more about his empire building."

"More than controlling England and being popular in Ireland?"

He smiled at my irony. "Recently, Earl Harold also backed a local noble who had challenged King Macbeth in Scotland, and the noble's son, having defeated Macbeth, became King Malcolm."

I found myself standing up to pace. "So, the King of Scotland is now a personal ally of Earl Harold of Wessex."

Onyame smiled. "I don't recall your being someone who paces."

"William paces, so I may have learned it from him. Just now, though, I remind myself of Edward when he used to pace back in Normandy."

"Do you know that King Edward sent Earl Harold to Wales twice?"

"I've heard that this is yet another territory where Harold is gaining support and a reputation as a wise leader."

"Then you know the history?"

"I know some of it," I said. "King Gruffydd of Wales, as Edward reminded us bitterly on several occasions, invaded England fifteen years ago, then ten years ago, and then again just after the conflict with Godwin's family was resolved. Gruffydd raided and escaped the first two times, but I think Harold himself forced him back into Wales the last time — with a minimum of force and a maximum of diplomacy."

"Yes, King Gruffydd did return this past autumn, and he raided Hereford. King Edward again ordered Earl Harold to confront him. Again, Earl Harold forced King Gruffydd back into Wales. While Harold could have pillaged the Welsh countryside as Gruffydd had pillaged Hereford, he chose instead to negotiate a peace."

I groaned. "So, the Welsh people, probably weary of the military adventures of their King, see Harold as a savior of their lives and livestock."

"In and around England, Earl Harold already has his empire."

I combined my training in visions with Young Moons' ideas about Harold and William. I spent many hours "visiting" those about whom I wanted to know more.

The dragon had warned me that I could not seek visions from mere curiosity: "Taking a great skill lightly will either reduce it or pervert it."

So, I learned to "see" only the major players in the unfolding story of Normandy and the North: King Harald Hardraada of Norway, King Sweyn of Denmark, King Edward of England, King Henry of France (this was more difficult, and the dragon said that the 'grasping' dragons were blocking my efforts to see Henry), Earl Harold of Wessex, and Earl Tostig of Northumbria.

Of course, I also "watched" William, Matilda, Voldred, Onyame, and Hervor. Hervor eventually said that if I did not stop annoying her, she would have Odin change the color of my blue robe to bright red whenever I was trying to hide.

When I was sure that I could use my vision-skill to see all those involved, I "visited" Garrad to discuss getting William and Harold in the same time and place doing the same things.

At first, Garrad did not trust the dragon, because, as he said, "There are dragons, and there are dragons, and not all are to be trusted."

When I told him that the Man Who Walks with Power had distinguished between trustworthy and non-trustworthy dragons, identifying mine as trustworthy, he relaxed.

He began by saying that, "We can both agree that William cannot meet Harold now. Harold is at the apex of his power in England, while William is struggling to survive as Duke here."

"Even more than that," I added, "Normandy itself may not survive, if King Henry has his way."

"Do you have any reason to assume that Henry will invade Normandy again? I don't trust his intentions, but I wonder if you've had a vision."

"The puoin here saw another attack in two or three years, and I had a vision which confirmed that. I saw Henry plotting with Geoffrey Martel, the Hammer of Anjou."

"That sounds right," Garrad said. "Though Geoffrey supplied friends for Henry's last attack on Normandy, he himself remained … conveniently absent."

"Henry must have been unhappy about that."

"Very unhappy. So, Geoffrey will need to regain Henry's favor, and Henry will need Anjou's soldiers. All they need do, though, is have one mutually supportive conversation for another invasion to be born."

"Should we plan for that?" I asked.

"No, I think William should. This is his strength. Let him use it. We need to focus on a more distant future and a more powerful opponent. Henry is unscrupulous and power-hungry, but he has no leadership skills. I do not think that he could ever defeat William."

"I see what you mean. Henry would have to outmaneuver William."

"He has proven himself incapable of doing that."

"So, we're planning for some event that throws William and Harold together."

"I think 'thrown together' is the correct term here, Cuin. Their meeting must seem to be chance."

"I agree."

"One characteristic that William and Harold share is their strategizing. While King Henry cannot strategize as well as William, Harold probably does."

"So, if they intentionally plan to meet each other, we will have nothing but a meeting of strategies, whereas we want them to meet as human beings."

"Yes, as fellow rulers with aims in common."

I paused, thinking. "This event is not going to be easy to plan, though I have some as yet unconnected ideas."

"No, this will not be easy, but you did help Edward keep his throne three years ago by convincing Godwin not to fight and convincing Hervor to give you a storm to keep two navies apart. Will this be any more difficult?"

I laughed. "Yes, because we will be planning around Harold and William. And they are not easily led."

That night, I continued to talk with Young Moons about Normandy.

She asked, "Do you think that your Duke and Harold of Wessex can be friends?"

I shrugged my shoulders. "I'm not sure I know Harold's character well enough to answer that."

"Do you need to know that?"

"His character? I would suppose so. Why do you ask?"

She looked at me seriously. "What you want them to do is talk together and hunt together. If you can help them do these things, then 'knowing their character,' as you say, may not be … required. So, what talking and hunting do you want them to do? That is what you need to create."

"You mean that I need only give them the opportunity to become friends and then let them take advantage of that opportunity."

"Yes."

A.D. 1056

When summer arrived, I accompanied Onyame to the islands, and we saw that the Icelanders continued to recover from their famine.

We found Hervor hiding in her cave — she had been told by Odin that we were coming and allowed us to find her — because she feared that she might be killed.

We sat in her cave as she reflected: "Some of the local inhabitants, good Christians all, suggested that they throw a few people off the cliffs to reduce the mouths to be fed. I'm sure I would have been popular for that activity, had they been able to find me."

I saw a pot simmering on her fire. "Where did you find food this past winter?"

"Odin warned me that the winter would be severe, so I collected and dried many things. They lined the entire entrance, and as you can see, they are gone now. I have used my entire winter stock. That is why I will accompany you to Normandy."

Onyame raised his eyebrows. "You'll travel with us?"

"Odin says that there will be another severe winter this year, so I will spend it in safe hands. That is, if you have no plans to hurl me over some cliff."

I looked at Onyame. "I don't think we have any cliffs in Normandy."

"We have them in Norway, so perhaps the problem is solved after all."

Hervor was shaking her head. "I don't know why I chose either of you disrespectful churls as students."

So we sailed with a seasick Hervor to the islands and Norway, where we stopped to express Hervor's gratitude for King Harald Hardraada's help with the famine in Iceland.

We intended only to leave a message, but Hardraada insisted on seeing both Hervor and me personally. We left Onyame out of the meeting, since his association with Thorir, who had remained with King Sweyn in Denmark, might endanger him.

Hardraada met with Hervor first, and they spent several hours together. I wondered what they might be talking about for so long. Hervor emerged from the great hall nodding and talking to herself.

She later told me that they had discussed Odin's accepting into Valhalla those slain in battle, even if they were Christians. She had reminded Hardraada that Thor still protected all people, and that Mjolnir, Thor's hammer, was the universal symbol of the North, the Christian cross simply being the hammer turned upside down.

I wondered what Hardraada might have thought about that. The image itself was all too familiar to me.

When I walked into the great hall with its fire roaring even in high summer, Hardraada stepped down from his high seat to greet me. He strode toward me and took my arm in the manner of Northern warriors greeting each other.

I saw new lines on his face and reminded myself that Hardraada would be forty years old at least. His voice still rang loudly through the hall, though, and he still seemed to be a giant emerging from one of the Nine Worlds of the Northern tales.

"So, my young friend, we meet once again!. I am delighted to see you in the flesh! I wondered whether that would happen before one of us left this world to feast in Valhalla."

The great warrior's strategies had not changed. Even as the Christian King of Norway, he would cite the Northern tales to see how I would react — since he must know by now that I was a student of Hervor. And by saying "in the flesh," did he mean to imply that he had detected me when I watched him in my visions?

I smiled and bowed to him. "As ever, my lord, I have no way of navigating the rivers your words create."

He laughed loudly. "Yet you just did! It is a warrior's delight to exchange words with you!"

"With the warrior in you satisfied, your majesty, how is the King faring?"

"I'm faring well! I thank you for asking, especially since I've discovered, in only whispered tones, of course, that you could be sitting on many thrones, in Normandy, in England, in Denmark, and even here in Norway, since Canute's reach stretched that far."

"However, your majesty, you and I know that Northern warriors, including Norman ones, choose leaders by their skills. And I have no skills that would fit my backside to any throne, especially yours."

He laughed again. "By God, it would be wonderful to have you as my emissary. Have you reconsidered my offer to represent Norway?"

"I have thought of little else, your majesty, but I cannot see my way clear to it with my wife so attached to her home on the other side of the world. Indeed, I too have become attached to it. Which reminds me to offer my gratitude for the help you gave the Icelanders. I have made friends there in my travels, and you saved many of their lives."

"They are my kinsmen," he said, waving me to a chair by the fire. "I would always help them if I could. Presently I can. The winter has been harsh here as well, but I have many resources to draw on." He smiled at me with a knowing look. "The war with Sweyn, your half-brother, has not drained me significantly."

"I am relieved to hear it, your majesty, though not surprised."

"To speak plainly, though I've had minor battles with Sweyn, I have enough stability here to maintain my resources. Every year I insist on reclaiming the throne of Denmark. Every year Sweyn refuses to give it to me. So I raid his coasts. That keeps my nobles content, since their soldiers claim spoils now and then, though I do not allow them to engage in wanton plunder."

"Duke William frowns on that among his troops as well."

"I've heard that."

I wondered how he had, and I knew I would have to rise to that challenge. "I hear that your majesty has secured local trade with a highly respected coin, which merchants do not clip."

He smiled. "You are well informed as always. Have you been watching me?"

"I always have an interest in your majesty's activities, since I admire them, and I have friends in most Northern countries." I added "most" to exclude my relation to Thorir.

"It's true that I have secured the coinage here and that trade has been good, even with Denmark. And of course, with the Southern countries." He turned toward me abruptly. "However, you have not come here to discuss my generosity and the state of Norway's coin, have you?"

"In truth, I came to express my gratitude, my lord."

"And?"

"And to see if I can do anything further to deepen your friendship with Duke William."

He paused for a long time. "Your friendship is what provides the depth of my friendship with your Duke. You're a remarkable young man, and I'm in earnest when I tell you that it's a delight to talk with you. There are few men with whom I can stand toe to toe."

I smiled. "I would not want to measure this friendship by the comparative heights that would emerge if we were to stand toe to toe, your majesty."

He returned the smile. "I thought that you could not resist remarking on that image. Nonetheless, even I had trouble pulling that bow of yours initially, though I hid it carefully when I saw how easily you pulled it. That was toe to toe, in some sense."

"Thank you, your majesty."

He leaned toward me and put his huge hand on my shoulder. "Now, Cuin. You would want to be certain of my support of Duke William because he's been attacked by his own King. Is that correct?"

"Your majesty is well informed about the events in the South, as I would expect. Yes, that is one reason."

He sat back and frowned. "It was a despicable invasion. Henry is a King, but he's not a great man. He was sworn to protect Duke William, as the Duke is sworn to fight for his King and never against him. Who did his duty, though? Your Duke, not that worm Henry." He sat back in his chair, shaking his head. "You probably know that this worm-King is married to my wife's sister."

"I do know that King Henry's wife is a daughter of Yaroslav, Grand Prince of Kiev, as is your wife."

"Yes, the worm-King is my brother-in-law, though I regret to say that our father-in-law died last year."

"I'm sorry to hear that, your majesty. Grand Prince Yaroslav was much admired. 'The Wise,' his nobles called him, did they not?"

"Yes, and he was wise politically to marry one of his daughters to King Henry. The alliance was useful. Those Frankish Kings, though, have always been weak, as their line is weak. There's no power or honor in it. No, what King Henry did to your Duke lacks all honor." He turned to me. "I will never support the worm invading those he is sworn to protect."

"Shall I receive that as a confirmation of your friendship?"

"Wholeheartedly. When I was part of the Varangian Guard in the Byzantine Empire, I fought along side Normans in Sicily. Later I fought against them when they resisted the Emperor. They seemed to be a noble race, upholding the standards of Northern warriors. Your Duke must be cut from that same cloth."

"Thank you, your majesty." I paused for a moment. "There's another question I would like to ask you. I know that your sons have raided England and that you've had some interaction with King Edward, since the question of royal succession in England involved you and King Magnus."

"You would know — no doubt from King Edward himself when you grew up with him in Normandy — that Hardecanute was the son of King Canute and Queen Emma."

"Yes, my lord, we heard a great deal about Emma from her Saxon sons while they were in Normandy."

He shook his head again. "Yes, Prince Alfred, who was so brutally killed. Hmm. When Hardecanute later became King of England, he was horrified by what had happened to Alfred. That was, I'm sure, a factor in his friendship with Alfred's brother."

"King Hardecanute was already King of Denmark and Norway when he was asked to be King of England, as I understand it."

"Yes, he was. Since he had to rule England and there was no one who could watch Denmark for him, he allied himself to Magnus, who as you know ruled Norway then. They agreed that whoever survived the longest would have the three thrones, England, Denmark, and Norway."

"The flaw in the plan developed, as I understand it, my lord, when Hardecanute invited Edward to share the throne with him."

"Yes, Hardecanute's decision complicated the succession. I understand why he brought Prince Edward from Normandy, of course. He needed someone who would help him secure the support of the Saxon nobles. When Hardecanute died suddenly, the Council wanted Edward to be King, while Magnus thought that the throne of England was his. He intended to invade England to get it."

"We know what happened, my lord, after Magnus, then both King of Norway and Denmark, asked Sweyn to watch Denmark for him."

"Yes, your half-brother seized the throne of Denmark for himself and still holds it, in spite of my raids."

"I do wonder about that, my lord, though I do not wish to seem impertinent."

He smiled at me. "Why have I not just invaded Sweyn and seized the country? Why I settle for raiding?"

I smiled in return. "He does lack your majesty's skills in battle."

"Your perceptions are correct. Your half-brother couldn't win a battle if the soldiers rolled on the ground with their bellies exposed."

I laughed. "He is just half a brother, your majesty."

He laughed with me.

"So," I continued, "you've restricted yourself to raiding ... to what end?"

"I don't need another country to rule now, Cuin, especially one in which I'm unpopular."

"I see. So Einar Paunch-Shaker and the others continue to resist your rule here."

"By the heavens, how do you come to get all this information about the North? Are you also a wizard in addition to being an archer and an emissary?"

"I'm afraid that the tension between you and Earl Einar's forces is not much of a secret, your majesty."

"Thank you for the 'your majesty' in that revelation." He sighed. "Yes, I'm still struggling to get complete control of Norway, and Einar and his friends are not making that easy."

"So, having to deal with opposition in yet another country, in this case Denmark, is not appealing."

"That is correct. As long as I keep my claim to Denmark alive with a few raids, I can always take the throne later — after I've secured my rule in Norway."

"I see. And you have negotiated with King Edward about the throne of England, have you not?"

"I'm sure King Edward would have told you about that. Since Magnus was to get the throne of England if Canute died, and since Magnus was King of Norway and Denmark, and since I am now King of Norway and Denmark — though both Magnus and I had to deal with Sweyn the usurper — the throne of England is legally mine, whatever the Council may think."

"So you have sent envoys to King Edward and allowed your sons the occasional raid to … keep your claim alive there, too?"

He shook his head and smiled. "You're too clever. Are you certain that you don't want to be my emissary? Even the Byzantine nobles, who could scheme and plot endlessly, were not as perceptive as you are. Yes, I'm keeping my claim alive there."

"Thank you, your majesty. I don't want to examine your motives regarding England, though. Rather, I am seeking your opinion and perhaps your advice."

"Indeed? Now, I am flattered. On what matter?"

"If I may ask, my lord: what is your perception of Earl Harold of Wessex?"

"He wants to become King of England and then rule the entire North and the South, including Normandy. What he can't control through diplomacy, he'll take by force."

I allowed myself to look surprised.

He smiled at that. "An intentional surprise look: thank you for the second compliment today. It is obvious, though, is it not? Before Canute divided England into the four earldoms, Wessex had produced great Saxon kings. Though Earl Godwin allied himself with Canute, there's no reason for his son to bow to the Danes."

"Or the Norwegians, my lord?"

He took a deep breath. "Or the Norwegians. Earl Harold grew up with power and wealth, and he's as ambitious as he is capable. I've heard him called the other-king of England, the real power behind King Edward. He has the drive and the ability to take the throne when Edward vacates it. The reason he does not seize it now is that he is carefully building alliances all over the North and the South. When Edward dies, Earl Harold becomes King, establishes his Northern empire, and then invades those regions in the South that he hasn't already won through negotiation. All this would be obvious to anyone who knows the prowess of the present Earl of Wessex and the history behind him."

"Now I'm impressed, your majesty. I had to overhear a conversation between Earl Harold and his late father to realize what he might want."

He looked at me closely and spoke seriously. "Remember, Cuin, I spent most of my life in and around the Byzantine Empire. I survived there by knowing my opponents and their character. And their ambitions." He paused. "Especially their ambitions. Ambitions are not always on the surface. You must read them in the characters of men ... and women."

"So, you see the ambition of Earl Harold, an ambition to rule the North and the South."

"I see Earl Harold building alliances everywhere. I have little doubt that he would invade all those countries that would not yield to him as their ruler."

"I overheard him say just that, but how have you become so certain about this?"

"I'm never certain about anything, so I keep watching. That's how I survive. Earl Harold has been reared with all that an ambitious man needs: wealth, power, influence, and admiration. What goals would he have, having grown up with all this? What's more, did you observe how he reacted when King Edward exiled his family?"

"He was furious. He gathered support from his allies in Ireland and invaded the west coast of England. A friend of mine with Berserker warriors could barely contain him, even though he had only a small force."

"What does this response tell you? Earl Harold feels that it is his right to be in power in England. He will tolerate no opposition to that right. The only possible goal he could set to test himself, to drive himself on — since he already has power in his own country — would be to rule other countries as well, to build an empire."

He stood up and walked toward the fire. "This country and Normandy stand in Earl Harold's way. Your Duke and I are the only rulers who could challenge Harold, and he knows that I will not allow him to be King."

I rose. "You will not, my lord?"

"Of course not. Any Northern ruler would have wanted Edward, chosen by King Hardecanute to become England's King, since he had both the unanimous support of the Council and no intention of ruling any region other than England. Now, though, every Northern ruler — and Southern ones — should look on Harold's kingship as a threat. Besides, my claim to England is stronger than Harold's."

"The Council will choose Harold if he wants the throne, your majesty."

"Yes, but the Council should be aware that Harold as King will want to rule an empire even larger than Canute's, an enterprise that will be very costly to England. Canute's empire, after all, will be the standard against which Harold measures his empire."

"Not King Alfred the Great?"

"Of course, Harold will measure himself against the great Saxon king, Alfred, but Harold is also half Dane. He will also measure himself against King Canute, especially since Canute's empire must be fresh in his memory."

"Yes, Canute died only twenty years ago, when I was a boy."

"I suspect that Harold will want to be as great as both kings. Even greater. If he builds alliances all around us, what does his ambition mean for Norway, Denmark, and Normandy?"

"When King Edward dies, all these territories are in danger."

He paused. "That is precisely why I cannot allow him to be King of England."

Back in Onyame's longship, I related my discussion with Hardraada. Hervor had recovered from seasickness and joined us.

"If Harold's plans are obvious to Hardraada," Onyame said, "then others will notice them as well."

Hervor shook her head. "I do not think so. I watched this young man when I was building the storm to keep him and his father apart — what was that, three years ago? — and he was determined even in his rage. He held his intentions closely in his mind and let few people know about anything except his anger. He is clever and guards himself internally."

Onyame watched her for a moment. "Do you think that he will hide his ambitions?"

I said, "Even to his father, he spoke secretly about his plans."

Hervor nodded. "That is your answer, Bear. He will conceal what he intentions. His empire-building will appear to be normal behavior, even doing his duty as his King commands."

"As in Wales," I said, nodding at Onyame.

Onyame summarized the Welsh incursions for Hervor. "After Harold subdued King Gruffydd, he won the admiration of the Welsh people by not pillaging Wales, even after Gruffydd had brutally attacked Hereford."

She nodded again. "Yes. That makes sense from what Odin has shown me of this man's character." She waved a finger in the air. "We must remember this. Harold will hide his ambitions under a cloak of ordinary intentions."

The following autumn, hiding his ambitions under other intentions was exactly what Harold did.

When the Holy Roman Emperor died in early October, Count Baldwin traveled to St. Omer to make his peace with the new regent, the mother of the new, very young Holy Roman Emperor.

As Baldwin later related in a private letter delivered to me, he was surprised to find Earl Harold of Wessex in attendance, "charming the new regent and promising his support to the Holy Roman Empire."

"Then," Baldwin's letter continued, "when the regent and I traveled to Cologne to meet Pope Victor II, who accompanied us unexpectedly? Earl Harold. Even you may be surprised at his next move. He invited himself to join the Pope's return trip to Rome, where he intended to spend Easter the following spring."

I was not surprised.

The letter went on: "He may have done himself little good in that respect, though. Pope Victor could see that behind Earl Harold's charm lay unrevealed intentions. The Pope worries that Earl Harold's power in England will do the Church little good. How do I know that? The Pope asked me privately before he left for Rome what sort of man Earl Harold was. He knew, of course, that Earl Harold's brother Tostig was married to my half-sister Judith. Before I could reply, he told me that Earl Harold had been seizing Church lands in England and that the Church does not consider Earl Harold a friend."

Baldwin closed with, "I hope that this information is helpful to you in your role as the emissary of my son-in-law, your Duke. Indeed, I am concerned for my son-in-law, as I have learned that the King in Paris is no longer friendly to him."

I wrote back to Baldwin, thanking him for his information and his concern, adding my own concern to his.

The following summer, King Henry invaded Normandy again.

A.D. 1057

William had kept me in Normandy through the year, insisting that I train his men in archery.

"They already know archery," I told him. "Besides, I'm just an emissary."

William assumed his ducal look, and I knew I could not convince him of my ineptitude as a teacher.

"All right," I said as he remained silent, "what do you want me to do?"

"Teach them how to pull the way you do, aim the way you do, and most importantly shoot their arrows quickly and in unison."

"You want them to have concentrated volleys of arrows, you mean."

"Precisely that. I already have the advantage of cavalry. Most of Henry's men fight on foot, and my knights, trained to fight on horseback, can intimidate them. If I have the best archers in the world, I will have every advantage in the field."

Soon, William did have every advantage. And he needed every one.

King Henry, with the aid of Geoffrey "the Hammer" Martel, Count of Anjou, invaded Normandy in August, plundering as they advanced on Falaise, where William was holding court.

He had sent me to Rouen, saying that he did "not want to risk my life at this time."

"So, you're planning to risk it in the future?" I asked, as I prepared to leave.

He smiled at me. "No, I plan to stage a narrow escape here. I will remain in Falaise until Henry and Geoffrey are almost upon the castle. Then I shall flee toward Bayeux."

"I'm not sure how that helps you.".

"I've already spread the word, among any French spy my messengers could discover, that I have a much smaller force than Henry or Geoffrey."

"So, you're an easy victory for them, with many spoils, including whatever they can get for your ransom."

"Yes. So, they must pursue me as I make for Bayeux. What they do not know is that I have already spoken with the local lords and commoners around Bayeux, asking for their help in defending their own lands against the French King and the Count of Anjou."

"I'm sure you described in grim detail how Henry and Geoffrey have plundered other Norman territories."

"Of course, and I was gratified to see the enthusiasm and anger of the Bayeux men."

"So, how does your smaller force deal with Henry and Geoffrey's larger force?"

"You know that in pursuing me, Henry and Geoffrey must cross the River Dives."

"Yes, near Varavilles."

"You've seen the bridge over the river."

"Yes, I have. It's sound, but it's narrow. I'm beginning to see what you have in mind. You cut the pursuing army in half."

"Correct. I let Henry and the vanguard pass over the bridge, cut off the rear guard, and then my men and the enthusiastic citizens of Bayeux surround and attack them, leaving Henry with a much weaker force."

The events happened exactly as William had planned. Henry and Geoffrey pursued him toward Bayeux, marching their men across the wooden bridge over the River Dives. The peasants and William's men cut off and attacked the rearguard of the invading army. Helplessly watching the peasants' revenge for their plundering, Henry and Geoffrey saw that they were defeated. They fled.

Garrad had been right. We did not need to aid William in dealing with King Henry. He was more than capable of handling the threat himself.

We did, however, need our own strategizing skills. Within weeks of King Henry's defeat, Harold made two empire-building moves.

The first required no response from us.

The one remaining bloodline heir to Edward's throne had been living in Hungary for twenty years. Son of an earlier king and Edward's own nephew, the heir abruptly decided to return to England.

His escort was Earl Harold of Wessex. Though Harold made sure that the heir arrived safely in England, he also made sure that before the heir could even see Edward, he was dead, a mysterious death, by all accounts.

Harold's second move did require our response.

The previous year's negotiations at St. Omer, which Count Baldwin's letter had described — where Baldwin had gone to make peace with the Holy Roman Empire — had attracted Earl Harold as an unexpected guest.

Also present was Normandy's northern neighbor, Guy, Count of Ponthieu, who then invited Earl Harold for a hunting trip whenever Harold was on our side of the Channel.

"Count Guy's relation to Normandy has been … uneven," Garrad said, as he and I sat in his hut, entertaining an unexpected guest, William. "He aided King Henry in his first invasion of Normandy."

I looked at William. "You have bad fortune with nobles named Guy. Your cousin first and now the Count of Ponthieu. Perhaps you should outlaw the name."

William only shook his head at me. "Guy was captured at Mortemer, and I imprisoned him here for two years."

Garrad nodded and poked the fire as I swung my feet closer to it. The evening felt unusually cold.

"As I recall," I said, wanting to redeem myself from the failed jest, "his uncle ruled as regent for those two years."

"Yes," William said. "I only released Guy so that he could be officially present as Count of Ponthieu for the meeting in St. Omer."

"The one that Count Baldwin wrote to me about," I said. "The one where Earl Harold of Wessex turned up unexpectedly."

"That event," William said, "was too important to ignore, even without Harold. Thanks to the Goliards I've had watching Harold, I knew he would be there. I sent Guy with a message to invite Harold to Ponthieu for hunting."

Garrad nodded. "It was a good strategy, even if it didn't work."

"It did work," William said. "As Guy recently informed me, Harold has accepted and plans to visit Ponthieu at the beginning of autumn."

"I see," Garrad said. "Harold could not ignore an opportunity to befriend one of your neighbors, allying himself to yet another region. Clever, William, clever."

"If Harold does visit," I said, "it presents us with an opportunity for you two to meet."

"I agree," William said. "So, I need to find a reason to be there. Or to be summoned there."

"A reason that does not arouse Harold's suspicions," Garrad added.

"Cuin," William said, "do you have any ideas?"

"I do. A plan has been forming in my mind for some years, since I first encountered a citizen of Ponthieu — living in the town of Eu, to be precise — a local physician, who also happens to be an expert in guiding ships onto the rocks and raiding them."

Garrad stared at me for a moment. "You mentioned this man to me. Fier is his name. Is that correct?"

"Yes. I think that Hervor could make certain that Harold's ship does not arrive on Ponthieu's coast until dark. Fier can do the rest."

"Do you intend to kill Harold," William asked, "or have me save him?"

Garrad shook his head and shrugged. "It must be said that either serves our purpose."

"Save him," I said.

"Will Hervor help?" William asked.

"She's remaining in Normandy to help you," I replied. "As she's reminded me, Odin is not an admirer of Harold and wants his empire blocked."

"I'm not sure about Odin's will," Garrad said, "but I appreciate that Hervor wants to help us. Her talents were a remarkable boon to Edward in peacefully ending the exile of Godwin."

"I need to add," I said, "that Fier's talents include not having sailors die in his wrecks. He prides himself on that. A broken leg or arm is fine with him. As a physician, he benefits from those. He claims, though, never to have killed anyone."

"So, Harold will be alive after his ship runs aground," William said.

"Which is what we want. If you save Harold from, say, capture and ransom, then he is indebted to you."

"So now," Garrad said, "we need to talk with Hervor and pay a visit to Fier."

Getting Hervor's agreement was easy.

Though Onyame had returned to the People in the spring, Hervor had accompanied me back to Falaise, still insisting that I would need her help during the year.

She had met Garrad, and to my surprise, they had liked each other immediately.

"If you'd told me that your teacher was the Icelandic prophetess I'd heard so much about in the North," Garrad had said, "I would have been less concerned about you. You have been less than clear, as usual. I think your emissary work includes too much secrecy."

Hervor had stayed in my hut near Falaise, traveling between the castle and the village, to the delight of both courtiers and villagers, who wanted to know more about a land that they considered almost as exotic as Eden.

William, too, had met Hervor with enthusiasm, and as I introduced him, she had said, "So, this is the leader in the South that Odin spends so much time watching." She looked him up and down. "Well, you're certainly tall enough."

William had bowed, closing the distance between his height and hers, since Hervor was even shorter than I was. Whether he had meant to reply to her comment with his bow, I could not determine. William's strategizing was becoming, like Hardraada's, impressive even in ordinary conversations.

"I welcome you to the Duchy of Normandy," he had said in his least harsh voice, "and I hope you enjoy your visit here."

She had nodded briskly. "I plan to. I have important work to do that includes using Normandy's resources, most especially your strength and charm."

"Be careful, William, that is the most civil she may be to you."

Hervor had waved my comment off and excused herself, muttering something about Odin's hat.

So, when I asked her to accompany us to Ponthieu, she nodded vigorously.

"This is something that Odin has foreseen, so I will join you. I will be happy to travel anywhere that does not involve a boat."

I also sent the Goliards to Eu with a letter for Fier, telling him to expect autumn guests, a ship bearing a noble, and a storm with his fortune in it.

As autumn approached, Rolf arrived with word that Earl Harold was putting to sea to visit Count Guy of Ponthieu.

Hervor, Garrad, and I headed north for Ponthieu, taking advantage of a cart William had lent us plus a good horse. I put blankets and every kind of padding I could think of on the cart's seat, which Hervor, who sat beside me, appreciated.

The roads and the weather being clear, we reached Eu within three days, arriving the evening of the third day. We located Fier's home, which had new thatching on it, so I deduced that the relic-forging and ship-wrecking trades were still supplementing his healing income.

Fier seemed delighted to see me again and especially pleased to meet Garrad and Hervor.

"Three healers visiting at one time," he said, as he greeted us and ushered us into his home. "I am unlikely to have this good fortune again as long as I live!"

Soon we were seated around a fire that had been prepared for the autumn evening's chill.

Fier asked about our trip, and we filled in the details while admiring the books, bones, and body charts that decorated his home. As I remembered the place, it was not huge, but it was spacious, now allowing room for all of us to sleep on the fresh-straw floor with mats that had been laid for our visit.

As we spoke, the light faded, and the room grew dark, so that all we saw was the firelight on each other's faces as we leaned forward and toward each other to talk. Shadows filled the corners of the house.

At one point, I imagined that the door, some distance behind us as we pulled closer to the fire, opened and closed silently, but I dismissed the thought.

As soon as I could, I turned the conversation to our plans.

"Fier, we know that a ship bearing a Saxon noble arrives here within two days. We have the ... ability ... to ensure that the ship does not arrive before we're ready to receive it."

"Who will be on this ship?"

"Earl Harold of Wessex, the most powerful man in England after the King."

"Even I have heard of the formidable Earl Harold. You're fishing large then."

"For a good reason."

"A reward from the Earl will be reason enough for me, but of course, I'm even more pleased if your reason is a noble one."

"It is."

"You can bring the ship here when you want and where you want?"

"Yes, and for your purposes, we can also ensure that it will arrive in a storm."

He frowned at me.

Hervor answered his unspoken question. "Cuin means that I have the ability to keep the wind against the ship until we're ready, and I can create a storm as it approaches here."

I expected Fier to be surprised, but instead he leaned toward Hervor.

"Can you make it arrive late at night as well? That would be ideal for my purposes."

She smiled at him. "Of course."

"We want you to guide the ship onto the rocks without killing anyone," I said.

He nodded. "As you know, I've never killed anyone in a wreck. Nor will I."

Suddenly a harsh voice came from the shadowy corner of the room nearest the door: "Your man is sure of his craft."

Only Fier leaped to his feet, startled. The rest of us recognized the voice and the figure that stepped from the shadows, clad in a dark green hooded riding cloak.

"Who are you?" Fier demanded.

The figure threw back his hood. "Duke William of Normandy, my friend, and I hope I haven't frightened you."

"No, my lord —" Fier began.

Hervor interrupted him. "Frightening him is just what you meant to do. You wanted to test his reactions."

William looked at her, raising his eyebrows. Then he turned back to Fier. "If I may join you at your fire, I'd like to be part of your conversation."

"You are most welcome, my lord," Fier replied and disappeared into a dark corner, returning with a chair for William. He motioned toward the chair. "Please, my lord."

William sat, and Fier looked uncomfortable for a moment.

"Please sit, my friend," William said. "Here we join to confront a demanding challenge." He looked around the room. "The methods to meet that challenge are extraordinary enough to make us equals before their power."

"I take that as a compliment," Hervor said, "even if it was not intended as one."

William smiled at her. "I never offer flattery where it's not deserved."

"Hmph. You're as slippery as your emissary." She turned to Fier. "Even in a storm strong enough to drive a ship onto rocks, you can be certain that no one will be killed?"

"No one ever has been."

She nodded once. "Good. Then let us plan what we will do and how we will do it."

Over the next two days, we went over the plan many times.

William's house guard, which included several Berserkers supplied by Voldred, arrived with extra supplies and gifts for Fier.

I noted that William always expressed lavish gratitude when anyone helped him.

When the evening of the second day arrived, we positioned ourselves at various points along the shoreline in keeping with our roles.

Garrad and I stood on the same rise where Onyame and I had first seen Fier almost ten years earlier. Our task was to spot the ship as early as possible and signal Fier.

Hervor sat not far from us, alternatively staring at the sky and then bowing her head, closing her eyes, and muttering to herself. Or to someone. Her tasks — wind and storm — were already complete.

William and his house guard had journeyed to one of Count Guy's homes nearby, where William would hide until needed to play his role. He left behind only one Berserker, who would return to William if anything went wrong.

The Berserker stood at the farthest point away from the coast where he could still see what was happening.

Fier had arranged for ten of his fellow townsmen to position themselves not far from where the ship would wreck. They would pose as looters. As the ship ran aground and the soldiers escaped it, the townsmen were to make themselves visible and then flee toward the town, as if something had frightened them.

I could see them in the distance, not far from Fier's line of fires, now small and flickering.

Soon Garrad and I saw a ship, almost a shadow in the darkening storm, approaching the coast.

Fier must have seen it, too, because before we could wave to signal him, his fires were already building. They began to lead the ship too far inland.

As I had years ago, I watched Fier dart between the fires, stirring one, then running to the next one, then stirring that one, and running to the next one. When he finished with the farthest one, he stared out to sea, studying the ship's progress. Then he dashed back down the line of fires, putting the farthest one out, restarting it even farther out, and then running to build each of the others to a blaze.

I saw Garrad shake his head. "How can he keep from killing the soldiers on that ship?" he asked, raising his voice above the wind.

"You heard what he said," I shouted back to him. "He claims never to have lost a life."

Garrad continued to shake his head. "We'll soon see."

We did not wait long. Soon the splintering of the ship and the cries of the men reached us. I saw Garrad grimace and realized that I was doing the same.

After that, everything happened just as we had planned.

The townspeople ran toward the ship, watched the men stumble from it, and then fled back to the town, the soldiers' curses following them.

The soldiers themselves did not follow, though. The injured could not, and those not injured were helping their comrades or trying to recover from the wreck.

I glanced at the fires, and Fier had disappeared. Soon, I heard running footfalls behind us, and he was with us, gasping for breath.

Garrad turned to him. "Are you sure no one has been killed?"

He smiled and said, still breathing heavily. "I am certain, as we shall soon discover."

We watched the men escape the ship and scatter themselves on the rocky shore. Soon a tall figure emerged among them and began shouting orders.

Earl Harold of Wessex.

Soon afterward, Fier said to us, "We can go down now. And we must run, as if we have been running from my house. We must be breathless."

So we ran, more quickly than we would have been able had we not practiced the run down the rocky slope many times in the past two days. In a short time, we reached the men and Earl Harold.

As before, several of the men seized us, thinking we were raiders.

I shouted at them as loudly as I could, "I'm Cuin of Falaise, and I know your lord, Earl Harold. I'm here to help! Tell him! Please!"

They did not have to. Harold heard my voice and ran toward us.

"By Valhalla!" he shouted. "Cuin, what are you doing here? Release these men. I know this one, and if he vouches for the others, they are under my protection."

"Thank you, my lord," I said loudly. "My original healing teacher, Garrad of Falaise, and I were visiting Eu's physician, Fier, when some townsmen informed us of the wreck. Since all of us are healers, we gathered what supplies we had and came as quickly as we could. I'm sorry that the wrecked ship is yours. Are you all right? May we help your men?"

He nodded. "I am unhurt, and I couldn't hope for better help." He turned to the soldiers. "See that no harm comes to these three healers, and help them in any way you can."

After that, we spent much of the night bandaging wounds and setting bones, though Garrad and Fier handled the bloodiest cuts. Not one person had been killed.

By morning, we had finished and sat on the beach, exhausted.

Harold found us there, and as he approached said, "Please don't rise. I'm coming to join you." He lowered himself onto the ground facing the three of us. "Thank God you were here, you three. I cannot think what might have happened had you not been."

"It was unfortunate that you were caught in a storm, my lord," I said, "but it was fortunate that we were in Eu. I've heard in England that some power watches over you — either God or Odin, depending on whoever was telling me this — and it appears to be true."

Harold nodded at the comment but moved quickly past it, apparently to keep his attention on us. "Did you say that you just happened to be visiting here?"

"I have known Fier, Eu's physician, for many years, my lord, and we have, over those years, exchanged many ideas about healing."

Harold glanced at Fier, who said, "Many useful ideas, my lord."

I continued, "I will confess, though, that I had heard from Fier that Count Guy had invited you for a hunting visit, and that you would be here sometime soon. Since I was hoping to see you, I took the opportunity to invite my first teacher, Garrad, to meet Fier. If I missed you, the three of us would at least have had a useful time talking about healing."

Garrad and Fier nodded their agreemen, as we had planned.

Harold looked at the three of us. "Why were you hoping to see me?"

"I was hoping that you would meet my Duke, William of Normandy."

Harold raised his eyebrows. "Duke William is here?"

"No, my lord, but he is at his castle in Fecamp, which is less than a day's ride from here. I could send a messenger, and Duke William could be here within two days."

"Is he involved in court or abbey business at Fecamp?"

Fortunately, I knew that since Godwin's exile, there had been a dispute involving Fecamp Abbey and a potential property belonging to it just across the channel in Steyning. Harold was trying to discover whether William was engaged in the dispute.

I wanted to use the dispute to show Harold that William was even-handed. So, I replied, "Only on court business, my lord. The Duke visits the abbey only for purposes of worship." To keep Harold from wondering further about the abbey affair, I added, "I will also confess, my lord, that I mentioned the possibility of your visit to Duke William. He said, with real enthusiasm, that he would be pleased to meet the Earl who, as he put it, 'has made King Edward's reign peaceful and perhaps even possible'."

Harold nodded and took a deep breath. Eventually he said, "I would like to meet your Duke, of course. I have heard much of him, especially from the Normans at court."

"Thank you, my lord. I will send a messenger today."

So it happened that William appeared within two days and met Harold.

I was surprised how quickly they became friendly with each other. As soon as the formal introductions had been made at one of Guy's homes — the one in which William had not been hiding — the two rulers began to have almost intimate exchanges.

William began. "What I've heard, Earl Harold, is that your diplomacy and charm have saved you many battles. Listening to your voice, I hear the first weapon you have for diplomacy. I cannot get my voice to sound less than harsh. Everyone tells me that. Yours, however, would soothe a startled horse."

Harold smiled. "It has aided me when I need to sound unthreatening. I used it again and again in Wales, where, as I learned, the quality of a voice is much studied. I believe that it allowed me to win the peace there twice."

William nodded. "Avoiding bloodshed. Admirable."

"I know that you don't allow your soldiers to plunder. It's an admirable trait. Also you prefer sieges to open battles."

"I saw too much local violence when I was young to want anything but less of it. I will strike hard when I need to, but only to prevent bloodshed later."

Harold nodded. "A good strategy and hard earned, as I've heard from King Edward. You had to survive many assassinations, and your method of ending them was astonishing. The King has told me the story more than once."

William smiled. "Edward loves to tell stories repeatedly."

Harold returned the smile. "I have noticed that, but it's a remarkable story, nonetheless. I genuinely do not think that I could have done what you did — to try that maneuver with an assassin riding on a large horse. To unseat him and then allow the other two assassins to return to their masters with your message. Remarkable. And effective. Much more so than if you had killed all three or had your men do so."

And so the exchange went on.

For the entire month that the two leaders hunted with an almost forgotten Guy.

By the time Harold sailed back to England, on a ship supplied by William, the two were close friends.

During one of their last conversations, I overheard a significant exchange.

William was commenting on the ambition of the Pope to control all the churches, abbeys, and clergy — disapprovingly.

"I don't deny that the Pope has overall authority," William said, "but I cannot see why he doesn't leave the local administration to the clergy and their overlords."

"I agree," Harold replied. "While I've tried to be friendly with Pope Victor, he seems similar to earlier popes in that he wants a say in how I administer my local churches as well as how I work with my local clergy."

"It's interference, and a ruler cannot look upon that with kindness."

"I worry, too, that as the power of the Church and the Holy Roman Empire grows, this interference will grow as well. Might our descendants in several generations wake up to find themselves vassals of the Pope?"

William nodded. "If rulers are not vigilant, that seems to be a real possibility."

"The problem with the way Pope Victor considers Christianity is that it has no honor. In that way, it is unlike Odin and Thor worship."

"I might share your view on that. What do you mean, exactly?"

"A warrior must have honor to fight in the world," Harold replied. "He may abandon his honor in an angry moment, or he may betray his honor for some lesser purpose. Honor, though, always remains his guiding star. A great warrior, one who becomes a great leader, must maintain his honor, follow that star, as ably as he can."

"That seems right to me."

"From what I've seen, though, the religion of the Pope and the Empire has no honor. While I understand the drive for power, I cannot approve of it in this religion. Christians approach their tasks with such fervor that, given some cause, no matter how base, they might stoop to any methods to achieve their ends. Honor would never be considered."

William nodded. "I understand your meaning. The religious zeal of King Olaf or even of Emperor Charlemagne meant torture and death to those who didn't agree with that zeal. Many were put to the sword."

"In a religion with a Healer and Peacemaker as exemplar."

There was a pause, and William said, "Honor is indeed a better guide, and it is often missing in Pope Victor's Christianity."

"If that spreads all over the world, God help us," Harold said. He was silent for a time. "I would like to see some empire set itself against this … power without honor."

"Ah, taking on the Pope! I admire your ambition, but … I could not do that."

"Why not?"

William sighed heavily. "He has a hold on me, at least for the present."

"What hold?"

"When I was young, while I had a few experiences in the ways of love, I didn't give my heart to anyone. Nor did I think I ever would. Ever. Then I met Matilda."

"Your wife."

"Yes. She captured my heart so completely that I could think of nothing else. It made me angry at first, to be so much in someone else's power. She didn't even want me at that time, so she didn't intend to have me in her power."

"It was just your heart being captured so completely …" Harold nodded. "Yes, I've had that once in my life."

"Well, it became almost my whole life, especially when she agreed to marry me. I was not useful to anyone or anything for months." I heard him laugh. "I cannot bear to think what judgements I must have given in court during those times."

Harold laughed with him. "This is a delightful problem, but how does the Pope fit in?"

Another sigh from William. "The former Pope Benedict, as you may know, never had good relations with the Normans, here or in southern Italy."

"Pope Benedict," Harold said, "never had good relations with anyone, except some of his soldiers and one of his mistresses."

"Benedict decided that Matilda and I were too closely related to be married."

"The consanguinity problem."

"I hate that word."

"In your case, I would assume that the word and the issue would both feel despicable."

William sighed again. "Yes, it was a political ploy to bring Normans to heel, using Normandy's leader as …"

"A pawn in a chess game of power?"

An odd sound from William. "Pope Victor kept the game going, so that the present uncertainty about a new Pope has not made my position any stronger."

"You two wed anyway."

"Yes, or course. Imagine, though, if a new Pope decides to excommunicate us? Who will follow a leader who has been excommunicated?"

"I see what you mean." There was silence for a moment. "You see, this is all the more reason that Popes and their empires should not be allowed to grow, to expand. Look at what this is doing to you."

Another silence. Then William's voice. "I never have or never could love a woman as much as I do Matilda. And I could never give her up. Even for Normandy."

Harold huffed. "Nor should you have to just to appease some Pope who is power mad and thinks that God gives him the right to be so."

Another long silence. Then William's voice. "Thank you, my friend."

"I've had some, perhaps even many, relationships with women," Harold said, "though there is one woman I have loved more than all the others."

"Is this Edith?"

"You have heard of her?" Harold sounded surprised.

"I have heard that she is a great beauty and that you two have children together."

"Ah, then," Harold said, "let me tell you about her."

And he began to do so.

I leaned heavily against the wall. The Duke of Normandy and the Earl of Wessex were friends.

Young Moons had been right.

CHAPTER 30

HIATUS

A.D. 1059 - 1064

The friendship with Earl Harold was the beginning of good fortune for William.

I remembered that Harold's ability to heal had run through my mind the night I had met him in his dying father's room. Perhaps he was a healing force, after all.

The year after Harold's visit, the new Pope, Nicholas II, came to office. He was backed by Hildebrand, the well known reformer about whom Lanfranc always commented positively — especially since, also in the year of Earl Harold's visit, Hildebrand had opposed former Pope Benedict, even attacking the castle in which Benedict was hiding.

Pope Nicholas had excommunicated Benedict and had also waged war against him in southern Italy, aided by the Norman lords living there.

Later that year, Nicholas officially approved the marriage of William and Matilda.

At the same time, he issued a Papal charter, which Lanfranc wanted to discuss with me.

While I was visiting Bec on a particularly rainy day in a particularly leaky room near where Lanfranc taught, he reviewed Nicholas' statement to impress upon me that it had just changed history.

"The Papal statement issued in April of this year," Lanfranc began, stroking one of the cats that always surrounded him, "declares that the election of the Pope is in the hands of the College of Cardinals. Only the College of Cardinals."

"I understand the implications," I said, "only insofar as Pope Nicholas removes the influence of the nobles who chose Benedict. Benedict was unlikable. The expression I've heard is that his mother might have liked him."

Lanfranc laughed. "What you've heard is true, though I know nothing of Benedict's mother."

"This is not about the character of a particular Pope or the decisions of particular nobles, though, is it?"

"It is not. Nicholas' charter means that for the first time, no ruler, noble or royal, will have an official role in who is to be Pope. The Church alone will hold that power, in this case within the College of Cardinals."

"That makes the Cardinals more powerful. Is that your concern?"

"Archdeacon Hildebrand supports anything that extends the Church's power. He supports this. And …" He stroked the cat a bit too vigorously, I thought. "This is an enormous expansion of Church power."

I thought for a moment about both William's and Harold's concerns about expanding Church power. "What worries you?"

"The Papal charter carries legal implications for the future that we cannot imagine. It changes the world in which future generations will live. Immediately, it expands the power of the office that holds Duke William hostage."

"I don't understand. William's marriage to Matilda has been blessed by the Pope."

"Yes, it has. With a condition."

"What condition?"

"That William spread the Church's power as far as he can. He and Matilda agreed to build monasteries to seal that … quiet contract."

"I thought the monasteries were a penance for marrying without papal approval."

"That's the public reason. The private one is more binding on both of them."

"Does this mean what I think it does? Could the Pope order William to … intrude in some Church matter, even if William had no personal interest in that matter?"

"Phrased like a diplomat. And exactly right. If the Pope wants something, he can treat William and the Norman lords as his personal army."

I leaned back in my chair. "I see. That's why using Normans as his army in southern Italy was important. Pope Nicholas didn't just want to get to the former Pope, Benedict. He wanted to enlist the southern Normans as his house guard."

"Yes, you grasp the implication that even William has missed: using the Normans in the south of Italy was just the beginning. Any Pope in the future may call on William in just the same way."

"And William cannot refuse."

He nodded. "Not without risking excommunication over the consanguinity issue and thus losing Matilda or Normandy or both."

When, two years later, a reform-minded student of Lanfranc's became Pope Alexander II, Lanfranc and I hoped that the new Pope would be too busy reforming to need William.

In the meantime, William's fortunes took another leap forward. In 1060 — two years after Earl Harold's visit — both King Henry in Paris and Count Geoffrey Martel of Anjou died. The two men who had invaded William twice were no more.

William immediately allied himself to the new rulers of Anjou, who became friendly neighbors.

In the meantime, the new King in Paris, Philip, too young to rule, was assigned a regent: Count Baldwin of Flanders, William's father-in-law.

Relieved, I sailed with Onyame to the People and to Young Moons, convinced that the efforts on William's behalf, including mine, has finally established him in a safe and prosperous Normandy.

To celebrate, I stayed with the People for several years, letting Onyame pick up and deliver his goods without me.

I continued to learn from the Man Who Walks with Power, working mostly on visions.

He also encouraged me to become more accurate and faster with my bow, which surprised me. I later learned that he had been a formidable archer himself. So I worked with the People's best archers, who increased both my speed and my accuracy.

Whenever I reflected on events, I found myself settling into what I was sure would be the rest of my life.

Indeed, when Harold paid William another friendly visit in A.D. 1064, again, meeting him in Ponthieu with Guy as host, I became convinced that my work securing William's position was ended.

When Onyame returned from his deliveries that year, we sat together near a vision stone in the forest, and he described how Harold and William had hunted together and traveled together.

"The hunting was for enjoyment," Onyame said. "The travel was more serious. Duke William and Earl Harold led a small army into Brittany, forcing the surrender of Count Conan."

"His surrender? That ends the long rivalry between Normandy and Brittany then. And secures yet another border for Normandy. Harold apparently is a force for good where William is concerned."

"You won't be surprised to hear then," Onyame said, "that not only did Earl Harold help Duke William with Conan, but he also saved two of the Duke's soldiers who had become mired in a bog, a sandy one, during the campaign."

"Did he?"

"The mire was not far from Mont Saint-Michel."

I smiled. "The soldiers may have even fallen into the same bog I did when I was a child, where Garrad taught me how to escape bogs."

"Well, it seems that Duke William expressed his gratitude by offering one of his daughters to Earl Harold."

I laughed. "I suppose that the offer was light-hearted. William knows that Harold has a passion for one particular woman."

"A formal alliance would help Normandy."

"So it would."

"At one meal they shared, Duke William and Earl Harold apparently laughed over becoming first friends and then eventually son and father-in-law."

I shrugged. "Perhaps I'm wrong then. Perhaps the two of them have better ideas than I do about formal alliances through marriage."

"There's something else. According to Rolf, who was there, Duke William and Earl Harold took oaths of mutual assistance."

"Oaths? Formal oaths? On relics?"

"They swore to support each other any way they could."

I leaned heavily against the stone. "So, the threat from Harold has vanished that easily."

Onyame laughed. "I wouldn't describe bringing these two together as easy, but yes."

I sighed deeply. "So my work in Normandy is complete."

"It seems so."

"As the People say, we may have many quiet seasons here."

But then everything changed.

A.D. 1065

The first cause of that change I saw in a vision brought by the dragon.

In the spring, Onyame had sailed east on his regular route, and I had remained with the People through the summer. On an early autumn afternoon, probably just after Michaelmas, I calculated, I was resting against a rock not far from the People's village when I heard the dragon hissing.

"We travel to the north of England, York," it said, "watch carefully."

A vision appeared.

In a large room, well over one hundred nobles shouted and pounded their axe and sword handles on the floor. Three nobles wound their way to the front of the hall, but they did not struggle to get there. They leaned toward many other nobles they passed, and many thumped them on their backs in gestures of support.

The three eventually reached the front of the hall and raised their battle axes. Soon, the hall became quiet, though I could still hear murmuring and an occasional axe handle pounding on the floor.

The three spoke for a time, but I could not hear what they said. Eventually, the voice of one of them reached me.

"So, we are agreed, my noble lords, that Earl Tostig has used his powers of taxation to steal from all of us! He has taken lands from us and the Church, so he has also robbed God! Worst of all, he has either murdered or caused to be murdered those whom he had sworn to protect during negotiations!"

A general uproar broke out again.

The noble waited a moment, and the hall became silent.

He continued, "This supposed Earl of Northumbria has never traveled here to offer leadership — other than leadership in villainy. Even now he hunts with the King in the south, a King who has never even traveled here. The King's own wife, Earl Tostig's sister, conspired with Earl Tostig in the recent deaths."

Another uproar.

The noble concluded: "Outlaw this Earl has shown himself to be, and outlaw we now declare him!"

The room filled with cries of "Outlaw!' and "Seize his property!" Someone in the back shouted something, and the nobles streamed from the hall.

The vision faded, and I concentrated to refocus the next scene: the same nobles rampaging through Tostig's palace in York, knocking over chairs and tables, filling their pouches with gold and silver, and further arming themselves with weapons stacked around the palace. I grimaced as seven servants and house-guards were killed.

As the scene faded, I saw the two Danish officers of the house guard hanging from an ash tree just outside the city walls.

I heard one noble pull another aside and say, "Now, we must inform Earl Harold that the plan to rebel has been successful, and his brother has been removed."

The other said, "It was an easy task. Such a hated ruler! But we must make Earl Harold believe that our efforts warranted the gold he gave us."

The voices were familiar. I focused hard on the vision, staring closely at the faces of the two men.

Ulf and Vandrad.

The last scene was a huge force of northern nobles marching through Northumbria, headed south. I noted Welsh banners among them.

"The Welsh," the dragon hissed.

I did not need to have it pointed out that Welsh soldiers, from a country that loved Harold, were helping to end Tostig's rule in the north of England.

The dragon's face appeared before me, and its body swirled in front of me. "Now we travel into the near future. Observe."

I watched another gathering, a huge one — apparently, from the religious banners, the Festival of St. Simon and St. Jude, one month into the future.

The dragon continued, "Earl Harold has already met with the northern nobles — the marauders we just saw — to confirm that Earl Tostig is now officially an outlaw, just as the northern nobles had demanded. Harold has also called a conference of northern and southern nobles to witness the freeing of Northumbria from Tostig's evil rule." The hissing grew louder. "Look at the site of the conference."

I drew my breath in sharply. Oxford.

Half a century earlier, King Canute had summoned his lords to a conference, often referred to as "the Great Reconciliation." Canute had insisted that his northern lords reconcile with his southern lords. And he was successful. The great conqueror became a peacemaker.

Canute's Great Reconciliation conference had been held at Oxford.

I watched Harold stand in front of the lords, issuing the King's commands: Earl Tostig must relinquish the earldom of Northumbria and leave the country. He would be replaced by an Earl of the northern lords' own choosing.

The northern lords shouted their approval. The southern lords praised the King but especially "the peacemaker Earl Harold of Wessex, because even though having to deal harshly with his own brother, he has prevented a civil war."

I especially heard two nobles crying loudly that, "Earl Harold has re-enacted, recreated, and reclaimed the laws of King Canute!"

The two "nobles" were Ulf and Vandrad.

Harold the formidable warrior lord had also become the peacemaker.

As a Saxon, he could already stand in the tradition of King Alfred the Great. Now he had taken on the mantle of the King Canute, the former Danish ruler of the entire North: England, Norway, and Denmark.

Two weeks later, the second event occurred to end my peaceful days with Young Moons and the People. Onyame sailed in with a message from William.

As we sat cross-legged on the blanket-covered floor of his home, Onyame looked at me for a long time and then spoke. "Duke William has received a message from the Pope, and he wants you back in Normandy as soon as possible."

"You just arrived here, and we risk autumn storms if we sail now."

"If we leave immediately, we avoid the worst storms, and Duke William insists that you return."

"I've read his letter, but all it tells me is that the Pope has ordered Norman emissaries to Rome. The issue is, as his scribe has written enigmatically, 'the service that Duke William owes the papal office'."

"What Duke William told me is that Pope Alexander has vision-seekers with skills similar to yours. They've seen the death of King Edward later this year, and they've seen Earl Harold take the throne."

I shook my head. "This is not an unexpected event, nor is it a disturbing one, since Harold and William are friends."

"The Pope does not see things in this light. He feels that Earl Harold as King of England will be a threat to the Church's power. Earl Harold, Pope Alexander says, insists that the English clergy are loyal first to him and only secondarily to the Church."

"As does William in Normandy."

"Duke William, however, does not steal Church lands and funds, while Earl Harold does, as you and I know. As the Pope knows. The Pope also suspects Harold of wanting to curtail the Church's empire as he builds an empire of his own, one that could eventually threaten the Church."

I sighed. "We've talked about this at length. All of us have, as you know. This is a threat we may have to face in the future, but until Harold provokes a response, we need not respond."

He paused. "From what Lanfranc says, it's not in the character of Pope Alexander to respond, to react. Rather, he acts. If he believes that Earl Harold is a threat to the Church's power, he wants that threat removed. Immediately. By force, if necessary."

"Popes do love to lead armies."

"This Pope can, but he wants Duke William to lead this army."

I groaned. "So, the consanguinity issue returns to haunt William."

"Pope Alexander prefers to say that, as head of the Church, he has served Duke William, and now Duke William must serve the Church."

"So, if William does not remove what the Pope perceives as a threat —"

He finished the thought, "The Pope will resurrect the threat to William's marriage and his rulership of Normandy."

"William is forced into action if or when Harold becomes King of England. And the Pope's vision-seekers tell him that Edward's death is imminent."

"Which is why Duke William wants you back in Normandy immediately."

After a sad good-bye to Young Moons and the People, I once again rowed and bailed my way back to Normandy. Though we returned safely, we encountered more storms than usual, and I arrived in Falaise exhausted.

While I recuperated with Garrad and Marie, William sent a message that I should join him in Rouen. So Garrad, Onyame, and I set out. With cold autumn rains making travel difficult, it took us three days to reach the castle.

William seemed happy to see us, and he apologized for insisting upon my return and an autumn sailing.

As we sat in a side chamber of Rouen Castle, he commented that I looked older but more relaxed and that life with the People and a beautiful wife seemed beneficial to my health.

I noted that although William had a few more lines in his face and some graying hairs, he otherwise appeared the same.

Watching me closely, he asked, "Have you had a vision of the death of King Edward?"

"Not for many years, so I don't know when the event happens, though Onyame told me that Pope Alexander believes it to be this year. I do know now that, true to my vision, Earl Harold becomes King after Edward."

"No one doubts that," William said, "but I've received disturbing reports about events in the north of England."

"Do you refer to Harold's plotting to have his brother removed, forcing Edward to oust Tostig, and becoming, in the minds of Saxons and Danes, King Alfred the Great and King Canute the Great combined?"

"How do you know that?" William asked. "I have fast spies, and they just delivered this message yesterday. Did you have a vision?"

"Yes." I described what I saw.

He got up to pace. "That's what disturbs me. Harold is a friend. I like him. I admire his abilities. But he has a drive for empire that exceeds any man I know."

"You mean" I added, "any man who is not running the Church or the Holy Roman Empire."

William allowed himself a harsh laugh. "Yes. It seems that empire builders cannot leave me in peace."

"It is not in the nature of empire builders to want peace," Onyame said.

William stared at him for a moment. "I think you're right. Harold ousting his own brother to gain favor with in northern England is troubling. The Saxons in the south already consider him their leader, but now the northern English lords do as well."

"I agree," I said. "The conference at Oxford would be troubling enough, but wanting the north's support, even at the cost of his brother's outlawry ..."

William breathed heavily and sat back down in his chair. "In Harold's defense, we know from the Goliards that Tostig was not a good ruler. His taxes in Northumbria were excessive. When he couldn't openly oppose an opponent, he had that opponent killed. One was murdered with the connivance of his sister, Queen Edith. As we consider all of this, Tostig's ouster was inevitable. Harold would consider Tostig an undesirable earl, during Edward's reign or his own to come. Harold would be doing what he thought was needed."

"Harold's benefiting so much from the ouster is what troubles you, is that right?" I said.

"Yes. He gained not only the entire country's support, but he also positioned himself as the ruler of the entire North, like Canute. England, Denmark, Norway. All of it. Harold's empire dreams have not lessened, I fear, but expanded with that move."

Onyame spoke quietly. "That is not your only problem, my lord, is it? Pope Alexander?"

William sank deeper into his chair. "The Pope sees Harold as a foe, and he wants me to be the weapon that destroys that foe."

"Surely the Pope cannot order you to kill a King," I said.

"He could order me to overthrow a usurper."

"Harold is hardly a usurper. Everyone knows that the Saxon Council will name him King as soon as Edward dies. The northern and southern English lords will support the decision wholeheartedly."

"Harold could be made to appear to be a usurper, though," Onyame said. "That's what you fear the Pope has in mind."

William looked him and nodded. "Yes."

There was silence for awhile.

Then I realized what the Pope wanted. "Nothing would please Pope Alexander more than to have you, William, defeat a usurper who steals Church property, further, a usurper who threatens the Church's own empire. What's more, you could put Pope Alexander's old teacher, Lanfranc, in charge of the English clergy, as Archbishop of Canterbury."

"That's been in my thoughts, too," William said.

Onyame allowed himself a surprised breath. "Living with the People, I often forget the power wars I witnessed in Norway and Denmark. The consequences of this, though, are greater ... for everyone."

William leaned toward me. "That's why, Cuin, I want you to get to England as soon as you can. Do what you can to ... I don't know. Just do what you can. You know what's happening."

I nodded. "I'll leave as soon as the preparations for the trip are completed. And I will keep you informed. Is Rolf around? May I take him and some of his Goliards with me?"

"Yes, I will also use them to keep you informed of anything I discover here."

As I rose to leave, he stood and put his hands on my shoulders. "You're the only person I trust with this. I also know that if anything can be done, you'll do it."

"I know the other half of your meaning. If nothing can be done, I'll send word to you as quickly as possible, so that you can plan for the worst."

"Yes. We pray for the best, but we prepare for the worst. It's the way you and I have always survived."

By the time Onyame delivered me to England, Christmas was only a week away, and Edward was already ailing, though no one could find a cause.

Some of his own physicians thought that he had been "brought down by his final defeat, the loss of Earl Tostig." Our early strategy of having Tostig befriend Edward had worked even better than we hoped, apparently.

I was not convinced, however, that this was the only cause of Edward's failing health. So I asked Onyame to stay near the court and keep a ship ready to sail back to Normandy.

For the Christmas court, Edward was once again at the royal palace on Thorne Isle in the Thames River, where, I was told, he would attend the consecration of the church he had worked so hard to see built, the Church of Saint Peter. The consecration was to be held three days after Christmas.

There were doubts, however, that the King would be able to attend. His physicians told me that he had been weak and occasionally delirious.

As they explained it, "Since Earl's Tostig's exile to Flanders began on the first of November, the King and his Queen, the Earl's sister, have been grief-stricken by the event."

The effects of Tostig's ouster could not have been more beneficial for Harold.

I found Edward in a large side room, resting quietly in a bed with red blankets trimmed in gold. The windows had been closed and curtained against the cold. A fire was constantly watched by a young boy, who kept it large and roaring, but who, given the size of the chamber, was probably the only warm person there.

I was reminded of the warmth of the People's homes, and the contrast made me feel even colder.

Two physicians and two house guards hovered over Edward, but since he seemed to be asleep, there was nothing for them to do but watch him.

I sat in a chair near the fire, waiting. Eventually Edward awoke and was informed of my presence.

He raised himself onto his pillows and asked for me. When I reached the bed, he smiled faintly and ordered all the others from the room, except the fire-tender.

When one of the house guards hesitated, Edward said, "Have no fear. I have known this healer since he was a child. I need to speak to him on most delicate matters, for which I prefer privacy. Please station yourself outside the door where you could hear a cry should I need you."

As Edward talked, I noticed that face was whiter than usual, almost bluish. His beard was as straggly as ever though now gray now and sparse.

Before I could speak, Edward smiled at me and grabbed at my hand. "Cuin, I am pleased to see you again. Thank you for coming." His voice sounded thin and raspy.

"The pleasure is mine, your majesty, but I would prefer to see you in better health."

He sighed deeply and waited for his breath to become even again. "I am not going to recover, Cuin. I have been poisoned. I will not live long now."

"Poisoned? Are you certain? What are your symptoms? Perhaps I can —"

"It is too late. I can feel my time. I am prepared to go." He shook his head weakly. "Anyway, whoever poisoned me would not have used a substance for which you could find a quick antidote."

"Who would have done …?" I began, but he raised his hand to wave the question away.

"There is something I want you to do for me."

"Anything, your majesty."

"I know that Duke William has ordered you here to help me and to watch the events that unfold after my death."

"That is true."

"I want you to leave now. As soon as you can."

"Why?"

He replied in a strained voice, "If you think like the diplomat that you are, you will realize." He paused, allowing his breathing to become normal again. "Earl Harold will become King after me."

"Yes, I know."

"I will ask Harold, as I bequeath him the throne, to allow any unpopular Normans to leave the country safely — *with* the goods they have acquired from me — but some Saxons, including those who conspired in my poisoning, may not allow them to leave. I do not know what sentiments will dominate here after I die."

I sighed. "I understand, your majesty. And I swear to you that I will be gone before Christmas."

He nodded with a weak smile. "Good. Tomorrow, if possible." He then put his hand under his pillow and pulled out a letter. He handed it to me. "This letter is for you and William. I want you to read it after you leave these shores, not before."

I took it and slipped it inside my tunic. "I will, your majesty."

His eyes closed, then reopened, focusing on me for a moment. "My young friend. You used to listen to me patiently back in Normandy. I would boast about all I would do once I returned to my home. In the end, I wonder whether I was as good a King as I told you I would be."

"You have been a great King, Edward."

He smiled and fell back against the pillow, closing his eyes.

The next day, I slipped away from the castle, located Onyame, and we headed back to Normandy.

Edward became more ill on Christmas Eve. He recovered enough to attend the Christmas Day festivities, the service in the abbey, and the banquet afterward. He even publicly told his wife that he might recover.

The day after Christmas, though, he fell gravely ill — perhaps from another dose of poison, I thought as I listened to the account — and he was too ill to attend the consecration of the Church of Saint Peter three days after Christmas.

From that time, he fell into a deep sleep, from which he awakened only a few times, once prophesying that, because the English nobles and clergy had wandered too far from God, the country would experience "fire and sword and be delivered to the enemy," though to what enemy he did not say.

He fell into a deep sleep again, awakening on the eve of the Epiphany to put the kingdom, his nobles, his wife, and all foreign, meaning Norman, vassals and servants in Harold's hands. He asked Harold to take care of all of them.

He requested the last rites, received them, and a few hours later, died. Edward, King of England, had passed into the other world.

Back in Normandy, I showed William the letter Edward had given me. It read:

"To my good friends, my family while I was in Normandy: I thank you for all the kindnesses you showed me while I was among you. I thank you for what you have done to help me rule this land and keep it safe. I know that you have taken steps to bring Normandy and England together in peace. I now pray that you, William, will unite with Harold to bring this country back to God.

"I fear that this will happen, however, only after a blood-sacrifice, and I know that you will limit that blood-sacrifice as much as you can. I have seen an omen, a hairy star, which will be God's sign that your time to act has come. Look for it. I know that you will use all your wisdom and all your strength to do the best you can for God's purposes.

"Farewell, my friends. I will meet you again in God's heaven."

CHAPTER 31

THE BATTLE

A.D. 1066

William, Garrad, and I agreed that one of us had to talk with Harold, who had been crowned King of England the day Edward was buried. We needed to discover whether King Harold's empire fever ran as hot as Earl Harold's had.

I was the obvious choice for the visit.

As soon as the winter weather allowed, I sailed for England. In Dover, I was told by two of Rolf's Goliards that King Harold was in Waltham visiting the abbey there. So I set out for Waltham.

The church at Waltham was the foundation of Harold's reputation as a supporter of the Church — a deceptive foundation.

In the reign of King Canute, Waltham had been a small village, ruled by the local lord, at whose wedding feast King Hardecanute had died in the spring of 1042, leaving the throne to Edward. Rather than being suspected of poisoning, though, this lord developed a reputation for religious piety, because he had been told in a dream that a sacred crucifix was buried somewhere on his estates.

He ordered men to dig for the holy relic, and indeed they found a large black flint cross. The diggers loaded the cross into an ox-cart to take to their lord, but the oxen would go only toward Waltham, several days journey away. So at Waltham, on the low grassland by the winding Lea River, the lord had built a church to house the cross. Pilgrims flocked to see the relic, and Waltham became a pilgrimage site.

Eventually, the town became a royal possession — the lord's son was in too much debt to hold onto the place — and King Edward had passed it on to Earl Harold of East Anglia.

The religiousness of the place predated Harold.

Further, Waltham became a favorite of Harold's only after he injured his back and temporarily lost use of his legs. The attending physician told him that the cure must come from the powers of Waltham's holy crucifix. Harold prayed before the crucifix and was healed.

He immediately decided to build a larger church, but with priests rather than monks, and a seminary where priests could be trained to be loyal to Harold. So, he built his church, founded his seminary, and put the physician in charge of it. In his later travels to Rome, he collected relics for the church.

The Pope, however, had not been impressed. He knew, as many people did, that Waltham Abbey represented Harold's gratitude for healing rather than his love for the Church. As the Pope told Lanfranc, "All the relics in the world, collected by Earl Harold for Waltham, will not prevent the Earl from stealing Church property."

Nonetheless, Waltham was the place Harold visited for respite from the demands of ruling. So, I hoped I would find him in his least aggressive temper.

He was in fact in the large stone church itself, sitting on a cushioned chair in the apse. He was slumped in the chair, staring at the altar, unmoving.

Though bare-headed, he was nonetheless dressed in the elegant style for which he was known, wearing a purple silk shirt and blue leggings. A jeweled knife was at his waist, and he wore soft slippers, which might have fit inside the polished black riding boots that I had seen sitting near the church entrance. Though his mustache retained its light color, his long blond hair now showed streaks of gray.

The guards and I waited for awhile, but he did not stir. Eventually one of them said, "Excuse me, your majesty. We have an emissary from Duke William of Normandy."

Harold sighed deeply and sat forward, slowly turning toward us.

"Yes." He stared hard at me for a moment. Then he nodded a thank you to the guards and said, "Cuin of Falaise, it's good to see you again."

I bowed slightly. "And you, your majesty."

He waved me into a nearby chair, smiling. "Of all people who don't have to stand in my presence, you are the most obvious."

"Thank you, your majesty."

"To what do I owe the honor of a visit from Duke William's distinguished emissary?"

I paused. "I must confess that I'm not sure how to express my purpose, your majesty. Duke William wishes to inquire about your intentions relative to Normandy and its neighbors."

He tilted his head. "You know that I have taken an oath to respect the borders of those territories."

"Yes, your majesty. The wording of the oath was precisely that. Again, though, I'm not sure how to express this, so if you can help me with a dialogue, I would be grateful."

"I am willing."

"Thank you. The oath that you and Duke William took was precisely worded to include within the meaning of the phrase "respect the borders" a broad interpretation, broad enough to include non-aggression, for instance."

He sat back in the chair and studied me. "I see. A less broad interpretation, by contrast, might be that I simply acknowledge the boundaries and do nothing to alter them. That would be an acceptable interpretation, would it not?"

"Yes, your majesty. An interpretation worthy of an emissary, if I may say so."

He smiled. "As you know, I had to develop diplomatic skills during the crises in Wales and Northumbria."

I returned the smile. "In Normandy as well. A lord shipwrecked on a foreign shore is not in a strong position."

He laughed briefly. "Astutely put. Nor was I in a strong position during my second visit when Duke William and I took the oath."

"I'm not sure I grasp your meaning, your majesty. You and Duke William met as friends, did you not?"

"Yes, but I was once again on foreign soil. Friend or not, the good Duke would not have been pleased had I refused to join him in our mutual vow.

So, an astute observer might note that I was in no position to refuse the oath, might he not?"

"He might, your majesty, but — and I mean this with no disrespect — it was an oath, nonetheless."

"An oath taken under duress, though, might be interpreted strictly rather than broadly."

"It might, your majesty."

"So, I would be bound only to recognize borders and to do nothing to change them."

"Is that how you interpret the oath, your majesty?"

"I have not thought about it before this moment, but I think that is my interpretation, yes."

"Then the oath does not exclude invasion?"

"Not as long as the borders of a region are maintained." He paused and then leaned forward again. "As King of this country, I must always do what is right for the people here. If that means claiming territory that ought to belong to England — even as I respect the borders of that territory — then I cannot exclude the possibility of invasion."

"Or even the likelihood of invasion?"

He became unusually serious. "Is the implication that English forces might invade Normandy or its neighbors?"

"I simply want to know whether I can rule out that possibility for Normandy's future."

"A fair request." He sat back and was quiet for a time. "The very least, I owe you, Cuin, is an answer, given what you have done for my family. And for me."

"I am not aware of any great service, your majesty."

"You helped my father when he was dying, and you helped to heal my men when I was shipwrecked in Ponthieu."

"I was happy to help, your majesty, and my service was not great."

"Nonetheless, I remember it."

"Thank you, your majesty. So the answer to my question is …?"

He took a deep breath. "Duke William cannot rule out that possibility of invasion, Cuin. I do not know the will of the Council, nor do I know what the future of this country demands. Already the Normans here have drained the native Saxons. Might the Saxon lords not want to take back some of what they have lost? Might I not be required, as their King, to comply with their wishes?"

"They might, and you might, which tells me all that I need to know. If your majesty will give me leave, I must return to Normandy with some haste."

"What is the source of your haste?"

I smiled. "Early next week is my birthday, your majesty, and I have promised to spend it with my families in Falaise."

"Then, by all means, take your leave, and I hope that you have a fine celebration next week."

"Thank you, your majesty."

As I rose to leave, he rose and stepped closer to me. "Cuin, you need not treat me as an enemy. Duke William need not treat me as an enemy. You should not consider me a passive friend, either."

I smiled. "I would consider your majesty neither of these, and I look forward to our next meeting."

When I arrived in Normandy, I went straight to Rouen, where William had planned his first meeting with his nobles, many of whom had already arrived. I found William in a room off the great hall.

"Cuin, I was just told that you'd returned."

I nodded and recounted my conversation with Harold.

"It's not what we hoped," he said.

"But it is what we expected."

He pulled me closer to the fire, speaking quietly. "I want you to contact Lanfranc, Osbern, and Garrad. We must consider our response to Harold."

"I can send messengers today."

"I don't want anyone to know about the meeting, which is why I want the messages to come from you. I'd prefer to meet in Garrad's hut, if he doesn't mind."

"He won't."

"I'll bring Matilda. No one must suspect that we're planning anything, though."

"Can we keep the meeting secret? Surely some nobles will notice your movements."

He smiled. "As you told King Harold, it is your birthday week. Matilda and I could be meeting you for that … Yes, that explanation will suffice. I'll see you in Garrad's hut in seven days. And I'll bring a gift."

A week later, we collected ourselves in Falaise. Lanfranc, who had been appointed Abbot of St. Stephen's Church in Caen, had an easy day trip and arrived early enough to visit with Garrad and Marie.

William and Matilda journeyed from Rouen, where Osbern had been visiting as well. My message had instructed Osbern — as William had requested — to travel separately to Falaise.

The evening that everyone arrived, Garrad and I prepared a supper, competing with each other for the most highly prized culinary offering. Marie watched us, smiling.

William offered his gift, a new, stronger carving knife with which I could make new bows.

I thanked him. "I appreciate the nature of the gift, since I'm also ordered by a demanding Duke to train his bowmen."

He smiled. "Now you're well prepared to meet that demand."

Garrad and Marie had arranged chairs and stools in front of a large fire. All of us sat, waiting for William to begin the conversation.

"You know the problem we face," he finally said. He turned to Osbern. "You, my friend, know less than the rest of us. In short, our plans aim at preventing the new King of England from empire-building."

"An empire which would include Normandy," Matilda added.

William nodded and continued speaking to Osbern, "Other details will be clear as we speak. As you will hear, we haven't discussed anything that you won't already have realized yourself."

I added, "I'd like to remind all of us that we've worked establishing alliances for over twenty years. Though we've had setbacks, Normandy now can claim Brittany, Maine, Anjou, Ponthieu, Boulogne, and Flanders as allies. Norway and Denmark are bound not to interfere with whatever we do. Finally, we have an ally in Harold's brother Tostig and any Saxons who will follow him."

"Tostig is presently in Flanders," Matilda said, "where my father has made him military ruler of St. Omer."

I nodded at her. "Tostig is convinced that Harold plotted to have him removed as the Earl of Northumbria last year, and he wants his earldom back. If he regains Northumbria, we gain an additional ally in the north of England."

William nodded at me and continued, "I don't want to say much myself tonight. I've thought about Harold's empire plans for some time. Now I need to hear from you. Not from my barons or knights or courtiers, but from you, who are not only my friends but also the wisest men and women in Normandy. So I ask you to speak frankly and as friends who share this crisis with me. How shall we respond to Harold?"

All of us looked at Lanfranc, who spoke first. "We now know that King Harold wants an empire. If he would maintain his imperial stance even in Cuin's presence, we know that he intends to pursue the imperial plans that Cuin discovered earlier."

"We need a response that avoids confrontation," Matilda said. "We do not want a war with King Harold."

"The threat of excommunication might stop him," Garrad said. "No excommunicate ruler would have the support of his lords or clergy, no matter how loyal they are to him."

"That's right," Lanfranc said. "Since the threat of excommunication would undermine King Harold's support in England, we should approach the Pope."

Osbern leaned forward. "Excommunication for what, though?"

"When Harold made his pilgrimage to Rome," I replied, "he met Pope Victor, who publicly complained that as Earl of East Anglia, Harold had seized property from the Church on no fewer than twenty occasions. The Pope also complained that Earl Harold was more nominally than substantially Christian. The present pope, Alexander, has the same complaint." I turned to Lanfranc. "Isn't that right?"

Lanfranc nodded. "Privately, Pope Alexander and Archdeacon Hildebrand — both former students of mine, so they speak frankly to me — consider King Harold dangerous. Harold does not support their reforms, and they feel that he allows the old religions too much freedom, while keeping a tight rein on the Christian clergy. Of course, they know, as Pope Victor did, that Harold appropriates Church property."

Garrad smiled. "I'm sure we could get both the Pope's and the mad reformer's support. Archdeacon Hildebrand has accused the English church of laxness as loudly and as often as he can."

Lanfranc nodded. "More than that, Peter's Pence hasn't been paid, and Hildebrand knows that the English churches are rich enough to pay it. If we agree that papal taxes should be collected in England regularly, Hildebrand will be drawn to our cause by both his reforming and financial ambitions."

He fell silent, looking at William.

"There's another side to the Pope's involvement," William said. "While the Pope considers Harold a threat, he wants me to contain that threat."

"By that you mean …?" Osbern asked.

"My husband is to be the Pope's instrument in dealing with Harold," Matilda replied.

William nodded. "That's why Lanfranc and the others are discussing exactly what the Pope wants Harold to do. I am ordered to make him do it."

Osbern stared at William. "How are you to accomplish such a task?"

"By whatever means that will force Harold to comply with the Pope's wishes."

Osbern leaned toward him. "Does he want you to invade England?"

"I would suppose so, yes."

Osbern glanced around the room. "Don't we need to avoid a war, as Duchess Matilda suggested?"

William sighed heavily. "If we can."

"I hope," Lanfranc said, "as we all hope, that papal condemnation of King Harold's practices will be enough for Harold and the Pope to come to terms. Regardless of the outcome of events, though, the Pope has chosen William to end Harold's threat to the Church."

Everyone fell silent.

William turned to Lanfranc. "Can you get a case written up and sent to Rome within the month?"

"Within the week," Lanfranc replied.

"Good. Thank you. I'll need you to go with me to France, though before you travel to Rome."

"We're going to ask young King Philip to join us?"

William shook his head. "Philip will not join us. He's too ambitious to join anyone. I will ask for his support, though. I need to hear his answer in person and watch his response."

"Even if he does not join you, he will surely he offer some support," Lanfranc said, "if only to keep an invader from his own shores."

"I'm not sure whether he will offer even meager support," William replied. "We'll see. There's another need, though, for which I need your influence. The churches and the monasteries. Can you ask them to help us pay for a campaign to England?"

"If it's necessary," Lanfranc said.

"The convents, too, can contribute," Matilda said. "Like the monasteries, they've grown rich during your father's reign and yours. They will support a righteous cause." She nodded at Lanfranc. "Especially if the Pope supports it."

"What if King Harold and the Pope do not come to terms?" Marie asked.

All of us glanced at each other.

William said, "Then I must end Harold's threat to the Church."

"Using force?" Marie asked.

William nodded.

There was silence again.

Garrad leaned toward William. "How much force would be necessary? Would we muster an army, prepare a fleet?"

"Of course," Osbern said.

William stared at Garrad and said nothing.

"Then," Garrad said, "we should raise the largest army that Normandy has ever seen. Or make everyone believe that is what we are doing."

"I agree," William said, "but I would hear what you advise."

"If you muster the men of Normandy," Garrad said, "if you call for help from the allies you named, and if you send for mercenaries, you may collect a force so large that Harold would not dare stand against it. It would be a wall against his plans to invade Normandy or its neighbors." He paused.

Matilda broke in. "I see what you mean, Garrad. Even if we can't raise that force, we could make Harold and his spies believe that we can."

Osbern held up his hand as if to slow the exchange. "Wouldn't all the soldiers that the lords owe you be enough to intimidate King Harold?"

I replied, "We must keep in mind that Harold can command a huge muster from the Saxon lords, and he would get eager help from the Welsh and Irish Kings, perhaps even the Scottish King."

William leaned toward Osbern, while continuing to watch Garrad. "I've already given that much thought. We can double the muster from the lords. Garrad and Matilda are right, though: we may not need to."

Osbern's mouth fell open. "Double?"

"Yes," William said. "We can amass a force at least as great as Harold's."

"Or," Matilda said, "we can be seen to be doing that."

"You mean," I said, "that Rolf and his Goliards and any other messengers we have can fool Harold's spies."

William and Matilda nodded at me.

"So, if we raise a huge force ..." I began.

William finished my thought, "Harold may not wish to risk his entire force. He may be forced to negotiate rather than invade or defend. Especially if he faces a threat in the north from his brother Tostig. He will face such a threat, will he not?"

"I'll know soon," I replied, "but yes, he most probably will."

William nodded to Garrad, indicating he wanted to hear whatever Garrad might want to add.

"If the monasteries can pay even mercenaries," Garrad said, "adding them to our force has two advantages. Initially, we will need to send word to every province to generate support."

"Which will make it seem that we are raising a huge force, even if we are not," Matilda said.

Garrad nodded at her. "Second, with such a widespread appeal for arms, Harold will know of the huge force and will realize that he's being challenged — before he has established his rule firmly enough in England to pursue his plans for empire. That may be enough to make him give up those plans."

"Or at least be in more of a mood to negotiate with Normandy and the Pope," Matilda said.

William nodded, still looking serious. "It's a good plan. I'll arrange a council for the muster and send for mercenaries."

"We'll need a fleet to accommodate this force," Osbern said, "if we really intend to sail it to England. King Harold will not fear an army without a fleet."

"You're right," William said. "That means building ships. Cuin and some Norman builders know the Norwegian and Danish methods, which are superior to our own. They can begin teaching others."

"I'll need help teaching," I began.

William ignored me. "We need to begin building as quickly as possible, so that Harold knows we're determined and believes that we're in a hot rage at him." He smiled. "I have a reputation for that, and it can serve us well. Besides, after what he said to Cuin, I am in a rage at him."

"Whatever numbers we get, my lord," Lanfranc added, "we must make them holy numbers. If we have seventy large ships or 700, counting the small ones, everyone would be struck by the holiness of our cause. If we have 700, 7,000 or 14,000 men, that too will help us."

"If the Lord provides—" began Matilda.

William smiled at her and touched her arm. "Even if he doesn't provide, we will. My men are religious. We need every force we can muster." He nodded to Lanfranc. "Make certain that the numbers that circulate are holy numbers, regardless of the count."

"We shall have holy numbers as we count," Lanfranc said. "I'm certain that the Lord will provide."

Within the same week, William sent me north with Rolf and several Goliards to find Hardraada and Tostig and to discover what plans they had regarding the new King of England.

We sent word to Tostig in St. Omer to meet us at the St. Vaast monastery, to which he agreed, since it reduced our travel by a day. We arrived at St. Vaast not long after Tostig and his wife Judith did.

While Rolf and his men headed for the kitchen — and I would like to have joined them — I went dutifully in search of Tostig. I happened upon him in conversation with Judith in one of the large side halls usually reserved for visitors.

"... betrayed and then ousted," he was saying loudly.

"There was not a single concern for your future." Judith was agreeing with him.

At that moment, they noticed that someone was at the other end of the hall. Squinting through the late afternoon sunlight coming in through the windows, Tostig recognized me.

He sprang out of his chair to greet me. "Great heavens — Cuin! Are you here already?"

I smiled as I approached them. "My lord, my lady, it is pleasant to see both of you again." I looked around. "We meet once again at St. Vaast."

"Yes," Judith, who had remained seated, smiled at me, "but you have managed to avoid an assassin's wounds this time. So I assume that your journey has been peaceful."

"It has been, my lady, thank you."

Tostig took my hand in greeting and pulled another chair close to theirs, waving me into it. I thanked him and moved it closer to the fire, since the hall was still cool and would get colder as night approached.

Tostig spoke again, "I assume you've come to talk with us about Harold."

"Yes. As you are a long-time friend, I will be direct: Duke William and I assume that you want to reclaim Northumbria now that Harold is King. Especially since Harold's interest in ousting you from the north seems clear: he wanted to be well liked there, so that he now has northern and southern support, something a Saxon King has not had since King Alfred the Great. His council at Oxford also gained for him a reputation as a peacemaker in the tradition of King Canute. He gained all this, though, at your expense. He may gain more at Normandy's expense. To prevent that happening, we need to have Earl Tostig back in Northumbria."

Judith raised her eyebrows.

I continued, "To regain your earldom, you need arms and men. And a candidate for the throne of England. The only person who can offer all of this is Harald Hardraada, King of Norway. So you need an introduction to him, which I can arrange."

Tostig smiled at his wife. "Judith, this man always knows what all of us are going to do and what we need to do it. I have no idea how he knows what he knows." He looked at me again. "Thank God you've never wanted a kingdom for yourself. With your abilities, you would be either the scourge of other rulers … or dead."

"I prefer to serve admirable rulers," I said, smiling. "I can assure you that I have none of the skills that you, Hardraada, or William have. So, I can only conclude that if I didn't prefer serving all of you, I'd be dead, by your account."

He laughed and glanced at Judith. "And this is how he answers us when we wonder how he knows what he knows — with non-answers and compliments."

Judith smiled. "He is a good diplomat."

Tostig paused and then said, "You're correct in all your assumptions. Everyone knows that I've been angry at my brother since he took Northumbria from me last year. Now that he is King, his manipulations are clear. As Earl of East Anglia, he did not need but nonetheless wanted support in the north, support he could draw on when he became King. I was a fool to go along with my removal at the time. I knew that he had schemed to have the nobles rebel against me."

"Edward was still King, though," I said, "and you and he were close friends. So when Harold insisted that Northumbria be taken from you — and Edward had no choice but to agree — you allowed yourself to be removed rather than cause difficulties for King Edward. That was a noble choice."

He huffed. "You may say so, and I don't disagree with you, but it left me here, helpless. So, yes, I do need the support of Norway's King." He gritted his teeth. "And his men and arms and money."

I paused for a moment. "Might I suggest that Hardraada needs you as much as you need him?"

Judith said, "Because my husband is a Saxon with Danish blood and could command the loyalty of the Saxons and Danes in England?"

I nodded. "Yes, my lady, that is precisely what I had in mind."

"Even more," she continued, "my husband knows more about England than Hardraada does and thus becomes a valuable ally when Hardraada takes the throne from Harold."

"Those, too, are important factors. Hardraada does have a claim to the throne, and he may well move to assert that now. Your husband as Earl of Northumbria would help him immensely, and a grateful Hardraada would likely offer him other territories."

Tostig leaned toward me. "How soon can you arrange a meeting with Hardraada? If he agrees to help, we still need to summon men, collect arms, and build a fleet. I have no desire to waste time."

"The trip by land and sea will take a little over a week. We can leave as early as tomorrow. I have already sent messengers north, and I know where to find Hardraada."

Tostig sat back. "Of course you do."

Hardraada had spent part of the winter in Oslo, a town founded at the beginning of the millennium. After becoming King of Norway, he had turned Oslo in to an active city and had built his royal chapel there within St. Mary's Church.

The wooden church was where we found him. Sections of it were still being built, and we made our way through noisy work that reminded me of Mont St. Michel when I was a child.

After the formal introductions were completed, all of us sat comfortably — Hardraada had arranged for thick cushions on tall-backed wooden chairs — around a fire, large enough to keep the winter chill from reaching us.

I mentioned that I had found King Harold of England in his favorite church in Waltham, and now I had found King Harald of Norway in his favorite church in Oslo.

Hardraada laughed, perhaps a bit too loudly for Lady Judith's taste, and said, "No doubt you know that neither of us is a very good Christian, though we have benefited much from Christianity's ... excess wealth."

I smiled. "You disappoint me, your majesty. All these years, I was sure that you would carry Christianity into Valhalla."

"I believe King Olaf has already done that," he replied, laughing again, "with sword in hand." He then became earnest and leaned forward in his chair. "And carrying swords is why you came to see me, is it not?"

"Yes, your majesty," I said. "You were one of the first men to mention Harold's ambition to me. His own brother has felt the sting of that."

Hardraada looked hard at Tostig. "Though we do not often get news of England here, many relatives of my subjects live in Northumbria. We heard of your ouster, Earl Tostig. Knowing what I do of your brother, I can say that I am saddened for you but not surprised by your brother's actions."

Tostig took this as his opening. "Then you are aware that my brother can be ruthless, your majesty."

Hardraada and I exchanged amused glances, since "ruthless" was one of the meanings of "hardraada," but he was earnest again immediately.

He nodded at Tostig and replied, "I believe that your brother is capable of anything that will further his goals. He has contracted the malady of empire-seeking." He leaned back in his chair. "I have a reputation for ruthlessness as well, but it was born first of necessity and second in the service of the Byzantine Empress. I do not seek an empire."

I saw an opening to further the dialogue. "I've been told, your majesty, that your concern is with ruling well rather than with ruling more. Even your political opponents admit that you've brought peace to Norway. And your raids into Denmark, which ended two years ago when you and King Sweyn declared peace, did not drain the country's resources. On the contrary, you've established a solid currency here, keeping your nobles rich and your farmers prosperous."

Hardraada tilted his head at me. "Sometimes, listening to you, Cuin, I almost believe that Norway shares borders with Normandy."

Tostig smiled and nodded. "I agree, your majesty. I cannot determine how he knows so much about all of our activities. He claims to be a Christian, but I think he may be a wizard."

"He has moved around the northern islands and the other side of the world," Hardraada added, "with a prophetess of the old religion, and he wears the blue-gray cloak associated with Odin. So, Cuin, your secret is revealed. The two ravens on Odin's shoulders bring information not only to him but also to you."

"I'm afraid that the explanation is much duller, your majesty," I said. "The Goliards are my informants. I believe that even you use them from time to time."

I gave Hardraada time to remain silent, since he would reveal as little as possible about his own sources.

Then I continued, "My informant about King Harold's imperial ambitions was Harold himself. I overheard him speaking with your father" — I gestured toward Tostig — "not long before his death."

Tostig leaned toward me. "I never knew this."

"Nor would you, while Edward was King," I said. "The last thing Harold would want you to know was the scope of his plans once your father and Edward had died. The astute King Harald of Norway, however, guessed Earl Harold's imperial plans the first time I spoke with him about Harold becoming King of England."

Tostig looked at Hardraada.

"You see, Earl Tostig," Hardraada said, "I have thought about your brother's ambitions for some time. So, I welcome planning a response with you, since you know your brother and England better than I ever will."

Tostig breathed deeply. "I'm pleased to hear you say that, your majesty. I am eager to get my earldom back, but to do that, I need resources."

"And you need to get your brother off the throne," Hardraada said.

Tostig drew a sharp breath. "Yes, I do."

"You cannot reclaim your earldom while your brother needs it to guarantee loyalty in the north of England," Hardraada said. "So you need a claimant to the throne who is at least acceptable to the leaders and citizens of your earldom. I am that claimant."

"I also need men and ships."

"Since I've declared peace with King Sweyn, I have those in abundance," Hardraada said, "including men who are eager for raiding and its spoils."

Tostig nodded. "Then let us plan together."

After the initial meeting, I said my good-byes, leaving Tostig, Judith, and Hardraada to work out their plans.

One day's sailing brought me to a village known as the Women's Fish Market, and there Rolf met me with three Goliards, carrying messages from William. He wanted me to know that he had summoned the nobles and that I needed to be back in Rouen within ten days.

The weather made traveling difficult, but we reached Rouen the day before the nobles were to arrive.

I headed immediately for William's chambers and found him there, pacing back and forth, wearing unusually plain colors, which he would normally wear for hunting. Or under armor.

"Cuin, good! I'm glad you're back. How did the meeting with Hardraada go?"

After I recounted the exchange, he nodded. "We have no surprises in Norway thus far." He paced and then returned to me. "You'll be in the meeting with the nobles tomorrow?"

"Yes, of course. Unless you want me elsewhere."

He leaned toward me, taking my arm. "I want you to watch the reactions of the nobles carefully."

"I'll read in them what I can."

"They will initially resist my plan. I would, too, if I were one of them. I only need to lay the groundwork for their acceptance, though. If I do that, the rest will happen naturally."

"I agree."

The next morning, we met again outside the great hall. Again, William was dressed in what might be considered battle clothes but without armor. He nodded at me but said nothing. He strode into the great hall, and I followed, seating myself to the side where I could see him and watch the nobles without having to turn in my chair.

"My lords," William addressed them. They were still restless. "We are here because of a threat of invasion from the North. A potentially deadly invasion, meaning even the end of Normandy as you know it and rule it."

William's voice was unusually harsh, and the room became silent.

"I want to address this matter and then let you return home to think about what to do."

The nobles sat back in their chairs and watched William closely.

"Earl Harold of East Anglia has seized the throne of England," he continued, "as you all know. This was not unexpected. Harold has been the power behind King Edward for the last decade. He was effective in battle and in diplomacy. His father, Earl Godwin of Wessex, was not of noble birth but came from a family of some rank and was a powerful noble under King Canute, while Harold's mother was from a noble Danish family. The Wessex rulers have given England a line of kings, including King Alfred the Great. So, knowing Harold's competence and that he was popular with commoners and nobles alike, the English Council elected him King without dissent."

He paused. "What you may not know is that King Harold secretly — and not so secretly — plans to build an empire, an empire greater than King Canute's, perhaps greater than any ruler since the Roman era. Normandy stands directly in his path."

The nobles murmured loudly to themselves and to each other.

William let them interact with each other for a long while and then spoke again. "We know that King Harold has the support of all of England. He was always popular where he ruled as Earl, and his handling of his brother's disastrous rule in Northumbria made him popular there as well. He has the backing of the Welsh people and their King, the Scottish people and their King, and the Irish people and their King. Few rulers before him have had this kind of support."

I watched the faces of the nobles as William paused again. Most of these men were close to William's age and owed their power to his administration of Normandy. They were loyal, most of them fiercely loyal, to him. They would take everything that he said seriously.

He continued, "Because our diplomatic efforts have been successful over the last two decades, we know that Denmark will not support Earl Harold as King of England. Denmark's King Sweyn remains friendly to us. We cannot take the threat of Danish raiders lightly, however, since Harold is half Danish and could even draw Danish raiders to him. As those who have met Harold know, he can be convincing when he wants to rally support. We also know that Viking raids are how Normandy came to be — and that later raids ravaged our towns and villages."

The nobles frowned and nodded. They knew the stories, similar to the ones I had heard back in Rouen when the tanner was protecting me from Voldred: the bodies of Normans had clogged the mills and the rivers.

"Nor can we ignore the threat of Norwegian raiders," William said. "King Harald of Norway, known as Hardraada, has long declared his friendship with Normandy, but that will not prevent Norwegians from aiding King Harold of England, if they see an opportunity for looting in the South."

He paused for a long time. "We simply cannot allow King Harold to build his empire."

William's half-brother, Robert of Mortain, spoke up. "Have we appealed to him diplomatically, my lord?"

Robert, of course, knew of my efforts, but he clearly intended that all other nobles should know of them as well.

"We have appealed to him diplomatically," William replied. "His reply was equivocal, but his intentions were clear. He has not given up his dreams of empire, even where Normandy is concerned. As soon as he has consolidated his rule in England, he will come for us."

Robert spoke again. "If King Harold is not open to negotiation, my lord, what means do we have to stop him?"

William breathed deeply. "A sudden threat of force. We do not allow him to consolidate his strength in England. And we do not allow him to leave England for an invasion."

The room fell silent.

Then Ralph of Tosny's deep voice echoed through the hall, "How?"

William nodded at him. "We announce as soon as possible that we're coming to his southern shores with a huge force, which will not leave his lands until he has sworn publicly never to invade us or any southern neighbor of ours."

The room became silent again.

"If we make our threat immediately," William said, "we may stop Harold immediately. He will not have time to rally support for his imperial ambitions."

He allowed a long pause and then continued. "The English nobles, Saxon and Danish, are not interested in war now. Having avoided civil war ten years ago when Harold's family was banished, and just having avoided civil war again last year with the rebellion against Tostig, the English nobles are unlikely to support imperial ambitions."

"Could Harold convince them to meet our force?" Ralph asked.

"If our force is simply defensive," William said, "if we are trying to stop Harold, he would have to explain why, and he would have to explain this to the leaders of England, Wales, Ireland, and Scotland. Our threat and its justification — to stop a foreign lord from invading us — would force Harold to reveal his plans. I doubt that any nobles would support those plans, especially this early in Harold's reign, and especially if our force is large enough."

The nobles dropped their heads or looked at each other.

"So," William concluded, "we create either a great land and sea force, or we create enough of that force that Harold and his nobles believe that we are prepared to block his imperial intentions."

The nobles murmured comments to each other.

"I do not want you to respond now," William said. "I simply want you to think about what King Harold is about to do and what we must do to stop him. I will speak with each of you individually to listen to what you have to say."

Osbern had to add something supportive of William. "Your strategies have never been defeated, my lord. I'm sure all of us will consider this one most seriously."

William smiled at him. "Thank you, Osbern. I appreciate that all of you, supportive friends, will ponder our situation. You know that each new strategy must be considered long and carefully."

He ended the formal part of the meeting. I knew that while few of the lords would support William's plan immediately, all would support it in the future. This part of the strategy had already succeeded.

In late winter, while I was busy in the North, making certain that King Sweyn still remembered his friendship with Normandy, William and Lanfranc traveled to Paris to ask for support from the new, very young but very ambitious King Philip.

As I passed through Flanders, I briefly visited Anette and her husband, who assured me that Count Baldwin remained neutral, something I knew from Baldwin himself, and that Tostig was popular enough in Flanders to get financial support from local lords.

"As a result," Anette said, "in addition to the promised wealth from King Harald of Norway, Earl Tostig now has the resources to raid England."

"Is that what he plans to do?"

"Yes," she replied. "He has made his intentions very public."

I thanked her and headed on to Denmark.

In Denmark, I had an audience with King Sweyn, though I spent most of my time visiting Thorir and Onyame, both of whom had helped me locate and communicate with the King.

Sweyn himself saw me just once, assuring me that he would not involve himself in any exchange between Harold and William and that Duke William was still considered a friend.

I watched him talk and move, finding it strange that this was another half-brother of mine, ruling another territory. I studied his movements and gestures, wondering whether I had any of those myself.

I knew that our shared mother, who served as Queen to the unmarried Sweyn, had died a few years earlier, and I wondered how she, too, might have appeared.

I kept my attention focused on Sweyn's positive relation to William, though, and I was assured that Denmark and Normandy were informal allies and certainly friends.

During one brief conversation we had, I asked Sweyn whether he would be willing to declare war on King Harold of England in the event of an invasion of the South from England.

He nodded. "If King Harold comes for you and succeeds, then he comes for us. If he comes for us, he will already have defeated both Duke William and King Harald of Norway. If that happens, we are doomed here. So, declaring war on him as soon as he launches his fleet toward the South would be our best defensive strategy."

Upon my return to Normandy, I learned that William and Lanfranc's visit had not gone as well as mine: Philip had refused any kind of support for William's efforts to contain Harold.

I thought Lanfranc might have returned to St. Stephen's Abbey in Caen, but he was still in Rouen when I visited the castle. So I headed for his chambers, where I found him, pacing and furious.

I had never seen Lanfranc angry before. It startled me.

"I've heard that Philip has denied William's appeal for help," I said. "While I find Philip's response irrational, I don't think we have lost much, have we, besides a few men and ships? As Philip must know, we can get all the French mercenaries we need by putting words in the right ears."

"Not only men are at stake," Lanfranc replied, still angry. "We had an opportunity to —" he held up his open hand and closed it "— pull the world together if Philip had agreed to the proposal."

"If William gains a foothold in England and Harold relents, why do we need Philip? Let him accuse Normandy of encroaching on France. If we're allied to England, he'll have an even bigger threat to fret over, but it won't bother us."

"Unification and the lack of it," Lanfranc said. Perhaps he recalled his own youth with its bitter political divisions. "What holds our civilization together? What keeps it from collapsing into the petty, feuding neighbors that the Northmen overran?"

I remained silent, listening.

He continued, "Here in Normandy, God's Providence gives us law-fascinated, aggressive, clever leaders, finally breeding the strongest of them all, Duke William. Not only does he build the most efficient, most united duchy on the continent, but he also builds relationships with his Norman lords, strong leaders loyal to him personally and to his ideals."

"I see that. He has created unusual unity here."

"Beyond our borders, he has also built support. His father-in-law holds Flanders. The Pope, trained in Normandy under me, backs him. As a result, every other province that fears excommunication is drawn into that community. He's pulled the world together. There's only one danger."

I began to follow him, thinking out loud. "If William has any presence in England, even a hand in ruling it, then his relation to the King of France becomes unclear."

"Dangerously unclear. If King Philip had agreed to aid our cause and if then William established some political foothold in England, William's relation to King Philip would be as both Duke of Normandy and as political representative of England."

"You mean that a hierarchy would be established. The relations of ruler to ruler and region to region would have a definite order, so that there would be far fewer occasions for quarreling … or for war."

"A legal order," he added. "The French King would, I believe, take legal precedence over the English King, especially if William's position in England were enlarged in the future. The Saxons might resist initially, as they usually do, but the ranking of the Kings would in practice affect them very little."

"And we Normans already consider the King of France our overlord."

Lanfranc nodded. "Normans love legal order. So they would submit to their Duke, even as a King or co-ruler in England, being subject to the King of France. They would appreciate the order, even if they grumbled, because they would see that their civilized community is at stake. Peace is at stake. I think that both Normans and Saxons would see that if they defied that legal order, the world could sink into the lawless savagery of war."

"I see what you mean. Without a definite ranking of their Kings, England and France could experience war after war."

Lanfranc shook his head angrily. "We had a legal order, a guarantee of peace, within our grasp. Then that stupid, selfish, small-minded boy in Paris worries about his petty borders and frets over William's strength. Just like his father at the end. Doesn't he see what he's done? Doesn't he know what may come of this? Any disgruntled lord or son of William will find an ally in Philip. And for what? For factions. And factions lead to war. Heaven help us, because now raiding and war on both sides of the English Channel could go on and on."

I watched him pace, like Edward and William.

He finally said, "God must forgive Philip the Fool, for I will not."

When I visited William, he echoed Lanfranc's sentiments, but he was less angry than Lanfranc.

"I didn't expect much from Philip," he said, sitting in a casual chair in a chilly side room, "but I did want him to know that we plan to curb Harold's empire-building ambitions."

"Hardraada called it 'the empire malady.'"

William smiled. "That's good. And it's exactly Harold's problem. Without it, he'd likely lead a quiet, prosperous life as King of England."

"You're satisfied then that Philip will not interfere, even if he will not help?"

"He's young, and he's a schemer, not a fighter. Since there is nothing to scheme about, he will remain quiet."

"For now."

"For now, which is all we need." He rose to put extra logs on the fire. "Cuin, I need to think through our plans again, especially after consulting with the nobles."

"How have they reacted?"

He stooped to rearrange the new logs. "Most were cautious but committed, especially after I related that you'd overheard Harold's plans to build an empire that swallows the South. So, we'll have little trouble getting their support."

"You're worried about what they're supporting, though."

He sat down again. "That's right. I know that the Pope wants me to build a huge invasion force."

"To avoid the threat of excommunication, you must either do that or make the Pope believe that you are doing that."

"Yes, just as we must make Harold believe the same."

I leaned toward him. "Do you favor a feigned force rather than a real one?"

"Think about it, Cuin. If we created a huge force, the nobles would have to support that force: many fighters, who would have to be armed, fed, and paid. We'd have to build ships to transport large numbers of horses and men. We'd need shipbuilders, weapon makers, carpenters, ditch-diggers, porters, horse handlers, saddle makers, woodsmen, seamen, cooks, and all the rest — and the means to pay for all of them."

"It would be better to make a show of this and make certain that Harold's spies think it's a real force."

"And the Pope's spies." He thought for a moment. "Didn't you tell me that when Harold raises an army, he doesn't provide for his men?"

"He allows them to raid the countryside, yes."

"And your friend, the Icelandic seer, can make storms."

"Hervor's skills lie with 'the gods of weather,' as she says. Do you have a plan?"

"Yes. First, we convince Harold that we have a large force on our coast, waiting to attack him. He moves his men to his coast to meet us, but Hervor blocks the channel."

"For how long?"

"If we time it right, we need only wait until his raiding strategy fails. Until his men can find no more food anywhere. Perhaps a month, six weeks at most."

"Six weeks? Channel weather changes every day or two. The most I've ever waited for a crossing is a day and a half."

"Listen, Cuin. I've thought this through. We build our supposedly huge fleet and position our supposedly huge fighting force on our northern coast, facing England, in late summer. Harold brings his force to his coast, where his men raid for provisions. However, storms and rising water and even sea monsters hold his men where they are."

"I see. In late summer, food is already becoming scarce, because the harvests have not yet been brought in."

"That's correct. Even with raiding, Harold's men will run out of provisions within six weeks. Perhaps earlier. Further, the men who owe Harold service will need to return home for the harvest."

"I see what you're thinking. His force abandons the coast, we land with our small force, coordinating that with the attack in the north by Tostig and Hardraada."

He nodded. "Exactly. For the storms, we need Hervor. For Tostig and Hardraada, we need you."

"Once all is accomplished, Harold has foes to his north and south."

"Yes. Harold is trapped in his own country and must back down. If the Pope backs me — and he's ordering me to invade England, so we can count on that — Harold faces two forces in his country, Tostig and Hardraada in the north and our forces in the south, as well as excommunication from the Pope."

"He'll be forced to negotiate. He'll have to abandon his plans for empire."

"As our last step, we need to ensure that he does abandon those plans. Tostig holds the north with Hardraada's help. So, we force Harold to name me as … what? You know some of the law."

"We should check with Lanfranc, but I would suppose that he should name you co-ruler, even though you would be a largely absent ruler. That way, he could not make any major move without your approval."

"Since the Pope backs me, expects me to keep England obedient to the Church …"

"… by logical extension, you and the Pope would be in reality co-rulers of Harold's domain. William, if this works …"

"Yes, all our problems, even any threats from the Church, disappear."

"Even more so, because Harold would have to yield at least part of Northumbria to Hardraada, who would become the third co-ruler of England."

William shook his head. "I'm not sure whether Harold would go that far, though he may. At the very least, he would have to offer Hardraada something. Perhaps Hardraada would settle for having one of his sons named as heir to the throne of England, a co-ruler with one of Harold's sons."

"That appears to be a better plan, yes. Once Harold feels trapped, I think I could get him to agree to that, especially since it guarantees a line of kings from Harold himself. He may not have an empire, but he will have a dynasty."

"Your diplomatic work has ensured that King Sweyn of Denmark will support us. That still holds?"

"Yes. Even more since Hardraada and Sweyn have made peace. Also, Sweyn is convinced that you are the wall between Denmark and Harold's imperial ambitions. Within Denmark itself, my friend Thorir will make certain that Sweyn is supportive." I paused. "That meeting with him all those years ago turns out to be more useful than I'd have ever supposed."

"Harold will be blocked everywhere, except perhaps in Ireland, Wales, and Scotland."

"I've learned something recently, William. Even King Malcolm in Scotland wants to claim the north of England. That means that he is less supportive of Harold than Harold believes. Indeed, the Goliards tell me that Tostig and Malcolm have made a pact to seize the north, if Hardraada fails to follow through."

"That's a fortunate development. With only Ireland at his back, Harold would be in a prison of his own making."

"The natural result of 'the empire-malady'."

William sat back and smiled. "Since he and I are friends, however, it would be a pleasant prison. We could hunt together."

"He might even come to enjoy it, you mean."

"It might just work out that way."

That night, while William and I went over the details of our plans, Providence intervened.

A guard ran into the chamber, breathless.

William leaped up, put his hand on his dagger, which was always at his side, and demanded, "What's happening?"

"There's no danger, my lord," the guard said, breathing heavily and pointing, "but the heavens are …"

Before he could finish, William dashed past him. I followed close behind. The guard followed both of us.

We reached the door of the castle to find ten other guards staring at the sky, their mouths open but wordless, their breathing creating smoke in the cold air but no sounds.

Above them was a huge glowing star with a fiery tale, revealing its direction as it streaked across the sky.

I recalled Edward's prophecy about a fiery star, a "hairy star."

I knew that William did not take omens seriously, but even he was staring upward, silently, still.

After a time, I said, "The spring equinox was not long ago, William. The balancing of day and night. Perhaps this is a symbol that reminds us that we must restore the balance that Harold's 'empire malady' has thrown off. Even you would notice that it appeared as we were planning to keep the world free of another Northern empire."

He waited for a while and then looked at me. "We make of omens what we choose, but this time, perhaps you're right." He stared into the sky again. "Perhaps that is what's happening."

During the spring and summer, I worked with the shipbuilders on the coast of Normandy to give the impression we were building a huge fleet. In reality, by late spring, we had built thirty-five oak ships with a planned total of seventy.

The number was religious, as William had requested, reflecting the Seven Days of Creation. More importantly, it was a large enough number to make anyone observing the fleet think that it was much larger. We even had the Goliards put out the idea that William had commissioned 700 ships, including local craft and boats hired from Flanders and Paris.

Matilda paid for William's flagship, the Mora, an elegant vessel with a leopard head at the prow. At the stern, a carved golden child turned to face forward, blowing a horn and holding a small lance with a banner hanging from it.

In May, the Mora joined seventy ships at the mouth of the Dives River.

At meetings in late spring and early summer, William publicly appealed to his nobles to join the enterprise and bring as many men as they could find. William's half-brothers, Robert and Odo, along with Ralph of Tosny and an enthusiastic Osbern, traveled around Normandy generating support, while also encouraging the lords to exaggerate the numbers of men to anyone who would listen.

The nobles found volunteers from Maine to Flanders and central France. Even some Normans from southern Italy made the trek north to join William.

By late summer, as far as I could tell, the world believed that William was amassing a force of tens of thousands. What we in fact planned for was a thousand men, including infantry, archers, and cavalry.

Most of the others recruited would be building forts when William landed in England — wooden structures built on mounds, easy to construct — that would make Harold feel the weight of the Norman presence.

To keep the Pope satisfied, William, Matilda, and other nobles made public endowments to religious houses in Normandy at Avranches, Caen, Fecamp, and Rouen.

To present the legal case to threaten Harold with excommunication, William gave Lanfranc's petition to a seasoned diplomat, Archdeacon Gilbert of Lisieux, and sent him to Rome in late spring.

Archdeacon Gilbert returned with a papal banner and relics of St. Peter — a hair and a tooth. When William showed them to me, both of us thought of Fier and smiled, wondering whether St. Peter had even a remote connection to these two items.

Publicly, the Pope formally blessed William's enterprise. Privately, he sent a message to William that, "bringing Harold into line with the Church's wishes would fulfill the service that William, Duke of Normandy, owes Alexander II, Pope of the Roman Catholic Church."

Then something unexpected happened.

We had arranged that Tostig and Hardraada would arrive in Northumbria just after the autumn equinox. After establishing themselves, they would send word to Harold that they intended to hold the north of England until he gave them control of it. If Harold refused, Hardraada would claim his right as King and march on London.

Giving Hardraada and Tostig time to take control of the northern part of England, William would then establish himself on England's southern coast.

Unfortunately for our plans, Tostig began to raid England in May, from the Isle of Wight to Sandwich, where he enlisted seamen and soldiers who had been loyal to his father. With a fleet of sixty ships, he then sailed north along the east coast of England, putting in at the mouth of the Humber River.

As he raided north Lincolnshire, just south of Northumbria, the local earl, Edwin of Mercia, soundly defeated his forces, and many of Tostig's followers deserted him. The Earl of Mercia celebrated this victory loudly and publicly, and the citizens of Mercia supported Earl Edwin in his dislike of Tostig.

With a mere twelve ships, Tostig made his way north to take refuge with King Malcolm of Scotland.

William met me at Caen to discuss the implications of Tostig's impatience. To be as private as possible, we met outside the city in a hastily constructed tent.

"I don't know what to make of Tostig's attacks," William said, "but I don't think that they help our cause."

"I agree. We're relying on Tostig and Hardraada to control the north of England. If the local lords don't support them, though — and the Earl of Mercia does not, as we now know — Harold has nothing to fear from the north."

"Our landing with a small force in the south is insufficient to deter him," William said. "Have you developed a strategy in response?"

"I've already sent Voldred north to meet with Hardraada. For Harold, Hardraada is still an unknown factor. And Hardraada may generate more support in the north than Tostig now does."

"Good."

"I've also sent Rolf and the Goliards to Scotland to urge Tostig — in your name — to stay with King Malcolm through the summer. And not to raid anywhere until he joins Hardraada in the autumn."

"Will Tostig comply?"

"I'll simply point out that the north and west of Scotland is still not in Malcolm's control."

"Is that true?"

"Yes, Malcolm's hold on Scotland is still weak. Further, many lords who resist him come from Norway and Denmark. I instructed the Goliards not only to speak to Tostig but also to remind King Malcolm that the Kings of Norway and Denmark — friends of Duke William, the source of this message — will offer support to Malcolm if he keeps Tostig quietly in Scotland until summer's end."

William smiled. "Well done."

"We need to watch closely what happens in the North, though. So after the fleet is assembled in Normandy, Voldred and I will join Hardraada and Tostig to make certain that our plan is carried out successfully in the north of England."

"Good. I will see that the two of you have a fast ship with strong rowers to deliver you there and bring you back quickly, since I may need you here, too."

For the rest of the spring and summer, we continued building, collecting men and supplies, while spreading reports everywhere about our hundreds of ships and thousands of warriors.

By mid-August, the ships, the men, the papal banner, and the hair and tooth, the latter strung around William's neck, arrived at the mouth of the Dives, not far from the spot where nine years earlier, William had defeated the combined forces of King Henry and Geoffery Martel of Anjou, both now dead for six years.

I smiled at the choice. As usual, William had chosen a site that spoke to the lords and to Harold of his earlier victories, even when he seemed outnumbered and out-maneuvered.

Then our deception gained an ally. Not far from the shipbuilding sheds, we caught the only remaining Saxon spy. The man expected to be executed.

Instead, William said to him, "Tell King Harold that all he needs to know he will discover when I land on his southern shore in 700 ships with 10,000 men in arms and thousands more to support them. And you may go. I don't kill spies or messengers."

The soldiers and workers remained near the mouth of the Dives for the summer, generously provisioned by William. With most of the work done, the atmosphere began to feel festive. Soldiers and workers both enjoyed themselves — William made certain that there was plenty of food and drink — while the local villagers openly expressed their gratitude that William's men left their crops and animals untouched.

All this while, Harold, who had rallied all the men that owed him service, waited in the south of England.

As we expected, he allowed his soldiers to raid and hoped that some battle would ensue before their service ended. Or before the food ran out.

We did not move from Normandy.

Meanwhile, Hervor, who had arrived in early August, made certain that no one could cross the Channel.

So, our side of the channel saw celebration and relaxation, as we leisurely checked that everything was prepared and continued to send misleading messages about the numbers of our men and ships.

By early September, the dragon gave me a vision showing that our plans had succeeded. Lacking food sources and a legal way to hold his men, Harold had to disband his forces. He returned with his house guard to London, leaving the south coast of England undefended.

In another move designed to get everyone's attention, William sailed his army and its fleet from the Dives to the mouth of the River Somme in Ponthieu.

Where Harold and William had met twice as friends.

The crossing to England was shorter from Ponthieu, so the move appeared strategic, but the move's message was as important as the reduced distance.

As the men settled on the shores of the Somme, Voldred and I took our leave. We boarded the ship William provided for us, with its extra rowers, and headed for the north of England.

Within a few days, we met Hardraada and Tostig at the mouth of the Humber, where Tostig had raided unsuccessfully in the spring.

We learned that a few weeks earlier, Hardraada had sailed down to the Humber from the Shetland and Orkney Islands, where he had gathered more men and ships. As he sailed south, he attacked a few towns, all of which submitted to him.

He had already begun his conquest.

He commanded a formidable force of over 100 ships carrying nearly 2,000 men, but he used the same tactic we had used: putting messengers ashore to carry word of the Norwegian King's "armada of 500 ships and 10,000 men."

Tostig had joined Hardraada with the force he had raised in Scotland, fewer than fifty ships and 200 men. He too sent messages ashore praising his "100 ships and 500 men."

From the mouth of the Humber, Hardraada and Tostig planned to march inland toward York, the capital of the English north.

Voldred and I arrived just as they were leaving. As the priests back in Falaise would have reminded me, this was the vigil of Saint Matthew, the twentieth day of September.

We watched the men marching away, clad in plain wool tunics and leggings tucked into heavy boots, shouldering single and double-bladed swords and axes. Many carried spears behind their metal-reinforced wooden shields.

As I had noticed often in the North, most of the shields were oblong, decorated with dragons and ravens, though now I saw a large number of smaller round shields, painted red, blue, yellow, and other bright colors, with weapons protruding from behind them at various angles. I supposed that the smaller shields were easier to wield in battle.

The men walked almost casually behind the brightly dressed nobles and the towering figure of Hardraada, next to whom flowed his banner, the crimson Land-Waster.

Voldred and I followed at a safe distance. Our job was to observe only. Even Voldred was not to fight, William had told us, especially since the only time Tostig had ever seen Voldred was when he saved me from the attack in St. Vaast, though both Voldred and I agreed that Tostig was unlikely to recognize him after all these years.

William's own personal Berserkers, six of whom guarded us now, were to remain outside any fray, so that they could escort us quickly back to William with the outcome of the invasion.

Wanting to avoid the sight of blood, I preferred to keep distance between us and any battle. So, it was from the returning Vikings and Hardraada and Tostig themselves that we learned of their victory.

Hardraada and Tostig had defeated the northern English Earls at a village south of York called Fulford. Hardraada and Tostig were triumphant, both believing that the Northumbrian resistance had been broken and that York was lying a short march away, theirs for the taking.

As we suspected, Tostig did not recognize Voldred and even offered to include him in a victory toast.

Later, I drew Voldred aside in one of the tents constructed for us and our Berserker bodyguards.

"You may recall that one of my visions foretold the defeat of the northern English Earls. This has just happened at Fulford. So, if we slip away now, we may be able to find the Earls of Mercia and Northumbria and forge some agreement with them."

"An agreement not to attack Duke William, should he invade England's southern shore?"

"Yes. Now that they've been defeated once, they may be in no mood to repeat the experience. They may agree not to join Harold's forces in the south."

"That would deprive King Harold of a significant force." He paused. "There is some risk of our being mistaken for spies."

"I'm well enough known as an emissary to avoid that. Anyway, the risk is worth the prize. I hope that we can carry word back to William that the north is won, and that even the Earls that opposed Hardraada and Tostig have agreed not to supply soldiers to Harold."

"All right. Let's take at least two of my fellow Berserkers with us, even though I hope that we can rely on your diplomatic reputation."

We slipped out of camp and with little effort located the two Earls just outside of York. I explained to the watchman who challenged us that we had messages from Duke William of Normandy.

Fortunately, the watchman, who did not recognize my name, nonetheless let us pass, noting that Duke William was not an enemy to the Northumbrians.

As we suspected, both northern Earls agreed to see us, because neither had any taste for further battle. They were even willing to swear an oath not to fight William, an oath on some of Fier's relics, which I had brought for such an occasion.

When I mentioned their defeat and the fact that they "had received no help from their new King," both Earls expressed their anger about the lack of support.

The Earl of Mercia even said, "I feel no need to send my battered soldiers to help the King with any of his battles. He may discover that the north of England is as far from the south as he thinks it is. The distance that kept his soldiers in the south when we needed them is the same distance that will keep our soldiers in the north when he needs them."

With this agreement, combined with Hardraada and Tostig's victory near York, Harold could command so few armed men that he would have to yield to Hardraada and Tostig in the north and William in the south.

Our plan was working exactly as we hoped it would.

For several days, Tostig and Hardraada marched in and out of York, gathering provisions and taking hostages. They also began to negotiate with the city's representatives.

I happened to pass Hardraada in the camp of makeshift tents where we all stayed. He was not otherwise engaged, and he greeted me with his usual enthusiasm.

When I asked him about his plans for York, he replied, "I've come here to win the cooperation of the northern towns and villages, beginning with York. So, I will not let my warriors loot the city or any neighboring town."

"A wise strategy, your majesty."

He smiled. "An obvious one, my friend."

"Not to some lords, your majesty, perhaps not even to Earl Tostig."

He stared in the direction of Tostig's tent in the distance. "You're right. He still wants revenge on any who aided the rebellion against him."

"How do you keep him in check?"

"I remind him that he should be angrier at his brother."

I smiled. "Another wise strategy."

He nodded. "And another obvious one. Now I must leave you, Cuin. I need to move all our forces to Stamford Bridge tomorrow for strategic advantage. It's less than a day's march away, which is far enough outside the city to avoid problems and close enough to our ships to ensure that no problems arise. I'll receive hostages from all over the shire and negotiate with the lords about our rule here."

I made a short bow and said, "A third obvious strategy, but wise nonetheless — like the other two."

He laughed and turned toward Tostig's tent.

The next day, as we were about to join the move to Stamford Bridge, Voldred and I received a troubling message.

One of Rolf's Goliards arrived breathlessly in camp, searching for us. He told us that King Harold was approaching from the south, gathering armed men as he marched.

"He marches both day and night," the Goliard said, "pushing north with a column of men, ponies, and wagons, clattering loudly through the villages to gain further support, while moving silently and quickly through the open spaces of the south."

"When will he arrive?" I asked.

"Tomorrow."

We thanked him and sent him south to inform William of Tostig and Hardraada's victory near York and Harold's advance. Then we informed Tostig and Hardraada of the new threat.

They thanked us and ordered us back to our tent.

Voldred and I agreed that, though we would march with the soldiers to Stamford Bridge the following day, we would stay close to the fleet. We were still under William's orders to observe only, and now a battle seemed likely.

"I will keep the events near Stamford Bridge within my sight," Voldred said, "but I advise you to remain with the Orkney Earls guarding the ships. They're led by one of Hardraada's sons, and you'll be safe with them, even if a battle ensues, especially if that battle turns against Tostig and Hardraada."

I agreed with his suggestion. "We expected the northern English Earls to be defeated by Hardraada and Tostig, and we were right. We assumed that the defeat would give Harold pause, but we were wrong."

"Harold is still a day away, and he's had a long march north," Voldred said.

"Yes, but Tostig and Hardraada's men are still recovering. They may have won their battle at Fulford, but many are wounded, and others are still exhausted."

"That is true, except for the Berserkers, of course."

"Of course. So, if Harold has come to fight rather than negotiate, the outcome of the battle is uncertain. Indeed, I think it very likely that the local people will support Harold."

"Do you think that they will support him in large enough numbers to defeat Tostig and Hardraada?"

"I don't know, but if Hardraada and Tostig are defeated, we need to get south as quickly as possible. Harold having a great victory in the north changes William's entire strategy."

Voldred paused. "William is still driven on by the Pope. We cannot change that."

"Nonetheless, we need to inform William about whatever happens here next."

"All right. As soon as I know whether there are negotiations or fighting and the outcome of either, I'll return here."

Before I made for the ships, I wanted a last world with Hardraada and Tostig.

I approached Tostig's tent, where the two of them sat outside, talking and drinking.

As I was trying to work out what to say, Tostig glimpsed me. He had just finished a horn of beer.

"Cuin! Come, join us!"

He motioned me to sit on a wooden stool and called for beer for me. I thanked him and remained silent.

Hardraada noticed my seriousness. "You have something to tell us?"

At first, my voice failed to issue any sound, so I coughed to clear my throat. "No, my lord." I hesitated. "I'm merely concerned."

"Concern!" Tostig cried, "We took Fulford with a few strokes of the sword, and soon we'll have York with a few negotiations!"

"I'm not certain of further victory, my lord, especially if your brother arrives with local forces as well as his own."

Tostig waved his hand. "Half the battle is won, and the other half certain. The north of England is ours. Even if Harold marches all the way here, he can't stand against our forces." He raised his drinking-horn in Hardraada's direction. "England, Norway, and Denmark will stand together for a hundred years!"

Hardraada continued to watch me. "What bothers you, Cuin?"

"I don't trust the resolve of the men of York, your majesty."

Tostig laughed. "A spy never trusts. Suspicion is his weapon. It's unnecessary here, though."

Hardraada ignored Tostig. "Why don't you trust them?"

I glanced at Tostig, but he continued to grin and shake his head at me.

I addressed myself to Hardraada. "I'm not certain about my concern. I can say what troubles me. The men of Northumbria are … Britons, Celts, Saxons, Danes, Norwegians, Christians, and Odin and Thor worshippers."

"Why does that trouble you?" Hardraada asked.

"They aren't a unified group. They more resemble ... a soup. Their allegiance is to no one, to no one religion and to no one lord. They live on the edge of rebellion. Armies have marched on them from the north, invaded them from the south. They have the skills of survivors, not subjects."

Tostig gestured at me again. "So they know what they need to survive. That will make them support us."

"They may know what they need to survive, but what is that in this case?" I gestured toward Hardraada. "Do they accept King Harald of Norway as their leader after a single battle? A foreign King with a small army? Or do they wait for the King they've already accepted, whom they've known for years before he was King, and who now commands a large army?"

"Ours isn't a small army," Hardraada said. "And these are Northern warriors."

"The whole country is the King's army, your majesty. The people of York know that. And they may have no love for Northern warriors."

"Many of the local families bear names from Norway and Denmark," Hardraada said. "Do you say that they hate a noble parentage of great fighters?"

"That is not what I intended to say, your majesty. The Danes and Norwegians who settled in and around York didn't come here for battle. They came for farming, for trading, for fishing. The warriors didn't stay. As for the others — the Britons, the Saxons and the Celts — what do they know of Norway and Denmark, but its assaults on their settled villages? Will they now take a Norwegian King? Will they throw off Harold, the new, strong King of England who promises them safety from Norway and Denmark, indeed, who plans to conquer those countries?"

Laughing and shaking his head, Tostig rose. "No more, Cuin! You've spent too many nights slinking through towns and forests. Join the feast and forget your concerns!" Drinking as he went, he strode away.

I found Hardraada studying me. "My young friend, you've done me good service before. This, too, is service, I know. You aren't the first to render it. Before I left Norway, my wife and daughter had dreams of my death, of my feasting with other warriors in Heaven or Valhalla."

I smiled at his jest.

He continued, "For a warrior, death is a possibility, and it may happen here and now. I do not know. The outcomes of wars are never certain. Perhaps we will die today. Perhaps your Duke will be defeated, and Tostig and I will conquer the entire north of England."

"Perhaps," I said, "but Duke William waits in Normandy, crossing into England only when he is sure of victory."

He leaned toward me, like a huge tree leaning in my direction. "In war, one is never sure of victory. War gods are changeable."

"You will take precautions then, your majesty?"

"I will take enough men to keep the good citizens of York and King Harold of England from running a knife into my back, but a warrior can do no more."

I slept that night on the fast ship William had given us, and I made sure the rowers were with me.

The next day I waited for Voldred to return from Stamford Bridge.

Later that afternoon, he came running toward the ships. I had never seen his face so pale.

"King Harold and his soldiers, joined by local men, as we suspected, attacked Tostig and Hardraada's forces. There was no negotiation. The King simply demanded that Tostig and Hardraada surrender to him." He paused to catch his breath. "The fighting was hard from the beginning, and there was much I couldn't see."

"Hardraada and Tostig?"

He shook his head. "As the fighting went on, it was clear that they would soon be surrounded. I saw King Harold himself with two men close in and slay Hardraada."

"Harold killed Hardraada himself?"

"Yes, as he would have to, for his men. They would need to see that their King is an invincible warrior."

"Tostig?"

"King Harold paused before him, as if he was giving Tostig an opportunity to escape, to flee, but Tostig attacked with a fury, and the King killed him. His own brother. I watched Harold stare down at Tostig's body and then step back to study the battle, to go where he was needed. It was finished right there, though. And I knew that I should get back here as quickly as possible."

I shook myself to focus on what needed to be done now. "Who returned with you?"

"I came alone, ahead of anyone else."

"We must ready our own ship for Normandy immediately."

"I agree. If King Harold's men pursue what's left of Hardraada's men back here, we're not safe."

As we sailed south, I leaned on the ship's side, staring back at the coast, recalling Tostig. The rough earl who had saved my life had now lost his. I thought that if this man could be killed, then nothing in England was safe. The thought was not logical, but it came nonetheless.

Then I thought of Norway. I imagined the poems that would be sung: King Harald Sigurdsson, called Hardraada, the Christian King of Norway, had died as a Viking warrior and now feasted with the Viking warrior gods in Valhalla.

At the last battle, Ragnarok, though, even the Viking gods would die, the old sagas said — the last death. I imagined Hardraada's huge form, waving his great sword and fighting under the Land-Waster, challenging his last foe.

We sailed first to the south of England, in case William had already crossed into England. If he had not, we could sail on to Normandy.

I used my vision skills to check on William, but even though the dragon appeared, saying "Here is where you go," all I saw was Rolf calling to his Goliards as they landed at Dover.

Since Dover was the closest port for a Norman crossing, we sailed there. The seas were not with us, but all of us rowed, so that we reached Dover within two days. At Dover's harbor, I spotted Rolf, sitting on a dock, staring out to sea, the striking white cliffs of the harbor behind him to the west.

As I approached, he leaped to his feet and said, "There you are!"

After Voldred and I greeted him, I asked, "How did you know we would be here?"

"Your Icelandic teacher, Hervor, appeared to me in a dream. She told me that as soon as Duke William began to prepare his men to sail, I should take a fast ship and make for Dover."

"Then William has begun his preparations?"

"This morning, as Hervor said he would."

I thought for a moment. "That means he should be in the Channel by nightfall and here before dawn."

Rolf nodded. "I agree."

"He will, then, land safely," Voldred said, "because the royal fleet has been reduced in the south. And King Harold is still in the north."

"What? Why?" Rolf asked.

"Then the messengers haven't yet reached you," I said. "We have troubling reports. King Harold received word of the attack on York and force-marched his soldiers north, gaining support along the way. Two days ago, he defeated Tostig and Hardraada's combined forces."

"The King and the Earl?" Rolf asked.

"King Harald of Norway and Earl Tostig are dead," Voldred said.

Rolf looked at me closely. "What does this mean for Duke William's plans?"

"I don't know," I said. "Though we have convinced the Earls of Mercia and Northumbria not to aid Harold immediately, we know that he controls the north of England. Half our plans are undone."

William did arrive in the morning — but later than we expected and not at Dover.

I discovered this while trying to rouse myself for a dawn meeting.

While working on being fully awake and using breakfast as my motivator, I was interrupted by a vision from Hervor.

"I see that you still sleep like a dead person," her voice broke in on my thoughts.

Immediately I had a vision of her standing with her hands on her hips. I could not see the surrounding countryside.

"Nor will you," she said.

"Will you please stop reading my thoughts?"

"Yes, when you stop invading my privacy with your visions. It is none of your concern where I am."

I stifled a yawn. "Fair enough. Why are you interrupting my quest for breakfast?"

"You must have noticed, if you have eyes for anything but food, that your Duke's ships are nowhere to be seen."

"I had noticed, but I supposed that he was late, held up in the Channel by some fog, perhaps even one of yours."

She huffed. "I opened the passage for him, so I made certain that there was no fog."

I yawned and stretched. "All right. No fog. What did happen, and where is he? I assume from your tone that he's not drowned."

"No, he's not drowned. Last night, during the crossing, his ship, which carried the lantern the others were following, sailed too far ahead. He lost those behind him."

"That's what William does."

"His crew panicked, thinking the entire endeavor was a failure. So Duke William pulled in his sails and had a leisurely supper until the other ships caught up to him."

"That's also what William does."

"He's developing a taste for food that rivals yours."

"Are you on the ship with him?"

"Of course not. Horrible thing, that narrow channel of water. No one should ever have to be on it. I am on land, and you need no more knowledge than that."

I yawned again, coming close to full wakefulness. "Where is William now, and what is it you want me to do?"

"At this moment, he is landing west of you at a small village. From what I can tell, it's called Pevensey. If you and Voldred get into the Channel soon, you should reach the place by late tonight, with rowers helping, of course."

"Is everything all right? Did he encounter resistance?"

"None. There was no royal fleet, and the local villagers were immediately in awe of the Norman Duke, about whom they've heard only terrifying stories."

"Good."

"Get your crew into the Channel."

"After my breakfast, I assume."

She was already gone.

We arrived at Pevensey later than Hervor said we would and found William's men building an inner rampart in the old Roman fort there. We knew that Harold's men had stayed near the Roman fort during the summer and had strengthened some of the old walls, digging ditches within them.

William himself was in a large tent with his half-brothers, Robert and Odo, and some of his closest advisors, including Ralph of Tosny and the ever present Osbern.

As Rolf, Voldred, and I waited at the tent entrance, we overheard William and the others discuss leaving a small force in Pevensey at the fort. They would move the main body of men and ships to Hastings, a town with a large enough harbor to maintain the illusion of a huge fleet and a huge force.

Hastings also contained an existing Saxon castle, which could become part of the line of castles William was creating along the south coast.

When William noticed us, he called us toward him.

"I'm relieved to see all three of you alive. What happened in the north?"

As we related the events, William stared at us, his face unchanged. Robert, Odo, Osbern, and the others, however, shook their heads.

When we finished, William said, "This was unexpected. We need to plan carefully now." He turned to the advisors. "I will need a moment alone with these three, please." As they turned to go, he said to them, "Have no fear. This only means that we strategize differently and more boldly. We will stop Harold."

When the advisors were gone, he turned to us. "Do you know where Harold is now?"

"No," Rolf said. "I have a companion shadowing his movements, but no one knows where I am, so they could not get a message to me."

William began to pace. "We need to discover Harold's movements. Rolf, take Voldred with you. Go to London. Harold is not likely to have stayed in the north, since he's been waiting for me all summer. He'll march for London, I think."

"Both of us can ride, my lord," Rolf said.

"I know, and I appreciate the suggestion. Take two fast horses from my cavalry. How long will it take you to get to London?"

"If the roads remain good," Rolf said, "a day and a half, perhaps two."

"Good," William said. "As soon as you know where Harold is, send a fast rider back to me. I need to know Harold's movements as soon as possible."

After they had gone, William said to me, "You and I need to sit together and rethink our plans. As you saw, the Norman lords, now that they've ventured beyond their own realms, turn fearful when anything unexpected happens. You and I, having grown up under the constant threat of assassins, respond more strategically."

"I did notice their reactions."

"You and I will now take a walk in the forest back here. Whatever passes between us stays between us."

I smiled. "Even if it's a brilliant idea?"

He smiled back and pulled me from the tent toward the forest. "Yes, because then I want to make certain that my men believe it was my idea."

We walked briefly in silence, and since the day was cool but sunny, I enjoyed the walk, especially feeling my feet on something that was not the bottom of a ship.

Eventually, I said, "The strategy to contain Harold must become an obstacle strategy now."

"No longer our imprisonment strategy, pressing Harold from two sides."

"That's right. While we expected the north and the south to be two hands pressing Harold, the northern hand is now missing. In its place is a hand that supports Harold, though the two northern Earls won't fight for him. As a consequence, the southern hand must present an obstacle."

William was silent for awhile longer and then asked, "Do you have ideas?"

"Let's think about what we have. The southern hand presently includes the men and the fleet, the castles you're building, and the Pope's banner, which threatens Harold with excommunication."

William stopped walking to look at me, which I appreciated since his longer legs were outpacing my shorter ones.

He said, "With no northern hand, we need to strengthen the southern one, but what you've listed as its strengths Harold already knows."

"Yes, so we need further strengthening, something Harold doesn't expect."

"The northern hand was perhaps stronger than the southern. Yet Harold felt strong enough to attack it, and he defeated it."

"What you're saying then, is that if both hands did not stop Harold, one will certainly not."

"That's how things appear."

"That's why I think that we must shape the southern hand into some great obstacle."

"It can't be just military. Or religious. Harold won't be intimidated by either. And we need him to be intimidated. To feel forced to negotiate."

"What is an obstacle that will stop him?"

William paused, and I saw his face change.

"You have something in mind," I said.

"I do. I take the throne from Harold."

I stared at him. "What …?"

To my dismay, William began walking again, which meant two things: he had a plan, and he was optimistic about its success.

"Let's consider, Cuin, what Harold really wants."

"He wants an empire to rival those of Kings Alfred and Canute."

"Yes, but to get that, he must have complete support for his reign in England. If doubts arise about that support, especially if the Pope raises them as well, he can't even begin to build an empire."

"I see. He'll have the same problem that Hardraada had in Norway. It took him so long to gain support of the Norwegian lords and the people that he never conquered Denmark."

"Precisely. So, first, we put out messages that I have a huge invasion force, which I'm using to make a legal claim to the throne of England."

"And the part about the Pope?"

"We send word to Harold that we've put the case before the Pope that I should be King of England, and the papal banner means that the Pope accepts the case."

"William, Harold can send messengers to Rome to discover that this is not true."

"Just as he can send spies to discover that we don't have a huge invasion force, but by that time, the outcome of our plan will already be assured."

"That outcome is?"

"We will already have confronted Harold — you and I privately — with our plan. We will force him to rethink his empire. More than that, we will force him into a confrontation that will determine how England is to be ruled."

"I don't understand. You're trying to avoid a battle with him."

"Not a battle. Single combat."

I stopped walking and made him return to me. "Single combat? How did you arrive at that form of confrontation? I know that you don't want to rule England. Besides, why would Harold agree to single combat? What if he kills you?"

William smiled. "He's a friend."

"Friendship will resolve this whole endeavor? Is that what you are saying? If so, we could have left everyone at home and invited Harold to Normandy for a hunting party."

"We know that Harold will agree to single combat because we know him." He turned again and threw back the comment, "And I can defeat him in single combat, something he does not know."

I hurried to catch up with him. "I'm going to reason through this just to be certain that you haven't gone mad."

"That's a good idea, anyway. We both need to think this through." He smiled again. "Though I am certain that it will work."

"All right, Harold is a friend, so instead of forcing him into a public confrontation, we — just you and I — talk with him privately."

"Yes."

"We tell him that you've landed here with a huge invasion force, which you brought with you only to make a legal claim to the throne of England, because …?"

"Because that's what the Pope insisted that I do. Or he would excommunicate me and denounce my marriage to Matilda."

"Hmm. That's good. He'll believe that."

"Of course he will. He knows that the Pope could undermine both my marriage and my rule of Normandy."

"So, we offer Harold single combat with you as a way to resolve the issue, to both avoid a legal battle with the Saxon Council —"

"Harold knows that I have Lanfranc, the most brilliant legal mind in Christendom in my camp. "

"And," I finished my own thought, "to avoid a huge battle over the English crown."

"Yes."

I continued, "We know that Harold is vulnerable where the law is concerned, because he doesn't have someone like Lanfranc. Further, he's illegally stolen Church lands and money."

"So, he'll do whatever he can to avoid a legal challenge."

"And to avoid a huge battle."

"Yes, he's a good enough warrior to know that strategy before a battle is better than strategy during a battle."

I nodded. "Harold negotiated in Wales rather than fight, and even though he was angry at the exile of his family, he nonetheless joined his father in negotiating a peace."

"That's right. He was angry enough to raid during the exile. When he and his father sailed together to London, however, he negotiated with Edward to avoid a civil war."

"He negotiated during the rebellion against Tostig, even though he'd helped to foment that very rebellion."

William shrugged. "He could have allowed that rebellion to break out into open warfare: the northern lords against the southern lords that Tostig and the King could summon. He chose instead to resolve the conflict, so that he would appear even more heroic."

"Yes, he convened the huge conference at Oxford, as Canute had once done, to avoid bloodshed."

"And to present himself as a law-loving peacemaker to the lords of both the north and south of England."

"This might work, William. He must accept the one strategy that allows him to avoid both a legal battle and a military battle."

William nodded emphatically. "Single combat."

It took Rolf's messenger a week to ride into our encampment with the report that Harold was a few days' march from London. His men were tired and discouraged. They had won a battle, but they had marched back to London after only a brief rest. Further, the two northern Earls — true to the oath they had taken in front of Voldred and me — refused to send soldiers.

The messenger said, "The King's men are grumbling that this King may be leading them into one battle after another."

William and I nodded at each other. Even among his fighting men, Harold was losing support for fighting.

After a brief session with his half-brothers and the rest of his advisors, William and I met with Rolf.

"I'd like you to ride north," William told Rolf, "to arrange a meeting with Harold. Perhaps in some small town south of London."

"I know a small village about half a day's march south of the city," Rolf said. "I will recommend that. A friend of mine lives there, and we may stay with him."

"Good. Take this to Harold, too." William pulled a ring from his finger. "He gave this to me himself, so he'll know the message is from me."

"I suggest," I said, "that we allow Harold to bring his house guard if he wishes. We want to reassure him that the visit will be peaceful. We'll even limit the number of our own men to, perhaps, twelve."

Rolf nodded, and William said, "I agree."

A few days after Rolf's departure, William and I headed north secretly, taking only Voldred, and eight Berserkers with us. William wore a peasant's disguise, and the Berserkers wore plain woolen cloaks. We traveled on foot with only two ponies to carry supplies, so that we would not be taken for knights or nobles.

When we arrived in the village, we were welcomed by Rolf's friend, who as I discovered also knew Garrad and had fought with him "in the early days." The man invited us to construct our tents outside of his hut on the south side of the village.

Rolf rode in the next day, informing us that Harold would arrive the following morning. He would travel, as we had, in disguise with twelve of his house guards.

Late the next morning, the new King of England and twelve of his house guards rode into town on the small English ponies that I admired, not the least for the reason that they had the good sense not to grow into huge horses.

After formal introductions and greetings, Harold turned to William and said, "I welcome this opportunity to visit a good friend again."

"As do I, your majesty," William said.

I noted that William's address as "your majesty" recognized Harold's right to be King. As William and I had discussed, Harold needed to feel that his position as King was secure.

It was only his imperial ambition that we intended to thwart.

William continued, "I wonder, your majesty, if we might speak privately?"

"Of course. As friends, you and I do not need guards at our sides as we talk."

"Thank you. The most private tent belongs to Cuin, who's never given up his habits as a hermit. So we may use that, if he will allow it."

Harold smiled. "I will have one guard follow me at a distance, of course. The house guard will insist on that. Shall Cuin be your guard?"

William laughed. "Yes, I'm sure to be safe with a small emissary at my side."

The three of us, followed by the head of Harold's house guards, walked a short distance away from the village into the clearing where my tent stood. It had been William's suggestion that I encamp away from the main party to provide a private meeting place.

The tent also backed up to a low rock cliff which ran from where the tent stood almost to the village. I had tried it before I constructed my tent in front of it: it was perfect for visions.

As the two of them entered the tent, I remained outside, but Harold turned back to me.

He smiled and said, "Well, Cuin, if you had become Duke of Normandy and taken all the thrones of the North, we would not be having this conversation, would we?"

I smiled in return. "No, your majesty. By now, trying to rule all four, I would have created such chaos that we'd be at someone's funeral, most likely mine."

He laughed. "Instead, you managed to get the rulers of Norway, Denmark, England, Normandy, and even Flanders talking to each other." He became serious and shook his head. "If my brother had not pulled Norway's King into his revenge, all of us might still be talking."

"I'm sorry about your brother and King Harald of Norway."

"So am I. Which brings me to this. I have something for you."

He reached into his tunic and pulled out a curved bladed knife with a long red line running down it. At first, it startled me.

Then I realized that the fourth knife of the Four Crowns Prophecy had found its way to the empire-building King Harold of England. If the King of England were to take over Norway, Denmark, Normandy, and then France, the prophecy would be fulfilled in a very different way.

"This really belongs to you now, does it not?" he said. "You did the work you were destined to do, after all. You lived long enough to see the Kings of Norway and Denmark make peace, to see King Edward of England have peaceful interactions with young King Philip of France through Duke William and through William's father-in-law and Philip's regent, Count Baldwin of Flanders."

"Thank you —" I began, but he interrupted me.

"It's remarkable, Cuin. The crowns of England, France, Norway, and Denmark all knew peace for a moment in history." He paused. "It's not your fault that it has come unraveled."

I stared at the knife and said, "Thank you, your majesty. I'm not sure how to respond to your gracious assessment. It's been my privilege to work with great leaders."

He stepped close to me to hand me the knife. Instead of feeling the fear I had felt before, I felt the odd sensation I had experienced in England when I first met Harold — a healing presence.

As he handed me the knife, he put out his hand to shake mine, saying, "It has been my privilege to know you, Cuin."

I felt the healing force from his hand as a noticeable power. I thanked him again.

He nodded and turned to William. "Here, my friend, is the ring I gave you during our second meeting in Ponthieu and our foray into Brittany. I want to make sure that you keep it as a sign of our friendship." He held the ring in his hand. "Our lasting friendship."

William took it and said, "Thank you, your majesty."

I decided to avoid a difficult moment by saying, "If you will excuse me, your majesty, I will leave you and Duke William to discuss the events at hand."

I left the tent and walked along the rock for twenty paces and then sat down in front of it. I cast my inner vision toward the tent, and the dragon appeared immediately. It led me down into the tent, so that I could both see and hear William and Harold talking.

William was speaking. "… friends," he was saying, and it was clear that it was at the end of a comment. "Now you see yourself now as the ruler of a large empire."

"I would say 'country,' not 'empire'," Harold replied.

William continued speaking. "I want to be clear, your majesty. I don't doubt that you would be a great ruler. Even a great ruler of many lands. You and I both know, however, that in the natural course of events, Normandy would become a political target, even a military one."

"Would it?

"Of course. Your empire would depend on bringing the northern countries together, which would be a challenge to both the Holy Roman Empire and the Pope. Even before you moved against any southern country, the Pope would consider you a threat. And as you know well, I am in the Pope's debt."

Harold shook his head. "If I am interested in an empire, Duke William, one reason is that Christian rulers, often at the behest of the Pope, have oppressed countries wherever they go. I am Christian, but I cannot condone torturing and killing those who would not convert to Christianity, the methods of Charlemagne, King Olaf, and even Pope Benedict. Wouldn't Normandy be willing to join an empire that opposes violence in the name of the Prince of Peace?"

"Would your empire be less violent, your majesty, when you wanted to expand it and met resistance?"

"I have always tried to negotiate for peace where I could."

"I know, but don't empires demand more than peaceful negotiations when you face an enemy? Your empire would require more than negotiations, since it would stand against the Pope, the Holy Roman Empire, and any country who joined them. I don't disagree with your complaints about aggressive conversions by the Church, but setting your empire against them ensures war."

Harold was silent for a long time, staring at William. "I wish I could answer you differently, my friend. You're right. I am determined to stand against that Church-controlled force and its allies."

"Even if it means bloodshed?"

"The Church's aggression has already meant bloodshed: stealing lands from those who would not submit, killing their families, torturing them. If this Church empire grows, what will it not be capable of? And what might it do, given free rein in the world?"

William dropped his head and was silent for a moment. Then he raised it again. "I don't know."

Harold leaned forward. "Then you agree, William, that it may create even more bloodshed in the future, even without my empire."

William nodded. "I see that possibility."

"Almost a certainty, I would say."

"No doubt you would. And I understand why you would." William paused. "You must see, though, that I would be forced to confront you, to stop you."

Harold leaned back and produced one of his charming smiles. "Why not just join me?"

"You're forgetting my obligation to the Pope, Harold. He holds my marriage and Normandy in his hand, as will any Pope who comes after him, as long as I live."

Harold tried to keep his light tone. "Doesn't this seem an intolerable slavery to you? Better to submit to my empire than that one, William. At least we're friends."

William remained serious. "At this moment, I'm not sure who will have to submit. Or to what conditions."

Harold stiffened in his chair. "Since we are friends, you know me well enough to know that I will never submit to the Pope as you do. And I will not give up England."

"I do know that. That is why I have a proposal that will avoid either of us having to submit to conditions we abhor."

"I'm eager to hear it."

"You know that I've been building a force in Normandy that now sits on your south coast."

"The rumors have reached me."

"Do you know why I've been building that force?"

"I am interested in your motives."

"If you have heard the rumors, you know already that the Pope has given me relics and more importantly, a banner."

"I've heard that."

"What you may not yet have discovered is that the Pope insists that I force you to surrender the English crown. If you do not yield it immediately, he wants me to make a legal case before the Saxon Council to have you replaced by me, either as King or as regent of … who is the next in the bloodline now, Edgar, the young atheling from Hungary?"

"Yes, Edgar."

"If that's not acceptable to you or the Council, the Pope insists that I take the throne by force, and he will excommunicate everyone who resists me, including you and the Council, so that I will be left the only non-excommunicate ruler in the country."

William paused. Then he continued, "Since I know that you won't give up the throne and won't yield to the Pope, I know that you're in a difficult position. I can make my way to London to put the Pope's instructions before the Council. If you try to stop me, I can use the force I've built, at the Pope's command, to fight my way to London. Many of our men will be killed, but I will make it to London. One way or another, I will address the Council."

Harold slumped in his chair. "So, my choices are to engage in battle with you, a valued friend, to prevent you from going to London, in which case, even if I win, the Pope excommunicates me. As a consequence, I can rule no Christian country that is subject to the Pope. Or I can let you go to London, so that both of us can argue our cases before the Council. Since you have Master Lanfranc as an advisor, I will likely lose the legal battle. Even if I win and if the Council agrees that I should keep the crown, the Pope still excommunicates me."

"The only advantage of the second option over the first is that the second avoids bloodshed."

"Either way, I am an excommunicate and cannot rule. So, these are battles I cannot win."

William nodded.

Harold sighed. "You said you had a proposal. At this moment, Duke William, I am open to any proposal that does not end with my excommunication and the loss of England."

"Shall we think this through together, your majesty? As friends?"

"I'm eager to do so."

"Let's start by noticing that your force is much reduced by your battle in the north. Also, the northern Earls have refused you any military service for the immediate future, giving as their excuse that they just fought a costly battle at Fulford."

Harold gave a light groan. "This will be the work of Cuin. That's the only way you could know about the two Earls so quickly."

William nodded. "Yes, this is from Cuin." He paused. "Let's also consider that my force is not as large as you believe. I've given my messengers and your spies numbers almost ten times as large as the force I have with me."

I was startled and almost lost the vision. Why was William telling Harold this?

Then it occurred to me: he's making them equals. Single combat must be between equals.

William continued, "So, we're evenly matched for battle. A battle that neither of us wants."

"I agree wholeheartedly, though I am surprised about your numbers. Everyone thinks, even now, that you have a massive force near Hastings."

William smiled. "Such impressions are the advantage and disadvantage of using spies, your majesty."

"I see what you mean."

"Let's also agree that even with reduced numbers, we need to show our soldiers and the people we rule that we are determined leaders and valiant warriors, men they can respect."

"I agree."

"So, we need a strategy that allows us to keep that respect, since both of us already have it, which is our good fortune."

Harold nodded. "We share that good fortune."

"At one extreme, we want to avoid a war. At the other extreme, we want to avoid a legal battle in the Council that ends badly, including a papal excommunication."

"Yes."

"The middle strategy is for us to meet one-on-one on the battlefield."

Harold leaned forward. "Single combat?"

"Yes. First, it avoids the war and enables us to keep the respect of our forces and our people. Second, it is a form of legal resolution that takes the place of a legal struggle with the Council. Third, we are evenly matched as fighters, and we are friends, so we could agree to fight for some considerable length of time, enough to be impressive, and arrive at no decisive conclusion."

"We would fight to a draw?"

"Yes, that provides the fourth and final outcome: you and I, having been unable to fight our way to a resolution, agree to terms that suit both of us. And the Pope. Perhaps a co-rulership, during which I make rare visits to England, appearing to advise you — the rarer the better, since I have to interest in ruling England, much less the ability to do so."

Harold sat silently for a long time, sometimes shaking his head, sometimes dropping it.

Then he lifted his head and began to smile. "William, this is an audacious plan. It's almost outrageous, but it's the only real course left to us."

William nodded and smiled. "I know what you're thinking: it may also work."

Harold's smile widened. "Yes, it could work. We — you and I — control all the conditions. If we plan carefully, nothing prevents this from working."

William nodded and put out his hand. "Are we agreed, your majesty?"

Harold took his hand. "Yes, Duke William, we are agreed."

I ended the vision and rested. I knew that the two rulers, the two friends, could make every detail work.

That night I slept soundly, though I kept hearing the dragon hissing, "Friday the 13th. Friday the 13th."

The next day, we headed south again, and William explained the plans he had made with Harold: after an interval that allowed William to move his forces to Hastings, Harold would gather an equal force and march on the town.

Then Harold would challenge William to single combat, and both would agree that this was an honorable way to spare the lives of their men, who would be grateful to avoid a battle, especially those of Harold's men who had fought at Stamford Bridge and had marched exhaustedly back to London.

William would move his force outside of Hastings, so that curious townspeople would be kept at a distance, while Harold encamped his forces nearby.

When William finished explaining the plans, I said, "If we can find a valley near the town, you and Harold should be able to put your armies on opposite sides of the valley at some distance from where you two will fight."

"That's a good idea. This ensures that neither soldiers nor townspeople can observe what happens."

"If any factors interfere with your plans, no local eyes will see how we deal with those factors."

William smiled at me. "Strategizing for unknown factors — that's one of the reasons I chose you to be an emissary."

I appreciated the compliment and said so, but I added, "Even single combat is fighting, William, and something might go wrong."

William did move the men and ships to the harbor town of Hastings, and a scout did find a valley that was a short march from the town, ideal for the single combat.

While we waited for Harold to arrive, William and his advisors planned where to position the fighting men. They had to be far enough away to ensure non-engagement but close enough in case Harold engaged in treachery.

Fortunately, small hills rimmed opposite sides of the valley, and the Norman and English forces could be positioned just under the crest of each hill away from the valley. That way, neither force could see what was happening in the valley itself.

Requesting one last planning meeting, William and Harold met once again at my tent, which sat a short distance away from the main body of tents. This time, I was asked to sit in on the meeting along with Leofwine, the youngest of Harold's brothers.

We reviewed the plans, and everyone agreed on the general strategies.

William suggested that he and Harold have a small contingent of men with them during the single combat.

"Six men should be sufficient," Harold said.

"I agree," William said.

"If I may add something," I said, "I suggest that you begin fighting well past dawn, so that both of you, as well as your men, will be well rested. Weary men may draw wrong conclusions from messages they receive while you two fight."

Harold smiled. "That's a good suggestion. It benefits everyone."

"May I also suggest, with some trepidation, since I am volunteering two noble lords for extended combat, that you fight until noon?"

Leofwine looked at Harold and William with clear concern and said, "For single combat, that's a huge effort."

"Since no fighting men will see what transpires," I replied, "we need only report that the fighting continued until noon. King Harold and Duke

William could be passing the time playing hnefatafl, for all the men would know."

Harold nodded. "The longer we fight, the more impressive the combat will be."

"Or seem to fight," William said.

"Fighting through midday," Harold said, "certainly justifies negotiations."

William smiled. "An entire morning of single combat sounds sufficiently heroic."

"May I ask about the details of that negotiation," I said, "or do you prefer to keep that to yourselves?"

"Not at all," Harold replied. "Having considered several possibilities, we decided to announce that we would share the throne."

"With King Hardecanute and King Edward as legal precedents?" I asked.

"Yes," William said, "Hardecanute inviting Edward to share the throne, though it happened twenty years ago, should provide adequate legal precedent when we approach the Saxon Council."

Harold laughed. "You Normans think elegantly in legal terms. I'm not sure whether you were all trained by Master Lanfranc or just born to think about law."

William smiled. "I don't know, either."

"What are your practical plans for ruling England?" I asked.

"Since I've already been crowned," Harold said, "Duke William will be crowned after the Council approves our plan."

"Will they approve it?"

"What choice will they have?" William replied. "No one really wants young Edgar to replace King Harold, who has already governed the country well for the past ten years, as he stood behind Edward's throne. Further, they see him as a great warrior and a peacekeeper."

Harold offered his charming smile. "Thank you, my friend. That was gracious."

"It has the added benefit of being true," William said.

"After William's coronation," Harold continued, "he will stay in the country just long enough to seem established —"

"Which will make the Pope happy," William said, "and end my service to him, I hope. Then I will return to Normandy, leaving Harold to handle the affairs of the country."

"William will make occasional visits to seem interested in England," Harold said, "so that the Pope and the Council are satisfied that joint rulership is working."

"I may even offer help with any problems involving Normans," William added.

Harold rose to leave, and William rose with him. He touched Harold's arm. "We tell our men none of this, is that right? Not about our plans, the real numbers of our men — any of it?"

"That's right," Harold said. "If anyone knew, my position as King would be undermined. How I came to retain the crown would be considered … dishonorable."

"Good," William said, though I thought his voice sounded too harsh.

To avoid any tension between them, I rose and asked, "Do you two want me in attendance tomorrow?"

"I do," Harold said, looking at William. "I will have my brothers with me as well as two of my house guards. We should have men around us whom we trust."

"I agree," William said. "Men we trust to tell our armies what we want them to hear. So, yes, Cuin, I want you, Osbern, Odo, and Robert with me."

"Each of us will have four men, then," Harold said, "including our brothers."

"Yes."

"It's settled then," Harold said, extending his hand.

William took it.

That night, I heard the dragon hissing in my dreams, "Friday the 13th, Friday the 13th."

For a moment I awoke to realize that we had been planning the next day's events on Friday, unlucky Friday. It was also the 13th day of October.

The next morning, William turned up at my tent not long after dawn. I moved from deep sleep to half sleep to the drowsy realization that someone was in my tent.

As William always could do, he waited patiently. When I was fully awake, I sat up and saw him staring out of the tent at the sky.

"Good morning, William. Is is everything all right?"

He turned to glance at me and then said, "Yes." He paused. "I have some … foreboding this morning."

I yawned and rubbed my hands over my face and hair. "The dragon awakened me last night to remind me that our planning day had been Friday, the 13th day of October."

"You know that I pay little attention to omens, Cuin."

"I know, but all the same, we should allow for the unexpected."

He turned fully toward me. "I recall now that Voldred's attacks on you happened on Fridays."

"Some on the 13th day of the month. I don't want to make too much of this, though. I simply think that we should be cautious."

"Are you awake yet?"

"Yes, yes, I am."

"Good. I want you to do something for me."

"Certainly. What is it? I'll be standing close to you as you fight, of course."

"I want you to have your bow with you. And four arrows."

"What? William, I've never killed anyone with my bow. I'm not sure that —"

"You will not have to use it. I just want you to have it with you. All those years ago when the assassins came for me, you were behind me with your bow. That… comforted me. It allowed me to focus. I would like to have that same focus today."

"Harold is not an assassin."

"I know that, but I do not know whether his house guards or his brothers might be. Let's remind ourselves that Harold is well loved in England. If any of the four men with him think that he is losing the crown, what might they do?"

"I see. They know nothing of our plans."

"Nor can they. If anyone thought the single combat was less than sincere, all our plans would come undone."

"All right. Will Harold think it is odd, though, that I have my bow?"

"All of us will have weapons, even though only Harold and I are supposed to use ours — on each other. Your bow will arouse no suspicions. I don't think your prowess with a bow is as well known in England as it is in Normandy, Norway, and Denmark. Besides, Osbern, Odo, and Robert will all have bows, which, by the way, you made for them."

"I'll stand behind you, then. With my bow."

The sun was well up when Harold and his men arrived. He maintained a serious demeanor, as did William, both giving the appearance of two men about to engage in a deadly struggle.

Both wore hauberks down to their mid-thighs, but the hauberks were made of leather, not mail. William and Harold had agreed that they could fight much longer without heavy mail. Accordingly, they also wore heavy leather leggings, the leggings running down to heavy shoes.

Neither wore helmets, and they had agreed to aim no blows at the head, even if those blows were slow enough to be deflected.

Harold had a gold tunic under his hauberk, while William wore a deep red tunic. I had overheard him earlier in the morning joking that, if he had any minor wounds, the tunic's color would mask them.

The two combatants met in a small clearing on the south side of the valley, the site we had chosen because of the tight groves of trees on either side of the clearing. The trees guaranteed that the day's events would be observed only by those in close proximity to the two fighters.

William and Harold approached each other, both wielding double-edged swords behind round shields. Harold's shield had the red dragon of Wessex painted on his, while William's displayed an attacking panther. They bowed briefly to each other and crossed swords.

Harold turned to nod to his two brothers and two house guards, who then seated themselves on makeshift benches, similar to ours, between two trees. William turned to nod to Osbern and his three half-brothers, Odo, Robert, and me.

As we had arranged, Osbern sat on my right, the two of us wedged in between two trees, while William's half-brothers, Odo and Robert, sat not far from Osbern, farther down on the right, also wedged between two trees.

My bow was behind the tree next to me, while Osbern kept his bow next to him, now straddling his lap. For their parts, Odo and Robert had leaned their weapons, two longbows with arrow quivers, gifts from William but crafted by me, against the tree next to them. Their swords lay behind them in their sheaths.

The fighting began.

At first, all of us followed every move of the fighters, every swing of the swords, and every block with the shields. We commented on the skills of Harold and William, their strength, and especially their quick reactions. William was clearly the stronger, but Harold could react to a blow faster than I could think about it.

Soon, however, the fighting began to take on a sense of sameness. I noticed that the other watchers on both sides relaxed and ceased jumping to their feet when either Harold or William went on the attack. For what seemed like almost the entire morning, it went on and on — the clanging of swords, the ringing of a sword on the metal bands of a wooden shield, and the occasional cry from an onlooker.

Periodically, one of the fighters would put up his sword, and the two would rest, putting down their shields and swords and taking water. After a long rest, they would resume.

Eventually, I began to wonder how long the two of them could keep fighting. I began to be amazed at their stamina.

I also realized that William was, as he had claimed, a better fighter than Harold. As the time went on, he attacked more and Harold yielded more, giving ground each time, until the two of them had drifted away from the center of the clearing, which was directly in front of me, and now fought much farther to my left.

Abruptly, William broke off his attack and turned to walk back into the middle of the clearing. I expected Harold to follow.

Harold, however, did not move.

At that moment, I thought I saw something. Almost like a leaf fluttering — the thought ran through my mind — but the movement was more than that.

At the same time, the dragon hissed loudly inside my head.

Without thinking, I reached for my bow and arrows, stood up, and slipped an arrow onto the bowstring.

Beside me, I saw Osbern rising, too, drawing back an arrow.

One of Harold's house guards had reached behind the tree next to him and produced a crossbow, which he lowered to tighten with his foot. As he raised the crossbow, he placed an arrow in its groove. That was the movement I had seen.

When the crossbow was fully raised, it would be aimed at William.

"William!" I shouted.

Without hesitating, William dropped to the ground, looking toward the house guard.

As he did, I released my first arrow, which jammed through the guard's right hand, causing him to drop the back of the crossbow. My second arrow thudded into front of the crossbow itself, driving it toward the earth.

As I reached for my third arrow, I saw out of the corner of my eye three movements. Osbern's arrow went through the throat of the other house guard, who had also pulled a crossbow from behind a tree.

Harold's brothers had seized the swords lying behind them, but as they rose to standing position, arrows from the bows of Odo and Robert were thudding into their chests.

Harold himself strode toward William, raising his sword.

I shouted, "Stop!" at him.

He turned to look at me as I released another arrow, aimed to pass in front of his face as he strode toward William.

However, he leaped toward William, my cry causing him to look in my direction. As he did, my arrow struck his left eye, close to the outer bone.

At the same time, he reacted with the speed we had witnessed all morning, his left hand seizing the shaft of the arrow, preventing it from penetrating further into his eye socket.

He spun to his left and stumbled backward, falling fell against one of the trees, groaning loudly.

Odo and Robert seized their swords and ran toward him, but William shouted, "No! Stop!"

The two of them turned from Harold to the wounded house guard and ran their swords through him. I looked away as they did.

From the next sound, I surmised that they were making certain that the other guard and Harold's brothers were dead.

They did not approach Harold, though. They stepped back toward William.

Then all of us seemed to freeze.

Soon, I heard a cry from Harold's men on the other side of the hill. About twenty of them appeared, racing down the hill toward us.

I was still stunned by the events, my mind trying to grasp what had happened. I heard myself shouting to Osbern, Odo, and Robert, and they returned with the cry, "Here!" They stood next to me, Osbern with his bow drawn, Odo and Robert with their bloody swords raised.

My bow was drawn, too, but my arms were beginning to shake.

At first Harold's men must have thought that William, lying on the ground, was dead, because they began to shout, "Long live King Harold! God save King Harold!"

They stopped when they saw Harold leaning against the tree, now on his knees, holding the arrow in his bleeding eye and groaning with pain. They also saw the four dead men beside him.

William leaped to his feet and gripped his sword with both hands.

"You see that your King is … defeated," he said, his voice harsh. "As is one of his house guards. The other guard and his two brothers are dead. If you take them and go now, you will be unharmed. If you attack us, I will kill you myself, even without the bowmen behind me."

The men hesitated, staring from William and us to Harold. One of them whispered something, and they raised open hands.

William lowered his sword, and I relaxed my bow. Osbern, Odo, and Robert did the same.

The men lifted Harold, still groaning and clinging to the arrow, onto their shoulders — and carried the King of England back up the hill.

We all stood in stunned silence for a time.

Then William said, "We rejoin the men. Quickly. Come."

We climbed the hill, checking behind us to make sure none of Harold's men appeared. None did.

Back in the camp, William said nothing to the men, waving off their questions.

To the three of us, he said, "To my tent."

We joined him and dropped into the chairs there, still unspeaking.

I found that my hands were shaking. In my mind, I could see the house guard's bleeding hand and Harold's bleeding eye. I could think of nothing else.

"Listen to me carefully," William said. "While we will have to deal with Harold's men, we need to think about our next step. The single combat has produced a victor, but the outcome is unacceptable. If Harold dies, I become a king-killer. This cannot happen. Harold was too loved in England. If I've killed him, I cannot negotiate with the Saxons. They will refuse to have any interaction with me. Do you understand this?"

All three of us slowly nodded.

Osbern said, "Do you think he will die, the King?"

"From that wound, he may. Did you all hear what I said? Harold's men do not know that we're not a huge force here. They will want to negotiate for peace and escape to their homes."

Odo finally spoke, "That's right, so we need to agree on what to tell them. We need some ... account of what happened that allows them to retreat without ..."

"Without thinking that William killed their King," Robert said, "which they will believe, since the single combat was with swords, and the King was hit with an arrow."

"That's right," Odo said. "So, what shall we tell them?"

"We need to decide quickly," William said. "We must go to them. They must not come here and see the real size of our forces. So, Odo, what ideas do you have? We need a deception, and this is what you do well."

Odo leaned forward in his chair. "First, I think, we need to engage them in a deception with us, or the real story emerges."

"What do you mean?" Robert asked.

"We tell them something they don't want to hear," Odo said, "so that they want to join us in a deception."

"Good," William said. "What shall we tell them?"

"We tell them something close to the truth," Odo said. "One of the house guards made a sudden move, and arrows flew. In the confusion, the guards were killed. The King was killed by accident. By a stray arrow."

I spoke up, but to myself my voice sounded weak. "I didn't mean to shoot him. I meant to put an arrow in front of his face, so that he wouldn't take another step …"

William rose and walked over to me, putting his hand on my shoulder. "Everyone knows that you didn't mean to kill him, Cuin. For your purposes, believe that God, who knows you didn't mean to kill, guided either your arrow or Harold's fatal step. That's enough for you now."

To Odo, William said, "Harold's men will not want their King to have died as the result of a mere accident. It's unheroic."

Odo nodded. "Yes, while they all sit behind a hill, their King faces single combat, only to die from a stray arrow. How would that sound in a battle song?"

"So," William said, "we have them agree on a more heroic account."

Odo hung his head for a moment and then looked up. "A grand battle. For arrows to be flying, there has to have been a great battle. Archers found the noble King — let's say because his banner stood next to him — and killed him."

"Only after much fighting," Robert added. "The King must be seen to have fought valiantly and killed many Normans."

"Agreed," Odo said. "Many dead Normans lie here. Duke William himself was almost killed. In the end, the Norman archers were too much for King Harold, even though many tried to kill him before the demon arrow found him."

"That will work," Robert said. "Harold's men know that we have the best archers in the world."

"They also know," William said, "that we brought many archers with us, hundreds, if our messengers were believed. They will agree to that story."

"We also have cavalry," Odo said, "while the Saxons have none. They always fight on foot. So the valiant King Harold withstood attacks from them as well, only to be killed by an archer from a distance. Even more heroic."

"Good," William said. "That's good. Odo, you and Robert must talk with Harold's men now. Take some men here with you, including archers and cavalry, but carry a flag of truce."

"Won't Cuin be coming with us?" Robert asked. "We could use his skills."

"No, Cuin must now disappear. His arrow has just killed a King, and while no one may know that, Harold may have lived long enough to utter Cuin's name. You must insist that Cuin was not here and that he will not be mentioned in any story you tell about a battle."

"You're right," Odo said. "A few people know his real identity, and if anyone claims that he killed a King, he would not be safe anywhere in the world. He would suddenly become too dangerous to leave alive."

"Exactly," William said.

Odo rose. "All right. We'll go to Harold's men as soon as we gather some archers and mounted knights."

"Take Osbern with you," William said, and he turned to Osbern. "You're too well known as an advisor to be left out of these negotiations."

Osbern rose and shook himself. "Yes, of course." To Odo and Robert he said, "I'm ready. Let's go."

The three of them strode from the tent.

William sat down on the chair next to me. "Cuin, are you all right?"

"Yes."

"You've never been good around blood."

"No."

"What I said to Odo and Robert is the truth. Any trace of your presence here must be removed. You cannot even be suspected of being the killer of the King."

"I know."

"This is the one time when your true identity can work against you. Fatally."

"Yes, I see that."

"For now, you need to rest. For tonight, I will place guards near your tent, so that nothing disturbs you."

"Thank you."

"Let me walk you to your tent."

That night I had trouble falling to sleep. The scenes of the day played in my memory again and again.

Then the dragon appeared and said, "A greater destiny has overtaken your life. Now all will change. You must sleep. Tomorrow you begin a different life."

I slept.

The next morning I awoke late. I could hear the sounds of the men moving through the encampment.

I found Odo close to his tent, and he assured me that Harold's men were more than willing to tell the story of a great battle. He was meeting with their leaders later in the day to talk through the specific events that all of us would report.

"The story will be embellished as it is told," Odo added, "so different versions will emerge, which works in our favor."

I agreed with him and asked, "Did you hear anything further about Harold?"

"Only that he is dead."

William found me wandering the camp and pulled me into his tent.

He put his hands on my shoulders and said, "I know that you must have heard about Harold's death. I want this to be clear to you, Cuin. I asked you to stand behind me, and you did. You saved my life."

That thought had not come to my mind.

William continued, "You also did it without killing anyone."

"Harold ...?"

"Listen to me. You wounded a guard to prevent his killing me. You aimed only a warning shot at Harold, but he stepped into it. You have killed no one."

"It's a shock to have killed someone, William."

"Yes, so I want you to rest here for a few days and return to yourself."

"All right. I will." And I did.

By the fourth morning, I was beginning to feel normal again. I even found myself making a half-hearted joke with Odo about the deteriorating quality of the breakfasts.

Later that day, I decided to take a longer walk away from the camps.

I checked with Odo first, because there had been sporadic fighting around the encampments of both armies. He directed me to a wooded area leading away from both camps, assuring me that no fighting would happen there, especially if I did not venture very far.

Since Odo and the sunny, slightly cool day seemed agreeable for the purpose, I threw on my blue-gray cloak and entered the forest.

As I moved from tree to tree, breathing more deeply with every step, I thought I heard footsteps behind me. I dismissed the sounds as trees rustling in the afternoon breeze.

Abruptly, though, the sound became running footsteps, the footfalls of more than one person. As I turned to see who was behind me, a swirl of robes closed around me, a hand pressed a cloth to my mouth, and I smelled mandrake.

I struggled only a moment until I felt myself slip away.

I awoke to feel a mossy, lumpy ground under me. I could see sparse and darkening leaves overhead. It was night, and a heavy blanket had been lain over me. I stirred, feeling unsteady but becoming progressively more alert.

I heard voices over me, and soon I saw two faces in front of me. As the faces became clearer, I groaned out loud. Ulf and Vandrad.

"Don't be alarmed," Vandrad said.

"Why not?" I asked.

"We mean you no harm," Ulf said.

I lifted up on my elbows to look at them. "Then why spirit me away like this? Is this some new form of negotiation? I predict that it will never be popular, except among thieves and murderers."

Ulf bent over me, squinting his eyes and looking more like a wolf than usual. "Cuin, listen to us, please. This is a serious matter. We need your skills."

I sat up and stared at them. "Being kidnapped by you two is a serious matter to me. Are you planning another poisoning, because I won't help this time, either."

Vandrad sat down beside me, rubbing the scar on his forehead. "The King needs you."

I looked at each of their faces. "The King is dead. He was killed ... what day is this?"

"He wasn't killed," Ulf said, "As for the day, we have brought you about a day's march away from Duke William's encampment. We kept you asleep."

"We hope that you will help heal the King," Vandrad said.

"I saw an arrow go into his eye. I even ..."

"An arrow did go into his eye," Ulf said, "but the King saw it coming and seized it just as it hit. We weren't there, but that's what we were told."

"He has lost his eye," Vandrad said, "but not his life."

I was stunned for a moment. Random thoughts began to form. "If I help Duke William's enemy, I'll be considered a traitor."

"That's why we kidnapped you," Vandrad said. "You have been carried away against your will. Thus you cannot be a traitor. We do hope, though, that you will help the King. You are a healer."

"We know that you're one of the best in the world," Ulf added.

"That sounds like the flattery you used in Norway all those years ago."

"We do not need a poisoner now," Vandrad said. "We need a healer."

"I need to be clear, to grasp this. The King didn't die from his wound, and his men have taken him ... where?"

"First," Ulf said, "will you help him?"

"Are you asking me to heal him, thus to put him back on his throne, where he can once again plot the invasion of Normandy? I am relieved — more than I can say — that he is not dead. How can I aid in his healing, though, without harming my own countrymen?"

They glanced at each other.

"When the King was carried back over the hill that day," Ulf began.

"Where the rest of his army waited," Vandrad said.

"Yes," Ulf continued. "He was bleeding from his eye and raving. He collapsed and became unconscious. The men close to him, fearing for his safety, exchanged his battle clothes with that of a common infantryman, and carried him to a wood not far from here."

"We had already made these plans in the event that the King was wounded," Vandrad said. "We also kept you in sight in case that happened. We had always planned to ask for your help."

"We also worried that you would refuse," Ulf said, "for obvious reasons. The King, however, did not regain consciousness the day after the battle or the day after that. Even today, he remains unconscious."

"His own healers have no idea why. Though … there may be other factors," Vandrad said.

They glanced at each other again.

"So, we told the King's healers that you were here," Ulf said. "They know of your abilities, of course, from the time you tended Godwin. They urged us to get you to help the King."

I paused to think. "Is he nearby?"

They nodded.

"You want me to heal him … to what end, if not to put him back on his throne?"

They glanced at each other once again.

"Will you stop doing that?" I said. "It's becoming annoying."

Vandrad finally spoke. "The men closest to the King have made a secret pact, just this morning, with Duke William, who is still camped about half a day from here."

"Though he is making plans to leave," Ulf added.

Vandrad nodded at him.

"A secret pact?"

"Yes," Vandrad said, "I spoke with the Duke myself. He even remembered me. You see, when the King did not regain consciousness, we knew that something had to be done. We could not move the King, though."

"Everyone knows," Ulf added, "that the King will be fighting no battles in the future. In fact, since we had saved his life by letting everyone believe that he is dead, we can keep him alive only by allowing that belief to continue."

"I told Duke William," Vandrad said, "that we had kidnapped you not for revenge, but because we needed a healer. If he would allow you to tend the King, the King and those closest to him would agree that he would never be a threat to Duke William or the southern realms again."

"How can you promise that? You don't know what Harold will do when he regains consciousness."

"We do," Vandrad said.

"How?"

"An old woman told us, a seer," Ulf said. "She appeared on the hill near the battlefield behind our soldiers just before the single combat —"

Vandrad interrupted him. "We refer to it only as a battle."

"Oh, that's right," Ulf said. "She appeared just before the … battle began. She told the nobles that King Harold would lose. He would not, however, be killed or harmed by Duke William. Instead, he would be wounded by an archer. An arrow would go into his eye, she said, and he would lose consciousness and not awaken for many days."

"She said that when he did reawaken …" Vandrad began.

"… finally," Ulf added.

"Yes, finally," Vandrad said, "He would devote his life to healing."

"You believed this old woman?" I said. "Harold's nobles took her seriously?"

"They held her under guard all morning," Vandrad said. "When everything unfolded as she said, we knew she was a genuine seer."

"The last thing she told us was to kidnap you and meet her where the King was being kept," Ulf said. "Indeed, she told us to tell you not to ask your usual stupid questions — her words, not mine."

I stared at them. "Hervor?"

"Yes, that's her name," Vandrad said, "and she told us that you would know it."

The hamlet where Harold was being hidden was, as Ulf and Vandrad had said, a short walk from where they had held me. We arrived within half a day. Several tents had been set up in a small circle, and guards stood everywhere, armed with axes and shields.

Ulf and Vandrad, along with two guards who had joined us when we arrived, escorted me to the largest tent, situated in the middle of the other tents. I leaned through the opening to find more guards stationed near the entrance, a fire burning in the middle of the area to keep the autumn chill at bay, and a low bed at the back with two chairs near it.

On the bed lay the unmoving form of Harold, former Earl of Wessex, now King of England.

In one of the chairs sat Hervor, who turned to greet me.

"Come, Cuin," she said. "This is our handiwork: your arrow and my sleeping charm. Sit next to me."

I sat on the other chair. "How is he?"

"Healing as he sleeps. Though I can use your skills."

"How did you come to be here?"

"You did not suppose that I was sitting quietly in Iceland while I controlled the ghastly English Channel and watched over you and your Duke, did you?"

"I don't understand. This was an unintended outcome. We thought —"

"Yes," she said, "you thought many things, some of them stupid. You thought that Hardraada, the King of Norway, would control northern England — with Tostig restored as Earl of Northumbria — despite the unpopularity of both men in northern England. You thought that King Harold could not defeat them, in spite of his extraordinary military prowess. You thought that Duke William would establish … what shall I call it? … a territorial foothold in southern England, which would give him control there, in spite of the unpopularity of Normans in that region. You thought that King Sweyn of Denmark, your half-brother, would defend Denmark against King Harold of England, but you had no idea how he might feel if the situation in England changed. With everything else you thought, you also believed that King Harold would give up his dreams of empire."

"Yes, I had the diplomatic successes to make it work, too."

"That is why I am here. Odin knew that Harold would not be so easily contained, that fate could not be so easily ignored. He sent me, and you see that I am needed. If Harold awakens before the right time, he will simply begin to rebuild his empire."

"I don't understand. His men have made everyone believe that he is dead, and they intend to keep it that way."

"Oh, Christians have never heard of resurrection."

"All right. I see what you mean." I stared at Harold, trying not to look at the blood-stained bandage over his eye. "How long can you keep him asleep? I can help him heal from his wound, but he needs to eat and drink."

She shook her head at me. "I know that, of course. I can awaken him anytime I wish. You know enough about herbs and healing to understand that."

"You also need to take him someplace safe from ambitious Norman warriors."

"Duke William has already agreed with you on this point, as I'm sure Ulf and Vandrad have informed you."

I leaned back in my chair. "This is going to be a difficult …" I couldn't think of the words to finish my thought.

"Diplomatic maneuver?"

"If it can be called that." I pointed behind me through the tent's door. "Just out there, not even a day's march away, William is trying to decide what to do, now that he has participated in a contest that ended with the public death of the King of England. His supporters are hoping for spoils, since they've been away from their homes for two months, even though they didn't have to fight. While the Saxon supporters of King Harold are … where? Scattered? Regrouping? Choosing a King, now that they think Harold is dead?"

She sighed. "You really can be tediously dull-witted. Duke William will, of course, take England now. What other choice does he have? If the Saxons, as you say, regroup, he needs to move quickly to establish his authority here."

"William take England? He wanted to avoid that."

"What should he do then? Go home and hope that the Saxon replacement for Harold will ignore what has happened?"

"Suppose that the Saxons have no candidate for King," I said. "Without Harold, would any other Saxon leader want to challenge William — or create Harold's empire? William could just return home then."

She continued to stare at me, giving me a disgusted look.

"All right," I said, "I see: William will not wait to discover whether another ambitious Saxon noble has plans for ruling England or not. Nor will William leave England open to an invader from Norway or Denmark."

"Finally, you arrive at the obvious. Of course he will not. You've grown up with this man and advised him for decades. Given his character and the state of the Northern kingdoms, how many paths are open to him?"

I sighed. "With Hardraada and Tostig dead and the Saxon nobles leaderless, he will march north to London and take the throne. He will also seize a significant number of towns before he arrives."

"His force is now the most powerful in England, and his nobles are interested in the spoils of war, even if that war was single combat. Their presence is part of what forced the combat, so they will want some reward."

I turned toward Harold, who still lay unmoving at the back of the tent. "So, William conquers England. We heal Harold and take him somewhere far enough away to be safe."

She nodded. "That is the rest of the obvious."

"Has Odin chosen a place, or shall we search the countryside for refuge?"

"Don't be irreverent. What contacts do you have in this country?"

"Not many, now that Edward is dead." I paused for a moment. "I do know someone. The nuns in Chester. I've heard that most of those I freed from slavery — some twenty years ago, I suppose — still reside in Chester Abbey. I am friendly with Sister Edyth, who runs the abbey. That reminds me: one of her nuns, Sister Agnes, is an excellent healer."

"Chester, hmm. Will anyone suspect that Harold would end up there?"

"It's far away and not particularly connected to Harold's supporters."

She nodded. "This sounds promising. How long will it take us to get there?"

"If we have good weather, no problem on the roads, and a cart that moves well, we should be there in five to seven days, I would guess."

She turned to Ulf and Vandrad and the guards near them. "Can you prepare for travel tomorrow?"

The next morning, we left for Chester. Aside from chilled nights, the weather remained good. We had light rain one day, but it was not enough to stop the cart in which Harold lay.

Hervor brought Harold out of his sleep twice a day to give him food and water and to allow both of us to tend him. Then she returned him to his unconscious state. By the fourth day on the road, she kept him conscious most of the day, lying or sitting in the cart.

"I don't want his full awareness to return until we arrive at Chester," she said. "He needs not just to recuperate. He needs to spend time in deep slumber, which is really time spent talking with the old kings of England and the warriors of Valhalla."

"What will come of that?"

"The leader of the warriors will be Odin, who will inform Harold that he is no longer to be King. Of anything."

"If I may ask, why is Odin involved in Harold's life?"

She smiled at me. "This is a question you may ask and not be annoying. First, Odin is interested in more than Harold's life. Along with Thor, he watches over the life of the North."

"I know what you mean, though I'm not sure the priests who trained me would agree."

"They have small ideas. Good intentions, I suppose." She held up her hands and moved them close together. "Narrow thinking, though. Anyway, if Harold and similar Kings, including Hardraada, had become powerful rulers, the entire North — England, Norway, Denmark, and the rest — would have become too violent. The ancient demons are still there, and many are bloodthirsty beyond what the world can survive now."

I did not understand all of what she was saying, but I asked, "Isn't Odin one of the ancient ... demons?"

She frowned at me. "Certainly not, though one demon has taken his name, which is why you're confused. The ancient demons prey on humans. On all life, for that matter. Odin is a warrior from the other realm who helps humans free themselves from ancient demons."

I pretended that I understood what she was saying. "How then is William's presence in England a positive turn?"

"Your Duke brings with him the Norman love of law, the same love we have in Iceland. He also brings the most brilliant scholar in the world, your friend Lanfranc, who will help bring peace and unity to the Northern and Southern worlds."

"With Lanfranc comes his reforming student, now Pope Alexander in Rome. Is that good? For Odin's purposes?"

"Just now, this reforming Pope means that the Christian Truce of God and Peace of God will, for a time at least, limit war and aggression."

"Odin knows all of this and thinks this is how things should be?"

She gave me another disgusted look. "If I were Odin, I could answer that question." She paused. "I do not think that even Odin knows how all things should be. I think that at this time, your Duke, even the way he handles the Church, is the best leader to unite the Northern and Southern lands."

I thought about this. "William does keeps the Church from establishing too much power, even as he champions reform in the religious houses in Normandy." I paused. "What is the second thing?"

"What second thing?"

"You said Odin was interested first in Harold's life and in the life of the North. What is his second interest?"

She stared at me. "You have a diplomat's memory. Odin's second interest is in Harold as a healer. The once-King is to become a hermit, one who heals and brings hope to people for as long as he lives."

"That's interesting. I've felt a healing presence around Harold."

"Of course you have."

As we approached Chester, Hervor kept Harold awake a few hours longer than usual, mostly just before darkness fell. He sat in the cart and stared wordlessly at the passing trees, bushes, and occasional farms, which in the fading light might have appeared as phantoms to him.

Hervor had draped him a blue-gray robe, and in the dusk, he seemed to disappear into a gray mist, as no doubt I did, too.

She had placed on his head a large, hood-like hat, blue-gray as well. The hat slouched down over his left eye, partially hiding the bandage, which had now been changed many times and had no sign of blood on it, a relief for me.

"In this clothing," Hervor had commented, "he remains invisible to anyone looking for a grand King who survived a huge battle."

As we approached the end of our week's journey, I found myself looking forward to reaching Chester, if only to get off my pony. My body had never become accustomed to riding, and I still preferred to walk when I could.

Several times, I lightly dozed while in the saddle and almost imagined myself back in Normandy, headed north with the Goliards. I could almost hear a Berserker cry in the distance.

Then I did hear a Berserker cry. I awoke, startled.

Everyone was staring down the road behind us. The guards had spurred their horses to form a tight circle around the cart, while Ulf and Vandrad positioned themselves close to Harold, their battle-axes raised.

Only Hervor distanced herself from the group and moved in the direction of the cry, her shoes and robe raising leaves and late-autumn dust as she walked.

The guards looked at each other in alarm and cried to her in a Wessex dialect, which she ignored.

As the cry became more shrill, a figure appeared on a horse, brandishing a sword. He was clad in a blue cloak with its hood blown back from his head, exposing graying hair and a heavy gray beard.

I got off the pony. The guards frowned at me, so I told them that they could lower their weapons.

"In the first place, he's one Berserker warrior, and there are more than ten of you. In the second place, he's old. Look at that gray hair." I paused as the cry began to fade. "Besides, he's losing his voice."

The Berserker warrior had now reached Hervor, and he jumped from his horse. He grabbed Hervor like a bear grabbing one of its cubs.

I could hear her exclaim in Icelandic: "Let go of me, you oaf!"

I glanced at the guards' faces and saw their perplexity.

The Berserker stood back and then saw me. He dashed toward me, issuing a short Berserker shriek.

"Must you always do that?"

He laughed out loud and then said, "I have every reason. Duke William told me that you'd been kidnapped. He sent me to rescue you."

"Alone?"

He looked around. "I didn't suppose that I would need anyone else."

Hervor stepped beside us. "You mean that you didn't think about needing anyone else."

He hesitated only a moment. "That's right." He stared at the guards, who remained unmoving. "I don't understand. You don't appear to be kidnapped."

Of course we've been kidnapped," I said. "At least, I have. Since Hervor planned it, Duke William connived in it, and these Saxon guards have been forced to go along with it, it's not the kidnapping you think it is."

"Duke William …" he began.

"Duke William," Hervor said, "is busy trying to determine what to do with England, so he's taking care of Cuin and Harold by sending you here." She turned to the guards. "By the way, my friends, this is Voldred, one of my students and a formidable Berserker warrior."

"In his day," I added.

Voldred shook his battle-axe mockingly. "I am still a formidable warrior." He looked beyond the guards at the cart. "Is King Harold really with you? There are rumors that he survived."

"Which I trust Duke William is denying," Hervor said.

Voldred nodded. "Yes, he is." He continued to search between the guards. "Is he here?"

"Yes," Hervor said. "He's under a sleeping charm, aided by my herbs, and he's just returning from a long unconsciousness. He will be fully awake by the time we reach Chester."

"Chester is where you're headed?"

"Yes," I said. "The nuns I bought out of slavery years ago have an abbey there. We needed to get Harold far away from the battlefield and from any Norman soldiers with an ambition for vengeance."

"Also away from the center of Saxon life in London," Hervor added.

Voldred nodded. "This certainly is far from the center of anything. You may not recall that I visited Chester to find out more about your birth, Cuin. I have even met the nuns you bought out of slavery."

"Do you know how far Chester is from our present position then?" Hervor asked.

"Probably another day's ride."

I pushed his axe, which he was still brandishing, down toward the ground. "Are you coming with us or returning to Duke William with news that we're not as kidnapped as we might have been?"

"I'm to stay with you until you rejoin the Duke."

"Good. You can give us news of William's progress."

We learned little from Voldred, though, because William had still been encamped near the battlefield when Voldred left.

We did discover, though, that small battles continued to break out around the two encampments. The Normans had not moved, and Harold's men had remained behind the hill overlooking what we now called "battle valley." Voldred estimated that a growing number of men would die as the skirmishes continued.

"I expect the fighting to continue," he said, "until some resolution emerges. Right now, it's not clear who rules England or what William's future role will be."

As we sat near the fire that evening, keeping the autumn chill at our backs, Voldred turned to me. "Do you have any idea about Duke William's strategy following the battle?"

I noted that he called the single combat "a battle." Out loud, I said, "No. Do you?"

"All I know," he said, "is that the Duke has retaliated against a village called Romney, because some of his troops were attacked by armed men from that village."

"If I know William," I said, "his response would have been severe."

"It was," Voldred said, "and the Duke sent messengers to Dover with an even more severe version of his response."

"He's headed to Dover now?" I asked.

Voldred nodded.

For Hervor, Ulf, and Vandrad I explained, "When anyone threatens William, he always responds ... viciously, I would say. Then he exaggerates the report of what he's done and spreads it as far as he can. Usually, any town hearing the report submits to him, avoiding further bloodshed."

"Has this always worked?" Ulf asked.

"Yes," I said. "I hope it works now as well, because, as Voldred knows, we didn't plan for any of this, and William's forces are not large enough for an invasion of England."

Voldred shook his head. "Though I was there to see it, I still cannot grasp that King Harold defeated Tostig and Hardraada in the North."

"I have the same near disbelief," I said. "It seems as if they are still in the North, poised to attack and rule Northumbria as they should."

Hervor huffed and muttered something about Odin, but both Voldred and I ignored her.

Voldred sat back and rested on his elbows, stretching his feet closer to the fire. "The North will be a different world with Hardraada gone. I wonder whether his sons will be able to hold Norway."

"I wonder, too," I said, "but for now, I wonder what England will make of William and what Harold will make of Chester."

The old Roman walls still surrounded Chester, though they had been widened and extended so that guards could walk along them.

Briefly, I recalled the walls around Hedeby and wondered whether it would ever be rebuilt.

Inside Chester's walls, we found the old stone building that served as the home for the Chester nuns. It sat back from the main entrance to the town, as if it had always been intended as a building set apart for prayer and healing.

The building's stones seemed especially old in some places, but in others, recent additions had been made. I could even see where the building had been extended to allow for more nuns.

Edyth was indeed still very much alive, looking older, but as vital as she had been back in St. Vaast. As she walked into the main room to greet what she took to be passing travelers, she stopped abruptly in front of me and gasped.

"By God's good graces, it's Brother Augustine!"

I smiled at her. "Yes, Sister Edyth, I've finally accepted your invitation to visit you in your beautiful home."

She stepped back to look at me. "You're not really a monk, though, are you? That's right. We learned later that you were Duke William's emissary, and that your name is ... something else. We've always thought of you, however, as the monk who saved us from slavery and then joined us in those evenings in St. Vaast, where we discussed so many wonderful things."

"I remember them vividly."

She shook her head, smiling broadly. "We've all become old, haven't we?"

"Wise, too, of course, Sister, since wisdom comes inevitably with age."

She laughed. "I remember your wit. It's a joy to see you again!"

I introduced Hervor to her, and to my surprise, Edyth bowed her head slightly and said, "We see few of the old prophetesses here, but we hear tales of you from Iceland. You have supported our Church there, and we are grateful."

Hervor thanked her and said, "Iceland's church is worth supporting, Sister, and I'm sure the same is true here."

Then I drew Voldred forward and said, "This introduction will lead to some questions, but this is Voldred, the Berserker warrior whose zeal put me in the St. Vaast infirmary."

Edyth stepped back and raised her eyebrows. "But I know this man. He visited here not long ago, asking about your birth. I thought he was a friend of yours."

"He is a friend," I said, "the history of which I shall relate during our visit."

Voldred bowed, and Edyth said, "I am pleased to meet you again, Voldred, especially as the friend of our young brother."

She turned to me. "We have just this day received word of a great battle in the south involving the King and your Duke. Is that what brings you here?"

"Yes. We need your house's sanctuary and healing skills." I turned to Voldred. "Will you bring him in, please?"

Voldred disappeared and reappeared, leading Harold with a guard on either side. Harold leaned heavily on the men, awake but groggy.

Edyth leaned forward, staring. "Who is this?"

"He is the man who used to be King Harold of England," Hervor said. "He is being kept semi-awake as he heals."

"The King? Why … I don't understand."

"He has come here to be transformed," Hervor said.

"Like Paul?" Edyth asked.

"Like Paul," I said. "No one must know that he is here, though."

Edyth seemed to understand immediately. "No one will learn anything from us, and he may remain, safely concealed, as long as he needs to."

"Is Sister Agnes still here? We may need her healing skills."

"She is. I will bring her to you." She nodded to the men. "Follow me, and I will show you a chamber where the King may rest."

She led us to a large room, containing four beds and a table. The external stone wall had both a fireplace and a narrow window which opened onto a small, tree-filled courtyard, the ground of which was now covered with colored leaves.

"This is where we tend the sick, so men are allowed here. This room and the one next to it should accommodate all the men in your party. The seer Hervor may stay with us." Her eyes went to Harold. "What has happened to the King's eye? Is he very ill?"

"He lost his eye in the battle," I said, "and while he will need to recover from that loss, he is otherwise whole."

"He should recover completely," Hervor said.

Edyth paused, still staring at Harold. "What will happen to him then?"

"That depends," Hervor said, "on what happens between now and the time he recovers."

Sister Agnes was happy to see me, and we talked for some time about what had transpired since we had last met. She soon moved to Harold's side, though — by now he was sleeping again — and began discussing his condition with Hervor.

The three of us decided that we would tend Harold for two more weeks before allowing him to be fully awake and wake him just before the full moon. We worked on him together during those weeks, noting that he was healing more quickly than we would have expected.

The morning of the full moon, Hervor, Agnes, and I stood in the room with him, along with Voldred, Ulf, Vandrad, and two of the King's guards. We watched as he opened his eyes.

Hervor was first to speak. "Do you know who you are?"

He turned his head slightly to stare at her. After a long pause, he said, "My name is ... Harold. Harold, yes. I am the son ... or leader ... of a powerful family. We ruled an ancient territory. Great kings came from that territory."

This is not a good start, I thought to myself.

Hervor continued, "Do you know where you are?"

Again, Harold stared at her a long while. "I am not certain. I have been asleep for a long time. Healing. I ... I was wounded." His hand went to his left eye, and he felt the patch there. "My eye. I was wounded in my eye. An arrow. I tried to stop it." He moved his left hand in the air as if to catch an invisible arrow.

"Your eye is gone," Hervor said. "You lost it when you were wounded." She nodded toward Agnes and me. "We healed you, but your eye was already gone."

"Yes, a piece of the world is missing, just beyond my vision. When I try to see that piece, I feel pain in my eye."

"That will pass with time," Agnes said.

"Your sight will change as the pain subsides," Hervor added. "You will adjust to seeing through only one eye."

Harold leaned toward her. "Who are you?"

"I am Hervor, last seer of the old religion of Odin in Iceland."

"Why are you here?"

"Because an old friend needed my help," she replied and waved her hand at me.

He looked in my direction and studied my face. After a long pause, he said, "Is it Cuin? Are you here, too?"

"Yes, my lord, I am. I aided in your healing, but there was little for me to do. Hervor's skill, Sister Agnes' skill, and your own body did most of the healing work."

His face, unmoving before, began to be more animated, and a slight smile appeared. "I recall something about you. Yes, you do that. You deflect praise from yourself to others. I do remember you, it seems."

Hervor leaned toward him. "What else do you remember — particularly while you were asleep?"

He was silent for a moment. "I think that … I was in … Valhalla. Yes, Valhalla. Warriors were there, including my father and my older brother. Even King Edward was there." He paused. "I was King of England. I remember that now. I was the King."

Hervor nodded. "You were the King of England, but you were told in Valhalla that your reign is over."

"Yes, I was told that. I had long talks with my family and with the old Kings. My two brothers, Gyrth and Leofwine, were there. They died recently. They told me everything was over."

"They died when you were wounded," Hervor said. "What else did you see in Valhalla?"

"I saw my brother Tostig, whom I killed. We wept together when I realized what I had done. I saw another warrior, Harald of Norway, who praised my strength and valor. Then I was shown many centuries of the past and many scenes of what is to come. I was told that my old world has ended. I have played my part as King. Now I am to be … someone different."

"You are to be a healer and a wise man," Hervor said.

"Yes … yes. I recall the ancient Kings, especially King Alfred, telling me that war was no longer a noble pursuit, that there are other tasks for me. Healing and offering wisdom. To the people. Sometimes even to the King." He looked confused. "How would I do that?"

Hervor sat back and smiled. "Easily. You travel around the country, even the world, if you wish, and let yourself be seen. You heal, and you let the people see you as a wise hermit."

Harold smiled faintly again. "It happens so easily?"

"It will take time, but yes, it does. The old Kings in Valhalla told you that."

"They did say that. I recall scenes they showed me of my travels. Many places, many people." He stared hard at her. "I seemed old, dressed in an old hat, a long robe, carrying a huge wooden staff — an odd traveler."

Hervor sat up again and leaned close to him. "The world is about to change, former King Harold. The ancient bloodthirsty gods will reappear in more vicious forms, and the people will suffer. They do not need another King now, but a wise man who reappears when they need him, to remind them that the suffering time will pass. Eventually, the bloodthirsty gods will disappear. Then the world will know peace."

"I would ask you how you know all of this ... but it is what I have seen while I was in Valhalla, so I know it to be the true course of the world."

"It's why they sent you back," she said.

"Yes."

I sighed quietly, relieved that the imperial ambition had faded.

Harold seemed to pick up my thought. He turned to me. "This life is like yours, isn't it?"

"I don't understand, my lord," I replied.

"I remember more. About you. Cuin. Many times I've wondered how you moved in the world. Without any interest in power or kingship, especially when ... kingship was your birthright, was it not?"

I noticed Ulf, Vandrad, and the guards looking at me.

"I was raised a commoner. I never had a vision of myself as powerful. Only helpful, if I could be. If you become someone similar, then we will share a fate."

"I was raised to be a powerful ruler. Now I wonder ... The warriors in Valhalla have a different perspective on power. It seems that all the power in the world is ... void of real power."

"If it will help," I said, "I was trained to be a healer, and I noticed that a healer's life lies outside the worldly power with which rulers must concern themselves. If you travel the world as a wise healer, the only power you command, besides your healing skills, is wisdom."

"And the grace of movement with the world," Hervor said.

Harold looked around at everyone in the room and returned his gaze to Hervor. "I'm not certain where to begin."

"You begin here. The Chester sisters have a deeper Christianity to teach you. I will teach you about the old ways. All of us will teach you about healing."

I was surprised, and Hervor must have picked up that thought, because she added, without taking her eyes from Harold, "Yes, I can hear you thinking, Cuin, and yes, I will break tradition and have an eighth student." Then she did turn to me. "Why should I not? I am the last of my kind."

I smiled. "I think it's an excellent idea."

"Good," she said, "Now, all of you go where you are needed, while Sister Edyth and I show a former King some paths to walk."

While many of the guards returned to London and Voldred headed back to his family in Norway, I remained at Chester. I had long talks with the sisters, which took me back to my days at St. Vaast.

I also had long talks with Harold. I needed to be assured that a powerful, ambitious King could become a healer, even if that healer was an advisor to Kings. Harold's visit to Valhalla, though, had changed him.

The teachings he received from Hervor especially convinced me that this was a different man.

He had never thought about other worlds, the powers of the natural world, and the powers of human beings to transform themselves and others. It was as if she initiated him into a new life where, as the Man Who Walks with Power always said to me, power is not found in fighting against the world but in walking with the world.

As I watched Harold in study with the Chester nuns and then with Hervor, he seemed to claim a different power, a healing power, easily.

Once again, I found him to be a formidable man.

I saw William once as we drifted into winter. He had sent a message in mid-December that he was to be crowned King of England at Christmastime in London. He particularly wanted to talk with me.

The messengers were Rolf and two of his Goliard companions, one of whom had been with me on my original trip north. As we left for London on a small cart, with adequate cushions and warm blankets, Rolf informed me about all that had happened.

"After you left, Duke William began to make plans to advance on London. He made his way to Dover, where he expected some resistance from the old hill fort there. The people, though, welcomed him. The news of his ferocity at Romney made them more than willing to submit to him."

"That's good," I said. "No blood shed there."

"Unfortunately, a few Norman soldiers were not convinced and forced some citizens out of their homes and set fire to the houses. Duke William was furious and publicly punished the soldiers, while paying the citizens handsomely for their lost property."

"Yes, William would do that and be more popular for it."

Rolf nodded his agreement. "There was some feeling that he had allowed the over-zealous soldiers some freedom, so that this kind of incident might occur, but I don't know whether the Duke schemes in that way or not."

I sighed. "I don't know either."

Rolf continued, "He and the men spent another week at Dover, where his men built another wooden castle, similar to the one they had built after the original landing at Pevensey. You know that, though."

"Yes."

"Dysentery afflicted some of the men," Rolf said, "so Duke William had to decide whether he could risk another delay in his march on London."

"Thus allowing another force to grow in the country and move against him — no, William would not want that."

"You're right. The Duke felt he needed to press on. He left a garrison at Dover and headed to Canterbury."

"He and I had discussed this, especially after we realized that our strategy to control the coast could not work. All the advisors agreed that William would march inland only if he knew he'd have to expand his presence in the country. This must have been discouraging."

"You know the Duke better than I do, but he had that determined look he gets when his plans go awry."

"I know that look. How did the citizens of Canterbury react?"

Rolf smiled. "The citizens of Canterbury sent a delegation to submit to the Duke before he even arrived at the city. It seemed as if the path to London might be smoother than any of us thought."

"Was it?"

Rolf shook his head. "At almost the same moment, we received word that the two Archbishops in London, including the infamous Stigand, with the support of the Earls of Mercia and Northumbria, had chosen young Edgar to be the new King. In London, they still believe that King Harold is dead."

"Edgar isn't even twelve years old yet, is he? Even Canute, with all his fierceness as a youth, could not hold the kingship at so young an age."

"Even if Edgar where older," Rolf said, "he's certainly not going to be as competent as King Harold."

I agreed. "By now, Harold is the standard for the Saxon Council. He was the power in England for over ten years."

"That's true. Duke William seemed to take the news hard, retiring to his tent. We soon learned, though, that he'd simply been stricken with dysentery himself."

"Oh, no. William does not handle sickness well."

"If you mean that he ignores it, you are correct. He remained as determined as ever to take London, but he changed his strategy and did not march on it directly."

I nodded. "That sounds like William. He never forces a confrontation if he's unsure of the outcome. That's why he's never been defeated."

"Instead of taking the few days he needed to recover, he led his men in a circuit around London. He divided the army into several groups and forced every town around the city to submit."

"William's strategy of intimidating his main opponent rather than attacking directly."

"It worked," Rolf said. "By the the time the Duke's forces arrived at Winchester, the city submitted immediately."

"Just like the others."

"Yes. At Wallingford, Archbishop Stigand himself came in to the camp to swear loyalty to the Duke."

"I thought you said that Stigand wanted Edgar as King."

"Stigand apparently wanted Duke William to know that Edgar's position had been thoroughly undermined."

"What of the northern Earls, Mercia and Northumbria?"

"They too submitted but made a hasty retreat north, assuming, I think, that the Duke would not pursue them there."

I smiled. "He wouldn't unless he were forced to."

"Of course, this meant that Duke William finally stood at what was Edward's throne in England. Should he take it or not? He walked around with that question in his mind for several days."

"Paced, no doubt."

"Almost unendingly. He and his advisors talked about the situation at length — always walking. Duke William worried that the Saxon leaders did not really desire him as their King. They simply had no one else, so they were capitulating. He also expressed concern about the peace. Would another army come against him?"

I sighed. "Even with Harold out of the picture, someone else may decide to become ambitious, even the local leaders in London. William is right to be cautious, especially where real diplomatic exchanges are lacking."

"His advisors, though — and you know all of them — thought that his not taking the crown would only add to the confusion, to the possibility of civil war."

"That's a good point. So, that's how William came to accept the crown?"

"He wanted to wait until Duchess Matilda could join him and be crowned with him."

I laughed. "The great giant always feels more secure with that tiny woman beside him."

Rolf joined the laugh. "In the end, though, his advisors and the army refused to hear any more about caution and waiting. So, the coronation was set ..."

"... for Christmas Day, the same day that Charlemagne was crowned Holy Roman Emperor over two hundred years ago."

"Yes. That's why I was sent to get you."

William and I met two days before the coronation. We found a quiet side chapel in the new cathedral, where the coronation would take place. The weather was not severe, but I felt the damp of the place and drew close to a temporary fire that had been built in a container not far from the altar.

William looked tired and was dressed in plain clothes that he might have worn for sleeping the previous night. Nonetheless, he greeted me cheerfully and thanked me for traveling all the way from Chester.

"How is Harold?" was his first question, as he settled into a chair by the fire.

"He's largely healed by now, though he's lost his left eye."

"Can he move around just as well without it?"

"He's learning how to do that, and he's adaptable. In truth, he seems unconcerned about it."

"I'm surprised to hear that. Why is he unconcerned?"

"I asked him, and he said that since he would neither need to fight or rule, his life would be a simpler business. So, the extra perception the eye would have given him was not needed."

William leaned forward toward me. "Has he really accepted that he is not to be King of England?"

"He appears to be a completely different person, William. If I hadn't been there as he came out of his long sleep, I wouldn't have believed that he would give up his ambitions for ruling."

"Or for empire?"

I looked at him closely. "He seems to have no interest in either."

William leaned back. "Could his response be some kind of deceit?"

I shrugged my shoulders. "If it were, what does he gain by it? He would have gained more by seizing the time after the battle when he still had Saxon support for the throne. Even if he was unsuccessful at gaining general support, he might have forced you to negotiate for part of England."

"He would have had general support. I had to maneuver determinedly just to get the Saxons in and around London to submit to me."

"I heard about the strategy, marching all around London until the entire countryside had submitted to you. Impressive."

He ignored the compliment. "So, Harold is really ... transformed."

"As he should be. He cannot remain a public figure while you are forced to rule his country."

William thought for a moment. "You're right, I think. It will be hard enough for me to determine how to rule the various parts of this country."

"I will say this carefully. If Harold had remained a public figure, every mistake laid at your doorstep would become a call for his return as sole King."

"You need not speak cautiously. I had the same thought. Here, in a foreign culture, I have no sense of governing easily. I will be beset by problems, and some of my solutions may be ineffective at best."

"I don't envy you the task. You may, however, have an advisor join you later who could be of some help."

"Do you mean Lanfranc?"

"No, though Lanfranc will be a great help. I'll keep the advisor's name to myself for now. Besides, no one will be able to help you in the immediate future."

He looked at me, sat back, and smiled. "So, clinging to your commoner upbringing and refusing any royal connection turns out to be a benefit here. Because you refused all crowns, you've been relieved of all the problems they would bring."

I smiled with him. "It seems so."

He became serious again. "Indeed, I think you have only one potential problem, one that you've carefully avoided up to now by remaining quietly behind the movements of rulers. If you suddenly become ... known, then even your presence on this side of the world presents you with a dangerous problem."

"I think I know what you mean."

"The world has just turned upside down. A Norman Duke is about to be crowned King of England. A probable successor, Tostig, is dead, as is Hardraada, the King of Norway. The King of Denmark is your half-brother and owes his throne, at least in some sense, to your efforts. If any ambitious person learns who you really are, your situation would not remain settled."

"I agree. It's still possible that some faction would pull me into a power struggle."

"Or kill you."

"That is also a possibility, one that we confronted constantly as children. So, we know it's a real possibility."

"There's more. Word has spread that Harold was killed by an archer. Many people know of your skill with a bow, and many of Harold's men know you were there."

"I've thought about that. As long as I remain here and remain active, especially as an archer, eventually I might be accused as a King-killer."

He looked at me seriously. "This side of the world may no longer safe for you."

"So, after all, the Land of the People is the best place for me."

He leaned toward me. "Does that place really feel like a home to you, Cuin?"

"Yes, it does."

He smiled. "Then I'm pleased that you'll be there and be safe. We shall miss you here. I especially will miss you. I'll never have a better emissary. Or a better brother."

Christmas Day dawned bright, except for a few clouds, and the city awoke to a rising noise that came from everyone being busy with the holiday and the new King, including the building of a new castle in the south-east corner of the surviving Roman walls.

I could not determine whether the noise, though, reflected busy acceptance or anxiety. As I sat in Westminster waiting for the coronation to begin, I wondered how the Saxons, even with Danish influence, would react to being ruled by a Norman.

The ceremony gave no hint of trouble at first, and William looked as royal as any King I had ever seen.

A new element had been added to the crowning, and I had heard William's supporters praising it. The new King was to be presented to the people in the church, and they were to acclaim him as their new ruler. Loudly.

When the moment came, I wondered what the attending Saxons might really feel.

The Saxon Archbishop Ealdred stepped toward the people and in English asked those present if they agreed that William of Normandy should be crowned King. Then Bishop Geoffrey de Mowbray of Coutances asked the same question in French.

To my astonishment, the acclamation cry was loud, almost raucous, and enthusiastic. I smiled to myself, thinking that this improbable event might actually succeed, and William might find a way to rule England.

Then a clamor arose outside the church. We heard men shouting, axes and swords clanging, and cries of women and children. Soon we could see flames through the church windows.

The attending dignitaries, men and women alike, began to cry out in dismay. They fled toward the doors to escape, thinking that that the church must have been set on fire by some attacking force.

As the huge doors swung open, we could see Norman knights and soldiers in the street outside. I pressed myself against a church wall and used a nearby stool to raise myself. I saw houses near the church on fire, but I saw no forces other than the Normans.

I caught a glimpse of William. As happened in times like this, he shook with determined anger. Whatever was happening was a threat.

He forced his way through the crowd, his head visible above the others, and shouted harshly at the soldiers. "What are you doing?"

The nearest knights looked at him, startled. I could hear nothing through the din, but I did see the Normans knights and soldiers stop and focus on William.

I heard him cry out, "Nothing is amiss here. Put out those fires, and attend to those whose homes you have damaged. You will have to deal with me later."

He turned and strode back into the church, but a few steps in, he turned back to the knights.

"From now on, you will take no action without my direct order. Ever."

Abruptly, the people in the church calmed.

As William strode back to the front of the church, the whispers reached me: "The Norman knights thought the acclamation was an attack on their Duke. So they set the surrounding houses on fire."

I caught some obviously Saxon side comments: "Ignorant, war-loving Normans."

As I watched Archbishop Ealdred administer the threefold oath to William, I thought that this King had a difficult task ahead of him.

Upon my return to Chester, I found Harold and the Chester nuns settled in for the cold season.

It was strange for me to watch the once powerful Earl and King in his winter seclusion in Chester, sitting in contemplation, engaging in theological and philosophical conversations with Hervor and the Chester nuns.

He even had questions for me about my life. When spring arrived, we had one last conversation.

We sat together in the clearing outside the monastery, watching the new flowers.

"You'll be leaving soon," he said.

"Yes, it's time for me to disappear and return to my wife on the other side of the world."

"I should like to see that world someday."

"You would be welcome. Onyame still makes voyages between the worlds."

He sighed and fell quiet. "I have already visited other worlds that I never dreamed existed. With Sister Edyth and Hervor. Now there is yours, on the other side of this world." He stared out the window. "My vision was so narrow."

I smiled. "A man who wanted a huge empire had a narrow vision?"

He laughed but said nothing.

"I know what you mean," I said. "Once I saw those other worlds, the world of crowns held no appeal for me."

He tilted his head and stared at me. "In that, you've had a more exciting life than I have, a richer one, a fuller one."

"I hadn't thought about it that way."

"I have." He became quiet again. "I have you and Duke William to thank for this, have I not?"

"Oh, yes. His sword and my bow have been nothing but beneficent to you."

He laughed again. "In a way, that's true."

We both fell silent for a time.

Then I said, "I do hope you visit my world sometime."

"So do I."

A.D. 1067

Finally, I received word that I was to leave. I sailed up the River Dee, at the mouth of which I found Onyame.

As so many times before, we sailed to the Shetland Islands, the Faeroe Islands, Iceland, Greenland, and eventually Vineland. I rowed and bailed during two storms. Once again, I watched the Great Lights over Iceland, as they shimmered green, blue, and purple above us.

The dragon visited me with one more vision of William in England, struggling to maintain himself as King there, while also ruling Normandy. He had encountered opposition to his rule initially then some acceptance, faced rebellions from the north, from an occasional ruler outside England, and even from his own son.

During that time, he had met a wise, one-eyed healer, who became his occasional advisor in England. Word spread that in the greatest crises, the people had a powerful healer to tend to them, and the new King had a wise man to guide him.

CHAPTER 32

THE TAPESTRY

A.D. 1077

I had been in the Land of the People for ten years when a message reached me from William. My presence was required, with that of my wife and Onyame, on the fourteenth day of the seventh month of the seventy-seventh year of the sixth millenium after creation.

The reason was that a tapestry would be hung in the Cathedral in Bayeux, depicting the events leading to the conquest of England by William, Duke of Normandy.

In attendance would be King William and Queen Matilda of England, Archbishop Lanfranc of Canterbury, and many nobles and bishops.

So, in the spring of 1077, Young Moons and I sailed with Onyame to the other side of the world.

Arriving in Normandy after an easy voyage — no storms and no bailing, since Onyame had engaged an extra man — Young Moons, Onyame, and I met Garrad and Marie outside Falaise.

Garrad looked a bit older. I realized that he was now the age I thought he was when I first met him. Marie had some gray in her hair as well. Aside from that, though, they were little changed, and both of them seemed lively and contented.

"We are," Garrad confirmed, "because we have little to challenge us these days, now that you're gone. No troublemakers visit Falaise anymore."

I laughed. "The dragon has kept me informed in visions. So I know that you're busy advising William about one challenge after another."

"Yes," Marie said, "but nothing like the excitement of your time here."

"We have a surprise for you," Garrad said. "We are well guarded in Falaise, and we will have an armed escort for part of our journey. The head of Duke William's Berserker guard will join us."

At that moment, Voldred appeared from behind a grove of trees and rode toward us, smiling. He seemed, if possible, taller than I remembered. Though his hair and beard were completely white and his face lined, he seemed somehow youthful in his exuberance to see us.

After we exchanged greetings, I asked him about his family and his work, to which he responded as we rode.

"I've been able to divide my time between my farm in Norway and training the Berserkers that guard the Duke here and the King in England."

"William has Berserkers in England as well?"

He nodded. "He has come to trust them, saying that his life is safe there only because the Berserkers keep the Saxons from murdering him."

"I'm sure he means that literally and figuratively. Your family and farm?"

"As you might suppose, they both thrive as a result of the skill of my wife. Both of my daughters are married now, as Onyame may have told you, and I have grandchildren to turn into little Berserkers. The only problem is that they are all girls, so they have difficulty swinging axes."

I was amused that Voldred had developed a sense of humor, and I said so.

"Well," he replied, "the second half of my life has turned out to be much lighter than the first half. I have even begun, in all seriousness now, to train one of my granddaughters in ritual."

"Good. Good. So, when will you join Onyame and bring them to the Land of the People so that we can meet them?"

"Perhaps sooner than you imagine. They are old enough for a sea journey, and Hervor has said that one of them will train in the rituals of the People."

"Has she? Wonderful. We'd be delighted to have you stay with us as long as you wish."

"Then expect me soon, and be warned: after the first visit, you may see us too often. If my granddaughters love the Land of the People, I cannot refuse them. Besides, they want to meet the man they call their second grandfather."

I smiled. "While I'm honored by the title, I'm not sure I'm flattered by being considered so aged."

We continued talking until Voldred had to ride back to Falaise to oversee the Berserker guard at the castle there.

His parting words were, "Look for me with several small female Viking invaders within a year or two. We have left you in peace long enough."

As we rode into Bayeux, we told each other stories of the last ten years, and I felt as if I had come home — but to a world that I had inhabited in a different lifetime.

At the ducal residence not far from Bayeux Cathedral, the five of us met William and Matilda in the great hall, which was now filling with people.

Matilda looked remarkably the same and as always, resembled a pillar of strength — although a small one, especially next to William. While he had gained only a few lines in his face, he had gained weight.

After formal greetings, I joked with him. "I see that you're not satisfied with just standing at a great height. You now intend to stand with great girth also."

He laughed. "Yes, I eat more than I should and sit too long in courts and on ships." He looked at me. "You look better than I've ever seen you, so the life with the People and your beautiful wife suits you."

Young Moons thanked him in Norman French, and William stepped aside to talk with her, as he said, "about my brother, to assure that he is a good husband to you."

Onyame and I turned back to Garrad and Marie, who had located Hervor, standing in one corner, talking with a long-haired, bearded, blue-cloaked man, his left eye patched.

As we approached, Hervor spotted us and said, "Now don't ask me something foolish, such as why I'm here. I wouldn't miss this event, even with the sea voyage it cost me."

We greeted her and turned to the blue-cloaked man, the former King Harold of England.

Before we could say anything, he said, "I am happy to see you again, my friends. If you are trying to figure out what to call me now, Cuin, I am the hermit, Harold of Chester, an occasional advisor to the King. I have no title. Since I am in William's confidence, though, I too have been invited."

We exchanged greetings and stories about the last ten years.

Eventually, I glanced at the tapestry hanging over our heads. "I see that Odo has had his tapestry makers recreate the battle with a great deal of … color."

Onyame had been studying it. "And imagination."

"The battle has expanded with every telling," Harold said. "Sometimes the Normans are the devils, sometimes the Saxons are. Sometimes William is the devil, sometimes I am. Every time, though, we are, every one of us, heroic. And well dressed."

I shook my head. "Were any of us, except the nobles, ever that well dressed?"

Harold shifted to look at me more closely. "I was, if you recall." He looked down at his clothes. "It's odd how contented I've become with this tunic and robe."

Garrad was squinting upward at the tapesty. "It's good that the scenes are … open to interpretation."

Harold laughed. "Assuredly."

I stared at the two of them. "So you two have met by now."

"How would the two advisors, one to the King and one to the Duke, not know each other?" Garrad said. "Yes, Harold and I have known each other for some time."

"As you may suppose, Cuin," Harold said, "we have had no small task helping this King govern well."

"Except for William's rebellious son and a few border disputes," Garrad said, "ruling Normandy is easier than it was when you were here. England, however … that's a different matter."

I nodded. "I never thought that William's rule in two realms would be easy. The main reason was that he would have no idea how to rule England. Without you, Harold, I think he may have given up by now." I smiled at them. "It's the reason I retired to the other side of the world."

"A wise choice, after all," Harold said. "By the way, do you know that Master Lanfranc is now Archbishop of Canterbury?"

"Yes."

"Did you see that in a vision?" Garrad asked.

"I saw it in William's invitation."

"I had already told him that after one of my voyages," Onyame said, "but now Cuin remembers nothing about this side of the world. He thinks only about studying with the elders of the People, fishing, wandering in the forests, eating good food, and spending too much time with his wife."

Hervor stepped in and took my arm, leading me away. "I am going to rescue you from these peasants. Come, I want to talk with you for a moment."

"Thank you, unless, of course, you mean to chide me for something."

"No, though I assume that you deserve chiding. No, I want to tell you that I shall make one last trip to Iceland. Then I think I will settle with the nuns in Chester."

"I'm surprised to hear you say that. Of course, you always did say that Iceland is not safe for Odin's prophetesses."

"I have, as I predicted, become the last one."

"So there's no reason for you to stay."

"That's right." She stared up at the tapestry for a time. "What do you think of this?"

I glanced up. "It's an elegant example of the art, and it disguises the truth just as elegantly. I like it. And you?"

She was silent for a time. "I don't know whether we have done well or not, whatever this depicts. Only Odin knows."

"The world did change, and this story is one way to remember that change."

"That is so, and I shall watch the aftermath of that change closely."

"You mean more than observing William, don't you?"

"Yes. When Duke William came to England, he brought with him the old Northern traditions as well as the traditions of the French and the Italians and the Church. I want to see what those threads look like woven together."

To my own surprise, I heard myself ask, "Do you think that we labored to some good end?" I waved my hand at the tapestry.

She looked at me. "Do you remember the Four Crowns Prophecy?"

"Good heavens, I'd almost forgotten that."

"In your lifetime, you saw the Kings of Norway, Denmark, and England forge a rough peace with each other. Do you recall that you carried King Magnus' dying message to your half-brother, Sweyn? Helped Hardraada become king of Norway?"

"I recall the former, but the latter …"

"You helped save him from assassins."

"Oh, that."

"You arranged for the Kings of Norway and Denmark to be friends of Duke William. And of King Edward. Even of Count Baldwin of Flanders. These men had challenges with each other, but they shared some peace. You helped them do it. Especially by not being a ruler yourself."

She paused and looked up at the tapestry again, especially at the battle scenes. "Though Odin is a warrior, only deluded rulers believe that power lies in war. Real power lies elsewhere — the kind of power you used, the kind that Onyame uses, the kind that Harold now uses. It's what the Man Who Walks with Power and I have used." She sighed deeply. "And loved, even when others did not."

She looked back down at me. "I will see you again one more time. Until then, take care. For now, I was told that the Archbishop of Canterbury has been looking for you."

"Lanfranc?"

"Yes, he's over there." She pointed. "With his famous student, Anselm, now Prior of Bec, a fine teacher in his own right." She gave me a push. "Away with you now."

I made my way through the crowd, and as I approached Lanfranc, he called out a greeting, "Cuin! By all that's holy, it's wonderful to see you! How have you been? Tell me everything."

We exchanged summaries of the last ten years, and then he drew me farther across the hall, where he introduced me to Prior Anselm, a serious looking young man dressed as plainly as an Abbot of Bec ever did.

"I'm happy to meet someone," I said to him, "who has the intelligence of Lanfranc and the good sense to stay at Bec Abbey."

Anselm replied, smiling, "I'm happy to meet you, since I've heard so much about a man who is, by all historical accounts, invisible."

I looked at Lanfranc. "I suppose that's true."

"It is so, my friend," Lanfranc said. "We've labored long to keep your identity secret."

I shook my head. "I've never been interested in being well known."

"No, you have not. That's probably how you came to achieve so much."

"I can't say that I achieved much, but I had wonderful moments here and wonderful friends and teachers, such as you."

Lanfranc glanced at Anselm. "This man can deflect a compliment like a warrior deflecting a sword's blow with a shield."

"I've heard that, too," Anselm said.

"So," I said, "what were the two of you discussing — in earnest, it appeared to me — before I interrupted you?"

"Freedom within the bounds of the Church," Anselm replied. "It has become a concern for us."

"In what way?"

"The Pope desires that Canterbury fall under his rule," Lanfranc said. "Neither the King nor I can allow that."

"Pope Gregory lacks nothing in energy," Anselm said.

Lanfranc nodded. "To stay free of the absolute rule of Rome will be a difficult struggle. Many monasteries are already losing independence. Bishops run them as they run churches. If this Pope forces this universal dominion, independence in Christianity will be lost."

"Bec Abbey alone stands free," Anselm said, "but I don't know how we can stem the tide of domination."

"This is an odd discussion for you two, isn't it? Wouldn't a unified Church help unify the world?"

"Yes," Lanfranc said, "if it were a true unity. Unified domination is mere tyranny."

"Surely, even a domineering Church would be preferable to a fragmented one."

"To what end?" Anselm asked.

"Peace and universal reform."

"Forced peace is not peace," Anselm replied.

Lanfranc had found a fine disciple, I thought.

"Gregory's a reformer and a good man," Lanfranc said., "but think like the diplomat that you are, Cuin. Wouldn't a united Western Church simply threaten the Eastern Church, the followers of Muhammad, and the nobles in every country? Far from peace, it might threaten war on a scale we've never seen."

"Shouldn't nobles be threatened occasionally?"

They laughed.

"I do see what you mean," I said. "So, now I wonder whether William's taking England wasn't about something else, something other than any of us thought."

Lanfranc sighed. "Everything is about something other than we think."

Returning to the theme, Anselm said, "I'm not convinced that papal domination would threaten nobles." And the two of them fell to debating the problem.

Lanfranc has lost none of his keenness. Looking at the lines on his face, I expected him to feel withdrawn with age, but I was wrong.

After a time, he caught my look. "How would you have it, Cuin?"

"I'm afraid I would have it end. I'd go to a monastery or become a hermit in the woods. As it is, I shall return to the People in a beautiful forest with a wife who gets more beautiful every year. And leave the solution of this problem to you two."

They laughed again.

"My heart is always at Bec Abbey," Lanfranc said, "but my mind and work are in the world."

"My faith, too, is in the world," Anselm said, "that is, in the future of the world."

"Yes," Lanfranc said, "It seems to be a new millennium after all. Now, I begin to believe that though there are many challenges, many things are possible."

Abruptly, a servant appeared and led Lanfranc and Anselm away to meet some dignitary, so they bowed a farewell.

At almost the same time, a hand grabbed my sleeve. I turned to see a swarthy face grinning at me from under a slanting leather cap.

Fier!" I extended my hand. "I'm delighted to see you."

He grasped my hand. "And I you, Sir whoever-you-are."

"I should have known you'd be here. Free food and wine."

Drawing me away from the others, he glanced around. "I still haven't been able to discover who you are."

"You know very well who I am."

"No one seems to know," he almost whispered, crouching toward me. "They say you're related to the Duke — I mean to say, the King — in some mysterious way and that you might be a great diplomat or healer or wizard. No one's certain about anything, though."

"Fier, can't you stop being a plotter long enough to enjoy a feast?"

He straightened and smiled. "How's the wine?"

I clapped his shoulder. "Not very good. Someone's put water in it, making off with the rest. Would you know anything about it?"

"Me? Of course not. I don't plan feasts." His head turned constantly. "Who's that?" He pointed.

I identified several monks and priests for him. I knew, though, the person he was searching for. I pointed. "Odo, the Bishop of Bayeux, William's half-brother, to whom you've sold bones and bodies, is over there."

"Quiet," he said, stooping over and then rising to stare at Odo. "Someone may hear."

"No one will know that I'm referring to relics."

He grimaced at me. "They will if you say it loudly enough." He continued staring around the room for a time. "Look at this assemblage. The grandeur of it." He turned back to me. "Your priests have done a fine job. Here stands the aristocracy of the churches and the realms."

"On the seventh day of the seventh month of the seventy-seventh year of the sixth millennium after creation," I said. "They planned that, too."

His head began to rotate again. "I'd certainly like to be standing here on the seventh day of the seventh month of the seventy-seventh year of the seventh millennium. That would be an event to be present for."

"Perhaps you'll be present as a relic."

At that moment, William strode toward us. Fier began to back away, but I held him in place.

"Just the man I was looking for," William said as he approached.

I had to hold Fier even more firmly.

Realizing that there was no escape, he bowed low. "Your majesty," he said.

William raised him up. "I want to thank you for the help you gave me" — he waved at the tapestry above us — "during this event and several others when I requested your help."

Fier looked surprised and relieved. "I … was happy … and am happy to help your majesty. Always. You need only ask."

"Thank you for the relics as well."

Fier bowed and mumbled some reply I did not hear.

I said to William, "You must have enough relics now to build your own saint."

William smiled and said to Fier, "You know, Cuin has never been the reverent Christian that the priests hoped he would be. Perhaps you should send him home with a relic, if only to diminish his unholy, doubting tendencies."

Fier smiled and said, "Whatever your majesty desires."

"Thank you," William replied. To me he said, "There's a loyal subject, Cuin. Immediately obedient. You could learn something from this man."

"It's too late."

"Will you excuse us, Fier?"

"Of course, your majesty."

William drew me aside and became serious. "I do not know how much time I will have to talk with you, Cuin, but I want to thank you again for all that you have done for me. And for Normandy."

"What about England? You can't be grateful for that, I think."

He groaned. "No. Ruling England has been a long path of troubles. I've had some successes, of course, but sometimes I wish Harold had … That reminds me, I have an advisor now, just as you said I would, a bearded, blue-cloaked hermit. He's been quietly helpful. I've needed his help with that rebellious country and all the mistakes I've made with the Saxons."

"I saw Harold. As for England — well, that was always going to be difficult, wasn't it? Edward had already established resentment of the Normans. Your reign after Harold's 'death' was never going to be free of crises."

"Even my own son is rebelling."

"I've heard. I'm sorry that I'm not here to help."

He stepped back and put his hands on my shoulders. "Well, I miss your help, but I'm relieved that you have your life. Your wife has told me how happy you are on the other side of the world. I'm happy for you."

"Thank you, William."

"Are you going back soon?"

"Yes, you planned this late enough in the year that, for Onyame and I to complete our rounds, we must leave within the week."

"I hope I shall see you again soon," he said.

"And I you."

"Until then, I shall miss my brother."

I rejoined Young Moons, waiting just outside the great hall.

We told Onyame that we would meet him back at the ship, so that we could ride leisurely through the countryside.

As we neared the river's mouth late that afternoon, we reached a promontory, from which we spied a small procession in the distance. A priest escorted a man and a woman into the forest. The woman carried a bundle.

I lost sight of them until they re-emerged onto the road. The bundle was gone. The man had his arm around the woman as they walked, while the priest swayed as if chanting.

Though I had never seen such a ritual before, I recognized it.

We urged our horses toward the place where the priest and the couple had entered the woods. We dismounted and retraced their path, easily visible from the crushed ferns and twigs. Soon we reached a clearing, just large enough for a single beam of sunlight to touch the ground. There lay the bundle.

It was a place where similar bundles had lain. I knew such places well when I was younger.

I approached and knelt down. Unwrapping the blanket, I found what I suspected I would: a black-haired Norman baby. This one was a boy-child, his legs curled up under him like closed fingers, one of his feet club-like, the other too short, even for his tiny legs.

I reacted the way his parents must have: his legs and feet were so badly deformed that they would be useless.

Young Moons said, "Perhaps, if he is not further damaged …"

She stretched her left hand toward him, and he closed his fingers around one of hers. I did the same, and he seized one of my fingers with his other hand.

He blinked at us, his black eyes moving back and forth on our faces. I touched his chin, and he stirred slightly.

Young Moons glanced at me. "His movements seem normal."

"Yes, the rest of his body is healthy."

"Would he …?"

"Would he survive a sea voyage to the Land of the People?" I looked down at him. "I don't know. I still have our hut in Falaise, though, near Garrad and Marie."

"Perhaps we can spend a year or two here."

I nodded. "Yes, until he is old enough."

"Onyame?"

"Let's leave a message at the ship."

I rewrapped the child, so that his face alone showed, his eyes still blinking. Carrying him back through the woods, we found our horses.

Holding the child, I waited for Young Moons to mount and then passed the child to her, while I remounted. Taking the reins of her horse, I urged both horses back toward the mouth of the river.

"The parents were wrong," I said.

She nodded. "Yes, they were. The child will walk."

ACKNOWLEDGEMENTS

I wish to thank my British "family," Cecil and Hilda Colson, who took me to Normandy to see the Bayeux Tapestry in 1987 and became my first readers. My original supporter for writing the novel was Denise Breton, while my last push came from Andrea Bosbach Largent, and I am deeply grateful to both of them. In between, I was encouraged by the late Paul Shockley and Kathy Bird as well by my early readers: Jim Clapp, my sister Linda Lladysmithe, and my late father, Robert Richard Largent. I am particularly grateful to Mary Anne Regan, Jill Snyder, Diane and Rob Mayer, and Tracy Halterman, who offered enthusiastic support and helpful comments on grammar and style. Finally, I thank my other readers: Elaine Burg, Tony Dobrowolski, Joan and Rob Gennarini, Dianne Harris and Tom McKay, Kallie Kendle, Mike Roberts, and my last surviving brother, Randy Largent.

To get an authentic 11th-Century voice for Cuin, I drew on a wide range of texts: from Ross and McLaughlin's 'The Portable Medieval Reader,' Baring-Gould's 'Curious Myths of the Middle Ages,' and George Whicher's 'The Goliard Poets' to St. Aelred of Rievaulx's 'Life of Edward the Confessor' (Bertram translation), Snorri Sturluson's "King Harald's Saga,' (Magnusson and Palsson translation), Clover and Gobson's 'The Letters of Lanfranc,' and 'Rodulfus Glaber Opera' from the Oxford Medieval Texts series.

The researchers on whom I drew for historical background include: Frank Barlow, Hillaire Belloc, David J. Bernstein, Johannes Bronsted, R. Allen Brown, Jesse Byock, David C. Douglas, Margaret Gibson, Frances and Joseph Gies, James Graham-Campbell, Christopher Hibbert, David Howarth,

Gwyn Jones, Alan Kendall, Alan Lloyd, Bruce D. Lyon, Olwyn Owen, Russell Phillips, Marjorie Rowling, George Slocombe, Edwin Tetlow, G.M.A. Trevelyan, Ian W. Walker, Sally N. Vaughn, Ruth Holmes Whitehead, and of course, David Wilson and his spectacular version of 'The Bayeux Tapestry.' I am grateful for their outstanding scholarship.

GLOSSARY OF CHARACTERS

Throughout the novel, I varied names to help the reader with clarity. For instance, Harold in England can be spelled the same as Harald of Norway, so I used a Norwegian variation for the latter (Harald not Harold) and referred to him by his famous nickname (though it is unclear how much it was used in his lifetime) Hardraada. Similarly, William of Normandy has the same name as his lifelong friend, William of Osbern, so the latter becomes Osbern. Herluin of Bec is distinguished from Herlwin of Conteville, though their names could have been spelled the same in their lifetimes. And so on.

An asterisk marks the characters or themes invented for the novel, though some of them may well have been actual characters or events.

Alfred (Prince Alfred of England, sent to Normandy as a child) is a young man when Cuin encounters him. He is Edward's brother, and Emma's son (by her first husband Ethelred), and he is brutally killed (blinded) when he returns to England at his mother's apparent request (her letter could have been from anyone and ends up being a trap). Edward never forgets that his brother was horribly killed, holds his mother Emma responsible for it, and mentions it even late in life, especially at the famous dinner where Earl Godwin, also implicated in Alfred's death, chokes on his food after Alfred is mentioned.

Anette* is the Norman healer whom Cuin meets during his recuperation in the St. Vaast Monastery in Flanders after he is attacked by Voldred. She's a companion of Matilda (the daughter of the powerful Count Baldwin of Flanders), and she helps Cuin heal from his wound and his limp. She is with him when he frees the Chester nuns from slavery, and she spends the winter with him discussing theology, philosophy, and history. She marries a Flemish man, Thiebaut,* and they help Cuin with several diplomatic projects.

Arlette, commoner mother of William (her father was a tanner), falls in love with Robert before he becomes Duke of Normandy but insists on being recognized publicly as his consort (Normans, like many Scandinavians, often cared little for Christian marriage). When Duke Robert dies on his pilgrimage, she marries Herlwin of Conteville and has two sons by him, Odo and Robert, William's famous half-brothers (who appear in the novel during William's marriage, the planning of 1066, and the battle between William and Harold).

Baldwin of Flanders (Count Baldwin) is the powerful and wealthy Flemish ruler whom Cuin is to contact when he heads north. While recuperating at St. Vaast after being attacked by Voldred, Cuin meets and is befriended by the Count. Baldwin's daughter is Matilda, who becomes William's wife, and Baldwin himself, though at odds with the Pope and especially the Holy Roman Empire when the novel opens, eventually makes peace with both and becomes regent to the new young King of France (Philip) when King Henry dies.

Berserkers are fierce Northern warriors, famous for fighting in a frenzy known as the Berserker Rage (the word "berserk" derives from this). The name derives in some way from "bear" and may refer to bear pelts the Berserkers wore into battle (they also wore wolfskins), significant because Odin, the leading god of the Old Religion can shape shift into a bear. Voldred is a Berserker and later brings Berserker warriors south to serve William in Normandy.

Canute, the Dane who controlled Denmark, Norway, parts of Sweden, and England when the story opens in 1035 (in fact, the year he dies), creates a Danish Empire in the North. We learn in the novel that he has arranged for his sister Estrith to marry Robert of Normandy (before Robert was Duke; his older brother Richard is the Duke at that time), but for some mysterious reason, Estrith is sent back. Canute, after defeating the English King Ethelred, then marries Ethelred's widow, Emma, and has children with her (her sons with Ethelred are Edward and Alfred, and her son by Canute who appears briefly in the novel is Hardecanute).

Cuin* (aliases Brother Augustine and Ambrose) is originally named "Lod," meaning "bastard" and here signifying a mysterious birth - which, though I originally thought I invented, might actually have taken place.

Edith, daughter of Godwin of Wessex, sister of Harold and Tostig, marries Edward when he becomes King Edward I of England, thus becoming Queen Edith. She is exiled to a nunnery by Edward in 1050-51, returns with her family a year later, and conspires as Queen with her brother Tostig to get rid of a political opponent, which leads to Tostig's ouster as Earl of Northumbria. She and Edward have no children, allowing Harold, Godwin's son to take the throne.

Edward, the half-Saxon, half-Norman Prince of England who becomes King of England, is sent to Normandy with his brother, Prince Alfred (who is brutally killed early in the novel when he returns to England). Edward blames their mother, Lady Emma and when he becomes King of England, strips her of her wealth. When the new Danish King Hardecanute (Emma's son by Canute) takes the English throne, he invites Edward to share it, but he dies soon afterward, so Edward becomes King Edward I of England (famous in history as Edward the Confessor and the king whose throne is still the official throne of England for coronation purposes). Forced to appease the powerful Earl Godwin of Wessex, Edward marries Godwin's daughter, Edith, though he sends her to a nunnery during the 1050-51 exile of Godwin's family. Edith returns as Queen when the family returns, but she and Edward have no offspring, leaving the throne open for Godwin's son, Harold.

Edyth* and her sister Chester nuns are bought out of slavery by Cuin during his recuperation at Flanders, after he is wounded by Voldred. Edyth and the Chester nuns spend the winter with Cuin at St. Vaast and join Cuin and

Anette in their discussions of theology. They reappear at the end of the novel - especially Edyth and the healer Sister Agnes - helping to heal a wounded Harold of Wessex.

Einar Paunch-Shaker, an impressive Norwegian earl, appears only briefly in the novel but is significant in that he leads the political opposition to Hardraada as King of Norway. after the death of King Magnus. When Hardraada becomes King and wants to invade Denmark immediately, Thorir and Einar trick him into putting his ambitions aside and traveling north with the body of King Magnus for a proper funeral. This allows King Sweyn of Denmark, to prepare himself for Hardraada's later attacks.

Emma, Queen of England and Norman mother of English Princes Edward and Alfred, is the former wife of Ethelred, the Saxon ruler of England. When her husband is defeated by the Danish King Canute, she sends her half-Saxon, half-Norman children (Edward and Alfred) to Normandy for safety and marries Canute, having more children by him, one of whom, Hardecanute (her favorite), becomes King of Denmark and also King of England, eventually inviting Edward to share the rulership of England. Edward, always suspecting that his mother Emma had something to do with Alfred's death, reduces her to poverty in England, where she dies many years later.

Estrith (who is only mentioned briefly in the novel), sister of King Canute, is sent to marry Robert of Normandy before he becomes Duke. Estrith and Robert are rumored to have a son, but Estrith is sent back to Canute, and the child never appears in history. She later marries a Danish noble and gives birth to Sweyn, becoming, when an unmarried Sweyn becomes King of Denmark, the Queen of Denmark.

Fier,* physician of Eu, a town in Ponthieu (a region ruled by Count Guy of Ponthieu), fakes relics and lures ships onto the rocks, so that he and his fellow villagers can benefit from the laws that allow them to claim whatever they find on the beach or whomever they can ransom. Cuin and Onyame stumble onto one of his luring adventures, befriend him, and later use his skills to lure

Harold's ship onto the rocks, so that William can save him. He also helps William and Cuin with fake relics and appears at the end of the novel at the hanging of the Bayeux Tapestry.

Four Crowns Prophecy* is from an Icelandic seer, who claims that the crowns of England, Denmark, and Norway will be united with some southern territory. When King Canute hears of the prophecy (at that time, he is the King of all three countries), he adds that the three Northern crowns will be united by the illegitimate son of a Norman duke, the son also being related to Canute himself (later the illegitimate son's lameness is added, but it's never clear by whom). This addition by Canute makes the original prophecy about three crowns the "Four Crowns Prophecy," though what Canute intends as the fourth crown is never clear (perhaps France). For each crown, Canute has a special knife made. At the beginning of the novel, one of these knives is in Voldred's possession, given to him by King Magnus, who also has one of the knives. Cuin learns that Harald Hardraada has the third knife, and he eventually discovers that the fourth one has made its way to Harold, son of Godwin. When King Magnus dies, he gives his knife to Cuin.

Garrad,* healer and hermit in Falaise, Normandy, is a former soldier whose arm was incapacitated in a battle with Berserkers, an advisor to Duke Robert of Normandy and later his son, William, a healer and a hermit, and Cuin's teacher. He marries a Falaise woman, Marie, who works with him occasionally. Rolf, the leader of the Goliards, is a longtime friend, who fought and studied with Garrad and now uses his Goliard identity to gather information for Garrad. Garrad is also, we later learn, the brother of Arlette and thus uncle and advisor to William. (Historical note: Garrad is a character I invented, but after I invented him, I discovered that Arlette's real brother, Walter - whom I include as a villager in the novel, one who helps Cuin after one of Voldred's early attacks - was in fact a hermit who did advise William.)

Geoffrey "the Hammer" Martel, Count of Maine is a minor character who is only mentioned, because he allies himself to King Henry of France against William - unsuccessfully - and dies in 1060.

Gilbert, Count of Brionne, gives the land for Bec Abbey to a former knight, Herluin (later Abbot Herluin) and is killed while a protector of William - Edward and Cuin witness his death. Afterward, Brionne Castle goes to Guy of Burgundy, William's cousin, who rebels against William and holds the castle during a long siege, which Cuin helps to end.

Goliards, the famous medieval defrocked, singing monks, accompany Cuin on his trip North to protect him and later aid him as messengers and information gatherers. Historically, Goliards were common from the 12th to the 14th Centuries, but I have backed them into the 11th Century to give Cuin colorful companions and the reader a sense of yet another reform within the Church.

Godwin, Earl of Wessex, though having a mysterious background, is nonetheless a major power in England during Canute's reign, Hardecanute's brief reign (during which Godwin is suspected of being complicit with Lady Emma in the brutal killing of Prince Alfred), and Edward's reign (by that time, his family controls almost all the earldoms in England, and his daughter Edith marries Edward, becoming Queen of England). Godwin has several famous sons, two of whom, Tostig and Harold, play major roles in Cuin's life and work. Cuin meets Godwin late in the elder Earl's life, first to ally with Godwin in ending the dangerous exile of his family and later to try to heal him. Cuin is with Godwin when he dies.

Harold, the handsome and charismatic son of Earl Godwin of Wessex, is an earl in his own right and a power with his father behind the thrones of King Hardecanute (of Norway, Denmark, and England), and especially King Edward of England. Exiled with his family in 1050-51, he raids England until his return from exile and then settles into expanding his connections all over the known world. He becomes friendly with Duke William, and he knows Cuin as a healer and a diplomat. In 1066, he becomes King of England.

Guy of Burgundy, a cousin of William, ridicules Cuin's singing and Cuin generally when both are young and as a young adult seizes Brionne Castle to challenge William's right to be Duke of Normandy. Cuin talks him out of Brionne Castle, ending a long siege.

Guy, Count of Ponthieu is a minor character who has earlier rebelled against Duke William (Ponthieu and Normandy have been allied for a generation by that time) and has been chastised but treated well by William. So, he helps Cuin, Fier (a physician in Guy's territory), and Garrad when they lure Harold, sailing from England, to Ponthieu to be rescued and then befriended by William.

Hardraada, or Harald Sigurdsson, also Prince Harald of Norway, later King Harald of Norway, nephew of King Olaf, is unusually tall, brilliant, and ferocious. His nickname means "hard counsel" or "ruthless." Wounded at a famous battle in his youth (his side loses), he flees through Russia to serve as a mercenary for Byzantine Emperors and an Empress, returning home later with great wealth. Because of his fierceness and ambition, his presence threatens the North and Normandy with new invasions. Cuin saves his life, but is implicated in an assassination plot and must flee, but upon his return, establishes a positive relationship with Hardraada, who by then is King of Norway, though Hardraada is initially unpopular, especially opposed by Einar Paunch-Shaker and his supporters. In 1066, Hardraada joins Tostig, son of Godwin and brother of Harold, in invading the north of England.

Henry, King of France, is William's overlord, who first supports the young Duke and then, fearing his power, allies with one of William's nemesis, Count Geoffrey Martel (nicknamed "the Hammer") of Maine, to twice invade Normandy. Both times, William out-maneuvers them. Henry and Geoffrey die in 1060, relieving William of two external pressures, and leaving the throne of France to young Philip, who has Count Baldwin of Flanders (William's father-in-law) as his regent.

Herluin, is a former warrior and Abbot of Bec Abbey, where Lanfranc retreats and becomes Prior. The land for Bec Abbey has been given to Herluin by his former lord, Count Gilbert of Brionne, who later becomes a protector of William.

Hervor is the last Volva, seer or priestess or prophetess of the Old Religion (focused on Odin, Thor, and Freya) in Iceland, who trains Cuin as her seventh student (Onyame is her sixth, and Voldred is "the failed one"). She accompanies Cuin and Onyame to the Land of the People and later helps Cuin deal with Godwin's exile and later with the wounded King Harold of England.

Lanfranc of Bec, originally Lanfranc of Pavia, is an internationally famous jurist and teacher, who leaves Italy because his family is dangerously embroiled in the politics there. Lanfranc has students in the North, and in the guise of visiting them, establishes ties in Normandy and relocates there. We first meet him in a monastery in Avranches, where Garrad, who has studied with him, goes for advice. Later Lanfranc retreats to Bec Abbey, becomes its Prior and its most famous teacher. Though later Abbot of St. Stephen in Caen, he turns up in the novel to advise Garrad and later to help William (and thus Matilda) with the problem of consanguinity, first appearing to support the Pope and then supporting William. Becoming a close advisor to William, he becomes Archbishop of Canterbury when William becomes King of England. His Italian students include the avid reformer Hildebrand and Pope Alexander II. At Bec, one of his students is Anselm, who appears at the hanging of the Bayeux Tapestry at the end of the story and who becomes the famous Christian theologian St. Anselm and later (though the novel has ended by then) succeeds Lanfranc as Archbishop of Canterbury.

Magnus, the son of the famous King Olaf (later St. Olaf), when the novel opens, is the young King of Norway and Denmark (the latter of which has been seized by Sweyn the usurper). He hears of the Four Crowns Prophecy and tricks Voldred into trying to kill the Norman boy who could make it come true. Magnus later regrets this and tries to free Voldred, but the task falls to Cuin, who has met Magnus earlier and is present at Magnus' death.

The Man Who Walks with Power* is the Mi'kmaq wise man or puoin who, with the help of Hervor trains Cuin's vision skills and helps Cuin in many ways. Though I invented this character, he is based on many native elders, teachers, and shamans of North America.

Marie,* is a Falaise villager and helper of Garrad when Cuin is young and a healer in her own right. She later marries Garrad.

Matilda of Flanders is the proud, brilliant, and short daughter of Count Baldwin of Flanders (her height being relevant because William is tall). A highly trained healer, she helps Cuin at St. Vaast Monastery after he is wounded by Voldred. Later, she becomes, after a rocky start, the wife of William - and the love of his life - and thus Duchess of Normandy and eventually Queen of England.

Olaf Trygvasson does not appear in the novel except by reference, but he is the famous St. Olaf, whose reputation for violent conversion of the North to Christianity sets a background tone for events in the novel. He is the father of King Magnus and appears to Magnus in a life-changing dream. He also turns up in one of Cuin's visions.

Onyame,* the African house-guard of Earl Thorir, becomes Cuin's friend and protector, helping him escape from Ulf and Vandrad (who have framed Cuin for a poisoning) by taking him by sea through the Northern islands to Iceland, where we discover that he is a student of Hervor, and eventually to the Land of the People (the Mi'kmaq), where he has his own family.

Osbern is a lifelong friend and tireless supporter of William. Early in the story, his father is poisoned on a snowy night while protecting young William. Cuin and Garrad help Osbern and at the same time fake William's death, so that the poisoner does not return. Osbern becomes an enthusiastic friend of Cuin's as well, and he appears when Cuin is being sent north and again during the planning of 1066.

Philip, the young King of France, is only referred to in the novel in that he becomes King at a young age when his father, Henry, dies in 1060. Count Baldwin of Flanders is his regent when Philip is very young. Philip's significance is related to his refusal to aid William in confronting King Harold in England in 1066, which William expects but which infuriates William's advisor, the famous teacher, Lanfranc.

Robert, Duke of Normandy (Duke Richard of Normandy, his older brother, was poisoned at a meal, so Robert became Duke), is William's father. In his late teens, he falls in love with Arlette (a commoner) and has William by her. When the novel opens, he is about to leave on a pilgrimage, which will claim his life. Before he leaves, he makes his nobles accept his bastard son, William, as the Duke of Normandy, should he fail to return from his pilgrimage. He is unusually friendly to Cuin, and Cuin admires him. One of Robert's close advisors is Garrad.

Rolf* is the leader of the Goliards, who accompany Cuin north. During the trip, Rolf reveals that he was once a warrior and student with Garrad. Disillusioned by the Church, he has become a Goliard, often helping Garrad and bringing him news of the world. Rolf becomes a messenger and information gatherer for Cuin as well.

Sweyn is the son of Canute's sister Estrith, who has Sweyn after she is sent back from her brief engagement with Robert of Normandy and marries a Danish lord. Asked by King Magnus of Norway and Denmark to watch Denmark for him, Sweyn seizes the throne of Denmark, so he is known initially as a usurper. Eventually, Sweyn receives the throne from Magnus, who, as he is dying, realizes that he must keep Hardraada from seizing all the Northern thrones. Sweyn as the official King of Denmark wars with Hardraada for many years before they finally make peace.

Thorir is the half-brother of King Magnus of Norway and an emissary for Magnus. He meets Cuin in the North, has a knife like Voldred's (one of the

Four Crowns Prophecy knives, which in this case, belongs to Magnus, but Thorir has been instructed by Magnus to offer it as a gift to Hardraada). He befriends and admires Cuin (in Cuin's disguise as Brother Augustine), taking Cuin to the Northern kings and introducing Cuin to Onyame, his African house-guard. Thorir later helps Cuin deliver the Danish crown to Sweyn when King Magnus dies.

Tostig, son of Godwin and brother of Harold, rescues Cuin from Voldred's attack in Flanders. Cuin mistakes Tostig for a courtier from Wessex, England, only to discover later that he is Earl Tostig, son of Earl Godwin of Wessex, and his older brother is the famous Earl Harold. It is his brother Harold who forces Tostig out of his own earldom and into exile, driving Tostig to join Hardraada in an attack on northern England when Harold becomes King of England. Tostig marries Judith, the half-sister of Count Baldwin of Flanders, and he is courting Judith while Cuin is recovering in St. Vaast Monastery in Flanders.

Ulf and Vandrad* befriend Cuin when he is taken to meet the Northern kings but later involve him in an assassination plot to benefit Hardraada. Professional spies, they end up working for several people, including King Henry, who gets them to spread the rumor that Edward is giving the throne to William, and Harold of Wessex, who uses them to get his brother Tostig removed as an earl. After the battle between William and Harold, they kidnap Cuin, so that he can help heal Harold.

Vagn* (and Sigvald*) are the rowers for Onyame. Vagn befriends Cuin, though initially he is frustrated by Cuin's lack of rowing ability.

Voldred is the Berserker and student of Hervor who is tricked by King Magnus into trying to kill the person referred to in the Four Crowns Prophecy.

Walter is a villager of Falaise, the head of one of Cuin's village families and thus feels a positive responsibility to Cuin. A minor character, he helps Cuin after an assassination attempt. In historical terms, the real Walter is Arlette's brother, a hermit who advises Arlette and later William - and Garrad is based on this character.

William is the boyhood friend of Cuin's - and gave him the name Cuin - who becomes Duke of Normandy in his teens and is later known as William the Conqueror. His half-brothers (his mother Arlette, after his father, Duke Robert, died, married Herlwin of Conteville and had two sons by him), Odo and Robert, though famous in Norman history, appear in the novel only in passing, in an amusing scene at William's marriage, at the planning in 1066, and at the fight with Harold. William marries Matilda of Flanders.

Young Moons* is one of the People (the Mi'kmaq), who for unknown reasons has no family and cannot have children. She is attracted to Cuin and later becomes his wife, traveling with him to Normandy several times.

ABOUT THE AUTHOR

Christopher Largent is the author of three critically acclaimed nonfiction books: *The Soul of Economies*; *The Paradigm Conspiracy*; and *Love, Soul, and Freedom: Dancing with Rumi on the Mystic Path*. Over the years, he has taught history of religion and philosophy, Shakespeare, English, the Arthurian cycle, and poetry.

He has also given public lectures on many historical subjects, run two micropresses, and worked as a marketing manager for a third, while also performing peer-review editing for four small houses. He is currently working on a novel set just after the death of Plato that reveals overlooked mysteries in the life of Alexander the Great.

He also teaches the history of philosophy and religion with his wife at his academy in southeastern Pennsylvania.

CPSIA information can be obtained
at www.ICGtesting.com
Printed in the USA
BVOW06s0125240517
485025BV00006B/77/P